P

IMPERIAL BLANDINGS:

AN OMNIBUS

P. G. Wodehouse was born in Guildford in 1881 and educated at Dulwich College. After working for the Hong Kong and Shanghai Bank for two years, he left to earn his living as a journalist and storywriter, writing the 'By the Way' column in the old *Globe*. He also contributed a series of school stories to a magazine for boys, the *Captain*, in one of which Psmith made his first appearance. Going to America before the First World War, he sold a serial to the *Saturday Evening Post* and for the next twenty-five years almost all his books appeared first in this magazine. He was part author and writer of the lyrics of eighteen musical comedies including *Kissing Time*; he married in 1914 and in 1955 took American citizenship. He wrote over ninety books and his work has won world-wide acclaim, being translated into many languages. *The Times* hailed him as 'a comic genius recognized in his lifetime as a classic and an old master of farce'.

P. G. Wodehouse said: 'I believe there are two ways of writing novels. One is mine, making a sort of musical comedy without music and ignoring real life altogether; the other is going right deep down into life and not caring a damn . . .' He was created a Knight of the British Empire in the New Year's Honours List in 1975. In a BBC interview he said that he had no ambitions left now that he had been knighted and there was a waxwork of him in Madame Tussaud's. He died on St Valentine's Day in 1975 at the age of ninety-three.

Contents

FULL MOON

1

PIGS HAVE WINGS

203

SERVICE WITH A SMILE

399

FULL MOON

Chapter 1

The refined moon which served Blandings Castle and district was nearly at its full, and the ancestral home of Clarence, ninth Earl of Emsworth, had for some hours now been flooded by its silver rays. They shone on turret and battlement; peeped respectfully in upon Lord Emsworth's sister, Lady Hermione Wedge, as she creamed her face in the Blue Room; and stole through the open window of the Red Room next door, where there was something really worth looking at – Veronica Wedge, to wit, Lady Hermione's outstandingly beautiful daughter, who was lying in bed staring at the ceiling and wishing she had some decent jewellery to wear at the forthcoming County Ball. A lovely girl needs, of course, no jewels but her youth and health and charm, but anybody who had wanted to make Veronica understand that would have had to work like a beaver.

Moving farther afield, the moon picked up Lord Emsworth's brother-in-law, Colonel Egbert Wedge, as he alighted from the station taxi at the front door; and moving still farther, it illuminated Lord Emsworth himself. The ninth earl was down by the pigsty near the kitchen garden, draped in his boneless way over the rail of the bijou residence of Empress of Blandings, his amiable sow, twice in successive years a popular winner in the Fat Pigs class at the Shropshire Agricultural Show.

The ecstasy which always came to the vague and woollen-headed peer when in the society of this noble animal was not quite complete, for she had withdrawn for the night to a sort of covered wigwam in the background and he could not see her. But he could hear her deep regular breathing, and he was drinking it in as absorbedly as if it had been something from the Queen's Hall conducted by Sir Henry Wood, when the scent of a powerful cigar told him that he was no longer alone. Adjusting his pince-nez, he was astonished to behold the soldierly figure of Colonel Wedge.

The reason he was astonished to behold Colonel Wedge was that he knew the other had gone to London on the previous day to lend his support to the annual banquet of the Loyal Sons of Shropshire. But it was not long before his astute mind had hit upon a possible explanation of his presence in the grounds of Blandings Castle – viz., that he might have come back. And such was indeed the case.

'Ah, Egbert,' he said, courteously uncoiling himself.

Going for a stroll to stretch his legs after his long journey, Colonel Wedge had supposed himself to be alone with Nature. The shock of discovering that what he had taken for a pile of old clothes was alive and a relation by marriage caused him to speak a little sharply.

'Good God, Clarence, is that you? What on earth are you doing out here at this time of night?'

Lord Emsworth had no secrets from his nearest and dearest. He replied that he was listening to his pig, and the statement caused his companion to wince as if some old wound had troubled him. Egbert Wedge had long held the view that the head of the family into which he had married approached more closely to the purely cuckoo every time he saw him, but this seemed to mark a bigger stride in that direction than usual.

'Listening to your pig?' he said, in an almost awestruck voice, and paused for a moment, digesting this information. 'You'd better come in and go to bed. You'll be getting lumbago again.'

'Perhaps you are right,' agreed Lord Emsworth, and fell into step at the other's side.

For a while they proceeded towards the house in a restful silence, each busy with his own thoughts. Then, as so often happens on these occasions, both spoke simultaneously, the colonel saying that he had run into Freddie last night and Lord Emsworth asking if his companion, when in London, had gone to see Mabel.

This puzzled the colonel.

'Mabel?'

'I mean Dora. I forgot her name for the moment. My sister Dora.'

'Oh, Dora? Good God, no. When I go to London for a day's pleasure, I don't waste my time seeing Dora.'

The sentiment was one of which Lord Emsworth thoroughly

approved. It made him feel that his brother-in-law was a man of taste and discernment.

'Of course not, my dear fellow, naturally not,' he hastened to say. 'Nobody in their senses would. Silly of me to have asked. I wrote to Dora the other day, asking her to find me an artist to paint the portrait of my pig, and she wrote back most rudely, telling me not to be ridiculous. Bless my soul, what a horrible collection of pests the female members of my family are. Dora is bad enough, but look at Constance, look at Julia. Above all, look at Hermione.'

'My wife,' said Colonel Wedge stiffly.

'Yes,' said Lord Emsworth, giving his arm a sympathetic little pat. 'Now why,' he mused, 'did I ask you if you had seen Dora! There was some reason. Ah, yes, Hermione had a letter from her this morning. Dora is very worried.'

'Why?'

'Oh, extremely worried.'

'What about?'

'I haven't a notion.'

'Didn't Hermione tell you?'

'Oh, she *told* me,' said Lord Emsworth, with the air of one conceding a minor point. 'She explained the circumstances fully. But what they were I have completely forgotten. Except that it was something to do with rabbits.'

'Rabbits?'

'So Hermione said.'

'Why the deuce should Dora be worried about rabbits?'

'Ah,' said Lord Emsworth, as if feeling that he was being taken into deep waters. Then, brightening: 'Perhaps they have been eating her lobelias.'

A sharp snort escaped Colonel Wedge.

'Your sister Dora,' he said, 'lives on the fourth floor of Wiltshire House, Grosvenor Square, a block of residential flats in the heart of London. So she has no lobelias.'

'Then it is difficult to see,' agreed Lord Emsworth, 'how rabbits can have entered into the thing. Tell me,' he proceeded, shelving a topic which had never really gripped his interest, 'did I hear you say that you had had a letter from Freddie?'

'I said I had met him.'

'Met him?'

'In Piccadilly. He was with a tight chap.'

'A tight chap?'

Colonel Wedge's temper was inclined to be short, and a *tête-à-tête* with the rambling old backwoodsman at his side never improved it. The latter's habit of behaving like a Swiss mountain echo or the member of the cross-talk team who asks the questions might well have irritated a more patient man.

'Yes, a tight chap. A young man under the influence of alcoholic liquor. You know what a tight chap is.'

'Oh, quite, quite. A tight chap, yes, certainly. But it couldn't have been Freddie, my dear fellow. No, not Freddie. Somebody else, perhaps.'

Colonel Wedge clenched his teeth. A weaker man might have gnashed them.

'It was Freddie, I tell you. Do you think I don't know Freddie when I see him? Why the devil shouldn't it have been Freddie?'

'He's in America.'

'He is not in America.'

'He is,' persisted Lord Emsworth stoutly. 'Don't you remember? He married the daughter of an American dog-biscuit manufacturer and went to live in America.'

'He's been back in England for weeks.'

'Bless my soul!'

'His father-in-law sent him over to whack up the English end of the concern.'

Once again Lord Emsworth blessed his soul. He found the idea of his younger son, the Hon. Freddie Threepwood, whacking up English ends of concerns almost incredible. Years of association with the boy had left him with the opinion that he had just about enough intelligence to open his mouth when he wanted to eat, but certainly no more.

'His wife came with him, but she has gone on to Paris. Freddie's coming down here tomorrow.'

Lord Emsworth gave a quick, convulsive leap, then became strangely rigid. Like so many fathers of the English upper classes, he was somewhat allergic to younger sons, and was never at his happiest when entertaining the one whom an unkind Fate had added to his quiver. Freddie, when at Blandings, had a way of mooning about looking like a bored and despairing sheep, with glassy eyes staring out over an eleven-inch cigarette holder, which had always been enough to bring a black frost into this Eden of his.

'Coming here? Freddie?' A numbness seemed to be paining his sense, as though of hemlock he had drunk. 'He won't be staying long, will he?' he asked, with a father's pathetic eagerness.

'Weeks and weeks and weeks, I gathered. If not months. In fact, he spoke as if he intended to stay indefinitely. Oh, and I forgot to mention it, he's bringing the tight chap with him. Good night, Clarence, good night,' said Colonel Wedge buoyantly. And, his cheerfulness completely restored by the reflection that he had ruined his relative's beauty sleep, he proceeded to the Blue Room to report to his wife, who had finished creaming her face and was now in bed, skimming the pages of a novel.

2

She glanced up as he entered with a pleased cry.

'Egbert!'

'Hullo, my dear.'

Unlike the rest of the female members of her family, who were tall and stately, Lady Hermione Wedge was short and dumpy and looked like a cook – in her softer moods, a cook well satisfied with her latest soufflé; when stirred to anger, a cook about to give notice; but always a cook of strong character. Nevertheless, for the eye of love is not affected by externals, it was with courtly devotion that her husband, avoiding the face cream, bent and kissed the top of her boudoir cap. They were a happy and united couple. Most of those who came into contact with this formidable woman shared Lord Emsworth's opinion of her, trembling – like Ben Bolt's Alice – with fear at her frown, but Colonel Wedge had never for an instant regretted having said: 'Eh? Oh, rather, yes, certainly,' in reply to the clergyman's: 'Wilt thou, Egbert, take this Hermione –?' Where others quailed before her commanding eye, he merely admired it.

'Well, here I am at last, old girl,' he said. 'The train was a bit late, and I've just been for a stroll in the garden. I ran into Clarence.'

'He wasn't out in the garden?'

'Yes, he was. Courting lumbago, and so I told him. What's all this Dora business? I met young Prudence this morning as I was passing through Grosvenor Square – she was airing those dogs of hers – but she never said a word about it. Clarence says you told him she was being worried by rabbits.'

Lady Hermione tut-tutted, as she had so often been compelled to tut-tut when her brother was the subject of the conversation.

'I wish Clarence would occasionally listen to one, instead of just gaping with his mouth open and not paying the slightest attention to what one is saying. What I told him was that Dora was worried because a man has been calling Prudence a dream rabbit.'

'Oh, was that it? Who was the man?'

'She hasn't the remotest idea. That is why she is so worried. It seems that yesterday her butler came and asked where Prudence was, as a gentleman wished to speak to her on the telephone. Prudence was out, so Dora went to the telephone, and a strange male voice said: "Hullo, my precious dream rabbit."'

'And what did she do?'

'Bungled everything, as you would expect her to do. Dora really has no sense whatever. Instead of waiting to hear more, she said that this was Prudence's mother speaking. Upon which the man gave a sort of gasp and rang off. Of course she questioned Prudence when she came in, and asked her who it was that called her a dream rabbit, and Prudence said it might have been anyone.'

'Something in that. Everyone seems to call everyone everything nowadays.'

'Not "dream rabbit".'

'You would consider that pretty strong stuff?'

'I know I should make the most searching inquiries about any young man whom I heard calling Veronica a dream rabbit. I don't wonder Dora is uneasy. She tells me Prudence has been seeing a great deal of Galahad recently, and goodness knows whom he may not have introduced to her. Galahad's idea of a suitable friend for an impressionable young girl might quite easily be a racecourse tout or a three-card-trick man.'

Colonel Wedge was exhibiting that slight sheepishness which comes to married men when the names of those whom they themselves esteem highly but of whom they are aware that their wives disapprove crop up in the course of conversation. He knew that his affection and admiration for Lord Emsworth's younger brother, the Hon. Galahad Threepwood, was not shared by the latter's sisters, who considered that *beau sabreur* and man about town a blot on the escutcheon of a proud family.

'Some of Gally's pals are queer fish,' he admitted. 'One of them once picked my pocket. He was at the dinner.'

'The pickpocket?'

'No, Gally.'

'He would be.'

'Oh, come, old girl, don't speak as if it had been an orgy. And whatever sort of a life Gally has led, by George it's agreed with him. I never saw a man looking fitter. He's coming here for Vee's birthday.'

'I know,' said Lady Hermione, without pleasure. 'And Freddie. Did Clarence tell you that Freddie would be here tomorrow with a friend?'

'Eh? No, I told him. I happened to run into Freddie in Piccadilly. You don't mean Clarence knew all the time? Well, I'm dashed. When I mentioned to him just now that Freddie was headed for the castle, the news came as a complete surprise and bowled him over.'

'His vagueness is really very trying.'

'Vagueness?' Colonel Wedge came of a long line of bluff military men who called spades spades. He would have none of these polite euphemisms. 'It isn't vagueness. It's sheer, gibbering lunacy. The fact is, old girl, we've got to face it, Clarence is dotty. He was dotty when I married you, twenty-four years ago, and he's been getting dottier and dottier ever since. Where do you think I found him just now? Down at the pigsty. I noticed something hanging over the rail, and thought the pig man must have left his overalls there, and then it suddenly reared itself up like a cobra and said, "Ah, Egbert." Gave me a nasty shock. I nearly swallowed my cigar. Questioned as to what the deuce he thought he was playing at, he said he was listening to his pig.'

'Listening to his pig?'

'I assure you. And what, you will ask, was the pig doing? Singing? Reciting "Dangerous Dan McGrew"? Nothing of the kind.

kind. Just breathing. I tell you, the idea of being cooped up at Blandings Castle at the time of the full moon with Clarence, Galahad, Freddie, and this fellow Plimsoll on the premises is one that frankly appals me. It'll be like being wrecked on a desert island with the Marx Brothers.'

'Plimsoll?'

'This chap Freddie's bringing down.'

'Is his name Plimsoll?'

'Well, I've only Freddie's word for it, of course. The chap himself was too blotto to utter. During our conversation he stood silently supporting himself with one hand against a cab shelter and catching invisible flies with the other, a sort of sweet, fixed smile on his face. I never saw a fellow so completely submerged.'

A wrinkle had come into Lady Hermione's forehead, as if she were trying to stimulate her memory.

'What was he like?'

'Tall, thin chap. About Clarence's build. In fact, if you can picture a young, intoxicated Clarence with a beaky nose and horn-rimmed spectacles, you will have a very fair idea of Plimsoll. Why, do you know him?'

'I'm trying to remember. I have certainly heard the name before. Did Freddie tell you anything about him?'

'He hadn't time. You know how it is when you meet Freddie. Your impulse is to hurry on. I just paused long enough for him to mention that he was coming to Blandings with this fly-catching chap and that the fly-catching chap's name was Tipton Plimsoll, and then I sprang into a cab.'

'Tipton! Of course! Now I remember.'

'You do know him?'

'We have never met, but he was pointed out to me in a restaurant just before we left London. He is a young American, educated in England, I believe, and very rich.'

'Rich?'

'Enormously rich.'

'Good God!'

There was a pause. They looked at each other. Then, as if by mutual consent, their eyes strayed to the wall on the left, behind which Veronica Wedge lay gazing at the ceiling. Lady Hermione's breathing had become more rapid, and on the colonel's face, as he sat silently playing 'This Little Pig Went to Market' with his consort's toes, there was the look of one who sees visions.

He coughed.

'He will be nice company for Vee.'

'Yes.'

'Do her all the good in the world.'

'Yes.'

'It's – er – an excellent thing for young people – in a place like this – depths of the country and all that – to have young people to talk to. Brightens them up.'

'Yes. Did he seem nice?'

'A charming personality, I thought. Allowing, of course, for the fact that he was as soused as a herring.'

'I don't attach much importance to that. He probably has not a very strong head.'

'No. And a fellow spending the evening with Freddie would naturally have to keep himself going. Besides, there is always this to bear in mind – Vee isn't hard to please.'

'What do you mean?'

'Well, dash it, when you reflect that she was once engaged to Freddie –'

'Oh, dear, I had forgotten that. I must tell her not to mention it. And you had better warn Clarence.'

'I'll go and see him now. Good night, old girl.'

'Good night, dear.'

There was a rather rapt look on Colonel Wedge's clean-cut face as he left the room. He was not a man given to any great extent to the dreaming of daydreams, but he had fallen into one now. He seemed to be standing in the library of Blandings Castle, his hand on the shoulder of a tall, thin young man in horn-rimmed spectacles who had asked if he could have a word with him in private.

'Pay your addresses to my daughter, Plimsoll?' he was saying. '*Certainly* you may pay your addresses to my daughter, my dear fellow.'

3

In the Red Room Veronica was still thinking about the County Ball, and not too optimistically. She would have liked to be in a position to attend that function glittering like a chandelier, but of this she felt there was little hope. For though she would be twenty-three years old in a few days, experience had taught her not to expect diamond necklaces on her birthday. The best the future seemed to hold was the brooch promised her by her uncle Galahad and an unspecified trinket at which her cousin Freddie had hinted.

Her reverie was interrupted by the opening of the door. The pencil of light beneath it had attracted Colonel Wedge's eye as he started forth on his mission. She raised her head from the pillow and rolled two enormous eyes in his direction. In a slow, pleasant voice, like clotted cream made audible, she said:

'Hullo, Dad-dee.'

'Hullo, my dear. How are you?'

'All right, Dad-dee.'

Colonel Wedge seated himself on the end of the bed, amazed afresh, as he always was when he saw this daughter of his, that two such parents as his wife and himself, mere selling platers in the way of looks, could have produced an offspring so spectacular. Veronica Wedge, if the dumbest, was certainly the most beautiful girl registered among the collateral branches in the pages of *Debrett's Peerage*. With the brains of a peahen, and one whose mental growth had been retarded by being dropped on its head when just out of the egg, she combined a radiant loveliness which made fashionable photographers fight for her custom. Every time you saw in the paper the headlines

WEST END AFFRAY

PHOTOGRAPHERS BRAWL WHILE

THOUSANDS CHEER

you could be pretty certain that trade rivalry concerning Veronica Wedge had caused the rift.

'When did you get back, Dad-dee?'

'Just now. Train was late.'

'Did you have a nice time in London?'

'Very nice. Quite a good dinner. Your uncle Galahad was there.'

'Uncle Gally's coming here for my birthday.'

'So he told me. And Freddie arrives tomorrow.'

'Yes.'

Veronica Wedge spoke without emotion. If the severing of her engagement to Frederick Threepwood and his union with another had ever pained her, it was clear that the agony had abated.

'He's bringing a friend with him. Chap named Tipton Plimsoll.'

'Oh, is that who it is?'

'You've met him?'

'No, but I was at Quaglino's with Mummie one day, and somebody pointed him out. He's frightfully rich. Does Mummie want me to marry him?'

There was an engaging simplicity and directness about his child which sometimes took Colonel Wedge's breath away. It did so now.

'Good God!' he said, when he had recovered it. 'What an extraordinary notion. I don't suppose such an idea so much as crossed her mind.'

Veronica lay thinking for a few moments. It was a thing she did very seldom and then only with the greatest difficulty, but this was a special occasion.

'I wouldn't mind,' she said. 'He didn't look a bad sort.'

Her words were not burning – Juliet, speaking of Romeo, would have put it better – but they came as music to Colonel Wedge. It was with uplifted heart that he kissed his daughter good night. He had reached the door, when it occurred to him that there was a subject he had intended to touch on the next time he saw her.

'Oh, by the way, Vee, has anyone ever called you a dream rabbit?'

'No, Dad-dee.'

'Would you consider it pretty significant if they did? Even nowadays, I mean, when everybody calls everyone every dashed thing under the sun – "darling" and "angel" and all that sort of thing?'

'Oh, yes, Dad-dee.'

'Ha!' said Colonel Wedge.

He returned to the Blue Room. The light had been switched off, and he spoke at a venture into the darkness.

'Old girl.'

'Oh, Egbert, I was nearly asleep.'

'I'm sorry. I thought you would like to hear that I've been talking to Vee about Plimsoll, and she seems interested. It appears that she was with you that time you saw him in the restaurant. She says she didn't think he looked a bad sort. I consider it promising.

Oh, and about that other matter. She says "dream rabbit" is dashed strong stuff. The real ginger. You'd better tell Dora. It seems to me that young Prudence wants watching. Good night, old girl. I'm off to see Clarence.'

4

Lord Emsworth was not asleep. He was lying in bed with a book on the treatment of pigs in sickness and in health. At the moment of his brother-in-law's entrance he had laid it down for a space, in order to brood on this awful thing which was about to befall him. To be compelled to play the host to his younger son Freddie was alone enough to unman him. Add a tight chap, and you had a situation at which the doughtiest earl might quail.

'Ah, Egbert,' he said dully.

'Shan't keep you a moment, Clarence. Just a trifling matter. You remember I told you Freddie was bringing his friend Plimsoll down here.'

Lord Emsworth quivered.

'As well as the tight chap?'

Colonel Wedge tutted a tut as impatient as any that had ever proceeded from the lips of his companion's female connections.

'Plimsoll *is* the tight chap. And what I came to say is, when you meet him, don't tell him Veronica used to be engaged to Freddie. Better write it down, or you'll go forgetting.'

'Certainly, my dear fellow, if you wish it. Have you a pencil?'

'Here you are.'

'Thank you, thank you,' said Lord Emsworth, and wrote on the flyleaf of the pig book, which was all he had at his bedside in the way of tablets. 'Good night,' he said, pocketing the pencil.

'Good night,' said Colonel Wedge, retrieving it.

He closed the door, and Lord Emsworth returned to his sombre thoughts.

5

Blandings Castle was in for the night. In the Clock Room, Colonel Wedge was dreaming of rich sons-in-law. In the Blue Room, Lady

Hermione, on the verge of sleep, was registering a mental note to ring her sister Dora up on the telephone first thing in the morning and warn her to keep a keen, motherly eye on her daughter Prudence. In the Red Room, Veronica was staring at the ceiling again, and now there was a soft smile on her lovely lips. It had just occurred to her that Tipton Plimsoll was exactly the sort of man who would provide her with jewels – in fact, cover her with them.

Lord Emsworth had picked up the pig book again and was peering through his pince-nez at the words on the flyleaf.

When Plimsoll arrives, tell him that Veronica used to be engaged to Freddie.

They perplexed him a little, for he could not understand why, if Colonel Wedge wished such a piece of information imparted to this tight Plimsoll, he should not impart it himself. But he had long given up trying to fathom the mental processes of those about him. Turning to page forty-seven, he began to reread its golden words on the subject of bran mash and was soon absorbed.

The moon beamed down on the turrets and battlements. It was not quite full yet, but would be in the course of the next few days.

Chapter 2

The hands of those of London's clocks which happened to be seeing eye to eye with Greenwich Observatory were pointing to twenty minutes past nine on the following morning, when the ornate front door of Wiltshire House, Grosvenor Square, flew open, and there came pouring out in close formation an old spaniel, a young spaniel, and a middle-aged Irish setter, followed by a girl in blue. She crossed the road to the railed-in gardens and unlocked the gate, and her associates streamed through; first the junior spaniel, then the senior spaniel, and finally the Irish setter, who had been detained for a moment by a passing smell.

It has never been authoritatively established what are the precise attributes which qualify a girl to rank as a dream rabbit, but few impartial judges would have cavilled at the application of the term to Prudence, only daughter of Dora, relict of the late Sir Everard Garland, KCB. For while she had none of that breath-taking beauty which caused photographers to fight over Veronica Wedge, she was quite alluring enough in her trim, slim, blue-eyed way to justify male acquaintances in so addressing her over the telephone. There was not much of her, but what there was was good.

Probably the chief thing about this attractive young half-portion that would have impressed itself upon an observer on the present occasion was the fact that she appeared extraordinarily happy. She had, indeed, the air of a girl who is thoroughly above herself. Her eyes were shining, her feet seemed to dance along the pavement, and from her lips there proceeded a gay song, not so loudly as to disturb the amenities of Grosvenor Square, but loudly enough to shock a monocled young man who had just come up behind her, causing him to prod her in the small of the back with an austere umbrella.

'Less of it, young Prue,' he said rebukingly. 'You can't do that there here.'

The clocks, as has been stated, showed that the time was only twenty minutes past nine. Nevertheless, this musical critic was Lord Emsworth's younger son, Freddie. Early though the hour was, Frederick Threepwood was up and about, giving selfless service to the firm which employed him. Sent over to London to whack up the English end of Donaldson's Inc., manufacturers of the world-famous Donaldson's Dog-Joy, he had come to catch his aunt Dora before she went out and give her a sales talk.

The thing was, of course, a mere incident in a busy man's routine. Lady Dora Garland was not, like some women, a sort of projecting rock in the midst of a foaming sea of dogs, and flags would not be run up over the firm's Long Island City factory if he booked her order; but as the managing director of two distinct spaniels and an Irish setter she was entitled to her place as a prospect. Allowing, say, twenty biscuits per day per spaniel and the same or possibly more per day per Irish setter, her custom per year per complete menagerie would be quite well worth securing. Your real go-getter, seething though his brain may be with gigantic schemes, does not disdain these minor coups, for he knows that every little bit added to what you've got makes just a little bit more.

The apparition of her cousin seemed to astonish Prudence as much as that of Colonel Wedge on the previous night had astonished Lord Emsworth.

'Golly, Freddie,' she cried, amazed. 'Up already?'

The poetic greeting plainly stung the young go-getter.

'Already? What do you mean, already? Why, over in Long Island City I leave the hay at seven sharp, and by nine-thirty we're generally half-way through our second conference.'

'You don't attend conferences?'

'You betcher I attend conferences.'

'Well, you could knock me down with a feather,' said Prudence composedly. 'I always thought you were a sort of office boy.'

'Me? Vice-president. Say, is Aunt Dora in?'

'She was just going to the phone when I came out. Somebody ringing up from Blandings.'

'Good. I want a talk with her. I've been trying to get around to it for days. It's about those dogs of yours. What do they live on?'

'The chairs most of the time.'

Freddie clicked his tongue. One smiles at these verbal pleasantries, but they clog the wheels of commerce.

'You know what I mean. What do you feed them?'

'I forget. Mother could tell you. Peterson's something.'

A quick shudder passed through Freddie's elegant frame. His air was that of a man who has been bitten in the leg.

'Not Peterson's Pup Food?'

'That's the name.'

'My God!' cried Freddie, dropping his monocle in his emotion. 'Is everybody over here nuts? This is the fifth case of Peterson's Pup Food I've come across in the last two weeks. And they call England a dog-loving nation. Do you want those hounds of yours to get rickets, rheumatism, sciatica, anaemia, and stomach trouble? Well, they jolly well will if you continue to poison them with a product lacking, I happen to know, in several of the most important vitamins. Peterson's Pup Food, forsooth! What they need, to make them the well-muscled, vital, one-hundred-per-cent he-dogs they ought to be, is Donaldson's Dog-Joy. Donaldson's Dog-Joy is God's gift to the kennel, whether it be in the gilded palace of the rich or the humble hovel of the poor. Dogs raised on Donaldson's Dog-Joy become fine, strong, upstanding dogs who go about with their chins up and both feet on the ground and look the world in the eye. Get your dog thinking the Donaldson way! Let Donaldson make your spaniel a super-spaniel! Place your Irish setter's paws on the broad Donaldson highroad and watch him scamper away to health, happiness, the clear eye, the cold nose, and the ever-wagging tail! Donaldson's Dog-Joy, which may be had in the five-shilling packet, the half-crown packet, and the –'

'Freddie!'

'Hullo?'

'Stop!'

'Stop?' said Freddie, who had only just begun.

Prudence Garland was exhibiting symptoms of being overcome.

'Yes, stop. Desist. Put a sock in it. Gosh, it's like a tidal wave. I'm beginning to believe you about those conferences. You must be the life and soul of them.'

Freddie straightened his tie.

'The boys generally seem to wish to hear my views,' he admitted modestly.

'And I'll bet they get their wish if you're within a mile of them.'

'Was I raising my voice?'

'You were yelling like a soul in torment.'

'One gets carried away.'

'You will be, by the constabulary, if you aren't careful. Do you mean to say you really are a success in business, Freddie?'

'Well, considering that the Big Chief has entrusted me with the task of gingering up the English branch, I must be fairly . . . Well, figure it out for yourself.'

'And you had had no previous experience.'

'None. It just seemed to come to me like a flash.'

Prudence drew in her breath sharply.

'Well, this settles it. If you can become a business man, anyone can.'

'I wouldn't say that.'

'I would. What a bit of luck, running into you like this. You've provided me with just the crushing argument I needed. I can now squelch Bill properly.'

'Bill?'

'He won't have a leg to stand on. You see, it's so obvious what happened. There were you, a perfectly ordinary sort of ass –'

'I beg your pardon?'

'– and you go and get married, and immediately turn into a terrific tycoon. That was what did the trick, your getting married.'

Freddie had no desire to contest this theory.

'Yes,' he agreed, 'I think one may say that. I have never attempted to disguise the fact that I owe everything to the little wo –'

'No man ever amounted to anything till he got married.'

'– man, my best pal and sev –'

'Look at Henry the Eighth.'

'– erest critic.'

'And Solomon. Once they started marrying, there was no holding them – you just sat back and watched their smoke. And it'll be the same with Bill. He keeps saying he wouldn't be any good at business, trying to come the dreamy artist over me, but that's all nonsense. Wait till you're married, I tell him, and then see how you'll blossom out. And now I'll be able to put you in as Exhibit A. "What price Freddie, Bill?" I shall say to him, and he won't know which way to look.'

'Who is this William?'

'A man I know. I met him through Uncle Gally. He's Uncle Gally's godson.' Prudence glanced cautiously about her; then, satisfied that no prying eyes intruded on their solitude, drew from the recesses of her costume a photograph. 'Here he is.'

The face that gazed from the picture was not that of a strictly handsome man. It was, indeed, that of one who would have had to receive a considerable number of bisques to make it worth his while to enter even the most minor of beauty contests. The nose was broad, the ears prominent, the chin prognathous. This might, in fact, have been the photograph of a kindly gorilla. Kindly, because even in this amateur snapshot one could discern the pleasant honesty and geniality of the eyes.

The body this face surmounted was very large and obviously a mass of the finest muscle. The whole, in short, was what a female novelist of the Victorian era would have called 'a magnificent ugly man', and Freddie's first feeling was a mild wonder that such a person should ever have consented to have his photograph taken.

Then this emotion changed to interest. Screwing his monocle more tightly into his eye, he examined the picture closely.

'Haven't I met this bird?'

'You know best.'

'Yes. I have met him.'

'Where?'

'At Oxford.'

'Bill wasn't at Oxford. He went to an art school.'

'I am not referring to the university of that name, but to a pub on the outskirts called the Mulberry Tree. I used to frequent it a good deal, and every time I went this bird was there. The story was that he was being paid to haunt the place.'

'It belonged to his uncle.'

'Did it? Then that explains why he was so glued to the premises. Well, what with him constantly being there and me constantly popping in for lunch, dinner, or possibly a drink, we became close cronies. Lister was his name.'

'It still is.'

'Bill Lister. We used to call him Blister. And he was, as you say, an artist. I remember thinking it rummy. Somehow the life artistic didn't seem to go with a face like that.'

'What do you mean, a face like that?'

'Well, it is, isn't it?'

'Your own dial, young Freddie,' said Prudence coldly, 'is nothing to write home about. I think Bill's lovely. How odd that you should be friends.'

'Not at all. Blister was loved by all who knew him.'

'I mean, how odd that you should have known him.'

'Not in the least. You couldn't look in at the Mulberry Tree without bumping into him. He seemed to fill up all the available space. And having bumped into him, one naturally fraternized. So his uncle owns that joint, does he?'

'Not now. He died the other day, and left it to Bill.'

'Any dogs there?'

'How on earth should I know?'

A keen look had come into Freddie's eyes.

'Ask Blister. And, if there are, put him in touch with me. Well,' said Freddie, returning to his breast pocket the notebook in which he had made a swift entry, 'this sounds like a bit of bunce for my old friend. Taking into consideration goodwill, fixtures, stock in cellar, and so forth, he should be able to sell out for a fairish sum.'

'But that's just the point. I don't want him to sell out. I want him to chuck being an artist and run the Mulberry Tree. It's the most wonderful opportunity. He'll never get anywhere, muddling along with his painting, and we could make a fortune out of a place like that. It's just the right distance from Oxford, which gives us a ready-made clientèle, and we could put in a squash court and a swimming pool and advertise it in the London papers, and it might become as popular as that place in Buckinghamshire that everybody goes to. Of course, we should need capital.'

Except when exercised in the interests of the dog biscuits so ably manufactured by the father of his charming wife, Freddie Threepwood's was not a particularly alert mind, but a duller man than he, listening to this speech, would have been able to detect an oddness in his companion's choice of pronouns.

'We?'

'Bill and I are going to be married.'

'Well, I'm blowed. You love this Blister?'

'Madly.'

'And he loves you?'

'Frightfully.'

'Well, I'm dashed. What does Aunt Dora think about it?'

'She hasn't heard about it yet.'

Freddie was looking grave. He was fond of this young peanut, and he feared for her happiness.

'I doubt if she's going to clap her little hands much.'

'No.'

'I wouldn't say a word against Aunt Dora, so I won't call her England's leading snob.'

'Mother's a darling.'

'A darling, maybe, though I confess I've never seen that side of her. But you can't say she isn't a bit acutely alive to the existence of class distinctions. And what I feel is that when you inform her that *i promessi sposi* had an uncle who ran a pub . . . But perhaps this uncle was just an unfortunate accident such as happens in the hottest families. Blister's father, you are possibly about to tell me, was of the *noblesse*?'

'He was a sporting journalist. Uncle Gally met him in a pub.'

'Pubs do seem to enter into this romance of yours, don't they? His mother?'

'A Strong Woman on the music-hall stage. One of Uncle Gally's dearest friends. She's been dead for a good many years, but he tells me that when she was in her prime she could take the poker and tie it into a lover's knot with one hand.'

'That's where Blister gets his physique?'

'I suppose so.'

Freddie removed his monocle and polished it. His face was graver than ever.

'Totting up the score, then, the best we can credit Blister with is a kind heart and a pub.'

'Yes.'

'For you, of course, that is enough. Kind hearts, you say to yourself, are more than coronets. But what of Aunt Dora? I have a feeling that the fact that Blister is Uncle Gally's godson won't carry much weight. I doubt if you can count on her blessing as an absolute snip.'

'The very thought that crossed my mind,' said Prudence.

'That's why we are having a quiet wedding this morning at the Brompton Road Registry Office without telling her.'

'What!'

'Yes.'

'Well, strike me pink!'

'I've got the whole thing worked out. What I feel is that we must confront the family with a . . . What's that French expression?'

'*Oo la la*?'

'*Fait accompli*. What I feel we need here is a *fait accompli*. When you confront people with *fait accompli*'s you've got 'em cold. You see, as I was saying, in order to develop this pub of Bill's as it should be developed, we shall need quite a bit of capital. That will have to come from Uncle Clarence.'

'You consider him the people's choice?'

'Well, he's the head of the family. A head of a family can't let his niece down. He's practically got to rally round her. So what I feel is, dish out the *fait accompli*, and then go to Uncle Clarence and say: "Here's this wonderful business opportunity, needing only a mere fraction of your heaped-up wealth to turn it into a bonanza. I'm your niece. Bill's just become your nephew. Blood is thicker than water. So how about it?" It seems to me that we're doing the only sane, prudent thing in getting married at the Brompton Road Registry Office.'

Her girlish enthusiasm had begun to infect Freddie. His, too, he could not but remember, had been a runaway match, and look what a ball of fire that had turned out. As he thought of the day when he and Niagara ('Aggie') Donaldson had skimmed around the corner and become man and wife, a wave of not unmanly sentiment poured over him.

'I guess you're about right, at that.'

'Oh, Freddie, you're a darling.' Prudence's blue eyes glowed with affection and gratitude for this cousinly support. She told herself that she had always been devoted to this prince of dog-biscuit pedlars, and a spasm of remorse shook her as she recalled that at the age of ten she had once knocked off his top hat with a well-directed half brick. 'Your sympathy and moral support mean so much to us. Are you doing anything this morning?'

'Nothing special. I want to have this conference with Aunt Dora, and then I've got to look in at Aspinall's in Bond Street. Apart from that I'm fairly free.'

'What are you doing at Aspinall's? Buying a birthday present for Vee?'

'I thought of getting her a pendant there. But what I'm really looking in about is Aggie's necklace. A rather unfortunate situation has arisen. She left the damn thing with me to take to Aspinall's to be cleaned, and what with one thing and another it's kept slipping my mind. She needs it, it seems, for the various routs and revels into which she has been plunged since her arrival in the gay city, and she's been wiring about it a good deal. The communication which reached me this morning was rather a stinker, and left me with the impression that further delay might be fatal. Why did you ask if I was doing anything this morning? Do you want me to roll up?'

'If you would. Bill's sure to forget to bring a witness. He's rather got the jumps, poor angel. And I don't want to have the driver of the taxi.'

'I know what you mean. When Aggie and I were put through it, we had to fall back on the charioteer, and he spoiled the party. A bit too broadly jocular for my taste, besides wanting to muscle in on the wedding breakfast. But won't Uncle Gally be on the spot! He seems to have been more or less the sponsor of this binge.'

'You don't expect Uncle Gally to be up by twelve, do you? He probably didn't get to bed till six or seven, poor lamb. No, it must be you. Do come, Freddie, my beautiful Freddie.'

'I'll be there. We Threepwoods stand by our pals. I shall have to bring a guy named Plimsoll.'

'Oh, why?'

'Imperative. I'm taking him down to Blandings later in the day, and I daren't let him out of my sight during the luncheon hour or he might vanish on a jag. I've got a colossal deal pending with the man.'

'Is he somebody special?'

'You bet he's somebody special. He's Tipton's.'

'What's that?'

'Haven't you ever heard of Tipton's? Shows you've not been in

America. Tipton's Stores have branches in every small town through-out the Middle West. They supply the local yokels with everything, including dog biscuits. I should estimate that the dog biscuits sold annually by Tipton's, if placed end to end, would reach from the rock-bound coast of Maine to the Everglades of Florida. Possibly further.'

'And Plimsoll is really Tipton in disguise? When I meet him and say: "Hullo there, Plimsoll," will he tear off his whiskers and shout: "April Fool! I'm Tipton"?'

Freddie was obliged to click his tongue once more.

'Plimsoll owns the controlling interest in Tipton's,' he explained austerely. 'And my aim is to talk him into giving Donaldson's Inc. the exclusive dog-biscuit concession throughout his vast system of chain stores. If I can swing it, it will be about the biggest thing we've ever pulled off.'

'Your father-in-law will be pretty bucked.'

'He'll go capering about Long Island City like a nautch girl.'

'I should think he would make you . . . Is there anything higher than a vice-president?'

'Well, as a matter of fact,' Freddie confessed, in a burst of candour, 'in most of these American concerns, as far as I've been able to make out, vice-president is about where you start. I fancy my guerdon ought to be something more on the lines of assistant sales manager.'

'Well, good luck, anyway. How do the prospects look?'

'Sometimes bright. Sometimes not so bright. You see, old Tippy only got control of his money a couple of months ago, and he has been celebrating almost without a break ever since.'

'He sounds the sort of man Uncle Gally would like. Twin souls.'

'And the difficulty I have had to contend with has been to catch him at the psychological moment for getting him to sign on the dotted line. He's either been too plastered to hold a pen, or else in the grip of the sort of hangover which makes a man lose interest in everything except bicarb of soda. That's why it's such a terrific strategic move having got him to let me take him to Blandings. He won't find the same facilities there as in London.'

'And he won't be able to get away, when you corner him and start yelling about the broad Donaldson high-road.'

'Exactly. I had omitted to take that into my calculations. Well, I mustn't stand talking to you all the morning, young dogface. Where did you say the fixture was?'

'Brompton Road Registry Office. It's just beyond the Park Hotel.'

'And the kick-off is timed for – ?'

'Twelve sharp.'

'Fine. That will give me nice time to sow the good seed with Aunt Dora and go to the jewel bin. Then a quick phone call to Tippy, telling him where and when to meet me, and I'll be with you.'

'Don't go dropping any incautious words to Mother.'

'My dear child! You know me. On the subject of your romance I shall of course seal my lips completely. And when I seal my lips,' said Freddie, 'they stay sealed.'

It was some twenty minutes later that he came out of Wiltshire House. When he did so, his face was grave and perplexed. The process of sowing the good seed with his aunt Dora had been attended by none of the success to which he had looked forward with such bright anticipation. True to his promise, he had sealed his lips regarding the forthcoming proceedings at the Brompton Road Registry Office, and it seemed to him that he might just as well have sealed them on the subject of dog biscuits.

To say that he had actually been given the sleeve across the windpipe by his relative would perhaps be too much. But he had found her in strange mood, her manner distrait and preoccupied and with more than a suggestion in it of wishing to be alone. The best he had been able to achieve had been an undertaking on her part that, if sent a free sample, she would give it a trial; and, as he returned to his headquarters after fulfilling his wife's commission and giving orders for Veronica's birthday present, he was realizing how those charmers must have felt who suffered from the sales resistance of the deaf adder.

Arrived at his rooms, he established telephonic communication with that haunt of the gilded rich, Barribault's Hotel in Brook Street, and asked to be connected with Mr Plimsoll. And presently a rather hoarse and roopy voice came to him over the wire, the voice of one who at no distant date has been wandering long and far across the hot sands.

'Hullo?'

'What ho, Tippy. This is Freddie.'

'Oh, hullo, Freddie. You caught me just in time. Another second, and I'd have been gone.'

'Where are you off to?'

'Going to see a doctor.'

Freddie cooed sympathetically.

'Feeling bad?'

'No, as a matter of fact I'm feeling extraordinarily well. Most amazingly well. You would be astounded if you knew how well I'm feeling. But a number of light pink spots appear to have sprouted on my chest. Have you ever had pink spots on your chest?'

'I don't think so.'

'It isn't a question of thinking. You've either got 'em or you haven't. There is no middle course. Mine are a curious rosy colour, like the first flush of the sky on a summer morning. I thought it might be as well to have the medicine man cock an eye at them. I never had measles as a child.'

'Why not?'

'Ah, that's what we would all like to know. I dare say, if the truth came out, it would rock civilization.'

'Well, can you meet me at twelve at the Brompton Road Registry Office? A pal of mine is getting married there.'

'Now, there's a sap's game, if you like. However, I hope he'll be happy. I don't say he will, mind you. It's just a kindly hope. Okay. Brompton Road Registry Office, twelve o'clock.'

'It's near the Park Hotel. I'll give you lunch there.'

'Excellent.'

'I'll come in the car, so bring your things. Then we can start straight off for Blandings afterwards.'

'Blandings?'

'I'd like to get there for dinner.'

'Blandings,' said Mr Plimsoll. 'Of course, yes, Blandings. I knew there was something I wanted to tell you. I'm not coming to Blandings.'

It was not easy to make Freddie Threepwood shake like an aspen.

Usually, in order to shatter his iron composure, you had to praise Peterson's Pup Food in his hearing. But he shook now perceptibly and just like an aspen.

'What!'

'No. Where's the sense in burying myself in the country when I'm feeling so extraordinarily well? The whole point of the scheme, if you remember, was that I should go there and tone up my system by breathing pure air. But now that it's gone and toned itself up, I don't need pure air. In fact, I'd rather not have it.'

'But, Tippy . . .'

'It's off,' said Mr Plimsoll firmly. 'We wash the project out. This other idea of yours, however, of standing me a bite of lunch, strikes me as admirable. I'll come dashing up, all fire and ginger. You'll know me by the rosy cheeks. I really am feeling astoundingly well. It's what I've always said – alcohol's a tonic. Where most fellows go wrong is that they don't take enough of it. Twelve o'clock at the what's-its-name. Good. Right. Fine. Swell. Capital. Excellent. Splendid,' said Mr Plimsoll, and rang off.

For some moments Freddie stood motionless. This shattering blow to his hopes and dreams had temporarily stunned him. He toyed with the idea of calling the other back and reasoning with him. Then he reflected that this could be better done quietly and at one's leisure across the luncheon table. He lit a cigarette, and there came into his face a look of stern determination. Donaldson's Inc. trains its vice-presidents well. They may be down, but they are never out.

As for Mr Plimsoll, he picked up hat and umbrella, balanced the latter buoyantly on his chin for an instant, then went out and rang for the elevator. A few minutes later he was being assisted into a taxi by the ex-King of Ruritania who patrolled the sidewalk in front of the main entrance.

'Harley Street,' he said to the driver. 'And don't spare the horses.'

Harley Street, as everybody knows, is where medical men collect in gangs, and almost every door you see has burst out into a sort of eczema of brass plates. At a house about half-way down the thoroughfare the following members of the healing profession had elected to mess in together: Hartley Rampling, P. P. Borstal, G. V. Cheesewright, Sir Abercrombie Fitch-Fitch, and E. Jimpson Murgatroyd. The one Tipton was after was E. Jimpson Murgatroyd.

Chapter 3

The great drawback to choosing a doctor at random out of the telephone directory just because you like his middle name – Tipton had once been engaged to a girl called Doris Jimpson – is that until you are in his consulting-room and it is too late to back out, you don't know what you are going to get. It may be a kindred soul, or it may be someone utterly alien and unsympathetic. You are taking a leap in the dark.

The moment Tipton set eyes on E. Jimpson Murgatroyd he knew that he had picked a lemon in the garden of medicine. What he had hoped for was a sunny practitioner who would prod him in the ribs with his stethoscope, compliment him on his amazing health, tell him an anecdote about a couple of Irishmen named Pat and Mike, give him some sort of ointment for the spots, and send him away in a whirl of good-fellowship. And E. Jimpson proved to be a gloomy man with side-whiskers, who smelled of iodoform and had obviously been looking on the black side of things since he was a slip of a boy.

Seeming not in the least impressed by Tipton's extraordinary fitness, he had asked him in a low, despondent voice to take a seat and show him his spots. And when he had seen them he shook his head and said he didn't like those spots. Tipton said he didn't like them either – which was fine, he pointed out, because if he was anti-spot and E. J. Murgatroyd was anti-spot, they could get together and do something about them. What brought home the bacon on these occasions, said Tipton, was team spirit and that shoulder-to-shoulder stuff. There was a song, he added, about the Boys of the Old Brigade, which illustrated what he had in mind.

Sighing rather heavily, E. J. Murgatroyd then fastened a sort of rubber contrivance about Tipton's biceps and started tightening it, keeping his eye the while upon what appeared to be some kind of score sheet on his desk. Releasing him from this, he said he didn't like Tipton's blood pressure. Tipton, surprised, for this was the first time he had heard of it, said had he a blood pressure? And E. J. Murgatroyd said yes, and a very high one, and Tipton said that was good, wasn't it, and E. J. Murgatroyd said no, not so good, and began to tap him a good deal. Then, having asked some rather personal and tactless questions concerning Tipton's general scheme of life, he delivered his verdict.

The spots, he said, considered purely as spots, were of no great importance. If there had been nothing wrong with him but the spots, Tipton could have sneered at them. But taken in conjunction with a number of other things which he had noticed in the course of his investigations, they made it clear to him that his patient was suffering from advanced alcoholic poisoning and in serious danger of being written off as a total loss. It was in vain that Tipton protested that he had never felt better in his life. E. J. Murgatroyd merely came back at him with the moody statement that that was often the way. Such a lull before the storm, he said, generally heralded the final breakdown.

And when Tipton asked him what he meant by 'final breakdown', E. J. Murgatroyd – his first name was Edward – came right out into the open and stated that if Tipton did not immediately abstain from alcoholic stimulants and retire to some quiet spot where he could live a life of perfect calm, breathing none but the best and purest air and catching up with his sleep, he would start seeing things.

Seeing things?

What sort of things?

Ah, said E. J. Murgatroyd, that was not easy to say. It might be one thing, or it might be another. Lizards . . . spiders . . . faces . . . Well, to give Tipton some sort of idea of what he meant, he instanced the case of a patient of aristocratic lineage who, after cutting much the same wide swath in the night-life of the metropolis as Tipton had been cutting, had supposed – erroneously – that he was being followed about by a little man with a black beard.

The interview had concluded with him getting into Tipton's ribs for three guineas.

As Tipton came out through the brass-plated door, there was a cloud on his erstwhile shining face, and he was muttering to himself. What he was muttering was: 'Three smackers. Chucked away. Just like that,' and his intonation was bitter. For, except when scattering it right and left in moments of revelry, he was inclined to be careful with his newly-acquired wealth. With a dark frown he hailed a cab and directed the driver to take him back to Barribault's. Reaching in his pocket for the materials for a soothing smoke, he had just discovered that he had left his cigarette case in his bedroom.

His mood was sceptical and defiant. His had not been a sheltered life, and he supposed that, taking it by and large, he had heard as much apple-sauce talked in his time as most people; but never in a career greatly devoted to listening to apple-sauce had his ears been affronted by such Grade A apple-sauce as that which E. Jimpson Murgatroyd had just been dishing out.

If E. Jimpson Murgatroyd had pulled a similar line of talk on one of those grey mornings when he had reclined limply in a chair with ice on his forehead and the bicarbonate of soda bottle within easy reach, he might have attached some credence to his wild theories. There had been times during the past two months when, if anyone had told Tipton Plimsoll that his only hope was to go into a monastery, he would have welcomed the suggestion as sound and decided to act upon it.

But to come across with that sort of stuff on a morning when the sun was shining and he was feeling like a million dollars was another matter altogether. And what he was saying to himself, as the cab drew up at the entrance of Barribault's, was that it was his moral duty to teach the man a sharp lesson which would make him more careful another time about talking through his hat in this irresponsible fashion.

Nor did it take him long to divine the correct procedure, to formulate the firm, spirited policy which would bathe E. J. Murgatroyd in confusion and cause him to feel about as silly as any Harley Street practitioner had felt since the invention of medicine bottles. And that was to make straight for Barribault's bar, push four or five nourishing drinks down the hatch, and then go back and confront the man all bursting with health, and say: 'Well Murgatroyd, dear old chap, it may interest you to learn that since I saw you last I've been mopping up the stuff like a vacuum cleaner, and I feel, if possible, better than ever. As for all that rot you talked about seeing faces, I haven't seen a sign of a face. What have you to say to that, Murgatroyd? Try that on your bazooka, E. Jimpson.'

With Tipton Plimsoll, to think was to act. It was with a song upon his lips that he established himself at the counter and told the man behind it to limber up his wrists and start pouring, for a big cash customer had arrived.

At about the same moment a young man who had been staring out into the street through the swing doors suddenly swerved away from them and came hurrying towards the bar. He was a massive young man who looked like a kindly gorilla and seemed to be labouring under some sort of nervous strain. His name was Lister, William Galahad, and he had come to Barribault's to book a table for his wedding breakfast.

2

When large earnest men with simple orderly minds fall desperately in love with small, reckless, impulsive girls whose motto is 'Anything goes', the result is not infrequently to make them feel as if their souls had been stirred up with a pole; and in conveying the impression that he was labouring under a nervous strain Bill Lister in no way deceived his public. Ever since the tempestuous entry into his life of Prudence Garland, he had been feeling almost without interruption rather as one might imagine a leaf to feel when caught up and whirled about in an autumn gale.

Bill's was essentially a simple, orderly mind. Nature had intended him to be one of those men to whom love, when it comes, comes gently and gradually, progressing in easy stages from the first meeting in rigidly conventional circumstances to the decorous wedding with the ushers showing friends and relatives into the ringside pews. If ever there was a man born to be the morning-coated central figure in a wedding group photograph, it was William Galahad Lister.

And here he was, after a month of hectic secret meetings and passionate secret correspondence, about to sneak off to a clandestine union at a registry office.

Not that he minded, of course. It was all right with him. If Prudence had wanted a Hollywood wedding with brass bands, cameras, and full floodlighting effects, he would have screwed his courage to the sticking point and gone through with it. For he had never lost sight of the fact that the nub of the thing, the aspect of the affair to keep the eye fixed on, was that she was going to be his wife. But there were moments when he could have wished that matters had arranged themselves somewhat differently, and one of the improvements which he could have suggested offhand would have been a change in venue for the wedding breakfast.

It is the boast of Barribault's Hotel, which caters principally to American millionaires and visiting maharajahs, that it can make the wrong sort of client feel more like a piece of cheese – and a cheap yellow piece of cheese at that – than any other similar establishment in the world. The personnel of its staff are selected primarily for their ability to curl the upper lip and raise the eyebrows just that extra quarter of an inch which makes all the difference.

Bill, as his photograph had shown, was a splendidly virile young man, and if you had had a mad bull you wished dealt with, you could have placed it in no better hands. But there are times when this business of being large and muscular pays no dividends, and in the superaristocratic interior of Barribault's you are better served by a slim elegance and up-to-the-minute tailoring.

By nature diffident, and conscious that his clothes, however admirably suited to some Bohemian revel at a Chelsea studio, were out of place in this temple of the best people, Bill had been reduced by his interview with a polished plenipotentiary in the dining-room to a state of almost soluble discomfort. It was all too plain to him that the plenipotentiary did not like his tie and was surprised and resentful that anyone in such baggy trousers should be proposing to lunch on the premises. He had tottered out feeling that his hands and feet had been affected by some sort of elephantiasis and that his outer appearance was that of a tramp cyclist.

And when he reached the swing doors which led to the street, there, standing on the sidewalk, was the uniformed exquisite who looked like an ex-King of Ruritania and who had glanced at him as he came in with such an obvious sneer. And it suddenly came over Bill like a wave that he was incapable of passing this man again unless he had a drink first, to fortify him. That was why he had swerved away and headed so abruptly for the bar.

Tipton Plimsoll at this moment had just disposed of his first and was watching the barman shake up another.

The thoughtful soul who built the bar at Barribault's Hotel constructed the upper half of its door of glass, so that young men about town, coming to slake their thirst, should be able to take a preliminary peep into its interior and assure themselves that it contained none of their creditors. Pressing his nose against this, Bill observed with regret that there was a tall thin fellow seated at the counter, and he drew back, thinking this over. He was not at all sure that in his present disordered condition he was capable of enduring the society of tall thin fellows.

A short while later, for the urge to get a couple of quick ones was very keen, he took another look. But once more he found himself unequal to entering. The tall thin fellow gave him the impression of being just the sort of man who would take one quick stare at the knees of his trousers and turn away with a short, sardonic laugh. He received this impression more strongly the third time he peered in, and still more strongly the fourth time.

It was as he was coming up for the second time that Tipton Plimsoll first became aware of him. Over the bar of Barribault's Hotel, reflecting the door, is a large mirror, tastefully fringed with bottles and advertisements of bottles. And it was suddenly borne in upon Tipton, as he sat sipping his third, that there kept appearing and disappearing in this mirror a hideous face.

At first the phenomenon occasioned him no concern. He directed the barman's attention to it with some amusement.

'Doesn't seem able to make up his mind,' he said.

'Sir?' said the barman.

Tipton explained that a bimbo with a face like a gorilla had started peeping in at the door and vanishing again, and the barman said that he had observed nothing. Tipton said 'Oh, hadn't he?' and for the first time became a little thoughtful. It suddenly occurred to him that the apparition's eyes, meeting his, had seemed to hold in them a sort of message or warning – at any rate, they had gazed at him with a singular fixity; and, recalling E. Jimpson Murgatroyd's words, he was conscious of a thrill of apprehension, faint for the moment, but beginning to gather strength.

'There,' he said, as Bill came into action for the fourth time.

'Where?' said the barman, looking up from his mixing.

'It's gone again,' said Tipton.

'Oh, yes, sir?' said the barman. 'Nice day,' he added, to keep the conversation going.

Tipton sat for a while in thought. That thrill of apprehension had now become quite a definite thrill. Then he reflected that there was a very simple way of easing his mind. He went to the door and opened it.

In the interval between Bill's fourth inspection and Tipton's courageous investigation a new factor had come into the affair – the awakening of the pride of the Listers. Quite suddenly there had come upon Bill a feeling of revulsion at the ignoble part he was playing. He saw himself for what he was, a poltroon who was allowing himself to be intimidated by a man in uniform. A spirit of defiance awoke in him. Was he, a finalist in the heavy-weight division of last year's Amateur Boxing Championship contests, to be scared by a mere doorkeeper, even if the latter was about eight feet in height and richly apparelled? Put like that, the question caused him to burn with shame. In the space of time – about forty seconds – in which Tipton had sat in thought, he had turned away with squared shoulders and pushed masterfully through the swing doors. And his bravery was rewarded. The ex-King happened at the moment to be scooping a duke or a marquess or some such person out of an automobile, so did not see him. Feeling a little like Shadrach, Meshach, and Abednego after their passage through the burning fiery furnace, Bill strode past and set off in the direction of the Brompton Road and its registry office.

And so it came about that Tipton, flinging wide the door and glancing sharply to right, to left, and in front of him, beheld only emptiness. And it was as if a hand of ice had been placed on his heart.

He returned to the counter, and the barman slapped down his latest effort before him. But he did not raise it to his lips. A new respect for E. Jimpson Murgatroyd had begun to burgeon within Tipton Plimsoll. No longer could he regard that medical Jeremiah in the old, off-hand, careless way as a talker of apple-sauce. You might not like E. Jimpson Murgatroyd. His whiskers and depressing outlook on life might jar your sensibilities. But you had to hand it to him in one respect. He knew his stuff.

3

Bill continued on his way to the Brompton Road. The momentary feeling of exaltation which had come upon him as the result of his defiance of the ex-King of Ruritania had passed, and he was again in the grip of that over-mastering desire for a couple of quick ones which had animated him in the lobby of Barribault's. Once more the mere quivering jelly of nerves he had been since he had woken to the realization that this was his wedding day, he panted for these quick ones as the hart pants for cooling streams when heated in the chase.

And it was as he drew abreast of the Park Hotel, which stands but a stone's throw from the Brompton Road Registry Office, that it came to him that here was his last chance of getting them. Once past the Park Hotel, moving westward, you are in the desert.

He went in, and sank gratefully on to a stool at the counter. And it was not five minutes later that Tipton Plimsoll, sighting the Park Hotel through the window of his cab, tapped on the glass.

'Hey!' he said to the driver, and the driver said: 'Hey?'

'Stop the machinery,' said Tipton. 'I'm getting off.'

It does not take a swift taxi more than about ten minutes to go from Barribault's to the Park Hotel, and this one of Tipton's had been exceptionally swift. But in ten minutes a strong man can easily rally from a shock and become himself again. As Tipton stood outside the Park Hotel, he was blushing hotly at the thought that he had left a cocktail untested simply because a face had happened to bob up and pop off again.

A dozen explanations of the face's coyness had now presented themselves, each a hundred times more plausible than the one which had first chilled him. It might suddenly have remembered an appointment, or a letter to post, or a telephone call to make, or – well, practically anything. The supposition that it had had no existence outside his imagination and was working in cahoots with E. Jimpson Murgatroyd was so absurd that it made him laugh – merrily, like the crackling of thorns under a pot. He was still chuckling as he reached the bar and pushed open the door.

Over the bar of the Park Hotel, as over that of Barribault's, there is a large mirror. And Tipton, directing a casual glance at this to see if his tie was straight, rocked back on his heels and stood spellbound. He had seen a face. And there was no getting away from it, it was the face of a young man who looked like a kindly gorilla.

4

To say of anyone's heart that it stood still is physiologically inexact. The heart does not stand still. It has to go right on working away at the old stand, irrespective of its proprietor's feelings. Tipton's, though he would scarcely have believed you if you had told him so, continued to beat. But the illusion that it had downed tools was extraordinarily vivid.

His eyes came out of his head like a snail's, and once more, as had happened at Barribault's, there swept over him the thought that E. Jimpson Murgatroyd, though not a man he liked or would ever invite to become his companion on a tour round the night-clubs, was there with his hair in a braid as a prophet or tipster. 'Uncanny' was the word that suggested itself as descriptive of the fellow's flair for predicting the future. For the space of about thirty seconds Tipton's attitude towards E. J. Murgatroyd was that of a reverent savage towards the tribal medicine man.

This being so, it may seem strange that a mere couple of minutes later he was back to his original view that the Sage of Harley Street was a poor fish, a wet smack, and a mere talker through the hat.

But what happened was that at the end of these thirty seconds he closed his eyes, kept them closed while he counted a hundred, and then opened them. And, when he did so, the face had vanished. Not a trace of it anywhere.

A profound relief stole over Tipton, accompanied by the above-mentioned hard thoughts regarding E. J. Murgatroyd, and the explanation of the whole unpleasant episode presented itself to him. He saw now what must have occurred. His experience at Barribault's had hit him harder than he had supposed, inducing a form of auto-hypnosis and causing him to fall a ready victim to some trick of the light. His spirits, which had been low, soared to new heights. From feeling like thirty cents he snapped back to the old level of a million dollars. It was with a cheery breeziness which seemed to bring the sunshine streaming into the bar that he pranced to the counter and opened negotiations with the man behind it.

Sipping his second, he mentioned to the barman that he was due at the Brompton Road Registry Office shortly and would be glad of a few words of advice from a friendly native as to how to get there. The barman said that that would be in Beaumont Street, and Tipton said 'Would it?' and the barman said it certainly would, and with the aid of a cherry and two cocktail sticks showed him how to set his course. Tipton thanked him with the sunny warmth which was endearing him to one and all this morning and went out, balancing the sticks and the cherry on the palm of his hand.

It was at about the same moment that Bill, who had found himself, even after his refreshment, too nervous to go on sitting at bars and had come out and started prowling feverishly up and down the Brompton Road, looked at his watch and decided that it was now time for him to go to the registry office and park himself in its waiting-room. It would never do for Prudence to arrive and find him missing. He turned eastward without delay.

The result was that Tipton, walking westward, got an excellent view of him just as he was about to turn into Beaumont Street, and his heart, after doing a few steps of a buck-and-wing dance, once more gave that illusion of standing still.

Adopting his old and tried policy, he closed his eyes. History repeated itself. When he opened them, the face had disappeared.

A few minutes earlier a similar occurrence had encouraged Tipton and calmed his fluttering nerves, but now it brought him no comfort whatsoever. It had become plain to him that this face which had suddenly come into his life was like the pea under the thimble – now you saw it and now you didn't – but it was always there or just lurking around the corner. This happened to be one of the occasions when it had melted into thin air; but it was a fat lot of good, he reflected very reasonably, faces melting into thin air, if they were going to come bobbing up again five minutes later. The vital fact which emerged was that, no matter to what extent this frightful face might play Peep-Bo, it was clearly from now on going to be his constant companion. The stuff, in short, had got him.

A sense of being unfairly discriminated against swept over Tipton

Plimsoll. The aristocratic patient, of whom E. Jimpson Murgatroyd had spoken, had apparently abused his system fully as energetically as had he, Tipton, and yet, according to E. J. Murgatroyd, he had got off with a little man with a black beard, a phenomenon which Tipton felt he could have taken in his stride. You might in time, he felt, come to make quite a pet of a little man with a black beard. To be haunted by a face like the face which had begun to haunt him was a vastly different matter.

He was feeling very low now, low and despondent, and taking all the circumstances into consideration it seemed to him that the best thing to do was to step into the park and take a look at the ducks on the Serpentine. He had often found the spectacle of these agreeable birds act as a sedative in times of mental stress, soothing the soul and bringing new life and courage. And, indeed, there is always something very restful about a duck. Whatever earthquakes and upheavals may be afflicting the general public, it stands aloof from them and just goes on being a duck.

He stepped into the park accordingly, and after a period of silent communion with the gaggle that lined the water front, returned to his quest of Beaumont Street. He found it and its registry office without difficulty, and walked into the waiting-room. It was a small, stuffy apartment, occupied at the moment only by a young man of powerful build who was sitting staring before him in the stuffed manner habitual with young men on their wedding mornings. His back was towards Tipton, and a kindly impulse came over the latter to tap him on the shoulder and urge him to escape while the going was good.

As he moved forward to do so, the young man looked round.

The next thing of which Tipton was conscious was that he was out in the street and that he was being spoken to by a voice that sounded vaguely familiar. The mists cleared away, and he perceived Freddie staring at him censoriously.

'What do you mean, you're feeling extraordinarily well?' demanded Freddie. 'I never saw you looking mouldier, not even on the morning after that night at the Angry Cheese, when you threw the soft-boiled eggs at the electric fan. You're crazy if you don't come to Blandings, Tippy.'

Tipton Plimsoll reached out a feeble hand and patted him on the arm.

'It's all right, Freddie o' man. I am coming to Blandings.'

'You are?'

'Yessir, I can't get there quick enough. And I should be glad if, while I am in residence, you would see that no alcoholic fluid of any description is served to me. I mean this, Freddie o' man. I have seen the light.' He paused for a moment with a quick shudder, remembering what else he had seen. 'And now excuse me. I have to go and look at the ducks on the Serpentine.'

'Why do you want to look at the ducks on the Serpentine?'

'There are moments in a man's life, Freddie o' fellow,' said Tipton gravely, 'when he has got to look at the ducks on the Serpentine. And about that lunch of ours. Cancel it. I'm going to lunch quietly at Barribault's on a rusk and a glass of milk. Pick me up there in the car when you're ready to start,' said Tipton, and walked off with bowed head.

Freddie, having followed his retreating form with a perplexed monocle till it was out of sight, turned and went into the registry office, where Bill was still sitting staring dully at nothing.

5

Into the early stages of the meeting between Frederick Threepwood and William Lister it is not necessary for the chronicler to go with any wealth of detail. It will be enough to say that they got together and picked up the threads. Few things are more affecting than these reunions of old buddies after long separation, but they involve too many queries as to what old What's-his-name is doing now and whatever became of old So-and-so to make good general reading.

We may pass, accordingly, to the moment when Bill, who had been rather less wholeheartedly absorbed in the fate of these once-familiar figures than his companion, looked at his watch and hazarded the suggestion that it was about time, surely, that the other contracting party to these proceedings showed up.

And Freddie, noting that the hands of the clock on the mantel-piece were now indicating half past twelve, was forced to agree that his cousin's failure to put in an appearance was not unrummy. One expects on these occasions that the bride, like a heavyweight champion defending his title, will let the groom get into the ring first, but Prudence should certainly have been here by now.

Bill, whose nerves for the last hour or so had been sticking out of his body, twisting themselves about like snakes and getting all knotted at the ends, took a grave view of the matter. Having gasped for air once or twice, he put his apprehension into words.

'Oh, gosh, you don't think she can have changed her mind?'

'My dear Blister!'

'She may have done.'

'Not a chance. I saw her this morning, and she was all in favour of the binge.'

'When was that?'

'Around about nine-thirty.'

'Three hours ago. Loads of time for her to have thought things over and decided to back out. As a matter of fact, I was rather expecting this. I've never been able to understand what she saw in me.'

'Tut, tut, Blister, this is mere weakness. Yours is a sterling character. I don't know a man I respect more.'

'I dare say, but look at my face.'

'I am looking at your face, Blister, and it's a fine, open, honest face. Not beautiful, perhaps, but what is beauty, after all? Skin deep, and you can quote me as saying so. Summing up, I consider that an undersized little half-pint like Prue is lucky to get such a mate.'

'Don't call her a half-pint!'

'Well, don't you be so dashed grovelling about her. She isn't the Queen of Sheba.'

'Yes, she is.'

'Pardon me.'

'Well, just as good, anyway.'

The thought came to Freddie that he had perhaps taken the wrong line in his endeavour to soothe and encourage. A silence fell, during which he sucked the knob of his umbrella thoughtfully while Bill, who had leaped from his chair as if it had been drawn to his attention that it was red hot, paced the room feverishly.

It was some moments before Freddie spoke. When he did there was a touch of diffidence in his manner.

'Here's a thought, Blister. Could someone have been telling her things about you?'

'How do you mean?'

42

'People do tell girls things about people. Some silly ass went and told Aggie I had once been engaged to my cousin Veronica, and I've never really heard the last of it since. Aggie is the sweetest girl in the world – an angel in human shape, you might say – but she still allows the subject to creep into her conversation at times, and I'm really taking a big chance giving Vee even the simplest of pendants for her birthday. Somebody may have been telling Prue about your private life.'

'My what?'

'Well, you know what I mean. Artists are artists. Or so I've always heard. Nameless orgies in the old studio, and all that sort of thing.'

'Don't be a damned fool. My life has always been –'

'Clean?'

'You could eat your dinner off it.'

Freddie took another chew at the knob of his umbrella.

'In that case,' he said, 'my theory falls to the ground. It was only a suggestion, anyway. What do you make the time?'

'A quarter to one.'

'Then that clock's right. I'm afraid you must brace yourself to face the worst, Blister. It begins to look, I fear, as if she wasn't coming.'

'Oh, my God!'

'Let me think this over,' said Freddie, applying himself once more to the umbrella. 'There's only one thing to be done,' he resumed some moments later. 'I will pop round to Grosvenor Square and make inquiries. You, meanwhile, go and wait for me at Barribault's.'

Bill paled.

'Barribault's?'

'I've got to go and see a man there. I'm taking him down to Blandings this afternoon, and I want to make sure he's fit to travel. His manner, when I saw him not long ago, was strange. I didn't like the way he said he was going to lunch on a rusk and a glass of milk. It gave me the impression that he was merely wearing the mask and trying to lull my vigilance. Wait in the lobby till I come. I'll be as quick as I can.'

'Not in the lobby,' said Bill, with a reminiscent shiver. It was in the lobby, on his way from the dining-room to the main exit, that he had bumped into a small boy in buttons, who might have been the heir of some ruling house, and had been given one of those quick, sharp, searing looks which the personnel of Barribault's staff, however junior, always give to louts of outsiders who trespass on the hotel's premises. 'I'll be waiting in the street,' he said. It meant, of course, having to brave the scrutiny of the ex-King of Ruritania, but that could not be avoided.

Nervous strain has different effects on different people. It caused Bill, who always walked everywhere, to take a cab to Barribault's; whereas Tipton Plimsoll, who always took cabs everywhere, decided to walk. The former, therefore, had already taken up his station at the entrance of the hotel when the latter arrived.

Bill, who was in a reverie, did not see Tipton. But Tipton saw Bill. He gave him a quick glance, then averted his eyes and hurried through the swing doors. The ex-King of Ruritania, touching his hat to him as he passed, noticed that his face was a rather pretty green and that he was shaking like a badly-set blancmange.

6

When two men are isolated together in a confined space, it generally happens that the social barriers eventually break down and they start to fraternize. The ex-King of Ruritania's position of official stander on the sidewalk outside Barribault's Hotel was one of splendour and importance, but life tended when business was slack to become a little lonely for him, and at such times his prejudice against hobnobbing with the proletariat weakened.

It was not long, accordingly, before he had decided to overlook the bagginess of Bill's trousers and was telling him condescendingly that it was a nice day, and Bill, whose need for human sympathy had now grown acute, was replying that the day might be nice enough as far as weather conditions were concerned, but that in certain other vital respects it fell far short of the ideal.

He asked the ex-King if he was married, and the ex-King said he was. Bill then said that he himself ought to have been by now, only the bride hadn't turned up, and the ex-King said that he doubted if a bit of luck like that would happen once in a hundred years. Bill had just asked the ex-King what he thought could have detained his betrothed, and the ex-King was offering to give him five to one that she had been run over by a lorry, when a cab whirled up, and Freddie stepped out.

Freddie's face was grave. He took Bill by the elbow and drew him aside. The ex-King, astounded that the latter should be on terms of intimacy with anyone so well dressed, gave his moustache a thoughtful twirl, said 'Cool', and went on standing.

'Well?' said Bill, clutching at Freddie's arm.

'Ouch!' said Freddie, writhing like a tortured snake. Men of his companion's physique generally have a grip like the bite of a crocodile when stirred, and his conversation with the ex-King had stirred Bill a good deal.

'Did you see her?'

'No,' said Freddie, rubbing his sleeve tenderly. 'And I'll tell you why. She wasn't there.'

'Not there?'

'Not there.'

'Then where was she?'

'Bowling along in a cab on her way to Paddington.'

'Why on earth did she want to go to Paddington?'

'She didn't want to go to Paddington. She was sent there, with gyves upon her wrists, in the custody of a stern-faced butler, who had instructions from my aunt Dora to bung her into the twelve-forty-two for Market Blandings, first stop Swindon. The fact is, Blister, my poor dear old egg, you've rather gone and made a hash of things. A wiser man would not have rung her up at her home address and called her a dream rabbit, or, if he did, he would have taken the elementary precaution of ascertaining, before doing so, that he was speaking to her and not to her mother.'

'Oh, my God!'

'Naturally, Aunt Dora's suspicions were aroused. Prudence, inter-rogated, proved furtive and evasive, and the upshot was that Aunt Dora sought counsel of an even bigger hellhound than herself – my aunt Hermione, now in residence at Blandings. Aunt Hermione was on the telephone first thing this morning, advising her to wait till Prue took the dogs out for their after-breakfast airing. Those dogs', said Freddie, 'have got rickets, or will have if they continue to eat

Peterson's Pup Food. Peterson's Pup Food, I don't mind telling you, Blister, is a product totally lacking in several of the most important – Ouch!'

He paused, and released his biceps from the steely fingers which had once more become riveted to it.

'Get on, blast you!' said Bill, in a low, quivering voice.

His demeanour was so menacing that Freddie, who had only touched the fringe of his critique of Peterson's degrading garbage, decided to postpone the bulk of his address to a more favourable moment. His companion was looking like a gorilla of testy and impatient habit from whom the keeper is withholding a banana. It would not have surprised Freddie greatly if he had suddenly started drumming on his chest with clenched fists.

'Of course, of course,' he said pacifically. 'I can quite understand your attitude. Naturally, you want the facts. In a nutshell, then, Aunt Hermione advised Aunt Dora to wait till Prue had popped out with the dumb chums and then go through her effects for possible compromising correspondence. She did so, and it was not long before she struck a rich lode – a bundle of about fifty letters from you, each fruitier than the last, tied round with lilso ribbon. Prue, grilled on her return, was forced to admit that you and she were that way, and further questioning elicited the confession that you were a bird short alike on Norman blood and cash. Ten minutes later her packing had begun; Aunt Dora supervising, she weeping bitterly.'

Bill clutched his hair. For an artist's, it was on the short side, but a determined man can clutch at anything.

'Weeping? I'd like to strangle that woman.'

'Aunt Dora is tough stuff,' assented Freddie. 'But, at that, you ought to see my aunt Constance, my aunt Julia, and my aunt Hermione, of whom I spoke just now. So there you are. Prue is now on her way to Blandings. I ought to mention that all the younger generation of my family get sent to Blandings when they fall in love with the wrong type of soul mate. It's a sort of Devil's Island. It seems only yesterday that I was trying to console my cousin Gertrude, who was in the cooler for wanting to marry a curate. And I'd have been sent to Blandings myself, when Aggie and I were walking out, only I happened to be there already. Yes,' said Freddie, 'they've slapped young Prudence in the jug, and what you are probably asking yourself is what's to be done about it.'

'Yes,' said Bill. This was the very question which had presented itself to his mind. He eyed his friend hopefully, as if awaiting some masterly exposition of strategy, but Freddie shook his head.

'It's no good looking at me like that, Blister. I have no constructive policy. You're making me feel the way my father-in-law does at conferences. You don't know my father-in-law, of course. He's a bird who looks like a Roman emperor and has a habit of hammering on the table during conferences and shouting: "Come on, come on, now. I'm waiting for suggestions." And I seldom have any. But I'll tell you what I have done. I remembered Prue telling me that you were Uncle Gally's godson, and I stopped off at a call-box and phoned him to meet us here. If anyone can think of the correct course to pursue, it will be this uncle. A man of infinite resource and sagacity. We may expect him shortly. In fact,' said Freddie, as a cab came to a halt with a grinding of brakes, 'here, if I mistake not, Watson, is our client now.'

Assisted by the ex-King of Ruritania, a trim, dapper, perky little gentleman in the middle fifties was emerging from the cab. He advanced towards them jauntily, his hat on the side of his head, a black-rimmed monocle gleaming in his right eye.

7

'Hullo there, Bill,' he said. 'Come along in and tell me all about it. I gather from Freddie that you're in a bit of trouble.'

He shook him warmly by the hand, and the ex-King of Ruritania gaped dazedly. He was feeling that he must have got his sense of values all wrong. Although he had stooped to converse with Bill, he had not abandoned his original impression that he was one of the dregs, even going so far as to suspect him of being an artist, and here the young deadbeat was getting the glad hand and the beaming smile from no less a celebrity than the eminent Gally Threepwood in person. It shook the ex-King and made him lose confidence in his judgement. For Gally was one of the nibs, one of the lights of London, one of the great figures at whom the world of the stage, the race-course, and the rowdier restaurants pointed with pride. In certain sections of the metropolis he had become a legend. If Joe Louis had stepped out of a cab and shaken hands with Bill, the ex-King could not have been more impressed.

The Hon. Galahad Threepwood was the only genuinely distinguished member of the family of which Lord Emsworth was the head. Lord Emsworth himself had once won a first prize for pumpkins, and his pig, as we know, had twice been awarded the silver medal for fatness at the Shropshire Agricultural Show; but you could not say that he had really risen to eminence in the public life of England. But Gally had made a name for himself. There were men in London – bookmakers, skittle sharps, jellied-eel sellers on race-courses, and men like that – who would have been puzzled to know whom you were referring to if you had mentioned Einstein, but they all knew Gally.

The chief thing anyone would have noticed about Galahad Threepwood in this, his fifty-seventh year, was his astounding fitness. After the life he had led, he had no right to burst with health, but he did. Even E. Jimpson Murgatroyd would have been obliged to concede that he was robust. Where most of his contemporaries had reluctantly thrown in the towel and retired to Harrogate and Buxton to nurse their gout, he had gone blithely on, ever rising on stepping-stones of dead whiskies and sodas to higher things. He had discovered the prime grand secret of eternal youth – to keep the decanter circulating and never to go to bed before four in the morning. His eye was not dimmed nor his natural force abated, his heart was of gold and in the right place, and he was loved by all except the female members of his family.

He led the way through the swing doors, the ex-King touching his hat forty times to the minute like a clockwork toy, and settled his little flock at a table in the lounge. After that first dazzling smile of greeting there had come upon him an air of gravity and intentness. Freddie had not told him much over the telephone, but he had told him enough to make it clear that a very serious hitch had occurred in the matrimonial plans of a young man whom he loved like a son. He had always been devoted to Bill. One of his earliest recollections was of drawing him aside at the age of ten, tipping him half a crown, and urging him in a confidential whisper to place it on the nose of Bounding Bertie in the two-thirty at Plumpton. And he had always been happy to remember that Bounding Bertie had romped home by three lengths at the very satisfactory odds of a hundred to eight.

'Now then,' he said, 'what's it all about?'

The statement which Freddie had made to Bill had been, as we have seen, admirably clear, omitting no detail, however slight. Repeated now, it impressed the facts with equal lucidity on the Hon. Galahad. He nodded intelligently from time to time as the narrative proceeded, and when it had wound to its conclusion made the comment that this was a nice bit of box fruit. And both Bill and Freddie agreed with him.

'Shipped her off to Blandings, have they?' said the Hon. Galahad, removing his eyeglass and polishing it meditatively. 'The old, old story, by gad. Years ago, before either of you kids was born, they shipped me off to Blandings, to stop me marrying a girl on the halls named Dolly Henderson.' He sat for a moment, his eyes dreamy, his thoughts in the past. He had touched briefly on the tragedy of his life. Then he gave himself a little shake and returned to the present. 'Well, it's obvious what you must do, Bill. Can't leave the poor child crying her eyes out, alone in the middle of a pack of wild aunts. You'll have to go to Blandings too.'

Freddie, great though his respect was for his gifted relative, shook his head dubiously.

'But, dash it, Uncle Gally, they'll give him the bum's rush the instant he sets foot inside the door.'

'Who said anything about setting feet inside doors? I see I haven't made myself clear. I shouldn't have said "Blandings". What I meant was "Market Blandings". You book a ticket to Market Blandings, Bill, and establish yourself at the Emsworth Arms. You'll like the Emsworth Arms. Good beer. I wonder if they've still got the same potboy they had last summer. Nice chap. Name of 'Erbert. Great friend of mine. No side about him. If he's there, give him my love.'

Freddie was still groping.

'I don't get it yet. What's Blister supposed to do at the Emsworth Arms?'

'Merely make it his headquarters. Got to sleep somewhere, hasn't he? During the day he'll be up at the castle, of course, painting the pig.'

'Painting the pig?'

'Ah, yes, I should have explained. I ought to have mentioned that your aunt Dora informed me the other day that your father had written to her, asking her to get him an artist to paint the portrait of his pig.'

'Gosh!' said Bill, light beginning to dawn.

'You may well say "Gosh!" Dora, as each and all of my sisters would have done in her place, ridiculed the request, scoffed at it, and took no further steps except to dash off a stinker to Clarence, telling him not to be a silly ass. No artist, accordingly, has been provided. You shall fill the long-felt want. How does that strike you?'

'Terrific,' said Bill.

'I told you he was good,' said Freddie.

'I assume that Clarence will accept my nominee.'

Freddie hastened to remove all doubts on this point.

'Have no anxiety, Uncle Gally. You wire the guv'nor that you're sending down an artist, and I'll do the rest. I go to the old shack this afternoon, and I will undertake to sell Blister to him before nightfall. A man who has talked some of the toughest prospects in America into buying Donaldson's Dog-Joy is scarcely likely to fail with the guv'nor. He will be clay in my hands from the start. You *can* paint pigs, Blister? Then take the next train, dig in at the Emsworth Arms, and expect to hear from me in due course. Bring paints, brushes, canvas, easels, palette knives, and what not.'

He broke off, seeing that he was not gripping Bill's attention. Bill was thanking Gally with a good deal of fervour, and Gally was saying no, no, my dear boy, not at all, not at all, adding that he was only too glad to have been of assistance.

'As I see it,' he said, 'it should not be long before you are able to find an opportunity of sneaking off with Prudence and taking up this marrying business at the point where you left off. You've got the licence? Well, tuck it away in an inside pocket and when the moment arrives, grab young Prue and slide off somewhere and get hitched up. Can you see a flaw?'

'No,' said Bill.

'Just one,' said Freddie. 'I have a bit of bad news for you, Blister. I would like to be on the spot to watch over you with a fatherly eye, but I can't fit it in. I've got to pay a series of business visits to various hot-shots in the neighbourhood and shall have to start these immediately. I'm due tomorrow at a joint in Cheshire.'

'It won't matter,' said Bill. 'I shall be all right.'

This airy confidence seemed to displease Freddie.

'You say you'll be all right,' he said sternly, 'but will you? There are a hundred pitfalls in your path.'

The Hon. Galahad nodded.

'I see what you mean. The name, for instance.'

'Exactly. One of the first confessions extracted from Prue, while undergoing the third degree, was that her heart-throb's name was William Lister. You'd better call yourself Messmore Breamworthy.'

'But I can't,' protested Bill, dismayed. 'There isn't such a name.'

'As it happens, it's the name of one of my fellow vice-presidents at Donaldson's Inc. That's why I thought of it.'

'"Messmore Breamworthy",' said the Hon. Galahad, giving his casting vote, 'will be admirable. And now we come to the important matter of disguise.'

'Disguise?'

'Essential, in my opinion. You can't go wrong, adopting a disguise. My old friend, Fruity Biffen, hasn't stirred abroad without one for years. His relations with the bookies are always a bit strained, poor chap.'

Freddie concurred.

'Must have a disguise, Blister.'

'But why? Nobody there has ever seen me.'

'Aunt Dora may have found a photograph of you and sent it to Aunt Hermione.'

'Prue's only got one photograph of me, and she carries that on her.'

'And if on arrival Aunt Hermione searches her to the skin?'

'You ought to allow for every contingency, my boy,' urged the Hon. Galahad. 'I advise a false beard. I have one I can lend you. Fruity Biffen borrowed it the other day, in order to be able to go to Hurst Park, but I can get it back.'

'I won't wear a false beard.'

'Think well. It's a sort of light mustard colour, and extraordinarily becoming. It made Fruity look like one of those Assyrian monarchs.'

'No!'

'That is your last word?'

'Yes. I won't wear a false beard. I'm frightfully grateful for helping me like this —'

'Not at all, not at all. Dash it, you're my godson. And I once saw your mother lift a dumb-bell weighing two hundred pounds. She did it after supper one night, simply to entertain me. That sort of thing puts a man under an obligation. Well, if you have this extraordinary prejudice against the beard, there is nothing more to be said. But I think you're running a grave risk. Don't blame me if my sister Hermione springs out from behind a bush and starts setting about you with her parasol. Still, if that's the way you feel, all right. We waive the beard. But the rest of it is all straight?'

'Absolutely.'

'Good. Well, I must be pushing along. I'm lunching with a confidence man at the Pig and Whistle in Rupert Street.'

'And I', said Freddie, 'must be going up and seeing that fellow I spoke of. Heaven send I don't find him with the bottle at his lips, stewed to the eyebrows.'

He need have had no concern. In his room on the third floor Tipton Plimsoll, having finished a strengthening rusk, was washing it down with a glass of milk, exactly as foreshadowed.

From time to time, in between the sips, he looked quickly over his shoulder. Then, seeming reassured, he resumed the lowering of the wholesome fluid.

Chapter 4

To travel from Paddington to Market Blandings takes a fast train about three hours and forty minutes. Prudence Garland, duly bunged into the twelve-forty-two by her mother's butler, reached her destination shortly before five, in nice time for a cup of tea and a good cry.

A prospective bride, torn from her betrothed on her wedding morning, is seldom really lively company, and Prudence provided no exception to this generalization. Tipton Plimsoll, now violently prejudiced against Bill Lister's face, might have wondered why anyone should be fussy about not being allowed to marry a man with such a map, but she could not see it that way. She made no secret of the fact that she viewed the situation with concern, and her deportment from the start would have cast a shadow on a Parisian Four Arts Ball.

It is not surprising, therefore, that Tipton's first impression of the ancient home of the Emsworths, when he arrived an hour or so later in the car with Freddie, should have been one of melancholy. Even though Prudence was absent at the moment, having taken her broken heart out for an airing in the grounds, an atmosphere of doom and gloom still pervaded the premises like the smell of boiling cabbage. Tipton was not acquainted with the writings of Edgar Allan Poe, and so had never heard of the House of Usher, but a more widely read man in his place might well have supposed himself to have crossed the threshold of that rather depressing establishment.

This note of sombreness was particularly manifest in Lord Emsworth. A kind-hearted man, he was always vaguely pained when one of his numerous nieces came to serve her sentence at Blandings for having loved not wisely but too well; and in addition to this almost the first of Prudence's broken utterances, as she toyed with her tea and muffins, had been the announcement that, life being now a blank for her, she proposed to devote herself to the doing of good works.

He knew what that meant. It meant that his study was going to be tidied again. True, all the stricken girl had actually said was that she intended to interest herself in the Infants' Bible Class down in Blandings Parva, but he knew the thing would go deeper than that. From superintending an Infants' Bible Class to becoming a Little Mother and tidying studies is but a step.

His niece Gertrude, while doing her stretch for wanting to marry the curate, had been, he recalled, a very virulent study tidier; and he saw no reason to suppose that Prudence, once she had settled down and hit her stride, would not equal, or even surpass, her cousin's excesses in this direction. For the moment she might slake her thirst for good works with Bible classes, but something told Lord Emsworth that in doing so she would be merely warming up, simply hitting fungoes.

Add to these nameless fears the fact that the sight of his younger son Frederick had had its usual effect on the sensitive peer, and one can understand why, during the committee of welcome's reception of Tipton Plimsoll, he should have sat hunched up in a corner with his head in his hands, shivering a good deal and taking no part in the conversation. One does not say that the perfect host might not have acted differently. All one says is that one can understand.

The despondency of Colonel Wedge and the Lady Hermione, his wife, almost equally pronounced, was due only in part to the miasma cast upon the Blandings scene by Prudence. Their outlook was darkened in addition by another tragedy. On this day of days, just when it was so vital for her to be in midseason form for making an impression on young millionaires, a gnat had bitten their daughter Veronica on the tip of her nose, the resultant swelling depreciating her radiant beauty by between sixty and seventy per cent.

All that Sugg's Soothine, highly recommended by the local chemist, could do was being done; but her parents, like Lord Emsworth, were not at their merriest, and it was not long before Tipton was wondering whether even the elimination from his life of the face would not be too dearly purchased at the cost of an extended sojourn in this medieval morgue. It was with something of the emotions of the beleaguered garrison of Lucknow on hearing the skirl of the Highland pipes that he came at long last out of a sort of despairing coma to the realization that the dressing gong was being beaten, and that for half an hour he would be alone.

This was at seven-thirty. At seven-fifty-five he started to make his way with dragging steps down to the drawing-room. And then, at seven-fifty-seven, the whole aspect of affairs abruptly changed. Gloom vanished, hope dawned, soft music seemed to fill the air, and that air became suddenly languorous with the scent of violets and roses.

'My daughter Veronica,' said a voice, and Tipton Plimsoll stood swaying gently, his eyes bulging behind their horn-rimmed spectacles.

Of Sugg, the man, one knows nothing. He may or may not have been a good man, kind to animals and respected by all who met him. In the absence of data, it is impossible to say. But of Sugg, the curative unguent king, one can speak with assurance. When it came to assembling curative unguent, he was there forty ways from the jack.

As Veronica Wedge stood gazing at Tipton Plimsoll with her enormous eyes, like a cow staring over a hedge at a mangel-wurzel, no one could have guessed that a few brief hours previously the nose beneath those eyes had been of a size and shape that had made her look like W. C. Fields's sister. Sugg had taken it in hand, and with his magic art rendered it once more a thing of perfection. Hats off to Sugg is about what it amounts to.

'My niece Prudence,' continued the voice, speaking now from the centre of a rosy mist to the accompaniment of harps, lutes, and sackbuts.

Tipton had no time for niece Prudence. Briefly noting that this one was a blue-eyed little squirt who appeared to be in the highest spirits, he returned to the scrutiny of Veronica. And the more he scrutinized her, the more she looked to him like something that had been constructed from his own blueprints. Love had come to Tipton Plimsoll, and, he realized, for the first time. What he had mistaken for the divine emotion in the case of Doris Jimpson and perhaps a couple of dozen others had, he now saw, been a mere pale imitation of the real thing, like one of those worthless substitutes against which Sugg so rightly warns the public.

He was still goggling with undiminished intensity when dinner was announced.

2

Too often, in English country houses, dinner is apt to prove a dull and uninspiring meal. If the ruling classes of the island kingdom have a fault, it is that they are inclined when at table to sit champing their food in a glassy-eyed silence, doing nothing to promote a feast of reason and a flow of soul. But tonight in the smaller of Blandings Castle's two dining-rooms a very different note was struck. One would not be going too far in describing the atmosphere at the board as one of rollicking gaiety.

The reactions of the wealthy guest to the charms of their child had not escaped the notice of Colonel Egbert and the Lady Hermione Wedge. Nor had they escaped the notice of the child. The emotions of all three members of the Wedge family may be briefly set down as those of a family which feels that it is batting .400.

As for the others, Prudence, having learned of her loved one's plans in the course of a conversation with Freddie shortly before the dressing gong sounded, was at the peak of her vivacity. Freddie, who always liked meeting the girls he had been engaged to, was delighted to renew his old friendship with Veronica, and spoke to her well and easily of dog biscuits. Lord Emsworth, informed by Prudence that on second thoughts she had changed her mind about doing good works, was as quietly happy as so excellent a man deserved to be. If he took but little part in the merry quips which flashed like lightning across the table, this was not due to any moodiness but simply to the fact that, having managed to elude his sister's vigilance for once, he had been able to bring his pig book in to dinner with him and was reading it under cover of the table.

And of all that gay throng, the gayest was Tipton Plimsoll. Not even his enforced abstinence and the circumstance that as the honoured guest he was seated beside his formidable hostess could check the flow of his spirits. From time to time his eye went swivelling round to where Veronica sat, and each time the sight of her seemed to tap in him a new vein of brilliance.

It was he who led the liveliest sallies. It was he who told the raciest anecdotes. It was he who, in between the soup and fish courses, entertained the company with a diverting balancing trick with a fork and a wineglass. For a time, in short, he was the spirit of Mirth incarnate.

For a time, one says. To be specific, up to the moment of the serving of the entrée. For it was just then that the figures in the tapestries on the walls noted that a strange silence had fallen upon the young master of the revels and that he refused the entrée in a manner that can only be described as Byronic. Something, it was clear, had suddenly gone amiss with Tipton Plimsoll.

The fact was that, taking another of his rapt looks at Veronica, he had been stunned to observe her slap Freddie roguishly on the wrist, at the same time telling him not to be so silly, and the spectacle had got right in among his vital organs and twisted them into a spiral.

For some time he had been aware that these two had seemed to be getting along pretty darned well together, but, struggling to preserve the open mind, he had told himself that a certain chumminess between cousins had always to be budgeted for. This wrist-slapping sequence, however, was another matter. It seemed to him to go far beyond mere cousinly good will. He was a man of strong passions, and the green-eyed monster ran up his leg and bit him to the bone.

'No, thank you,' he said coldly to the footman who was trying to interest him in chicken livers and pastry.

And yet, had he but known it, in what had caused Veronica to slap Freddie on the wrist there had been nothing to bring the blush of shame to the cheek of modesty. All that had happened was that Freddie had told her in a confidential undertone that a Donaldson's dog biscuit was so superbly wholesome as to be actually fit for human consumption. Upon which, as a girl of her mentality might have been expected to do, she had slapped him playfully on the wrist and told him not to be so silly.

But Tipton, not being in possession of the facts, writhed from stem to stern and relapsed into a dark silence. And this so concerned Lady Hermione that she sought for first causes. Following his sidelong glances, she understood the position of affairs, and registered a resolve to have a heart-to-heart talk with Freddie at the conclusion of the meal. She also promised herself a word with her daughter.

The latter of these two tasks she was able to perform when the female members of the party rose and left the men to their port. And so well did she perform it that the first thing Tipton beheld on entering the drawing-room was Veronica Wedge advancing towards him, a fleecy wrap about her lovely shoulders.

'Mummie says would you like to see the garden by moonlight,' she said, in her direct way.

A moment before Tipton had been feeling that life was a hollow thing, for on top of the spectacle of this girl slapping the wrists of other men there had come the agony of watching his host, his host's son, and his host's brother-in-law lowering port by the pailful while he was forced to remain aloof from the revels. But at these words that soft music started to play again, and once more the air seemed redolent of violets and roses. As for the pink mist, he could hardly see through it.

He snorted ecstatically: 'Would I!'

'Would you?'

'I'll say I would.'

'Darned chilly,' said Freddie judicially. 'You wouldn't catch me going into any bally gardens. Stay snugly indoors is my advice. How about a game of backgammon, Vee?'

Breeding tells. Lady Hermione Wedge might look like a cook, but there ran in her veins the blood of a hundred earls. She overcame the sudden, quick desire to strike her nephew over his fat head with the nearest blunt instrument.

'It is not in the least chilly,' she said. 'It is a lovely summer night. You will not even need a hat, Mr Plimsoll.'

'Not a single, solitary suspicion of a hat,' assented Tipton with enthusiasm. 'Let's go!'

He passed with his fair companion through the french window, and Lady Hermione turned to Freddie.

'Freddie,' she said.

Her manner was grim and purposeful, the manner of an aunt who rolls up her sleeves and spits on her hands and prepares to give a nephew the works.

*

At about the same moment, down at the Emsworth Arms in Market Blandings, Bill Lister, comfortably relaxed after a square meal in the coffee room, was reclining in a deck chair in the inn's back garden, gazing at the moon and thinking of Prudence.

It had just occurred to him that on a night like this it would be a sound move to walk the two miles to the castle and gaze up at her window.

3

In dealing with the first romantic stroll together of Tipton Plimsoll and Veronica Wedge, the chronicler finds himself faced by the same necessity for pause and reflection which confronted him when he had the opportunity of describing the reunion between Freddie Threepwood and Bill Lister. It would be possible for him to record their conversation verbatim, but it is to be doubted whether this would interest, elevate, and instruct the discriminating public for whom he is writing. It is wiser, therefore, merely to give briefly the general idea.

Tipton started off well enough by saying that the garden looked pretty in the moonlight, and Veronica said, 'Yes, doesn't it?' He followed this up with the remark that gardens always look kind of prettier when there is a moon – sort of – than when, as it were, there isn't a moon, and Veronica said, 'Yes, don't they?' So far, the exchanges would not have disgraced a *salon* such as that of Madame Récamier. But at this point Tipton ran suddenly dry of inspiration, and a prolonged silence followed.

The fact was that Tipton Plimsoll was one of those young men who while capable, when well primed, of setting on a roar a table composed of males of their own age and mental outlook for whose refreshment they are paying, tend to lose their grip when alone with girls. And in the case of the girl with whom he was now marooned on the moonlit terrace, this was particularly so. His great love, her overwhelming beauty, and the fact that at dinner he had drunk nothing but barley water combined to render him ill at ease.

Some little while later Veronica, starting the conversational ball rolling once more, said that she had been bitten on the nose that afternoon by a gnat. Tipton, shuddering at this, said that he had never liked gnats. Veronica said that she, too, did not like gnats, but that they were better than bats. Yes, assented Tipton, oh, sure, yes, a good deal better than bats. Of cats Veronica said she was fond, and Tipton agreed that cats as a class were swell. On the subject of rats they were also at one, both holding strong views regarding their lack of charm.

The ice thus broken, the talk flowed pretty easily until Veronica said that perhaps they had better be going in now. Tipton said, 'Oh, shoot!' and Veronica said, 'I think we'd better,' and Tipton said, 'Well, okay, if we must.' His heart was racing and bounding as he accompanied her to the drawing-room. If there had ever been any doubt in his mind that this girl and he were twin souls, it no longer existed. It seemed to him absolutely amazing that two people should think so alike on everything – on gnats, bats, cats, rats, in fact absolutely everything. And, as for that episode at dinner, he was now prepared to condone that. True, she had certainly appeared to slosh Freddie roguishly on the wrist, but that could be explained away on the supposition that her hand had slipped.

His elation persisted all through the long, quiet home evening, causing him to feel right up to bedtime as he generally felt only when about half-way through the second quart. So much so, indeed, that when the ten-thirty tray of whisky and its accessories was brought in, he took his barley water without a qualm. It surprised him a little that Freddie and Colonel Wedge should feel the need of anything stronger.

At eleven o'clock Lady Hermione headed a general exodus, and at eleven-ten Tipton was in his room on the second floor, gazing out at the moonlight and still in the grip of that strange, febrile excitement which comes to young men who have recently for the first time encountered a twin soul of the opposite sex.

It seemed to him absurd to think of going to bed when he was feeling like this. He gazed out at the moonlight, and it seemed to beckon to him.

Five minutes later he was unfastening the french window of the drawing-room and stepping out on to the terrace.

As he did so, a voice said, 'Bless my soul!' and he perceived Lord Emsworth at his elbow.

4

In moments of emotion Lord Emsworth's pince-nez always sprang from their base, dancing sportively at the end of their string. The sight of a stealthy figure emerging from the window of the drawing-room caused them to do so now, for he took it for granted that it must be that of a burglar. Then he reflected that burglars do not come out, they go in, and it was in a calmer frame of mind that he reached for the dangling glasses, hauled in the slack, and replaced them on his nose.

He then saw that the other was no midnight marauder, but merely his guest Popkins or Perkins or Wilbraham – the exact name had escaped his memory.

'Ah, Mr Er,' he said genially.

As a rule, the *seigneur* of Blandings Castle was not very fond of the society of his juniors. In fact, the only time he ever moved with any real rapidity and nimbleness was when endeavouring to avoid them. But tonight he was feeling a kindly benevolence towards the whole human species.

To this Prudence's change of heart had, of course, contributed, but it was principally owing to the fact that in the course of the conversation over the port his son Frederick had mentioned that this time he would not, as had always happened before, be sticking to Blandings Castle like a limpet on a rock, but rather using it simply as a base for operations in the neighbourhood. Shropshire and its adjoining counties are peculiarly rich in landowners with well-stocked kennels, and it was Freddie's intention to pay flying visits to these, sometimes staying the night, sometimes inflicting himself on his unfortunate prey for days at a time.

No father could help but be uplifted by such news, and Lord Emsworth's manner, as he proceeded, was very cordial and winning.

'Going out for a little walk, Mr Ah?' he said.

Tipton said that he was, adding in rather a defensive way that it was such a swell night.

'Beautiful,' agreed Lord Emsworth, and then, for he was a man who always liked to make his meaning quite clear, added, 'Beautiful, beautiful, beautiful, beautiful. There is a moon,' he went on, directing his young friend's attention to this added attraction with a wave of the hand.

Tipton said he had noticed the moon.

'Bright,' said Lord Emsworth.

'Very bright,' said Tipton.

'Very bright, indeed,' said Lord Emsworth. 'Oh, extremely bright. Are you', he asked, changing the subject, 'interested in pigs, Mr Er – Ah – Umph?'.

'Plimsoll,' said Tipton.

'Pigs,' said Lord Emsworth, raising his voice a little and enunciating the word more distinctly.

Plimsoll explained that what he had been intending to convey was that his name was Plimsoll.

'Oh, is it?' said Lord Emsworth, and paused awhile in thought. He had a vague recollection that someone had once told him to do something – what, he could not at the moment recall – about someone of that name. 'Well, as I was about to say, I am just going down to the sty to listen to my pig.'

'Oh, yes?'

'Her name is Plimsoll.'

'Is that so?' said Tipton, surprised at this coincidence.

'I mean Empress of Blandings. She has won the silver medal in the Fat Pigs class at the Shropshire Agricultural Show twice –'

'Gee!'

'– in successive years.'

'Gosh!'

'A thing no pig has ever done before.'

'Well, I'll be darned.'

'Yes, it was an astounding feat. She is very fat.'

'She must be fat.'

'She is. Extraordinarily fat.'

'Yessir, I'll bet she's fat,' said Tipton, groaning in spirit. No lover, who has come out to walk in the moonlight and dream of the girl he adores, likes to find himself sidetracked on to the subject of pigs, however obese. 'Well, I mustn't keep you. You want to see your pig.'

'I thought you would,' said Lord Emsworth. 'We go down this path.'

He grasped Tipton's arm, but there was really no necessity for thus taking him into custody. Tipton had resigned himself to going quietly. He had had no experience in the difficult art of shaking off adhesive peers, and it was too late to start learning now. Merely registering a silent wish that his companion would trip over a moonbeam and break his neck, he accompanied him without resistance.

As usual at this hour, the Empress had retired for the night. It was only possible at the moment, accordingly, for Lord Emsworth to give his guest a mere word-picture of her charms. But he held out the promise of better things to come.

'I will take you to see her tomorrow morning,' he said. 'Or, rather, in the afternoon, for I shall be busy in the morning arranging matters with this artist of Galahad's. My son Freddie,' he explained, 'tells me that my brother Galahad is sending down an artist to paint the Empress's portrait. It is an idea I have long had in mind. I wrote to my sister Dora, asking her to find me an artist, but she answered very rudely, telling me not to be absurd, and my sister Hermione was also opposed to the project. They seemed to dislike the idea of a pig appearing in the family portrait gallery. That was Hermione you sat next to at dinner. The girl sitting next to Freddie was her daughter Veronica.'

For the first time Tipton began to feel that something might be saved from the wreck of his moonlight walk.

'I thought she was very charming,' he said, limbering himself up for a good long talk on his favourite topic.

'Charming?' said Lord Emsworth, surprised, 'Hermione?'

'Miss Wedge.'

'I don't think I know her,' said Lord Emsworth. 'But I was speaking of my niece Veronica. A nice girl, with many good qualities.'

'Ah!' breathed Tipton reverently.

'She has an excellent heart, and seems fond of pigs. I saw her once go out of her way to pick up and drop back into the sty a potato which the Empress had nosed beneath the bars. I was very pleased. Not every girl would have been so considerate.'

Tipton was so overcome by this evidence of the pure-white soul of the goddess he worshipped that for a moment he was incapable of speech. Then he said 'Gosh!'

'My son Freddie, I remember, who was present – '

Lord Emsworth broke off abruptly. This third mention of his younger son had had the effect of stirring his memory. Something seemed to be coming to the surface.

Ah, yes. He had it now. His bedroom . . . Egbert bursting in . . . himself jotting down that memorandum in his pig book.

'Freddie, yes,' he went on. 'Of course, yes, Freddie. I knew there was something I wanted to tell you about him. He and Veronica were once engaged to be married.'

'What!'

'Yes. It was broken off – why, I cannot at the moment recall – possibly it was because Freddie married somebody else – but they are still devoted to each other. They always were, even as children. My wife, I recollect, used to speak of Veronica as Freddie's little sweetheart. My wife was alive at that time,' explained Lord Emsworth, careful to make it clear this was no question of a voice from the tomb.

Although any possible misunderstanding had thus been avoided, Tipton's brow remained drawn and furrowed. Spiritually, he was gasping for air. At a boisterous reunion in a speakeasy someone had once hit him on the bridge of the nose with an order of planked steak. As he had felt then, so did he feel now. The same sensation of standing insecurely in a tottering and disintegrating universe.

Many lovers in his position might have consoled themselves with the reflection that Freddie, being now a married man, was presumably out of the race for Veronica Wedge's hand and heart. But Tipton had had the wrong sort of upbringing to permit of his drawing comfort from any thought like that. The son of parents who after marrying each other had almost immediately started marrying other people with a perseverance worthy of a better cause, his had been one of those childhoods where the faintly bewildered offspring finds himself passed from hand to hand like a medicine ball. And, grown to riper years, he had seen among his friends and acquaintances far too much of that Ex-Wife's Heart Balm Society Love Tangle stuff to be a believer in the durability of the married state.

That very Doris Jimpson, of whom he had once supposed himself enamoured, had become Doris Boole, Doris Busbridge, and

Doris Applejohn in such rapid succession that the quickness of the hand almost deceived the eye.

So the fact that Veronica's little sweetheart was now a married man by no means seemed to Tipton to render him automatically a non-starter. Freddie, he assumed, having wearied of Mrs Freddie, had sent her off to Paris to secure one of the divorces which that city supplies with such a lavish hand; and now, giving himself a preliminary shake preparatory to starting all over again, he was about to make a pass at his old love. That low-voiced remark of his at dinner, which had caused the girl to slap his wrist and tell him not to be silly, had, of course, been something in the nature of a sighting shot.

That was how Tipton summed up the situation, and while the moon did not actually go out with a pop, like a stage moon when some hitch occurs in the lighting effects, it seemed to him to have done so.

'I guess I'll be turning in,' he said hollowly. 'Getting kind of late.'

As he made his way back to the drawing-room, one coherent thought held sway in his seething mind; and that was that, faces or no faces, he had got to have a bracer. He was convinced that even E. J. Murgatroyd, had the facts been placed before him, would have patted him on the shoulder and bidden him go to it. He would never, Murgatroyd would reason, were he standing beside him now, need a drop of the right stuff more than at this shattering moment; and, after all, the clear-thinking medico would go on to point out, since two o'clock that afternoon he had been leading a quiet regular life, thus reducing risk to a minimum.

The decanter was still on the drawing-room table, fully half of its precious contents intact. To seize it and take a long, invigorating snort was with Tipton the work of an instant. Then, as a prudent man's will, his thoughts turned to the future. Owing to those insane instructions which he had given Freddie, that only non-alcoholic beverages should be served to him while at the castle, this, unless he took steps, was the last life-saver he would get till he returned to civilization. A prospect at which imagination boggled.

Swift action was required, and he acted swiftly. Hastening to his room, he found the large flask without which he never travelled, and which he had brought along this time partly from habit and partly out of sentiment. He took it down to the drawing-room and filled it. Then, feeling that he had done all that man could do to make the future safe, he returned to his bedchamber.

Probably owing to his prompt measures, the moon had now begun to shine again, and Tipton, leaning on the window sill looking down over the meadows and spinneys which it illuminated so tastefully, was sufficiently himself once more to regard its activities with approval. The fact that he was sharing the same planet with Freddie still aggrieved him, but he no longer feared the other as a rival. That gargle from the decanter had made him feel capable of cutting out a dozen Freddies, and it now occurred to him that a gargle from the flask might help the good work along still further.

He took one, accordingly, and was about to take another, when he suddenly checked the progress of his hand towards his lips and leaned forward, peering. A moving something on the lawn below had caught his eye.

It seemed to be a human figure.

It was a human figure – that of Bill Lister, who had carried out his intention of walking to the castle and gazing up at Prudence's window. The fact that he had no means of knowing which of these many windows was hers in no way deterred him. He was planning to gaze up at them all and so make sure. And, as a matter of fact, he had made an extraordinarily accurate shot. Her room was next door to Tipton's, the one with the balcony.

He had been gazing up at it a moment before, and he now moved along and gazed up at Tipton's. And as the moonlight fell full on his face, Tipton shot backwards into the room, groped for the bed, and sank bonelessly upon it.

It was some minutes before he could nerve himself to return to the window and take another look. When he did so, the face was no longer there. Having appeared and leered, it had vanished. This, he now realized, was its set routine. He went back to the bed and sat down again, his chin on his hand, motionless. He looked like Rodin's *Penseur*.

Some little while later, Lord Emsworth, pottering upstairs to his bedroom, was aware of a long, thin form confronting him on the landing. A ghost, was his first impression, though he would have expected a White Lady or a man in armour with his head under his arm rather than a string-beanlike young man wearing horn-rimmed spectacles. Then, as had happened before, a little intensive blinking enabled him to identify the agreeable young fellow who had been so interested in pigs, his guest Mr Er or Mr Ah or possibly Mr Umph.

'Say,' said the apparition, speaking in a low, emotional voice, 'would you do me a favour?'

'You would like to listen to my pig again? It is a little late, but if you really –'

'Look,' said Tipton. 'Will you take this flask and put it away somewhere?'

'Flask? Flask? Flask? Eh? What? Put it away somewhere? Certainly, my dear fellow, certainly, certainly, certainly,' said Lord Emsworth, for such a task was well within his scope.

'Thanks,' said Tipton. 'Good night.'

'Eh? Oh, good night? Yes indeed,' said Lord Emsworth. 'Oh, quite, quite, quite.'

Chapter 5

The Emsworth Arms, that old-world hostelry at which Bill Lister had established himself with his paints, brushes, canvas, easel, palette knives, and what not, stands in the picturesque High Street of the little town of Market Blandings; and towards the quiet evenfall of the third day after his arrival there a solitary two-seater might have been observed dashing up to its front entrance. The brakes squealed, a cat saved its life by a split second, the car stopped, and Freddie Threepwood alighted. Having given a couple of nights to the Cheshire Brackenburys, he was on his way to stay with the equally deserving Worcestershire Fanshawe-Chadwicks.

His visit to Cogwych Hall, Cogwych-in-the-Marsh, Cheshire, the seat of Sir Rupert Brackenbury, MFH, had left Freddie in a mood of effervescent elation. He had gone there with the intention of talking Sir Rupert into playing ball, and he had done so. His subtle sales talks had made this MFH a devout convert to Donaldson's Dog-Joy. And when you bore in mind the fact that the initials MFH stand for Master of Fox Hounds, you could see what that meant.

Chaps from neighbouring counties would come to hunt with the Cogwych pack and be stunned by the glowing health of its personnel. 'Egad, Sir Rupert,' they would say, 'those hounds of yours look dashed fit.' To which Sir Rupert would reply, 'And no wonder, considering that they are tucking into Donaldson's Dog-Joy all the time, a bone-forming product peculiarly rich in Vitamins A, B, and C.' 'Donaldson's Dog-Joy, eh?' the chaps would say, and they would make a note to lay in a stock for their own four-leggers. And in due season other chaps would call on these chaps and say, 'Egad . . .' Well, you could see how the thing would spread. Like a forest fire.

As he passed through the portal of the Emsworth Arms, he was whistling cheerily. Not the slightest presentiment came to him that he would find the affairs of Bill Lister in anything but apple-pie order. By this time the foundations of a beautiful friendship between Blister and the guv'nor should have been securely laid. 'Call me Uncle Clarence,' he could hear the guv'nor saying.

It was accordingly with a crushing bolt-from-the-blueness that the information which he received at the reception desk descended upon him. He had to clutch at a passing knives-and-boots boy to support himself.

'Leaving?'

'Yes, sir.'

'*Leaving?*' repeated Freddie incredulously. 'But, dash it, he's only just come. He was supposed to be here for weeks. Are you sure?'

'Oh, yes, sir. The gentleman has paid his bill, and the cab is ordered for the six-o'clock train for London.'

'Is he in his room?'

'No, sir. The gentleman went for a walk.'

Freddie released the knives-and-boots boy, who thanked him and passed on. With pursed lips and drawn brows he returned to the two-seater. He was deeply concerned. Unless all the signs deceived him, something had gone seriously wrong with the works, and it was imperative, he felt, that he look into the matter without delay.

A promising line of inquiry occurred to him almost immediately, for the young men of Donaldson's Inc. are trained to think like lightning and it is seldom that they are baffled for more than about a minute and a quarter. If anyone could cast a light on this mystery, it would be his cousin Prudence. She surely must be an authoritative source. A man who has sweated four hours by train to a one-horse town in the country simply in order to be near the girl he loves does not, he reasoned, suddenly leg it back to where he started without a word of explanation to her.

A few moments later he was speeding on his way to the castle. No one could have been more acutely alive than he to the fact that this was going to be a nasty jar for the Worcestershire Fanshawe-Chadwicks, who would not get him quite so soon as they had expected, but that could not be helped. Into each life some rain must fall, and the Fanshawe-Chadwicks would have to stiffen the upper lip and stick it like men. As Bill's patron and backer, duty called him to proceed to the fountain-head and obtain the low-down from the horse's mouth.

The two-seater was a car which could do seventy-five at the height of its fever, and he reached the castle gates in record time. But turning through them into the drive he slackened his speed. He had observed ahead of him a familiar figure.

He put a finger on the tooter and tooted a toot or two.

'What ho, Tippy!' he called. He was in a hurry, but one cannot pass an old buddy by with a mere wave of the hand after being away from him for two days.

Tipton Plimsoll stopped, looked over his shoulder, and seeing who it was that had spoken frowned darkly. For some little while he had been pacing the drive, deep in his thoughts. And among the thoughts he had been deep in had been several particularly hard ones relating to this tooting ex-friend.

Ex, one says, for where he had once beheld in Frederick Threepwood a congenial crony and a side-kick with whom it had been a pleasure to flit from high spot to high spot, he now saw only a rival in love, and a sinister, crafty, horn-swoggling rival at that, one who could be classified without hesitation as a snake. At least, if you couldn't pigeon-hole among the snakes bimbos who went about the place making passes at innocent girls after discarding their wives like old tubes of toothpaste, Tipton was at a loss to know into what category they did fall.

'Guk,' he said reservedly. A man has to answer snakes when they speak to him, but he is under no obligation to be sunny.

His gloom did not pass unnoticed. It could scarcely have done so except at a funeral. But Freddie, placing an erroneous interpretation upon it, was pleased rather than wounded. In a man who suddenly abstains from the alcoholic beverages which were once his principal form of nourishment a certain moodiness is to be expected, and all that this Hamlet-like despondency suggested to him was that his former playmate was still on the wagon, and he honoured him for it. His only comment on the other's bleakness of front was to lower his voice sympathetically, as he would have done at some stricken bedside.

'Seen Prue anywhere?' he asked, in a hushed whisper.

Tipton frowned.

'You got a sore throat?' he inquired with some asperity.

'Eh? No, Tippy, no sore throat.'

'Then why the hell are you talking like a suffocating mosquito? What did you say?'

'I asked if you had seen Prue anywhere.'

'Prue?' Tipton's frown deepened. 'Oh, you mean the squirt?'

'I don't know that I would call her a squirt, Tippy.'

'She looks like a squirt to me,' said Tipton firmly. 'Ruddy little midget.'

'She isn't a tall girl,' Freddie conceded pacifically. 'Never has been. Some girls are, of course, and some aren't. You've got to face it. Still, putting all that on one side for the nonce, do you know where I can find her?'

'You can't find her. She's gone with your aunt to call on some people named Brimble.'

Freddie clicked his tongue. He knew what these afternoon calls in the country were. By the time you had had tea and been shown round the garden and told how wonderful it had looked a month ago and come back to the house and glanced through the photograph album, it was getting on for the dinner hour. Useless, therefore, to wait for Prudence. Apart from anything else, there is a limit to the agony of suspense which you can inflict on Worcestershire Fanshawe-Chadwicks. You don't want to get the poor devils feeling like Mariana at the moated grange.

He performed complicated backing and filling manoeuvres with the car. As he got its nose pointed down the drive, the idea struck him that Prudence might have confided in her cousin Veronica.

'Where's Vee?' he asked.

A quick tremor passed through Tipton Plimsoll. He had been expecting this. All that eyewash about wanting to see the squirt Prudence had not deceived him for an instant. The coldness of his manner became intensified.

'She went too. Why?'

'I just wanted a word with her.'

'What about?'

'Nothing important.'

'I could give her a message.'

'Oh, no, that's all right.'

There followed a silence, and it was unfortunate that during it Freddie should suddenly have recalled the powerful harangue which his aunt Hermione had delivered in the drawing-room after dinner on the night of his arrival. He saw now that he had come near to missing an opportunity of speaking the word in season.

In disembowelling her nephew on the occasion referred to, Lady Hermione Wedge had made it abundantly clear to him that the idea of a union between Tipton Plimsoll and her daughter was one that was very near her heart. And Freddie, considering the thing, had also been decidedly in favour of it. It would, he had perceived, fit in admirably with his plans if the man who owned the controlling interest in Tipton's Stores should marry a wife who could be relied on to use her influence to promote the interests of Donaldson's dog biscuits. And he knew that good old Vee, who had practically written the words and music of *Auld Lang Syne*, could be trusted to do her bit. Wondering how he could have been so remiss as not to have strained every nerve to push this good thing along earlier, he now addressed himself to repairing his negligence, beginning by observing that Veronica, in his opinion, was a ripper and a corker and a topper and didn't Tipton agree with him?

To this, looking like Othello and speaking like a trapped wolf, Tipton replied: 'Yup.'

'Dashed attractive, what?'

'Yup.'

'Her profile. Lovely, don't you think?'

'Yup.'

'And her eyes. Super-colossal. And such a sweet girl, too. I mean as regards character and disposition and soul and all that sort of thing.'

A man trained over a considerable period of time to become lyrical about dog biscuits at the drop of the hat never finds any difficulty in reaching heights of eloquence on the subject of a beautiful girl. For some minutes Freddie continued to speak with an enthusiasm and choice of phrase which would have excited the envy of a court poet. There was deep feeling behind his every word, and it was not long before Tipton was writhing like an Ouled Nail stomach dancer. He had known, of course, that this human snake was that way about the girl he worshipped, but he had not suspected that the thing had gone so far.

'Well,' said Freddie, pausing at length, 'I must be getting along. I shall be back in a few days.'

'Oh?' said Tipton.

'Yes,' Freddie assured him. 'Not more than two or three at the outside.'

And having delivered these words of cheer, he trod on the self-starter and put the two-seater into first. It seemed to him, as he did so, that the gears were a bit noisy. But it was only Tipton Plimsoll grinding his teeth.

2

Better news awaited Freddie on his return to the Emsworth Arms. Bill Lister had come in from his walk and was up in his room, packing. Taking the stairs three at a time, he burst in without formality.

Although at the moment of his entry all that was visible of his friend was the seat of his trousers as he bent over a suitcase, Freddie, though not a particularly close observer, had no difficulty in discerning that he stood in the presence of a man into whose life tragedy has stalked. The face which now looked up into his was one which harmonized perfectly with the trouser seat. It was the face, as the trouser seat had been the trouser seat, of a tortured soul.

'Blister!' he cried.

'Hullo, Freddie. You back?'

'Just passing through, merely passing through. What's all this about your leaving, Blister?'

'I am leaving.'

'I know you're leaving. They told me downstairs. The point – follow me closely here – is why are you leaving?'

Bill placed an undervest in the suitcase like a man laying a wreath on the grave of an old friend and straightened himself wearily. He looked like a gorilla which has bitten into a bad coconut.

'I've got the push,' he said.

Deeply concerned, Freddie was nevertheless not particularly surprised. The possibility, even the probability, of something like this happening if he went away and ceased to keep the other's affairs under his personal eye had always been in his mind.

'I feared this, Blister,' he said gravely. 'I should have remained at your side to counsel and advise. What came unstuck? Didn't the guv'nor like the portrait?'

'No.'

'But surely you haven't finished it already?'

A flicker of life came into Bill's set face. He packed a pair of pyjamas with something approaching spirit.

'Of course I haven't. That's just what I tried to make him understand. So far it's the merest sketch. I kept telling the old blighter . . . Sorry.'

'Not at all. I know whom you mean.'

'I kept telling him that a portrait of a pig must be judged as a whole. But the more I tried to make him see it, the more he kept giving me the push.'

'Have you got it here?'

'It's on the bed.'

'Let's have a – My God, Blister!'

Freddie, hastening to the bed and gazing down at the canvas which lay upon it, had started back like one who sees some dreadful sight. He was now replacing his monocle in his eye, preparatory to trying again, and Bill looked at him dully.

'You notice something wrong too?'

'Wrong? My dear old bird!'

'Don't forget it's not finished.'

Freddie shook his head.

'It's no good taking that line, Blister. Thank heaven it isn't. One wouldn't want a thing like that to spread any further. What on earth made you depict this porker as tight?'

'Tight?'

'The pig I see here is a pig that has obviously been on the toot of a lifetime for days on end. Those glassy eyes. That weak smile. I've seen old Tippy look just like that. I'll tell you what it reminds me of. One of those comic pigs you see in Christmas numbers.'

Bill was shaken. The artistic temperament can stand only just so much destructive criticism. He, too, approached the bed and examining his handiwork was compelled to recognize a certain crude justice in the other's words. He had not noticed it before, but in the Empress's mild face, as it leered from the canvas, there was a

74

distinct suggestion of inebriation. Her whole aspect was that of a
pig which had been seeing the new year in.

'That's odd,' he said, frowning thoughtfully.

'Worse than odd,' corrected Freddie. 'I don't wonder the guv'nor
was stirred to his depths.'

'I think where I must have gone wrong,' said Bill, stepping back
and closing one eye, 'was in trying to get some animation into her
face. You've no notion, Freddie, how disheartening it is for an
artist to come up against a sitter like that. She just lay on her side
with her eyes shut and bits of potato dribbling out of the corner of
her mouth. Velasquez would have been baffled. It seemed to me
that I had somehow got to create a bit of sparkle, so I prodded her
with a stick and shoved the result down like lightning before she
could go to sleep again. But I see what you mean. The expression
isn't right.'

'Nor the shape. You've made her oblong.'

'Oh, that's nothing. I should probably have altered that. I have
been experimenting in the cubist form lately, and I just tried it as an
idea. Purely tentative.'

Freddie looked at his watch, and was shocked at the position of
the hands. Already the wretched Fanshawe-Chadwicks must be
suffering agonies, which would inevitably become more and more
severe. But he could not leave matters as they stood. He sighed and
forced the picture of the Fanshawe-Chadwicks from his mind.

'Tell me exactly what took place, Blister. Up to a certain point, of
course, I can visualize the scene. You at your easel, plying the brush; the
guv'nor toddling up, adjusting his pince-nez. He stands behind you.
He peers over your shoulder. He starts back with a hoarse cry. What
then? Was what he proceeded to dish out undisguisedly the raspberry?'

'Yes.'

'No avenue was left open that might have led to a peaceful settlement?'

'No.'

'It would be no use your offering to rub it out and try again?'

'No. You see, I'm afraid I lost my temper a bit. I forget what I
said exactly, but it was to the effect that if I had known he wanted
the pretty-pretty, chocolate-box sort of thing, I would never have
accepted the commission. That and something about stifling the

freedom of expression of the artist. Oh, yes, and I told him to go and boil his head.'

'You did? H'm,' said Freddie. 'Ha. 'Myes. Um. This isn't too good, Blister.'

'No.'

'Prue may be upset.'

Bill shuddered.

'She is.'

'You've seen her, then?'

Bill shuddered again.

'Yes,' he said, in a low voice. 'I've seen her. She was with your father, and she stayed on after he left.'

'What was her attitude?'

'She was furious, and broke off the engagement.'

'You astound me, Blister. You couldn't have understood her.'

'I don't think so. She said she never wanted to see me again, and was going to devote herself to good works.'

'To which you replied – ?'

'I hadn't time to reply. She streaked off like an electric hare, laughing hysterically.'

'She did, did she? Laughed hysterically, eh? The unbridled little cheese mite. I sometimes think that child is *non compos*.'

A look of menace came into Bill's strained face.

'Do you want your head bashed in?' he asked.

'No,' said Freddie, having considered the question. 'No, I don't think so. Why?'

'Then don't call Prue a cheese mite.'

'Don't you like me calling her a cheese mite?'

'No.'

'This would almost seem as if love still lingered.'

'Of course it lingers.'

'I should have thought you would have considered yourself well rid of a girl who hands you the mitten just because you failed to make a solid success of painting the portrait of a pig – an enterprise fraught, as you yourself have shown, with many difficulties.'

Bill quivered irritably.

'It wasn't that at all.'

'Then your story has misled me.'

'The real trouble was that she asked me to give up painting, and I wouldn't.'

'Oh, I see. You mean that pub business.'

'You know about that?'

'She told me that morning I met her in Grosvenor Square. She said you had inherited the Mulberry Tree, and she wanted you to run it as a going concern.'

'That's right. We've been arguing about it for weeks.'

'I must say I agree with her that you ought to have a pop at it. There's gold in them thar hills, Blister. You might clean up big as a jolly innkeeper. And as for giving up your art – well, why not? It's obviously lousy.'

'I feel that, now that I've had time to think it over. Seeing her leg it like that sort of opened my eyes. Have you ever seen the girl you love sprinting away from you having hysterics?'

'No, now you mention it, I can't say I have. I've known Aggie to throw her weight about on occasion, but always in a fairly static manner. Unpleasant, I should imagine.'

'It does something to you, Freddie. It makes you realize that you've been a brute and a cad and a swine.'

'I see what you mean. Remorse.'

'I'm ready now to do anything she wants. If she feels that I ought to give up painting, I'll never touch a brush again.'

'Well, that's fine.'

'I'm going to write and tell her so.'

'And have Aunt Hermione intercept the letter?'

'I never thought of that. Would she?'

'Unquestionably. When the younger female members of the family are sent up the river to Blandings, their correspondence is always closely watched.'

'You could slip her a note.'

'No, I couldn't. I told you I was merely passing through. I'll tell you what I will do, though. I'll nip up to the penitentiary now, and if Prue's got back, I'll place the facts before her. Wait here. I shan't be long. At least, I hope I shan't,' said Freddie, his mind sliding back to that painful vision of the Worcestershire Fanshawe-Chadwicks with their noses pressed against the windowpane and their haggard eyes staring yearningly out at an empty drive.

3

It was not so very long before Freddie once again presented himself in Bill's room, the latter's estimate of his absence at an hour and a half being erroneous and due to strained nerves. In response to his friend's passionate complaint that there had been no need for him to stop by the roadside and make daisy chains, he waved a soothing hand.

'I've been as quick as was humanly possible, Blister,' he assured him. 'If I am late, it is merely because I was working in your interests. There were one or two little tasks I had to perform before I could return.'

'Is everything all right?'

'If you mean did I see Prue and square you with her, the answer is no. She hadn't got back from calling on some people she was calling on. The Brimbles, if you want to keep the record straight. They live out Shrewsbury way. Extraordinary, this rural practice of driving miles on a hot day to pay calls. You spend hours dressing in your most uncomfortable clothes, you tool across the countryside under a blazing sun, you eventually win through to Shrewsbury, and when you do, what have you got! The Brimbles. However,' proceeded Freddie, observing in his audience signs of impatience, 'you will want to know what steps I have taken, Prue being unavoidably absent. But before I slip you the lowdown, let me first get this thing straight. You really desire this reconciliation? I mean, in order to achieve it, you are prepared to creep, to crawl, to yield on every point?'

'Yes.'

'Realizing – I merely mention it in passing – that this will be a hell of a start for your married life, if and when, reducing your chances of ever being the dominant partner practically to zero?'

'Yes.'

'I wouldn't be too hasty about it, Blister. I know young Prue better than you do. She's like all these cheese – these small girls – bossy. Give her a thingummy, and she'll take a what's-its-name. The reason I've always found her civil and respectful is that I've never relaxed the iron hand. Small girls are like female Pekinese. Have you ever seen a man in the thrall of a female Pekinese? Can't call his soul his own. He –'

'Get on,' said Bill. 'Get on, get on, get on, get on!'

'Right,' said Freddie. 'Well, if that's the way you feel, we can proceed to the agenda. The first thing I did on reaching the hoosegow and discovering that Prue was not in her cell was to put in a trunk call to Uncle Gally.'

'To Gally?'

'None other. I knew that if anyone could spear an idea out of the void, it would be he. Nor was I mistaken. Within two minutes of hearing the facts, assisted only by a single whisky and soda while I held the line, he came across with a pippin.'

'God bless him!'

'And so say all of us. Did he ever tell you that he got my cousin, Ronnie Fish, married to a chorus girl in the teeth of the united opposition of a bristling phalanx of aunts?'

'No, did he?'

'He did indeed. There are practically no limits to the powers of this wonder man. You're lucky to have him in your corner.'

'I know I am. What was his idea?'

'It was a pippin,' repeated Freddie, rolling the word round his tongue. 'I wonder if you have ever reflected, Blister, that an employer of labour on an extensive scale, like my guv'nor, never really knows how many human souls he's got on the pay-roll. Take gardeners, for example. He is aware that the honest fellows abound on his property, but he doesn't know half of them from Adam. If he's strolling around of a morning and sees one leaning on a spade, he doesn't say to himself, "Ah, there's good old George sweating himself to the bone," or old Joe or old Percy, or Peter or Thomas or Cyril, as the case may be. He just says, "Oh, what ho, a gardener," and passes by with a wave of the hand and a careless, "Okay, gardener, carry on." And so –'

For some moments Bill had been clenching and unclenching his hands in a rather febrile manner. He now spoke.

'Get on, get on, can't you? Get on, get on, get on. What's all this drivel about gardeners?'

'Not drivel, Blister,' said Freddie, pained.

'I'm waiting to hear what Gally suggested.'

'Well, I'm telling you as quick as I can, dash it. The point Uncle Gally made, when consulted over the long-distance telephone, was that anyone who liked could come and garden at the old homestead, and no questions asked. You get this trend? Of course you do. A child couldn't miss it. If you want to oil into the premises, you can do so by affecting to be a gardener. And if you're going to say you don't know anything about gardening, I reply that you don't have to. All you've got to do is just wander around with a rake or hoe, looking zealous. Rakes and hoes may be purchased at Smithson's in the High Street.'

The immensity of the idea, coming suddenly home to Bill, held him speechless for a moment. Then obstacles began to present themselves.

'But isn't there a head gardener, or someone of that sort, who keeps an eye on the gardeners?'

'There is. One McAllister. It was in order to square him that I had to dally awhile. It's all fixed now. A fiver changed hands. You can settle up at your leisure. So if an elderly Scotsman who looks like a minor prophet comes up and gives you the eye, don't be alarmed. Just nod and say the gardens are a credit to him. If you see the guv'nor, touch your hat a good deal.'

Bill had now no hesitation in endorsing his companion's description of the scheme as a pippin. The word, indeed, seemed to him rather a weak one.

'It's terrific, Freddie.'

'I told you it was.'

'I can hang about –'

'– till Prue comes along –'

'– and have a talk with her –'

'– thus healing the rift and arriving at a perfect understanding. And if she doesn't come along, some scullion or what not is sure to, and you can slip him a couple of bob and a carefully-written note to give to Prue, which of course you will have in readiness on your person. What's the matter, Blister?'

Bill's face had suddenly darkened. Anguish and despair were once more limned upon it.

'Oh, my God!'

'Something wrong?'

'It won't work. Your father has seen me.'

Freddie raised his eyebrows. His manner was amused and indulgent.

'You don't suppose Uncle Gally overlooked a point like that? My dear chap! He's sending it down by the next post.'

'It?'

'It.'

A hideous suspicion smote Bill. He paled.

'Not – *it*?' he quavered.

'He was starting off to see Fruity Biffen immediately and get it back. Honestly, Blister, I can't see why you have this extraordinary prejudice against the thing. I haven't seen it myself, of course, but if it made old Biffen look like an Assyrian monarch, it must be dignified and striking. Well, anyway, you've got to have some rude disguise or you can't be a gardener, so stick it like a man is my advice. And now, old bird,' said Freddie, 'I must fly. Good-bye, good luck, and God bless you.'

Chapter 6

'Tchah!' said Colonel Wedge.

He spoke the word as it should be spoken, if it is to have its proper value, crisply and explosively from between clenched teeth. He had been sitting at the foot of his wife's bed, conversing with her while she breakfasted, as was his companionable habit of a morning. He now rose, and walking to the window stood staring out, jingling his keys irritably in his pocket.

'Good God! I never saw such a chap!'

Had there been some sympathetic friend standing at his side and following the direction of his moody gaze, such a one might have supposed the object of his remark to have been the gardener who was toying with a rake on the lawn below, and he would probably have felt the criticism to be fully justified. Nature has framed strange fellows in her time, and this was one of them, a gardener of vast physique and rendered more than ordinarily noticeable by the mustard-coloured beard of Assyrian cut which partially obscured his features.

It was not, however, to this fungus-covered son of the soil that the colonel alluded. He had seen him hanging about the place this last couple of days but had never given him more than a passing thought. When the heart is bowed down with weight of woe, we have little leisure for brooding on gardeners, however profusely bearded. The chap to whom he referred was Tipton Plimsoll.

There are fathers, not a few of them, who tend to regard suitors for their daughter's hand with a jaundiced and unfriendly eye, like shepherds about to be deprived of a ewe lamb. Colonel Wedge did not belong to this class. Nor was he one of those parents who, when their child has made an evidently deep impression upon a young millionaire, are content to sit back with folded hands and wait patiently for the situation to develop in a slow, orderly manner. He wanted action. He had observed the love light in Tipton Plimsoll's eyes, and what he wished to see in the fellow now was a spot of the Young Lochinvar spirit.

'What's he waiting for?' he demanded querulously, turning back to the bed. 'Anyone can see he's head over ears in love with the girl. Then why not tell her so?'

Lady Hermione nodded mournfully. She, too, was all in favour of dash and impetuosity. Looking like a cook who smells something burning, she agreed that the Plimsoll self-control was odd.

'Odd? It's maddening.'

'Yes,' agreed Lady Hermione, accepting the emendation. 'I don't know when I have been so upset. Everything seemed to be going so well. I'm sure it is affecting Veronica's spirits. She has not seemed at all herself these last few days.'

'You've noticed that? So have I. Goes into long silences.'

'As if she were brooding.'

'The exact word. She reminds me of that girl in Shakespeare who . . . How does it go? I know there's something about worms, and it ends up with something cheek. Of course, yes. "She never said a word about her love, but let concealment, like a worm i' the bud, feed on her damned cheek." Of course she's brooding. What girl wouldn't? Bowled over by a fellow at first sight; feels pretty sure he's bowled over too; everything pointing to the happy ending; and then suddenly, without any reason, fellow starts hemming and hawing and taking no further steps. It's a tragedy. Did I tell you what Freddie told me that day he arrived?' said Colonel Wedge, lowering his voice with the awe that befitted the revelation he was about to make. 'He told me that this young Plimsoll holds the controlling interest in one of the largest systems of chain stores in America. Well, you know what that means.'

Lady Hermione nodded, even more sadly than before – the cook who has discovered what it was that was burning, and too late now to do anything about it.

'And such a nice boy too,' she said. 'So different from what you led me to expect. Nothing could have been quieter and more correct than his behaviour. I noticed particularly that he had drunk nothing but barley water since he came here. What is it, Egbert?'

The solicitous query had been provoked by the sudden, sharp cry which had proceeded from her husband's lips. Colonel Wedge, except for the fact that he was fully clothed, was looking like Archimedes when he discovered his famous Principle and sprang from his bath, shouting 'Eureka!'

'Good God, old girl, you've hit it. You've put your finger on the whole dashed seat of the trouble. Barley water. Of course! That's what's at the root of the chap's extraordinary behaviour. How the deuce can a young fellow be expected to perform one of the most testing, exacting tasks in life on barley water? Why, before I could work up my nerve to propose to you, I remember, I had to knock back nearly a quart of mixed champagne and stout. Well, this settles it,' said Colonel Wedge. 'I go straight to this young Plimsoll, put my hand on his shoulder in a fatherly way, and tell him to take a quick snort and charge ahead.'

'Egbert! You can't!'

'Eh? Why not?'

'Of course you can't.'

Colonel Wedge seemed discouraged. The fine, fresh enthusiasm died out of his face.

'No, I suppose it would hardly do,' he admitted. 'But somebody ought to give the boy a hint. Happiness of two young people at stake, I mean, and all that sort of thing. It isn't fair to Vee to let this shilly-shallying continue.'

Lady Hermione sat up suddenly, spilling her tea. She, too, looked like Archimedes – a female Archimedes.

'Prudence!'

'Prudence?'

'She could do it.'

'Oh, you mean young Prue? Couldn't think what you were talking about.'

'She could do it quite easily. It would not seem odd, coming from her.'

'Something in that. Prudence, eh?' Colonel Wedge mused. 'I see what you mean. Warmhearted, impulsive girl . . . Devoted to her cousin . . . Can't bear to see her unhappy . . . "I wonder if you would be offended if I said something to you, Mr Plimsoll." . . . Yes, there's a thought there. But would she do it?'

'I'm sure she would. I don't know if you have noticed it, but

Prudence has changed very much for the better since she came to Blandings. She seems quieter, more thoughtful and considerate, as if she were going out of her way to do good to people. You heard what she was saying yesterday about helping the vicar with his jumble sale. I thought that very significant.'

'Most. Girls don't help vicars with jumble sales unless their hearts are in the right place.'

'You might go and talk to her now.'

'I will.'

'You will probably find her in Clarence's study,' said Lady Hermione, refilling her cup and stirring its contents with a new animation. 'She told me last night that she was going to give it a thorough tidying this morning.'

2

'The stately homes of England,' sang the poetess Hemans, who liked them, 'how beautiful they stand'; and about the ancient seat of the ninth Earl of Emsworth there was nothing, as far as its exterior was concerned, which would have caused her to modify this view. Huge and grey and majestic, flanked by rolling parkland and bright gardens, with the lake glittering in the foreground and his lordship's personal flag fluttering gaily from the topmost battlement, it unquestionably caught the eye. Even Tipton Plimsoll, though not as a rule given to poetic rhapsodies, had become lyrical on first beholding the impressive pile, making a noise with his tongue like the popping of a cork and saying: 'Some joint!'

But, as is so often the case with England's stately homes, it was when you got inside and met the folks that you saw where the catch lay. This morning, as he mooned morosely on the terrace, Tipton Plimsoll, though still admiring the place as a place, found himself in complete sympathy with its residents. What a crew, he felt, what a gosh-awful aggregation of prunes. Tick them off on your fingers, he meant to say.

Lord Emsworth	*A Wash-Out*
Colonel Wedge	*A Piece of Cheese*
Lady Hermione	*A Chunk of Baloney*

Prudence   *A Squirt*
Freddie   *A Snake*
Veronica Wedge

Here he was obliged to pause in his cataloguing. Even in this bitter mood of his, when he was feeling like some prophet of Israel judging the sins of the people, he could not bring himself to chalk up against the name of that lovely girl the sort of opprobrious epithet which in the case of the others had sprung so nimbly to his lips. She, and she alone, must be spared.

Not, mind you, but what he was letting her off a darned sight more easily than she deserved, for if a girl who could bring herself to stoop to a Frederick Threepwood did not merit something notably scorching in the way of opprobrious epithets, it was difficult to see what she did merit. And that she had fallen a victim to Freddie's insidious charms was clearly proved by her dejected aspect since his departure. You had only to look at her to see that she was pining for the fellow.

But the trouble was, and he did not attempt to conceal it from himself, he loved her in spite of all. King Arthur, it will be remembered, had the same experience with Guinevere.

With a muffled curse on his fatal weakness, Tipton made for the french windows of the drawing-room. It had occurred to him that the vultures which were gnawing at his bosom might be staved off, if only temporarily, by a look at the Racing Prospects in the morning paper. And as he approached them somebody came out, and he saw that it was the squirt Prudence.

'Oh, hullo, Mr Plimsoll,' said the squirt.

'Hullo,' said Tipton.

He spoke with about the minimum of pleasure in his voice which was compatible with politeness. Never ever at the best of times fond of squirts, he found the prospect of this girl's society at such a moment intolerable. And it is probable that he would have passed hurriedly on with some remark about fetching something from his room had she not fixed her mournful eyes upon him and said that she had been looking for him and wondered if she could speak to him for a minute.

A man of gentle upbringing cannot straight-arm members of the opposite sex and flit by when they address him thus. Tipton's 'Oh, sure,' could have been more blithely spoken, but he said it, and they moved to the low stone wall of the terrace and sat there, Prudence gazing at Tipton, Tipton staring at a cow in the park.

Prudence was the first to break a rather strained silence.

'Mr Plimsoll,' she said, in a low, saintlike voice.

'Hullo?'

'There is something I want to say to you.'

'Oh, yes?'

'I hope you won't be very angry.'

'Eh?'

'And tell me to mind my own business. Because it's about Vee.'

Tipton removed his gaze from the cow. As a matter of fact, he had seen about as much of it as he wanted to see. A fine animal, but, as is so often the case with cows, not much happening. He found this conversational opening unexpectedly promising. His first impression, when this girl accosted him, had been that she wanted to touch him for something for the vicar's jumble sale, an enterprise in which he knew her to be interested.

'Ur?' he said inquiringly.

Prudence was silent for a moment. The rupture of her relations with the man she loved had left her feeling like some nun for whom nothing remains in this life but the doing of good to others, but she was wondering if she had acted quite wisely in so readily accepting the assignment which her uncle Egbert had given her just now. She had become conscious of a feeling that she was laying herself open to the snub of a lifetime.

But she did not lack courage. Shutting her eyes to assist speech, she had at it.

'You're in love with Vee, aren't you, Mr Plimsoll?'

A noise beside her made her open her eyes. Sudden emotion had caused Tipton to fall off the wall.

'I know you are,' she resumed, having helped to put him right end up again with a civil 'Upsy-daisy'. 'Anyone could see it.'

'Is that so?' said Tipton, in a rather nasty voice. He was stung. Like most young men whose thoughts are an open book to the populace, he supposed that if there was one thing more than another for which he was remarkable, it was his iron inscrutability.

'Of course. It sticks out like a sore thumb. The way you look at her. And what beats me is why you don't tell her so. She hasn't actually said anything to me, but I know you're making her very unhappy.'

Tipton's resentment faded. This was no time for wounded dignity. He gaped at her like a goldfish.

'You mean you think I've got a chance?'

'A chance? It's a snip.'

Tipton gulped, goggled, and nearly fell off the wall again.

'A snip?' he repeated dazedly.

'Definitely. Today's Safety Bet.'

'But how about Freddie?'

'Freddie?'

'Isn't she in love with Freddie?'

'What an extraordinary idea! What makes you think so?'

'That first night, at dinner, she slapped his wrist.'

'I expect there was a mosquito on it.'

Tipton started. He had never thought of that, and the theory, when you came to examine it, was extraordinarily plausible. In the dining-room that night there had unquestionably been mosquitoes among those present. He had squashed a couple himself. A great weight seemed to roll off his mind. His eye rested for a moment on the cow, and he thought what a jolly, lovable-looking cow it was, the sort of cow you would like to go on a walking tour with.

Then the weight rolled back again. He shook his head.

'No,' he said, 'it was something he whispered to her. She told him not to be so silly.'

'Oh, that time, you mean? I heard what he said. It was about those dog biscuits of his being so wholesome that human beings could eat them.'

'Gosh!'

'There's nothing between Vee and Freddie.'

'She used to be engaged to him.'

'Yes, but he's married now.'

'Sure,' said Tipton, and smiled darkly. 'Married, yes. Married, ha!'

'And they were only engaged about a couple of weeks. I was at Blandings when it happened. It was raining all the time, and I suppose it was a way of passing the day. You get sick of backgammon. Honestly, I wouldn't worry about Vee being in love with other people, Mr Plimsoll. I'm sure she's in love with you. You should have heard her raving about that balancing trick you did at dinner with the fork and the wineglass.'

'She liked it?' cried Tipton eagerly.

'The way she spoke of it, I think it absolutely bowled her over. Vee's the sort of girl who admires men who do things.'

'This opens up a new line of thought,' said Tipton, and was silent for a space, adjusting himself to it.

'If I were you, I'd ask her to marry me right away.'

'Would you?' said Tipton. His eyes rested on Prudence and in them now there was nothing but affection, gratitude, and esteem. It amazed him that he could ever have placed her among the squirts. An extraordinarily bad bit of casting. What had caused him to do so, of course, had been her lack of inches, and he realized now that in docketing the other sex what you had to go by was not size, but soul. A girl physically in the peanut division steps automatically out of her class if she has the opalescent soul of a ministering angel.

'Gosh!' he said. 'Would you?'

'I wouldn't waste another minute. Let me go and tell her that you want to see her, as you have something most important to say to her. Then you can put the thing through before lunch. Here is the set-up as I see it. I don't want to influence you if you have other ideas, but my suggestion would be that you ask her to come and confer with you behind the rhododendrons, and then, when she shows up, you reach out and grab her and kiss her a good deal and say: "My woman!" So much better, I mean, than messing about with a lot of talk. You get the whole thing straight that way, right from the start.'

The motion picture she conjured up made a profound appeal to Tipton Plimsoll, and for some moments he sat running it off in his mind's eye. Then he shook his head.

'It couldn't be done.'

'Why not?'

'I shouldn't have the nerve. I'd have to have a drink first.'

'Well, have a drink. That's just the point I was going to touch on. I've been watching you pretty closely, and you haven't drunk anything since you got here but barley water. That's what's been holding you back. Have a good, stiff noggin.'

'Ah, but if I do, what happens? Up bobs that blasted face.'

'Face? How do you mean?'

Tipton saw that it would be necessary to explain the peculiar situation in which he had been placed, and he proceeded to do so. Looking on this girl, as he now did, as a sort of loved sister and knowing that he could count on her sympathy, he experienced no difficulty in making his confession. With admirable clearness he took her through the entire continuity – the acquisition of his money, the urge to celebrate, the two months' revelry, the spots, the visit to E. Jimpson Murgatroyd's consulting room, E. Jimpson's words of doom, the first appearance of the face, the second appearance of the face, the third, fourth, fifth, and sixth appearances of the face. He told his story well, and a far less intelligent listener than Prudence would have had no difficulty in following the run of the plot. When he had finished, she sat in thoughtful silence, staring at the cow.

'I see what you mean,' she said. 'It can't be at all pleasant for you.'

'It isn't,' Tipton assured her. 'I don't like it.'

'Nobody would.'

'It would be quite different if it were a little man with a black beard. This face is something frightful.'

'But you haven't seen it since the first night you were here?'

'No.'

'Well, then.'

Tipton asked what she meant by the expression 'Well, then,' and Prudence said that she had intended to advance the theory that the thing had probably packed up and gone out of business. To this Tipton demurred. Was it not more probable, he reasoned, that it was just lurking – simply biding its time as it were? No, said Prudence, her view was that, discouraged by Tipton's incessant barley water, it had definitely turned in its union card and that Tipton would be running virtually no risk in priming himself – within moderation, of course – for the declaration of his love.

She spoke with so much authority, so like somebody who knew all about phantom faces and had studied their psychology, that

Tipton drew strength from her words. There was a firm, determined set to his lips as he rose.

'Okay,' he said. 'Then I'll have a quick snootful.'

He did not mention it, but what had helped to crystallize his resolution was the thought that in this matter of getting Veronica Wedge signed up, speed was of the essence. He had Prudence's assurance that the girl was still reeling under the effects of that balancing trick with the fork and the wineglass, but he was a clear-thinking man and knew that the glamour of balancing tricks does not last for ever. Furthermore, there was the menace of Freddie to be taken into account. His little friend had scouted the idea that there was any phonus-bolonus afoot between Veronica Wedge and this prominent Anglo-American snake, but though she had been convincing at the moment, doubts had once more begun to vex him, and he was now very strongly of the opinion that the contract must be sewed up before his former friend could return and resume his sinister wooing.

'If you'll excuse me,' he said, 'I'll pop up to my room. I've got a . . . No, by golly, I haven't.'

'What were you going to say?'

'I'd started to say I'd got a flask there. But I remember now I gave it to Lord Emsworth. You see, that time I saw this old face out of the window I kind of thought it would be better if somebody took charge of that flask for me, and I met His Nibs going to his room and gave it to him.'

'It's in Uncle Clarence's bedroom?'

'I guess so.'

'I'll go and get it for you.'

'Giving you a lot of trouble.'

'Not a bit. I was just going to tidy Uncle Clarence's bedroom. I've done his study. I'll bring it to your room.'

'It's darned good of you.'

'No, no.'

'Darned good,' insisted Tipton. 'White, I call it.'

'But I think one ought to help people, don't you?' said Prudence, with a faint, gentle smile like that of Florence Nightingale bending over a sick-bed. 'I think that's the only thing in life, trying to do good to others.'

'I wish there was something I could do for you.'

'You can give me something for the vicar's jumble sale.'

'Count on me for a princely donation,' said Tipton. 'And now I'll be getting up to my room. If you wouldn't mind contacting Miss Wedge and telling her to be behind the rhododendrons in about twenty minutes and bringing me the good old flask, you can leave the rest of the preliminaries to me.'

3

In the bearing of Tipton Plimsoll, as some quarter of an hour later he took up station at the tryst, there was no trace of the old diffidence and lack of spirit. He was jaunty and confident. The elixir, coursing through his veins, had given his system just that fillip which a lover's system needs when he is planning to seize girls in his arms and say, 'My woman!' to them. You could have described Tipton at this moment as the dominant male with the comfortable certainty of having found the *mot juste*. He exuded the will to win.

He looked at the sky sternly, as if daring it to start something. In the quick glance which he gave at the rhododendrons there was the implication that they knew what they might expect if they tried any funny business. He straightened his tie. He flicked a speck of dust off his coat sleeve. He toyed with the idea of substituting 'My mate!' for 'My woman!' but discarded it as having too nautical a ring.

A caveman, testing the heft of his club before revealing his love to the girl of his choice, would have shaken hands with Tipton in his present mood and recognized him as a member of the lodge.

Nevertheless, it would be falsifying the facts to say that beneath his intrepid exterior there did not lurk an uneasiness. Though feeling more like some great overwhelming force of nature than a mere man in horn-rimmed spectacles, he could not but remember that he had rather thrown down the challenge to that face. Far less provocation than he had just been giving it had in the past brought it out with a whoop and a holler, and Prudence's encouraging words had not wholly removed the apprehension lest it might report for duty now. And if it did, of course, phut went all his carefully reasoned plans. A man cannot put through a delicate operation like a proposal of marriage with non-existent faces floating at his elbow. Then, if ever, it is essential that he be alone with the adored object.

But as the minutes passed and nothing happened hope began to burgeon. His experience of this face had taught him that the one thing it prided itself on was giving quick service. That time in his bedroom, for instance, he had scarcely swallowed the stuff before it was up and doing. Nor had it been noticeably slower off the mark on other occasions. He could not but feel that this dilatoriness on its part now was promising.

He had just decided that he would give it a couple more minutes before finally embracing Prudence's theory that it had gone on the pension list, when a sharp whistle in his rear caused him to look around, and one glance put an end to his hopes.

On the other side of the drive, screening the lawn, was a mass of tangled bushes. And there it was, leering out from them. It was wearing a sort of Assyrian beard this time, as if it had just come from a fancy-dress ball, but he had no difficulty in recognizing it, and a dull despair seemed to crush him like a physical burden. Useless now to think of awaiting Veronica's arrival and going into the routine which Prudence had sketched out. He knew his limitations. With spectral faces watching him and probably giving him the horse's laugh to boot, he was utterly incapable of reaching out and grabbing the girl he loved. He turned on his heel and strode off down the drive. The whistling continued, and he rather thought he caught the word 'Hi!' but he did not look back. He would not, it appeared, avoid seeing this face, but it was some slight consolation to feel that he could cut it.

He was scarcely out of sight when Veronica Wedge came tripping joyously from the direction of the house.

Veronica, like Tipton five minutes earlier, was in excellent fettle. For the past few days she had been perplexed and saddened, as her father and mother had been, by the spectacle of an obviously enamoured suitor slowing down after a promising start. That moonlight walk on the terrace had left her with the impression that she had found her mate and that striking developments might be expected as early as the next day. But the next day had come and gone, and the days after that, and Tipton had continued to preserve his strange aloofness. And Melancholy was marking her for its own when along came Prudence with her sensational story of his wish to meet her behind the rhododendrons.

Veronica Wedge was, as has been indicated, not a very intelligent girl, but she was capable, if you gave her time and did not bustle her, of a rudimentary process of ratiocination. This, she told herself, could mean but one thing. Men do not lightly and carelessly meet girls behind rhododendrons. The man who asks a girl to meet him behind rhododendrons is a man who intends to get down to it and talk turkey. Or so reasoned Veronica Wedge. And now, as she hastened to the tryst, she was in buoyant mood. Her cheeks glowed, her eyes sparkled. A photographer, seeing her, would have uttered a cry of rapture.

A few moments later her animation had waned a little. Arriving at the rhododendrons and discovering that she was alone, she experienced a feeling of flatness and disappointment. She halted, looking this way and that. She saw plenty of rhododendrons but no Plimsoll, and she found this shortage perplexing.

However, she was not accorded leisure to brood on it, for at this point it was borne in upon her that she was not alone, after all. There came to her ears the sound of a low whistle, and a voice said 'Hi!' Assuming that this was her missing Romeo and wondering a little why he should have chosen to open an emotional scene in this rather prosaic manner, she spun around. And having done so she stood staring, aghast.

From out of the bushes on the other side of the drive a bearded face was protruding, its eyes glaring into hers.

'Eeek!' she cried, recoiling.

It would have pained Bill Lister, the kindliest and most chivalrous of men, could he have read the *News of the World* headlines which were racing through her mind – FIEND DISMEMBERS BEAUTIFUL GIRL the mildest of them. Preoccupied with the thought of the note which he wished conveyed to his loved one, he had forgotten what a hideous menace the beard lent to his honest features. Even when clean-shaved, he was, as has been shown, not everybody's money. Peering out from behind Fruity Biffen's beard, he presented an appearance that might have caused even Joan of Arc a momentary qualm.

But he had overlooked this. All he was thinking was that here at last was somebody who could oblige him by acting as a messenger.

His original intention had been to entrust the note to the tall, horn-rimmed spectacled chap who had been here a moment ago. He had seen him coming down the drive and, feeling that he looked a good sort who would be charmed to do a man a kindness, he had hurried across the lawn and intercepted him. And the fellow had merely given him a cold stare and proceeded on his way. Veronica's sudden appearance a few moments later had seemed to him sent from heaven. Girls, he reasoned, have softer hearts than men in horn-rimmed spectacles.

For a meeting with Prudence herself Bill had ceased to hope. If she sauntered about the grounds of Blandings Castle, it was not in the part of them in which he had established himself. And in any case the note put what he wanted to say to her so much more clearly and fluently than tongue could be trusted to do. He knew himself to be an unready speaker.

He wished he had some means of ascertaining this girl's name, for there was something a little abrupt in just saying 'Hi!' But there seemed no other way of embarking on the conversation, so he said it again, this time emerging from the bushes and advancing towards her.

It was most unfortunate that in doing so he should have caught his foot in an unseen root, for this caused him to come out at a staggering run, clutching the air with waving hands, the last thing calculated to restore Veronica's already shaken morale. If he had practised for weeks, he could not have given a more realistic and convincing impersonation of a Fiend starting out to dismember a beautiful girl.

'BLANDINGS CASTLE HORROR,' thought Veronica, paling beneath her Blush of Roses make-up. 'MANGLED BEYOND RECOGNITION. HEADLESS BODY DISCOVERED IN RHODODENDRONS.'

Daughter of a soldier though she was, there was nothing of the heroine about Veronica Wedge. Where other, tougher soldiers' daughters might have stood their ground and raised their eyebrows with a cold 'Sir!' she broke in panic. The paralysis which had been affecting her lower limbs gave way, and she raced up the drive like a blonde whippet. She heard a clatter of feet behind her; then it ceased and she was in sight of home and safety.

Her mother – a girl's best friend – was strolling on the terrace. She flung herself into her arms, squeaking with agitation.

4

Bill went back to his lawn. There are moments in life when everything seems to be against one, and this was such a moment. He felt moody and discouraged.

Freddie had talked of smuggling a note to Prudence as if it were the easiest and simplest of tasks, and it was beginning to look like one calculated to tax the most Machiavellian ingenuity. And it was not as if he had got unlimited time at his disposal. At any moment some accuser might rise to confront him with the charge of being no genuine gardener, but merely a synthetic substitute.

This very morning he had thought that the moment had come, when Lord Emsworth had pottered up and engaged him in a lengthy conversation about flowers of which he had never so much as heard the names. And while he had fought off the challenge with a masterly series of 'Yes, m'lords' and 'Ah, m'lords' and once an inspired 'Ah, that zu zurely be zo, m'lord,' leaving to the other the burden of exchanges, could this happen again without disaster? His acquaintance with the ninth Earl of Emsworth, though brief, had left him with the impression that the latter's mind was not of a razor-like keenness, but would not even he, should another such encounter take place, become alive to the fact that here was a very peculiar gardener and one whose credentials could do with a bit of examination?

It was imperative that he find – and that, if possible, ere yonder sun had set – some kindly collaborator to take that note to Prudence. And where he had gone wrong, it seemed to him, had been in trying to enlist the services of horn-rimmed spectacled guests of the castle who merely glared and passed on and neurotic females of the leisured class who ran like rabbits the moment he spoke to them. What he required, he now saw, was an emissary lower down in the social scale, to whom he could put the thing as a commercial proposition – one, for instance, of those scullions or what not of whom Freddie had spoken, who would be delighted to see the whole thing through for a couple of bob.

And scarcely had this thought floated into his mind when he espied coming across the lawn towards him a dumpy female figure, so obviously that of the castle cook out for her day off that his heart leaped up as if he had beheld a rainbow in the sky. Grasping the note in one hand and half a crown in the other, he hurried to meet her. A short while before he had supposed Veronica Wedge to have been sent from heaven. He was now making the same mistake with regard to her mother.

The error into which he had fallen was not an unusual one. Nearly everybody, seeing her for the first time, took Lady Hermione Wedge for a cook. Where Bill had gone wrong was in his assumption that she was a kindly cook, a genial cook, a cook compact of sweetness and light who would spring to the task of assisting a lover in distress. He had not observed that her demeanour was that of an angry cook, whose deepest feelings had been outraged and who intends to look into the matter without delay.

Her daughter's tearful outpourings had left Lady Hermione Wedge so full of anti-bearded-gardener sentiment that she felt choked. The meekest mother resents having her child chivvied by the outdoor help, and she was far from being meek. As she drew near to Bill, her face was a royal purple, and there were so many things she wanted to say first that she had to pause to make selection.

And it was as she paused that Bill thrust the note and the half-crown into her hand, begging her to trouser the latter and sneak the former to Miss Prudence Garland, being careful – he stressed this – not to let Lady Hermione Wedge see her do it.

'One of the worst,' said Bill. 'A hellhound of the vilest description. But you know that, I expect,' he added sympathetically, for he could imagine that this worthy soul must have had many a battle over the roasts and hashes with Prue's demon aunt.

A strange rigidity had come upon Lady Hermione.

'Who are you?' she demanded in a low, hoarse voice.

'Oh, that's all right,' said Bill reassuringly. He liked her all the better for this concern for the proprieties. 'It's all perfectly on the level. My name is Lister. Miss Garland and I are engaged. And this blighted Wedge woman is keeping her under lock and key and watching her every move. A devil of a female. What she needs is a spoonful of arsenic in her soup one of these evenings. You couldn't attend to that, I suppose?' he said genially, for now that everything was going so smoothly he was in merry mood.

5

The soft-voiced clock over the stables had just struck twelve in the smooth, deferential manner of a butler announcing that dinner is served, when the sunlit beauty of the grounds of Blandings Castle was rendered still lovelier by the arrival of Freddie Threepwood in his two-seater. He had concluded his visit to the Worcestershire Fanshawe-Chadwicks. One assumes that the parting must have been a painful one, but he had torn himself away remorselessly, for he was due for a night at the Shropshire Finches. To look in at the castle *en route* he had had to make a wide detour, but he was anxious to see Bill and learn how he had been getting along in his absence.

A search through the grounds failed to reveal the object of his quest, but it enabled him to pass the time of day with his father. Lord Emsworth, respectably – even ornately – clad in a dark suit of metropolitan cut and a shirt with a stiff collar, was leaning on the rail of the pigsty, communing with his pig.

Accustomed to seeing the author of his being in concertina trousers and an old shooting jacket with holes in the elbows, Freddie was unable to repress a gasp of astonishment, loud enough to arrest the other's attention. Lord Emsworth turned, adjusting his pince-nez, and what he saw through them, when he had got them focused, drew from him, too, a sudden gasp.

'Freddie! Bless my soul, I thought you were staying with some people. Have you come back for long?' he asked in quick alarm, his father's heart beating apprehensively.

Freddie stilled his fears.

'Just passing through, Guv'nor. I'm due at the Finches for lunch. I say, Guv'nor, why the fancy dress?'

'Eh?'

'The clothes. The gent's reach-me-downs.'

'Ah,' said Lord Emsworth, comprehending. 'I am leaving for London on the twelve-forty train.'

'Must be something pretty important to take you up to London in weather like this.'

'It is. Most important. I am going to see your uncle Galahad about another artist to paint the portrait of my pig. That first fellow . . .' Here Lord Emsworth was obliged to pause, in order to wrestle with his feelings.

'But why don't you wire him or just ring him up?'

'Wire him? Ring him up?' It was plain that Lord Emsworth had not thought of these ingenious alternatives. 'Bless my soul, I could have done that, couldn't I? But it's too late now,' he sighed. 'I most unfortunately forgot that it is Veronica's birthday tomorrow, and so have purchased no present for her, and her mother insists upon my going to London and repairing the omission.'

Something flashed in the sunlight. It was Freddie's monocle leaping from the parent eye-socket.

'Good Lord!' he ejaculated. 'Vee's birthday? So it is. I say, I'm glad you reminded me. It had absolutely slipped my mind. Look here, Guv'nor, will you do something for me?'

'What?' asked Lord Emsworth cautiously.

'What were you thinking of buying Vee?'

'I had in mind some little inexpensive trinket, such as girls like to wear. A wrist-watch was your aunt's suggestion.'

'Good. That fits my plans like the paper on the wall. Go to Aspinall's in Bond Street. They have wrist-watches of all descriptions. And when you get there, tell them that you are empowered to act for F. Threepwood. I left Aggie's necklace with them to be cleaned, and at the same time ordered a pendant for Vee. Tell them to send the necklace to . . . Are you following me, Guv'nor?'

'No,' said Lord Emsworth.

'It's quite simple. On the one hand, the necklace; on the other, the pendant. Tell them to send the necklace to Aggie at the Ritz Hotel, Paris –'

'Who,' asked Lord Emsworth, mildly interested, 'is Aggie?'

'Come, come, Guv'nor. This is not the old form. My wife.'

'I thought your wife's name was Frances.'

'Well, it isn't. It's Niagara.'

'What a peculiar name.'

'Her parents spent their honeymoon at the Niagara Falls Hotel.'

'Niagara is a town in America, is it not?'

'Not so much a town as a rather heavy downpour.'

'A town, I always understood.'

'You were misled by your advisers, Guv'nor. But do you mind if we get back to the *res*. Time presses. Tell these Aspinall birds to mail the necklace to Aggie at the Ritz Hotel, Paris, and bring back the pendant with you. Have no fear that you will be left holding the baby –'

Again Lord Emsworth was interested. This was the first he had heard of this.

'Have you a baby? Is it a boy? How old is he? What do you call him? Is he at all like you?' he asked, with a sudden pang of pity for the unfortunate suckling.

'I was speaking figuratively, Guv'nor,' said Freddie patiently. 'When I said, "Have no fear that you will be left holding the baby," I meant, "Entertain no alarm lest they may shove the bill off on you." The score is all paid up. Have you got it straight?'

'Certainly.'

'Let me hear the story in your own words.'

'There is a necklace and a pendant –'

'Don't go getting them mixed.'

'I never get anything mixed. You wish me to have the pendant sent to your wife and to bring back –'

'No, no, the other way round.'

'Or rather, as I was just about to say, the other way round. It is all perfectly clear. Tell me,' said Lord Emsworth, returning to the subject which really interested him, 'why is Frances nicknamed Niagara?'

'Her name isn't Frances, and she isn't.'

'Isn't what?'

'Nicknamed Niagara.'

'You told me she was. Has she taken the baby to Paris with her?'

Freddie produced a light blue handkerchief from his sleeve and passed it over his forehead.

'Look here, Guv'nor, do you mind if we call the whole thing off? Not the necklace and pendant sequence, but all this stuff about Frances and babies –'

'I like the name Frances.'

'Me, too. Music to the ears. But shall we just let it go, just forget all about it? We shall both feel easier and happier.'

Lord Emsworth uttered a pleased exclamation.

'Chicago!'

'Eh?'

'Not Niagara. Chicago. This is the town I was thinking of. There is a town in America called Chicago.'

'There was when I left. Well, anything been happening around here lately?' asked Freddie, determined that the subject should be changed before his progenitor started asking why he had had the baby christened Indianapolis.

Lord Emsworth reflected. He had recently revised the Empress's diet, with the happiest results, but something told him that this was not the sort of news item likely to intrigue his younger son, who had always lacked depth. Delving into the foggy recesses of his mind, he recalled a conversation which he had had with his brother-in-law, Colonel Wedge, some half-hour earlier.

'Your uncle Egbert is very much annoyed.'

'What about?'

'He says the gardeners have been chasing Veronica.'

This startled Freddie and, though he was no prude, shocked him a little. His cousin Veronica, true, was a very alluring girl, but he would have credited the British gardener with more self-control.

'Chasing her? The gardeners? Do you mean in a sort of pack?'

'No, now I come to remember, it was not all the gardeners – only one. And it seems, though I cannot quite follow the story, that he was not really a gardener, but the young fellow who is in love with your cousin Prudence.'

'What!'

Freddie, reeling, had fetched up against the rail of the sty. Supporting himself against this, he groped dazedly for his monocle, which had once more become AWOL.

'So Egbert assures me. But it seems odd. One would have expected him to chase Prùdence. Veronica ran to your aunt Hermi-one, who immediately went to ask the man what he meant by such behaviour, and he gave her a letter and half a crown. That part of the story, also,' Lord Emsworth admitted, 'is not very clear to me. I cannot see why, if this man is in love with Prudence, he should have been conducting a clandestine correspondence with Hermione, nor why he should have given her half a crown. Hermione has plenty of money. Still, there it is.'

'If you'll excuse me, Guv'nor,' said Freddie, in a strangled voice, 'I'll be reeling off. Got some rather heavy thinking to do.'

He fished out the handkerchief again and once more applied it to his brow. The affair, perplexing to Lord Emsworth, held no element of mystery for him. For the second time, he saw, poor old Blister had gone and made a floater, putting the kibosh on the carefully-laid plans which had been devised for his benefit. The guv'nor had not mentioned it, but he assumed that the episode had concluded with his aunt Hermione slinging his unfortunate friend out on his ear. By this time, no doubt, the latter was in his room at the Emsworth Arms putting the finishing touches to his packing. But it was impossible to go there and confer with him. The delay involved would mean his being absent from the Finch luncheon table. And you cannot play fast and loose with Shropshire Finches any more than you can with Worcestershire Fanshawe-Chadwicks.

He passed slowly on his way, and he had not gone far before he beheld in front of him one of those rustic benches which manage to get themselves scattered about the grounds of country houses.

To a man whose mind is burdened with weight of care, rustic benches – *qua* rustic benches – make little appeal. He just gives them a glance and passes on, wrapped in thought. And this one would certainly not have arrested Freddie's progress had he not observed seated upon it his cousin, Veronica Wedge. And even as he gazed an emotional sniff rent the air and he saw that she was weeping. It was the one spectacle which could have taken his thoughts off the problem of Bill. He was not the man to stride heedlessly by when Beauty was in distress.

'Why, hullo, Vee,' he said, hurrying forward. 'Something up?'

A sympathetic listener, with whom she could discuss in detail the peculiar behaviour of Tipton Plimsoll in making assignations behind rhododendron bushes and then allowing her to keep them alone and be harried by wild gardeners, was precisely what Veronica Wedge had been wanting. She poured out her story in impassioned words, and it was not long before Freddie, who had a feeling heart, was placing a cousinly arm about her waist; and not long after that before he was bestowing on her a series of cousinly kisses. Her story being done, he gave her for her pains a world of sighs: he swore, in faith, 'twas strange, 'twas passing strange; 'twas pitiful, 'twas wondrous pitiful — at the same time kissing her a good deal more.

From behind a tree some distance away Tipton Plimsoll, feeling as if some strong hand had struck him shrewdly behind the ear with a stuffed eelskin, stared bleakly at this lovers' reunion.

6

Lord Emsworth reached London shortly before five, and took a cab to the Senior Conservative Club, where he proposed to book a room for the night. Bill, arriving in the metropolis at the same time, for he had travelled on the same train, made his way immediately to the headquarters of the Hon. Galahad Threepwood in Duke Street, St James's. From the instant when Lady Hermione Wedge, exploding like a popped paper bag, had revealed her identity, he had seen that his was a situation calling above all else for a conference with that resourceful man of the world. For though a review of the position of affairs had left him with the feeling that he was beyond human aid, it might just possibly be that the brain which had got Ronnie Fish married to a chorus girl in the teeth of the opposition of a thousand slavering aunts would function now with all its pristine brilliance, dishing out some ingenious solution of his problem.

He found the Hon. Galahad standing by his car at the front door, chatting with the chauffeur. An uncle's obligations were sacred to this good man, and he was just about to start off for Blandings Castle to attend the birthday festivities of his niece Veronica.

Seeing Bill, he first blinked incredulously, then experienced a quick concern. Something, he felt, in the nature of a disaster must have occurred. To a mind as intelligent as his, the appearance in Duke Street of a young man who ought to have been messing about with a rake in the gardens of Blandings Castle could not fail to suggest this.

'Good Lord, Bill,' he cried. 'What are you doing here?'

'Can I have a word with you in private, Gally?' said Bill, with an unfriendly glance at the chauffeur, whose large pink ears were sticking up like a giraffe's and whose whole demeanour indicated genial interest and a kindly willingness to hear all.

'Step this way,' said the Hon. Galahad, and drew him out of earshot down the street. 'Now, then, what's all this about? Why aren't you at Blandings? Don't tell me you've made another bloomer and got the push again?'

'Yes, I have, as a matter of fact. But it wasn't my fault. How was I to know she wasn't the cook? Anyone would have been misled.'

Although still fogged as to what had occurred, the Hon. Galahad had no difficulty in divining who it was at Blandings Castle who had been taken for a cook.

'You are speaking of my sister Hermione?'

'Yes.'

'You thought she was the cook?'

'Yes.'

'Whereupon –?'

'I gave her half a crown and asked her to smuggle a note to Prudence.'

'I see. Yes, I grasp the thing now. And she whipped out the flaming sword and drove you from the garden?'

'Yes.'

'Odd,' said the Hon. Galahad. 'Strange. A precisely similar thing happened thirty years ago to my old friend Stiffy Bates, only he mistook the girl's father for the butler. Did Hermione keep your half-crown?'

'No. She threw it at me.'

'You were luckier than Stiffy. He tipped the father ten bob, and the old boy stuck to it like glue. It used to rankle with Stiffy a good deal, I remember, the thought that he had paid ten shillings just to be chased through a quickset hedge with a gardening fork. He was always a chap who liked to get value for money. But how did you happen to come across Hermione?'

'She came to tick me off for chasing her daughter.'

'You mean her niece.'

'No, her daughter, A tall, half-witted girl with goggly eyes.'

The Hon. Galahad drew his breath in sharply.

'So that was how Veronica struck you, was it? Yours is an

unusual outlook, Bill. It is more customary for males of her acquaintance to allude to her as a goddess with the kind of face that
launches a thousand ships. Still, perhaps it is all for the best. It
would have complicated an already complicated state of affairs if
there had been any danger of your suddenly switching your affections to her. But if the appeal she made to you was so tepid, why
did you run after her?'

'I wanted her to take the note to Prue.'

'Ah, I see. Yes, of course. What was there in this note?'

'It was to tell her that I was ready to do everything she wanted –
give up painting and settle down and run that pub of mine. Perhaps
Freddie told you about that?'

'He gave me a sort of outline. Well, as far as the note is concerned, don't worry. I'm just off to Blandings. I'll see that she gets
it.'

'That's awfully good of you.'

'Not at all. Is that it?' said the Hon. Galahad, taking the envelope
which Bill had produced from an inner pocket like a rabbit from a
hat. 'A bit wet with honest sweat,' he said, surveying it critically
through his eye-glass, 'but I don't suppose she'll mind that. So you
have decided to run the Mulberry Tree, have you? I think you're
wise. You don't want to mess about with art these days. Hitch your
wagon to some sound commercial proposition. I see no reason why
you shouldn't make a very good thing out of the Mulberry Tree.
Especially if you modernized it a bit.'

'That's what Prue wants to do. Swimming pools and squash
courts and all that sort of thing.'

'Of course you'd need capital.'

'That's the snag.'

'I wish I could supply some. I'd give it to you like a shot if I had
it, but I subsist on a younger son's allowance from the estate. Have
you anyone in mind whose ear you might bite?'

'Prue thought Lord Emsworth might cough up. After we were
married, of course. But the trouble is, I told him to boil his head.'

'And you were right. Clarence ought to boil his head. What of
it?'

'He didn't like it much.'

'I still cannot see your point.'

'Well, don't you think it dishes my chance of getting his support?'

'Of course not. Clarence never remembers ten minutes afterwards what people say to him.'

'But he would recognize me when he saw me again.'

'As the chap who made a mess of painting his pig? He might have a vague sort of idea that he had seen you before somewhere, but that would be all.'

'Do you mean that?'

'Certainly.'

'Then why,' demanded Bill hotly, quivering with self-pity at the thought of what he had endured, 'did you make me wear that blasted beard?'

'Purely from character-building motives. Every young man starting out in life ought to wear a false beard, if only for a day or two. It stiffens the fibre, teaches him that we were not put into this world for pleasure alone. And don't forget, while we are on the subject, that it is extremely fortunate, as you happened to run into my sister Hermione, that you did wear that beard. Now she won't recognize you when she sees you without it.'

'How do you mean?'

'When you appear at the castle tomorrow.'

'When I – what?'

'Ah, I didn't tell you, did I? While we have been talking,' explained the Hon. Galahad, 'I have hit on the absurdly simple solution of your little problem. Clarence is coming to consult me about getting another artist to paint the Empress. He wired me from Market Blandings station that he would be calling here soon after five. When he arrives, I shall present you as my selection for today. That will solve all your difficulties.'

Bill gaped. He found it difficult to speak. One reverences these master minds, but they take the breath away.

'You'll never be able to get away with it.'

'Of course I shall. I shall be vastly surprised if there is the slightest hitch in the negotiations from start to finish. My dear boy, I have been closely associated with my brother Clarence for more than half a century, and I know him from caviare to nuts. His IQ is about thirty points lower than that of a not too agile-minded jelly-fish. The only point on which I am at all dubious is your ability to give satisfaction for the limited period of time which must elapse before the opportunity presents itself for scooping Prudence out of the castle and taking her off and marrying her. You seem to have fallen down badly at your first attempt.'

Bill assured him that that was all right – he had learned a lesson. The Hon. Galahad said he hoped it was a drawing lesson. And it was at this moment that Lord Emsworth came pottering round the corner from St James's Street, and Bill, sighting him, was aware of a sudden access of hope. The scheme which his benefactor had propounded called for a vague and woollen-headed party of the second part, and the ninth Earl of Emsworth unquestionably had the appearance of being that and more.

London, with its roar and bustle and people who bumped into you and omnibuses which seemed to chase you like stoats after a rabbit, always had a disintegrating effect on the master of Blandings Castle, reducing his mental powers to a level even below that of the jellyfish to which his brother had compared him. As he stood in the entrance of Duke Street now, groping for the pince-nez which the perilous crossing of the main thoroughfare had caused to leap from their place, his mouth was open, his hat askew, and his eyes vacant. A confidence man would have seen in him an excellent prospect, and he also looked good to Bill.

'Ah, here he is,' said Gally. 'Now follow me carefully. Wait till he comes up, and then say you've got to be getting along. Walk slowly as far as St James's Palace and slowly back again. Leave the rest to me. If you feel you want an excuse for coming back, you can ask me what it was I told you was good for the two o'clock at Sandown tomorrow. Hullo, Clarence.'

'Ah, Galahad,' said Lord Emsworth.

'Well, I must be getting along,' said Bill, wincing a little as the newcomer's pince-nez rested upon him. Despite his mentor's assurances, he could not repress a certain nervousness and embarrassment on finding himself once more face to face with a man with whom his previous encounters had been so painful.

His mind was still far from being at rest as he returned to Duke Street after the brief perambulation which he had been directed to make, and he found the cheery insouciance of the Hon. Galahad's greeting encouraging.

'Ah, my dear fellow,' said Gally. 'Back again? Capital. Saves me having to ring you up from the country. I wonder if you know my brother? Lord Emsworth, Mr Landseer.'

'How do you do?' said Lord Emsworth.

'How do you do?' said Bill uneasily. Once more he was feeling nervous and embarrassed. It would have been exaggerating to say that the ninth earl was directing a keen glance at him, for it was not within the power of the weak-eyed peer to direct keen looks, but he was certainly staring somewhat intently. And, indeed, it had just occurred to Lord Emsworth that somewhere, at some time and place, he had seen Bill before. Possibly at the club.

'Your face seems familiar, Mr Landseer,' he said.

'Oh, yes?' said Bill.

'Well, naturally,' said Gally. 'Dashed celebrated chap, Landseer. Photograph always in the papers. Tell me, my dear Landseer, are you very busy just now?'

'Oh, no,' said Bill.

'You could undertake a commission?'

'Oh, yes,' said Bill.

'Splendid. You see, my brother was wondering if he could induce you to come to Blandings with him tomorrow and paint the portrait of his pig. You've probably heard of the Empress of Blandings?'

'Oh, rather,' said Bill.

'You have?' said Lord Emsworth eagerly.

'My dear chap,' said Gally, smiling a little, 'of course. It's part of Landseer's job as England's leading animal painter to keep an eye on all the prominent pigs in the country. I dare say he's been studying photographs of the Empress for a long time.'

'For years,' said Bill.

'Have you ever seen a finer animal?'

'Never.'

'She is the fattest pig in Shropshire,' said Gally, 'except for Lord Burslem, who lives over Bridgnorth way. You'll enjoy painting her. When did you say you were going back to Blandings, Clarence?'

'Tomorrow on the twelve-forty-two train. Perhaps you could meet me at Paddington, Mr Landseer? Capital. And now I fear I must be leaving you. I have to go to a jeweller's in Bond Street.'

He shambled off, and Gally turned to Bill with pardonable complacency.

'There you are, my boy. What did I tell you?'

Bill was panting a little, like a man who has passed through an emotional ordeal.

'Why Landseer?' he asked at length.

'Clarence has always admired your Stag at Bay,' said the Hon. Galahad. 'I made it my talking point.'

Chapter 7

The morning following Lord Emsworth's departure for London
found Blandings Castle basking in the warmth of a superb summer
day. A sun which had risen with the milk and gathered strength
hourly shone from a sky of purest sapphire, gilding the grounds
and messuages and turning the lake into a sheet of silver flame. Bees
buzzed among the flowers, insects droned, birds mopped their
foreheads in the shrubberies, gardeners perspired at every pore.

About the only spot into which the golden beams did not
penetrate was the small smoking-room off the hall. It never got the
sun till late in the afternoon, and it was for this reason that Tipton
Plimsoll, having breakfasted frugally on a cup of coffee and his
thoughts, had gone there to brood over the tragedy which had
shattered his life. He was not in the market for sunshine. Given his
choice, he would have scrapped this glorious morning, flattering
the mountain tops with sovereign eye, and substituted for it something more nearly resembling the weather conditions of King Lear,
Act Two.

It does not take much to depress a young man in love, and
yesterday's spectacle of Veronica Wedge and Freddie hobnobbing
on the rustic bench had reduced Tipton's vivacity to its lowest ebb.
As he sat in the small smoking-room, listlessly thumbing one of
those illustrated weekly papers for which their proprietors have the
crust to charge a shilling, he was experiencing all the effects of a
severe hangover without having had to go to the trouble and expense
of manufacturing it. E. Jimpson Murgatroyd, had he beheld him,
would have been shocked and disappointed, assuming the worst.

Nor did the periodical through which he was glancing do anything to induce a sprightlier trend of thought. Its contents consisted
almost entirely of photographs of female members of the ruling
classes, and it mystified him that the public should be expected to

disburse hard cash in order to hurt its eyes by scrutinizing such gargoyles. The one on which his gaze was now resting showed three grinning young women in fancy dress – reading from right to left, Miss 'Cuckoo' Banks, Miss 'Beetles' Bessemer, and Lady 'Toots' Fosdyke – and he thought he had never seen anything more fundamentally loathsome. He turned the page hastily and found himself confronted by a camera study of an actress leering over her shoulder with a rose in her mouth.

And he was about to fling the thing from him with a stifled cry, when his heart gave a sudden bound. A second and narrower look had shown him that this was no actress but Veronica Wedge herself. What had misled him was the rose in the mouth. Nothing in his association with Veronica had given him the idea that she was a female Nebuchadnezzar.

There were unshed tears in Tipton's eyes as they stared down at this counterfeit presentment of the girl he loved. What a face to sit opposite to at breakfast through the years. What a sweet, tender, fascinating, stimulating face. And at the same time, of course, if you looked at it from another angle, what a hell of a pan, with its wide-eyed innocence and all that sort of thing misleading honest suitors into supposing that everything was on the up and up, when all the while it was planning to slip round the corner and neck with serpents on rustic benches. So chaotic were Tipton Plimsoll's emotions as he scanned those lovely features with burning spectacles, that he would have been at a loss to say, if asked, whether he would have preferred to kiss this camera study or give it a good poke in the eye.

Fortunately, perhaps, he had not time to arrive at a decision on the point. A cheery voice said, 'Hullo, hullo. Good morning, good morning,' and he saw framed in the window the head and shoulders of a dapper little man in a grey flannel suit.

'Beautiful morning,' said this person, surveying him benevolently through a black-rimmed monocle.

'Grrh,' said Tipton, with the same reserve of manner which he had employed some days earlier when saying 'Guk' to Freddie Threepwood.

The newcomer was a stranger to him, but he assumed from a recollection of conversation overheard at the breakfast table that he must be Veronica's uncle Gally, who had arrived overnight too late to mix with the company. Nor was he in error. The Hon. Galahad, having stopped at a roadside inn for a leisurely dinner and a game of darts and subsequently having got into an argument with a local patriarch about the Corbett-Fitzsimmons fight, had reached the castle after closing time. This morning he had been rambling about in his amiable way, seeing the old faces, making the acquaintance of new ones, and generally picking up the threads. His arrival at the home of his ancestors always resembled the return of some genial monarch to his dominions after long absence at the Crusades.

'Hot,' he said. 'Very hot.'

'What?' said Tipton.

'It's hot.'

'What's hot?'

'The weather.'

'Oh,' said Tipton, his eyes straying back to the weekly illustrated paper.

'Regular scorcher it's going to be. Like the day when the engine driver had to get inside his furnace to keep cool.'

'What?'

'The engine driver. Out in America. It was so hot that the only way he could keep cool was by crawling into his furnace and staying there. Arising from that,' said the Hon. Galahad, 'have you heard the one about the three stockbrokers and the female snake-charmer?'

Tipton said he had not – at least he made a strangled noise at the back of his throat which gave Gally the impression that he had said that he had not, so he told it to him. When he had finished, there was a silence.

'Well,' said Gally, discouraged, for a raconteur of established reputation expects something better than silence when he comes to the pay-off of one of his best stories, 'I'll be pushing along. See you at lunch.'

'What?'

'I said I would see you at lunch.'

'Guk,' said Tipton, and resumed his scrutiny of the camera study.

2

On the occasions of his intermittent visits to Blandings Castle, the mental attitude of the Hon. Galahad Threepwood, as has been said, resembled that of a genial monarch pottering about his kingdom after having been away for a number of years battling with the Paynim overseas; and like such a monarch in such circumstances what he wanted was to see smiling faces about him.

The moroseness of the young man he had just left had, in consequence, made a deep impression upon him. He was still musing upon it and seeking to account for it when he came upon Colonel Egbert Wedge, sunning himself in the rose garden.

As Gally always breakfasted in bed and the colonel would have scorned to do anything so effete, this was the first time they had met since the banquet of the Loyal Sons of Shropshire, and their conversation for a few moments dealt with reminiscences of that function. Colonel Wedge said that in all his experience, which was a wide one, he had never heard a more footling after-dinner speech than old Bodger had made on that occasion. Gally, demurring, asked what price the one delivered half an hour later by old Todger. The colonel conceded that Todger had been pretty ghastly, but not so ghastly as Bodger. Gally, unwilling to mar this beautiful morning with argument, said perhaps he was right, adding that in his opinion both these territorial magnates had been as tight as owls.

A silence followed. Gally broke it by putting the question which had been exercising his mind at the moment of their meeting.

'Tell me, Egbert,' he said, 'who would a tall, thin chap be?'

Colonel Wedge replied truly enough that he might be anyone – except, of course, a short, stout chap, and Gally became more explicit.

'I was talking to him just now in the small smoking-room. Tall, thin chap with horn-rimmed spectacles. American, if I'm not mistaken. Oddly enough, he reminded me of a man I used to know in New York. Tall, thin, young, with a hell of a grouch and horn-rimmed spectacles all over his face.'

Colonel Wedge's eyebrows came together in a frown. He no longer found any difficulty in assisting the process of identification.

'That is a young fellow named Tipton Plimsoll. Freddie brought him here. And if you ask me, he ought to have taken him to a lunatic asylum instead of to Blandings Castle. Not', he was obliged to add, 'that there's much difference.'

It was plain that the name had touched a chord in Gally's mind.

'*Tipton* Plimsoll? You don't happen to know if he has anything to do with a racket over in the States called Tipton's Stores?'

'Anything to do with them?' Colonel Wedge was a strong man, so he did not groan hollowly, but his face was contorted with pain. 'Freddie tells me he practically owns them.'

'Then that is why his appearance struck me as familiar. He must be the nephew of old Chet Tipton, the man I was speaking of. I seem to remember Chet mentioning a nephew. One of my dearest friends out there,' explained Gally. 'Dead now, poor chap, but when in circulation as fine a fellow as ever out-talked a taxi-driver in his own language. Had one peculiar characteristic. Was as rich as dammit, but liked to get his drinks for nothing. It was his sole economy, and he had worked out rather an ingenious system. He would go into a speakeasy, and mention casually to the barman that he had got smallpox. The barman would dive for the street, followed by the customers, and there Chet was, right in among the bottles with a free hand. Colossal brain. So this young Plimsoll is Chet's nephew, is he? For Chet's sake, I am prepared to love him like a son. What's he grouchy about?'

Colonel Wedge made a despairing gesture.

'God knows. The boy's mentality is a sealed book to me.'

'And why do you say he ought to be in a loony bin?'

Colonel Wedge's pent-up feelings expressed themselves in a snort so vehement that a bee which had just settled on a nearby lavender bush fell over backwards and went off to bestow its custom elsewhere.

'Because he must be stark, staring mad. It's the only possible explanation of his extraordinary behaviour.'

'What's he been doing? Biting someone in the leg?'

Colonel Wedge was glad to have found a confidant into whose receptive ear he could pour the story of the great sorrow which was embittering the lives of himself, his wife, and his daughter Veronica. Out it all came, accompanied by gestures, and by the time he arrived at the final, inexplicable episode of Tipton's failure to clock in behind the rhododendrons, Gally was shaking his head in manifest concern.

'I don't like it, Egbert,' he said gravely. 'It sounds to me un-natural and unwholesome. Why, if old Chet had heard that there were girls in the rhododendrons, he would have been diving into them head foremost before you could say "What ho." If there is anything in heredity, I can't believe that it was the true Tipton Plimsoll who hung back on the occasion you mention. There's something wrong here.'

'Well, I wish you'd put it right,' said Colonel Wedge sombrely. 'I don't mind telling you, Gally, that it's a dashed unpleasant thing for a father to have to watch his – only child slowly going into a decline with a broken heart. At dinner last night Vee refused a second helping of roast duckling and green peas. That'll show you.'

3

As the Hon. Galahad resumed his stroll, setting a course for the sun-bathed terrace, his amiable face was wrinkled with lines of deep thought. The poignant story to which he had been listening had stirred him profoundly. It seemed to him that Fate, not for the first time in his relations with the younger generation, had cast him in the role of God from the Machine. Someone had got to accelerate the publication of the banns of Tipton Plimsoll and Veronica Wedge, and there could be no more suitable person for such a task than himself. Veronica was a niece of whom, though yielding to no one in his recognition of her outstanding dumbness, he had always been fond, and Tipton was the nephew of one of his oldest friends. Plainly it was up to him to wave the magic wand. He seemed to hear Chet's voice whispering in his ear: 'Come on, Gally. Li'l speed.'

It was possibly this stimulation of his mental processes from beyond the veil that enabled him to hit upon a solution of the problem. At any rate, he was just stepping on to the terrace when his face suddenly cleared. He had found the way.

And it was at this moment that a two-seater came bowling past with Freddie at the wheel back at the old home after his night with the Shropshire Finches. He whizzed by and rounded the corner leading to the stables with a debonair flick of the wrist, and Gally lost no time in following him. In the enterprise which he was planning he required the cooperation of an assistant. He found the young go-getter, his two-seater safely garaged and a cigarette in its eleven-inch holder between his lips, blowing smoke rings.

Freddie's visit to Sudbury Grange, the seat of Major R. B. and Lady Emily Finch, had proved one of his most notable triumphs. He had found Sudbury Grange given over to the damnable cult of Todd's Tail-Waggers' Tidbits, an even fouler product than Peterson's Pup Food, and it had been no easy task to induce his host and hostess to become saved and start thinking the Donaldson way. But he had done it. A substantial order had been booked, and during the drive to Blandings the exhilaration of success had kept his spirits at a high level.

But with the end of the journey, there had come the sobering thought that though his own heart might be light there were others in its immediate circle that ached like billy-o. Bill Lister's, for one. Prue's, for another. Veronica Wedge's, for a third. So now, when he blew smoke rings, they were grave smoke rings.

At the moment of Gally's appearance he had been thinking of Veronica, but the sight of his uncle caused Bill's unhappy case to supplant hers in the forefront of his mind, and he started to go into it without delay.

'Oh, hullo, Uncle Gally,' he said. 'What ho, Uncle Gally? I say, Uncle Gally, brace yourself for a bit of bad news. Poor old Bill –'

'I know, I know.'

'You've heard about him being given the bum's rush again?'

'I've seen him. Don't you worry about Bill,' said Gally, who believed in concentrating on one thing at a time. 'I have his case well in hand. Bill's all right. What we've got to rivet our attention on now, Freddie, my boy, is this mysterious business of young Plimsoll and Veronica.'

'You've heard about that too?'

'I've just been talking to her father. He seems baffled. You're a friend of this young Plimsoll. I am hoping that he may have confided in you or at least let fall something which may afford a clue to the reason for this strange despondency of his. I saw him for the first time just now, and was much struck by his resemblance to a rainy Sunday at a South Coast seaside resort. He is in love with Veronica, I presume?'

'All the nibs seem to think so.'

'And yet he takes no steps to push the thing along. Indeed, he actually gives her the miss in baulk when she goes and waits for him in the rhododendrons. This must mean something.'

'Cold feet?'

Gally shook his head.

'I doubt it. This young man is the nephew of my old friend Chet Tipton, and blood must surely tell. Chet never got cold feet in his life when there were girls around. The reverse, in fact. You had to hold him back with ropes. On the other hand, he did experience strange fits of despondency, when he would sit with his feet on the mantelpiece examining his soul. Another old friend of mine, Plug Basham, was the same. Very moody chap. However, I managed to snap Plug out of it, and I am inclined to think that the same method would be successful with this young Plimsoll. By great good luck we have the animal all ready to hand.'

'Animal?'

'Your father's pig. The worst attack of despondency from which I ever remember Plug suffering occurred when a few of us were at a house in Norfolk for the pheasants. We talked it over and came to the decision that what he wanted was a shock. Nothing serious, you understand, just something that would arrest his attention and take his mind off his liver. So we borrowed a pig from a neighbouring farm, smeared it with a liberal coating of phosphorus, and put it in his bedroom. It worked like magic.'

A certain concern had manifested itself in Freddie's aspect. His eyes bulged and his jaw dropped a little.

'You aren't going to put the guv'nor's pig in Tippy's bedroom?'

'I think it would be rash not to. They've given me the Garden Suite this time, with french windows opening on the lawn, so there will be no difficulty in introducing the animal. It almost seems as though it were meant.'

'But, Uncle Gally –'

'Something on your mind, my boy?'

'Would you really recommend this course?'

'It proved extraordinarily efficacious in Plug's case. He went into his room in the dark, and the thing caught him right in the eyeball. We heard a cry, obviously coming straight from the heart, and then he was pelting downstairs three stairs at a time, wanting to know what the procedure was when a fellow had made up his mind to sign the pledge – how much it cost, where you had to go to put in your application, did you need a proposer and seconder, and so forth.'

'But it might have worked the other way round.'

'I don't follow you.'

'What I mean is, if he'd been on the wagon already, it might have prompted him to take the snifter of a lifetime.'

'Plug wasn't on the wagon.'

'No, but Tippy is.'

Gally started. He was surprised and shocked.

'What? Chet Tipton's nephew a teetotaller?'

'Only in the past few days,' explained Freddie, who was the last man to wish to put a friend in a dubious light. 'Before that he was one of our leading quaffers. But after being on a solid toot for two months he has now signed off for some reason which he has not revealed to me, and at moment of going to press absorbs little except milk and barley water. It's a thing his best friends would have advised, and honestly, Uncle Gally, I doubt if you ought to do anything that might turn his thoughts back in the direction of the decanter.'

The Hon. Galahad's was a quick, alert mind. He could appreciate sound reasoning as readily as the next man.

'I see what you mean,' he said. 'Yes, I take your point. I'm glad you told me. This calls for a radical alteration in our plans. Let me think.'

He took a turn about the stable yard, his head bowed, his hands behind his back. Presently Freddie, watching from afar, saw him remove his monocle and polish it with the satisfied air of one who has thought his way through a perplexing problem.

'I've got it,' he said, returning. 'The solution came to me in a flash. We will put the pig in Veronica's room.'

A rather anxious expression stole into Freddie's face. Of the broad general principle of putting pigs in girls' rooms he of course approved, but he did not like that word 'we'.

'Here, I say!' he exclaimed. 'You're not going to lug me into this?'

The Hon. Galahad stared.

'Lug?' he said. 'What do you mean lug? The word "lug" appears to me singularly ill-chosen. I should have supposed that as a friend of this young Plimsoll and a cousin of Veronica you would have been all eagerness to do your share.'

'Well, yes, of course, definitely, but I mean to say –'

'Especially as that share is so trivial. All I want you to do is go ahead and see that the coast is clear. I will attend to the rough work.'

His words left Freddie easier in his mind. But that mind, what there was of it, was still fogged.

'But where's the percentage?'

'I beg your pardon?'

'What's the good of putting pigs in Vee's room?'

'My dear fellow, have you no imagination? What happens when a girl finds a pig in her room?'

'I should think she'd yell her head off.'

'Precisely. I confidently expect Veronica to raise the roof. Whereupon, up dashes young Plimsoll to her rescue. If you can think of a better way of bringing two young people together, I should be interested to hear it.'

'But how do you know Tippy will be in the vicinity?'

'Because I shall see to it that he is. Immediately after lunch I shall seek him out and engage him in conversation. You, meanwhile, will attach yourself to Veronica. You will find some pretext for sending her to her room. What pretext? Let me think.'

'She was threatening the other day to show me her album of school snapshots. I could ask her to fetch it.'

'Admirable. And the moment the starter's flag has dropped, give the gong in the hall a good hard bang. That will serve as my cue for unleashing young Plimsoll. I think we have synchronized everything?'

Freddie said he thought so.

'And the guv'nor being in London,' he pointed out with some relief, 'you will be able to restore the animal to its sty without him knowing to what uses it has been put in his absence.'

'True.'

'A rather important point, that. Any funny business involving the ancestral porker is apt to wake the sleeping tiger in him.'

'Quite. That shall be attended to. One does not wish to cause Clarence pain. I suppose the best time to inject this pig would be after the gang have settled in at lunch. You won't mind being ten minutes late for lunch?'

'Try to make it five,' said Freddie, who liked his meals.

'And now,' said Gally, 'to find Prudence. I have a note to give her from Bill which, unless I am greatly mistaken, will send her singing about the premises like a skylark in summer. Where would she be, I wonder? I've been looking for her everywhere.'

Freddie was able to assist him.

'I met her in the village as I was driving through. She said she was going to see the vicar about his jumble sale.'

'Then I will stroll down and meet her,' said Gally.

With a parting instruction to his nephew to be on his toes the moment he heard the luncheon gong go, he sauntered off. His mood was one of quiet happiness. If there was one thing this good man liked, it was scattering light and sweetness, and today, it seemed to him, he was about to scatter light and sweetness with no uncertain hand.

4

Tipton Plimsoll stood on the terrace, moodily regarding the rolling parkland that spread itself before his lacklustre eyes. As usual in this smiling expanse of green turf and noble trees, a certain number of cows, some brown, some piebald, were stoking up and getting their vitamins, and he glowered at them like a man who had got something against cows. And when a bee buzzed past his nose, his gesture of annoyance showed that he was not any too sold on bees either. The hour was half past two, and lunch had come to an end some few minutes earlier.

It had proved a melancholy meal for Tipton. A light breakfaster, he generally made up leeway at the midday repast, but on this occasion he had more or less pushed his food away untasted. Nothing in the company or the conversation at the board had tended to dispel the dark mood in which he had started the morning. He had been glad when the ritual of coffee-drinking was over and he was at liberty to take himself elsewhere.

His initial move, as we say, had been to the terrace, for he needed air and solitude. He got the air all right but missed out on the solitude. He had been looking at the cows for scarcely a minute and a quarter with growing disfavour, when a monocle gleamed in the sunshine and the Hon. Galahad was at his side.

Most people found Gally Threepwood a stimulating and entertaining companion and were glad of his society, but Tipton goggled at him with concealed loathing. And when one says 'concealed', that is perhaps the wrong word. All through lunch this man had insisted on forcing upon him a genial flow of talk about his late Uncle Chet, and as far as Tipton was concerned Uncle Chet had reached saturation point. He felt that he had heard all that any nephew could possibly wish to hear about an uncle.

So now, starting away like some wild creature frightened by human approach, he was off the terrace and into the house before his companion could so much as be reminded of a story. The gloom of the small smoking-room drew him like a magnet, and he had fled there and was reaching out a limp hand for the weekly illustrated paper containing the camera study when the door opened.

'Aha!' said Gally. 'So here you are, eh?'

There is this to be said for the English country-house party, whatever its drawbacks, which are very numerous – when you have had as much of the gay whirl as you can endure, you can always do a sneak to your bedroom. Two minutes later Tipton was in his. And two minutes after that he found that he had been mistaken in supposing that he was alone at last. There was a knock on the door, the robust and confident knock of one who is sure of his welcome, and a dapper, grey-flannelled form sauntered in.

Anybody who wishes to be clear on Tipton Plimsoll's feelings at this juncture has only to skim through the pages of Masefield's *Reynard the Fox*. The sense of being a hunted thing was strong upon him. And mingled with it was resentment at the monstrous injustice of this persecution. If a country-house visitor is not safe in his bedroom, one might just as well admit that civilization has failed and that the whole fabric of society is tottering.

Agony of spirit made him abrupt.

'Say, you chasing something?' he demanded dangerously.

It would have required a dull man to be unconscious of the hostility of his attitude, and it did not escape Gally's notice that his young friend was rapidly coming to the boil. But he ignored the sullen fire behind the horn-rimmed spectacles.

'We do keep meeting, don't we?' he replied with the suave geniality which had so often disarmed belligerent bookmakers. 'The fact is, my boy, I want a long talk with you.'

'You just had one.'

'A long, intimate talk on a matter closely affecting your happiness and well-being. You are the nephew of my old friend Chet Tipton –'

'You already told me that.'

'– and I decline, I positively refuse to see Chet Tipton's nephew ruining his future and bunging golden prospects of roseate bliss where the soldier bunged the pudding, when I can put the whole thing right in half a minute with a few simple words. Come now, my dear fellow, we needn't beat about the bush. You love my niece Veronica.'

A convulsive start shook Tipton Plimsoll. His impulse was to deny the statement hotly. But even as he opened his mouth to do so, he found himself gazing at the lovely features of the camera study. Actually, the camera study was still in the small smoking-room, but he seemed to see it now, the rose dangling from its lips, and he had not the heart to speak. Instead, he gave a quick, low gulp like a bulldog choking on a piece of gristle, causing Gally to pat his shoulder five or six times in a fatherly manner.

'Of course you do,' said Gally. 'No argument about that. You love her like a ton of bricks. The whole neighbourhood is ringing with the story of your passion. Then why on earth, my dear chap, are you behaving in this extraordinary way?'

'What do you mean, extraordinary way?' said Tipton, weakly defensive.

'You know what I mean,' said Gally, impatient of evasion. 'Many people would say you were playing fast and loose with the girl.'

'Fast and loose?' said Tipton, shocked.

'Fast *and* loose,' repeated Gally firmly. 'And you know what the verdict of men of honour is on chaps who play fast and loose with girls. I have often heard your uncle Chet express himself particularly strongly on the subject.'

The words 'To hell with my uncle Chet' trembled on Tipton's lips, but he forced them back in favour of others more germane to the subject under discussion.

'Well, what price her playing fast and loose with me?' he cried. 'Leading me on and then starting the old army game, the two-timing Jezebel.'

'Don't you mean Delilah?'

'Do I?' said Tipton, dubious.

'I think so,' said Gally, none too sure himself. 'Jezebel was the one who got eaten by dogs.'

'What a beastly idea.'

'Not pleasant,' agreed Gally. 'Must have hurt like the dickens. However, the point is,' he said, a stern look coming into his face, 'that you are speaking of my niece and bringing a very serious accusation against her. What, exactly, do you imply by the expression "the old army game"?'

'I mean she's giving me the run-around.'

'I fail to understand you.'

'Well, what would you call it if a girl let it be generally known that you were the blue-eyed boy and then you found her necking on benches with that heel Freddie?'

This shook Gally.

'Necking on benches? With Freddie?'

'I saw them. He was kissing her. She was crying, and he was kissing her like nobody's business.'

'When was this?'

'Yesterday.'

Daylight flooded in upon the Hon. Galahad. He was a man who could put two and two together.

'Before you had failed to meet her behind the rhododendrons,' he asked keenly, 'or after?'

'After,' said Tipton, and having spoken allowed his mouth to remain open like that of a sea lion expecting another fish. 'Gee! Do you think that was why she was crying?'

'Of course it was. My dear chap, you're a man of the world and you know perfectly well that you can't go about the place telling girls to meet you behind rhododendrons and then not turning up without gashing their sensitive natures to the quick. One sees the whole picture. Having drawn blank in the rhododendrons, Veronica would naturally totter to the nearest bench and weep bitterly. Along comes Freddie, finds her in tears, and in a cousinly spirit kisses her.'

'Cousinly spirit? You think that was it?'

'Unquestionably. A purely cousinly spirit. They have known each other all their lives.'

'Yes,' said Tipton moodily. 'People used to call her his little sweetheart.'

'Who told you that?'

'Lord Emsworth.'

Gally clicked his tongue.

'My dear fellow, one of the first lessons you have to learn, if you intend to preserve your sanity in Blandings Castle, is to pay no attention whatsoever to anything my brother Clarence says. He has been talking through the back of his neck for nearly sixty years. I never heard anyone call Veronica Freddie's little sweetheart.'

'He used to be engaged to her.'

'Well, weren't we all? I don't mean engaged to Veronica, but to somebody. Weren't you?'

'Why, yes,' Tipton was forced to admit. 'I've been engaged about half a dozen times.'

'And they mean nothing to you now, these momentary *tendresses*?'

'Momentary what?'

'Oh, get on with it,' said Gally. 'You don't care a damn for the girls now, what?'

'I wouldn't say a damn,' said Tipton meditatively. 'There was one named Doris Jimpson . . . Yes, I would too. No, I don't care a damn for any of them.'

'Exactly. Well, there you are. You needn't worry about Freddie. He's devoted to his wife.'

Hope dawned in his young friend's face.

'You mean that?'

'Certainly. A thoroughly happy marriage. They bill and coo incessantly.'

'Gosh,' said Tipton, and mused awhile. 'Of course cousins do kiss cousins, don't they?'

'They're at it all the time.'

'And it doesn't mean a thing?'

'Not a thing. Tell me, my dear chap,' said Gally, feeling that the sooner this point was settled the quicker the conference would begin to get results. 'Why did you hang back from that rhododendron tryst?'

'Well, it's a long story,' said Tipton.

It was not often that the Hon. Galahad found himself commending the shrewdness and intelligence of a nephew whom from infancy he had always looked upon as half-witted, but he did so now, as the tale of the face unfolded itself. In the course of a longish life spent in London's more Bohemian circles it had been his privilege to enjoy the friendship of quite a number of men who saw things, and he knew how sensitive and highly strung those so afflicted were, and how readily they had recourse to the bottle to ease the strain. Unquestionably, Freddie had been right. It would have been an error of the gravest nature to have put the pig in Tipton Plimsoll's sleeping quarters.

'I see,' he said thoughtfully, as the narrative drew to its conclusion. 'This face peered at you from the bushes?'

'Not so much peered,' said Tipton, who liked to get things straight, 'as leered. And I rather think it said "Hi!"'

'And had you given it any encouragement?'

'Well, I did take a short snort from my flask.'

'Ah! You have it here, this flask?'

'It's in that drawer over there.'

The Hon. Galahad cocked a dubious eyebrow at the drawer.

'Hadn't you better let me take charge of that?'

Tipton chewed his lip. It was as if the suggestion had been made to a drowning man that he part with his life-belt.

'It is not the sort of thing you ought to have handy. And you won't need it. Believe me, my boy, this is going to be a walkover. I know for a fact that Veronica is head over ears in love with you. No earthly need to buck yourself up before proposing.'

'The squirt thought otherwise.'

'The squirt?'

'That small, blue-eyed girl they call Prudence.'

'She advised a gargle?'

'A quick one.'

'I think she was wrong. You could do it on lime juice.'

Tipton continued dubious, but before any settlement could be reached, the debate was interrupted. From the hall below there burst upon their ears the sound of booming brass. Gally, who had been prepared for it, showed no concern, but Tipton, to whom it came as a complete surprise and who for a moment had mistaken it for the Last Trump, rose an inch or two into the air.

'What the devil was that?' he asked, becoming calmer.

'Just someone fooling about,' said Gally reassuringly. 'Probably Freddie. Pay no attention. Go right up to Veronica's room and get the thing over.'

'To her room?'

'I have an idea I saw her going there.'

'But I can't muscle into a girl's room.'

'Certainly not. Just knock, and ask her to come out and speak to you. Do it now,' said the Hon. Galahad.

5

It is a truism to say that the best-laid plans are often disarranged and sometimes even defeated by the occurrence of some small unforeseen hitch in the programme. The poet Burns, it will be remembered, specifically warns the public to budget for this possibility. The gong sequence now under our notice provides a case in point.

What the Hon. Galahad had failed to allow for in arranging for Freddie to beat the gong as a signal that Veronica Wedge was on her way up to her room was that there is a certain type of girl, to which Veronica belonged, who on hearing gongs beaten when they are half-way upstairs come down again and start asking those who have beaten them why they have beaten them. Freddie was just replacing the stick on its hook with the gratifying feeling of having completed a good bit of work when he observed a pair of enormous eyes staring into his and realized that the starter's flag had dropped prematurely.

The following dialogue took place:

'Fred-dee, was that you?'

'Was what me?'

'Did you beat the gong?'

'The gong? Oh, yes. Yes, I beat the gong.'

'Why did you beat the gong?'

'Oh, I don't know. I thought I would.'

'But what did you beat the gong *for*?'

This sort of thing was theatening to go on for some time when Lady Hermione came out of the drawing-room.

Lady Hermione said:

'Who beat the gong?'

To which Veronica replied: 'Fred-dee beat the gong.'

'Did you beat the gong, Freddie?'

'Er – yes. Yes, I beat the gong.'

Lady Hermione swooped on this damaging admission like a cross-examining counsel.

'*Why* did you beat the gong?'

Veronica said that that was just what she had been asking him.

'I was going up to my room to get my album of snapshots, Mum-mee, and he suddenly beat the gong.'

Beach, the butler, appeared through the green baize door at the end of the hall.

'Did somebody beat the gong, m'lady?'

'Mr Frederick beat the gong.'

'Very good, m'lady.'

Beach withdrew, and the debate continued. It came out in the end that Freddie had beaten the gong just for a whim. A what? A *whim*! Dash it, you know how you get whims sometimes. He had got this sudden whim to beat the gong, so he had beaten the gong. He said he was blowed if he could see what all the fuss was about, and Veronica said: 'But, Fred-dee,' and Lady Hermione said that America appeared to have made him even weaker in the head than he had been before crossing the Atlantic, and Veronica was just about to resume her progress up the stairs (still feeling that it was peculiar that her cousin should have beaten gongs), when it occurred to Lady Hermione that she had forgotten to tell Bellamy, her maid, to change the shoulder straps on her brassiere and that this was a task which could be very well undertaken by Veronica.

Veronica, always dutiful, said: 'Yes, Mum-mee,' and set out for the room next to the servants' hall where Bellamy did her sewing. Lady Hermione went back to the drawing-room. Freddie, feeling that the situation had got beyond him, took refuge in the billiard room, and started thinking of dog biscuits.

So that when the Hon. Galahad, misled by the beating of the gong, supposed that his niece was on her way up to her bedroom, she was really headed in a different direction altogether, and the chances of Tipton Plimsoll rescuing her from pigs and clasping her trembling form to his bosom and asking her to be his wife were for the moment nil. It was not until quite some little time later that Veronica, having delivered her message to Bellamy, turned her thoughts once more towards the fetching of snapshot albums.

Tipton, meanwhile, having reached the Red Room, had paused before its closed door. He was breathing rather stertorously, and he balanced himself first on one leg, then on the other.

In scouting Freddie's suggestion that a nephew of the late Chet Tipton might be suffering from cold feet in his relations with the opposite sex, the Hon. Galahad had erred. Nephews do not always inherit their uncles' dash and fire. You might have had to hold Chet back with ropes when there were girls around, but not Tipton. In spite of the encouragement which he had received both from Gally and the squirt Prudence, he was conscious now of a very low temperature in his extremities. Also, his heart was throbbing like a motor-cycle, and he experienced a strange difficulty in breathing. And the more he thought the situation over, the more convinced he became that a preliminary stimulant was essential to the task he had in hand.

A look of decision crept into his face. He strode from the door and hurried back to his room. The flask was still in the drawer – he shuddered to think how near he had come in a moment of weakness to yielding to Gally's offer to take charge of it – and he raised it to his lips and threw his head back.

The treatment was instantaneously effective. Resolution and courage seemed to run through his veins like fire. Defiantly he looked about the room, expecting to see the face and prepared to look it in the eye and make it wilt. But no face appeared. And this final bit of good luck set the seal on his feeling of well-being.

Three minutes later he was outside the Red Room again, strong now and confident, and he lost no time in raising a hand and driving the knuckles against the panel.

It was the sort of buffet which might have been expected to produce instant results, for in his uplifted mood he had put so much follow-through into it that he had nearly broken the skin. But no voice answered from within. And this struck Tipton as odd, for there could be no question that the girl was there. He could hear her moving about. Indeed, as he paused for a reply, there came a sudden crash, suggesting that she had bumped into a table or something with china on it.

He knocked again.

'Say!' he said, putting his lips to the woodwork and speaking in a voice tense with emotion.

This time his efforts were rewarded. From the other side of the door there came an odd sound, rather like a grunt, and he took it for an invitation to enter. He had not actually expected the girl he loved to grunt, but he was not unduly surprised that she had done so. He assumed that she must have something in her mouth. Girls, he knew, often did put things in their mouths – hairpins and things like that. Doris Jimpson had frequently done this.

He turned the handle . . .

It was a few minutes later that Beach, the butler, passing through the baize doors into the hall on one of those errands which take butlers through baize doors into halls, was aware of a voice from above that said, 'Hey!' and, glancing up, perceived that he was being addressed by the young American gentleman whom Mr Frederick had brought to the castle.

'Sir?' said Beach.

Tipton Plimsoll's manner betrayed unmistakable agitation. His face was pale, and the eyes behind the horn-rimmed spectacles seemed heavy with some secret sorrow. His breathing would have interested an asthma specialist.

'Say, listen,' he said. 'Which is Mr Threepwood's room?'

'Mr Frederick Threepwood, sir?'

'No, the other one. The guy they call Gally.'

'Mr Galahad is occupying the Garden Suite, sir. It is on the right side of the passage which you see before you. But I fancy he is out in the grounds at the moment, sir.'

'That's all right,' said Tipton. 'I don't want to see him, just to leave something in his room. Thanks.'

He made his way with faltering footsteps to the sitting-room of the Garden Suite and, drawing the flask from his pocket, placed it on the table with something of the sad resignation of a Russian peasant regretfully throwing his infant son to a pursuing wolf pack. This done, he came slowly out and slowly started to walk upstairs once more.

And he had just reached the first landing, still in low gear, when something occurred that caused him to go abruptly into high, something that made him throw his head back like a warhorse at the sound of the bugle, square his shoulders, and skim up the stairs three at a time.

From above, seeming to proceed from the direction of the Red Room, a girl's voice had spoken, and he recognized it as that of Veronica Wedge.

'EEEEEEEEEEE!!!' it was saying.

6

A girl with good lungs cannot exclaim 'EEEEEEEEEEE!!!' to the fullest extent of those lungs on the second floor of a country house during the quiet period which follows the consumption of lunch without exciting attention and interest. The afternoon being so fine, most of the residents of Blandings Castle were out in the open – Gally for one; Colonel Wedge for another; Prudence for a third; and Freddie, who had found the billiard room stuffy and had gone off to the stables to have a look at his two-seater, for a fourth. But Lady Hermione, who was in the drawing-room, got it nicely.

At the moment when the drowsy summer stillness was ripped into a million quivering fragments, Lady Hermione had been reading for the third time a telegram which had just been brought to her on a silver salver by Beach, the butler. Signed 'Clarence' and despatched from Paddington Station at 12.40, it ran as follows:

ARRIVING TEA TIME WITH LANDLADY

When Lord Emsworth composed telegrams in railway stations

two minutes before his train was due to leave, his handwriting, never at the best of times copperplate, always degenerated into something which would have interested a Professor of Hieroglyphics. The operator at Paddington, after a puzzled scrutiny, had substituted on his own responsibility 'Arriving' for 'Ariosto' and 'tea time' for what appeared to be 'totem' but the concluding word had beaten him completely. It had seemed to him a choice between 'lingfear', 'leprosy', and 'landlady'. He had discarded the first because there is no such word as 'lingfear'; the second because, though not a medical expert, he was pretty sure that Lord Emsworth had not got leprosy; and had fallen back on the third. He hoped that it would convey some meaning at the other end.

He had been too optimistic. Lady Hermione stared at the missive blankly. Its surface import – that the head of the family, when he showed up for the afternoon cup of tea, would be accompanied by something stout in a sealskin coat and a Sunday bonnet – she rejected. If it had been her brother Galahad who had so telegraphed, it would have been another matter. Galahad, being the sort of man he was, might quite conceivably have decided to present himself at Blandings Castle with a landlady, or even a bevy of landladies, explaining that they had been dear friends of his years ago when they used to do clog dances on the halls. But not Clarence. She had never been blind to the fact that the head of the family was eccentric, but she knew him to be averse to feminine society. Landladies who wanted a breath of country air would never get it on his invitation.

She was just wondering if the word could possibly be a misprint for 'laryngitis', a malady from which the ninth earl occasionally suffered, when Veronica went on the air.

To refresh the reader's memory, in case he has forgotten, what Veronica was saying was 'EEEEEEEEEEE!!!' and as soon as she had made certain that the top of her head had not come off Lady Hermione found the cry speaking to her very depths. A moment's startled rigidity and she was racing up the stairs at a speed not much inferior to that recently shown by Tipton. It is a callous mother who can remain in a drawing-room when her child is squealing 'EEEEEEEEEEE!!!' on the second floor.

Her pace was still good as she rounded into the straight, but as she came in sight of the door of the Red Room she braked sharply. There had met her eyes a spectacle so arresting, so entrancing, so calculated to uplift a mother's heart and make her want to turn cartwheels along the corridor that she feared for an instant that it might be a mirage. Blinking and looking again, she saw that she had not been deceived.

There, half-way down the corridor, one of the richest young men in America was clasping her daughter to his chest, and even as she gazed he bestowed upon that daughter a kiss so ardent that there could be no mistaking its meaning.

'Veronica!' she cried. A lesser woman would have said 'Whoopee!'

Tipton, tensely occupied, had been unaware till now that he was not alone with his future wife. Turning to include his future mother-in-law in the conversation, his immediate impulse, for he was an American gentleman, was to make it clear to her that this was the real stuff and not one of those licentious scenes which Philadelphia censors cut out of pictures.

'It's quite OK,' he hastened to assure her. 'We're engaged.'

Her dash up the stairs had left Lady Hermione a little touched in the wind, and for a space she remained panting. Eventually she was able to say: 'Oh, Tipton!'

'You are not losing a daughter,' said Tipton, having had time to think of a good one. 'You are gaining a son.'

Any doubts which he might have entertained as to the popularity of his romance in the circles most immediately interested were at once removed. It was abundantly clear that the arrangement which he had outlined was one that had Lady Hermione's sympathy and support. Her breath now recovered, she kissed him with a warmth that left no room for misunderstanding.

'Oh, Tipton!' she said again. 'I am delighted. You must be very happy, Veronica.'

'Yes, Mum-mee.'

'Such a lovely birthday present for you, darling,' said Lady Hermione.

Her words got right in amongst Tipton Plimsoll. He started as if a whole platoon of faces had suddenly manifested themselves before his eyes. He remembered now that at breakfast somebody had been saying something about it being somebody's birthday, but he had been moody and abstracted and had not thought to inquire into the matter. A vague impression had been left upon his mind that they had been talking about the squirt Prudence.

Remorse shot through him like a red-hot skewer. It seemed incredible to him that preoccupation should have caused him to remain in ignorance of this vital fact.

'Jiminy Christmas!' he cried, aghast. 'Is this your birthday? And I haven't got you a present. I must get you a present. Where can I get you a present?'

'Shrewsbury,' said Veronica. She was at her best when answering simple, straightforward questions like that.

Tipton's air was now that of one straining at the leash.

'How long does it take you to get to Shrewsbury?'

'About three quarters of an hour in a car.'

'Are there shops there?'

'Oh, yes.'

'Jewellers' shops?'

'Oh, *yes*!'

'Then meet me in the rhododendrons in about a couple of hours and anticipate a pleasant surprise. I'll go swipe a car. Oh, say,' said Tipton, recollecting something which, though of minor importance compared with birthday presents for the girl he loved, deserved, he felt, a passing mention. 'There's a pig in there.'

'A pig?'

'Yes, Mum-mee, there's a pig in my bedroom.'

'Most extraordinary,' said Lady Hermione, and might have been sceptical had not the Empress selected this moment for thrusting a mild and inquiring face round the door.

'There you are,' said Tipton. 'One pig, as stated.'

He left her to cope with it. He felt that the matter could be in no better hands. On flying feet he hastened to the stables.

Freddie was in the yard, tinkering with his two-seater.

7

There had been a time, and that not so long ago, when, finding Freddie in stable yards tinkering with two-seaters, Tipton Plimsoll would have drawn himself to his full height and passed by with a cold stare. But now that he had wooed and won the most beautiful girl in the world he was in softer, kindlier mood. He had erased the other's name from his list of snakes and saw him for what he was – a blameless cousin.

Later on, no doubt, they would have to come to some arrangement about the other's habit of bestowing cousinly kisses on the future Mrs Plimsoll, but for the moment there was no jarring note to cause a discord between them. Filled to the brim with the milk of human kindness, Tipton regarded Freddie once more as a pal and a buddy. And when you are sitting on top of the world, the first people you apprise of the fact are pals and buddies. He lost no time in announcing the great news.

'Say, Freddie,' he said, 'guess what? I'm engaged!'

'Engaged?'

'Yup.'

'To Vee?'

'Sure. Just signed on the dotted line.'

'Well, I'm dashed,' said Freddie. 'Put it there, pardner.'

So beaming was his smile, so cordial his handshake, that Tipton found his last doubts removed. And so beaming was *his* smile, so instinct with benevolence his whole demeanour, that Freddie decided that the moment had arrived to put his fate to the test, to win or lose it all.

This necessitated a somewhat abrupt change of subject, but he was feeling too tense to lead the conversation around to the thing in easy stages.

'Oh, by the way, old man,' he said.

'Yes, old man?' said Tipton.

'There's something I've been meaning to ask you for some time, old man,' said Freddie, 'only it kept slipping my mind. Will you give the Tipton's Stores dog-biscuit concession to Donaldson's Dog-Joy, old man?'

'Why, sure, old man,' said Tipton, looking like something out of Dickens. 'I was going to suggest it myself.'

The stable yard seemed to reel before Freddie's eyes. He stood silent for an instant, struggling with his emotion. In his mind he was sketching out the cable which he would despatch that night to

Long Island City, informing his father-in-law of this outstanding triumph which he had achieved in the interests of the dog biscuits he loved so well. He could picture the old buster opening the envelope and going into a hootchy-kootchy dance all over the office.

He drew a long breath.

'Old man,' he said reverently, 'they don't come any whiter than you. I've always said so.'

'Have you, old man?'

'I certainly have. And I hope you'll be very, very happy, old man.'

'Thanks, old man. Say, can I borrow your car? I want to go to Shrewsbury and buy Veronica a birthday present.'

'I'll drive you there, old man.'

'That's darned good of you, old man.'

'Not at all, old man, not at all,' said Freddie.

He seated himself at the wheel and placed a suede-clad shoe on the self-starter. It occurred to him as a passing thought that all was for the best in this best of all possible worlds.

Chapter 8

A man who likes to see the young folks happy always finds it agreeable to be able to reflect that owing to his ministrations joy among the younger set is reigning unconfined; and the events of the summer afternoon had left the Hon. Galahad Threepwood feeling at the peak of his form.

He had just met his niece Veronica on her way to the rhododendrons and had been informed by her of the signal good fortune which had befallen the house of Wedge. And before that he had come upon his niece Prudence palely loitering in the drive and had given her Bill's letter, thereby bringing the roses back to her cheeks and causing her to revise her views on the sadness of life from the bottom up. As he came out of the sunshine into the dim coolness of the hall he was walking jauntily and humming beneath his breath a gay music-hall ballad of his youth.

It was now the hour when the fragrance of tea and the warm, heartening scent of buttered toast begin to float like a benediction over the English home, and Beach and his capable assistants had already set out the makings in the drawing-room. He proceeded to trip thither, but more from sociability than with any idea of becoming an active participant in the feast. He never drank tea, having always had a prejudice against the stuff since his friend Buffy Struggles back in the nineties had taken to it as a substitute for alcohol and had perished miserably as a result. (Actually what had led to the late Mr Struggles's turning in his dinner pail had been a collision in Piccadilly with a hansom cab, but Gally had always felt that this could have been avoided if the poor dear old chap had not undermined his constitution by swilling a beverage whose dangers are recognized by every competent medical authority.)

The drawing-room was empty except for his sister Hermione,

who was seated behind the teapot, ready to get into action the instant the call came. She stiffened as he entered and directed at him a stern and accusing glare, like a well-bred basilisk.

'So there you are, Galahad,' she said, coming to the point in the direct way characteristic of sisters all the world over. 'Galahad, what do you mean by putting that beastly pig in Veronica's bedroom?'

This was not clairvoyance. Lady Hermione had reached her conclusion by a careful process of character analysis. Probing into the natures and dispositions of her little circle, she had decided that there was only one person on the premises capable of putting pigs in bedrooms and that that person stood before her now.

The arrival of Beach at this moment with a bowl of strawberries, followed by a footman bearing cream and another staggering under the weight of powdered sugar, prevented an immediate reply to the question. When the procession had filed out, Beach in transit booking an order for a whisky and soda, Gally was able to speak.

'So you've heard about that?' he said airily.

'Heard about it? The loathsome animal was galloping all over the corridor.'

'It was a clever idea,' said Gally, with modest pride. 'Yes, though I say it myself, clever. Egbert was weeping on my shoulder this morning about the way young Plimsoll was shilly-shallying. I saw that it was no time for half-measures. I acted. To whisk the Empress from her sty and put her in the forefront of the battle was with me the work of an instant. Did Veronica yowl?'

'She screamed,' corrected his sister coldly. 'The poor child received a very severe shock.'

'And Plimsoll, I gather, dashed up and came to the rescue. The ice was broken. He lost his reserve. He folded her in his arms and spoke his love, and a wedding has been arranged and will shortly take place. Just as I foresaw. Precisely as I had anticipated. The whole operation from start to finish went according to plan, and the curtain fell on the happy ending. So what you're blinding and stiffing about,' said Gally, who, unlike Lord Emsworth, was not the man to be browbeaten by sisters, 'I fail to understand.'

Lady Hermione denied the charge that she was blinding and stiffing. She was, she said, extremely annoyed.

'Annoyed? What the dickens is there to be annoyed about?'

'The animal ate one of Veronica's new camisoles.'

'Well, finding itself in the bedroom, it would naturally assume that it had been invited to take pot luck. Stick to the point, which is that you can't get away from it that but for my subtle strategy business would never have resulted. Dash it, which would the girl rather have – a mouldy camisole or a wealthy and devoted husband whose only thought will be to gratify her lightest wish? Young Plimsoll will be able to provide Veronica with diamond camisoles, if she wants them. So stop cursing and swearing like a bargee, and let's see that sunny smile of yours. Can't you realize that this is the maddest, merriest day of all the glad New Year?'

The soundness of his reasoning was so manifest that Lady Hermione was obliged to relax her austerity. She did not actually smile her sunny smile, but a trace of softness crept into her demeanour, which up till now had resembled that of a rather unusually stern governess.

'Well, I have no doubt that your motives were excellent, but I hope you will not do it again.'

'You don't suppose a busy man like me makes a practice of putting pigs in girls' rooms? What became of the animal in the final issue?'

'The pig man removed it.'

'I must remember to fling him a purse of gold, or he'll go squealing to Clarence. What would you say was the market price of a pig man's silence? How did you get in touch with him?'

'I rang for Beach, who sent a footman to fetch him. A little gnome of a man with no roof to his mouth, who smelled worse than the pig.'

'Niffy, eh? It probably covered an honest heart. Niffiness often does. And we can't all have roofs to our mouths. When are you expecting Clarence back?'

'He wired that he would be here for tea.'

'Odd how he enjoys his cup of tea. Can't think why. Horrible muck. Polished off poor old Buffy Struggles as clean as a whistle.'

'Here's his telegram. It arrived just before Veronica received that terrible shock.'

In Gally's opinion this remark came under the heading of harping on the dead past.

'I wish you wouldn't keep burbling on about Veronica receiving shocks,' he said impatiently. 'You talk as if finding a simple pig in her room were enough to disintegrate her entire nervous system. I don't suppose that after her first natural surprise she experienced any discomfort whatsoever. What did Clarence say in his telegram?'

'That he would be arriving at tea-time with landlady.'

'With what?'

'Read it for yourself.'

Gally fixed his black-rimmed monocle more firmly in his eye and scrutinized the document. His face cleared.

'I can tell you what this means. What he was trying to say in that vile handwriting of his was that he would be accompanied by Landseer.'

'Landseer?'

'The artist.'

'Landseer is dead.'

'He wasn't when I met him yesterday.'

'Do you mean the Landseer who painted stags?'

'No. I mean the Landseer who paints pigs.'

'I never heard of him.'

'Well, cheer up. You're hearing of him now. And you'll be meeting him in a few minutes. Clarence has commissioned him on my recommendation to do the Empress's portrait.'

Lady Hermione uttered a sharp cry.

'You have not been encouraging Clarence in that idiotic idea of his?'

'He didn't need any encouraging. He came up to London full of iron resolution, determined to procure an artist of some kind. All I did was to assist him in his choice. You'll like this fellow. Charming chap.'

'A friend of yours?'

'Yes,' replied Gally, with spirit. 'A very dear friend of mine. What did you say?'

Lady Hermione said that she had not spoken. Nor had she. She had merely sniffed. But in certain circumstances a sniff can be as wounding as the bitterest repartee, and Gally was about to comment on hers in a militant manner, for his lifelong policy had been to be very firm with sniffing sisters, when there came the sound of wheels grinding to a standstill on the gravel outside the front door.

'Clarence,' said Gally.

'And Mr Landseer.'

'Don't say "And Mr Landseer" in that soupy tone of voice,' said Gally sternly. 'He hasn't come to steal the spoons.'

'If he is a friend of yours, I should imagine that he is quite capable of doing so. Is he wanted by the police?'

'No, he is not wanted by the police.'

'How I sympathize with the police,' said Lady Hermione. 'I know just how they feel.'

From the hall the reedy tenor voice of Lord Emsworth cut in upon a conversation which was threatening to become acrimonious.

'Beach will show you your room, my dear fellow,' he was saying, addressing an unseen companion. 'Tell you where it is and so forth. Come along to the drawing-room when you're ready.'

And presently the *seigneur* of Blandings Castle entered, inhaling the grateful odour that rose from the teapot and beaming vaguely through his pince-nez.

'Ah,' he said. 'Tea, eh? Tea. Capital, capital. Tea.' Then, following his custom of making his meaning thoroughly clear, added the word 'Tea', repeating it three times. The dullest listener would have divined that he was aware of the presence of tea and would be glad of a cup, and Lady Hermione, pausing only to sniff, poured him out one.

'Tea,' said Lord Emsworth again, clearing the whole situation up and getting everything straight. 'Thank you, my dear.' He took the cup, cleverly added milk and sugar, stirred, and drank. 'Ha!' he ejaculated, refreshed. 'Well, here I am, Galahad.'

'You never spoke a truer word, Clarence,' his brother agreed. 'I can see you with the naked eye. Did you bring Landseer?'

'Who is Landseer? Oh, of course, yes, Landseer. I was forgetting. That was Landseer I was talking to in the hall. Landseer', explained Lord Emsworth, addressing his sister, 'is an artist who has come to paint the Empress.'

'So Galahad was telling me,' said Lady Hermione.

Her tone was so free from joyous animation that Gally felt constrained to supply a footnote.

'Hermione is anti-Landseer. She has taken one of her absurd prejudices against the poor chap.'

'I have done nothing of the kind,' said Lady Hermione. 'I preserve an open mind on the subject of Mr Landseer. I am quite prepared to find him reasonably respectable, even though he is a friend of yours. I merely feel, as I have always felt, that it is a ridiculous waste of money to have that pig's portrait painted.'

Lord Emsworth stiffened. He was shocked, not only by the sentiment but by the allusion to his ewe lamb as 'that pig'. He felt it to be lacking in respect.

'The Empress has twice in successive years won the silver medal in the Fat Pigs' class at the Shrewsbury Show,' he reminded her coldly.

'Exactly,' said Gally. 'The only celebrity we have ever produced. She has a far better right to be in the family portrait gallery than half those bearded bounders who disfigure it.'

Lady Hermione became rigid. Like her sister, she revered her ancestors with an almost Chinese fervour and had always resented the casual attitude towards them of the male members of the family.

'Well, we will not discuss it,' she said, closing the debate. 'I hope you remembered to buy Veronica her birthday present, Clarence?'

From sheer force of habit Lord Emsworth started guiltily. And he was just about to assume the weak, blustering manner customary with him on these occasions and to demand how the dickens a man like himself, with a hundred calls on his time, could be expected to remember to buy birthday presents, when he recollected that he had done so.

'Certainly I did,' he replied with dignity. 'A most excellent wrist watch. I have it in my pocket.'

He produced it as he spoke with quiet pride, and with it another package also bearing the famous label of the Bond Street firm of Aspinall, at which he peered perplexedly.

'Now what the deuce is this?' he queried. 'Ah, yes, I remember. It is something Freddie asked me to pick up at the shop. His present for Veronica, I understand. Where is Freddie?' he asked, scanning the furniture vaguely as if expecting to see his younger son lurking behind some chair or settee.

'I saw him going hell for leather down the drive in that car of his about two hours ago,' said Gally. 'He had young Plimsoll with him. I don't know where they were off to.'

'Shrewsbury,' said Lady Hermione. 'Tipton wanted to buy Veronica a birthday present. They are engaged, Clarence.'

'Eh?'

'They are engaged.'

'Ah,' said Lord Emsworth, becoming interested in a plate of cucumber sandwiches. 'Sandwiches, eh? Sandwiches, sandwiches. Sandwiches,' he added, taking one.

'They are engaged,' said Lady Hermione, raising her voice.

'Who?'

'Veronica and dear Tipton.'

'Who is dear Tipton?'

'"Dear Tipton"', explained Gally, 'is Hermione's nickname for young Plimsoll.'

'Plimsoll? Plimsoll? Plimsoll? Oh, *Plimsoll*? I remember him,' said Lord Emsworth, pleased at his quick intelligence. 'You mean the young man with those extraordinary spectacles. What about him?'

'I am trying to tell you', said Lady Hermione patiently, 'that he and Veronica are engaged.'

'God bless my soul!' said Lord Emsworth, a look of startled concern coming into his face. 'I didn't know these sandwiches were cucumber. I thought they were potted meat. I would never have eaten one if I'd known they were cucumber.'

'Oh, Clarence!'

'Can't digest cucumber. Never could.'

'Well, really, Clarence. I thought you might take a little interest in your niece.'

'What's she been doing?'

'They keep these things from you, Clarence,' said Gally sympathetically. 'You ought to be told. Veronica and young Plimsoll are engaged.'

'Ah,' said Lord Emsworth, now thoroughly abreast of the position of affairs. 'Well, that's all right. No harm in that. I like him. He is sound on pigs.'

'And Hermione likes him because he's a millionaire,' said Gally. 'So you're all happy.'

Lady Hermione was asserting with some warmth that her fondness for Tipton Plimsoll was due entirely to the fact that he was a charming, cultured young man and devoted to Veronica, and Gally was challenging her to deny that at least a portion of the Plimsoll glamour proceeded from the circumstance of his having got the stuff in sackfuls, and Lord Emsworth was saying again that he would never have eaten that cucumber sandwich if he had known it was cucumber, because cucumbers did something to his inside, when Freddie appeared in the french windows.

'Hullo, Guv'nor. Hullo, Aunt Hermione. Hullo, Uncle Gally,' said Freddie. 'Hope I'm not too late for a beaker. We rather overstayed our time in Shrewsbury owing to Tippy insisting on buying up the whole place. The two-seater returned laden with apes, ivory, and peacocks like a camel of the epoch of King Solomon. Did you remember to pick up that little thing of mine at Aspinall's, Guv'nor?'

Secure in the fact that he was holding it in his hand, Lord Emsworth permitted himself to become testy.

'Certainly I did. Everybody asks me if I have remembered something. I never forget anything. Here it is.'

'Thanks, Guv'nor. A quick cup of tea, and I'll go and give it to her.'

'Where is Veronica?' asked Lady Hermione.

'Tippy was expecting to locate her in the rhododendrons. They had a date there, I understand.'

'Go and tell them to come in to tea. Poor Tipton must be exhausted after his long drive.'

'He didn't seem to be. He was panting emotionally and breathing flame through the nostrils. God bless my soul,' said Freddie, 'how it brings back one's bachelor days, does it not, to think of young lovers hobnobbing in shrubberies. I often used to forgather with Aggie in the local undergrowth in my courting days, I recollect. Well, I will do my best to get your kindly message through to him, Aunt Hermione, but always with the proviso that I am not muscling in on a sacred moment. If in my judgement he doesn't want to be interrupted, I shall tip-toe away and leave him. See you later, folks. Pip-pip, Guv'nor; don't take any wooden nickels.'

He drained his cup and departed, and Lord Emsworth had just begun to say that since his younger son had returned from America he had observed in him a sort of horrible briskness and jumpiness which he deplored, when there came from without the sound of some heavy body tripping over a rug, and Bill came in.

2

Bill was looking fresher than might have been expected after a four-hour railway journey with Lord Emsworth, the explanation of this being that the latter always slept in the train, so that he had had nothing to do but lie back and look out of the window and think long thoughts of Prudence.

These had been not only loving, but optimistic. Well in advance of his arrival, he presumed, Gally would have given her that letter of his, and from its perusal he confidently expected the happiest results. He had put his whole heart into the communication, and when a man with a heart as large as his does that, something has got to give. The Prue whom he would shortly meet would, he anticipated, be a vastly different Prue from the scornful girl who had called him a fathead, broken the engagement, and whizzed off like a jack rabbit before he could even start to appeal to her better nature.

But though such reflections as these had unquestionably tended to raise his spirits, it would be too much to say that William Lister, as he clumped across the threshold of the drawing-room of Blandings Castle, was feeling completely carefree. He was in the pink, yes, but not so entirely in the pink as to preclude a certain wariness and anxiety. His mental attitude might be compared to that of a cat entering a strange alley whose resident population may or may not be possessed of half-bricks and inspired with the urge to heave them.

To the discomfort of being in the society of an elderly gentleman whom in a moment of pique he had once told to go and boil his head he had become inured. He no longer regarded Lord Emsworth as a potential obstacle in his path. The occasional puzzled stares which the other had bestowed upon him in the train before stretching out his legs and closing his eyes and starting to grunt and gurgle had fallen off him like blunted arrows. That the thought behind these stares was that Lord Emsworth was conscious of a nebulous feeling that his face was somehow familiar, he was aware; but basing his trust on the statement of the Hon. Galahad that the ninth earl had an IQ thirty points lower than a jellyfish he had been enabled to meet with an easy nonchalance the pince-nez-ed eyes that gazed perplexedly into his.

But the formidable woman seated behind the teapot was a different proposition. Here, beyond a question, danger lurked. You might not admire Lady Hermione Wedge as you would admire Helen of Troy, or the current Miss America, but there was no gainsaying her intelligence. It would have to be an exceptionally up-and-coming jellyfish which could even contemplate challenging her IQ. He could only hope that at their previous encounter the beard had done its silent work well, obscuring his features beyond recognition.

Her greeting, if you could call it a greeting, seemed to suggest that everything was all right so far. She was unable entirely to conceal the fact that she regarded him as a pest and an intruder who if she had had her way would have been dumped at the Emsworth Arms and not allowed to inflict his beastly presence on a decent castle; but she directed at him no quick, suspicious stare, uttered no sharp cry of denunciation. She said: 'How do you do, Mr Landseer,' in a voice that suggested that she hoped he was going to tell her that the doctors had given him three weeks to live, and supplied him with a cup of tea. Bill knocked over a cake table, and they all settled down to make a cosy evening of it.

Conversation became general. Lord Emsworth, sniffing the scented breeze which floated in through the open windows, said that it was nice to be back in civilized surroundings after a visit to London, and Gally said that he had never been able to understand his brother's objections to London, a city which he himself had always found an earthly Paradise. He applied to Bill to support him in this view, and Bill, who had fallen into a dream about Prudence, started convulsively and kicked over the small table on which he had placed his cup. In response to his apologies Lady Hermione assured him that it did not matter in the least. Anybody who had not caught her eye, as Bill did, would have supposed her to be one of those broad-minded hostesses who prefer tea on their carpets.

Lord Emsworth then said that his distaste for London was due to the circumstance of it being a nasty, noisy, filthy, smelly hole, full of the most frightful cads, and Gally said that they were probably all charming chaps once you got to know them, instancing the case of a one-eyed three-card-trick man back in the early days of the century to whom he had taken an unreasoning dislike at their first meeting, only to discover, after they had been on a binge together one evening, that the fellow was the salt of the earth.

Lady Hermione, who deprecated the introduction into the tea-table conversation in her drawing-room of reminiscences of one-eyed three-card-trick men, however sound their hearts, changed the subject by asking Bill if this was his first visit to Shropshire, and the latter, shaken to his foundations by the innocent query, once more kicked over the cake table. The fact was that Bill, though an admirable character, was always a little large for any room in which he was confined. To ensure his not kicking over cake tables, you would have had to place him in the Gobi Desert.

Gally in his genial way had just offered, if Bill wanted to make a nice clean job of smashing up the premises, to bring him an axe, and was asking Lord Emsworth if he remembered the time when their mutual uncle, Harold, who had never been quite himself after that touch of sunstroke in the East, had wrecked this same drawing-room with a borrowed meat-chopper in an attempt to kill a wasp, when Lady Hermione, who had been regarding Bill with quiet loathing, suddenly gave a start and intensified her scrutiny.

It had just occurred to her, as it had occurred to Lord Emsworth in Duke Street, that somewhere, at some time and place, she had seen him before.

'Your face seems oddly familiar, Mr Landseer,' she said, gazing at it with a raptness which only Tipton Plimsoll could have surpassed.

Lord Emsworth peered through his pince-nez, intrigued.

'Just what I said when I met him. Struck me at once. It's a peculiar face,' he said, scanning it closely and noting that it had now turned a rich vermilion. 'Sort of face that stamps itself on the memory. Galahad's suggestion was that I must have seen his photograph in the papers.'

'Does Mr Landseer's photograph appear in the papers?' asked Lady Hermione, her tone suggesting that, if so, it lowered her opinion of the British Press.

'Of course it does,' said Gally, correctly divining that Bill would appreciate a helping hand. 'Repeatedly. As I told Clarence, Landseer is a dashed celebrated chap.'

Lord Emsworth endorsed this view.

'He painted the Stag at Bay,' he said admiringly.

There was a special sound which Lady Hermione often found it convenient to employ when conversing with her elder brother and feeling the need of relieving her feelings. It was not exactly a sniff and not precisely a snort, but a sort of blend of the two. It proceeded from her now.

'Mr Landseer did not paint the Stag at Bay. It was painted by Sir Edwin Landseer, who has been dead for years.'

'That's odd. Galahad told me it was this chap who painted the Stag at Bay.'

Gally laughed indulgently.

'You've muddled the whole thing as usual, Clarence. I said the Pig at Bay.'

'The *Pig* at Bay?'

'Yes. A very different thing.'

Lord Emsworth digested this. A question occurred to him almost immediately.

'But are pigs at bay?'

'This one was.'

'It seems most unusual.'

'Not when you remember, as you would if you were a travelled man, that Bée is a village in the Pyrenees famous for its pigs. If Landseer goes to Bée on a sketching tour one summer and sees a pig there and paints it and, hunting round for a title, decides to call it the Pig at Bée, it seems to me quite a natural sequence of events. I don't see what all the argument is about, anyway. The only thing that matters, to my mind, is that you have got hold of a man who knows his pigs and can be relied on to turn out a speaking likeness of the Empress. You ought to be rejoicing unstintedly.'

'Oh, I am,' said Lord Emsworth. 'Oh, yes, indeed. It's a great relief to feel that Mr Landseer is going to attend to the thing. I'm sure he will be an enormous improvement on the other fellow. By George!' cried Lord Emsworth with sudden animation. 'God bless my soul! Now I know why I thought I'd seen him before. He's the living image of that other fellow – the frightful chap you sent down a few days ago, the one who did a horrible caricature of the Empress and then told me to go and boil my head because I ventured on the mildest of criticisms. What was his name?'

'Messmore Breamworthy.' Gally eyed Bill with mild interest.

'Yes, there is resemblance,' he agreed. 'Quite understandably, of course, considering that they are half-brothers.'

'Eh?'

'Landseer's widowed mother married a man named Breamworthy. The union culminated in young Messmore. A good enough chap in his way, but I would never have sent him down if I had known that Landseer was available. No comparison between the two men as artists.'

'Odd that they should both be artists.'

'Would you say that? Surely these things often run in families.'

'That's true,' agreed Lord Emsworth. 'There's a man living near here who breeds cocker spaniels, and he has a brother in Kent who breeds sealyhams.'

During these exchanges Lady Hermione had been silent. It was the burgeoning within her of a monstrous suspicion that had made her so. Slowly and by degrees this suspicion was gathering strength. Indeed, the only barrier to a complete understanding on her part was the feeling that there must surely be some things of which her brother Galahad was not capable. She knew him to be a man possessed to an impressive degree of the gall of an army mule, but even an army mule, she considered, would hesitate to smuggle into Blandings Castle an ineligible suitor from whose society one of its sacred nieces was being rigorously withheld.

She looked at Bill and closed her eyes, trying to conjure up that interview on the lawn. She wished she could be sure . . .

Too little, the chronicler realizes, has been said about that beard of Fruity Biffen's, and it may be that its concealing properties have not been adequately stressed. But reading between the lines, the public must have gathered an impression of its density. The Fruities of this world, when they are endeavouring to baffle the scrutiny of keen-eyed bookmakers, do not skimp in the matter of face fungus. The man behind this beard was not so much a man wearing a beard as a pair of eyes staring out of an impenetrable jungle; and, try as she might, Lady Hermione was unable to recall any more definite picture than just that.

She sat back in her chair frowning. The whole thing turned, of course, on whether her brother Galahad was or was not capable of drawing the line somewhere. She mused on this, and the conversation flowed about her unheard.

As a matter of fact, there was nothing in it particularly worth hearing. Lord Emsworth said that he had been wrong in asserting that the man who lived near here bred cocker spaniels – he had meant retrievers. And as the mention of dogs of any breed could scarcely fail to remind Gally of a rather amusing story which might possibly be new to those present, he told one.

He had finished it and was starting another, begging them to stop him if they had heard it before, when Lord Emsworth, who had been showing signs of restlessness, said that he thought he ought to be going down and seeing Pott, his pig man, in case the latter should have anything of interest to report concerning the affairs of the Empress during his absence.

The words brought Gally to an abrupt halt in his narrative. They reminded him that he had still to see this Pott and purchase his silence. If Lord Emsworth were to contact the fellow before this was done, who knew what sensational confidences might not be poured into his quivering ear. Gally was extremely fond of his brother and shrank from having him upset. He also disliked arguments and discussions.

Policy plainly called to him to race off and sweeten Pott. But this involved leaving Bill. And was it safe to leave Bill to cope unsupported with a situation which he was quite aware was delicate and difficult?

The point was very moot, and for a moment he hesitated. What finally decided him was Lady Hermione's trancelike demeanour. She seemed to have withdrawn into a meditative coma, and as long as this persisted there could surely be no peril. And, after all, it does not take the whole evening to whizz down to a pigsty, stop the pig man's mouth with gold, and whizz back again. He would be able to return in a quarter of an hour at the outside.

Rising, accordingly, with a muttered statement about having forgotten something, he passed through the french windows and disappeared; and a few moments later Lord Emsworth, who always took a little time to collect his hands and feet when about to potter from any given spot, followed him. With much the same unpleasant shock which must have come to the boy who stood on the burning deck, Bill awoke from a reverie on his favourite subject of Prudence to the realization that all but he had fled and that he was alone with his hostess.

A silence ensued. When a young man of shy disposition, accustomed to the more Bohemian society of Chelsea, finds himself alone on her home ground with a daughter of a hundred earls and cannot forget that at their last meeting he mistook her for the cook and tipped her half a crown; and when the daughter of the hundred earls, already strongly prejudiced against the young man as an intruder, has begun to suspect that he is the miscreant who recently chivvied her only child and is doing his best to marry her niece against the wishes of the family, it is almost too much to expect that the conversation will proceed from the first with an easy flow.

Her friends had sometimes said of Lady Hermione, who was a well-read, well-educated woman with an interest in most of the problems of the day, that if she wanted to she could found a modern *salon*. At the moment, it seemed, she did not want to, at any rate with Bill as the nucleus of it.

The two were still eyeing each other with embarrassment on the one side and an ever-increasing suspicion on the other, when their *tête-à-tête* was interrupted. A shadow fell on the pool of sunlight in the french windows, and Freddie came curvetting in.

'No dice,' announced Freddie, addressing his aunt. 'I found them linked in a close embrace, and I hadn't the heart to interrupt them.'

At this point he observed that his father and his uncle were no longer in the room, but that a newcomer had been added in the shape of a large individual who was sitting with his long legs twined round those of a chair. Coming out of the sunshine, he experienced a momentary difficulty in seeing this substantial bird steadily and seeing him whole, and for an instant supposed himself to be gazing upon a stranger. The thought occurred to him that it might be possible to interest the man in a good dog biscuit.

Then, as his eyes adjusted themselves to the subdued light, they suddenly widened in an incredulous stare and his mouth, as was its habit in time of emotion, fell open like a letter box.

To his uncle Galahad he later put two simple questions, explaining that on these he rested his case.

They were:

(a) How the dickens could he have been expected to know? and, arising from this,

(b) Why had he not been kept informed?

It stands to reason, argued Freddie, that if a chap has been widely publicized as a pariah and an outcast and then you suddenly come upon him sitting at his ease in the drawing-room, having a cosy dish of tea with the spearhead of the opposition, you naturally assume that the red light has turned to green and that he has been taken to the family's bosom. Particularly, he added with quiet reproach, if you have been expressly told that he is 'all right' and that you need not worry about him because the speaker assures you that he has his case 'well in hand'.

It was on those phrases, he said, that he took his stand. Had his uncle Gally used them, or had he not? Had he or had he not practically stated in so many words that the ban on poor old Blister had been lifted and that his future need cause his friends and well-wishers no concern? Very well, then, there you were. The point he was making was that it was unjust and absurd to apply such a term as 'cloth-headed young imbecile' to himself and to hurl at him the reproach of being a spiller of beans and a bunger of spanners into works.

What had brought about the disaster, he urged, was the Hon. Galahad's extraordinary policy of silence and secretiveness. A word to the effect that he was planning to introduce Bill Lister into the house surreptitiously, and all would have been well. In these affairs, he pointed out, cooperation is of the essence. Without cooperation and a frank pooling of information, no dividends can be expected to result.

Thus Freddie later. What he said now was:

'Blister!'

The word rang through the drawing-room like a bugle, and Lady Hermione, on whose heart the name 'Lister' was deeply graven, leaped in her chair.

'Well, well, well!' said Freddie, beaming profusely. 'Well, well, well, well, well! Well, this is fine, this is splendid. So you've seen reason, Aunt Hermione? I was hoping your sterling good sense would assert itself. I take it that you have talked Aunt Dora over, or propose to do so at an early date. Now that you are wholeheart-edly on the side of love's young dream, I anticipate no trouble in that quarter. She will be wax in your hands. Tell her from me, in case she starts beefing, that Prue could find no worthier mate than good old Bill Lister. One of the best and brightest. I've known him for years. And if he chucks his art, as he has guaranteed to do, and goes into the pub-keeping business, I see no reason why the financial future of the young couple should not be extremely bright. There's money in pubs. They will need a spot of capital, of course, but that can be supplied. I suggest a family round-table conference, at which the thing can be thoroughly gone into and threshed out in all its aspects. Cheerio, Blister. Heartiest congratulations.'

Throughout this well-phrased harangue Lady Hermione had been sitting with twitching hands and gleaming eyes. It had not occurred to the speaker that there was anything ominous in her demeanour, but a more observant nephew would have noted her strong resemblance to the puma of the Indian jungle about to pounce upon its prey.

She eyed him inquiringly.

'Have you quite finished, Freddie?'

'Eh? Yes, I think that about covers the subject.'

'Then I should be glad', said Lady Hermione, 'if you would go and see Beach and tell him to pack Mr Lister's things, if they are already unpacked, and send them to the Emsworth Arms. Mr Lister will be leaving the castle immediately.'

Chapter 9

Accustomed from earliest years to carry out with promptness and civility the wishes of his aunts, a nephew's automatic reaction to a command from one of the platoon, even after he has become a solid married man with an important executive post in America's leading firm of dog-biscuit manufacturers, is to jump to it. Ordered by his aunt Hermione to go and see Beach, Freddie did not draw himself up and reply that if she desired to get in touch with her staff she could jolly well ring for them; he started off immediately.

It was only when he was almost at the door of the butler's pantry that it occurred to him that this errand-boy stuff was a bit *infra dig* for a vice-president, and he halted. And having halted he realized that where he ought to be was back in the drawing-room, which he should never have left, trying to break down with silver-tongued eloquence his relative's sales resistance to poor old Blister. A testing task, of course, but one not, he fancied, beyond the scope of a man who had recently played on Major R. B. and Lady Emily Finch as on a couple of stringed instruments.

Reaching the drawing-room, he found that in the brief interval since his departure Bill had left, presumably with bowed head, through the french windows. But, restoring the quota of lovers to its previous level, Prudence had arrived, and her aspect showed only too plainly that she had been made acquainted with the position of affairs. Her eyes were dark with pain, and she was eating buttered toast in a crushed sort of way.

Lady Hermione was still sitting behind the teapot, as rigidly erect as if some sculptor had persuaded her to pose for his Statue of an Aunt. In all the long years during which they had been associated, it seemed to Freddie that he had never seen her looking so undisguisedly the Aunt, the whole Aunt, and nothing but the Aunt, and in spite of himself his heart sank a little. Even Lady Emily Finch, though her mental outlook was that of a strong-minded mule, an animal which she resembled in features as well as temperament, had been an easier prospect.

'Blister gone?' he said, and marshalled a telling phrase or two in his mind for use later.

'Gone,' said Prudence, through a bitter mouthful of buttered toast. 'Gone without a cry. Driven into the snow before I could so much as set eyes on him. Golly, if a few people around this joint had hearts, Blandings Castle would be a better, sweeter place.'

'Well spoken, young half-portion,' said Freddie approvingly. 'I thoroughly concur. What the old dosshouse needs is a splash of the milk of human kindness. Switch it on, Aunt Hermione, is my advice.'

Lady Hermione, disregarding this appeal, asked if he had seen Beach, and Freddie said no, he had not seen Beach and he would tell her why. It was because he had hoped that better counsels would prevail, and if his aunt would give him a couple of minutes of her valuable time he would like to put forward a few arguments which might induce her to look with a kindlier eye on these young lovers who were being kept asunder.

Lady Hermione, who was somewhat addicted to homely phrases, said: 'Stuff and nonsense.' Freddie, shaking his head, said that this was hardly the spirit he had hoped to see. And Prudence, who had been sighing rather heavily at intervals, brought the names of Simon Legree and Torquemada into the conversation, speculating as to why people always made such a song and dance about their brutal inhuman inhumanity when there were others (whom she was prepared to name on request) who could give them six strokes in eighteen holes and be dormy two on the seventeenth tee.

Lady Hermione said: 'That is quite enough, Prudence,' and Freddie contested this view.

'It is not enough, Aunt Hermione. Far from it. We will now go into executive session and thresh the whole thing out. What have you got against poor old Blister? That is the question I should like to begin by asking you.'

'And this', said Lady Hermione, 'is the question I should like to begin by asking *you*. Were you a party to this abominable trick of Galahad's?'

'Eh?'

'You know perfectly well what I mean. Bringing that young man into the house under a false name.'

'Oh, that?' said Freddie. 'Well, I'll tell you. I was not actually hep to the stratagem you mention, or I would never have dropped the brick I did. But if you are asking me: "Am I heart and soul in Blister's cause?" the answer is in the affirmative. I consider that a union between him and this young prune here would be in the best and deepest sense a bit of all right.'

'Att-a boy, Freddie,' said the prune, well pleased with this sentiment.

'Stuff and nonsense,' said Lady Hermione, with whom it had not gone over so big. 'The man looks like a gorilla.'

'Bill does not look like a gorilla!' cried Prudence.

'Yes, he does,' said Freddie, who, though partisan, was fair. 'As far as the outer crust goes, good old Blister could walk straight into any zoo, and they would lay down the red carpet for him. But the point seems to me to have little or no bearing upon the case at issue. There is nothing in the book of rules, as far as I am aware, that prevents a man looking like a gorilla and still having what it takes when it is a question of being a good husband, and a loving father, if you'll excuse me mentioning it, Prue. Just peeping into Vol. Two for a moment.'

'Quite all right,' said Prudence. 'Carry on. You're doing fine.'

'Where you have made your bloomer, Aunt Hermione, is in allowing yourself to be influenced too much by appearances. You cock an eye at Blister and you say to yourself, "Gosh! I'd hate to meet that bird down a lonely alley on a dark night," overlooking the fact that beneath that sinister exterior there beats one of the most outsize hearts you're likely to find in a month of Sundays. It isn't faces that matter, it's honest worth, and in that department Blister is a specialist.'

'Freddie?'

'Hullo?'

'Will you be quiet!'

'No, Aunt Hermione,' said the splendid young dog-biscuit vendor stoutly. 'I will not be quiet. The time has come to speak out. Blister, as I told you before, is one of the best. And I believe I mentioned that he is the owner of a pub which only needs a bit of capital to make it a gold mine.'

Lady Hermione shuddered. She was not a woman who had ever been fond of public houses.

'The fact that this young man may have a bright future as a potboy', she said, 'does not seem to me an argument in favour of his marrying my niece. I wish to hear no more about Mr Lister.'

The wish was not fulfilled. There was a patter of feet outside the french windows, and Gally tripped in, looking well satisfied with himself. He did not know what the European record was for a two-hundred-yard dash to a pigsty, the bribing to silence of the pig man, and the two-hundred-yard dash back, but he rather fancied that he had clipped a few seconds off it. It seemed to him most improbable that in such a brief period of time anything could have gone wrong with his protégé's affairs, and the first flicker of apprehension which disturbed his equanimity came when he glanced about the room and noted his absence.

'Hullo,' he said. 'Where's Landseer?'

Lady Hermione was looking like a cook about to give notice on the evening of the big dinner party.

'If you are referring to Mr Lister, your public-house friend, he has gone.'

A deep sigh escaped Prudence.

'Aunt Hermione bunged him out, Uncle Gally.'

'What!'

'She found out who he was.'

Gally stared at his sister, stunned by this evidence of what seemed to him a scarcely human penetration.

'How the dickens', he asked, awed, 'did you do that?'

'Freddie was obliging enough to tell me.'

Gally turned to his nephew, and his monocle shot forth flame.

'You cloth-headed young imbecile!'

It was at this point that Freddie put the two questions to which allusion has been made earlier, and followed them up with the train of reasoning which has already been outlined. He spoke eloquently and well, and as his uncle also spoke eloquently and well at the same time, a certain uproar and confusion resulted. Simultaneously Prudence was adding her mite, protesting in her clear soprano voice that she intended to marry the man she loved, no matter what anybody said and no matter how often her flinty-hearted relatives might see fit to throw the poor angel out on his ear; and Lady Hermione's position became roughly that of a chairman at a stormy meeting of shareholders.

She was endeavouring to restore order by beating on the table with a teaspoon when Veronica came in through the french windows, and at the sight of her the uproar ceased. People who knew her always stopped arguing when Veronica came along, because she was sure to want them to explain what they were arguing about and, when they had explained, to ask them to start at the beginning and explain again. And when nerves are frayed that sort of thing is annoying.

Gally stopped calling Freddie names. Freddie stopped waving his hands and appealing to the other's simple sense of justice. Prudence stopped saying they would all look pretty silly when they found her drowned in the lake one morning. And Lady Hermione stopped hammering on the table with the teaspoon. It was like a lightning strike in a boiler factory.

Veronica was radiant. Not even in the photograph taken after the Pageant in Aid of Distressed Public School Men and showing her as the Spirit of the Playing Fields of Eton had she exhibited a more boneheaded loveliness. She seemed to have developed a sort of elephantiasis of the eyes and front teeth, and her cheeks glowed with the light that never was on land or sea. She was wearing on her right wrist the best bracelet which Shrewsbury could produce at a moment's notice, and there were other ornaments on her person. But she made it plain at once that her thirst for *bijouterie* was by no means slaked.

'Oh, Fred-dee,' she said, 'has Uncle Clarence got back yet?'

Freddie passed a careworn hand over his brow. He had had the sense of being just about to triumph in the argument which her arrival had brought to a close, and this interruption irked him.

'Eh? Yes, the guv'nor is on the premises. You'll find him in the pigsty, I imagine.'

'Did you bring your present?'

'Oh, the present? The gift? Yes, I have it here. Here you are, with oomps and good wishes.'

'Oh, thank you, Fred-dee,' said Veronica, and withdrew into a corner to inspect it.

As a rule, as has been said, people stopped arguing when this girl came in, and they had done so now. But so gripping were the various subjects on the agenda paper that it was only a moment before the discussion broke out again. At first it was conducted in whispers, but gradually these gathered strength, until presently the boiler factory was in full swing once more.

Gally said that while he had always held a low opinion of his nephew's mentality and would never have cared to risk important money on him in an intelligence contest against a child of three with water on the brain, this latest manifestation of his ingrowing imbecility had come as a profound and painful shock, seeming, as it did, to extend the bounds of possibility. Years ago, he recalled, when shown the infant Frederick in his cradle, he had been seized by a strong conviction that the sensible thing for his parents to have done would have been to write off their losses and drown him in a bucket, and to this view he still adhered. Much misery might thus have been averted.

Freddie said that it began to look to him as if there were no such thing as justice in this world. If ever a fellow had been allowed to wander into a snare through lack of inter-office communication, that fellow was himself. Why had he not been told? Why had he not been put abreast? A simple memo would have done the trick, and no memo had been forthcoming. If the verdict of posterity was not that the whole thing was the fault of his uncle and that he himself was blameless and innocent, he would be surprised and astonished – in fact, amazed and stunned.

Prudence said that the idea of drowning herself in the lake was beginning to grow on her. It had floated into her mind just now as a rather attractive daydream, and the more she examined the project, the better it looked. She would prefer, of course, life as Mrs William Lister, but if that avenue were to be closed and poor darling Bill thrown out on the back of his neck every time he tried to get a couple of words with her, she could not see that there was anything bizarre about wanting to drown herself in the lake. It seemed to her the obvious policy to pursue. She went on to draw rather an interesting picture of Lord Emsworth diving in one morning for his before-breakfast swim and bumping his head against her swollen corpse. She said it would make him think a bit, and no doubt she was right.

Lady Hermione said nothing, but continued to bang the table with the teaspoon.

What results this spoon work might eventually have produced, one cannot say. No doubt ere long the rhythmic thrumming would have influenced the tone of the discussion and done something to restore the decencies of debate. But before it had had time to make its presence felt there cut into the confused welter of competing voices a sudden observation from Veronica.

'EEEEEEEEEEE!!!' said Veronica.

The chronicler has already had occasion to show this girl saying 'EEEEEEEEEEE!!!' and it will not have been forgotten how instantaneously arresting was the effect of the word on her lips. Whatever you were doing when you heard it, your tendency was to drop it and listen.

It was so now. Gally, who had been comparing Freddie to his disadvantage with a half-witted whelk-seller whom he had met at Hurst Park the year Sandringham won the Jubilee Cup, stopped in mid-sentence. Freddie, who by way of giving some idea of what he meant by cooperation, had started to describe the filing system in vogue at the offices of Donaldson's Inc., broke off with a gasp. Prudence, who, still toying with the idea of suicide by drowning, had just remembered the notable precedent of Ophelia and was asking what Ophelia had got that she hadn't got, gave a startled jump and was silent. Lady Hermione dropped her teaspoon.

They all turned and gazed in the speaker's direction, and Freddie uttered a piercing cry.

Veronica, looking like a lovely young mother at the cot-side of her newborn child, was holding aloft a superb and expensive diamond necklace.

'Oh, Fred-dee!' she said.

2

The cry which Freddie had uttered had proceeded straight from a strong man's heart. It was, as has been stated, piercing, and it had every reason to be so.

It is always exasperating for a son who has given his father the clearest possible instructions as to how to proceed in a certain matter to find that the latter has gone and got them muddled up after all, and once again, as had happened during the recent unpleasantness with his uncle Galahad, Freddie found himself chafing at the apparent impossibility of ever obtaining cooperation in the country of his birth. He sighed for the happier conditions prevailing in the United States of northern America, where you got it at every turn.

But what had seared his soul so agonizingly when he beheld the necklace in Veronica's hands was the thought of the delay which must now inevitably ensue before it could be shipped off to Aggie. As he had explained to Prudence in their conversation in Grosvenor Square, Aggie needed the thing in a hurry. She had said so in her first wire and repeated the statement in her second, third, and fourth wires; and as the days went by and it failed to reach her, an unmistakably peevish note had crept into her communications. Niagara Threepwood (*née* Donaldson) was the sweetest of women, and there was no argument about her being the light of her husband's life and the moon of his delight, but she had inherited from her father the slightly impatient temper which led the latter at conferences to hammer on the table and shout: 'Come on, come on now!'

Thinking of the fifth wire, which might now be expected at any moment, Freddie found himself shuddering in anticipation. Going by the form book, it should be a pipterino. Even the fourth had been good, fruity stuff.

'Hell's bells!' he cried, deeply moved.

The reactions of the rest of the company to the spectacle of the glittering bauble, though differing from his in their nature, were almost equally pronounced. Gally said: 'Good Lord!' Prudence, forgetting Ophelia for the moment, said: 'Golly!' Lady Hermione said: 'Veronica! Where *did* you get that lovely necklace?'

Veronica was cooing like a dove in springtime.

'It's Freddie's present,' she explained. 'Oh, Fred-dee! How sur-*sweet* of you! I never dreamed that you meant to give me anything like this.'

It always pains a chivalrous man to be compelled to dash the cup of joy from the lips of Beauty. The resemblance of his cousin to a young mother crooning over her new-born child had not escaped Freddie, and he was aware that what he had to say would cause chagrin and disappointment. But he did not hesitate. On these occasions the surgeon's knife is best.

'I didn't,' he said crisply. 'Not by a ruddy jugful. What you draw is a pendant.'

'A pendant?'

'A pendant,' said Freddie, who wished to leave no loophole for misunderstanding. 'It will be delivered shortly. Accept it with best wishes from the undersigned.'

Veronica's eyes widened. She seemed perplexed.

'But I'd much rather have this than a pendant. Really I would.'

'I dare say,' said Freddie, regretful but firm. 'So would most people. But that necklace happens to belong to Aggie. The story is a long and complicated one, and throws a blinding light on the guv'nor's extraordinary mentality. Boiling it down, I asked him to have the necklace mailed to Aggie in Paris and to bring back the pendant for you, and he went and got the wires crossed, though having assured me in set terms that he thoroughly understood and that there was no possibility of a hitch in the routine. I may say – and this is official – it's the last time I ever get the guv'nor to do anything for me. I believe if you sent him out to buy apples, he'd come back with an elephant.'

Lady Hermione made a noise like the hissing of fat in a saucepan.

'Isn't that Clarence!' she said, and her brother Galahad agreed that that was Clarence.

'Really,' said Lady Hermione, 'I often think he ought to be certified.'

Freddie nodded. Filial respect had prevented him putting the thought into speech, but it had crossed his mind. There were undoubtedly moments when one felt that the guv'nor's true environment was a padded cell at Colney Hatch.

'Such a disappointment for you, darling,' said Lady Hermione.

'Too bad,' said Gally.

'Tough luck, Vee,' said Prudence.

'Deepest symp,' said Freddie. 'One knows how you feel. Must be agony.'

It was only slowly that anything ever penetrated to Veronica's consciousness, and for some moments she had been standing be-wildered, unable to grasp the trend of affairs. But this wave of commiseration seemed to accelerate her thought processes.

'Do you mean', she said, beginning to understand, 'that I'm not to keep this necklace?'

Freddie replied that that was it in a nutshell.

'Can't I wear it at the County Ball?'

The question caused Lady Hermione to brighten. It seemed to her that the cup of joy need not be dashed completely from her child's lips after all. She might not be in a position to drain it to the bottom, but the arrangement she had suggested would enable her at least to take a sip or two.

'Why, of course,' she said. 'That would be lovely, darling.'

'Splendid idea,' agreed Gally. 'Compromise satisfactory to all parties. Wear it at the County Ball, and then turn it in and Freddie can ship it off.'

'You'll look wonderful in it, Vee,' said Prudence. 'I shan't be there to see you, because I shall have drowned myself in the lake, but I know you'll look marvellous.'

Once more Freddie was reluctantly compelled to apply the sur-geon's knife.

'Imposs, I fear,' he said, with a manly pity that became him well. 'I'm sorry, Vee, old girl, but that idea's out too. The jamboree to which you allude does not take place for another fortnight, and Aggie wants the thing at once. She has already wired four times for it, and I am expecting telegram number five tomorrow or the day after. And I don't mind telling you that it promises to be hot stuff. At the thought of what she would say if I kept her waiting another fortnight the imagination boggles.'

The Hon. Galahad snorted sharply. Himself a bachelor, he was unable to understand and sympathize with what seemed to him a nephew's contemptible pusillanimity. There is often this unbridgable gulf between the outlook of single and married men.

'Are you afraid of your wife?' he demanded. 'Are you man or mouse? She can't eat you.'

'She'd have a jolly good try,' said Freddie. 'What you don't appear to realize is that Aggie is the daughter of an American millionaire, and if you'd ever met an American millionaire –'

'I've met dozens.'

'Then you ought to know that they bring their daughters up to expect a certain docility in the male. Aggie got the idea into her nut at about the age of six that her word was law and never lost it, and it was always understood that there was a sort of gentleman's agreement that the bird who married her would roll over and jump through hoops on demand. There are few, if any, sweeter girls on earth than good old Aggie, but if you ask me: "Is she a bit on the imperious side from time to time?" I answer frankly that you have rung the bell and are entitled to the cigar or coconut. I love her with a devotion which defies human speech, but if you were to place before me the alternatives of disregarding her lightest behest and walking up to a traffic cop and socking him on the maxillary bones, you would find me choosing the cop every time. And it's no good calling me a bally young serf,' said Freddie, addressing the Hon. Galahad, who had done so. 'That's the posish, and I like it. I fully understood what I was letting myself in for when the registrar was doing his stuff.'

There was a silence. It was broken by Veronica making a suggestion.

'You could tell Aggie you had lent the necklace to me.'

'I could,' agreed Freddie, 'and I would if I wanted hell's foundations to quiver and something like the San Francisco earthquake to break loose. You all seem to have overlooked another important point, which, though delicate, I can touch on as we're all members of the family here. Some silly ass went and told Aggie that Vee and I were once engaged, and ever since she has viewed Vee with concern. She suspects her every move.'

'Ridiculous!' said Lady Hermione. 'A mere boy-and-girl affair.'

'Blew over years ago,' said Gally.

'I dare say,' said Freddie. 'But to listen to Aggie, when the topic crops up, you'd think it had happened yesterday. So I'm jolly well not going to lend you that necklace, Vee, and I will now ask you – regretfully, and fully appreciating your natural disappointment and all that sort of thing – to look slippy and hand it over.'

'Oh, Fred-dee!'

'I'm sorry, but there you are. That's life.'

Veronica's hand stole out. There was a quiver on her lovely lips

and moisture in her beautiful eyes, but her hand holding the
necklace stole out. When a man trained in eloquence in the testing
school of Donaldson's Inc. of Long Island City employs that
eloquence at its full voltage, it is enough to make any girl's hand
steal out.

'Thanks,' said Freddie.

He had spoken too soon. It was as if some sudden vision of the
County Ball had come to Veronica Wedge, with herself in the foreground feeling practically naked without those shining diamonds
about her neck. Her lips ceased to quiver and set in a firm and
determined line. The moisture left her eyes, to be replaced by a
fanatic gleam of defiance. She drew back her hand.

'No,' she said.

'Eh?' said Freddie weakly.

A strange bonelessness had come upon him. The situation was
one which he had not anticipated, and he was asking himself how
he was going to cope with it. The man of sentiment cannot leap at
girls and choke necklaces out of them.

'No,' repeated Veronica. 'You gave me this as a birthday present
and I'm going to keep it.'

'Keep it? You don't mean absolutely freeze on to it permanently?'

'Yes, I do.'

'But it's Aggie's!'

'She can buy another.'

This happy solution restored Lady Hermione's composure completely.

'Of course she can. How sensible of you, darling. I'm surprised
you didn't think of that, Freddie.'

'Sounds to me an admirable way out,' agreed Gally. 'You can
always get round these difficulties if you use your head.'

Freddie's was now reeling as it had not reeled since those bygone
nights with Tipton Plimsoll in his pre-Jimpson Murgatroyd period,
but he endeavoured to make these people see the light of reason. It
amazed him that nobody seemed to realize the spot he was in.

'But don't you understand? Didn't you grasp what I was saying
just now? Aggie will go up in the air like a rocket when she hears
I've given Vee – Vee of all people! – her necklace. She'll divorce
me.'

'Nonsense.'

'She will, I tell you. American wives are like that. Let the slightest thing ruffle their equanimity, and *bingo*! Ask Tippy. His mother divorced his guv'nor because he got her to the station at ten-seven to catch a train that had started at seven-ten.'

The Hon. Galahad's eye lit up.

'That reminds me of a rather amusing story –'

But the story of which he had been reminded was not to be told on this occasion – though, knowing Gally, one cannot believe that it was lost to the world forever. A sharp cough from his sister drew his attention to the fact that Tipton Plimsoll was entering the room.

3

Tipton was unmistakably effervescent, his manner and appearance alike completely exploding his hostess's theory that he must be exhausted after his long drive. His spectacles were gleaming, and he seemed to float on air.

There is a widely advertised patent medicine which promises to its purchasers a wonderful sense of peace, poise, neural solidity, and organic integrity, and guarantees to free them from all nervous irritability, finger-drumming, teeth-grinding, and foot-tapping. This specific Tipton Plimsoll might have been taking for weeks, and the poet Coleridge, had he been present, would have jerked a thumb at him with a low-voiced: 'Don't look now, but that fellow over there will give you some idea of what I had in mind when I wrote about the man who on honeydew had fed and drunk the milk of Paradise.'

'Hi, ya!' he cried, the first time he had used the expression in Blandings Castle.

But it has been well said that it is precisely these moments when we are feeling that ours is the world and everything that's in it that Fate selects for sneaking up on us with the rock in the stocking. Scarcely had Tipton floated half a dozen feet when he was brought up short by the sight of Veronica dandling the necklace, and it was as if a blunt instrument had descended on the base of his skull.

'What's that?' he cried, tottering. He did not actually clutch his brow, but anyone could have seen that it was a very near thing. 'Who gave you that?' he demanded tensely.

Lady Hermione awoke to a sudden sense of peril. She had not forgotten the night of her wealthy future son-in-law's arrival at the castle and his strongly-marked reaction to the spectacle of Veronica slapping Freddie on the wrist and telling him not to be so silly, and the look of quick suspicion which he had just cast at the last named told her that he still feared his fatal fascination. Let him learn that this ornate piece of jewellery was a gift from Freddie and who knew what horrors might not ensue? A vision of the owner of the controlling interest in Tipton's Stores stalking out, leaving a broken engagement behind him, made her feel for a moment quite faint.

She was wondering how, without actually drawing her into a corner and slowly and carefully explaining to her for about forty minutes, she could impress upon her child the absolutely vital necessity for secrecy and evasion, when Veronica spoke.

'Freddie gave it me for my birthday,' she said.

From Tipton's lips, starting from the lower reaches of his soul, there came a low, soft, hollow, grunting sound. Lord Emsworth, had he been there to hear, would have recognized it as familiar. It closely resembled the noise which sometimes proceeded from the Empress when she was trying to get a potato which had rolled beyond her reach. He tottered again, more noticeably than the first time.

'Yes, Tip-pee.'

When we last saw Tipton Plimsoll, he was, it will be remembered, all straightened out on the snake question. The frank delight with which Freddie had received the news of his engagement and the hearty manner in which he had shaken his hand had finally dispelled the uneasy suspicions which had been oppressing him for so long. We faded out, it will be recalled, on a medium shot of him erasing the young dog biscuiteer's name from his list of snakes and according to him the honourable status of an innocent cousin.

Now, his heart sinking till it seemed to be all mixed up with his socks, he saw that the slitherer, when exhibiting joy at the news of his engagement, had been but acting a part. The handshake which he had mistaken for that of a pal had been the handshake of a serpent, and of a serpent who had, the moment his back was turned, intended to go on playing the old army game with the girl he loved. No wonder Tipton tottered. Anyone would have tottered.

It was the licentious lavishness of the gift that made the whole ghastly set-up so hideously plain. If Freddie had presented Veronica with a modest wrist-watch or a simple pendant, he would have had no criticism to make. Quite in order, he would have said, as from cousin to cousin. But a necklace that must have cost a packet was a very different matter. Cousins do not blow their substance on expensive diamond necklaces and give them to girls on their birthdays. Snakes, in sharp contradistinction, do.

'Cheese!' he muttered, using this expression, too, for the first time on these refined premises.

Freddie, meanwhile, had paled beneath his tan. He could read what was passing in Tipton's mind as clearly as if it had been the top line on an oculist's chart, and the thought that unless prompt steps were taken through the proper channels the exclusive concession which the other, speaking for Tipton's Stores, had granted to Donaldson's Dog-Joy might go west chilled him to the marrow.

'It's my wife's!' he cried.

He would have done better to remain silent. The cynical confession set the seal on Tipton's horror and disgust. For while we may pardon, if only with difficulty, the snake which seeks to undermine a young girl's principles at its own expense, at the snake which swipes its wife's jewellery as a means to this end we look askance, and rightly.

'What I mean –'

A smooth voice cut in on Freddie's broken stammer. It was the voice of one whose suave diplomacy had a hundred times reconciled brawling race-course touts and acted like oil upon troubled waters when feelings ran high between jellied-eel sellers.

'Just a moment, Freddie.'

The Hon. Galahad's was essentially a kindly soul. He was a man who liked to see everybody happy and comfortable. It had not escaped his notice that his sister Hermione was looking like an interested bystander waiting for a time bomb to explode, and it seemed to him that the moment had arrived for a polished man of the world to take the situation in hand.

'What Freddie is trying to say, my dear fellow, is that the thing originally belonged to his wife. Having no more use for it, she handed it over to him to do what he liked with. Why should there be anything to cause remark in the fact that he gave the little trinket to Veronica?'

Tipton stared.

'You call that a little trinket? It must have cost ten thousand smackers.'

'Ten thousand smackers?' There was genuine amusement in the Hon. Galahad's jolly laugh. 'My dear chap! Don't tell me you've got the idea into your mind that it's real? As if any man with Freddie's scrupulous sense of the fitness of things would go giving a ten-thousand-dollar necklace to a girl who has just become engaged to his friend. There are some things that are not done. Mrs Freddie bought that necklace at the five-and-ten-cent store. Or did I misunderstand you when you told me that, Freddie?'

'Perfectly correct, Uncle Gally.'

Tipton's brow became wrinkled.

'She bought it at the five-and-ten-cent store?'

'That's right.'

'Just for a gag, you mean?'

'Exactly. A woman's whim. I wonder if you have ever heard the one about the man whose wife had a whim of iron? He was going down the street one day —'

Tipton was not interested in men with iron-whimmed wives. He was pondering on this new angle and finding the explanation plausible. He had known wealthy female compatriots of his to buy some odd things. Doris Jimpson had once bought twelve coloured balloons, and they had popped them with their cigarettes on the way home in the car. His sombre face began to clear, and one noted a relaxation in the tenseness of his bearing.

It was unfortunate, therefore, that Veronica should have chosen this moment to give tongue. You could generally rely on Veronica to say the wrong thing, and she did so now.

'I'm going to wear it at the County Ball, Tip-pee.'

An instant before, it had seemed as though Tipton Plimsoll were about to become again the carefree soul who had entered the room with a merry 'Hi, ya!' His eye, resting on Freddie, had not had actual brotherly love in it, but it had been reasonably free from horrified suspicion and loathing disgust and seemed likely to become freer. The caveman in Tipton Plimsoll, you would have said, was preparing to put up the shutters and close down.

But at these words his brow darkened once more and a haughty gleam shot from his horn-rimmed spectacles. Veronica had touched his pride.

'Is that so?' he said formidably. 'Wear it at the County Ball, huh? You think I'm going to have my future wife wearing fake five-and-ten-cent store jewellery at any by golly County Ball? I'll say I'm not. I'm the fellow who'll buy you all the stuff you need for the County Ball. Me!' said Tipton, pointing with his left hand at his torso and with his right jerking the necklace from her grasp.

'Hey!' he said.

His eye, sweeping the room, had fallen on Prudence. Wearying of a discussion whose din and uproar were preventing her thinking of lakes, she had begun to move towards the door.

'You off?'

'I am going to my room,' said Prudence.

Tipton stopped her with an imperious gesture.

'Juss-a-moment. You were saying yesterday you needed something for that jumble sale of yours. Take this,' said Tipton.

'Right ho,' said Prudence listlessly. 'Thanks.'

She passed through the door, leaving a throbbing silence behind her.

4

Prudence's room was at the back of the castle, next door to Tipton Plimsoll's. Its balcony looked down on meadows and trees, and so a few minutes later did Prudence. For on leaving the drawing-room she had gone to lean on the rail, her sad eyes roaming over the spreading woodland, her bruised spirit seeking to obtain some solace from the contemplation of the peaceful scene. She eyed the copses and spinneys from much the same general motives as had led Tipton on a memorable occasion to go and look at the ducks on the Serpentine.

But when a spirit is as bruised as hers, there is not much percentage in gazing at scenery. Presently she went back into the room with a weary sigh, which changed abruptly to a startled squeak.

She had seen a human form sitting in the armchair, and it had made her jump.

'Hullo, my dear,' said her uncle Galahad genially. 'I saw you out there but didn't like to disturb you. Your air was that of a girl deep in meditation. Did you think I was a burglar?'

'I thought you were Freddie.'

'Do I look like Freddie?' said Gally, wounded.

'I thought it was Freddie come for the necklace.'

There was a grave expression on Gally's face as he adjusted his monocle and focused it upon her.

'It is extremely fortunate that it wasn't, considering that you had left the thing lying right out in the open on your dressing-table. You might have ruined everything. Oh, it's all right now. I've got it in my pocket. Don't you realize, my dear child, what the possession of this necklace means to you?'

Prudence made a tired gesture, like a Christian martyr who has got a bit fed up with lions.

'It doesn't mean anything to me. Nothing means anything to me if I can't have Bill.'

Gally rose and patted her on the head. It meant leaving the armchair, which was a very comfortable one, but he did it. A man with a big heart is always ready to put up with discomfort when it is a case of consoling a favourite niece. At the same time he regarded her with frank astonishment. He had supposed her mind to be nimbler than this.

'You're going to have Bill,' he said. 'I fully expect to be dancing at your wedding at an early date. Haven't you grasped the position of affairs yet? Why, you might be Veronica.'

'What do you mean?'

'This necklace is the talisman which is going to unlock the gates of happiness for you. Freeze on to it like flypaper and refuse to give it up no matter what threats and cajoleries may be employed, and all you will have to worry about is where to spend the honeymoon. Can't you understand that you have been handed the whole situation on a plate? What's going to happen when you refuse to part with this necklace? The opposition will have to come to terms, and we shall dictate those terms.'

The Hon. Galahad removed his monocle, breathed on it, polished it with his handkerchief, and put it back.

'Let me tell you', he said, 'what happened after you left the drawing-room. Plimsoll took Veronica off for a stroll, leaving the rest of us to our general meeting. Freddie was the first to take the floor. He told us rather eloquently what Aggie was going to do to him if she didn't get her necklace. His speech was accorded only a rather tepid reception. Your aunt Hermione seemed to think that the disaster to which he alluded was exclusively Freddie's headache. My ready wit had saved the situation, leaving Plimsoll soothed and happy, and that was all she cared about. As far as she was concerned, the incident was closed.'

'Well, wasn't it?'

'It might have been, if Freddie had not ripped it wide open again. America's done something to that boy. It's made him think on his feet and get constructive ideas. This time he held his audience spellbound.'

'What did he say?'

'I'll tell you. He threatened, unless the necklace was in his hands by nightfall, to blow the gaff. He said he would tell Plimsoll what it was really worth and add that he had given it to Veronica as a birthday present and leave the rest to him. He said that this would probably mean the loss of some concession or other which Plimsoll had promised him, but that if he was going to have a headache he intended others to share it with him. His remarks caused a sensation. I don't think I have ever seen Hermione so purple. She is convinced that if Plimsoll ever finds out that necklace is genuine he will break off the engagement and stalk out of Veronica's life. It appears that he is madly jealous of Freddie.'

Prudence gave an awed gasp.

'Golly!' she said. 'I see what you mean.'

'I thought you would. Hermione's anguish was painful to witness, and Clarence, who dropped in with your uncle Egbert just in time to join the conference at this point, put the lid on it by revealing that he had told young Plimsoll that Freddie and Veronica were once engaged. He said Egbert had told him to. Egbert says he told him *not* to. I left them arguing the point.'

Prudence's eyes had rolled to the ceiling. She seemed to be offering silent thanks to Heaven for a notable display of benevolence to a damsel in distress.

'But, Uncle Gally, this is marvellous!'

'Solves everything.'

'They'll have to let me marry Bill.'

'Exactly. That is our price. We stick to it.'

'We won't weaken.'

'Not an iota. If they come bothering you, refer them to your agent. Tell them I've got the thing.'

'But then they'll bother you.'

'My dear child, mine has been a long life, in the course of which I have frequently been bothered by experts. And always without effect. Bothering passes me by as the idle wind, which I respect not.'

'That's Shakespeare, isn't it?'

'I shouldn't wonder. Most of the good gags are.'

Prudence drew a deep breath.

'You're a great man to have on one's side, Uncle Gally.'

'I like to stick up for my pals.'

'What a bit of luck Bill getting you for a godfather.'

'So I said at the time. There was a school of thought which held otherwise. Well, I'm going to my room to hide the swag.'

'Hide it carefully.'

'I'll put it in a place where no one would dream of looking. After that I thought of going for a saunter in the cool of the evening. Care to join me?'

'I'd love to, but I've got to write to Bill. I say, Uncle Gally,' said Prudence, struck with a sudden thought. 'All this is a bit tough on Freddie, isn't it?'

The same thing had occurred to the Hon. Galahad.

'A little, I suppose. Possibly just a trifle. But you can't make an omelette without breaking eggs. Not Shakespeare,' said the Hon. Galahad. 'One of my own. Unless I heard it somewhere. Besides, Freddie's agony will be only temporary. Hermione will have to throw in the towel. No alternative. I told her so in set terms, and left her to think it over.'

Chapter 10

If Prudence had had keener ears – or, rather, if her hearing had not at the moment been dulled by grief – she might have heard, while leaning on the rail of her balcony, a sound from below which would have registered itself on her consciousness as a gasping cry. And if she had been looking more narrowly at the meadows and spinneys – if, that is to say, her eyes had not been blurred with unshed tears – she would have noticed that it proceeded from Bill Lister, who was sitting on a tree stump outside the second spinney to the right.

But being preoccupied she missed him, and Bill, who had sprung to his feet and was about to start waving his arms like a semaphore in the hope of attracting her attention, had the chagrin of seeing her vanish like some goddess in a dream. The best he was able to do was to take careful note of the spot at which she had made her brief appearance and go off to see if he could find a ladder.

In supposing that Bill had left the drawing-room with bowed head during his absence, Freddie had been quite correct. After a rather one-sided exchange of remarks with Lady Hermione he had seen that there was nothing to keep him, and pausing only to knock over a chair and upset the cake table again he had tottered forth into the sunshine. Any anxiety he might have felt about the disposition of his luggage was dispelled by his hostess's assurance that it would be thrown out after him and would in due course find its way to the Emsworth Arms.

The emotions of a man who, arriving at a country house for a long visit, finds himself kicked out at the end of the first twenty minutes are necessarily chaotic, but on one point Bill was pretty clear – that he had plenty of time on his hands. It was not yet six o'clock, and the day seemed to stretch before him endlessly. By way of getting through it somehow he started on a desultory tour of the grounds, and instinctively avoiding those in the front of the house, where the danger of running into Lady Hermione again would be more acute, he had come at length to the second spinney on the right of Prudence's balcony. There he had sat down to review his position and to endeavour to assess his chances of ever seeing again the girl he loved.

And such is the whimsicality of Fortune that he had seen her again within the first couple of minutes. True, she had come and gone like something out of a cuckoo clock, but he had seen her. And, as we say, he had marked the spot carefully and gone off to find a ladder.

That his mind should have turned so immediately in the direction of ladders is not really surprising. Romeo's would have done the same and so, if the Hon. Galahad's diagnosis of his temperament had been a correct one, would that of Tipton Plimsoll's Uncle Chet. Uncle Chet, like Romeo, had been a man who thought on his feet and did it now when there were girls around, and Bill was as full of ardour and impetuosity as either of them. The primary impulse of every lover, on seeing the adored object on a balcony, is to shin up and join her.

One of the things which may be placed to the credit side of the English country house is that if you want a ladder when you are in its grounds, you can generally find one. It may take time, as it did on this occasion, but the search is seldom fruitless. Bill eventually found his propped up against a tree, where somebody seemed to have been doing a bit of pruning, and it was here that his powerful physique, which had been of such negligible value to him in the interior of Barribault's Hotel and, for the matter of that, in the Blandings Castle drawing-room, began to show returns. A ladder, even the medium-sized one which he had found, is not a light burden, but he made nothing of it. He carried it like a clouded cane. There were moments when he came near to flicking it.

He placed it against the wall, steadied it, and began to climb. Love lent him wings. Massive though he was, he skimmed up the rungs like a featherweight. He reached the balcony. He hurried into the room. And down below Colonel Egbert Wedge, who at the conclusion of the general meeting had decided that only a brisk walk could restore a mental poise rudely shaken by his exchanges with Lord Emsworth, rounded the corner of the house and stood staring.

The impression left on Colonel Wedge's mind by the general meeting, and particularly by his brother-in-law's share in it, had been that he had already undergone the maximum which a retired colonel of a cavalry unit could reasonably be expected to endure. If you had buttonholed him as he stalked out of the drawing-room and said to him: 'Tell me, Colonel Wedge, have you drained the bitter cup?' he would have replied: 'Yes, dash it, certainly. To the dregs.' And now, on top of all that, here was a beastly bounder of a burglar having the cool effrontery to break into the house in broad daylight.

It was this that was causing his blood pressure to rise in a manner which would have made E. Jimpson Murgatroyd shake his head. At night, yes. He could have understood that. If this had happened in the small hours or even round about the time of the final whisky and soda, he might not actually have approved of the blasted fellow's activities, but he could have put himself to a certain extent in his place. But at a moment when the household had not yet digested its five-o'clock tea and buttered toast . . .

'Tchsh!' said Colonel Wedge, revolted, and gave the ladder a petulant jerk.

It measured its length on the turf, and he hurried off to GHQ to put in his report and make arrangements for reinforcements.

2

After the departure of her uncle Galahad, Prudence had not lingered long in her room. A girl in love, remorseful for having wounded the man of her choice and pouring out her heart to him with a fountain pen, writes nearly as quickly as Lord Emsworth sending off telegrams at Paddington Station with his train puffing in the background. She had finished the letter and addressed it to W. Lister, Esq., at the Emsworth Arms and licked the gum and fastened it up long before Bill had come anywhere near his ladder.

It was her intention to get in touch with one of the under-housemaids with whom she had struck up an acquaintance, warm enough perhaps to be called a friendship, and to fee her to take it down by hand after dinner; and she set out now to find her.

And so it came about that Bill, entering the room with beating heart, found it empty and was for an instant downcast.

But a moment later he had perceived that though he had missed Prudence, he had found the next best thing. The letter was lying on the dressing-table, where its author had thought it wisest to leave it while she conducted her negotiations with the under-housemaid. In the present unsettled conditions at Blandings Castle, to have taken it with her would have been too much like carrying despatches through the enemy's lines in war-time.

It was with trembling fingers that Bill opened the envelope. In the course of their romantic love affair he had received in all forty-seven letters from this girl, but while the sight of her handwriting had always affected him powerfully, it had never affected him so powerfully as now. So much hung on this communication. The other forty-six had been mere variations on the theme 'I love you', and very pleasant reading they had made! But this one – the room swam before him as the thought shot through his soul like a red-hot skewer – might quite possibly be the bird. It was the answer to his well-expressed note pleading for a reconciliation, and who knew what scornful rebuffs it might not contain?

Through the mist which flickered before his eyes he read the words

My own precious darling beautiful Bill

and he felt as he had sometimes felt on stricken football fields when a number of large, well-fed members of the opposition team had risen from their seat on his stomach. Reason told him that a girl whose intention it was to rebuff and to administer the bird would scarcely have chosen this preamble.

'Woof!' he breathed, and with swelling heart settled down to a steady perusal.

It was a wonderful letter. Indeed, off-hand, he did not see how it could well have been improved upon. Its gist was that she loved him as of yore – in fact, even more than of yore. She made that clear in paragraph one, and clearer still in the pages which followed. She was, indeed, so complimentary about him that somebody like Lady Hermione, had she perused the eulogy, would have supposed that there was some mistake and that she must be thinking of a couple of other fellows. Even Bill, though he had read the same sort of thing forty-six times before, found a difficulty in realizing that this godlike being whose virtues provoked such enthusiasm in her was himself.

On page four the tone of the letter changed. At first a mere outpouring of worship and affection, it now became more like some crisp despatch from the Front. For it was here that the writer began to outline for his attention the saga of the necklace. And, as he read, his heart bounded within him. So clearly had she set forth the salient points that he was able to follow the scenario step by step to its triumphant conclusion without any difficulty, and he recognized that what had happened was what Freddie would have called in the best and deepest sense a bit of all right. Rout had been turned to victory.

The thought did strike him, as it had struck Prudence, that it was all perhaps a bit tough on Freddie, who seemed through no fault of his own to have become a sort of football of Fate; but it was not long before he was consoling himself with the philosophical reflection which had enabled the Hon. Galahad to bear up – viz., that the breaking of eggs is an inseparable adjunct to the making of omelettes and that in any case his old friend's agony would be only temporary. 'Hermione', Gally had said, 'will have to throw in the towel', and this was the bracing conclusion to which Bill, too, came. It would have been difficult at this moment for anything to have increased his happiness.

But something now happened which definitely diminished it. From outside in the corridor there came the sudden sound of voices, and he leaped up and stood rigid, listening.

Nor was his agitation without reason. One of the voices was that of Lady Hermione Wedge, and such had been his relations with her that her lightest word was enough to make him tremble.

'Are you sure?' she was saying.

The voice which replied was strange to Bill, for he had not yet had the privilege of meeting Colonel Wedge.

'Quite sure, old girl. No possibility of error. He propped a beastly great ladder against the wall, and before my very eyes he shinned up it like a lamplighter. I can show you the ladder. Here, come and look. Down there.'

There was an interval of silence, during which the unseen speakers had apparently gone to gaze out of one of the corridor windows. Then Lady Hermione spoke.

'Most extraordinary,' she said. 'Yes, I see the ladder.'

'He climbed up to a bally balcony,' said Colonel Wedge, like some member of the Capulet family speaking of Romeo.

'And he can't have climbed down.'

'Exactly. And if he had come down the stairs, we should have met him. We arrive, then, at the irresistible conclusion that the bounder is lurking in one of these rooms, and I shall now search them one by one.'

'Oh, Egbert, no!'

'Eh? Why not? I've got my service revolver.'

'No. You might get hurt. Wait till Charles and Thomas come. They ought to have been here long ago.'

'Well, all right. After all, there's no hurry. The blighter can't get away. One can proceed at one's leisure.'

In every difficult situation, when the spirit has been placed upon the rack and peril seems to threaten from every quarter, there inevitably comes soon or late to the interested party at the centre of the proceedings a conviction that things are getting too hot. Stags at bay have this feeling. So have Red Indians at the stake. It came now to Bill.

Who Charles and Thomas might be, he did not know. As a matter of fact, they were respectively the Blandings Castle first and second footmen. We saw them before, it may be remembered, toiling into the drawing-room with cream and powdered sugar. They were now restoring their tissues in the Servants' Hall and listening without enthusiasm to the details of the assignment which was being sketched out for them by Beach, the butler. The delay in their arrival was owing to the slowness with which Beach was putting across the idea which he was trying to sell them; they holding, properly enough, that it was not their place to go and overpower burglars right in the middle of their meat tea.

To Bill, as we say, their names were unfamiliar; but whoever they were, and however long they might take in reaching the front line, it seemed pretty clear to him that they might be expected eventually, and he had no desire to remain and make their acquaintance. It was not that a man of his thews and courage shrank from a turn-up with a hundred Charleses and Thomases, any more than he paled at the menace of a thousand colonels with service revolvers. What urged him to retreat was the thought of having to meet Lady Hermione again. It stimulated him to action like a cactus in the trouser seat.

Having decided to leave, his first move was to lock the door so as to ensure himself at least a respite when the big push started. This done, he hastened out on to the balcony.

It has been Colonel Wedge's view that there was no need for hurry, because the blighter could not get away, and Bill would have been the first to acknowledge that the loss of the ladder had struck a very serious blow at his line of communications. But that he was actually encircled he would have disputed. What the colonel had not allowed for was the extraordinary stimulus which the prospect of having to meet his wife gave to blighters' mental powers. The brain of a blighter faced with the imminent prospect of an encounter with a woman of the type of Lady Hermione Wedge works like lightning, and it was almost no time before Bill was telling himself that on the walls of houses there are generally water pipes down which a venturesome man may slide.

A moment later he had seen one. And as his eye, sweeping the castle wall, fell upon it, his stout heart sank. It was a matter of some dozen feet away from him.

To a performing flea, of course, a standing broad jump of a dozen feet would have been child's play. Such a flea in Bill's place would have bowed to the audience, smiled at personal friends in the front row, dusted off its antennae, and made the leap with a careless 'Allay-oop!' Bill did not even contemplate its possibility. He knew his limitations. There was once a young man on the flying trapeze who flew through the air with the greatest of ease, but he had presumably had years of training. Bill was a novice.

It was as he stood there with a silent 'What to do?' on his lips that he suddenly saw that there was still hope. Running along the wall was a narrow ledge. Furthermore, Blandings Castle having been in existence a great number of years, ivy had grown upon its surface in some profusion. And a man anxious to remove himself from a balcony here to a water pipe over there can do a great deal with the assistance of a ledge and some ivy.

What held Bill motionless for a while, wrinkling his forehead and chewing the lower lip a little, was a growing doubt as to whether he wanted to be that man. There was a pleasantly solid look about that ivy; its strands were stout and gnarled and certainly had the appearance of being strong enough to support him; but you can never be quite sure about ivy. It puts up an impressive front and then, just when it is the time for all good ivy to come to the aid of the party, it lets you down. That was the thought which was causing Bill to hesitate. Like Freddie, he yearned for cooperation, and he wanted to be quite certain that he was going to get it.

There was no question that failure on the part of that ivy to give one-hundred-per-cent service would mean a quick, sticky finish for the man who had put his trust in it. He would go straight down and not stop till he had hit the lawn, and it did not escape Bill's notice that that lawn had a hard, unyielding look. He could see himself bouncing – once, twice, possibly thrice – and then lying lifeless, like the man in 'Excelsior'.

He was still weighing the pros and cons when there cut abruptly into his meditations the sound of a woman's voice, sharpened by the excitement of the chase.

'This door is locked. He must be in here. Break down this door, Charles.'

Worse things can happen to a man than lying lifeless on lawns. Bill scrambled over the balcony rail and set his foot on the ledge.

Simultaneously, Tipton Plimsoll hurried past the group in the corridor and shot into his bedroom like a homing rabbit.

3

Tipton lowered himself into a chair with a satisfied grunt, his air that of a man glad to be at journey's end. He was breathing a little jerkily, for he had come up the stairs at a smart pace. A spectator, had one been present, would have observed that beneath his coat there was some bulky object, spoiling the set of it. It was as if he had grown a large tumour on his left side.

At about the moment when Bill, having heard all he wanted to hear on the subject of Charleses, Thomases, and service revolvers, retreated to the balcony and started looking around for water pipes, Tipton had been leaving the Hon. Galahad's suite on the ground floor in the furtive manner of a stag which, while not yet actually at bay, is conscious of a certain embarrassment and a desire to avoid attention. He had been to fetch the flask which he had been mad enough to allow out of his possession, foolishly overlooking the fact that the time was bound to come when he would need it, and need it sorely.

It was the presence of this flask on his person which had caused him to whizz so nimbly past the group in the corridor. He had seen that the gathering consisted of Colonel Wedge, Lady Hermione Wedge, Beach, the butler, and a brace of footmen, and at any other time — for the affair undoubtedly presented certain features of interest — he would have paused to ask questions. But with that bulge under his coat he shrank from establishing communication with his fellows, who might ask questions in their turn. The fact that this assorted mob was gathered about the door next to his own and seemed to be gazing at it with great intentness filled him not with curiosity but with thankfulness. It meant that their backs were turned, thus enabling him to pass by unseen.

Safe in his refuge, he now produced the flask, looking at it with affection and an anticipatory gleam in his eye. His manner had ceased to betray anxiety and embarrassment. If he still resembled a stag, it was a stag at eve, about to drink its fill. His tongue stole out and passed lightly over his lips.

In the period which had passed since he last appeared on the Blandings scene a complete change had taken place in Tipton Plimsoll's mood. He had quite got over that momentary spasm of bad temper which had led him to snatch the necklace from Veronica's grasp and fling it scornfully to Prudence as a contribution towards the vicar's jumble sale. Five minutes in the rose garden with the girl he loved had made another man of him.

He was now filled to the brim with a benevolence so wide in its scope that it even embraced Freddie. He had got back to his old idea of Freddie as a man and a brother, and was glad he had given him that concession for his blasted dog biscuits. He saw that he had wronged Freddie. After all, it is surely straining a regard for the proprieties absurdly to object to a male cousin giving a female cousin a trifle of five-and-ten-cent store jewellery on her birthday.

But there were other and weightier reasons for his desire to celebrate than a mere conviction of the blamelessness of one whom he had once been reluctantly compelled to class among the rattlesnakes and black mambas. Apart from the intoxicating feeling of being betrothed to the only girl in the world, there was the realization that he had passed through the valley of the shadow and come up smiling on the other side. Even E. Jimpson Murgatroyd would now be compelled in common honesty to give him a clean bill of health.

For mark what had happened. In order to brace himself up to tell his love he had taken a snifter. And what had ensued? He had seen a pig in a bedroom. Yes, but a real pig, a genuine pig, a pig that was equally visible to such unbiased eyes as those of Veronica and her mother. E. Jimpson Murgatroyd himself in his place would have seen precisely what he had seen. No amount of quibbling on his part could get around that.

And another thing which must have impressed E. J. Murgatroyd very deeply, had he been apprised of it, was that from start to finish there had not been a sign of the face. For the first time in his association with it, it had been subjected to the test and had failed to deliver.

To what conclusion, then, was one forced? One was forced to the conclusion that he had turned the corner. The pure air of Shropshire had done its work, and he was now cured and in a position to go ahead and drink to his happiness as it should be drunk to.

And he was proceeding to do so when he saw something out of the corner of his eye and, turning, realized that he had underestimated the face's tenacity and will to win. What had kept it away earlier this afternoon he could not say – some appointment elsewhere, perhaps; but in lightheartedly assuming that it had retired from business he had been sadly mistaken.

There it was, pressed against the windowpane, that same fixed, intent expression in its eyes. It seemed to be trying to say something to him.

4

The reason Bill's eyes were fixed and intent was that the sight of Tipton through the window had come to him like that of a sail on the horizon to a shipwrecked mariner. And what he was trying to say to him was that he would be glad if Tipton would at his earliest convenience open the window and let him in.

There is this about climbing along ledges towards water pipes, that by the time you have reached your water pipe and have come to the point where you are going to slide down it the whole idea of sliding down water pipes is apt to have lost any charm which it may have possessed at the outset of your journey. Bill, facing the last leg of his trip, was feeling the same lack of faith in the trustworthiness of the water pipe as he had formerly felt in that of the ivy.

Arriving at the window, therefore, and seeing Tipton, he decided abruptly to alter his whole scheme of campaign. He had recognized the other immediately as the tall, thin chap who had showed himself so aloof on the occasion of their encounter in the rhododendrons, but he was hoping that in the special circumstances he might be induced to unbend a bit. In Tipton he saw one of those men who dislike talking to strangers and raise their eyebrows and pass on if accosted by them; but, after all, when it is a question of saving a human life, the aloofest of tall, thin chaps may reasonably be expected to stretch a point.

What he wanted Tipton to do was to let him in and allow him to remain in modest seclusion under the bed or somewhere until the fever of the chase had spent itself in the bosoms of Charles, whoever he was, of Thomas, whoever *he* was, of the unidentified person with the service revolver, and of Lady Hermione. He did not want to talk to Tipton or bore him in any way, and he was prepared to give him a guarantee that he would not dream of presuming on this enforced acquaintance. He was perfectly willing that Tipton, if he desired to do so, should cut him next time they met, provided that he would extend the hand of assistance now.

It was a difficult idea to put through a closed window, but by way of starting the negotiations he placed his lips to the pane and said:

'Hi!'

He could have made no more unfortunate move. Recalling as it did so strongly to Tipton the circumstances of their last meeting, the monosyllable set the seal on the latter's gloom and depression. Bill did not, of course, know it, but it was that 'Hi!' of his at their previous encounter which had affected the man behind the flask even more powerfully than the mere sight of his face. Broadly, what Tipton felt about phantom faces was that a man capable of taking the rough with the smooth could put up with them provided they kept silent. Wired for sound, they went too far.

He gave Bill one long, reproachful look such as St Sebastian might have given his persecutors, and left the room in a marked manner.

To Bill it was as if he had been one of a beleaguered garrison and the United States Marines, having arrived, had simply turned on their heels and gone off again. For some moments he continued standing where he was, his nose pressed against the pane; then reluctantly he grasped the water pipe and started to lower himself. He was oppressed by a bitter feeling that this was the last time he would put his faith in tall, thin chaps. 'Let me have men about me that are fat,' thought Bill, as he worked his way cautiously downwards.

The water pipe was magnificent. It could easily, if it had had the distorted sense of humour of some water pipes, have come apart from the wall and let him shoot down like a falling star, but it stood as firm as a rock. It did not even wabble. And Bill's heart, which had been in his mouth, gradually returned to its base. Something resembling elation crept into his mood. He might have missed seeing Prudence, but he had outsmarted Lady Hermione Wedge, the man with the service revolver, the unseen Thomas, and the mysterious Charles. They had pitted their wits against his, and he must have made them feel uncommonly foolish.

This elation reached its peak as he felt the solid earth beneath his feet. But it did not maintain its new high for long. Almost immediately there was a sharp drop, and his heart, rocketing up once more, returned to his mouth. A rich smell of pig assailed his nostrils, and a thin, piping voice spoke behind him.

'Wah yah dah?' said the voice.

5

The speaker was a very small man in corduroy trousers, niffy to a degree and well stricken in years. He might have been either a smelly centenarian or an octogenarian who had been prematurely aged by trouble. A stranger to Bill, he would have been recognized immediately by Lady Hermione Wedge, to whom both his appearance and aroma were familiar. He was Lord Emsworth's pig man, Edwin Pott, and the reason he said 'Wah yah dah?' when he meant 'What are you doing?' was that he had no roof to his mouth. One does not blame him for this. As Gally had said to Lady Hermione, we can't all have roofs to our mouths. One simply mentions it.

The point is perhaps a moot one, but it is probably better, when you are caught sliding down water pipes outside other people's houses, if your captor is a man with a roof to his mouth and not one lacking this useful property. In the former case, some sort of exchange of ideas is possible, in the latter not. When Edwin Pott said 'Wah yah dah?' Bill could not follow him.

He made, accordingly, no reply, and the other, seeming to feel that the burden of the conversation was up to him, said: 'Car yar, har?' To this question, too, Bill made no response. He would have been, in any event, disinclined for talk. What he wanted to do was to remove himself as speedily as possible, and with this end in view he began to move round his companion like a large steamer circling a small buoy.

His progress was arrested. When Edwin Pott had said, 'Car yar, har?' he had meant 'Cotched you, have I?' and he now proceeded to suit action to words by clutching at Bill's coat and seizing it in a senile grasp. Bill endeavoured to release himself, but the hand held firm.

It was a situation with which Bill frankly did not know how to cope. We have spoken of him as a young man whose name would have come high up on the list of anyone looking for a deputy to tackle a mad bull for him, and with a mad bull he would have known where he was. Nor would he have been at a loss if Edwin Pott had been some powerful thug. With such antagonists he could have expressed himself.

But this was different. Here he was confronted by a poor human wreck with one foot in the grave and the other sliding towards it, a frail wisp of a creature whose white hairs, such of them as still lingered on his egg-shaped head, claimed chivalry and respect. He could have recommended Edwin Pott a good lung tonic. He could not haul off and sock him on the jaw.

Once more he tried chivalrously and respectfully to loosen the clutching hand. It was in vain. 'Come one, come all, this rock shall

fly from its firm base as soon as I,' Edwin Pott seemed to be saying.
The situation had arrived at what is commonly known as a deadlock.
Bill wanted to get away but was unable to do so. Edwin Pott
wanted to shout for assistance but could produce only a thin, shrill
sound like the whistling of gas in a pipe. (His vocal cords had never
been the same since the evening during the last General Election
when he had strained them while addressing the crowd at the public
bar of the Emsworth Arms in the Conservative interest.)

It was on this picture in still life that Colonel Wedge now intruded with his service revolver.

In supposing that by climbing down the water pipe he had
outsmarted Colonel Wedge Bill had been laughably in error. You
might outsmart captains by such tactics, and perhaps majors, but
not colonels. The possibility of the existence of such a pipe had
flashed upon Egbert Wedge at the moment when Charles, enjoying
himself for the first time, for every footman likes smashing his
employer's property, had started to break down Prudence's door,
and it had sent him racing for the stairs. You do not have to tell a
military man anything about the importance of cutting off the
enemy's retreat.

His first emotion on beholding the group before him was a stern
joy mingled with cordial appreciation of his cleverness and foresight;
his second a strong feeling of relief that he had got his service
revolver with him. Seen at close range, this marauding blighter
looked an unpleasantly tough marauding blighter, the very type of
marauding blighter for whose undoing you need all the service
revolvers you can get. He found himself marvelling that Edwin
Pott had had the intrepidity to engage in hand-to-hand combat so
extraordinarily well-nourished a specimen of the criminal classes,
and immediately decided that he personally was not going to do
anything so damn silly.

'Hands up, you feller!' he cried, opening the proceedings at a
comfortable distance. He had intended to say 'scoundrel', but the
word had escaped him in the heat of the moment.

'Ar car har,' said Edwin Pott rather smugly, and Colonel Wedge,
who was something of a linguist, correctly understanding him to
have explained that it was he who had cotched the miscreant, gave
credit where credit was due.

'Smart work, Pott,' he said. 'Right ho, Pott, stand aside. I'm going to march him up to the house.'

Although he had anticipated some such development, Bill could not restrain a cry.

'Silence!' barked Colonel Wedge in his parade voice. 'Rightabout turn, quick march, and don't try any of your larks. This revolver's loaded.'

With an imperious gesture he motioned Bill to precede him, and Bill, feeling that any show of disinclination on his part would be classed by this severe critic under the head of trying larks, did so. Colonel Wedge followed, his weapon at the ready, and Edwin Pott, in his capacity of principal witness for the prosecution, brought up the rear. The procession moved round the corner of the house and approached the terrace.

The Hon. Galahad was standing on the terrace, apparently in a reverie. He looked up as they drew near, having become aware of Edwin Pott, from whose direction a light breeze was blowing. At the sight of Bill, the revolver, the colonel, and the pig man, a surprised expression came into his face. He had been wondering what had become of his young friend, but he had never expected that anything like this had happened to him.

'Good Lord, Bill,' he ejaculated, screwing his monocle more tightly into his eye. 'What's all this?'

Colonel Wedge was surprised in his turn. He had not known that burglars moved in such influential circles.

'Bill? Do you know this frightful chap?'

'Know him? Many a time I've dandled him on my knee.'

'You couldn't have done,' said Colonel Wedge, running his eye over Bill's substantial frame. 'There wouldn't have been room.'

'When he was a baby,' explained Gally.

'Oh, when he was a baby? You mean you knew him as a baby?'

'Intimately.'

'What sort of baby was he?'

'Delightful.'

'Well, he's changed a lot since then,' said Colonel Wedge, breaking the bad news regretfully. 'He's become the most ghastly outsider. Burgles houses at six o'clock in the evening.'

'Ar car har,' said Edwin Pott.

'Pott cotched him,' translated the colonel. 'The chap was sliding down a water pipe.'

Bill felt it time to put in a word.

'I wanted to find Prue, Gally. I saw her standing on a balcony, and I went and fetched a ladder.'

'Quite right,' said Gally approvingly. 'Did you have a nice talk?'

'She wasn't there. But she had left a letter for me. It's all right, Gally. She still loves me.'

'So she gave me to understand when I was chatting with her. Well, that's fine.'

Enlightenment had come upon Colonel Wedge.

'Good God! Is this the chap Hermione was telling me about?'

'Yes, this is Prue's demon lover.'

'Well, I'm dashed. I took him for a burglar. I'm sorry.'

'Not at all,' said Bill.

'Afraid you must have thought me a bit abrupt just now.'

'No, no,' said Bill. 'Quite all right.'

Colonel Wedge found himself in something of a quandary. A romantic at heart, his wife's revelations of the tangled love affair of his niece Prudence had left him sensible of a sneaking sympathy for the young man of her choice. Unpleasant it must have been for the chap, he felt, to have his bride whisked away on the wedding morning, and kept in storage under lock and key. Not the sort of thing he would have liked himself. He was also an admirer of spirit in the young of the male sex, and Bill's thrustful policy in the matter of ladders and water pipes appealed to him.

On the other hand, he was a loyal husband and he knew that his wife felt very strongly on the subject of the fellow. Not once but many times she had spoken of him in terms which left no room for misunderstanding.

'Do you know, Gally,' he said, 'I think I'll be popping off. I don't want to be mixed up with this. See what I mean?'

The Hon. Galahad saw what he meant and thought his policy prudent.

'Yes, no need for you to stick around, Egbert. Buzz off. And', he added, indicating Edwin Pott, who had withdrawn respectfully into the background until his offices as a witness should be required, 'take that odoriferous gargoyle with you. I've something to say to Bill in private.'

Colonel Wedge strode off, followed by Edwin Pott, and a grave look came into Gally's face.

'Bill,' he began, 'I'm sorry to tell you that a rather unfortunate thing has happened. Oh, blast it,' he broke off, for he saw that they were about to be interrupted.

Tipton Plimsoll had appeared on the terrace.

'There's someone coming,' he said, jerking an explanatory thumb.

Bill looked round. And as he saw the tall, thin chap who had so signally fallen short at their last meeting in hospitality and indeed in the first principles of humanity, his face darkened. His was as a rule a mild and equable nature, but Tipton's behaviour on that occasion had aroused his indignation. He wanted a word with him.

'Hi!' he said, advancing.

There had crept into Tipton Plimsoll's face a sudden expression of grim determination. It was the sort of look you might have seen on the faces of the Light Brigade when the order came to charge. He had not thought of it before, but it came to him now that there was a special technique which knowledgeable people employed with phantoms. They walked through them. He had read stories where fellows had done this, and always with the happiest results. The phantoms, realizing that they had run up against something hot, faltered, lost their nerve, and withdrew from the unequal contest.

If there had been any other avenue to a peaceful settlement, he would have taken it, for it was a thing he was not at all anxious to do. But there seemed no alternative. You have got to be firm with phantoms.

Commending his soul to God, he lowered his head and drove forward at Bill's midriff.

'Oof!' said Bill.

'Cheese!' said Tipton.

It would not be easy to say which of the two was the more astonished, or which the more filled with honest indignation. But Bill being occupied with the task of recovering his breath, Tipton was the first to give expression to his feelings.

'Well, how was I to know he was real?' he demanded, turning to Gally as a fair-minded non-partisan who would be able to view the situation objectively. 'This guy's been following me around for days, dodging in and out of registry offices, popping around corners, leering at me out of shrubberies. And it isn't more than about half a minute ago that he was snooping in at my window. If he thinks I'm going to stand for that sort of thing, he's darned well mistaken. There's a limit,' said Tipton, summing up.

Once more the congenial task of pouring oil on troubled waters had fallen to the Hon. Galahad. Tipton's revelations in his bedroom on the previous day had placed him in the position of being able to understand what he might otherwise have found a perplexing state of affairs.

'You don't mean to tell me it's Bill you've been seeing all this time? How very remarkable. This is my godson, Bill Lister. Tipton Plimsoll, Bill, nephew of my old friend Chet Tipton. When did you two first meet? At Barribault's Hotel, was it not?'

'He came rubbering through the glass door when I was in the bar.'

'Well, I wanted a drink,' said Bill defensively. 'I was being married that morning.'

'Married?' Tipton was beginning to understand all and to be in a position to forgive all. 'Was that why you were at that registry office?'

'Yes.'

'Well, I'm darned.'

'The whole matter', said Gally, 'is susceptible of a ready explanation. His bride, my niece Prudence, was arrested by the authorities before she could get to the registry office and sent down here. Bill followed. That was how you happened to meet.'

Tipton's whole manner had softened. He had even begun to smile. But now the recollection of a particular grievance hardened him again.

'There was no need for him to wear that gosh-awful beard,' he said.

'There was every need,' said Gally. 'He had to avoid recognition. And when he made faces outside your window, I imagine he was just coming from my niece's room, which adjoins yours. Am I right, Bill?'

'Yes. I was walking along a sort of ledge and I saw him in his room and I wanted him to let me in. But he just stared at me and went out.'

'And now, of course, you appreciate his motives in doing so. I remember a dear old friend of mine, Boko Bagshott – dead now, I'm sorry to say, cirrhosis of the liver – who frequently saw faces at windows, and he was always off like a scalded cat the moment they appeared. In fairness I don't think we can blame Plimsoll.'

'I suppose not,' said Bill, though grudgingly.

'One must always try to put oneself in the other fellow's place. You could hardly have expected him in the circumstances to extend a warm southern welcome.'

'I suppose not,' said Bill, less grudgingly.

As far as Tipton Plimsoll was concerned, the whole unpleasant matter was now forgotten. The smile which had stolen into his face and receded returned with increased brilliance. It became a grin which would have made an excellent substitute for the evening sunlight, if the latter had for any reason decided to cease to illuminate the terrace.

'Gosh,' he said, 'this is a weight off my mind. This is where I begin to live. You don't know what it's been like this last week, never being able to take the slightest snifter without seeing a hideous – without seeing a face bob up in the offing. I couldn't have stuck it out much longer. Mind you, now that I'm going to be married –'

'Are you going to be married?'

'You betcher.'

'Congratulations,' said Bill.

'Thanks, old man,' said Tipton.

'I hope you will be very, very happy, old man,' said Bill.

'I'll do just that little thing, old man,' said Tipton. 'As I was saying,' he went on, resuming his remarks, 'now that I'm going to be married, I've finished with all the rough stuff and I don't suppose I shall go on another real toot for the rest of my life, except of course on New Year's Eve –'

'Of course,' said Bill.

'– and Boat Race Night –'

'Naturally,' said Bill.

'– and special occasions like that,' said Tipton. 'But it's nice to know that one will be able to lower the stuff in strict moderation. It makes you feel so darned silly, swigging barley water when the rest of the boys are having highballs. Yes, it's certainly been a life-saver, running into you.'

' "Running into" is right,' said Bill.

'Ha, ha,' said Tipton, laughing heartily.

'Ha, ha,' said Bill, also laughing heartily.

Tipton slapped Bill's back. Bill slapped Tipton's. The Hon. Galahad beamed with growing approval on this delightful scene of cordiality and good feeling. He now asked Tipton if he would be offended if he were to take his godson to one side and impart to him something which was exclusively for his personal ear; and Tipton said: 'Go ahead, go right ahead.' Gally said they would be only half a minute, and Tipton said: 'Take your time, take your time, take your time.'

'Bill,' said Gally, leading him to the terrace wall and speaking in a low, urgent voice, 'we have come to a crisis in your affairs. It's most unfortunate that you should have formed such a warm friendship with this chap Plimsoll.'

'He seems a good sort.'

'A capital young fellow. Grouchy when I first met him, but now the living image of his uncle Chet, who was the most carefree soul who ever wrecked a restaurant. Very rich.'

'Is he?'

'Enormously. And I feel he likes you.'

'I thought he was matey.'

'Yes, I think you have made an excellent first impression. And everything now depends on him.'

'How do you mean?'

A rather sombre look had come into the Hon. Galahad's monocle.

'I was telling you, when he came up, that an unfortunate thing had happened. Prue's original plan, if you remember, was to get the capital for modernizing and running the Mulberry Tree from my brother Clarence. And with that necklace under our belts this could have been done. Prue told you about the necklace in her letter?'

'Yes. It struck me as the goods.'

'It was the goods. With it in our possession, we should have been able to dictate terms. Most unfortunately, I've lost it.'

'What!'

'It has been pinched. I went to my room just now, to make sure it was there, and it wasn't.'

'Oh, my aunt!'

Gally shook his head.

'It isn't your aunt that matters, it's Prue's. There is just a chance that it isn't Hermione who has got the thing, but if she has, our flank is turned and only one hope remains. We must try to get that capital from young Plimsoll.'

'But I can't. We've only just met.'

'Quite. But his feelings towards you are obviously warm. I got the impression that he was so much obliged to you for not being a spectre that you would be able to ask of him anything you wished, even unto half his kingdom. At any rate, his are the ribs we must endeavour to get into. Tails up, and leave the talking to me. Dash it,' said Gally, with much the same gallant spirit as had animated Freddie when about to broach the subject of Donaldson's Dog-Joy to Major R. B. and Lady Emily Finch, 'I've talked the hind legs off the toughest bookies in my time and defeated in debate bouncers at all the principal bars both in London and New York. I should not fail now.'

6

'Tell me, my dear Plimsoll,' said Gally. 'Or may I call you Tipton?'

'Why, sure,' said Tipton. 'Or, rather, Tippy. You, too,' he added handsomely.

'Thanks, Tippy,' said Bill.

'Not at all,' said Tipton. 'Delighted.'

The Hon. Galahad allowed his monocle to play upon him like a sunbeam, well pleased that such a delightful atmosphere of cama-raderie should have been established at the very outset of the negotiations.

'What I was about to ask you, my dear Tippy,' he said, 'was, have you ever given a thought to modern trends?'

'Well, I'll tell you,' said Tipton, learning for the first time that these existed, 'what with one thing and another, no.'

'When I say "modern trends",' proceeded Gally, 'I am thinking at the moment of the amusement world. Amazing how people's tastes have altered since I was your age. *Tempora mutantur, nos et mutamur in illis.'*

'You betcher,' said Tipton, fogged but courteous.

'Take the simple matter of having a drink. In my young days one just went down the street to a bar.'

'And not at all a bad thing to do,' said Tipton.

'Quite. But see how the motor-car has changed all that. The cry now is all for the great outdoors. The fellow with a thirst grabs the nearest girl, dumps her in his automobile, and ho for the open spaces. Instead of suffocating in some smelly bar in London they take their refreshment on the cool terrace swept by the healthy breezes of a country inn outside Oxford.'

'Oxford?'

'Oxford.'

'Why Oxford particularly?' asked Tipton.

'Because', said Gally, 'that is the modern trend. Oxford is a nice easy distance, and you are right away from all the stuffiness of London. A man who owns an inn anywhere near Oxford is a man to be envied.'

'I guess so,' said Tipton.

'Such a man, to take an instance, as Bill.'

'Bill?'

'Bill.'

'This Bill?'

'That's the one,' said Gally. 'He is the proprietor of a picturesque inn not far from Oxford, and what I have been telling him is that if he branches out and turns the place into what they call in your country a roadhouse with all the modern improvements, he has a gold mine. You probably agree with me?'

'Oh, sure.'

'I thought you would. Properly developed, this inn of Bill's would be a bonanza.'

'I'll say.'

'It is situated in the most delightful spot of one of England's most delightful counties. People would come from miles around merely to look at the scenery. Add a first-class cellar, squash racket courts, a jazz band, and really fine cooking, perfectly served – out of doors on the terrace in good weather, in the richly panelled dining-room when it was wet – and you would have something which would draw the automobile trade like a magnet.'

'Is the dining-room richly panelled?'

'Not yet. I was going to touch on that point. To develop this place – the Mulberry Tree is its name – will require capital.'

'Sure. You can't branch out without capital.'

'I close my eyes,' said Gally, doing so, 'and I seem to see the Mulberry Tree as it will be when all the improvements are completed. Turning in off the main road, we drive through a fairylike garden studded with coloured lanterns.'

'With a fountain in the middle.'

'With, of course, a fountain in the middle.'

'Lit up with coloured lights.'

'Lit up, as you say, with coloured lights. I really am delighted at the way you are taking hold, my dear Tippy. I knew that I should interest you.'

'Oh, you do. Where were we?'

'We had reached the fountain. To our right are wide, spreading gardens, rich in every variety of flower; to our left, through the dim, mysterious trees, we catch a glimpse of shimmering silver.'

'Do we?' said Tipton. 'Why's that?'

'The swimming pool,' explained Gally.

'There's a swimming pool, is there?'

'There will be – once we have got the capital.'

Tipton reflected.

'I'd have artificial waves.'

'An admirable idea.'

'Artificial waves make such a difference.'

'All the difference. Make a note of artificial waves, Bill.'

'Right ho, Gally.'

'We then approach the terrace.'

'That's where the dinner is?'

'If the night is fine.'

'Look,' said Tipton, beginning to take fire, 'I'll tell you about that terrace. Make it a bower of roses.'

'We will.'

'You want one of those things you have over things. What *are* those things you have over things?'

'Umbrellas?' hazarded Bill.

'Bill!' said Gally reproachfully. 'You can't get an umbrella to smell like roses. You know that. The word Tippy is searching for, I imagine, is "pergolas".'

'Pergolas. That's right. You've got to have a rose-covered pergola, and you hide your jazz band behind a mass of luxurious honeysuckle. Gosh, it'll be great,' said Tipton, snapping his fingers. 'How much per head for dinner?'

'Eight shillings, I thought.'

'Make it ten bob. No one will ever know the difference. Well, look. Call it on an average night two hundred dinners at ten bob a nob, that's a hundred quid right out of the box. And when you reflect that that's going on all through the summer . . . And then there are the drinks. Don't forget the drinks. That's where the big profit comes in. Cocktails would be served on little tables around the fountain.'

'And on the brink of the swimming pool.'

Tipton had begun to pace up and down, expressing his emotion in sweeping gestures.

'Bill,' he said, 'you're on to a big thing.'

'I think so, Tippy.'

'Yessir, big. Folks'll come from all over the country. You won't be able to keep them away with an injunction. They'll have to tell off a special squad of cops to handle the traffic. You'll be a millionaire before you know where you are.'

'That's what I tell him,' said Gally. 'Really, one sees no limits to the enterprise.'

'None,' agreed Tipton.

'There only remains this trifling matter of the capital.'

'The capital. Sure.'

'Get the capital, and we can start tomorrow.'

'Get the capital, and you're home.'

'Three thousand might do it.'

'Four would be safer.'

'Or five.'

'Yes, maybe five. Yes, five's the figure I see.'

Gally laid an affectionate hand on Tipton's shoulder and massaged it.

'You would really be prepared to put up five thousand pounds?' he asked tenderly.

Tipton stared.

'Me? Put up five thousand pounds? I'm not going to put up anything,' he said, chuckling a little at the bizarreness of the idea. 'Why, I might lose my money. But I guess you'll get your capital all right. Ask around. And now you'll have to excuse me. I promised to take Vee for a row on the lake.'

He gambolled off, the picture of youth and life and happiness. It is possible that he may have known that he was leaving aching hearts behind him, but not probable. Tipton Plimsoll was a rather self-centred young man.

7

Gally looked at Bill. Bill looked at Gally. For a moment neither spoke, their thoughts being too deep for words. Then Gally made an observation which he had once heard from the lips of a disappointed punter at a suburban race meeting on the occasion of his finding that the bookmaker with whom he had wagered on the winner of the last race had packed up and disappeared, leaving no address. It seemed to relieve him. His manner became calmer.

'Well, that's that, Bill.'

'That's that, Gally.'

'An extraordinarily similar thing happened to an old friend of mine many years ago, when he was trying to interest a wealthy young man in a club which he was planning to open. He told me with tears in his eyes, I remember, that he could have betted his entire fortune, if he had had one, that the chap was just about to reach for his cheque book. These things do happen. One must accept them with grim fortitude. We now come back to Clarence. I'd give anything to know if Hermione has got that necklace. If she hasn't, it may be possible to achieve the happy ending by means of a little inspired bluffing. Ah, here she comes.'

Bill leaped like a hooked worm.

'Eh? What? Where?' He cast a feverish eye towards the house and saw that the bad news was only too true. Lady Hermione, accompanied by Lord Emsworth, had just come through the french windows of the drawing-room. 'Gally, I'm off.'

The Hon. Galahad nodded.

'Yes, I think perhaps it would be best if you left me to handle the negotiations. If I were you, I'd go and have a chat with Prue. I saw her just now going in the direction of the rose garden. You will find the rose garden over there,' said Gally, pointing. 'I'll join you later,' he said, and turned to meet his flesh and blood, who were now making their way towards him across the terrace. His face was hard and determined. His monocle gleamed with quiet resolution. He looked like a featherweight contender entering the ring to do battle with the champion.

It was as his sister drew near and he was able to study her face that a sudden quick hope strengthened his doughty heart. Hers, it seemed to him, was not the air of a woman who by getting her hooks on necklaces has outgeneralled the opposition. It was unmistakably one of gloom.

'Tails up!' said Gally to his heart, and his heart replied, 'You betcher.'

In supposing Lady Hermione to be gloomy, Gally had been right. It is fortunately only very rarely that in any given family in the English upper classes you will find two members of it who have drained the bitter cup in a single afternoon. The average of mental anguish is as a rule lower. But this had happened today. We have shown Colonel Wedge frankly confessing that he had done so, and Lady Hermione, if questioned, would have been obliged to make the same admission. As she came on to the terrace, her spirits were at a very low ebb and she was recognizing the outlook as unsettled.

To the best of her knowledge, the necklace still remained in her brother Galahad's possession, and his prediction that she would be compelled to throw in the towel still rang in her ears. The more she contemplated the position of affairs, the more sadly convinced did she become that he was right, and a proud woman dislikes having to throw in towels. But she could see no way out of it.

Freddie, delivering his ultimatum at the general meeting, had seemed to her to speak with the voice of doom. Were he to carry out his threat of telling all to Tipton Plimsoll, disaster must ensue. She had been deeply impressed by the haughty and imperious spirit which Tipton had shown when switching necklaces from spot to spot in the drawing-room. There, she had felt, stood a man who would stand no nonsense. Let him discover that he had been deceived, and he would break off the engagement. And at the thought of her child losing such a mate, she quailed.

It would be but a poor consolation to her in later years, when people were congratulating her on Veronica's marriage to the reasonably eligible husband whom the future would no doubt produce, to tell them that they ought to have seen the one that got away.

Reflections such as these had weakened her once iron will. She was beginning to think that there were more important things in life than checking the impulse of her sister Dora's daughter to marry into the Underworld. She had not revised her opinion that Bill was the dregs of humanity, but there had begun to steal over her the feeling that it was Dora's place, not hers, to do the worrying.

She was, in short, but a shell of her former self. She had become a defeatist.

Gally was a man who believed in brisk attack. He wasted no time in preliminaries.

'Well?' he said.

Lady Hermione quivered, but was silent.

'Made up your mind?' said Gally.

There was almost a pleading note in Lady Hermione's voice as she endeavoured to reason with him.

'But, Galahad, you can't want your niece to marry a penniless artist?'

'He isn't a penniless artist. He's the owner of what will be the finest roadhouse in England as soon as Clarence has put up the capital for modernization and improvements.'

'Eh?' said Lord Emsworth, whose thoughts had wandered.

'Listen, Clarence,' said Gally. 'Do you want to make a lot of money?'

'I've got a lot of money,' said Lord Emsworth.

'You can always do with a bit more.'

'True.'

'Picture to yourself, Clarence,' said Gally, 'a fair countryside, and in that countryside a smiling inn. Its grounds', he hurried on, for he could see that his brother was about to ask why the inn was smiling, 'are dotted – very profusely dotted – with groups sucking down cocktails at a couple of bob a go. Its terrace is a solid mass of diners enjoying the ten-shilling dinner under a bower of roses. There are lanterns. There is a fountain, lit by coloured lights. There is a swimming pool with – mark this, Clarence – artificial waves. It is, in short, the most popular place of its kind in the country, the turnover being terrific.'

Lord Emsworth said it sounded nice, and Gally assured him that he had found the *mot juste*.

'A gold mine,' he said. 'And a half share in it, Clarence, is yours for five thousand pounds.'

'Five thousand pounds?'

'You can hardly believe it, can you? A mere pittance. And no need', said Gally, seeing that the other had become meditative, 'to dig up the money on the nail. All I want from you is a letter to my godson, Bill Lister, promising to cough up in due course.'

Lord Emsworth had begun to fiddle with his pince-nez – a bad sign, in Gally's opinion. He had often seen bank managers fiddle with their pince-nez when he looked in to arrange about an overdraft.

'Well, I don't know, Galahad.'

'Come, come, Clarence.'

'Five thousand pounds is a great deal of money.'

'A sprat to catch a whale. You'll see it back at the end of the first year. Did I mention that there would be a first-class jazz orchestra playing behind a mass of honeysuckle?'

Lord Emsworth shook his head.

'I'm sorry, Galahad –'

Gally's face hardened.

'All right,' he said. 'Then mark the alternative. I stick to that necklace, and what ensues? Ruin and misery and desolation. Young Plimsoll breaks off his engagement to Veronica. Mrs Freddie divorces Freddie.'

'Eh?'

'And poor old Freddie, I suppose, comes to eke out the sad remainder of his days at Blandings Castle.'

'What!'

'It seems the logical thing for him to do. The wounded bird creeping back to the old nest. You'll like having Freddie at Blandings. Nice company for your declining years.'

Lord Emsworth recovered the pince-nez which had leaped from his nose. On his face, as he replaced them, there was the look of one who has come to a decision.

'I'll go and write that letter at once,' he said. 'The name is Lister?'

'William Lister,' said Gally. 'L for Laryngitis, I for Ipecacuanha, S for —'

But Lord Emsworth had gone.

'He!' said Gally, removing his hat and fanning with it a brow which had become a little heated.

His sister Hermione, too, seemed to be under a sense of strain. Her eyes were bulging, and there was a tinge of purple in her cheeks.

'And now, perhaps, Galahad,' she said, 'you will be good enough to give me that necklace.'

There was a brief pause. It was as if the Hon. Galahad shrank from saying what he feared might wound.

'I haven't got it.'

'What!'

'I'm sorry. Not my fault. I'll tell you exactly what happened,' said Gally, with manly regret. 'From motives of safety, in case you might feel the urge to come and hunt about in my room, I put it in a place where I thought you wouldn't dream of looking. Yesterday young Plimsoll gave me his flask to keep for him — a large, roomy flask —'

He paused. A stricken cry had rung through the quiet garden. Lady Hermione was looking like a cook who has seen a black beetle in her kitchen and the last of the beetle powder used up yesterday.

'You put the necklace in Tipton's flask?'

'A dashed shrewd hiding-place, I thought. But I'm sorry to say the bally thing has been removed. Who has got it now I can't tell you.'

'I can,' said Lady Hermione. 'He gave it to me. I met him coming out of my room just now, and he pressed it into my hand with a strange, wild look in his eyes, and asked me to take care of it for him.'

Her voice trailed away in a sigh that was like the wind blowing through the cracks in a broken heart.

'Galahad,' she said, 'you ought to have been a confidence man.'

'So people have told me,' said Gally, flattered. 'Well, that's fine. If you've got the thing, you can give it to Freddie, and the matter is closed. Everybody happy, loving young hearts united, nothing to worry about. And now I'll go and see how Clarence is getting on with that letter. After that, I have to go and meet a couple of people in the rose garden.'

He trotted off towards the house, going hippety-hippety-hop like an elderly Christopher Robin.

PIGS HAVE WINGS

Chapter 1

Beach the butler, wheezing a little after navigating the stairs, for he was not the streamlined young under-footman he had been thirty years ago, entered the library of Blandings Castle, a salver piled with letters in his hand.

'The afternoon post, m'lord,' he announced, and Lord Emsworth, looking up from his book – he was reading Whiffle on *The Care Of The Pig* – said: 'Ah, the afternoon post? The afternoon post, eh? Quite. Quite.' His sister, Lady Constance Keeble, might, and frequently did, complain of his vagueness – ('Oh, for goodness' sake, Clarence, don't *gape* like that!') – but he could on occasion be as quick at the uptake as the next man.

'Yes, yes, to be sure, the afternoon post,' he said, fully abreast. 'Capital. Thank you, Beach. Put it on the table.'

'Very good, m'lord. Pardon me, m'lord, can you see Sir Gregory Parsloe?'

'No,' said Lord Emsworth, having glanced about the room and failed to do so. 'Where is he?'

'Sir Gregory telephoned a few moments ago to say that he would be glad of a word with your lordship. He informed me that he was about to walk to the castle.'

Lord Emsworth blinked.

'Walk?'

'So Sir Gregory gave me to understand, m'lord.'

'What does he want to walk for?'

'I could not say, m'lord.'

'It's three miles each way, and about the hottest day we've had this summer. The man's an ass.'

To such an observation the well-trained butler, however sympathetic, does not reply 'Whoopee!' or 'You said it, pal!' Beach merely allowed his upper lip to twitch slightly by way of indication that his heart was in the right place, and Lord Emsworth fell into a reverie. He was thinking about Sir Gregory Parsloe-Parsloe, Bart, of Matchingham Hall.

To most of us, casual observers given to snap judgements, the lot of an Earl dwelling in marble halls with vassals and serfs at his side probably seems an enviable one. 'A lucky stiff,' we say to ourselves as we drive off in our charabanc after paying half a crown to be shown over the marble halls, and in many cases, of course, we would be right.

But not in that of Clarence, ninth Earl of Emsworth. There was a snake in his Garden of Eden, a crumpled leaf in his bed of roses, a grain of sand in his spiritual spinach. He had good health, a large income and a first-class ancestral home with gravel soil, rolling parkland and all the conveniences, but these blessings were rendered null and void by the fact that the pure air of the district in which he lived was polluted by the presence of a man like Sir Gregory Parsloe – a man who, he was convinced, had evil designs on that pre-eminent pig, Empress of Blandings.

Empress of Blandings was the apple of Lord Emsworth's eye. Twice in successive years winner in the Fat Pigs class at the Shropshire Agricultural Show, she was confidently expected this year to triumph for the third time, provided – always provided – that this Parsloe, who owned her closest rival, Pride of Matchingham, did not hatch some fearful plot for her undoing.

Two years before, by tempting him with his gold, this sinister Baronet had lured away into his own employment Lord Emsworth's pig man, the superbly gifted George Cyril Wellbeloved, and it was the opinion of the Hon. Galahad Threepwood, Lord Emsworth's younger brother, strongly expressed, that this bit of sharp practice was to be considered just a preliminary to blacker crimes, a mere flexing of the muscles, as it were, preparatory to dishing out the real rough stuff. Dash it all, said Galahad, reasoning closely, when you get a fellow like young Parsloe, a chap who for years before he came into the title was knocking about London without a bean in his pocket, living God knows how and always one jump ahead of the gendarmerie, is it extravagant to suppose that he will stick at nothing? If such a man has a pig entered for the Fat Pigs contest and sees a chance of making the thing a certainty for his own candidate by nobbling the favourite, he is dashed well going to jump at it. That was the view of the Hon. Galahad Threepwood.

'Parsloe!' he said. 'I've known young Parsloe since we were both in the early twenties, and he was always so crooked he sliced bread with a corkscrew. When they saw Parsloe coming in the old days, strong men used to wince and hide their valuables. That's the sort of fellow he was, and you can't tell me he's any different now. You watch that pig of yours like a hawk, Clarence, or before you know where you are, this fiend in human shape will be slipping pineapple bombs into her bran mash.'

The words had sunk in, as such words would scarcely have failed to do, and they had caused Lord Emsworth to entertain towards Sir Gregory feelings similar to, though less cordial than, those of Sherlock Holmes toward Professor Moriarty. So now he sat brooding on him darkly, and would probably have gone on brooding for some considerable time, had not Beach, who wanted to get back to his pantry and rest his feet, uttered a significant cough.

'Eh?' said Lord Emsworth, coming out of his coma.

'Would there be anything further, m'lord?'

'Further? Oh, I see what you mean. Further. No, nothing further, Beach.'

'Thank you, m'lord.'

Beach withdrew in that stately, ponderous way of his that always reminded travellers who knew their Far East of an elephant sauntering through an Indian jungle, and Lord Emsworth resumed his reading. The butler's entry had interrupted him in the middle of that great chapter of Whiffle's which relates how a pig, if aiming at the old mid-season form, must consume daily nourishment amounting to not less than fifty-seven thousand eight hundred calories, these calories to consist of barley meal, maize meal, linseed meal, potatoes, and separated buttermilk.

But this was not his lucky afternoon. Scarcely had his eye rested on the page when the door opened again, this time to admit a handsome woman of imperious aspect in whom – after blinking once or twice through his pince-nez – he recognized his sister, Lady Constance Keeble.

2

He eyed her apprehensively, like some rat of the underworld cornered by G-men. Painful experience had taught him that visits from Connie meant trouble, and he braced himself, as always, to meet with stout denial whatever charge she might be about to hurl at him. He was a great believer in stout denial and was very good at it.

For once, however, her errand appeared to be pacific. Her manner was serene, even amiable.

'Oh, Clarence,' she said, 'have you seen Penelope anywhere?'

'Eh?'

'Penelope Donaldson.'

'Who,' asked Lord Emsworth courteously, 'is Penelope Donaldson?'

Lady Constance sighed. Had she not been the daughter of a hundred Earls, she would have snorted. Her manner lost its amiability. She struck her forehead with a jewelled hand and rolled her eyes heavenward for a moment.

'Penelope Donaldson,' she said, speaking with the strained sweetness of a woman striving to be patient while conversing with one of the less intelligent of the Jukes family, 'is the younger daughter of the Mr Donaldson of Long Island City in the United States of America whose elder daughter is married to your son Frederick. To refresh your memory, you have two sons – your heir, Bosham, and a younger son, Frederick. Frederick married the elder Miss Donaldson. The younger Miss Donaldson – her name is Penelope – is staying with us now at Blandings Castle – this is Blandings Castle – and what I am asking you is . . . Have you seen her? And I do wish, Clarence, that you would not let your mouth hang open when I am talking to you. It makes you look like a goldfish.'

It has already been mentioned that there were moments when Lord Emsworth could be as quick as a flash.

'Ah!' he cried, enlightened. 'When you say Penelope Donaldson, you mean Penelope Donaldson. Quite. Quite. And have I seen her, you ask. Yes, I saw her with Galahad just now. I was looking out of the window and they came past. Going for a walk or something. They were walking,' explained Lord Emsworth, making it clear that his brother and the young visitor from America had not been mounted on pogo-sticks.

Lady Constance uttered a sound which resembled that caused by placing a wet thumb on a hot stove lid.

'It's too bad of Galahad. Ever since she came to the castle he has simply monopolized the girl. He ought to have more sense. He must know that the whole point of her being here is that I wanted to bring her and Orlo Vosper together.'

'Who –?'

'Oh, Clarence!'

'What's the matter now?'

'If you say "Who is Orlo Vosper?", I shall hit you with something. I believe this vagueness of yours is just a pose. You put it on simply to madden people. You know perfectly well who Orlo Vosper is.'

Lord Emsworth nodded intelligently.

'Yes, I've got him placed now. Fellow who looks like a screen star. He's staying here,' he said, imparting a valuable piece of inside information.

'I am aware of it. And Penelope seems to be deliberately avoiding him.'

'Sensible girl. He's a dull chap.'

'He is nothing of the kind. Most entertaining.'

'He doesn't entertain me.'

'Possibly not, as he does not talk about pigs all the time.'

'He's unsound on pigs. When I showed him the Empress, he yawned.'

'He is evidently very much attracted by Penelope.'

'Tried to hide it behind his hand, but I saw it. A yawn.'

'And it would be a wonderful marriage for her.'

'What would?'

'This.'

'Which?'

'Oh, Clarence!'

'Well, how do you expect me to follow you, dash it, when you beat about the bush like – er – like someone beating about the bush? Be plain. Be clear. Be frank and straightforward. Who's marrying who?'

Lady Constance went into her wet-thumb-on-stove routine again.

'I am merely telling you,' she said wearily, 'that Orlo Vosper is obviously attracted by Penelope and that it would please Mr Donaldson very much if she were to marry him. One of the oldest families in England and plenty of money, too. But what can he do if she spends all her time with Galahad? Still, I am taking her to London tomorrow, and Orlo is driving us in his car. Something may come of that. Do *listen*, Clarence!'

'I'm listening. You said Penelope was going to London with Mr Donaldson.'

'Oh, Clar-*ence*!'

'Or rather with Vosper. What's she going to London for in weather like this? Silly idea.'

'She has a fitting. Her dress for the County Ball. And Orlo has to see his lawyer about his income tax.'

'Income tax!' cried Lord Emsworth, staring like a war horse at the sound of the bugle. Pigs and income tax were the only two subjects that really stirred him. 'Let me tell you –'

'I haven't time to listen,' said Lady Constance, and swept from the room. These chats with the head of the family nearly always ended in her sweeping from the room. Unless, of course, they took place out of doors, when she merely swept away.

Left alone, Lord Emsworth sat for awhile savouring that delicious sense of peace which comes to men of quiet tastes when their womenfolk have said their say and departed. Then, just as he was about to turn to Whiffle again, his eye fell on the pile of correspondence on the table, and he took it up and began glancing through it. And he had read and put aside perhaps half a dozen of the dullest letters ever penned by human hand, when he came upon something of quite a different nature, something that sent his eyebrows shooting up and brought a surprised 'Bless my soul!' to his lips.

It was a picture postcard, one of those brightly coloured picture postcards at which we of the intelligentsia click our tongues, but which afford pleasure and entertainment to quite a number of the lower-browed. It represented a nude lady, presumably Venus, rising from the waves at a seashore resort with a cheery 'I'm in the pink, kid' coming out of her mouth in the form of a balloon, and beneath this figure, in a bold feminine hand, were the words 'Hey hey, today's the day, what, what? Many happy returns, old dear. Love and kisses. Maudie.'

It puzzled Lord Emsworth, as it might have puzzled an even deeper thinker. To the best of his knowledge he was not acquainted with any Maudie, let alone one capable of this almost Oriental warmth of feeling. Unlike that *beau sabreur* and man about town, his brother Galahad, who had spent a lifetime courting the society of the breezier type of female and in his younger days had never been happier than when knee-deep in barmaids and ballet girls, he had always taken considerable pains to avoid the Maudies of this world.

Recovering his pince-nez, which, as always in times of emotion, had fallen off and were dangling at the end of their string, he slipped the card absently into his pocket and reached out for his book. But it was too late. The moment had passed. What with butlers babbling about Parsloes and Connies babbling about Vospers and mystery women sending him love and kisses, he had temporarily lost the power to appreciate Whiffle's mighty line.

There was only one thing to be done, if he hoped to recover calm of spirit. He straightened his pince-nez, and went off to the piggeries to have a look at Empress of Blandings.

3

The Empress lived in a bijou residence not far from the kitchen garden, and when Lord Emsworth arrived at her boudoir she was engaged, as pretty nearly always when you dropped in on her, in hoisting into her vast interior those fifty-seven thousand and eight hundred calories on which Whiffle insists. Monica Simmons, the pig girl, had done her well in the way of barley meal, maize meal, linseed meal, potatoes, and separated buttermilk, and she was digging in and getting hers in a manner calculated to inspire the brightest confidence in the bosoms of her friends and admirers.

Monica Simmons was standing at the rail as Lord Emsworth pottered up, a stalwart girl in a smock and breeches who looked like what in fact she was, one of the six daughters of a rural Vicar all of whom had played hockey for Roedean. She was not a great favourite with Lord Emsworth, who suspected her of a lack of reverence for the Empress. Of this fundamental flaw in her character she instantly afforded ghastly proof.

'Hullo, Lord Emsworth,' she said. 'Hot, what? Have you come to see the piggy-wiggy? Well, now you're here, I'll be buzzing off and getting my tea and shrimps. I've a thirst I wouldn't sell for fifty quid. Cheerio.'

She strode off, her large feet spurning the antic hay, and Lord Emsworth, who had quivered like an aspen and was supporting himself on the rail, gazed after her with a smouldering eye. He was thinking nostalgically of former custodians of his pig supreme – of George Cyril Wellbeloved, now in the enemy's camp; of Percy Pirbright, George Cyril's successor, last heard of in Canada; and of Edwin Pott, who, holding portfolio after Percy, had retired into private life on winning a football pool. None of these would have alluded to Empress of Blandings as 'the piggy-wiggy'. Edwin Pott, as a matter of fact, would not have been able to do so, even had he wished, for he had no roof to his mouth.

Ichabod, felt Lord Emsworth, and was still in a disturbed state of mind, though gradually becoming soothed by listening to that sweetest of all music, the sound of the Empress restoring her tissues, when there appeared at his side, leaning on the rail and surveying the champ through a black-rimmed monocle, a slim, trim, dapper little gentleman in his late fifties, whom he greeted with a cordial 'Ah, Galahad.'

'Ah, to you, Clarence old bird, with knobs on,' responded the newcomer, equally cordial.

The Hon. Galahad Threepwood was the only genuinely distinguished member of the family of which Lord Emsworth was the head. The world, it is said, knows little of its greatest men, but everyone connected with the world of clubs, bars, theatres, restaurants, and racecourses knew Gally, if only by reputation. He was one of that determined little band who, feeling that London would look better painted red, had devoted themselves at an early age to the task of giving it that cheerful colour. A pain in the neck to his sister Constance, his sister Julia, his sister Dora, and all his other sisters, he was universally esteemed in less austere quarters, for his heart was of gold and his soul overflowing with the milk of human kindness.

As he stood gazing at the Empress, something between a gulp and a groan at his side caused him to transfer his scrutiny to his elder brother, and he was concerned to note that there was a twisted look on those loved features, as if the head of the family had just swallowed something acid.

'Hullo, Clarence!' he said. 'The old heart seems a bit bowed down. What's the matter? Not brooding on that incident at the Emsworth Arms, are you?'

'Eh? Incident? What incident was that?'

'Has no word of it reached your ears? I had it from Beach, who had it from the scullery maid, who had it from the chauffeur. It appears that that butler of Parsloe's – Binstead is his name, I believe – was swanking about in the tap room of the Emsworth Arms last night, offering five to one on Parsloe's pig.'

Lord Emsworth stared.

'On Pride of Matchingham? The fellow's insane. How can Pride of Matchingham possibly have a chance against the Empress?'

'That's what I felt. It puzzled me, too. The simple explanation is, I suppose, that Binstead had got a snootful and was talking through his hat. Well, if that's not what's worrying you, what is? Why are you looking like a bereaved tapeworm?'

Lord Emsworth was only too glad to explain to a sympathetic ear what had caused the resemblance.

'That girl Simmons upset me, Galahad. You will scarcely credit it, but she called the Empress a piggy-wiggy.'

'She did?'

'I assure you. "Hullo, Lord Emsworth," she said. "Have you come to see the piggy-wiggy?"'

Gally frowned.

'Bad,' he agreed. 'The wrong tone. If this is true, it seems to show that the child is much too frivolous in her outlook to hold the responsible position she does. I may mention that this is the view which Beach takes. He has put a considerable slice of his savings on the Empress's nose to cop at the forthcoming Agricultural Show, and he is uneasy. He asks himself apprehensively is La Simmons fitted for her sacred task? And I don't blame him. For mark this, Clarence, and mark it well. The girl who carelessly dismisses Empress of Blandings as a piggy-wiggy today is a girl who may quite easily forget to give her lunch tomorrow. Whatever induced you, my dear fellow, to entrust a job that calls for the executive qualities of a Pierpont Morgan to the pop-eyed daughter of a rural vicar?'

Lord Emsworth did not actually wring his hands, but he came very near to it.

'It was not my doing,' he protested. 'Connie insisted on my engaging her. She is some sort of protégé of Connie's. Related to someone she wanted to oblige, or something like that. Blame Connie for the whole terrible situation.'

'Connie!' said Gally. 'The more I see of this joint, the more clearly do I realize that what Blandings Castle needs, to make it an earthly Paradise, is fewer and better Connies. Sisters are a mistake, Clarence. You should have set your face against them at the outset.'

'True,' said Lord Emsworth. 'True.'

Silence fell, as nearly as silence could ever fall in the neighbourhood of a trough at which Empress of Blandings was feeding. It was broken by Lord Emsworth, who was peering about him with the air of a man who senses something missing in his surroundings.

'Where,' he asked, 'is Alice?'

'Eh?'

'Or, rather, Penelope. Penelope Donaldson. I thought you were out for a walk together.'

'Oh, Penny? Yes, we have been strolling hither and thither, chewing the fat. There's a nice girl, Clarence.'

'Charming.'

'Not only easy on the eye and a conversationalist who holds you spellbound on a wide variety of subjects, but kind-hearted. I happened to express a wish for a whisky-and-soda, and she immediately trotted off to tell Beach to bring me one, to save me trudging to the house.'

'You are going to have a whisky-and-soda?'

'You follow me like a bloodhound. It will bring the roses back to my cheeks, which is always so desirable, and it will enable me to drink Beach's health with a hey-nonny-nonny and a hot-cha-cha. It's his birthday.'

'Beach's birthday?'

'That's right.'

'God bless my soul.'

Lord Emsworth was fumbling in his pocket.

'By the afternoon post, Galahad, I received an extraordinary communication. Most extraordinary. It was one of those picture postcards. It said "Many happy returns, old dear. Love and kisses", and it was signed Maudie. Now that you tell me it is Beach's birthday, I am wondering . . . Yes, as I thought. It was intended for Beach and must have got mixed up with my letters. Look.'

Gally took the card and scrutinized it through his monocle. On the reverse side were the words:

> Mr Sebastian Beach,
> Blandings Castle,
> Shropshire

A grave look came into his face.

'We must inquire into this,' he said. 'How long has Beach been at the castle? Eighteen years? Nineteen? Well, the exact time is immaterial. The point is that he has been here long enough for me to have grown to regard him as a son, and any son of mine who gets picture postcards of nude Venuses from girls named Maudie has got to do some brisk explaining. We can't have Sex rearing its ugly head in the butler's pantry. Hoy, Beach!'

Sebastian Beach was approaching, his customary measured step rather more measured than usual owing to the fact that he was bearing a tall glass filled to the brim with amber liquid. Beside him tripped a small, slender girl with fair hair who looked as if she might have been a wood nymph the butler had picked up on his way through the grounds. Actually, she was the younger daughter of an American manufacturer of dog biscuits.

'Here come the United States Marines, Gally,' she said, and Gally, having replied with a good deal of satisfaction that he could see them with the naked eye, took the glass and drank deeply.

'Happy birthday, Beach.'

'Thank you, Mr Galahad.'

'A sip for you, Penny?'

'No, thanks.'

'Clarence?'

'Eh? No, no thank you.'

'Right,' said Gally, finishing the contents of the glass. 'And now to approach a painful task. Beach!'

'Sir?'

'Peruse this card.'

Beach took the postcard. As his gooseberry eyes scanned it, his lips moved the fraction of an inch. He looked like a butler who for two pins, had he not been restrained by the rigid rules of the Butlers' Guild, might have smiled.

'Well, Beach? We are waiting. Who is this Maudie?'

'My niece, Mr Galahad.'

'That is your story, is it?'

'My brother's daughter, Mr Galahad. She is what might be termed the Bohemian member of the family. As a young girl she ran away from home and became a barmaid in London.'

Gally pricked up his ears, like a specialist whose particular subject has come up in the course of conversation. It was as if razor blades had been mentioned in the presence of Mr Gillette.

'A barmaid, eh? Where?'

'At the Criterion, Mr Galahad.'

'I must have known her, then. I knew them all at the Criterion. Though I don't remember any Maudie Beach.'

'For business purposes she adopted the *nom de guerre* of Montrose, sir.'

Gally uttered a glad cry.

'Maudie Montrose? Is that who she was ? Good heavens, of course I knew her. Charming girl with blue eyes and hair like a golden bird's nest. Many is the buttered rum I have accepted at her hands. What's become of her? Is she still working the old beer engine?'

'Oh no, Mr Galahad. She married and retired.'

'I hope her husband appreciates her many sterling qualities.'

'He is no longer with us, sir. He contracted double pneumonia, standing outside a restaurant in the rain.'

'What on earth did he do that for?'

'It was in pursuance of his professional duties, sir. He was the proprietor of a private investigation bureau, Digby's Day and Night Detectives. Now that he has passed on, my niece conducts the business herself, and I believe gives general satisfaction.'

Penny gave an interested squeak.

'You mean she's a sleuth? One of the bloodstain and magnifying glass brigade?'

'Substantially that, miss. I gather that she leaves the rougher work to her subordinates.'

'Still she's a genuine private eye. Golly, it takes all sorts to make a world, doesn't it?'

'So I have been given to understand, miss,' said Beach indulgently. He turned to Lord Emsworth, who, finding the Maudie topic one that did not grip, had started to scratch the Empress's back with a piece of stick. 'I should have mentioned, m'lord, that Sir Gregory has arrived.'

'Oh, dash it. Where is he?'

'I left him in the morning-room, m'lord, taking off his shoes. I received the impression that his feet were paining him. He expressed a desire to see your lordship at your lordship's earliest convenience.'

Lord Emsworth became peevish.

'What on earth does the man want, coming here? He knows that I regard him with the deepest suspicion. But I suppose I shall have to see him. If I don't, it will only mean an unpleasant scene with Connie. She is always telling me I must be neighbourly.'

'Thank goodness I don't have to be,' said Gally. 'I can look young Parsloe in the eye and make him wilt. That's the advantage of not having a position to keep up. That was interesting, what Beach was telling us, Clarence.'

'Eh?'

'About Maudie.'

'Who is Maudie?'

'All right, master-mind, let it go. Trot along and see what that thug wants.'

Lord Emsworth ambled off, followed at just the right respectful distance by his faithful butler, and Gally looked after them musingly.

'Amazing,' he said. 'Do you know how long I have known Beach? Eighteen years, or it may have been nineteen, ever since I was a slip of a boy of forty. And only today have I discovered that his name is Sebastian. The same thing happened with Fruity Biffen. I don't think you met my old friend Fruity Biffen, did you? He was living down here at a house along the Shrewsbury road till a short time ago, but he left before you arrived. In the old days he used to sign his IOU's George J. Biffen, and it was only after the lapse of several years, one night when we were having supper together at Romano's and he had lost some of his reserve owing to having mixed stout, *Crème de menthe*, and old brandy, to see what it tasted like, that he revealed that the J. stood for —'

'Gally,' said Penny, who for some moments had been tracing arabesques on the turf with her shoe and giving other indications of nerving herself to an embarrassing task, 'can you lend me two thousand pounds?'

4

It was never an easy matter to disconcert the Hon. Galahad. For half a century nursemaids, governesses, tutors, schoolmasters, Oxford dons, bookmakers, three-card-trick men, jellied-eel sellers, skittle sharps, racecourse touts and members of the metropolitan police force had tried to do it, and all had failed. It was an axiom of the old Pelican Club that, no matter what slings and arrows outrageous fortune might launch in his direction, Gally Threepwood could be counted upon to preserve the calm insouciance of a pig on ice. But at these words a spasm definitely shook him, causing his black-rimmed monocle to leap as nimbly from his eye as the pince-nez had ever leaped from the nose of his brother Clarence. His look, as he stared at the girl, was the look of a man unable to believe his ears.

'Two thousand pounds?'

'It's sorely needed.'

Gally gave a little sigh. He took her hand and patted it.

'My child, I'm a pauper. I'm a younger son. In English families the heir scoops in the jackpot and all the runners-up get are the few crumbs that fall from his table. I could no more raise two thousand pounds than balance that pig there on the tip of my nose.'

'I see. I was afraid you mightn't be able to. All right, let's forget about it.'

Gally looked at her, astounded. Did she really think that Galahad Threepwood, one of the most inquisitive men who ever knocked back a Scotch and soda, a man who wished he had a quid, or even ten shillings, for every time he had been called a damned old Nosey Parker, was as easily put off as this?

'But, good heavens, aren't you going to explain?'

'Shall I? It depends whether you can keep a secret.'

'Of course I can keep a secret. Why, if I were to reveal one tithe of the things I know about my circle of acquaintance, it would rock civilization. You can confide in me without a tremor.'

'It would be a relief, I must say. Don't you hate bottling things up?'

'I prefer unbottling them. Go on. What's all this about two thousand pounds? What on earth do you want it for?'

'Well, it isn't exactly for me. It's for a man I know. It's the old, old story, Gally. I'm in love.'

'Aha!'

'Aha to you. Why shouldn't I be in love? People do fall in love, don't they?'

'I've known of cases.'

'Well, I'm in love with Jerry.'

'Jerry what?'

'Jerry Vail.'

'Never heard of him.'

'Well, I don't suppose he's ever heard of you.'

Gally was indignant.

'What do you mean, he's never heard of me? Of course he's heard of me. England's been ringing with my name for the last thirty years. If you weren't a benighted Yank on your first visit to the British Isles, you would have my life history at your finger-tips and treat me with the respect I deserve. But to return to the dream man. From the fact that you are going about trying to bite people's ears on his behalf, I deduce that he is short of cash. A bit strapped for the ready, eh? What is sometimes called an impecunious suitor?'

'Well, he gets by. He's self-supporting.'

'What does he do?'

'He's an author.'

'Good heavens! Oh, well, I suppose authors are also God's creatures.'

'He writes thrillers. But you know the old gag. "Crime doesn't pay . . . enough." We couldn't possibly get married on what he makes, even in a good year.'

'But your father, the well-to-do millionaire. Won't he provide?'

'Not for an impecunious suitor. If I were to write and tell Father I wanted to marry someone with an annual income of about thirty cents, he would whisk me back to America by the next boat, and I should be extremely lucky if I didn't get interned at my old grandmother's in Ohio.'

'Stern parent stuff, eh? I thought all that sort of thing went out in the eighties.'

'Yes, but they forgot to tell Father. And anyway, Jerry's much too full of high principles and what have you to let himself be supported by his wife.'

'You could talk him out of that.'

'I wouldn't want to. I admire him for it. If you'd seen some of the fortune-hunting dead-beats I've had to keep off with a stick since I ripened into womanhood, you could understand my thinking it's a pleasant change to meet someone like Jerry. He's swell, Gally. He has to be seen to be believed. And if only he can get this two thousand pounds . . .'

'You might give me the inside stuff on that. Does he want it for some particular reason, or is it just that he likes two thousand pounds?'

'He has a friend, a doctor, who wants to start one of those health places. Did you ever hear of Muldoon's in America?'

'Of course. I was always popping in and out of America in the old days.'

'This would be something on the same sort of lines, only, being in England, more . . . what's the word?'

'Posh?'

'I was going to say plushy. It would cater for tired Dukes and weary millionaires, all paying terrific fees. There's a place like it up in Wales, Jerry tells me, which simply coins money. This would be the same sort of thing, only easier to get at because the house Jerry's doctor friend has his eye on is in Surrey or Sussex or somewhere, much nearer London. The idea is that if Jerry could raise this two thousand pounds and buy in, he would become a junior partner. The boy friend would feel the patients' pulses and prescribe diets and so on, and Jerry would take them out riding and play tennis and golf with them and generally be the life and soul of the party. It's the sort of thing that would suit him down to the ground, and he would be awfully good at it. And he would have time to write his great novel.'

'Is he writing a great novel?'

'Well, naturally he hasn't been able to start it yet, being so busy winning bread, but he says it's all there, tucked away behind the frontal bone, and give him a little leisure, he says, a few quiet hours each day with nothing to distract him, and he'll have it jumping through hoops and snapping sugar off its nose. Why are you looking like a stuffed frog?'

'If you mean why am I looking like Rodin's *Le Penseur*, I was wondering how the dickens you ever managed to get acquainted with this chap. Connie met you when you landed at Southampton, and after a single night in London brought you down here, where you have been ever since. I don't see where you fitted in your billing and cooing.'

'Think, Gally. Use the bean.'

'No, it beats me.'

'He was on the boat, chump. Jerry's got vision. He realized that the only way for a writer to make a packet nowadays is to muscle in on the American market, so he took time off and dashed over to study it.'

'How do you study an American market?'

'I suppose you . . . well, study it, as it were.'

'I see. Study it.'

'That's right. And when he had finished studying it, he hopped on the boat and came home.'

'And who should be on the boat but you?'

'Exactly. We met the second day out, and never looked back. Ah, those moonlight nights!'

'Was there a moon?'

'You bet there was a moon.'

Gally scratched his chin. He removed his monocle and polished it thoughtfully.

'Well, I don't know quite what to say. You have rather stunned your grey-haired old friend. You really love this chap?'

'Haven't you been listening?'

'But you can't have known him for more than about four days?'

'So what?'

'Well, I was just thinking . . . Heaven knows I'm not the man to counsel prudence and all that sort of thing. The only woman I ever wanted to marry was a music-hall serio who sang songs in pink tights. But –'

'Well?'

'I think I'd watch my step, if I were you, young Penny. There are some queer birds knocking around in this world. You can't always go by what fellows say on ocean liners. Many a man who swears eternal devotion on the boat deck undergoes a striking change in his outlook when he hits dry land and gets among the blondes.'

'Gally, you make me sick.'

'I'm sorry. Just thought I'd mention it. Facts of life and all that sort of thing.'

'If I found Jerry was like that, I'd give him the air in a second, though it would break my heart into a million quivering pieces. We Donaldsons have our pride.'

'You betcher.'

'But he isn't. He's a baa-lamb. And you can't say a baa-lamb isn't a nice thing to have around the house.'

'Nothing could be nicer.'

'Very well, then.'

The Empress uttered a plaintive grunt. A potato, full of calories, had detached itself from the rest of her ration and rolled outside the sty. Gally returned it courteously, and the noble animal thanked him with a brief snuffle.

'But if he's a baa-lamb, it makes it all the worse. I mean, it must be agony for you being parted from such a paragon. Here you are at Blandings, and there he is in London. Don't you chafe?'

'I did until today.'

'Why until today?'

'Because this morning sunshine broke through the clouds. Lady Constance told me she is taking me to London tomorrow for a fitting. Lord Vosper is driving us in his car.'

'What do you think of Vosper?'

'I like him.'

'He likes you.'

'Yes, so I've noticed.'

'Good-looking chap.'

'Very. But I was telling you. The expedition arrives in London tomorrow afternoon, so tomorrow night I shall be dining with my Jerry.'

Gally gazed at her in amazement. Her childish optimism gave him a pang.

'With Connie keeping her fishy eye on you? Not a hope.'

'Oh yes, because there's an old friend of Father's in London, and Father would never forgive me if I didn't take this opportunity of slapping her on the back and saying hello. So I shall dine with her.'

'And she will bring your young man along?'

'Well, between us girls, Gally, she doesn't really exist. I'm like the poet in Shakespeare, I'm giving to airy nothing a local habitation and a name. Did you ever see *The Importance of being Earnest*?'

'Don't wander from the point.'

'I'm not wandering from the point. Do you remember Bunbury, the friend the hero invented? This is his mother, Mrs Bunbury. You can always arrange these things with a little tact. Well, I must be going in. I've got to write to Jerry.'

'But if you're seeing him tomorrow —'

'Really, Gally, for an experienced man, you seem to know very little about these things. I shall read him the letter over the dinner table, and he will read me the one he's probably writing now. I sent him a telegram this morning, saying I was coming up and staying the night with Lady Garland — your sister Dora, in case you've forgotten — and telling him to meet me at the Savoy at eight.'

Penny hurried away, walking on the light feet of love, and Gally, whose youth had been passed in a world where girls, except when working behind bars or doing *entrechats* at the Alhambra, had been less resourceful, gave himself up to meditation on the spirit and enterprise of their present-day successors. There was no question that the current younger generation knew how to handle those little problems with which the growing girl is so often confronted. This was particularly so, it appeared, if their formative years had been passed in the United States of Northern America.

Having reached the conclusion that the advice of an elderly greybeard counselling prudence and look-before-you-leap-ing would be something of a drug on the market where the younger daughter of Mr Donaldson of Donaldson's Dog-Joy was concerned, he was resuming his study of the Empress, when a bleating noise in his rear caused him to turn. Lord Emsworth was approaching, on his face that dying duck look which was so often there in times of stress. Something, it was plain to him, had occurred to upset poor old Clarence.

5

His intuition had not deceived him. Poor old Clarence was patently all of a doodah. Eyeing him as he tottered up, Gally was reminded of his old friend Fruity Biffen on the occasion when that ill-starred sportsman had gone into Tattersall's ring at Hurst Park wearing a long Assyrian beard in order to avoid identification by the half-dozen bookmakers there to whom he owed money, and then the beard had fallen off. The same visible emotion.

'Strike me pink, Clarence,' he exclaimed, 'you look like something out of a Russian novel. What's on your mind? And what have you done with Parsloe? Did you murder him, and are you worried because you don't know how to get rid of the body?'

Lord Emsworth found speech.

'I left him in the morning-room, putting on his shoes. Galahad, an appalling thing has happened. I hardly know how to tell you. Let me begin,' said Lord Emsworth, groping his way to the rail of the sty and drooping over it like a wet sock, 'by saying that Sir Gregory Parsloe is nothing short of a rogue and a swindler.'

'We all knew that. Get on.'

'Don't bustle me.'

'Well, I want to hear what all the agitation's about. When last seen, you were on your way to the house to confront this bulging Baronet. Right. You reached the house, found him in the morning-room with his shoes off, gave him a cold look and said stiffly: "To what am I indebted for the honour of this visit?", to which Parsloe, twiddling his toes, replied . . . what? To what *were* you indebted for the honour of his visit?'

Lord Emsworth became a little calmer. His eyes were resting on the Empress, and he seemed to draw strength from her massive stolidity.

'Do you ever have presentiments, Galahad?'

'Don't ramble, Clarence.'

'I am not rambling,' said Lord Emsworth peevishly. 'I am telling you that I had one the moment I entered the morning-room and saw Parsloe sitting there. Something seemed to whisper to me that the man was preparing an unpleasant surprise for me. There was a nasty smirk on his face, and I didn't like the sinister way he said "Good afternoon, Emsworth." And his next words told me that my presentiment had been right. From an inside pocket he produced a photograph and said: "Cast an eye on this, old cock."'

'A photograph? What of?'

Lord Emsworth was obliged to fortify himself with another look at the Empress, who was now at about her fifty-fourth thousandth calorie.

'Galahad,' he said, sinking his voice almost to a whisper, 'it was the photograph of an enormous pig! He thrust it under my nose with an evil leer and said: "Emsworth, old cocky-wax, meet the winner of this year's Fat Pig medal at the Shropshire Agricultural Show." His very words.'

Gally found himself unable to follow this. It seemed to him that he was in the presence of an elder brother who spoke in riddles.

'You mean it was a photograph of Pride of Matchingham?'

'No, no, no. God bless my soul, no. This animal would make two of Pride of Matchingham. Don't you understand? This is a new pig. He imported it a day or two ago from a farm in Kent. Queen of Matchingham, he calls it. Galahad,' said Lord Emsworth, his voice vibrating with emotion, 'with this Queen of Matchingham in the field, Empress of Blandings will have to strain every nerve to repeat her triumphs of the last two years.'

'You don't mean it's fatter than the Empress?' said Gally, cocking an eye at the stable's nominee and marvelling that such a thing could be possible.

Lord Emsworth looked shocked.

'I would not say that. No, no, I certainly would not say that. But the contest will now become a desperately close one. It may be a matter of ounces.'

Gally whistled. He was fully alive at last to the gravity of the situation. Apart from his fondness for old Clarence and a natural brotherly distaste for seeing him in the depths, the thing touched him financially. As he had told Penny, he was not a rich man, but, like Beach, he had his mite on the Empress and it appeared now that there was a grave peril that his modest investment would go down the drain.

'So that's why Binstead was going about the place with his five to one! He knew something. But is this hornswoggling high-binder allowed to import pigs? I thought the competition was purely for native sons?'

'There has always been an unwritten law to that effect, a gentleman's agreement, but Parsloe informs me that there exists no actual rule. Naturally the possibility of such a thing happening never occurred to those who drew up the conditions governing these contests. It's abominable!'

'Monstrous,' agreed Gally with all the warmth of a man who, having slapped down his cash on what he supposed to be a sure thing, finds the sure thing in danger of coming unstuck.

'And the ghastliest part of it all is that, faced with this hideous menace, I am forced to rely on the services of that Simmons girl to prepare the Empress for the struggle.'

A stern look came into Gally's face. A jellied-eel seller who had seen it would have picked up his jellied eels and sought refuge in flight, like one who fears to be struck by lightning.

'Simmons must go!' he said.

Lord Emsworth blinked.

'But Connie –'

'Connie be blowed! We can't afford to humour Connie's whims at a time like this. Leave Connie to me. I'll see that she ceases to bung spanners into the machinery by loading you up with incompetent pig girls when there are a thousand irreproachable pig men who will spring to the task of fattening the Empress for the big day. And while I'm about it, I'll have a word with young Parsloe and warn him that anything in the nature of funny business on his part will not be tolerated for an instant. For don't overlook that aspect of the matter, Clarence. Parsloe, with this new pig under his belt, is certain to get ideas into his head. Unless sternly notified that his every move will be met with ruthless reprisals, he will leave no stone unturned and no avenue unexplored to nobble the Empress.'

'Good heavens, Galahad!'

'But don't worry. I have the situation well in hand. My first task is to put the fear of God into Connie. Where is she? At this time of day, poisoning her system with tea, I suppose. Right. I'll go and talk to her like a Dutch uncle.'

Lord Emsworth drew a deep breath.

'You're such a comfort, Galahad.'

'I try to be, Clarence, I try to be,' said Gally.

He screwed the monocle more firmly into his eye, and set off on his mission, resolution on his every feature. Lord Emsworth watched him out of sight with a thrill of admiration. How a man about to talk to Connie like a Dutch uncle could be looking like that, he was unable to understand.

But Galahad was Galahad.

Chapter 2

Up at the castle, Sir Gregory Parsloe, having put on his shoes, was standing at the window of the morning-room, looking out.

If you like your baronets slender and willowy, you would not have cared much for Sir Gregory Parsloe. He was a large, stout man in the middle fifties who resembled in appearance one of those florid bucks of the old Regency days. Like Beach, he had long lost that streamlined look, and the fact that, just as you could have made two pretty good butlers out of Beach, so could you have made two quite adequate baronets out of Sir Gregory was due to the change in his financial position since the days when, as Gally had put it, he had knocked about London without a bean in his pocket.

A man with a fondness for the fleshpots and a weakness for wines and spirits who, after many lean years, suddenly inherits a great deal of money and an extensive cellar finds himself faced with temptations which it is hard to resist. Arrived in the land of milk and honey, his disposition is to square his elbows and let himself go till his eyes bubble. He remembers the days when he often did not know where his next chump chop was coming from, and settles down to make up leeway. This is what had happened to Sir Gregory Parsloe. Only an iron will could have saved him from accumulating excess weight in large quantities, and he had not an iron will. Day by day in every way he had got fatter and fatter.

Outside the morning-room window the terrace shimmered in the afternoon sun, but at the farther end of it a spreading tree cast its shade, and in this cool retreat a tea-table had been set up. Presiding over it sat Lady Constance Keeble, reading a letter, and an imperative urge to join her came over Sir Gregory. After his gruelling three-mile hike, a cup of tea was what he most needed.

As he made for the terrace, limping a little, for he had a blister on his right foot, it might have been supposed that his thoughts would have been on the impending refreshment, but they were not. A week or two ago he had become engaged to be married, and he was thinking of Gloria Salt, his betrothed. And if anyone is feeling that this was rather pretty and touching of him, we must reluctantly add that he was thinking of her bitterly and coming very near to regretting that mad moment when, swept off his feet by her radiant beauty, he had said to her 'I say, old girl – er – how about it, eh, what?' It would be too much perhaps to say that the scales had fallen from his eyes as regarded Gloria Salt, but unquestionably he had had revealed to him in the past few days certain aspects of her character and outlook which had materially diminished her charm.

Sighting him on the horizon, Lady Constance put down the letter she was reading, one of a number which had come for her by the afternoon post, and greeted him with a bright smile. Unlike her brothers Clarence and Galahad, she was fond of this man.

'Why, Sir Gregory,' she said, beaming hospitably, 'how nice to see you. I didn't hear your car drive up.'

Sir Gregory explained that he had walked from Matchingham Hall, and Lady Constance twittered with amazement at the feat.

'Good gracious. Aren't you exhausted?'

'Shan't be sorry to rest for a bit. Got a blister on my right foot.'

'Oh, dear. When you get home, you must prick it.'

'Yes.'

'With a needle.'

'Yes.'

'Not a pin. Well, sit down and I'll give you a cup of tea. Won't you have a muffin?'

Sir Gregory took the muffin, gave it a long, strange, sad look, sighed and put it down on his plate. Lady Constance picked up her letter.

'From Gloria,' she said.

'Ah,' said Sir Gregory in a rather guarded manner, like one who has not quite made up his mind about Gloria.

'She says she will be motoring here the day after tomorrow, and it's all right about the secretary.'

'Eh?'

'For Clarence. You remember you said you would ring her up and ask her to get a secretary for Clarence before she left London.'

'Oh, yes. And she's getting one? That's good.'

It was a piece of news which would have lowered Lord Ems-worth's already low spirits, had he been present to hear it. Connie was always encouraging ghastly spectacled young men with knobbly foreheads and a knowledge of shorthand to infest the castle and make life a burden to him, but there had been such a long interval since the departure of the latest of these that he was hoping the disease had run its course.

'She says she knows just the man.'

This again would have shaken Lord Emsworth to his foundations. The last thing he wanted on the premises was anyone who could be described as just the man, with all that phrase implied of fussing him and bothering him, and wanting him to sign things and do things.

'Clarence is so helpless without someone to look after his affairs. He gets vaguer every day. It was sweet of Gloria to bother. What a delightful girl she is.'

'Ah,' said Sir Gregory, again in that odd, guarded manner.

'I do admire those athletic girls. So wholesome. Has she been winning any tennis tournaments lately?'

Sir Gregory did not reply. His eyes were on the muffin, as it swam in butter before him, and once more he heaved that heavy sigh. Following his gaze, Lady Constance uttered a concerned cry. The hostess in her had been piqued.

'Why, Sir Gregory, you are eating nothing. Don't you like muffins?'

This time the sound that emerged from the Baronet, seeming to come up from the very soles of his feet, was nothing so mild as a sigh. It was unmistakably a groan, the sort of groan that might have been wrung from the reluctant lips of a Red Indian at the stake.

'I love 'em,' he said in a low voice that shook with feeling. 'But Gloria says I've got to cut them out.'

'Gloria? I don't understand.'

Until this moment, like the Spartan boy who allowed the fox to gnaw his vitals without mentioning it to a soul, Sir Gregory had kept his tragedy a secret from the world. Rightly or wrongly, he thought it made a fellow look such an ass. Chaps, he felt, chaps being what they were, would, if informed that he was mortifying the flesh at the whim of a woman, be inclined to laugh their silly heads off at a chap. But now the urge to confide in this sympathetic friend was too strong for him.

'She says I'm too fat, and if I don't reduce a bit the engagement's off. She says she positively refuses to stand at the altar rails with someone who looks like ... well, she was definitely outspoken about it. You know what girls are, especially these athletic girls who dash about tennis courts shouting "Forty love" and all that. They're all for the lean, keen, trained-to-the-last-ounce stuff. Dam' silly, of course, the whole thing. I put it to her straight. I said: "Dash it, old girl, what's all this about? I'm not proposing to enter for the six-day bicycle race or something," but nothing would move her. She said unless I ceased to resemble a captive balloon poised for its flight into the clouds, those wedding bells would not ring out. She said she was as fond of a laugh as the next girl, but that there were limits. I quote her verbatim.'

'Good gracious!'

Now that he had started to pour out his soul, Sir Gregory found it coming easier. His hostess was gazing at him wide-eyed, as if swearing, in faith, 'twas strange, 'twas passing strange, 'twas pitiful, 'twas wondrous pitiful, and there came upon him something of the easy fluency which had enabled Othello on a similar occasion to make such a good story of his misfortunes.

'So, the upshot is no butter, no sugar, no bread, no alcohol, no soups, no sauces, and I'm not allowed to swallow so much as a single potato. And that's not all. She's mapped out a whole chart of bally exercises for me. Up in the morning. Breathe deeply. Touch the toes. Light breakfast. Brisk walk. Chop down a tree or two. Light lunch. Another brisk walk. That's the one I'm taking now, and how I'm to get home under my own steam with this blister ... Ah well,' said Sir Gregory, summoning all his manhood to his aid, 'I mustn't bore you with all this stuff. Merely observing that I am going through hell, I will now withdraw. No, no more tea, thanks. She specifies a single cup.'

He rose heavily and made his way across the terrace. As he walked, he was thinking of that new pig of his. Pretty dashed ironical, he was feeling, that whereas he was under these strict orders to get thinner and thinner, Queen of Matchingham was encouraged – egged on with word and gesture, by gad – to get fatter and fatter. Why should there be one law for pigs and another for Baronets?

Musing thus, he had reached the top of the drive and was congratulating himself on the fact that from there onwards for the next three-quarters of a mile it would be all downhill, when he heard his name called in a sharp, imperious voice and, turning, perceived the Hon. Galahad Threepwood.

2

Gally was looking cold and stern.

'A word with you, young Parsloe,' he said.

Sir Gregory's full height was six foot one. He drew himself to it. Even in the days when they had been lads about town together, he had never liked Gally Threepwood, and more recent association with him had done nothing to inaugurate a beautiful friendship.

'I have no desire to speak to you, my good man,' he said.

Gally's monocle flashed fire.

'Oh, you haven't? Well, I'm dashed well going to speak to *you*. Parsloe, it was the raw work of slippery customers of your kidney that led to the destruction of the cities of the plain and the decline and fall of the Roman Empire. What's all this about your new pig?'

'What about it?'

'Clarence says you imported it from Kent.'

'Well?'

'A low trick.'

'Perfectly legitimate. Show me the rule that says I mustn't.'

'There are higher things than rules, young Parsloe. There is an ethical code.'

'A what?'

'Yes, I thought you wouldn't know what that meant. Let it pass. You are really proposing to enter this porker of yours in the Fat Pigs class at the Agricultural Show?'

'I have already done so.'

'I see. And now, no doubt, your subtle brain is weaving plots and schemes. You're getting ready to start the funny business, just as you used to do in the old days.'

'I don't know what you're talking about.'

Gally gave a short, hard, unpleasant laugh.

'He doesn't know what I'm talking about! I will ask you, Parsloe, to throw your mind back a number of years to a certain evening at the Black Footman public-house in Gossiter Street. You and I were young then, and in the exuberance of youth I had matched my dog Towser against your dog Banjo for a substantial sum in a rat contest. And when the rats were brought on and all should have been bustle and activity on Towser's part, where was he? Dozing in a corner with his stomach bulging like an alderman's. I whistled him . . . called him . . . Towser, Towser . . . No good. Fast asleep. And why? Because you had drawn him aside just before the starting bell was due to go and filled him up past the Plimsoll mark with steak and onions, thus rendering his interest in rats negligible and enabling your Banjo to win by default.'

'I deny it!'

'It's no good standing there saying "I deny it". I am perfectly aware that I am not able to prove it, but you and I know that that is what happened. Somebody had inserted steak and onions in that dog – I sniffed his breath, and it was like opening the door of a Soho chop-house on a summer night – and the verdict of History will be that it was you. You were the world's worst twister in the old days, a man who would stick at nothing to gain his evil ends. And . . . now I approach the nub . . . you still are. Even as we stand here, you are asking yourself "How can I nobble the Empress and leave the field clear for my entry?" Oh, yes, you are. I remember saying to Clarence once, "Clarence," I said, "I have known young Parsloe for thirty years and I solemnly state that if his grandmother was entered in a competition for fat pigs and his commitments made it desirable for him to get her out of the way, he would dope her bran mash and acorns without a moment's hesitation." Well, let me tell you that that is a game two can play at. Your every move will be met with ruthless reprisals. You try to nobble our pig, and we'll nobble yours. One poisoned potato in the Empress's dinner pail, and there will be six poisoned potatoes in Queen of Matchingham's. That is all I wanted to say. A very hearty good afternoon to you, Parsloe,' said Gally, turning on his heel.

Sir Gregory, who had been gulping, recovered speech.

'Hey!'

'Well?'

'Come back!'

'Who, me? Certainly not. I have no desire to speak to you, my good man,' said Gally, and continued his progress in the direction of the terrace.

Lady Constance was dipping her aristocratic nose in her teacup as he approached the table. At the sound of his footsteps, she looked up.

'Oh, it's you?' she said, and her tone made it abundantly clear that no sudden gush of affection had caused her to alter the opinion she had so long held that this brother of hers was a blot on the Blandings scene. 'I thought it was Sir Gregory. Have you seen Sir Gregory?'

'The man Parsloe? Yes. He has just slunk off.'

'What do you mean, slunk off?'

'I mean slunk off.'

'If you are referring to the fact that Sir Gregory was limping, he has a blister on his foot. There was something I was going to tell him. I must wait and telephone when he gets home. Do you want tea?'

'Never touch the muck.'

'Then what do you want?'

Gally screwed his monocle more firmly into his eye.

'To talk to you, Constance,' he said. 'To talk to you very seriously about this Simmons disaster, this incompetent ex-Roedean hockey-knocker whom you have foisted upon Clarence in the capacity of pig girl. Clarence and I have been discussing it, and we are in complete agreement that Simmons must be given the old heave-ho. The time has come to take her by the seat of her breeches and cast her into outer darkness where there is wailing and gnashing of teeth. Good God, are you prepared to stand before the bar of world opinion as the woman who, by putting up with your bally Simmonses, jeopardized the Empress's chance of performing the unheard-of feat of winning the Fat Pigs medal for the third year in succession? A pig man, and the finest pig man money can procure, must place his hand upon the tiller in her stead. No argument, Constance. This is final.'

3

It is always a disturbing thing to be threatened. In an unpublished story by Gerald Vail there is a scene where a character with a criminal face sidles up to the hero as he pauses on Broadway to light a cigarette and hisses in his ear 'Say, listen, youse! Youse'll get out of this town if youse knows what's good for youse!', and the hero realizing from this that Louis The Lip's Black Moustache gang have become aware of the investigations he has been making into the bumping off of the man in the green fedora, draws in his breath sharply and, though a most intrepid young man, is conscious of a distinct chill down the spine.

Precisely the same sort of chill was cooling off the spine of Sir Gregory Parsloe as he limped back to Matchingham Hall. His encounter with Gally had shaken him. He was not an imaginative man, but a man did not have to be very imaginative to read into Gally's words the threat of unilateral action against Queen of Matchingham. True, the fellow had spoken of 'reprisals', as though to imply that hostilities would not be initiated by the Blandings Castle gang, but Sir Gregory's mental retort to this was 'Reprisals my left eyeball'. The Galahad Threepwood type of man does not wait politely for the enemy to make the first move. It acts, and acts swiftly and without warning, and the only thing to do is to mobilize your defences and be prepared.

His first act, accordingly, on arriving at Matchingham Hall, sinking into an armchair and taking off his shoes, was to ring the bell and desire his butler to inform George Cyril Wellbeloved, his pig man, that his presence was desired for a conference. And in due season a rich smell of pig came floating in, closely followed by George Cyril in person.

George Cyril Wellbeloved was a long, lean, red-haired man with strabismus in the left eye. This rendered his left eye rather unpleasant to look at, and as even the right eye was nothing to cause lovers of the beautiful to turn handsprings, one can readily understand why Sir Gregory during the chat which followed preferred to avert his gaze as much as possible.

But, after all, what is beauty? Skin deep, you might say. His OC Pigs had a mouth like a halibut's, a broken nose acquired during a political discussion at the Emsworth Arms and lots of mud all over him, but when you are engaging a pig man, Sir Gregory felt, you don't want a sort of male Miss America, you want someone who knows about pigs. And what George Cyril Wellbeloved did not know about pigs could have been written on one of Maudie Montrose's picture postcards.

In terse, nervous English Sir Gregory related the substance of his interview with Gally, stressing that bit about the poisoned potatoes, and George Cyril listened with a gravity which became him well.

'So there you are,' said Sir Gregory, having completed his tale. 'What do you make of it?'

George Cyril Wellbeloved was a man who went in for a certain verbal polish in his conversation.

'To speak expleasantly, sir,' he said, 'I think the old — means to do the dirty on us.'

It would perhaps have been more fitting had Sir Gregory at this point said 'Come, come, my man, be more careful with your language,' but the noun — expressed so exactly what he himself was thinking of the Hon. Galahad Threepwood that he could not bring himself to chide and rebuke. As a matter of fact, though — is admittedly strong stuff, he had gone even farther than his companion, labelling Gally in his mind as a ****** and a !!!!!!.

'Precisely what I think myself,' he agreed. 'From now on, Wellbeloved, ceaseless vigilance.'

'Yes, sir.'

'We cannot afford to relax for an instant.'

'No, sir. The Hun is at the gate.'

'The what's where?'

'The Hun, sir. At the gate, sir. Or putting it another way,' said George Cyril Wellbeloved, who had attended Sunday School in Market Blandings as a boy and still retained a smattering of what he had learned in the days when he was trailing clouds of glory, 'See the troops of Midian prowl and prowl around.'

Sir Gregory thought this over.

'Yes. Yes, I see what you mean. Troops of Midian, yes. Nasty fellers. You did say Midian?'

'Yes, sir. Midian, troops of. Christian, dost thou hear them on the holy ground? Christian, up and smite them!'

'Quite. Yes. Precisely. Just what I was about to suggest myself. You will need a shot-gun. Have you a shot-gun?'

'No, sir.'

'I will give you one. Keep it beside you, never let it out of your hands, and if the occasion arises, use it. Mind you, I am not saying commit a murder and render yourself liable to the extreme penalty of the law, but if one of these nights some bally bounder – I name no names – comes sneaking around Queen of Matchingham's sty, there's nothing to prevent you giving him a dashed good peppering in the seat of the pants.'

'Nothing whatever, sir,' assented George Cyril Wellbeloved cordially.

'If he asks for it, let him have it.'

'I will, sir. With both barrels.'

The conference had gone with such a swing up to this point, overlord and vassal being so patently two minds with but a single thought, that it was a pity that Sir Gregory should now have struck a jarring note. A sudden idea had occurred to him, and he gave it utterance with all the relish of a man whose betrothed has put him on a strict teetotal regimen. Misery loves company.

'And another thing,' he said. 'From this moment you abstain from all alcoholic beverages.'

'Sir!'

'You heard. No more fuddling yourself in tap rooms. I want you keen, alert, up on your toes.'

George Cyril Wellbeloved swallowed painfully, like an ostrich swallowing a brass door-knob.

'When you say alcoholic beverages, sir, you don't mean beer?'

'I do mean beer.'

'No beer?'

'No beer.'

'No *beer*?'

'Not a drop.'

George Cyril Wellbeloved opened his mouth, and for a moment it seemed as if burning words were about to proceed from it. Then, as though struck by a thought, he checked himself.

'Very good, sir,' he said meekly.

Sir Gregory gave him a keen glance.

'Yes, I know what you're thinking,' he said. 'You're thinking you'll be able to sneak off on the sly and lower yourself to the level of the beasts of the field without my knowing it. Well, you won't. I shall give strict orders to the landlords of the various public-houses in Market Blandings that you are not to be served, and as I am on the licensing board, I think these orders will be respected. What beats me,' said Sir Gregory virtuously, 'is why you fellers want to go about swilling and soaking. Look at me. I never touch the stuff. All right, that's all. Push off.'

Droopingly, like a man on whose horizon there is no ray of light, George Cyril Wellbeloved, having given his employer one long, sad, reproachful look, left the room, taking some, but not all, of the pig smell with him. A few moments after the door had closed behind him, Lady Constance's telephone call came through.

'Matchingham 8-30?'

'Yes.'

'Sir Gregory?'

'Yes.'

'Are you there?'

'Yes.'

'Is your blister still painful?'

'Yes.'

'I did tell you to prick it, didn't I?'

'Yes.'

'With a needle. Not a pin. Pins are poisonous. I think they are made of brass, though I must say they don't *look* as if they were made of brass. But what I rang up about was this other trouble of yours. Gloria, you know. The dieting, you know. The exercises, you know.'

Sir Gregory said he knew.

'All that sort of thing cannot be good for you at your age.'

Sir Gregory, who was touchy on the subject, would have liked to ask what she meant by the expression 'your age', but he was given no opportunity to do so. Like most female telephonists, Lady Constance was not easy to interrupt.

'I couldn't bear to think of you having to go through all that dieting and exercising, because I do think it is so dangerous for a man of your age. A man of your age needs plenty of nourishing food, and there is always the risk of straining yourself seriously. A distant connexion of ours, one of the Hampshire Wilberforces, started touching his toes before breakfast, and he had some sort of a fit. Well, I don't know how I came to forget it when you were here this afternoon, but just after you had left, I suddenly remembered seeing an advertisement in the paper the other day of a new preparation someone had just invented for reducing the weight. Have you heard of it? Slimmo they call it, and it sounds excellent. Apparently it contains no noxious or habit-forming drugs and is endorsed by leading doctors, who are united in describing it as a safe and agreeable medium for getting rid of superfluous flesh. It seems to me that, if it is as good as they say, you would be able to do what Gloria wants without all that dieting and exercising which had such a bad effect on that distant connexion of ours. Rupert Wilberforce it was – a sort of second cousin I suppose you would have called him – he married one of the Devonshire Fairbairns. He was a man getting on in years – about your age – and when he found he was putting on weight, he allowed himself to be persuaded by a thoughtless friend to touch his toes fifty times before breakfast every morning. And on the third morning he did not come down to breakfast, and they went up to his room, and there he was writhing on the floor in dreadful agonies. His heart had run into his liver. Slimmo. It comes in the small bottles and the large economy size. I do wish you would try it. You can get it in Market Blandings, for by an odd coincidence the very day I read about it in the paper I saw some bottles in Bulstrode's window, the chemist in the High Street. It's curious how often that happens, isn't it? I mean, seeing a thing and then seeing it again almost directly afterwards. Oh, Clarence! I was speaking to Clarence, Sir Gregory. He has just come in and is bleating about something. What *is* it, Clarence? You want what? He wants to use the telephone, Sir Gregory, so I must ring off. Good-bye. You won't forget the name, will you. Slimmo. I suggest the large economy size.'

Sir Gregory removed his aching ear from the receiver and hung up.

For some moments after silence had come like a poultice to heal the blows of sound, all that occupied his mind was the thought of what pests the gentler sex were when they got hold of a telephone.

The instrument seemed to go to their heads like a drug. Connie Keeble, for instance. Nice sensible woman when you talked to her face to face, never tried to collar the conversation and all that, but the moment she got on the telephone, it was gab, gab, gab, and all about nothing.

Then suddenly he was asking himself whether his late hostess's spate of words had, after all, been so devoid of significance as in his haste he had supposed. Like most men trapped on the telephone by a woman, he had allowed his attention to wander a good deal during the recent monologue, but his subconscious self had apparently been drinking it in all the time, for now it brought up for his inspection the word Slimmo and then a whole lot of interesting stuff about what Slimmo was and what it did. And it was not long before it had put him completely abreast of the thing.

The idea of achieving his ends by means of an anti-fat specific had not previously occurred to Sir Gregory. But now that this alternative had presented itself, it became more attractive the longer he mused on it. The picture of himself, with a tankard of Slimmo at his elbow, sailing into the starchy foods with impunity intoxicated him.

There was but one obstacle in the way of this felicity. Briefly, in order to start filling the wassail bowl with Slimmo, you have first to get the bally stuff, and Sir Gregory, a sensitive man, shrank from going into a shop and asking for it. He feared the quick look of surprise, the furtive glance at the waist-line and the suppressed – or possibly not suppressed – giggle.

Then what to do?

'Ha!' said Sir Gregory, suddenly inspired.

He pressed the bell, and a few moments later Binstead, his butler, entered.

We have heard of Binstead before, it will be remembered. He was the effervescent sportsman who electrified the tap room of the Emsworth Arms by bounding in and offering five to one on his employer's pig. It is interesting to meet him now in person.

Scrutinizing him, however, we find ourselves unimpressed. This Binstead was one of those young, sprightly butlers, encountering whom one feels that in the deepest and holiest sense they are not butlers at all, but merely glorified footmen. He had none of Beach's measured majesty, but was slim and perky. He looked – though, to do him justice, he had never yet actually proceeded to that awful extreme – as if at any moment he might start turning cart-wheels or sliding down the banisters. And when we say that he was often to be found of an evening playing ha'penny nap with George Cyril Wellbeloved and similar social outcasts and allowing them to address him as 'Herb', we think we have said everything.

'Sir?' said this inadequate juvenile.

Sir Gregory coughed. Even now it was not going to be easy.

'Er, Binstead,' he said. 'Have you ever heard of Slimmo?'

'No, sir.'

'It's some sort of stuff you take. Kind of medicine, if you see what I mean, endorsed by leading doctors. A distant connexion of mine . . . one of the Hampshire Wilberforces . . . has asked me to get him some of it. I want you to telephone to Bulstrode in the High Street and tell him to send up half a dozen bottles.'

'Very good, sir.'

'Tell him the large economy size,' said Sir Gregory.

4

There had been a grave, set look on the face of the Hon. Galahad Threepwood as he stumped away from the tea table on the terrace, and it was still there when, after considerable moody meditation in the grounds, he turned into the corridor that led to Beach's pantry. In the battle of wills which had recently terminated he had not come off any too well. The trouble about talking to a sister like a Dutch uncle is that she is very apt to come right back at you and start talking to you like a Dutch aunt. This is what had happened to Gally at his interview with Lady Constance, and an immediate exchange of ideas with Shropshire's shrewdest butler seemed to him essential.

Entering the pantry, he found only Penny there. Her letter finished, she had gone off, as she so often did, to sit at the feet of one whose society, ever since she had come to the castle, had been a constant inspiration to her. Right from the start of her visit to Blandings Castle, the younger daughter of Mr Donaldson of Donaldson's Dog-Joy had recognized in Sebastian Beach a soul-mate and a buddy.

In the butler's absence she was endeavouring to fraternize with his bullfinch, a bird of deep reserves who lived in a cage on the table in the corner. So far, however, she had been unsuccessful in her efforts to find a formula.

'Oh, hello, Gally,' she said. 'Listen, what do you say to a bullfinch?'

'How are you, bullfinch?'

'To make it whistle, I mean.'

'Ah, there you take me into deep waters. But I didn't come here to talk about bullfinches, whether whistling or strongly silent. Where's Beach?'

'Gone into Market Blandings. The chauffeur took him.'

'Dash the man. What did he want to go gadding off to Market Blandings for?'

'Why shouldn't he go gadding off to Market Blandings? The poor guy's got a right to see a little life now and then. He'll be back soon.'

'He should never have left his post.'

'Why, what's the matter?'

'This pig situation.'

'What pig situation would that be?'

Gally passed a careworn hand over his brow.

'I'd forgotten you weren't there when Clarence broke the big story. You had left to go and write to that young man of yours . . . Dale, Hale, Gale, whatever his name is.'

'Vail.'

'Oh, Vail.'

'One of the Loamshire Vails. You must learn to call him Jerry. So what happened after I left?'

'Clarence appeared, buffeted by the waves and leaking at every seam like the Wreck of the Hesperus. He had just been talking to that hell-hound.'

'What hell-hound?'

'Sir Gregory Parsloe.'

'Oh yes, the character who keeps taking off his shoes. Who is Sir Gregory Parsloe?'

'Good God! Don't you know that?'

'I'm a stranger in these parts.'

'I'd better begin at the beginning.'

'Much better.'

If there was one thing Gally prided himself on – and justly – it was his ability to tell a story. Step by step he unfolded his tale, omitting no detail however slight, and it was not long before Penny had as complete a grasp of the position of affairs as any raconteur could have wished. When, after stressing the blackness of Sir Gregory Parsloe's soul in a striking passage, he introduced the Queen of Matchingham motif into his narrative and spoke of the guerrilla warfare which must now inevitably ensue, fraught with brooding peril not only to Lord Emsworth's dreams and ambitions but to the bank balances of himself and Beach, she expressed her concern freely.

'This Parsloe sounds a hot number.'

'As hot as mustard. Always was. Remind me to tell you some time how he nobbled my dog Towser on the night of the rat contest. But you have not heard the worst. We now come to the Simmons menace.'

'What's that?'

'In your ramblings about the grounds and messuages do you happen to have seen a large young female in trousers who looks like an all-in wrestler? That is Monica Simmons, Clarence's pig girl. Her high mission is to look after the Empress. Until recently the latter's custodian was a gnomelike but competent old buffer of the name of Pott. But he won a football pool and turned in his seal of office, upon which my sister Connie produced the above Simmons out of her hat and insisted on Clarence engaging her. When this Queen of Matchingham thing came up, Clarence and I agreed that it would be insanity to leave the Empress's fortunes in the hands of a girl like that. Simmons must go, we decided, and as Clarence hadn't the nerve to tackle Connie about it, I said I would. I've just been tackling her.'

'With what result?'

'None. She dug her feet in and put her ears back and generally carried on like a Grade A deaf adder. And what do you think?'

'What?'

'Clarence had told me that Connie's interest in this Simmons was due to the fact that she, the Simmons, was tied up in some way with someone Connie wanted to oblige. Who do you suppose that someone is?'

'Not Parsloe?'

'None other. Parsloe himself. In person, not a picture. The girl is his cousin.'

'Gosh!'

'You may well say "Gosh!". The peril would be ghastly enough if we were merely up against a Parsloe weaving his subtle schemes in his lair at Matchingham Hall. But Parsloe with a cousin in our very citadel, a cousin enjoying free access to the Empress, a cousin whose job it is to provide the Empress with her daily bread . . . Well, dash it, if you see what I mean.'

'I certainly do see what you mean. Dash it is right.'

'What simpler than for Parsloe to issue his orders to this minion and for the minion to carry them out?'

'Easy as falling off a log.'

'It's an appalling state of things.'

'Precipitates a grave crisis. What are you going to do?'

'That's what I came to see Beach about. We've got to have a staff conference. Ah, here he comes, thank goodness.'

Outside, there had become audible the booming sound of a bulky butler making good time along a stone-flagged corridor. The bull-finch, recognizing the tread of loved feet, burst into liquid song.

5

But Beach, as he entered, was not taking the bass. A glance was enough to tell them that he was in no mood for singing. His moon-like face was twisted with mental agony, his gooseberry eyes bulging from their sockets. Even such a man so faint, so spiritless, so dead, so dull in look, so woebegone, drew Priam's curtain in the dead of night and would have told him half his Troy was burned – or so it seemed to Penny, and she squeaked in amazement. Hers had been a sheltered life, and she had never before seen a butler with the heeby-jeebies.

'Beach!' she cried, deeply stirred. 'What is it? Tell Mother.'

'Good Lord, Beach,' said Gally. 'Then you've heard, too?'

'Sir?'

'About the Simmons girl being Parsloe's cousin.'

Beach's jaw fell another notch.

'Sir Gregory's cousin, Mr Galahad?'

'Didn't you know?'

'I had no inkling, Mr Galahad.'

'Then what are you sticking straws in your hair for?'

With trembling fingers Beach put a green baize cloth over the bullfinch's cage. It was as if a Prime Minister in the House of Commons had blown the whistle for a secret session.

'Mr Galahad,' he said. 'I can hardly tell you.'

'What?'

'No, sir, I can hardly tell you.'

'Snap into it, Beach,' said Penny. 'Have your fit later.'

Beach tottered to a cupboard.

'I think, Mr Galahad, if you will excuse me, I must take a drop of port.'

'Double that order,' said Gally.

'Treble it,' said Penny. 'A beaker of the old familiar juice for each of the shareholders, Beach. And fill mine to the brim.'

Beach filled them all to the brim, and further evidence of his agitation, if such were needed, was afforded by the fact that he drained his glass at a gulp, though in happier times a sipper who sipped slowly, rolling the precious fluid round his tongue.

The restorative had its effect. He was able to speak.

'Sir . . . and Madam . . .'

'Have another,' said Penny.

'Thank you, miss. I believe I will. I think you should, too, Mr Galahad, for what I am about to say will come as a great shock.'

'Get on, Beach. Don't take all night about it.'

'I know a man named Jerry Vail, a young author of sensational fiction,' said Penny chattily, 'who starts his stories just like this. You never know till Page Twenty-three what it's all about. Suspense, he calls it.'

'Cough it up, Beach, this instant, and no more delay. You hear me? I don't want to be compelled to plug you in the eye.'

'Very good, Mr Galahad.'

With a powerful effort the butler forced himself to begin his tale.

'I have just returned from Market Blandings, Mr Galahad. I went there for the purpose of making a certain purchase. I don't know if you have happened to notice it, sir, but recently I have been putting on a little weight, due no doubt to the sedentary nature of a butler's –'

'Beach!'

'Let him work up to it,' said Penny. 'The Vail method. Building for the climax. Go on, Beach. You're doing fine.'

'Thank you, miss. Well, as I say, I have recently become somewhat worried about this increase in my weight, and I chanced to see in the paper an advertisement of a new preparation called Slimmo, guaranteed to reduce superfluous flesh, which was stated to contain no noxious or habit-forming drugs and to be endorsed by leading doctors. So I thought I would look in at Bulstrode's in the High Street and buy a bottle. It was somewhat embarrassing walking into the shop and asking for it, and I thought I noticed Bulstrode's young assistant give me a sort of sharp look as much as to say "Oho!" but I nerved myself to the ordeal, and Bulstrode's young assistant wrapped the bottle up in paper and fastened the loose ends with a little pink sealing wax.'

'Beach, you have been warned!'

'Do be quiet, Gally. And that was that, eh?'

A spasm shook Beach.

'If I may employ a vulgarism, miss, you do not know the half of it.'

'More coming?'

'Much, much more, miss.'

'Well, here I am, Beach, with the old ear trumpet right at the ear.'

'Thank you, miss.'

Beach closed his eyes for a moment, as if praying for strength.

'I had scarcely paid for my purchase and received my change when the telephone bell rang. Bulstrode's young assistant went to the instrument.'

'And a dead body fell out?'

'Miss?'

'Sorry. My mind was on Mr Vail's stories. Carry on. You have the floor. What happened?'

'He spoke a few words into the instrument. "Okeydoke", I remember, was one of them, and "Righty-ho", from which I gathered that he was speaking to a customer of the lower middle class, what is sometimes called the burjoisy. Then he turned to me with a smile and observed "Well, that is what I call a proper co-incidence, Mr Beach. Never rains but it pours, does it? That was Herbert Binstead. And know what he wants? Six bottles of Slimmo, the large economy size."'

Gally started as if he had been bitten in the leg by Baronets.

'What!'

'Yes, Mr Galahad.'

'That fellow Binstead was buying Slimmo?'

'Yes, Mr Galahad.'

'Good God!'

Penny looked from one to the other, perplexed.

'But why shouldn't he buy Slimmo? Maybe he's a leading doctor.'

Gally spoke in a voice of doom.

'Herbert Binstead is Gregory Parsloe's butler. And if you have the idea that he may have been buying this anti-fat for his own personal use, correct that view. He's as thin as a herring. His motive is obvious. One reads the man like a book. Acting under Parsloe's instructions, he plans to pass this Slimmo on to the accomplice Simmons, who will slip it privily into the Empress's daily ration, thus causing her to lose weight, thus handing the race on a plate to Queen of Matchingham. Am I right, Beach?'

'I fear so, Mr Galahad. It was the first thought that entered my mind when Bulstrode's young assistant revealed to me the gist of his telephone conversation.'

'No explanation other than the one that I have outlined will fit the facts. I told you Parsloe was mustard, Penny. He moves in a mysterious way his wonders to perform.'

Silence fell, one of those deep, uneasy silences which occur when all good men realize that now is the time for them to come to the aid of the party but are unable to figure out just how to set about doing so.

But it was not in the nature of the Hon. Galahad to be baffled for long. A brain like his, honed to razor-like sharpness by years of association with the members of the Pelican Club, is never at a loss for more than a moment.

'Well, there you are,' he said. 'The first shot of the campaign has been fired, and soon the battle will be joined. We must consider our plan of action.'

'Which is what?' said Penny. 'I don't see where you go from here. I take it the idea is to keep an eye on this Simmons beazel, but how is it to be done? You can't watch her all the time.'

'Exactly. So we must engage the services of someone who can, someone trained to the task, someone whose profession it is to keep an eye on the criminal classes, and most fortunately we are able to lay our hand on just such a person. The guiding spirit of Digby's Day and Night Detectives.'

Beach gave a start which set both his chins quivering.

'Maudie, Mr Galahad? My niece, Mr Galahad?'

'None other. Is she Mrs Digby?'

'No, sir. Mrs Stubbs. Digby is a trade name. But –'

'But what?'

'I am in perfect agreement with what you say with regard to the necessity of employing a trained observer to scrutinize Miss Simmons's movements, Mr Galahad, but you are surely not thinking of bringing my niece Maudie here? Her appearance –'

'I remember her as looking rather like Mae West.'

'Precisely, sir. It would never do.'

'I don't follow you, Beach.'

'I was thinking of Lady Constance, sir. I have known her ladyship to be somewhat difficult at times where guests were concerned. I gravely doubt whether her reactions would be wholly favourable, were you to introduce into the castle a private investigator who is the niece of her butler and looks like Miss Mae West.'

'I am not proposing to do so.'

'Indeed, sir? I gathered from what you were saying –'

'The visitor who arrives at Blandings Castle and sings out to the varlets and scurvy knaves within to lower the portcullis and look slippy about it will be a Mrs Bunbury, a lifelong friend of your father, Penny. You remember that charming Mrs Bunbury?'

Penny drew a deep breath.

'You're a quick thinker, Gally.'

'You have to think quick when a man like Gregory Parsloe is spitting on his hands preparatory to going about seeking whom he may devour. By the way, Beach, not a word of all this to Lord Emsworth. We don't want him worrying himself into a decline, nor do we want him giving the whole thing away in the first ten minutes, as he infallibly would if he knew about it. An excellent fellow, Clarence, but a rotten conspirator. You follow me, Beach?'

'Oh yes, indeed, Mr Galahad.'

'Penny?'

'He shall never learn from me.'

'Good girl. Too much is at stake for us to take any chances. The hopes and dreams of my brother Clarence depend on Maudie, and so, Beach, does the little bit of stuff which you and I have invested on the Empress. Get her on the telephone at once.'

'Is the Empress on the telephone?' asked Penny, surprised, though feeling that something like this might have been expected of that wonder-pig.

Gally frowned.

'I allude to Maudie Beach Montrose Digby Stubbs Bunbury. Get on to her without delay and instruct her to pack her toothbrush and magnifying glass and be with us at her earliest convenience.'

'Very good, Mr Galahad.'

'Pitch it strong. Make her see how urgent the matter is. Play up the attractive aspects of Blandings Castle, and tell her that she will find there not only a loved uncle but one of her warmest admirers of the old Criterion days.'

'Yes, Mr Galahad.'

'I will now go and inform my sister Constance that at the urgent request of Miss Penelope Donaldson I am inviting the latter's father's close crony Mrs Bunbury to put in a week or two with us. I do not anticipate objections on the part of my sister Constance, but should she give me any lip or back chat I shall crush her as I would a worm.'

'Do you crush worms?' asked Penny, interested.

'Frequently,' said Gally, and trotted out, to return a few minutes later beaming satisfaction through his monocle.

'All set. She right-hoed like a lamb. She seems to have an overwhelming respect for your father, Penny, no doubt because of his disgusting wealth. And now,' said Gally, 'now that what you might call the preliminary spadework is completed and we are able to relax for a bit, I think a drop more port might be in order. For you, Penny?'

'Let it flow like water, as far as I'm concerned.'

'And you, Beach?'

'Thank you, Mr Galahad. A little port would be most refreshing.'

'Then reach for the bottle and start pouring. And as you pour,' said Gally, 'keep saying to yourself that tempests may lower and storm clouds brood, but if your affairs are in the hands of Galahad Threepwood, you're all right.'

Chapter 3

Although it is the fashion in this twentieth century of ours to speak disparagingly of the modern machine age, to sneer at its gadgets and gimmicks and labour-saving devices and to sigh for the days when life was simpler, these gimmicks and gadgets unquestionably have their advantages.

If Penny Donaldson had been a princess in ancient Egypt desirous of communicating with the man she loved, she would have had to write a long letter on papyrus, all animals' heads and things, and send it off by a Nubian slave, and there is no telling when Jerry Vail would have got it, for the only time those Nubian slaves hurried themselves was when someone was behind them with a spiked stick. Living in modern times, she had been able to telegraph, and scarcely two hours elapsed before Jerry, in his modest flat in Battersea Park Road, London, SW, received the heart-stirring news that she would be with him on the morrow.

Sudden joy affects different people in different ways. Some laugh and sing. Some leap. Others go about being kind to dogs. Jerry Vail sat down and started writing a story designed for one of the American magazines if one of the American magazines would meet him half-way, about a New York private detective who was full of Scotch whisky and sex appeal and got mixed up with a lot of characters with names like Otto the Ox and Bertha the Body.

He was just finishing it on the following afternoon – for stories about New York private detectives, involving as they do almost no conscious cerebration, take very little time to write – when the telephone bell stopped him in the middle of a sentence.

There is always something intriguing and stimulating about the ringing of a telephone bell. Will this, we ask ourselves, be the girl we love, or will it be somebody named Ed, who, all eagerness to establish communication with somebody named Charlie, has had the misfortune to get the wrong number? Jerry, though always glad to chat with people who got the wrong number, hoped it would be Penny.

'Hullo?' he said, putting a wealth of pent-up feeling into the word, just in case.

'Hullo, Jerry. This is Gloria.'

'Eh?'

'Gloria Salt, ass,' said the voice at the other end of the wire with a touch of petulance.

There had been a time when Jerry Vail's heart would have leaped at the sound of that name. Between Gloria Salt and himself there had been some tender passages in the days gone by, passages which might have been tenderer still if the lady had not had one of those level business heads which restrain girls from becoming too involved with young men who, however attractive, are short of cash. Gloria Salt, though she had little else in common with Mr Donaldson of Donaldson's Dog-Joy, shared that good man's aloof and wary attitude toward the impecunious suitor.

But though, like the Fairy Queen in Iolanthe, on fire that glows with heat intense she had turned the hose of common sense, and though on Jerry's side that fire had long since become a mere heap of embers, their relations had remained cordial. From time to time they would play a round of golf together, and from time to time they would lunch together. One of these nice unsentimental friendships it had come to be, and it was with hearty good will that he now spoke.

'Why, hullo, Gloria. I haven't heard from you for ages. What have you been doing with yourself?'

'Just messing around. Playing a bit of tennis. Playing a bit of golf. Ridin' a bit, swimmin' a bit. Oh yes, and I've got engaged,' said Miss Salt as an afterthought.

Jerry was delighted to hear the news.

'Well, well. That's the stuff. I like to see you young folks settling down. Who's the other half of the sketch? Orlo the Ox, I presume?'

'Who?'

'I'm sorry. I was thinking of something else. My lord Vosper, I mean.'

There was a momentary silence. Then Gloria Salt spoke in an odd, metallic voice.

'No, not my lord Vosper, thank you very much. I wouldn't marry Orlo by golly Vosper to please a dying grandmother. If I found myself standing with that pill at the altar rails and the clergyman said to me "How about it, Gloria, old sport? Wilt thou, Gloria, take this Orlo?", I would reply "Not in a million years, laddie, not to win a substantial wager. If you were suggesting that I might like to attend his funeral," I would proceed, developing the theme, "that would be another matter, but if, as I think, the idea at the back of your mind is that I shall become his wedded wife, let me inform you, my dear old man of God, that I would rather be dead in a ditch." Orlo Vosper, egad! I should jolly well say not.'

Jerry was concerned. Here was tragedy. Mystery, too. Like most of her circle, he had always supposed that it was only a matter of time before these twain sent out the wedding announcements. Affinities, they had seemed to be, always being 'seen' together at Cannes or 'glimpsed' together at Ascot or 'noticed' together playing in the mixed doubles at some seaside tennis tournament. To hear Gloria Salt talking in this acid strain about Orlo, Lord Vosper, was as surprising as if one had heard Swan knocking Edgar or Rodgers saying nasty things about Hammerstein.

'But, good Lord, I always thought –'

'I dare say you did. Nevertheless, the facts are as I have stated. I have returned Orlo Vosper to store and shall shortly – wind and weather permitting – become the bride of Sir Gregory Parsloe, Bart, of Matchingham Hall, Much Matchingham, in the county of Shropshire.'

'But what happened?'

'It's too long to go into over the phone. I'll tell you when we meet, which will be tonight. I want you to give me dinner at Mario's.'

'Tonight, did you say?'

'Tonight. Are you getting deaf in your old age?'

Jerry was not deaf, but he was deeply agitated, and in the circumstances the toughest baa-lamb might have been excused for being so. This night of nights was earmarked for his dinner with Penny. He had been counting the minutes to that sacred reunion, scrutinizing his boiled shirts, sorting out his white ties, seeing to it that the patent leather shoes and the old top hat had the perfect gloss which such an occasion called for, and what he was thinking now was that, if you have been torn from the only girl that matters and have got an utterly unforeseen chance of having a bite to eat with her at the Savoy, of gazing into her eyes at the Savoy and holding her little hand at the Savoy, it is a pretty state of things when other girls, however old friends they may be, come muscling in, wanting to divert you to Mario's.

'But listen, old thing. I can't possibly manage tonight. Won't tomorrow do?'

'No, it won't. I'm leaving for the country tomorrow. I don't want to see you just for the pleasure of your society, stupendous though that is. I want to do you a good turn. Do you remember telling me once that you were trying to raise two thousand pounds to buy in on some private loony bin?'

The actual project for which Jerry required the sum mentioned was not, as we have seen, the securing of a share in the management of a home for the mentally unbalanced, but this was no moment for going into long explanations. He gasped, and the room flickered before his eyes.

'You don't mean – ?'

'Yes, I think I can put you in the way of getting it.'

'Good Lord! Gloria, you're a marvel. When pain and anguish rack the brow, a ministering angel thou. Let's have full details.'

'Tonight. It's much too long to tell you now. Eight sharp at Mario's. And I'm going to dress. Because if you aren't dressed at Mario's, they shove you up in the balcony, a thing my proud spirit would never endure. Have you a dickey and celluloid cuffs?'

'But, Gloria, half a second –'

'That's all there is, there isn't any more. Good-bye. I must rush. Got to see a man about a tennis racquet.'

For some time after the line had gone dead, an observer, had one been present in Flat Twenty-three, Prince of Wales Mansions, Battersea Park Road, would have been able to see what a young man standing at the crossroads looked like, for during that period Gerald Anstruther Vail sat wrestling with himself, torn this way and that, a living ganglion of conflicting emotions.

The thought of cancelling his dinner with Penny, of not seeing her after all, of not gazing into her eyes, of not holding her little hand, was about as unpleasing a thought as had ever entered his mind. It is not too much to say that it gashed the very fibres of his being.

On the other hand, if Gloria had meant what she said, if by conferring with her at Mario's, there was really a chance of learning a method of getting his hooks on that two thousand, would it not be madness to pass it up?

Aeons later he decided that it would. The money was his passport to Paradise, and he knew Gloria Salt well enough to be aware that, though a girl of kind impulses, she was touchy. Spurn her, and she stayed spurned. To refuse to meet her at Mario's and hear her plan for conjuring two thousand pounds out of thin air, which seemed to be what she had in mind, would mean pique, resentment and dudgeon. She would drop the subject entirely and decline to open it again.

Heavily, for the load on his heart weighed him down, he rose and began to turn the pages of the telephone book. Chez Lady Garland, whoever she might be, Penny had said she would be during her brief stay in the great city, and there was a Garland, Lady, with a Grosvenor Square address among the G's. He dialled the number, and hooked what sounded like a butler.

'Could I speak to Miss Donaldson?'

He could not. Penny, it appeared, was out having a fit. A what? Oh, a fitting? Yes, I see. Any idea when she will be back? No, sir, I am unable to say. Would you care to leave a message, sir?

'Yes. Will you tell Miss Donaldson that Mr Gerald Vail is terribly sorry but he will be unable to give her dinner tonight owing to a very important business matter that has come up.'

'Business matter, sir?'

'That's right. A most important business matter.'

'Very good, sir.'

And that was that. But oh, the agony of it. Replacing the receiver, Jerry slumped into a chair with a distinct illusion that mocking fiends were detaching large portions of his soul with red-hot pincers.

At Wiltshire House, Grosvenor Square, residence of Dora, relict of the late Sir Everard Garland, KCB, Lady Constance Keeble was not feeling any too good herself. Jerry had made his call at the moment when Riggs, the butler, was bringing tea for herself and Lord Vosper, who had looked in hoping for buttered toast and a chat with Penny, and it had taken her attention right off the pleasures of the table.

'Sinister' was the word that flashed through Lady Constance's mind. 'Sir,' Riggs had said, indicating that the mysterious caller was of the male sex, and she was at a loss to comprehend how – unless the girl had told him – any mysterious male could know that Penny was in London. And if she had told him, it implied an intimacy which froze her blood.

'Who was that, Riggs?'

'A Mr Gerald Vail, m'lady, regretting his inability to entertain Miss Donaldson at dinner tonight.'

Training tells. 'Ladies never betray emotion, Connie dear,' an early governess of Lady Constance's had often impressed upon her, and the maxim had guided her through life. Where a woman less carefully schooled might have keeled over in her chair, possibly with a startled 'Golly!', she merely quivered a little.

'I see. Thank you, Riggs.'

She picked up the cake with jam in the middle which had fallen from her nerveless fingers and ate it in a sort of trance. The discovery that on the pretext of dining with her father's old friend Mrs Bunbury, Penelope Donaldson had been planning to sneak off and revel with a young man who, from the fact that she had never mentioned his name, must be somebody quite impossible appalled her. It revealed the child as what her brother Galahad would have called a hornswoggling highbinder, and anyone who has anything to do with highbinders knows that that is the very worst sort.

It was with relief that she remembered that by tomorrow evening Penelope Donaldson would be safely back at Blandings Castle, well away from the Vail sphere of influence.

What a haven and refuge Blandings Castle was, to be sure, felt Lady Constance. It seemed to her to have everything. Bracing air, picturesque scenery, old world peace and – best of all – not a Vail to be seen for miles.

2

When girls like Gloria Salt, planning dinner with an old friend, say they are going to dress, they use the word in its deepest and fullest sense, meaning that they propose to extend themselves and that such of the populace as are sharing the *salle-à-manger* with them will be well advised to wear smoked glasses. Jerry, waiting in the lobby of Mario's restaurant some three hours later, was momentarily stunned by what came floating in through the revolving door twenty minutes or so after the time appointed for the tryst. Owing to the fact that their meetings for some years had been confined to the golf links and the luncheon table, he had forgotten how spectacular this girl could be when arrayed for the evening meal.

Gloria Salt was tall and slim and the last word in languorous elegance. Though capable of pasting a golf ball two hundred yards and creating, when serving at tennis, the illusion that it was raining thunderbolts, her dark beauty made her look like a serpent of old Nile. A nervous host, encountering her on her way to dine, might have been excused for wondering whether to offer her a dry martini or an asp.

He would have been wrong in either case. She would have declined the asp, and she now declined Jerry's suggestion of a cocktail.

'Never touch 'em. Can't keep fit if you put that foul stuff into you. That's what I told my future lord and master,' said Gloria, as they seated themselves at their table. 'Lay off those pink gins, Greg, I said, avoid those whisky sours, and while you're about it cut out the starchy foods and take regular daily exercises, because a girl who marries a man who looks like you do at moment of going to press is going to have an uneasy feeling that she's committing bigamy.'

'How did he take that?'

'He laughed at the wit. The satire didn't go so well.'

'He is stout, this Parsloe?'

'He certainly gets his pennyworth out of a weighing machine.'

Jerry was, not unnaturally, anxious to condense preliminaries to a minimum and come to the real business of the evening, but a host must be civil. He cannot plunge into business over the smoked salmon. He was, moreover, extremely curious to learn the inside story of the rift within the lute at which his guest had hinted – if hinted is the word – when speaking earlier in the day of Orlo, Lord Vosper. Jerry, who had known that handsomest ornament of the

Peerage from boyhood days and was very fond of him, had been saddened by her tale of sundered hearts.

'A bit of a change from the old Wasp,' he ventured.

'What old wasp?'

'Boyish nickname for Vosper. I was at school with him.'

'You were, were you? Borstal, I presume? Did you kick him?'

'Of course I didn't kick him. I loved him like a brother.'

'The chance of a lifetime thrown away,' said Miss Salt with bitterness. 'If Orlo Vosper in his formative years had been thoroughly kicked twice a day, Sundays included, he might not have grown up the overbearing louse he has become.'

'Would you call him an overbearing louse?'

'I did. To his face.'

'When was this?'

'On the tennis court at Eastbourne, and again when entering the clubhouse. I'd have done it in the dressing-room, too, only he wasn't there. They separate the sexes. Of all the overbearing lice that ever overbore, I told him, you are the undisputed champion, and I gave him back his ring.'

'Oh, you were engaged?'

'Don't rub it in. We all make mistakes.'

'I didn't see anything about it in the papers.'

'We were going to announce it just before Wimbledon.'

'What did he do to incur your displeasure?'

'I'll tell you. We were playing in the mixed doubles, and I admit that I may have been slightly off my game, but that was no reason why, after we had dropped the first set, he should have started barging into my half of the court, taking my shots for me as if I were some elderly aunt with arthritis in both legs who had learned tennis in the previous week at a correspondence school. "Mine!" he kept yelling. "Mine, mine!", and where was Gloria? Crouching in a corner, looking at him with wide, admiring eyes and saying "My hero!"? No, sir. I told him that if he didn't stop his damned poaching, I would brain him, if he had a brain. That held him for awhile. After that, he kept himself to himself, as it were. But every time I missed a shot, and a girl with an emotional nature couldn't be expected not to miss a few after an ordeal like that, he raised his eyebrows in a superior kind of way and gave a sort of nasty dry snigger and kept saying "Too bad, too bad." And when it was over and we had lost — two six, three six — he said what a pity it all was and if only I had left it to him . . . Well, that was when we parted brass rags. Shortly afterwards I got engaged to Greg Parsloe.'

Jerry clicked his tongue, and when his guest inquired with some asperity why he was making that idiotic noise, and did he think he was riding in the Grand National and encouraging his horse to jump Beecher's Brook, explained that her story had distressed him. As, indeed, it had. Nobody likes to hear of these rifts between old friends. He had been devoted to Lord Vosper since the days when they had thrown inked darts at one another, while for Gloria Salt he felt that gentle affection which men feel for women who could have married them and didn't.

'Has the Wasp heard about it?'

'I suppose so. It was in *The Times*.'

'It must have given him a jolt.'

'One hopes so.'

'Where is he now?'

'Goodness knows. I don't. And for heaven's sake let's stop talking about him. I should have thought you would have shown some interest in what I said to you over the phone this afternoon. I pictured you running up to me the moment I came in, all full of eager questions. And you haven't so much as mentioned it.'

Jerry was dismayed to think that she should have got so wrong an impression from his gentlemanly reserve.

'Good Lord, of course I'm interested. But I thought you would get around to that when you felt like it. I didn't want you to think that was the only reason I wanted to dine with you.'

'Did you want to dine with me?'

'Of course I did.'

'You didn't sound too pleased.'

'Well, you see, actually I had another date for tonight, and I was feeling it might be awkward breaking it.'

'A girl?'

It was a loose way of describing the divinest of her species, but Jerry let it pass.

'Yes, a girl.'

Gloria Salt's eyes grew soft and sympathetic. She leaned across the table and patted his cheek.

'I'm terribly sorry, Jerry. I didn't know. Is this love? Yes, I can see it is from the way your eyes are goggling. Well, well. When did this happen?'

'Not so long ago. I dashed over to New York the other day, and she was on the boat coming back.'

'When are you going to get married?'

'Never, unless I can raise that two thousand pounds.'

'It's like that, is it? Don't you make anything with your writing?'

'Not half enough.'

'I see. Well, as I say, I'm sorry I had to come butting in, but this was my last chance of getting hold of you. I'm motoring down to Shropshire tomorrow, to stay at a place called Blandings Castle.'

Jerry started.

'Blandings Castle?'

'You know it?'

Jerry hesitated. Should he tell her all about Penny? On the whole, he thought, no. The fewer people who knew, the better.

'I've heard of it,' he said. 'Nice place, I believe.'

'So they all tell me. It's only a mile or two from where Gregory hangs out, so we'll be able to see something of each other. I imagine that's why Lady Constance invited me. Well, keep the words "Blandings Castle" steadily in your mind, because they are the heart of the matter. I will now approach the heart of the matter.'

A waiter brought roast beef, underdone, and she took a thin slice. Jerry took two slices, with potatoes, and Gloria in her austere way advised him to be very careful how he tucked into those things, because she was convinced that it was a lifelong passion for potatoes that had made Sir Gregory Parsloe the man he was . . . or, rather, she added, for she was a girl who liked exactness, the two men he was.

'Where were we?' she asked, as the waiter withdrew.

'You were about to approach the heart of the matter.'

'That's right. So I was. Well, here it comes. Listen attentively, for what I have to say will interest you strangely.'

She ate a Brussels sprout. It is the virtue of Brussels sprouts that you can wolf them freely without running any risk of becoming like

Sir Gregory Parsloe, Bart, of Matchingham Hall, Much Matchingham.

'I don't know about the flora of Blandings Castle,' she said, 'though no doubt they are varied and beautiful, but its fauna consist of – amongst others – Clarence, ninth Earl of Emsworth, and his sister, Lady Constance. What the relations are between the noble lord and my betrothed I cannot say, but Lady Constance and he appear to be on matey terms, so much so that when the other day she wanted to get a new secretary for Lord Emsworth, she asked if he could do anything to help. "Charmed, dear lady," said Greg, and got me on the phone and told me to attend to it, if it was not giving me too much trouble. "No trouble at all, my king," I said. "As a matter of fact, I know a man." You're the man.'

Jerry gasped. The roast beef swam before his eyes.

'You don't mean –?'

'The job's yours, if you care to take it, and I strongly advise you to take it, because there is more in this than meets the eye and the plot is shortly about to thicken. But I suppose you're going to come over all haughty and say that the Vails don't take jobs as secretaries.'

Jerry laughed. The thought of being too proud to allow himself to be employed in a house which contained Penny, a house probably stiff with rose gardens and other secluded nooks where he and Penny could meet and talk of this and that, was an amusing one. Had it been required of him, he would have accepted office as the boy who cleaned the knives and boots.

'I'll be there. You couldn't have suggested anything that would have suited me better.'

'That's all right, then. And now for the thickening of the plot. About a year ago I ran into a lad I used to go dancing with in the days of Edward the Confessor, a youth named Hugo Carmody, and he gave me lunch and told me all about Blandings Castle. It seems that he was Lord Emsworth's secretary at one time, and he had me in stitches with his diverting stories about the old boy. Are you listening?'

'You bet I'm listening.'

'I had completely forgotten Hugo and his saga till Greg rang me up, and then the word "secretary", taken in conjunction with the words "Blandings Castle", brought it all back to me, and I saw that this was where I could do my day's good deed. The gist of what Hugo had told me was that the old bird – I allude to the ninth Earl – is practically dotty on the subject of pigs. He has a prize pig called Empress of Blandings to which he is devoted. In fact, you might say he thinks of nothing else. Hugo's tenure of his job was very rocky off and on, but he told me he could always stabilize it by talking pig to Lord Emsworth. There were times, he said, when he was at the top of his form as a pig talker, when he got the impression that Lord Emsworth would have given him all he had, even unto half his kingdom. And when Greg told me about this secretary thing and I thought of you, it was because it suddenly struck me that it was quite possible that if you went to Blandings and showed yourself sufficiently pig-conscious, old Emsworth might be induced to advance you that two thousand you require. Naturally I don't say it's a snip. Lots of elderly men, however fond they may have become of an eager youngster, wince and shrink back when the latter shows a disposition to climb on their laps and help himself out of their pockets. But in your case it wouldn't be a straight touch. All you would be asking for would be a loan, and not too risky a loan considering what pots of money these cure places make. You would put it up to him as a business proposition. "Lord Emsworth," you would say, "do you want to make a bit? Because, if so, I can swing it for you," and then you would go into your sales talk and offer him a large interest on his money. An old bird like that probably has all his cash salted away in Government bonds at three per cent, and you would sneer at Government bonds, and ask if he wouldn't prefer a safe ten. I think he would drop. Mind you, I'm not saying that you could walk into Blandings Castle tomorrow and expect to get a cheque for two thousand of the best before bedtime, but after the lapse of some weeks, after you had softened him up with your encyclopaedic knowledge of pigs, I don't see why you shouldn't have a sporting chance. Think it over.'

Jerry was doing so, and now he came up with an objection.

'But I haven't an encyclopaedic knowledge of pigs.'

'There are a million books you can get it from. Good heavens! Go to the British Museum and ask for everything they have on the subject. If I were in your place, I'd guarantee to become an authority in a couple of days. You don't suppose Hugo Carmody knew anything about pigs do you? He had never met a pig except informally over the dish of breakfast bacon. Whenever the sack seemed to him to be looming, when he could hear the beating of its wings, so to speak, he used to sneak down at night to Lord Emsworth's library and bone up on the subject till breakfast time. By then, he tells me, though a little apt to fall asleep where he sat, he did know about pigs. What Hugo could do, you can do. Or are you a spineless worm incapable of honest effort?'

So might the Cleopatra she so closely resembled in appearance have addressed one of her soldiers who seemed in need of a pep talk before the Battle of Actium. And just as this soldier would have sprung to his feet with flashing eyes, so did Jerry Vail leap with flashing eyes from his chair.

'Want to dance?' said Gloria.

Jerry quivered.

'What I really want is to fold you in my arms and cover your upturned face with burning kisses.'

'You can't do that there here. And you seem to be forgetting that we're both engaged to somebody else.'

'You don't get the idea. These would be kisses of gratitude, the sort of kisses a brother would bestow on a sister who deserved well of him. I simply don't know what to say, Gloria, old thing. You spoke of doing your day's good deed. What you have done this night is sufficient to carry you over till a couple of years from now, even if you do no good deeds in the meantime. Well, I suppose all I can say is "Thank you."'

She patted his cheek.

'Don't mention it,' she said. 'Come on, let's dance.'

3

In her bedroom in her neat little house in the suburb of Valley Fields, Maudie Stubbs, *née* Beach, was enjoying a last cigarette before turning in for the night.

All her arrangements for tomorrow's exodus were completed – her packing done, her hair waved, her cat Freddie lodged with a friend down the road, and now she was musing dreamily on something her Uncle Sebastian had said over the telephone yesterday.

The story he had told had of necessity been brief and sketchy, and she had still to learn in detail exactly what was expected of her on arrival at this Blandings Castle of which she had heard so much, but in the course of his remarks Uncle Sebastian had mentioned as the menace to the well-being of himself and associates a Sir Gregory Parsloe.

She wondered if this could possibly be the Tubby Parsloe she had known so well in the days when she had been Maudie Montrose.

Chapter 4

With the possible exception of Mrs Emily Post, a few of the haughtier Duchesses and the late Cornelia, mother of the Gracchi, the British barmaid, trained from earliest years to behave with queenly dignity under the most testing conditions, stands alone in the matter of poise.

It was no timid and fluttering Maudie Stubbs who stepped off the train next day at Market Blandings station. Where another representative of what is sometimes termed the burjoisy might have quailed at the thought of being plunged into so posh – or plushy – a nest of the aristocracy as Blandings Castle, she faced the prospect with equanimity, remaining as calm and composed as she would have been if entering a den of lions like the prophet Daniel or a burning fiery furnace like Shadrach, Meshack and Abednego. In her professional capacity, she had seen far too many members of the Peerage thrown out of the bar over which she presided for blue blood to mean anything to her.

Gally, all eagerness to renew a friendship interrupted by time and change, had walked in to meet the train, and there was an affecting reunion on the station platform. After which, he had taken her off to the Emsworth Arms for a spot of refreshment. He felt she must be in need of it after her long journey, and apart from the altruistic desire to keep an old crony from fainting by the wayside, he thought it would be no bad thing to have a quick run-through before the rise of the curtain, just to make sure that she was letter perfect in her part.

When two old friends get together after long separation, the proceedings always begin with a picking up of threads. The first old friend asks the second old friend for news of Jimmy So-and-so, while the second old friend asks the first old friend what has been heard of Billy Such-and-such. Inquiries are also instituted regarding

Tom This, Dick That and Harry The Other, with speculations as to whatever became of old Joe What's-his-name, the chap who always used to do an imitation of a cat fight after his third whisky and splash.

These routine preliminaries had been disposed of during the walk from the station, and now, as they sat at a rustic table in the garden behind the inn, sipping the beer for which the Emsworth Arms is so justly renowned, they were at liberty to speak of other things. To a man as gallant as the Hon. Galahad a compliment with reference to his companion's appearance naturally suggested itself first, and he proceeded to pay it.

'Well, well, well,' he said, gazing at her with undisguised admiration. 'Do you know you positively don't look a dashed day older, Maudie? It's amazing.'

And indeed the years had dealt lightly with the erstwhile Maudie Montrose. A little more matronly, perhaps, than the girl with the hourglass figure who had played the Saint Bernard dog to the thirsty wayfarers at the old Criterion, she still made a distinct impression on the eye, and the landlord of the Emsworth Arms, his growing son Percy, and the half-dozen Shropshire lads who were propping up the establishment's outer wall had stamped her with the seal of their popeyed approval. Her entrance had been in the nature of a social triumph.

'It's astounding,' said Gally. 'One gasps. Put you in a bathing suit, add you to the line of contestants in any seaside beauty competition, and you would still have the judges whooping and blowing kisses and asking you if you were doing anything next Saturday night.'

It was the sort of tribute a thousand mellowed clients had paid her across the bar in the old days, and Maudie, who had simpered indulgently then, simpered indulgently now.

'Thank you, dear,' she said. 'I call that very nice of you. You don't look so bad yourself,' she added, with that touch of surprise which always came into the voices of those who, meeting Gally after a lapse of years, found him so bright and rosy.

This man's fitness was one of the eternal mysteries. Speaking of him, a historian of Blandings Castle had once written: 'A thoroughly mis-spent life had left the Hon. Galahad Threepwood, contrary to the most elementary justice, in what appeared to be perfect, even exuberantly perfect physical condition. How a man who ought to have had the liver of the century could look as he did was a constant source of perplexity to his associates. It seemed incredible that anyone who had had such an extraordinarily good time all his life should, in the evening of that life, be so superbly robust.'

Striking words, but well justified. Instead of the blot on a proud family which his sister Constance, his sister Julia, his sister Dora and all his other sisters considered him, he might have been a youngish teetotaller who had subsisted from boyhood on yoghurt, yeast, wheat germ and blackstrap molasses. He himself attributed his health to steady smoking, plenty of alcohol and his lifelong belief that it was bad form to go to bed before three in the morning.

'I keep pretty well,' he agreed complacently. 'Life in the country suits me.'

'I should have thought you'd have been bored stiff.'

'No, I like it. It's all a matter of taste. Poor old Fruity Biffen, now, he couldn't cope with the local conditions at all. You remember Fruity Biffen? He was down here till a few days ago, but he couldn't take it, and left. A great loss. He would have been of invaluable assistance to us in this task of ours of foiling Parsloe. Your Uncle Sebastian, though a good chap, lacks a certain something. Not the sort of fellow to put in the forefront of the battle. What one wants in a crisis like that through which we are now passing is one of those young, tough, butlers, spitting out of the side of the mouth and ready for anything.'

'How is Uncle Sebastian?'

'Very well, considering everything. Worried, naturally. The dark circles which you will notice under his eyes are due to anxiety regarding the Empress's future. The Agricultural Show is approaching, and he has invested far more on her than he cares to lose. Me too. I also am heavily involved. So we are relying on you, Maudie, to do your bit. Watch the girl Simmons unblinkingly, for it is from that quarter that peril looms. Did your Uncle Sebastian explain the situation fully?'

'Not what you would call fully. But I understand most of it.'

'The pig contest? The danger that threatens? The need for constant vigilance?'

'Yes, all that. But who is this Mrs Bunbury I'm supposed to be?'

'The lifelong friend of a Mr Donaldson, father of a Miss Penelope Donaldson who is a guest at the castle, a merchant prince who provides the American dog with its daily biscuit. So when Connie starts talking about him, don't be like Clarence and say "Who is Mr Donaldson?" Clarence is my brother, Lord Emsworth, and Connie is my sister, Lady Constance Keeble. She is the menace in the treatment.'

'I thought this Sir Gregory Parsloe was the menace.'

'Aided and abetted by Connie. Not that a twister like Tubby Parsloe needs any aiding and abetting.'

Maudie sat up with a jerk.

'Tubby?'

'That's odd,' said Gally. 'I don't suppose I've called him that for thirty years. Meeting you again like this seems to have put the clock back. Tubby was his nickname in the old days, due to his obscene obesity. Did you ever run across him when you were at the Criterion?'

Maudie was breathing emotionally. A strange light had come into her blue eyes.

'Did I ever run across him! Why, I was going to marry him.'

'What!'

'Only he never turned up.'

'Never turned up?'

'Never turned up. I waited an hour and a quarter at the church with my bunch of lilies of the valley in my hand, and then I came away.'

Gally was not one of those monocled men who are always taking their monocle out of their eye and polishing it. He reserved this gesture for occasions when he was much moved. This was one of them. For perhaps half a minute he sat in silence, thoughtfully passing his handkerchief over the crystal, while his guest, her mind back in the past, heaved gently, from time to time drinking beer in a manner that betrayed the overwrought soul.

'Too bad,' he said at length.

'Yes, it annoyed me a good deal, I must say.'

'I'm not surprised. Enough to upset anyone. A rather similar thing happened to Mariana of the Moated Grange, and she was as sick as mud. You really mean he never showed up?'

'Not a sign of him. It's my belief he blew the honeymoon money in at the races and hadn't the nerve to tell me. Because it was all settled. He was living down at Shepperton-on-Thames at that time, and I'd had a letter from him making all the arrangements. I can remember every word of it as if it was yesterday. Be at St Saviour's, Pimlico, two o'clock sharp June the seventh, he said. Nothing could be plainer than that, could it? And then all the stuff about going to Paris for the honeymoon. Well, I don't know how you feel about it, but I think there's something not quite nice in telling a girl to meet you at the church and you'll get married and then not showing up,' said Maudie with a touch of austerity. 'That sort of thing sounded funny, I admit, when you heard Vesta Victoria singing about it . . . Remember?'

Gally nodded.

'I remember. "There was I, waiting at the church . . ."'

'Waiting at the church . . .'

'Waiting at the church . . .'

'For he'd gone and left me in the lurch. Lord how it did upset me . . .'

'—set me.'

'Yes,' said Maudie, suspending the community singing, 'that sort of thing's funny enough in a music hall song, but it's no joke when it happens to you, you can take it from me. Makes a girl feel silly. So he's Sir Gregory Parsloe now?'

'Sir Gregory Parsloe, Bart. A cousin of his died, and he came into the title. Did you ever see him again?'

'No.'

'Did he write?'

'Not a word.'

'Just faded away like a dream at daybreak? Well, that's Parsloe,' said Gally philosophically. 'What else could you expect of a man capable of loading my dog Towser up with steak and onions on the night of the rat contest? But I can readily understand that it must have been an unpleasant experience for you, old girl. Must have given you a jaundiced idea of the male sex. Still, you got over it.'

'Oh, I got over it.'

'You were well out of it, if you ask me. Were you happy with the late Stubbs?'

'Yes, Cedric and I were very happy.'

'There you are, then,' said Gally buoyantly. 'All's well that ends well. No good brooding over what might have been. Let the dead past bury its dead, and all that sort of thing. Well, I'm glad you told me this, Maudie, because it stimulates and encourages me. If young Parsloe did you down in that scurvy fashion, you will be up and doing with a heart for any fate, unremitting in your efforts to get a bit of your own back on the son of a bachelor, straining every nerve to foil his evil schemes. Which is precisely the spirit we want to see in you at this juncture. More beer?'

'No, thanks.'

'Then we might be strolling along and picking up the station taxi, Jno. Robinson proprietor. I suppose it's about time I sprang you on the old folks. Keep calm when you meet Connie. And when you see Beach, for goodness' sake don't go losing your head and flinging yourself into his arms with a "Hey, hey, Uncle Sebastian!"' said Gally. 'Treat him with distant hauteur, and if you can manage an occasional "Ah, my good man" or "Ha, Beach, my honest fellow," it will help the general composition greatly.'

2

In all properly regulated country houses the hours between tea and dinner are set aside for letter writing. The strength of the company retire to their rooms, heavy with muffins, and settle down to a leisurely disposal of their correspondence. Those who fall asleep try again next day.

Lady Constance Keeble, having a boudoir of her own as well as a bedroom, had gone there as soon as tea on the terrace was over, to relay the latest from Blandings Castle to Mr Donaldson of Long Island City. She had just finished, and was relaxing over a cigarette, when the door opened and her brother Galahad came in.

'Yes?' she said, in a voice in which sisters like her do say 'Yes?' to brothers like Gally. She also raised her eyebrows.

Her intrepid visitor was not the man to be quelled by this sort of thing.

'Step out of the frame, Mona Lisa,' he said briskly. 'I came to hear what you think of this Mrs Bunbury.'

It was a point on which he was most anxious to obtain first-hand information. On presenting Maudie to Lady Constance at the tea table, he had observed the chatelaine of Blandings Castle blink twice, rapidly, rather in the manner of a woman who has been slapped between the eyes with a wet fish, and the spectacle had momentarily disconcerted him. He had not needed Beach to tell him that his sister's standards in the matter of guests were exacting, and there was unquestionably quite a good deal of that passed-for-adults-only stuff about Maudie. He had been forced to ask himself if she had made the grade.

But after that first electric moment it seemed to him that everything had gone with a swing, nor in arriving at this conclusion had he erred. Confronted with Maudie, Lady Constance had certainly blinked, but almost immediately had reminded herself that this guest of hers was American. One always, she knew, has to budget for a touch of the spectacular in the outer crust of the American Society woman. This concession made, she had speedily been won over by the polished elegance of Maudie's deportment, which, as always, was considerable, with the result that the letter to Mr Donaldson now lying on her desk was a definitely enthusiastic one. In her view of the presiding genius of Digby's Day and Night Detectives she was seeing eye to eye with the Shropshire lads, the landlord of the Emsworth Arms and the latter's growing son Percy.

'Nice woman, I thought.'

'Very. I have just been writing to Mr Donaldson to tell him how much I like her.'

'That's fine. That's splendid. That's the way to talk.'

'I don't see why you are so interested.'

Gally gave her a rebuking look.

'My dear Connie,' he said, 'I am interested, as you put it, because I am extremely fond of Penny Donaldson and would not have liked her to be upset. This Mrs Bunbury is a close friend of her father, and she is naturally anxious for her to get the green light. Picture the poor child's feelings if you had drawn yourself up in that sniffy way of yours and come the *grande dame* over Ma Bunbury. And it might easily have happened. If I've caught you being the haughty English aristocrat once, I've caught you a hundred times. It gets you greatly disliked on all sides.'

'Let me relieve your mind. Mrs Bunbury is a little odd-looking, but I think she is quite attractive.'

'So do I.'

'Not that that matters. Well, good-bye, Galahad.'

'And so does Clarence, by Jove. I've never seen him take to a member of the opposite sex so wholeheartedly. Usually, if you try to make Clarence say What ho to a female of the species, he's off over the horizon like a jackrabbit. But you would not be putting it too strongly if you said that he took this Mrs Bunbury to his bosom. He was all over her. Watching them go off together to see the Empress, I was reminded of a couple of sailors on shore leave at Marseilles. Astounding!'

'I am rather busy, Galahad.'

'Eh?'

'I say I am rather busy.'

'You're not in the least busy. When I came in, you were smoking a gasper with your feet on the mantelpiece.'

'My feet were not on the mantelpiece.'

'And in another minute you'd have been asleep, snoring your head off.'

'How dare you say I snore? I never snore.'

'That is not the point at issue,' said Gally. 'The point at issue is the way you have been behaving since I blew in. Your manner has been most peculiar. It has wounded me a good deal. If your own brother can't come and pay you a friendly visit without having you blinding and stiffing at him like a bargee, things have reached a pretty pass in English family life.'

The conversation was approaching a stage where it might easily have developed into one of those distressing brother-and-sister brawls, for both participants were of high spirit, but at this moment Lord Emsworth appeared, giving tongue immediately in the high, plaintive tenor which he used when he felt ill-treated.

'Stamps!' said Lord Emsworth. 'I am writing a letter and I have no stamps. Have you been taking my stamps, Constance?'

'I have not been taking your stamps,' said Lady Constance wearily. 'You keep letting your box get empty and forgetting to tell Beach to have it filled. You can have one of mine, if you like.'

'Thank you,' said Lord Emsworth, pacified. 'That will be capital,

capital. I am writing to the Shropshire, Herefordshire and South Wales Pig-Breeders' Association.'

'Is it their birthday?' asked Gally, interested.

'Eh? No, not that I know of. But I had a letter from them yesterday, asking me to deliver an address on certain aspects of the Empress. Very flattering, I thought it. I am looking forward to . . . My God!' said Lord Emsworth in sudden alarm. 'Shall I have to wear a top hat?'

'Of course you will.'

'And a stiff collar?'

'Well, really, Clarence, do you expect to address these people in pyjamas?'

Lord Emsworth considered this.

'No. No, I see what you mean. No, possibly not pyjamas. But a stiff collar in weather like this!'

'*Noblesse oblige*,' said Gally.

'Eh?'

'I presume what Galahad means is that you have a certain position to keep up.'

'Exactly,' said Gally. 'You've got to impress these pig-breeding blighters. Give 'em the morning coat, the sponge-bag trousers, the stiff collar and the old top hat, and you have them saying to themselves "Golly, these Earls are hot stuff!". Whereas, seeing you dressed as you are now, they would give you the bird and probably start a revolution. You must cow them, Clarence, overawe them, make them say "The half was not told me," like the Queen of Sheba when she met King Solomon. This cannot be done in a ten-year-old shooting coat with holes in the elbows.'

'And flannel trousers that have not been pressed for weeks,' added Lady Constance. 'You look like a tramp. I cannot imagine what Mrs Bunbury thought of you.'

Lord Emsworth started. A quick look of concern came into his face.

'Do you think Mrs Bunbury thought I looked like a tramp?'

'Everything turns,' said Gally, 'on whether she thrust a penny into your hand and told you not to spend it on drink. Did she?'

'No. No, I don't remember her doing that.'

'Then all may be well. Nice woman, that, Clarence.'

'Delightful.'

'You seemed to be getting along with her all right.'

'Oh, capitally.'

'Yes,' said Gally. He wandered to the window and stood looking out. 'I was telling Connie that you reminded me of a couple of . . . Hullo.'

'What's the matter?'

'A strange young man is crossing the terrace.'

'A strange young man?'

'Look for yourself.'

Lord Emsworth joined him at the window.

'Where? I don't see any . . . Ah yes, I was looking in the wrong direction. That is not a strange young man. That is my new secretary.'

'I didn't know you had a new secretary.'

'Nor did I till just now, dash it.'

'You'd better go and pass the time of day with him.'

'I have passed the time of day with him, and I must say that, much as I resent having these infernal secretaries thrust upon me, this time the outlook seems considerably brighter than usual. By a most happy chance, this fellow turns out to be a mine of information on the subject of pigs, and we got along capitally together. We were exchanging the customary civilities, when he suddenly said "I wonder if you are interested in pigs, Lord Emsworth?" "God bless my soul, yes," I replied. "Are you?" "They are a passion with me," he said. "I'm afraid I'm rather inclined to bore people about pigs," he went on with a little laugh, and then he told me all sorts of things I didn't know myself. He was most informative about pigs in ancient Egypt. It appears that the ancient Egyptians believed that pigs brought good crops and appeased evil spirits.'

'You could hardly ask more of them than that.'

'With regard to the pig in the time of Christopher Columbus —'

Lady Constance rapped the table.

'Clarence!'

'Yes?'

'Go away!'

'Eh?'

'I came to this room to be alone. Am I not to have a moment of privacy?'

'Yes, come along, Clarence,' said Gally. 'Connie is in a strange mood. We are not wanted here, and I am anxious to meet this gifted youth. What's his name?'

'Whose name?'

'The gifted youth's.'

'What gifted youth?'

'Listen, Clarence,' said Gally patiently. 'You have a new secretary. You concede that?'

'Oh, certainly, certainly.'

'Well, I want to know what his name is.'

'Oh, his name? You mean his *name*. Quite. Quite. It's . . . no, I've forgotten.'

'Smith? Jones? Brown? Cholmondeley-Marjoribanks? Vavasour-Dalrymple? Ernle-Plunkett-Drax-Plunkett?'

Lord Emsworth stood in thought.

'No . . . Ah, I have it. It's Vail.'

'Vail!'

'Gerald Vail. He asked me to call him Jerry.'

The door closed behind them. The sharp, wordless cry which had proceeded from Lady Constance they attributed to a creaking hinge.

3

Having walked as far as the end of the corridor together, in pleasant conversation on such topics as top hats, secretaries and what a pest their sister Constance was, the brothers parted with mutual expressions of good will, Lord Emsworth to go to the library for a quick look at Whiffle on *The Care Of The Pig*, Gally to toddle out into the gloaming for a breath of air.

As he toddled, he was feeling deeply stirred. It was possible, of course, that there were several Gerald Vails in the world and the one now in residence one of the wrong ones, but it seemed unlikely. The way it looked to Gally was that somehow, by the exercise of he knew not what girlish wiles and stratagems, Penny Donaldson had succeeded in smuggling into the home circle the quite unsuitable young man to whom she had given her heart, and he was filled with a profound respect for the resource and enterprise of the present generation. Where the Emmelines and Ermyntrudes of his Victorian youth, parted from ineligible suitors, had merely dropped a tear and eventually married along lines more in keeping with the trend of parental thought, the Pennys of today, full of the rebel spirit, pulled up their socks and got things done.

Her behaviour appealed to everything in this deplorable buccaneer of the nineties which made his sister Constance, his sister Julia, his sister Dora, and all his other sisters wince when they saw him and purse their lips when his name was mentioned, and he was still aglow with admiration, proud that such a girl should have honoured him with her friendship, when he bumped into something solid, and saw that it was the dream man in person.

'Oh, sorry,' said Jerry.

'Not at all,' said Gally courteously. 'A pleasure.'

Seeing the object of Penny's affections at close range, he found himself favourably impressed. For an author Jerry Vail was rather nice-looking, most authors, as is widely known, resembling in appearance the more degraded types of fish, unless they look like birds, when they could pass as vultures and no questions asked. His face, while never likely to launch a thousand ships, was not at all a bad sort of face, and Gally could readily picture it casting a spell in a dim light on a boat deck. Looking at him, he found it easy to understand why Penny should have described him as a baa-lamb. From a cursory inspection he seemed well entitled to membership in that limited class.

Jerry, meanwhile, drinking Gally in, had discovered that this was no stranger he had rammed.

'Why, hullo, Mr Threepwood,' he said. 'You won't remember me, but we've met before. I was introduced to you once by Admiral Biffen.'

Gally retained no recollection of this previous encounter, but the mention of that honoured name stirred him like a bugle.

'You know Fruity Biffen?'

'I've known him all my life. He's a great friend of an uncle of mine. Major Basham.'

Any doubts Gally might have entertained as to the suitability of this young man as a husband for a girl on whom he looked as a daughter were dispelled. The name of Major Basham was equally as honoured as that of Fruity Biffen.

'You mean Plug Basham is your uncle? God bless my soul, as my brother Clarence would say. One of my oldest friends.'

'Yes, I've often heard him speak of you.'

'We've always been like Damon and what's-his-name. I once put a pig in his bedroom.'

'Really? What made you do that?'

'Oh, it struck me as a good idea. It was the night of the Bachelor's Ball at Hammer's Easton. Old Wivenhoe's pig. Puffy Benger and I borrowed it and put it in Plug's room. I had to leave early next morning, so never learned what happened when he met it. No doubt they got together across a round table and threshed things out. Plug Basham, by Jove! I once saw Plug throw a side of beef at a fellow in Romano's. Laid him out cold, and all the undertakers present making bids for the body. How is he these days?'

'Going as strong as ever.'

'Fruity and I were talking about him only a week ago. Fruity was down here. Not staying at the castle – he can't stand my sister Constance, and I don't blame him. I got him to take a little house along the Shrewsbury road not far from here because I met him in London and he seemed a bit run down and I thought a breath of country air would do him good. But he couldn't stick it out. Too much noise. He said there was a bunch of assorted bugs and insects in his front garden which seemed to be seeing the new year in all night, and he went back to Piccadilly, where he said a man could get a bit of peace. I miss him. Did he ever tell about the time when he and I –'

Gally paused. The story he had been about to relate was a good one, but he was a kindly man and realized that this was no time for stories, however entertaining.

'But I mustn't keep you here talking. You'll be wanting to find Penny. Oh, I know all about you and Penny,' said Gally, noticing that his young friend had leaped skywards as if a red-hot iron had been applied to the seat of his trousers. 'She confided in me.'

Jerry became calmer. He was still not sure how he liked the idea of anyone sharing his sacred secret, but this old boy was so obviously friendly that perhaps in his case one could stretch a point.

'I was just thinking, when you came along,' said Gally, 'what a really exceptional girl she must be to have sneaked you in here as Clarence's secretary without my sister Constance entertaining a single suspicion. Good brains there. How the dickens did she work it?'

'But Penny doesn't know I'm here.'

'What! Then how –?'

'It was a girl called Gloria Salt who got me the job.'

'Gloria Salt? Oh yes, I remember. She's coming here.'

'She's here already. She drove me down in her car. She's an old friend of mine.' Jerry hesitated. Then he decided to keep nothing back. 'She thought that if I became Lord Emsworth's secretary, I might . . . Did Penny ever say anything to you about a scheme I had for –'

'She told me all. In fact, she tried to touch me for that two thousand.'

'Oh, good Lord, she shouldn't have done that.'

'Quite all right. I enjoyed the novel experience of having someone suppose that I had two thousand pounds. Yes, I know all about that health cure place idea of yours, and I think it's a good one. The problem, as always, is how to get the cash. How are you coming along with regard to that? Any likely prospects in view?'

'I was just going to tell you. Gloria thought –'

'Because if you have nobody on your list who looks like a snip, you could do far worse than consider my brother Clarence.'

'Why, that's just what Gloria –'

'My brother Clarence,' proceeded Gally, 'is a peculiar chap. He eats, sleeps, and dreams pig, and he was telling us just now how extraordinarily pig-minded you were. You positively stunned him with your fund of information on the subject.'

'Yes, you see I –'

'And the thought that crossed my mind was that, if you played your cards right, you might quite easily put yourself in a position where you could go to him, when acquaintance had ripened into friendship, and sting him for the sum you need. Yes, I know,' said Gally catching his audience's eye and observing that it was bulging. 'It seems to you a bizarre idea. Far-fetched. Potty. The picture you are forming in your mind of me is that of a man talking through the back of his neck. But I know Clarence. Not an easy partner in normal circumstances, he would, I am convinced, lend a ready ear to the blandishments of a fellow pig-lover. You wait and see if I'm not right.'

Jerry was looking like the Soul's Awakening. He stammered with emotion.

'What an amazing coincidence!' he said. 'That's exactly what Gloria told me.'

'You mean she suggested touching Clarence?'

'That's why she wanted me to come here as his secretary.'

'So that you could join him in slapping his pig on the backside and let your light so shine that eventually you would be in a position to put the bite on him?'

'That's right.'

'Sounds an intelligent girl.'

'Oh, she is. Most intelligent. She –'

Jerry broke off. Gally, eyeing him, saw that his face had lighted up as if someone had pressed a switch. Turning, for what had caused this ecstasy was apparently something that was happening behind him, he perceived Penny approaching.

'Ah!' he said, understanding.

The only flaw in what should have been a moment of unalloyed joy was that Penny was not alone. Walking at her side was a tall, superbly built young man whose dark, Byronic beauty made him look like something that had eluded the vigilance of the front office and escaped from the Metro-Goldwyn lot. Having met him at meals for more than two weeks, Gally had no difficulty in identifying him as Orlo, Lord Vosper.

Penny seemed listless. Her eyes, as she walked, were on the ground. It may have been merely maiden meditation, but it looked to Gally more like the pip, and he wondered what was amiss. He whooped welcomingly, and she looked up. Having done so, she stood staring, the colour draining from her face. She reminded Gally of a girl named Mabel something who, walking with him at a Buckingham Palace garden party in the year 1906, had suddenly become aware that there was a beetle down her back.

'Ah, Penny,' he said, subtle as always, 'I want you to meet Clarence's new secretary. His name is – What did you say your name was?'

'Vail,' said Jerry huskily.

'Vail,' said Gally. 'Nice chap. Draw him out on the subject of pigs. Mr Vail, Lord Vosper.'

Lord Vosper, like Penny, seemed not to be in the highest spirits. He nodded dully at Jerry.

'Oh, we know each other. School together. Hullo, Jerry.'

'Hullo, Wasp. You here?'

'That's right. You here, too?'

'Yes.'

'I thought so,' said Lord Vosper, and returned to his meditations.

He was still occupied with them, and the silence which had fallen was still unbroken, when Sebastian Beach appeared, heading in their direction.

'Pardon me, m'lord,' said Beach. 'A Mr Wapshott is on the telephone, desirous of speaking to you. He implied that the matter was of importance –'

Lord Vosper came out of his trance.

'Wapshott?'

'Yes, m'lord. He stated that he represented the firm of Wapshott, Wapshott, Wapshott, and Wapshott.'

'Reminds me,' said Gally, who never let an opportunity like this pass, 'of the story of the chap in New York who rang up the legal firm of Shapiro, Shapiro, Shapiro, and Shapiro. "Hello," he says, "can I speak to Mr Shapiro?" "Mr Shapiro is in court." "Then I'll talk to Mr Shapiro." "Mr Shapiro is in conference with an important client." "Then connect me with Mr Shapiro." "I'm sorry, but Mr Shapiro has taken the day off to play golf." "Oh, all right, then I'll talk to Mr Shapiro." "*Speaking*." Who is this Wapshott?'

'My income tax chap,' said Lord Vosper. 'Fellow who looks after my income tax,' he added, clarifying the situation still further. 'Better go and see what he wants, I suppose.'

He walked away, followed by Beach, and Gally stared after them. It seemed to him that Beach was looking careworn, and it made him uneasy. These were the times that tried men's souls, and at such times one does not like to see a careworn butler, if that butler is a butler with whom one is sitting in on a campaign that calls for alertness and efficiency on the part of all concerned.

Turning, he saw that Penny was still gazing at Jerry in that odd, dumb way. He came to himself with a start.

'Good Lord, I'm sorry,' he said. 'I'm in the way. I see just how it is, Penny. With every fibre of your being you yearn to do a swan dive into this bimbo's arms, but modesty forbids. "How," you are saying, "can I fulfil and express myself with this old image goggling at me through his eyeglass as if he were sitting in the front row at the circus with his all-day sucker and his bag of peanuts?" It's all right. I'll look the other way.'

There is a type of short, sharp, bitter laugh which is like a yelp of agony and does no good to man or beast. Lady Constance sometimes employed it when she heard someone say what a charming man her brother Galahad was. It was a laugh of this kind that now proceeded from Penny Donaldson, and for the first time there began to steal over Jerry a suspicion that he had been mistaken in supposing this the maddest merriest day of all the glad new year and the world in which he moved the best of all possible worlds.

'Please don't bother, Gally,' she said. 'I have not the slightest wish to dive into Mr Vail's arms. I wonder if you would care to hear a little story?'

'Story? Of course, of course. Go ahead. But what's all this "Mr Vail" stuff?'

'You remember me telling you that I was to have had dinner last night with Mr Vail?'

'Certainly. But –'

Penny went on, still speaking in a strange metallic voice that reminded Jerry of Gloria Salt fulfilling and expressing herself on the subject of Lord Vosper.

'We had arranged to meet at the Savoy at eight. I had a fitting in the afternoon, and when I came home at about six I found a telephone message waiting for me. It said that Mr Vail regretted that he would be unable to dine tonight as an important business matter had come up. I was naturally disappointed –'

She choked, and a tear stole down her cheek. Jerry, seeing it, writhed with remorse. He realized how a good-hearted executioner at an Oriental court must feel after strangling an odalisque with a bowstring.

'But, Penny –'

'Please!' She gave him a fleeting look, the sort of look a good woman gives a caterpillar on finding it in her salad, and turned back to Gally. 'I was naturally disappointed, of course, because I had been looking forward very much to seeing him, but I quite understood that these things happen —'

Gally nodded.

'Sent to try us.'

'I quite understood that these things happen —'

'Probably meant to make us more spiritual.'

'I say I quite understood that these things happen,' proceeded Penny, raising her voice and giving Gally a look similar in quality to the one she had just given Jerry, 'and I said to myself that naturally, if Mr Vail had important business, he couldn't be expected to neglect it just for me.'

'But, Penny —'

'So, when Lord Vosper, who was there, suggested that he should give me dinner, I thought it would be a nice way of passing the evening. Lord Vosper, it seems, is very fond of a restaurant called Mario's. He took me there.'

She paused again, this time because Jerry, his eyes leaping from their sockets, had uttered a sound not unlike the howl of a trapped timber wolf.

'We didn't dress,' she resumed, 'so they put us up in the balcony. Do you know Mario's, Gally?'

'Since my time.'

'It's quite nice up in the balcony there. You get a good view of the main floor. And one of the first things I saw on that main floor was Mr Vail attending to his important business. It consisted of dining with a girl who looked like a snake with hips and from time to time having his face patted by her.'

Gally's monocle came swinging round at Jerry like the eye of a fire-breathing dragon. His face was hard and set.

'You abysmal young wart-hog!'

'Oh, you mustn't say that, Gally,' said Penny, gently rebuking. 'I'm sure Mr Vail has a perfectly satisfactory explanation. Probably the girl was the editor of some magazine, discussing a series of stories with him. I believe editors always pat contributors' faces. It creates a friendly atmosphere.'

It cost Jerry an effort to raise his chin and square his shoulders, but he did it. The consciousness of being a good man unjustly accused always helps to stiffen the spinal vertebrae.

'I can explain everything.'

'Why is it,' inquired Penny – she seemed to be addressing a passing butterfly, 'that men always say that?'

'I say it,' said Jerry stoutly, 'because it's true. The girl you saw me dining with was Gloria Salt.'

'Pretty name. A friend of yours?'

'A very dear friend of mine.'

'I thought you seemed on good terms.'

'She patted my face twice.'

'I should have said oftener. Of course, I hadn't a score card with me.'

'Twice,' repeated Jerry firmly. 'And I'll tell you why. Let us take these pats in their order. Pat One was a congratulatory pat when I told her how much I loved you. Pat Two occurred when I was thanking her for having suggested a way by which I might be able to raise that two thousand pounds which I need in order to marry you. So much for your face patting! And if,' Jerry went on, addressing the Hon. Galahad, 'you call me an abysmal young wart-hog again, I shall forget the respect due to your grey hairs and haul off and let you have one right on the maxillary bone. Abysmal young wart-hog, indeed! My motives were pure to the last drop. Gloria Salt rang me up in the afternoon to say she wanted me to give her dinner, promising over the meal to spill this scheme of hers for connecting with the cash, because it was too long, she said, to tell me on the phone. Reluctantly, for it made me feel as if my soul were being passed through a wringer, I broke our date. I dined with her at Mario's. She told me her scheme. I thanked her brokenly, and she patted my face. I may mention that when she patted it, it was as though a kindly sister had patted the face of a blameless brother. So I should be much obliged if you would stop looking at me as if you had caught me stealing pennies from a blind man.'

Penny had already done so. Her lips parted, and she was gazing at him, wide-eyed. There was no suggestion in her expression that she had found him enriching himself at the expense of the blind.

'Furthermore,' said Jerry, now thundering, 'if additional proof is required to drive into your nut the fact that the last thing in the minds of either of us was anything in the nature of funny business, I may mention that Miss Salt – besides being, like myself, pure to the last drop, if not further – is engaged to be married. She is shortly to become the bride of a certain Sir Gregory Parsloe, who, I believe, resides in this vicinity.'

Gally's monocle flew from his eye.

'Parsloe!'

'Parsloe.'

Gally recovered his monocle. But as he replaced it, his hand was trembling. He was a man who prided himself on his British fortitude. Come the three corners of the world in arms and we shall shock them, he had said in effect to Beach and Penny when speaking of the Binstead-Simmons threat, and he had been quite prepared to cope gallantly with a pig girl in the Parsloe pay and a Parsloe minion who went about buying bottles of anti-fat, the large economy size. But add to that pig girl and that minion a Parsloe fiancée, and it seemed to him that things were becoming too hot. No wonder, he felt, that Beach just now had looked careworn. The faithful fellow, possibly listening at some key-hole whilst this Salt girl traded confidences with Lady Constance, must just have had the bad news.

'Oh Lord and butter!' he exclaimed, moved to his depths, and without further speech hastened off in the direction of the butler's pantry. It was obvious to him that the crisis called for another of those staff conferences.

'So there you are,' said Jerry. He stepped forward masterfully. 'I shall now kiss you.'

'Oh, heavens, what a mess!' wailed Penny.

Jerry paused.

'Mess? You believe what I was saying?'

'Of course I believe it.'

'You love me?'

'Of course I love you.'

'All right, then. What are we waiting for? Let's go.'

Penny stepped back.

'Jerry darling, I'm afraid things are more complicated than you think. You see, when I saw that girl pat your face –'

'In a sisterly manner.'

'Yes, but the point is that it didn't *look* sisterly, and I got the wrong angle. So when, just as we were finishing dinner, Orlo Vosper asked me to marry him—'

'Oh, my God!'

'Yes,' said Penny in a small voice. 'He asked me to marry him, and I said I would.'

Chapter 5

But what, meanwhile, it will be asked, of George Cyril Wellbeloved, whom we left with his tongue hanging out, the future stretching bleakly before him like some grim Sahara? Why is it, we seem to hear a million indignant voices demanding, that no further mention has been made of that reluctant teetotaller?

The matter is susceptible of a ready explanation. It is one of the chief drawbacks to the lot of the conscientious historian that in pursuance of his duties he is compelled to leave in obscurity many of those to whom he would greatly prefer to give star billing. His task being to present a panoramic picture of the actions of a number of protagonists, he is not at liberty to concentrate his attention on any one individual, however much the latter's hard case may touch him personally. When Edward Gibbon, half-way through his *Decline and Fall of the Roman Empire* complained to Doctor Johnson one night in a mood of discouragement that it – meaning the lot of the conscientious historian – shouldn't happen to a dog, it was to this aspect of it that he was referring.

In this macédoine of tragic happenings in and around Blandings Castle, designed to purge the souls of a discriminating public with pity and terror, it has been necessary to devote so much space to Jerry Vail, Penny Donaldson, Lord Emsworth and the rest of them that George Cyril Wellbeloved, we are fully aware, has been neglected almost entirely. Except for one brief appearance early in the proceedings, he might as well, for all practical purposes, have been painted on the back drop.

It is with genuine satisfaction that the minstrel, tuning his harp, now prepares to sing of this stricken pig man.

There is no agony like the agony of the man who wants a couple of quick ones and cannot get them and in the days that followed his interview with Sir Gregory Parsloe, George Cyril Wellbeloved may be said to have plumbed the depths. It would, however, be inaccurate to describe him as running the gamut of the emotions, for he had had but one emotion, a dull despair as there crept slowly upon him the realization of the completeness with which his overlord had blocked all avenues to a peaceful settlement. He was in the distressing position of finding himself foiled at every point.

Although nobody who had met him would have been likely to get George Cyril Wellbeloved confused with the poet Keats, it was extraordinary on what similar lines the two men's minds worked. 'Oh, for a beaker full of the warm South, full of the true, the blushful Hippocrene!' sang Keats, licking his lips, and 'Oh, for a mug of beer with, if possible, a spot of gin in it!' sighed George Cyril Wellbeloved, licking his; and in quest of the elixir he had visited in turn the Emsworth Arms, the Wheatsheaf, the Waggoner's Rest, the Beetle and Wedge, the Stitch in Time, the Jolly Cricketers and all the other hostelries at which Market Blandings pointed with so much pride.

But everywhere the story was the same. Barmaids had been given their instructions, potboys warned to be on the alert. They had placed at his disposal ginger beer, ginger ale, sarsaparilla, lime juice and on one occasion milk, but his request for the cup that clears today of past regrets and future fears was met with a firm *nolle prosequi*. Staunch and incorruptible, the barmaids and the potboys refused to serve him with anything that would have interested Omar Khayam, and he had come away parched and saddened.

But it has been well said of pig men as a class that though crushed to earth, they will rise again. You plot and plan and think you have baffled a pig man, but all the while his quick brain had been working, and it has shown him the way out. It was so with George Cyril Wellbeloved. Just when the thought of the Hon. Galahad Threepwood came stealing into his mind, he could not have said, but it did so steal, and it was as though a light had shone upon his darkness. That dull despair gave way to a flaming hope. Glimmering in the distance, he seemed to see the happy ending.

Although during his term of office at Blandings Castle his opportunities of meeting Gally socially had been rather limited, George Cyril knew all about him. Gally, he was aware, was a man with a feeling heart, a man who could be relied upon to look indulgently on such of his fellow men as wanted a gargle and wanted it quick. According to those who knew him best, his whole life since reaching years of what may loosely be called discretion had been devoted to seeing that the other chap did not die of thirst. Would such a man turn his back on even a comparative stranger, if the comparative stranger were in a position to prove by ocular demonstration that his tongue was blackening at the roots? Most unlikely, thought George Cyril Wellbeloved, and if there was even a sporting chance of securing the services of this human drinking fountain, it was his duty, he felt, not to neglect it.

With pig men, to think is to act. Dinner over and his employer safely in his study with his coffee and cigar, he got out his bicycle and started pedalling through the scented summer night.

The welcome he received at the back door of Blandings Castle could in no sense have been termed a gushing one. Beach, informed that there was a gentleman asking for him and finding that the person thus described was a pig man whom he had never liked and who in his opinion smelled to heaven, was at his most formal. He might have been a prominent Christian receiving an unexpected call from one of the troops of Midian.

George Cyril, in sharp contradistinction, was all bounce and breeziness. Unlike most of those who met that godlike man, he stood in no awe of Beach. He held the view, and had voiced it fearlessly many a time in the tap room of the Emsworth Arms, that Beach was an old stuffed shirt.

'Hoy, cocky,' he said, incredible as such a mode of address might seem. 'Where's Mr Galahad?'

Ice formed on the butler's upper slopes.

'Mr Galahad is in the amber drawing-room with the rest of the household,' he replied austerely.

'Then go and hoik him out of it,' said George Cyril Wellbeloved, his splendid spirit unsubdued. 'I want to see him. Tell him it's important.'

2

In stating that Gally was in the amber drawing-room with the rest of the household, Beach had spoken with an imperfect knowledge of the facts. He had been in the amber drawing-room, but he was now just outside it, seated on the terrace with his friend Maudie, and an observer, had one been present, would have received the impression that both he and his companion had much on their minds. In a situation where it might have been expected that reminiscences of the old days would have been flashing merrily to and fro, they had fallen into a silence, busy with their thoughts.

It is possible that there are in the world women of meek and angelic disposition who, deserted by gentlemen friends at the church door, are capable of accepting the betrayal tranquilly, saying to themselves that boys will be boys, but Maudie was not one of them. Hers was a high and mettlesome spirit, and a sense of grievance still burned within her. For years she had been storing up a number of good things which she proposed to say to her faithful lover, should they meet, and it was bitter to think that now, with only three miles separating them, this meeting seemed as far away as ever. Situated as she was, she could hardly ask for the car to drive her over to Matchingham Hall, and she shrank from the thought of walking there in this sultry summer weather, her views on pedestrianism being much the same as those of Sir Gregory Parsloe.

On the premises of Blandings Castle, as of even date, there were to be found stricken souls in large numbers – it would, indeed, have been almost impossible to have thrown a brick without hitting one – and that of Maudie Stubbs, alias Bunbury, came high up on the list.

Gally's moodiness is equally easily explained. With the man Parsloe's cousin closeted daily with the Empress, the man Parsloe's fiancée established in the house and the man Parsloe himself rubbing his hands and singing 'Yo ho ho and a bottle of Slimmo', a consistent cheerfulness on his part was hardly to be expected. Add to this the tragedy which had darkened the lives of Penny Donaldson and this excellent young fellow Vail, and add to that the telephone conversation he had had with Sir Gregory shortly before dinner, and it cannot be wondered at that he was not his usual effervescent self.

How long the silence might have lasted, it is impossible to say. But at this point the spell was broken by the arrival of Lord Emsworth, who came pottering out of the drawing-room with the air of a man looking for somebody. Having observed Maudie making for the terrace, it had seemed to him that here was a capital opportunity of having a quick word with her outside the orbit of his sister Connie's watchful eye. Conditions for such a *tête-à-tête* could scarcely have been more suitable. The moon was riding serenely in the sky, the air was fragrant with the scent of night-blooming flowers, Lord Vosper, who in addition to playing a red-hot game of tennis had a nice tenor voice, was at the piano singing a song with lots of sentimental stomp in it, and what Lord Emsworth felt was that ten minutes of roaming in the gloaming with Maudie would just about top it off.

Ever since his brother Galahad had introduced him to the relict of the late Cedric Stubbs on this same terrace, strange and novel emotions had been stirring in Lord Emsworth's bosom. He was a man who since the death of his wife twenty years ago had made something of a lifework of avoiding women. He could not, of course, hope to avoid them altogether, for women have a nasty way of popping up at unexpected moments, but he was quick on his feet and his policy of suddenly disappearing like a diving duck had had excellent results. It was now pretty generally accepted by his little circle that the ninth Earl of Emsworth was not a ladies' man and that any woman who tried to get a civil word out of him did so at her own risk.

To Maudie, however, he had felt from the start strangely drawn. He admired her looks. Her personality appealed to him. 'Alluring' was the word that suggested itself. When he caught Maudie's eye, it was as though he had caught the eye of a woman who was silently saying 'Come up and see me some time', and this – oddly enough – struck him as an admirable idea. So now he had pottered out on to the terrace in the hope of a pleasant exchange of views with her.

But these things never work out perfectly. Here was the terrace, bathed in moonlight, and here was she, bathed in moonlight, too, but here in addition, he now saw, was his brother Galahad, also bathed in moonlight, and the sight brought a quick 'Oh, ah' to his lips. The presence of a third party chilled his romantic mood.

'Hullo, Clarence,' said Gally. 'How's the boy?'

'Quite, quite,' said Lord Emsworth, and drifted back into the drawing-room like a family spectre disappointed with the room it had been told off to haunt.

Maudie came out of her thoughts.

'Was that Lord Emsworth?' she said, for from the corner of her eye she seemed to have seen something flickering.

'Yes, there he spouted,' said Gally. 'But he buzzed off, mumbling incoherently. Walking in his sleep, probably.'

'He's absent-minded, isn't he?'

'Yes, I think one could fairly call him that. If he has a mind, it is very seldom there. Did I ever tell you the story of Clarence and the Arkwright wedding?'

'I don't think so.'

'Odd. It happened about the time when I was a regular client of yours at the Criterion and I told it to everybody else. I wonder why I discriminated against you. The Arkwrights lived out Bridgnorth way, and their daughter Amelia was getting married, so Clarence tied a knot in his handkerchief to remind him to send the bride's mother a telegram on the happy day.'

'And he forgot?'

'Oh, no, he sent it. "My heartfelt congratulations to you on this joyous occasion," he said.'

'Well, wasn't that all right?'

'It was fine. Couldn't have been improved on. Only the trouble was that in one of his distrait moments he sent it, not to Mrs Arkwright but to another friend of his, a Mrs Cartwright, and her husband had happened to die that morning. Diabetes. Very sad. We were all very sorry about it, but no doubt the telegram cheered her up. Did I ever tell you about Clarence and the salad?'

'No.'

'I don't seem to have told you any of my best stories. It was in the days when he was younger and used to let me take him about London a bit. Well, of course, even then it wasn't easy to get him absolutely shining and glittering in lively society and being the belle of the ball, but he did have one unique gift. He could mix a superb salad. As his public relations man, I played this up on all occasions. When men came to me and said "Tell me, Gally, am I correct in supposing that this brother of yours you're lugging around town is about as outstanding a dumb brick and fathead as ever broke biscuit?" I would reply "To a certain extent, my dear Smith or Jones, or whatever the name might be, the facts are as you state.

Clarence has his limitations as a social ball of fire – except when it comes to mixing salads. You just get him to mix you a salad one of these days." So his fame grew. People would point him out in the streets and say "That's Emsworth, the chap who mixes salads." And came a day when I took him to the Pelican Club, feeling like the impresario of a performing flea on an opening night, and they handed him the lettuce and the tomatoes and the oil and the vinegar and the chives and all the rest of it, and he started in.'

'And made a mess of it?'

'Not at all. He was a sensational success. He had cut his finger that morning and was wearing a finger-stall, and I feared that this might cramp his style, but no, it didn't seem to hamper him a bit. He chopped and mixed and mixed and chopped, with here a drop of oil and there a drop of vinegar, and in due season the salad was prepared in a lordly bowl and those present flung themselves on it like starving wolves.'

'And they liked it?'

'They loved it. They devoured it to the last morsel. There wasn't so much as a shred of lettuce or a solitary chive left in the bowl. And then, when everyone was fawning on Clarence and slapping his back, it was noticed that he was looking disturbed and unhappy. "What's the matter, old man?" I asked. "Is something wrong?" "Oh, no," he said. "Everything is capital, capital . . . only I seem to have lost my finger-stall." That's Clarence. A sterling fellow whom I love as if he were my own brother, which he is, of course, but a little on the dreamy side. I remember my nephew Freddie saying once that if you sent him out to buy apples, he would come back with an elephant, and there was considerable justice in the remark. He dodders. He goes off into trances. And you're seeing him at his worst these days, for he has much on his mind. He has a speech to make tomorrow which involves a stiff collar and a top hat, and he's naturally worried about his pig and the machinations of the man Parsloe. The shadow of Parsloe broods over him like a London fog. You've seen that dark girl with the serpentine figure who's just blown in here?'

'Miss Salt?'

'That's the one. Parsloe's fiancée. Makes you think a bit, eh? They're closing in on us, old girl, closing in on us. The iron ring is narrowing. It won't be long now ... Oh, dash it, here comes someone else,' said Gally, clicking his tongue. 'The curse of Blandings Castle, no privacy. Oh, no, it's all right. I think it's Penny.'

It was Penny. In the amber drawing-room Lord Vosper, having finished his torch song, had started another with even more heartbreak to the cubic inch, and it had been too much for the poor girl. Rising with a stifled sob, she had made a dive for the French windows and was now coming towards them, looking like Ophelia.

'Hullo, there,' said Gally. 'Come and join the party. Nice night.'

Penny sank into a chair.

'Is it?' she said listlessly.

'Come, come,' said Gally. 'Tails up, my child. You mustn't let yourself get downhearted. There's too much defeatism in this joint. I've been meaning to speak to you about that, Maudie. I've noticed in you, too, a dropping of the spirits. When I told you that story of Clarence and the salad, which should have had you rolling in the aisle, gasping with merriment, you were gazing at me mournfully all the time. What's the matter? Don't you like it here?'

Maudie sighed. Blandings Castle had been a place of enchantment to her.

'It's wonderful. But I feel I'm not doing anything to help. I'm about as much use as a cold in the head.'

'Come, come.'

'It's true. Uncle Sebastian —'

'Not so loud. Castles have ears.'

'Uncle Sebastian,' Maudie went on, lowering her voice, 'was all wrong when he told you about me. He seems to have given you the idea that I was a sort of Sherlock Holmes or something. All I've done since Cedric passed on has been to kind of look after the agency — answer letters and send out the bills and sort of keep an eye on things. I don't do any of the detective work. I wouldn't know how to begin. That's all done by Mr North and Mr Connor and Mr Fauntleroy. I mean, suppose you wanted divorce evidence or something, you would come and see me, and I'd say Okay, we'll attend to it and it'll be so much as a retainer and so much per week and all that, but then I would hand everything over to Mr Fauntleroy and Mr Connor and Mr North. I don't see any point in my staying on here.'

Gally patted her hand.

'Of course you must stay, my dear child. Your moral support is invaluable. And one of these days you're sure to come up with some terrific idea which will solve all our difficulties. A brainy girl like you? Don't tell me. I shouldn't be surprised if there wasn't one fermenting inside you at this very moment.'

'Well, as a matter of fact –'

'I told you so.'

'I was just going to suggest something when Miss Donaldson came along.'

'You may speak freely before Miss Donaldson, who has been associated with me in a number of my cases.'

Maudie looked about her cautiously. They were alone and unobserved. In the drawing-room Lord Vosper was now singing something so full – judging by the sound – of anguish that they were fortunate in not being able to distinguish the words. Even the melody was affecting Penny unpleasantly.

'What I thought was this. Why don't you steal Tubby's old pig?'

'What!'

A momentary fear that she had said something unladylike flitted through Maudie's mind, but she dismissed it. She had known Gally too long to suppose that he was capable of being shocked.

'Well, he seems to be doing everything he can to queer your old pig, so why shouldn't you start? Attack . . . what's that thing you hear people say?'

'Attack is the best form of defence?'

'That's right. If I were you, I'd sneak over to his house and wait till there was nobody around –'

Gally patted her hand again.

'What you propose, my dear Maudie,' he said, 'would, of course, be the ideal solution, and the suggestion strengthens the high opinion I had already formed of your resource and intelligence. But there are obstacles in the way. The catch is that there would be somebody around.'

'How do you know that?'

'I have it from an authoritative source. Just before dinner I was called to the telephone. It was young Parsloe. He had rung me up, he said, to warn me that if I was contemplating any off-colour work, I would do well to think twice, because he had provided his pig man, Wellbeloved, with a stout shot-gun and Wellbeloved had a roving commission to blaze away with it at all intruders. So there the matter rests. I don't know how accurate a marksman the blighter is, but I certainly don't propose to ascertain by personal inquiry. It would be foreign to my policy to have to take all my meals standing up for the next few weeks because George Cyril Wellbeloved had planted a charge of small shot in my . . . well, that is neither here nor there. As I was saying, with the broad, general idea of pinching Parsloe's pig I am wholly in sympathy. We could put it in that gamekeeper's shack in the west wood and keep it incommunicado there indefinitely. But things being as they are –'

Maudie nodded.

'I see. Then there's nothing to be done?'

'Nothing, I'm afraid, so long as George Cyril Wellbeloved –'

He broke off. The voice of Sebastian Beach had spoken at his elbow, causing him to leap like a lamb in springtime. Absorbed in his remarks, he had had no inkling that there were butlers present.

'You made me bite my tongue, Beach,' he said reproachfully.

'I am sorry, Mr Galahad. I should have coughed.'

'Or tooted your horn. What is it?'

'A person has called, asking to see you, sir. The man Wellbeloved, Mr Galahad.'

'Wellbeloved?' Gally stiffened formidably. 'You mean that this renegade pig man, this latter-day Benedict Arnold, this degraded specimen of pond life, is *here*?'

'I left him in my pantry, sir. He expressed himself as very desirous of having a word with you. The matter, he said, was one of urgency.'

An idea struck Gally. He slapped his forehead. 'My God! Perhaps he has come to betray Parsloe. Perhaps he wants to change sides again. Like Long John Silver. Did you ever read *Treasure Island*, Beach?'

'No, sir.'

'Ass! Or do you think he is here as a spy? No,' said Gally, having mused a moment, 'it can't be that, or why does he want to see me? Would a spy in the pay of Napoleon Bonaparte have come to the British camp before the battle of Waterloo, asking for a word with the Duke of Wellington? I doubt it. Well, I must certainly hear what he has to say. Lead on, Beach, lead on.'

'If you will step this way, Mr Galahad.'

The departure of the most gifted conversationalist of the little group caused another of those long silences. Maudie was a woman who seldom spoke unless spoken to, and any disposition Penny might have had towards small talk was checked by the wailing of Lord Vosper's reedy tenor. He was now singing something about 'You're breaking my heart, we're drifting apart, as I knew at the start it would be,' and no girl who is headed for the altar with the wrong man can prattle when she hears that sort of thing.

Once again it was Lord Emsworth who broke the spell. Hopeful that by now his brother Galahad might have removed himself, he came out of the drawing-room to have another try for that *tête-à-tête*, only to discover that though the terrace was free from Galahads, it had become all stocked up with Penny Donaldsons. He paused, and said 'Er'.

There was another longish silence.

'The moon,' said Lord Emsworth, indicating it.

'Yes,' said Maudie.

'Bright,' said Lord Emsworth, paying it a well-deserved tribute.

'Yes,' said Maudie.

'Very bright,' said Lord Emsworth. 'Oh, very, very bright,' and seemed for a moment about to converse with easy fluency. But inspiration failed him, and with a 'Quite, quite. Capital', he disappeared again.

Penny regarded his retreating back with a listless eye.

'Do you think he's had a couple?' she asked.

It was precisely what had suggested itself to Maudie. In her Criterion days she had encountered many a customer who had behaved in just such a manner, and her seasoned eye could detect little difference between her host and the scores of exuberant young men whom she had seen in the old days conducted gently from her bar with the bouncer's hand caressing their elbow.

Then a more charitable view supervened.

'Of course, he's very absent-minded.'

'Yes, I believe he is.'

'Gally was saying so only just now.'

'Oh, yes?'

Maudie hesitated.

'Talking of Gally,' she said, 'he was telling me yesterday that you –'

'Yes?'

'He was telling me about you. He said you had gone and got engaged to the wrong young man.'

'Quite true.'

Maudie felt relieved. Like all women, she took a passionate interest in the love lives of other women and was longing for a cosy talk about Penny's and she feared that she might have spoken out of turn and given offence.

'Well, that's how it goes,' she said. 'That happened to me once. Someone rang me up on the telephone one morning and said "Hoy!", and I said "Yes?", and he said "This is Tubby", and I said "Hullo, Tubby", and he said "Hullo, Maudie – I say, will you marry me?", and I said "Rather, of course I will", because I was very much in love with him at the time and quite pleased that he had mentioned it. And it was only after we had made all the plans for the honeymoon that I found it wasn't the Tubby I'd thought it was, but another Tubby whom I didn't like at all. And there I was, engaged to him. I often laugh when I think of it.'

'What did you do?'

'Oh, I gave him the bird. I told him to go fry an egg.'

'Lucky you could.'

'Why, any girl can break off an engagement, can't they?'

'I can't.'

'Why not?'

'Because if I did, Lady Constance would write and tell Father, and Father would have me shipped back to America on the next boat, and I would never see Jerry again. He can't keep coming over to America with ocean liners charging the earth, the way they do.'

'I see what you mean. You would be sundered by the seas.'

'Sundered like nobody's business.'

'Well, that *is* a nice bit of box fruit, isn't it?'

Penny was agreeing that the expression 'A nice bit of box fruit' unquestionably summed up the position of affairs, when out came Lord Emsworth again. For centuries the Emsworths had been

noted for their dogged courage, and this time he was resolved that
Operation Maudie should be carried through.

'Er,' said Lord Emsworth.

'Er, Mrs Bunbury,' said Lord Emsworth.

'Er, Mrs Bunbury, I – ah – I am just going down to have a look
at the Empress,' said Lord Emsworth. 'I wonder if you would care
to join me?'

'I'd love to,' said Maudie.

'Capital, capital,' said Lord Emsworth. 'Capital, capital, capital,
capital.'

They had scarcely gone, when there was a patter of feet and Gally
appeared.

Even in the uncertain light cast by the moon it was easy to see
that Gally was in radiant spirits. His eyes were sparkling, his whole
demeanour that of a man who has found the blue bird. Whatever
had passed between him and George Cyril Wellbeloved, it was plain
that it had acted on him like a tonic.

His opening words left no room for doubt on this point.

'I do believe in fairies!' he said. 'There *is* a Santa Claus! Penny, do
you know what?'

'What?'

'Listen attentively. This gargoyle Wellbeloved has been pouring
out his heart to me. It appears that Parsloe, wishing to keep the
fellow alert and on his toes, ruthlessly ordered him to go on the
wagon, and furthermore gave instructions to all the pubs in Market
Blandings that they weren't to serve him. Did this blot the sunshine
from Wellbeloved's life, you ask? It did. The poor chap was in
despair. Then he remembered that I was a man with a feeling heart,
and he came over here to ask me to do something about it.'

'You mean plead with Parsloe?'

'No, no, no. You can't plead with a hard nut like Parsloe. The
man has no bowels of compassion. He wanted me to give him a
drink. You see the tremendous significance of this?'

'No.'

'You disappoint me. I'd have thought you would have grasped it
in an instant. Why, dash it, it means that the coast is clear. The menace
of that shot-gun has ceased to function. I have instructed Beach to
lush this Wellbeloved up in his pantry, and he will continue to lush

him up till the stuff comes trickling out of the top of his head, while I, taking the car, nip over to Parsloe's lair and remove his pig to that shack in the west wood of which I spoke. Any questions?'

'Yes,' said Penny. 'Isn't Parsloe's pig pretty big?'

'Enormous. It bestrides the narrow world like a Colossus.'

'Then how are you going to remove it?'

'My dear child, pigs have rings through their noses. This facilitates pulling and hauling.'

'You'll never be able to do it.'

'What do you mean, I'll never be able to do it? Of course I'll be able to do it. When Puffy Benger and I stole old Wivenhoe's pig the night of the Bachelors' Ball at Hammer's Easton, we had to get it up three flights of stairs before we could put it in Plug Basham's bedroom, and we found the task an absurdly easy one. A little child could have led it. Why, my nephew Ronald, from motives which I have not the leisure to go into now, once stole the Empress, and I resent the suggestion that I am incapable of performing a task within the scope of a young poop like Ronnie Fish. Never be able to do it, forsooth!' said Gally, burning with honest indignation. 'I can do it on my head. I can do it blindfolded, with one arm tied behind me. So if you wish to be in this, Penny Donaldson, get moving. Come, Watson, come. The game is afoot!'

3

It was some ten minutes later that Gloria Salt, who had been sitting silent and pensive in the amber drawing-room, rose from her chair and said that if Lady Constance didn't mind, she would say good night. One or two things to attend to before turning in, she explained, and glided out.

For a long instant after she had left, Lord Vosper, who had gallantly opened the door for her, stood motionless, the handle in his hand, a strange light in his eyes. The sound of her voice, the scent of her perfume, the sight of her so near to him that he could have slapped her between the shoulder-blades – not that he would have, of course – had affected him powerfully. Standing there, he was wrestling with an almost overmastering urge to dash after her and fold her in his arms and beg her to let bygones be bygones.

It is too often the way. A girl whom we have set on a pedestal calls us an overbearing louse, and love dies. Good-bye to all that, we say to ourselves, wondering what we could ever have seen in her. And then she suddenly pops up out of a trap at the house where we are staying, and before we can say 'What ho!' love has sprung from the obituary column and is working away at the old stand more briskly than ever.

Lord Vosper became calmer. What a writer of radio drama would have called the moment of madness, sheer madness, passed and Reason returned to her throne. He rebuked himself for having allowed his thoughts to wander in such a dubious direction. He had received his early education at Harrow, and Old Harrovians, he reminded himself, when they have plighted their troth to Girl A, do not go about folding Girl B in their arms. Old Etonians, yes. Old Rugbeians, possibly. But not Old Harrovians. With a sigh and a gesture of resignation he closed the door and returned to the piano. Resuming his seat on the music stool, he began to sing once more.

'The sun is dark (*tiddle-om*) . . . The skies are grey (*tiddle-om*) . . . since my sweetie (*pom*) . . . went away,' sang Orlo Vosper, and Gloria Salt, in her bedroom above, clenched her hands as the words came floating in through the open window and stared before her with unseeing eyes.

Youth, according to most authorities, is the season for gaiety and happiness, but one glance at this girl would have been enough to show that nobody was likely to sell that idea to her. Her lovely face was twisted with pain, her dark eyes dull with anguish. If she had appeared, looking as she was looking now, in one of the old silent films, there would have been flashed on the screen some such caption as:

BUT CAME A DAY WHEN REMORSE GNAWED GLORIA SALT. THINK-ING OF WHAT MIGHT HAVE BEEN HER PROUD HEART ACHES.

And such a caption would have been roughly correct.

To Gloria Salt, as well as to Lord Vosper, the past few days had been days of severe strain, filling her with emotions so violent that she had become more like a volcano than a girl with a handicap of six at St Andrews. Arriving at Blandings Castle and finding herself confronted first crack out of the box by a man whom in that very instant she realized that she loved more passionately than ever, she had received a severe shock. Nor was the turmoil in her soul in any way lessened by the discovery that, since last heard of, he had gone and got engaged to that saffron-haired midget one saw bobbing about the place, answering, she understood, to the name of Penelope Donaldson.

Forced, this afternoon, to play mixed doubles with Jerry Vail against her lost lover, partnered by the midget, she had drained the bitter cup, the ordeal being rendered still more testing by the fact that the midget, displaying unexpected form at the net, had kept killing her warmest returns. And tonight she had been listening to Orlo Vosper's singing.

It was, in short, the last moment when a man with as many chins as Sir Gregory Parsloe should have thrust himself on her notice. And this he now unfortunately did. We have said that Gloria Salt's eyes, as she stared before her, were unseeing, but at this juncture the mists cleared and they began to focus. And the first thing they saw was the photograph of Sir Gregory on the dressing-table.

Strolling through the jungles of Brazil, the traveller sometimes sees a barefoot native halt with a look of horror, his body rigid except for a faint vibration of the toes. He has seen a scorpion in his path. It was with just such a look of horror that Gloria gazed at the photograph of Sir Gregory Parsloe. Very imprudently, he had had himself taken side face and, eyeing those chins, she winced and caught her breath sharply. She took another look, and her mind was made up. She had thought it could be done, but she saw now that it could not be done. There are shots which are on the board, and shots which are not. It might be that some day some girl, veiled in white, would stand at the altar rails beside this vast expanse of Baronet while the organ played 'The Voice That Breathed O'er Eden', but that girl would not be G. Salt.

With a sudden, impulsive movement she snatched the photograph from its frame and with a quick flick of the wrist sent it skimming through the open window. Then, hurrying to the desk, she took pen and paper and began to write.

Half an hour later Sebastian Beach, crossing the hall, heard his name spoken and, turning, saw that what had come into his life was a sinuous form clad in some clinging material which accentuated rather than hid its graceful outlines.

'Miss?' he said.

This, he knew, was the fiancée of the Professor Moriarty of Matchingham Hall and as such to be viewed with concern and apprehension, but twenty years of butling had trained him to wear the mask, and there was nothing in his manner to suggest that he was feeling like a nervous character in a Gerald Vail story trapped in a ruined mill by one-eyed Chinamen.

'I want this note taken to Sir Gregory Parsloe,' said Gloria. 'Could someone go over with it in the morning?'

Sinister, felt Beach, very sinister. Despatches, probably in code. But he replied with his customary courtesy.

'The communication can be delivered tonight, miss. Sir Gregory's pig man is at this moment in my pantry. I will entrust it to his care.'

'Thank you, Beach.'

'Not at all, miss. The individual will be leaving shortly on his bicycle.'

If, thought Beach, he is able to ride a bicycle with all that stuff in him. He moved ponderously off. He was on his way to the cellar for a bottle of Bollinger. Mr Galahad's instructions had been that in the matter of entertaining their guest the sky was to be regarded as the limit, and George Cyril Wellbeloved had expressed a desire for that beverage. He had heard it mentioned, he said, by Sir Gregory's butler, his friend Herbert Binstead, and had often wondered what it was and wished he could have a pop at it.

4

The process of going to have a look at the Empress was always, when you did it in Lord Emsworth's company, a lengthy one, and nearly forty minutes elapsed before Maudie and her host returned to the terrace.

Lord Emsworth had employed these forty minutes shrewdly and well. Playing on his companion's womanly sympathy by telling her of the agonies he was enduring, having to make this dashed speech to these dashed Shropshire, Herefordshire, and South Wales Pig-Breeders chaps, he had won from her a promise that she would accompany him next day and see him through his ordeal. It made such a difference to someone, he explained, if someone had someone

someone could sort of lean on at times like this, and Maudie said she quite understood. They would have to make a pretty early start, he warned her, because Shropshire, Herefordshire, and South Wales Pig-Breeders were assembling in Wolverhampton of all ghastly places, and Maudie said she liked early starts and spoke of seeing Wolverhampton as if it had been a lifelong dream of hers. In short, by the time they reached the terrace, their relations were practically those of Tristan and Isolde.

They found the terrace empty, for Penny had accepted Gally's invitation to go off with him in the car. She might be heartbroken, but she was not so heartbroken as to hold herself aloof from an enterprise which involved stealing pigs. Except for the winged creatures of the night which haunt English country house terraces when the shadows have fallen, nothing was to be seen except a small oblong object lying in the fairway. It looked like a photograph, and Lord Emsworth, picking it up, found that it was a photograph.

'God bless my soul!' he said. 'How very peculiar.'

'What is it?' asked Maudie.

'It is a photograph of a neighbour of mine, a Sir Gregory Parsloe. Lives out Matchingham way. Somebody must have dropped it out of the window. Though what anyone would want with a photograph of Sir Gregory Parsloe I cannot understand,' said Lord Emsworth, marvelling at the eccentric tastes of his fellow men.

Maudie took it from him, and gazed at it in silence. And as her eyes fell, for the first time in ten years, upon those once familiar features, her bosom seethed with feelings too deep for utterance. Like Gloria Salt, she had become a volcano.

Her once coherent thought, apart from the reflexion that this old love of hers had put on a bit of weight since she had seen him last, was that, even if it meant a three-mile walk there and a three-mile walk back, she intended to go to Matchingham Hall at the earliest opportunity and tell Tubby Parsloe what she thought of him.

5

Beach need have had no anxiety as to his guest's ability to negotiate without disaster the three miles that separated him from home. George Cyril Wellbeloved, even when as brilliantly illuminated as he was when he started his journey, did not fall off bicycles. He might swoop from side to side of the road like a swallow in pursuit of mayfly, but the old skill was all there and he remained in the saddle. In due season he arrived at the back door of Matchingham Hall, singing 'When Irish Eyes Are Smiling' in a pleasant light baritone, and proceeded to Sir Gregory's study to deliver Gloria Salt's note. It would have been far more fitting, of course, for him to have given it to Binstead, to be taken to the presence on a silver salver, but he was in merry mood and welcomed this opportunity of a chat with his employer.

The latter was reading a cookery book as he entered. Some hold the view that a sorrow's crown of sorrow is remembering happier things, but Sir Gregory found that it gave him a melancholy pleasure to be wafted back into the golden past by perusing the details of the sort of dishes where you start off with a dozen eggs and use plenty of suet for the pastry. At the moment he was deep in the chapter about Chocolate Soufflé. And he had just got to the part where the heroine takes two tablespoonfuls of butter and three ounces of Sunshine Sauce and was wondering how it all came out in the end, when he had a feeling that the air in the room had become a little close and, looking up, saw that he had a visitor.

'What the devil are you doing here?' was his kindly greeting, and George Cyril Wellbeloved, smiling a pebble-beached smile of indescribable suavity, replied that he had come to bring him a note. By a hair's breadth he avoided calling Sir Gregory 'cocky', but only by a hair's breadth, and the other gave him one of those keen looks of his.

'You've been drinking!' said Sir Gregory, an able diagnostician.

George Cyril Wellbeloved was amazed.

'Drinking, sir? Me, sir? No, sir. Where would I get a drink, sir?'

'You're as tight as an owl.'

This was a wholly unjustified slur on a most respectable breed of bird, for owls are as abstemious as the most bigoted temperance advocate could wish, and at another time George Cyril Wellbeloved might have been tempted to take up the cudgels on their behalf. But his employer's charge had cut him to the quick, and he sank into a chair and brushed a tear from his eye.

'Sir,' he said, 'you will regret those words, regret 'em on your dying bed you will. On that last awful day, when we are all called to render account before the judgement seat, you'll be sorry you spoke so harsh. I'm not angry – just terribly, terribly hurt . . .'

'Stop drivelling. What's all this about a note? Who from?'

'That I am unable to tell you, sir, not knowing. It was entrusted to me by Butsch the beetler at Blandings Castle. Or, rather,' said George Cyril Wellbeloved, for he liked to get these things right, 'by Beet the bushler –'

'And might I ask what you were doing at Blandings Castle?'

George Cyril, though intoxicated, was able to dodge that one.

'I was revisiting the scenes of the past, sir. Nos-something, they call it. I spent many a happy year at Blandings Castle, and I wanted to see what the old place looked like. I don't know if you are familiar with the poem that begins "How dear to this heart are the scenes of my childhood, when fond recollection presents them to view." I learned it at Sunday school. It goes on about an old oaken bucket.'

There was something in the manner in which Sir Gregory damned and blasted not only his companion but the latter's Sunday school and the poems he had learned there that wounded the sensitive pig man afresh. He relapsed into a hurt silence, and Sir Gregory took the letter. He opened it, and the next moment a startled cry was echoing through the room.

'Bad news, old man?' asked George Cyril sympathetically, rising and leaning negligently on the arm of his host's chair.

Sir Gregory had sprung to the telephone and was busy getting the number of Blandings Castle.

'Beach? . . . This is Sir Gregory Parsloe . . . Never mind whether it's a good evening or not. I want to speak to Miss Salt . . . Eh? . . . I don't care if she has retired to her room. Go and fetch her. Tell her I want to speak to her about her letter –'

'Let *me* see that letter,' said George Cyril Wellbeloved, curtly.

He twitched it out of Sir Gregory's hand and with a little difficulty, for his eyes for some reason were not at their best tonight, spelled his way through it with now a 'Humph' and anon a 'Tut, tut', while Sir Gregory at the telephone continued his unsuccessful efforts to establish communication with Miss Salt.

'I tell you . . . Oh, hell!' shouted Sir Gregory, and replaced the receiver with a bang.

George Cyril Wellbeloved laid down the letter.

'And now,' he said, 'I suppose you're waiting to hear what *I* think of all this.'

Sir Gregory, aware for the first time that his private correspondence had been read by a pig man, and a smelly pig man at that, was able for the moment merely to stare with bulging eyes, and George Cyril proceeded.

'Well, I'll tell you. It's the bird all right. What you've been doing to bruise that gentle heart, I don't know. That is a matter between you and your own conscience. But there's no two questions about it, she's given you the raspberry. If you've ordered your trousseau, cocky, cancel it.'

An animal howl burst from Sir Gregory Parsloe.

'What the devil do you mean by reading my letters? Get out! You're sacked!'

George Cyril's eyebrows rose.

'Did I hear you employ the word "sacked"?'

'Yes, you did. Get out of here, you foul blot, and be off the place first thing tomorrow.'

It is at moments like this that you catch a pig man at his best. Nothing could have been more impressive in its quiet dignity than George Cyril Wellbeloved's manner as he spoke.

'Very good,' he said. 'Have it your own way.' He paused on the verge of trying to say 'It's wholly immaterial to me,' but wiser counsels prevailed and he substituted the more prudent 'Okey doke'. 'The Alligural Show'll be along at any minute now, and if you want to dispense with my services and see your ruddy pig fobbed off with an hon. mention, do so. But drop the pilot now, Sir Gregory Parsloe, and Queener Mash'n hasn't a hope. Not a nope,' said George Cyril Wellbeloved, and rested his case.

In these days when changes in the public taste have led to the passing from the theatre of the old-fashioned melodrama, it is not often that one sees a baffled Baronet. But anyone who had chanced to glance in at the window of Sir Gregory Parsloe's study now would have been able to enjoy that spectacle. In the old melodramas the baffled Baronet used to grab at his moustache and twirl it. Sir Gregory, having no moustache, was unable to do this, but in every other respect he followed tradition.

He recognized the truth of this man's words. Pigs are temperamental. With them, things have to be just so. Remove the custodian to whose society they have become accustomed and substitute a stranger, and they refuse their meals and pine away. Incredible as it seemed to Sir Gregory that a level-headed pig could detect charm in George Cyril Wellbeloved, he knew that it was so, and when he took out his handkerchief and blew his nose, that fluttering handkerchief was the white flag.

'We'll talk about it tomorrow,' he said. 'Go away and sleep it off,' he added, a little offensively, and George Cyril Wellbeloved zigzagged to the door and left him to his thoughts.

Whether it was the gipsy in him, calling him out into the great open spaces, or merely a desire to cool a head heated almost to bursting point by his recent excesses, one cannot say. But now, zigzagging from the study and zigzagging to the front door, George Cyril Wellbeloved zigzagged out into the grounds of Matchingham Hall and presently found himself at Queen of Matchingham's sty.

Grasping the rail, he chirruped. After that unpleasant scene with his employer, a few words with a personal friend like Queen of Matchingham were just what he needed to restore his composure.

Usually he had but to stand here and start chirruping, and the first chirrup brought the noble animal out at a gallop, all eagerness for the feast of reason and flow of soul. But now all was silence. Not a movement could be heard from within the shed where the Queen retired for the night. He chirruped again. No response. A little annoyed at this absence of the get-together spirit, he climbed the rail, not without difficulty, and peered in at the entrance of the shed. The next moment he had uttered a wordless gasp. If that gasp had had words, those words would have been 'Gone! Gone without a cry!' For the outstanding feature of the interior of that shed was its complete freedom from pigs of any description.

Nothing is more sobering than a sudden, severe shock. An instant before, George Cyril Wellbeloved had been a jovial roisterer, Bollinger swishing about inside him and the vine leaves in his hair. An instant later, it was as though he had spent the evening drinking the lime juice they had tried to push off on him at the Beetle and Wedge or the milk with which he had been insulted at the Jolly Cricketers.

Bravely and forcefully though George Cyril had spoken to Sir Gregory Parsloe in their recent interview when the subject of the sack had come up, his words had been dictated by the beer, whisky, gin, and champagne surging in his interior. Now that they had withdrawn their support, he quailed as he thought of what must befall when Sir Gregory discovered that he was a pig short. The last thing he desired was to lose his excellent position.

How long he stood there, leaning against the empty sty, he would not have been able to say. But after an extended period of limp stupefaction life slowly returned to his drooping limbs. His face pale and drawn, he tottered to the house and made for the butler's pantry. There are moments when a fellow needs a friend, and his best friend on the premises of Matchingham Hall was Herbert Binstead.

6

When a man has gone about Market Blandings offering five to one on his employer's pig and, having booked a number of bets at those odds with the younger sporting set, learns that the pig has vanished like a Cheshire cat, it is excusable for him to show a little emotion. Binstead, who was reading the morning paper when George Cyril arrived with the bad news, tore it in half with a convulsive jerk and leaped from his chair as if a red-hot skewer had come through its seat.

'Pinched?' he gasped.

'R.,' said George Cyril, and added, prefacing the latter's name with some rather regrettable adjectives, that this was the work of the Hon. Galahad Threepwood. He mentioned some of the things, mostly of a crudely surgical nature, which, if given a free hand, he would have liked to do to that ingenious old gentleman.

Having said all he could think of on the spur of the moment with reference to Gally, he paused and looked at Herbert Binstead, not exactly confidently but with a faint touch of hope. It might be, he felt, that the other would have something to suggest. Binstead was one of those fox-faced, quick-witted young men who generally have something to suggest.

His trust had not been misplaced. A considerable time elapsed before his companion was able to point the way, but eventually a sudden gleam in his eye showed that he had received the necessary inspiration.

'Look,' said Binstead. 'Do you know where this pig of old Emsworth's is?'

George Cyril said the Empress was at Blandings Castle, and Binstead clicked his tongue impatiently.

'Whereabouts at Blandings Castle?'

'Down by the kitchen garden.'

'And she knows you?'

'Of course she knows me. I looked after her for a year or more.'

'So if you went and snitched her, she wouldn't make a fuss about it?'

'Coo!' said George Cyril, stunned as the brilliancy of the idea hit him. He had known all along, he told himself, that good old Herb would be equal to the emergency.

'She would let you take her?'

'Like a lamb,' said George Cyril. 'Without so much as a grunt.'

Binstead was now the big executive, the man who gets things done.

'Then come along,' he said. 'We can sneak the car from the garage. We'll load her in at the back.'

George Cyril Wellbeloved expelled a deep breath. The outlook was still a little dark, but one major point had been established. When on the morrow Sir Gregory Parsloe came to the sty for his morning visit of inspection, he was going to find a pig in it.

Chapter 6

The following day dawned bright and clear. The skies were blue, the birds twittered, all Nature smiled. But Nature's example was not followed by Lord Emsworth. Apart from the galling necessity of having to put on a stiff collar and a top hat and make the early start of which he had spoken, he had caught a cold. Sneezes and snuffles punctuated the unmanly complaints with which he damped all spirits at the breakfast table. Even the thought of having Maudie at his side seemed to do little to alleviate his gloom.

They got him off eventually, though Lady Constance had to exercise the full force of her personality to stop him going down to take a last farewell of the Empress, and Gally was restoring himself with a cigar on the terrace, when he observed Lord Vosper approaching. It seemed to be Lord Vosper's wish to have speech with him.

And this was odd, for their relations had never been intimate. There was little in the characters of the two that could serve as a common meeting-ground. Orlo Vosper, who was an earnest young man with political ambitions, given, when not slamming them back over the net, to reading white papers and studying social conditions, thought Gally frivolous; and Gally thought Orlo Vosper, as he thought most of his juniors in these degenerate days, a bit of a poop and not at all the sort of fellow he would have cared to take into the old Pelican Club.

But though a man one would have hesitated to introduce to Fruity Biffen, Plug Basham and the rest of the boys at the Pelican, Orlo Vosper belonged to the human race, and all members of the human race were to Gally a potential audience for his stories. It was possible, he felt, that the young man had not heard the one about the duke, the bottle of champagne and the female contortionist, so he welcomed him now with a cordial wave of his cigar.

'Nice day,' he said. 'Going to be hotter than ever. Well, we got old Clarence off.'

'That's right.'

'Never an easy task. Launching Clarence on one of these expeditions is like launching a battleship. I sometimes feel we ought to break a bottle of champagne over his head. Arising from that, have you heard the one about the duke, the bottle of champagne and the female contortionist?'

'No,' said Lord Vosper. 'Have you any smelling salts on you?'

Gally blinked. He found himself unable to follow the other's train of thought.

'Smelling salts?'

'That's right.'

'I'm sorry,' said Gally. 'I seem to have come out without mine this morning. Careless. What do you want smelling salts for?'

'I understand one uses them when women have hysterics.'

'Hysterics?'

'That's right.'

'Who's having hysterics?'

'That large girl in the trousers. Looks after the pigs.'

'Simmons?'

'Is that the name?'

'Monica Simmons, the pride of Roedean. Is she having hysterics?'

'That's right.'

'Why is she having hysterics?'

Lord Vosper seemed glad that his companion had put that question.

'Ah,' he said, 'that's what I asked myself. And, what's more, I asked her. I happened to be down in the vicinity of the pig bin just now and found her there, and it seemed to me rather peculiar that she should be laughing and crying and wringing her hands and all that, so I put it to her straight. "Is something the matter?" I said.'

'Came right to the point, didn't you? And was there?'

'Yes, as I had suspected from the outset, there was. She was a bit incoherent at first, gasping and gurgling and calling on the name of her Maker and so forth, but the gist gradually emerged. She had had a bereavement. It appears that that pig of Lord Emsworth's, the one they call the Empress, is missing.'

At any other moment Gally would have said 'On how many cylinders?', for he liked his joke of a morning, but these devastating words put whimsical comedy out of the question. It was as though he had been hit over the head with a blunt instrument. He stood yammering speechlessly, and Lord Vosper thought his emotion did him credit.

'Bad show, what?' he said. 'One needs smelling salts.'

Gally spoke in a low, grating voice.

'You mean the Empress isn't there? She's gone?'

'That's right. Gone with the wind. Or so this Simmons tells me. According to the Simmons, her room was empty and her bed had not been slept in. The pig's bed, I mean, not the Simmons's. I know nothing of the Simmons's bed. For all I've heard to the contrary, it was slept in like billy-o. The point I am making –'

He would have proceeded to elucidate the matter further, rendering it clear to the meanest intelligence, but it would have meant soliloquizing, for Gally had left him. His dapper form was flashing along the terrace, and now it disappeared from view, moving rapidly.

'Odd,' thought Lord Vosper. 'Most extraordinary.'

He went off to see if Lady Constance had smelling salts. He was convinced that in some way smelling salts ought to enter into the thing.

2

Over at Matchingham Hall, Sir Gregory Parsloe was in his study doing *The Times* crossword puzzle, his brow wrinkled as he tried to think what a word in three letters, beginning with E and signifying a large Australian bird, could possibly be. He liked crossword puzzles, but was not very expert at them. Anything more abstruse than the Sun God Ra generally had him baffled.

To those who recall his overnight anguish, it may seem odd that this jilted lover should have been occupying himself with large Australian birds on the morning after the shattering of his romance. But British Baronets, like British pig men, are resilient. They rise on stepping-stones of their dead selves to higher things and are quick to discern the silver lining in the clouds. A night's sleep had done wonders for the Squire of Matchingham. We left him a broken man. We find him now mended, in fact practically as good as new.

When a man of Sir Gregory's age and temperament is informed by his prospective bride shortly before the date fixed for their union that she has made other plans and that there will be no wedding bells for him, he is naturally annoyed, but his chagrin is never so deep or so enduring as would be that of someone like Romeo in similar circumstances. Passion, as it is understood by the Romeos, seldom touches the Sir Gregory Parsloes of this world. What passes for love with them is really not much more than a tepid preference. The poet Berlin, seeking material for another 'What'll I do?' would have had to go elsewhere for inspiration, if he had come looking for it from Sir Gregory Parsloe.

Sir Gregory was mildly fond of Gloria Salt, and had been on the whole rather attracted by the idea of marrying her, but it had not taken him long to see that there was a lot to be said in favour of the celibate life. What was enabling him to bear his loss with such fortitude was the realization that, now that she had gone and broken off the dashed engagement, there was no longer any need for all that bally dieting and exercising nonsense. Once more he was the master of his fate, the captain of his soul, and if he felt like widening his waistline, could jolly well widen it, and no kick coming from any quarter. For days he had been yearning for beer with an almost Wellbelovedian intensity, and he was now in a position to yield to the craving. A tankard stood beside him at this very moment, and in the manner in which he raised it to his lips there was something gay and swashbuckling. A woman is only a woman, he seemed to be saying, but a frothing pint is a drink.

And so, even more so, are two frothing pints. He pressed the bell, and Binstead appeared.

'Hey!' said Sir Gregory. 'Another of those.'

'Very good, sir.'

'Hey!' said Sir Gregory, when a few minutes later the butler returned with the life-giving fluid. He had just remembered something. 'Where did you put that Slimmo stuff?' he asked.

'I placed it in the store-room cupboard, sir. Should I fetch a bottle, sir?'

'No. I don't want . . . I've heard from my distant connexion, and he doesn't want the stuff. Pour it down the sink.'

'Or should I return it to the chemist, sir? He would possibly be willing to refund the money.'

'All right. Do that, if you like. If you can get anything out of him, you can keep it.'

'Thank you very much, sir,' said Binstead. There might not be much in the transaction, but there ought to be something. And every little bit added to what you've got makes just a little bit more.

It was now approaching the hour when it was Sir Gregory's custom to go and pay his respects to Queen of Matchingham, and as he had finished his beer and saw no prospect of ever solving the mystery of that large Australian bird, he rose, lit a fresh cigar with a debonair flourish and made his way to the sty.

The first thing he beheld on arrival was George Cyril Wellbeloved propped up against a tree, obviously in the grip of one of those hangovers that mark epochs, the sort of hangover you tell your grandchildren about when they come clustering round your knee. He looked like the things you find in dust-bins, which are passed over with a disdainful jerk of the head by the discriminating alley cat, and so repellent was his aspect that after a brief 'Good morning' – and even that caused the pig man to quiver like a smitten blancmange – Sir Gregory averted his gaze and transferred it to the occupant of the sty.

And as he did so, he suddenly stiffened, blinked, gasped, dropped his cigar and stood staring.

'What?' he stammered. 'What? What? What?'

The next moment, it seemed to George Cyril Wellbeloved that the end of the world had come and Judgement Day set in with unusual severity. Actually, it was only his employer shouting his name, but that was the illusion it created.

'Sir?' he whispered feebly, clutching his temples, through which some practical joker was driving white-hot spikes.

'Come here!' bellowed Sir Gregory.

George Cyril obeyed his master's voice, but reluctantly. Sir Gregory, he had not failed to observe, in addition to being yellow in colour and flickering at the edges, was looking like a touchy tribal god who, dissatisfied with the day's human sacrifice, is preparing to say it with thunderbolts. He feared the shape of things to come.

'What's all this?' the employer roared.

'Sir?'

'What's been going on here?'

'Sir?'

'Don't stand there bleating like a sheep, you loathsome excrescence. You know perfectly well what I mean, blister your insides. Where's my pig? This isn't my pig. What's become of Queen of Matchingham, and what's this damned animal doing here? You've removed my pig and substituted a blasted changeling.'

Except for Lord Emsworth, on whose capabilities in that direction we have already touched, there was not in all Shropshire – and probably not in Herefordshire and South Wales – a more gifted exponent of stout denial than George Cyril Wellbeloved, and in this moment of peril a special effort might have been expected from him. But, in order to deny with the adequate measure of stoutness, a man has to be feeling at the top of his form, and we have been strangely remiss if we have left our public with the impression that George Cyril was at the top of his. He was but a shadow of his former self, his once alert brain a mere mass of inert porridge.

'WELL?'

George Cyril Wellbeloved cracked beneath the strain. One last futile attempt to find an explanation that would cover the facts, at the same time leaving him with an unsullied reputation, and he was telling all, omitting no detail however slight.

It went considerably better than he had anticipated. True, his audience punctuated the narrative by calling him a number of derogatory names, but he was not torn limb from limb, as at one point had seemed likely. Encouraged, he became fluent, and the story went better than ever. As he told of his journey to Blandings Castle and the theft of the Empress, something like a faint smile of approval seemed to flicker across his employer's face.

And, indeed, Sir Gregory was not ill pleased. He began to see daylight. It seemed to him that the position of affairs was somewhat similar to that which would have prevailed in the Malemute saloon if Dangerous Dan McGrew and one of his friends had got the drop on each other simultaneously. And on such occasions compromise and bargaining become possible. Moreover, if he now despatched this pig man of his to scout around in the grounds of Blandings Castle, it might be possible to ascertain where the hellhounds of the opposition had hidden the Queen. That knowledge acquired, what simpler than to send an expeditionary force to the rescue?

A few minutes later, accordingly, George Cyril Wellbeloved, relieved to find himself still in one piece, was bicycling once more along the old familiar road, while Sir Gregory went to the garage to get out his car. It was his intention to beard Lord Emsworth and that old image, his brother Galahad, in their lair, and tell them one or two things about the facts of life.

'Lord Emsworth in?' he asked, having reached journey's end.

Beach was courtly, but distant.

'His lordship has gone to Wolverhampton, sir.'

'Where's Mr Threepwood?'

'Mr Galahad is also absent.'

'H'm,' said Sir Gregory, wondering what to do for the best, and as he spoke Lady Constance came through the hall.

'Why, good morning, Sir Gregory,' said Lady Constance. 'Have you come to see Clarence?'

'Eh? Oh, good morning. Yes. Wanted to speak to him about something.'

'He won't be back till tonight, I'm afraid. He has gone to Wolverhampton.'

'So Beach was saying.'

'He is making a speech there to some sort of pig-breeding society. But you will stay to lunch, won't you?'

Sir Gregory considered. Lunch? Not a bad idea. He had a solid respect for the artistry of the castle cook, and now that Gloria Salt had given him the old heave-ho, there was no obstacle to his enjoyment of it.

'Kind of you,' he said. 'Delighted.'

He looked forward to filling himself to the brim under Gloria's eyes, defiantly sailing into the potatoes and generally raising hell with the calories. That, in his opinion, would show her she wasn't everybody.

3

When Gally had left Lord Vosper so abruptly in the middle of their conversation on the terrace, it was with the intention of hastening to Matchingham Hall and confronting its proprietor, and such was his agitation of spirit that he was half-way there before he realized

that a sensible man would have taken the car instead of walking. It
being too late to turn back now, he completed the journey on foot,
using the short cut across the fields, and reached his destination in a
state of considerable warmth.

Binstead's manner, as he imparted the information that Sir Gregory was not at home, should have cooled him, for it was frigid in
the extreme. It was impossible for so young a butler to be as glacial
as Beach would have been in similar circumstances, but he was as
glacial as he knew how to be, and it disappointed him that this
visiting pig stealer appeared quite oblivious to his chilliness. Gally
was much too exhausted by his hike to make a close study of butlers
and notice whether they were hot or cold.

'I'll come in and wait,' he said, and Binstead, though in inward
revolt against the suggestion, did not see what he could do to
prevent the intrusion. Reluctantly he conducted Gally to the study,
and Gally, making for the sofa, put his feet up with a contented
sigh. He then outraged Binstead's feelings still further by asking for
a whisky and soda.

'A good strong one,' said Gally, and such was the magic of his
personality that the butler, who had stiffened from head to foot,
relaxed with a meek 'Yes, sir'.

When he returned with the restorative, Gally had settled down to
The Times crossword puzzle.

'Thanks,' he said. 'You don't know what a large Australian bird
in three letters beginning with E is, do you?'

'I do not, sir,' said Binstead icily, and withdrew.

For some minutes after he was alone, Gally gave himself up to
the crossword puzzle, concentrating tensely. But crossword puzzles
are only a palliative. They do not really cure the aching heart. Soon
his mind was straying back to the burden that weighed on it, and he
put the paper down with a weary sigh and gave himself up to
thought.

It might have been supposed that a man who had himself
purloined a pig on the previous night would have looked with an
indulgent eye on the pig-stealing activities of others, on the principle
that a fellow-feeling makes one wondrous kind. But there was
nothing resembling tolerant sympathy in Gally's mind as he sat
there brooding on Sir Gregory Parsloe. The blackness of the other's

villainy appalled him. He could see no excuse for the fellow. Still, there it was and no use thinking about it. He tried to envisage the outcome, were the man to stick to his guns and refuse to restore the Empress.

A superficial thinker would have said in his haste that the thing was a stand-off. If Empress of Blandings had been removed from circulation, he would have reasoned, so had Queen of Matchingham. Here, in other words, were two pigs, both missing, and these two pigs cancelled each other out.

But Gally saw more deeply into the matter, and shuddered at what he saw. What the superficial thinker was overlooking was the fact that while the Empress was the solitary jewel in Lord Emsworth's crown, the man Parsloe had another pig up his sleeve which he could thrust into the arena at a moment's notice. In the whirl of recent events, Pride of Matchingham, the original Parsloe entry, had rather receded into the background, but it was still there, a unit in the Parsloe stable, and if necessary it could do its stuff.

And with what hideous effectiveness! For two years Pride of Matchingham had been runner-up in the contest, and in the absence of the Empress its triumph was assured. In other words, all the man Parsloe had to do was to hang on to the Empress, and he would flourish like a green bay tree. If there was a bitterer thought than that, Gally would have been interested to learn what it was. It was the sudden realization of this angle that had caused Sir Gregory to perk up so noticeably towards the end of his interview with George Cyril Wellbeloved.

After a three-mile walk on a hot summer morning, followed by a stiffish whisky-and-soda in a comfortable arm chair, a man who is getting on in years tends to become drowsy, and at this point in his meditations Gally's head began to nod.

For a long time the study remained hushed and still except for an occasional gurgle, like that of a leaky radiator. Then the telephone bell rang, and Gally sat up with a jerk.

He lifted the receiver. Somebody at the other end of the wire was saying 'Sir' – huskily, like a voice speaking from the tomb.

'Who's that?'

'Wellbeloved, Sir Gregory.'

The last mists of sleep cleared from Gally's mind. He became keen and alert. He was a man of the world, and he knew that pig men do not call their employers on the telephone unless they have something urgent to say. Plainly this Wellbeloved was about to plot, and he was consequently in the position of a Private Eye who is listening in on the intimate agenda of the Secret Nine.

'Where are you?'

'I'm phoning from the Beetle and Wedge, Sir Gregory. And I was wondering, Sir Gregory,' proceeded George Cyril Wellbeloved, a pleading note creeping into his voice, 'if under the circs, it being such a warm day and me all worn out from toiling in your interests, I might have a glass of beer.'

'Certainly, certainly,' said Gally heartily. 'Have all you want and tell them to charge it to me.'

There was a silence. It seemed for a moment that the pig man had swooned. When he resumed, it was plain from the new animation with which he spoke that he was feeling that there had been a great improvement in his employer since they had last met. This, he seemed to be saying to himself, was something like sweetness and light.

'Well, sir,' he said, sunnily, 'I've found her.'

'Eh?'

'The Queen, sir.'

Gally reeled. The words had been like a blow between his eyes. He had been so sure that his secret was safe from the world, and here he was, unmasked by a pig man. For a long instant he stood speechless. Then he managed to utter.

'Good God!'

'Yes, sir, it took a bit of doing, but I did it, and I came along here to the Beetle and Wedge to apprise you of her whereabouts. Following your instructions, sir, I proceeded to Blandings Castle . . . About that beer,' said George Cyril Wellbeloved, digressing for a moment. 'Would it run to a spot of gin in it, sir?'

'Yes, yes, yes.'

'Thank you, sir. I find it improves the flavour. Well, sir, as I was saying, I proceeded to Blandings Castle and proceeded to lurk unseen. What had occurred to me, thinking it over, was that if the Queen was being held in durance vile – that's an expression they use, sir, I don't know if it's familiar to you – somebody would have to be feeding her pretty soon, and this, I presumed, would be done by an underling, if you understand the word, effecting an egress through the back door. So I lurked near the back door, and sure enough out came Mr Beach, the butler, carrying in his hand a substantial pail and glancing very nervous from side to side as much as to say "Am I observed?" Well, sir, to cut a long story short, he proceeded to proceed to what is known as the west wood – which is a wood lying in a westerly direction – and there fetched up at an edifice which I assumed to have been at one time the residence of one of the gamekeepers. He went in. He effected an entrance,' said George Cyril Wellbeloved, correcting himself, 'and I crope up secretly and looked in through the window, and there was the Queen, sir, as large as life. And then I took my departure and proceeded here and rang you up on the telephone so as to apprise you of what had transpired and leave it to you to take what steps you may consider germane to the issue, trusting I have given satisfaction as is my constant endeavour. And, now, sir, with your permission, I will be ringing off and going and securing the beer you have so kindly donated. Thank you, sir.'

'Hey!' shouted Gally.

'Sir?'

'Where's the Empress?'

'Why, just where we left her, sir,' said George Cyril Wellbeloved, surprised, and hung up.

Gally replaced the receiver, and stood dazed and numb. He was thinking hard thoughts of George Cyril Wellbeloved and wondering a little that such men were permitted to roam at large in a civilized country. If at that moment he had learned that George Cyril Wellbeloved had tripped over a hole in the Beetle and Wedge's linoleum and broken his neck, he would, like Pollyanna, have been glad, glad, glad.

But men of the stamp of the Hon. Galahad Threepwood do not remain dazed and numb for long. Another moment, and he was lifting the receiver and asking for the number of Blandings Castle. And presently Beach's voice came over the wire.

'Hullo? Lord Emsworth's residence. Beach, the butler, speaking.'

'Beach,' said Gally, wasting no time in courteous preliminaries, 'pick up those flat feet of yours and race like a mustang to the west wood and remove that pig. That blasted Wellbeloved was tailing you up when you went to feed the animal, and has just been making his report to me, thinking that I was the man Parsloe. We've got to find another resting-place for it before he realizes his error, and most fortunately I know of one that will be ideal. Do you remember Fruity Biffen? Don't be an ass, Beach, of course you remember Fruity Biffen. My friend Admiral Biffen. Until a few days ago he was living in a house on the Shrewsbury road. You can't mistake it. It's got a red roof, and it's called Sunnybrae. Take this pig there and deposit it in the kitchen. What do you mean, what will Admiral Biffen say? He isn't there. He went back to London, leaving the place empty. So put the pig . . . What's that? *How*? Use a wheelbarrow, man, use a wheelbarrow.'

4

In his office in Long Island City, NY, Mr Donaldson of Donaldson's Dog-Joy was dictating a cable to his secretary.

'Lady Constance Keeble, Blandings Castle, Shropshire, England. Got that?'

'Yes, Mr Donaldson.'

Mr Donaldson thought for a moment. The divine afflatus descended on him, and he spoke rapidly.

'"Cannot understand your letter just received saying you find my old friend Mrs Bunbury so charming. Stop. Where do you get that old friend Mrs Bunbury stuff. Query mark. I never had an old friend Mrs Bunbury. Stop. If person calling self Mrs Bunbury has insinuated self into Blandings Castle claiming to be old friend of mine, comma, she is a goshdarned impostor and strongly advocate throwing her out on her . . ." What's the word, Miss Horwitt?'

'Keister, Mr Donaldson.'

'Thank you, Miss Horwitt. "Strongly advocate throwing her out on her keister or calling police reserves. Stop. Old friend of mine forsooth. Stop. The idea. Stop. Never heard of such a thing. Stop."'

'Shall I add "Hoity-toity", Mr Donaldson?'

'No. Just kindest regards.'

'Yes, Mr Donaldson.'

'Right. Send it direct.'

Chapter 7

The annual binge or jamboree of the Shropshire, Herefordshire and South Wales Pig Breeders' Association is always rather a long time breaking up. Pig breeders are of an affectionate nature and hate to tear themselves away from other pig breeders. The proceedings concluded, they like to linger and light pipes and stand around asking the boys if they know the one about the young man of Calcutta. It was consequently not till late in the afternoon that the car which had taken Lord Emsworth and Maudie to Wolverhampton – Alfred Voules, chauffeur, at the wheel – began its return journey.

Stress was laid earlier in this narrative on the fact that the conscientious historian, when recording any given series of events, is not at liberty to wander off down byways, however attractive, but is compelled to keep plodding steadily along the dusty high road of his story, and this must now be emphasized again to explain why the chronicler does not at this point diverge from his tale to give a word for word transcript of Lord Emsworth's speech. It would have been a congenial task, calling out all the best in him, but it cannot be done. Fortunately the loss to Literature is not irreparable. A full report will be found in the *Bridgnorth, Shifnal and Albrighton Argus* (with which is incorporated the *Wheat Growers' Intelligencer and Stock Breeders' Gazetteer*), which is in every home.

Nor is he able to reveal the details of the conversation in the car, because there was no conversation in the car. It was Lord Emsworth's custom, when travelling, to fall asleep at the start of the journey and remain asleep throughout. Possibly on a special occasion like this a strong man's passion might have kept him awake, at least for the first mile or two, but the cold from which he was suffering lowered his resistance and he had had a tiring day trying to keep his top hat balanced on his head. So Nature took its toll, and Maudie, watching him, was well pleased, for his insensibility fitted in neatly with her plans. She was contemplating a course of action which she would have found difficult to carry out with a wakeful host prattling at her side.

As the car neared the home stretch and his thoughts, like drifting thistledown, had begun to turn to supper and beer, Alfred Voules heard the glass panel slide back behind him and a hushed voice say 'Hey!'

'Listen,' whispered Maudie. 'Do you know a place called Matchingham Hall? And don't yell, or you'll wake Lord Emsworth.'

Alfred Voules knew Matchingham Hall well. He replied in a hoarse undertone that it was just round the next bend in the road and they would be coming to it in a couple of ticks.

'Stop there, will you. I want to see Sir Gregory Parsloe about something.'

'Shall I wait, ma'am?'

'No, don't wait. I don't know how long I shall be,' said Maudie, feeling that hours – nay days – might well elapse before she had finished saying to Tubby Parsloe all the good things which had been accumulating inside her through the years. Hell hath no fury like a woman scorned, and when a woman scorned starts talking, she likes to take plenty of time. She does not want to have to be watching the clock all the while.

The car slowed down and slid to a halt outside massive iron gates flanked by stone posts with heraldic animals on top of them. Beyond the gates were opulent-looking grounds and at the end of the long driveway a home of England so stately that Maudie drew her breath in with a quick 'Coo!' of awe. Tubby, it was plain, had struck it rich and come a long way since the old Criterion days when he used to plead with her to chalk the price of his modest refreshment up on the slate, explaining that credit was the life-blood of Commerce, without which the marts of trade could have no elasticity.

'This'll do,' she said. 'Drop me here.'

2

Sir Gregory Parsloe had just sat down at the dinner table when the door bell rang. He had had three excellent cocktails and was looking forward with bright anticipation to a meal of the sort that sticks to the ribs and brings beads of perspiration to the forehead. He had ordered it specially that morning, taking no little trouble over his selections. Some men, when jilted, take to drink. Sir Gregory was taking to food. Freed from the thrall of Gloria Salt, he intended to make up for past privations.

Le Diner
Smoked Salmon
Mushroom Soup
Filet of Sole
Hungarian Goulash
Mashed Potatoes
Buttered Beets
Buttered Beans
Asparagus with Mayonnaise
Ambrosia Chiffon Pie
Cheese
Fruit
Petits Fours

Ambrosia Chiffon Pie is the stuff you make with whipped cream, white of egg, powdered sugar, seeded grapes, sponge cake, shredded coconut and orange gelatin, and it had been planned by the backsliding Baronet as the final supreme gesture of independence. A man who has been ordered by his fiancée to diet and defiantly tucks into Ambrosia Chiffon Pie has formally cast off the shackles.

He had unfastened the lower buttons of his waistcoat and was in the act of squeezing lemon juice over his smoked salmon, when the hubbub at the front door broke out. It was caused by Maudie demanding to see Sir Gregory Parsloe immediately and Binstead explaining – politely at first, then, as the argument grew more heated, in a loud and hostile voice – that Sir Gregory was at dinner and could not be disturbed. And the latter was about to intervene in the debate with a stentorian 'What the devil's all that noise going on out there?' when the door flew open and Maudie burst in, with Binstead fluttering in her wake.

The butler had given up the unequal struggle. He knew when he was licked.

'Mrs Stubbs,' he announced aloofly, and went off, washing his hands of the whole unpleasant affair and leaving his employer to deal with the situation as he thought best.

Sir Gregory stood staring, the smoked salmon frozen on its fork. It is always disconcerting when an unexpected guest arrives at dinner time, and particularly so when such a guest is a spectre from the dead past. The historic instance, of course, of this sort of thing is the occasion when the ghost of Banquo dropped in to take pot luck with Macbeth. It gave Macbeth a start, and it was plain from Sir Gregory's demeanour that he also had had one.

'What? What? What? What? What?' he gasped, for he was a confirmed what-whatter in times of emotion.

Maudie's blue eyes were burning with a dangerous light.

'So there you are!' she said, having given her teeth a little click. 'I wonder you can look me in the face, Tubby Parsloe.'

Sir Gregory blinked.

'Me?'

'Yes, you.'

It occurred to Sir Gregory that another go at the smoked salmon might do something to fortify a brain which was feeling as if a charge of trinitrotoluol had been touched off under it. Fish, he had heard or read somewhere, was good for the brain. He took a forkful, hoping for the best, but nothing happened. His mind still whirled. Probably smoked salmon was not the right sort of fish.

Maudie, having achieved the meeting for which she had been waiting for ten years, wasted no time beating about the bush. She got down to the *res* without preamble.

'A nice thing that was you did to me, Tubby Parsloe,' she said, speaking like the voice of conscience.

'Eh?'

'Leaving me waiting at the church like that!'

Once more Sir Gregory had to fight down a suspicion that his mind was darkening.

'*I* left *you* waiting at the church? I don't know what you're talking about.'

'Don't try that stuff on me. Did you or did you not write me a letter ten years ago telling me to come and get married at St Saviour's, Pimlico, at two o'clock sharp on June the seventh?'

'June the what?'

'You heard.'

'I did nothing of the sort. You're crazy.'

Maudie laughed a hard, bitter laugh. She had been expecting some such attitude as this. Trust Tubby Parsloe to try to wriggle out of it. Fortunately she had come armed to the teeth with indisputable evidence, and she now produced it from her bag.

'You didn't, eh? Well, here's the letter. I kept it all these years in case I ever ran into you. Here you are. Look for yourself.'

Sir Gregory studied the document dazedly.

'Is that your handwriting?'

'Yes, that's my handwriting.'

'Well, read what it says.'

'"Darling Maudie –"'

'Not that. Over the page.'

Sir Gregory turned the page.

'There you are. "Two o'clock sharp, June seven".'

Sir Gregory uttered a cry.

'You're cockeyed, old girl.'

'How do you mean, I'm cockeyed?'

'That's not a seven.'

'What's not a seven?'

'That thing there.'

'Why isn't it a seven?'

'Because it's a four. June 4, as plain as a pikestaff. Anyone who could take it for a . . . Lord love a duck! You don't mean you went to that church on June the seventh?'

'Certainly I went to that church on June the seventh.'

With a hollow groan Sir Gregory took another forkful of smoked salmon. A blinding light had shone upon him, and he realized how unjustified had been those hard thoughts he had been thinking about this woman all these years. He had supposed that she had betrayed him with a cold, mocking callousness which had shaken his faith in the female sex to its foundations. He saw now that what had happened had been one of those unfortunate misunderstandings which are so apt to sunder hearts, the sort of thing Thomas Hardy used to write about.

'I was there on June the fourth,' he said.

'What!'

Sir Gregory nodded sombrely. He was not a man of great sensibility, but he could appreciate the terrific drama of the thing.

'In a top hat,' he went on, his voice trembling, 'and, what's more, a top hat which I had had pressed or blocked or whatever they call it and in addition had rubbed with stout to make it glossy. And when you didn't show up and after about a couple of hours it suddenly struck me that you weren't going to show up, I took that hat off and jumped on it. I was dashed annoyed about the whole business. I mean to say, when a man tells a girl to meet a fellow at two o'clock sharp on June the fourth at St Saviour's, Pimlico, and marry him and so on, and he gets there and there isn't a sign of her, can a chap be blamed for feeling a bit upset? Well, as I was saying, I jumped on the hat, reducing it to a mere wreck of its former self, and went off to Paris on one of the tickets I'd bought for the honeymoon. I was luckily able to get a refund on the other. I had quite a good time in Paris, I remember. Missed you, of course,' said Sir Gregory gallantly.

Maudie was staring, round-eyed, the tip of her nose wiggling.

'Is that true?'

'Of course it's true. Dash it all, you don't suppose I could make up a story like that on the spur of the moment? You don't think I'm a ruddy novelist or something, do you?'

This was so reasonable that Maudie's last doubts were resolved. She gulped, her eyes wet with unshed tears, and when he offered her a piece of smoked salmon, waved it away with a broken cry.

'Oh, Tubby! How awful!'

'Yes. Unfortunate, the whole thing.'

'I thought you had blown the honeymoon money at the races.'

'Well, I did venture a portion of it at Sandown Park, as a matter of fact, now you mention it, but by great good luck I picked a winner. Bounding Bertie in the two-thirty at twenty to one. What a beauty! I won a hundred quid. That is what enabled me to buy that hat. The money came in handy in Paris, too. Very expensive city, Paris. Never believe anyone who tells you living's cheap there. They soak you at every turn. Though, mark you, the food's worth it, the way they cook it over there.'

There was a silence. Maudie, like Gloria Salt, was thinking of what might have been, and Sir Gregory, his mind back in the days of his solitary honeymoon, was trying to remember the name of that little restaurant behind the Madeleine, where he had had the most amazingly good dinner one night. The first time, he recalled, that he had ever tasted bouillabaisse.

Binstead, who had spent the last ten minutes panting feebly in his pantry, for Acts of God like Maudie had never before come bursting into his placid life and he was feeling somewhat unnerved, had at last succeeded in restoring his aplomb sufficiently to enable him to resume his butlerine duties. He now entered, bearing a tureen, and Sir Gregory was recalled with a start to a sense of his obligations as a host.

'What ho, the soup!' he said, welcoming it with a bright smile. 'I say, now you're here, you'll stay and have a bite of dinner, old girl, what? Eh? Got to be getting along? Don't be silly. You can't turn up after all these years and just say "Hullo, there" and dash off like a ruddy jack rabbit. We've got to have a long talk about all sorts of things. My chauffeur can take you back to wherever you're staying. Where are you staying, by the way, and how on earth do you happen to be in these parts? You could have knocked me down with a toothpick when you suddenly popped up out of a clear sky like that. Mrs Stubbs and I are old friends, Binstead.'

'Indeed, Sir Gregory?'

'Knew each other years and years ago.'

'Is that so, Sir Gregory?'

'You didn't tell me where you were hanging out, Maudie.'

'I'm at Blandings Castle.'

'How the devil did you get there?'

'Gally Threepwood invited me.'

Sir Gregory puffed his cheeks out austerely.

'That gumboil!'

'Why, Tubby, he's nice.'

'Nice, my foot! He's a louse in human shape. Well, come along and sit down,' said Sir Gregory, abandoning the distasteful subject. 'There's a Hungarian goulash due at any moment which I think you'll appreciate, and I stake my all on the Ambrosia Chiffon Pie. It's made of whipped cream, white of egg, powdered sugar, seeded grapes, sponge cake, shredded coconut, and orange gelatin, and I shall be vastly surprised if it doesn't melt in the mouth.'

The presence of Binstead, hovering in the background with his large ears pricked up, obviously hoping to hear something worth including in his Memoirs, prevented anything in the nature of intimate exchanges during the meal. But when he had served the coffee and retired, Sir Gregory, heaving a sentimental sigh, struck the tender note.

'Dashed good, that goulash,' he said. 'It isn't every cook in this country who knows how to prepare it. The paprika has to be judged to a nicety, and there are other subtleties into which I need not go at the moment. Which reminds me. I wonder, old girl, if you remember me standing you dinner one evening years ago – or, rather, you standing me, as it turned out, because I was compelled to stick you with the bill – at a little place in Soho where they dished up a perfectly astounding Hungarian goulash?'

'I remember. It was in the spring.'

'Yes. A lovely spring evening, with a gentle breeze blowing from the west, the twilight falling, and a new moon glimmering in the sky. And we went to this restaurant and there was the goulash.'

'You had three helpings.'

'And you the same, if memory serves me aright. With a jam omelette to follow. That's what I always admired about you, Maudie, you never went in for this dieting nonsense. You enjoyed your food, and when you had had it, you reached out for more, and to hell with what it did to your hips. Too many girls nowadays are mad about athletics and keeping themselves fit and all that, and if you ask me, they're a worse menace to the peaceful life of the countryside than botts, glanders, and foot-and-mouth disease. An example of this type of feminine pestilence that springs to the mind is my late fiancée, Gloria Salt. Physical fitness was her gospel, and she spread disaster and desolation on every side like a sower going forth sowing.'

'Aren't you still engaged to Miss Salt?'

'Not any more. She sent me round a note last night telling me to go and boil my head. And a very good thing, too. I should never have asked her to marry me. A rash act. One does these foolish things.'

'Didn't you love her?'

'Don't be silly. Of course I didn't love her. There was some slight feeling of attraction, possibly, due to her lissom figure, but you couldn't call it love, not by a jugful. I've never loved anyone but you, Maudie.'

'Oh, Tubby!'

'You ought to know that. I told you often enough.'

'But that was years ago.'

'Years don't make any difference when a fellow really bestows his bally heart. Yes, dash it, I love you, old girl. I fought against it, mark you. Thinking you had let me down, I tried to blot your image from my mind, if you follow what I mean. But when you came in at that door, looking as beautiful as ever, I knew it was no good struggling any longer. My goose was cooked. It was just as though I had been taken back to the old days and was leaning against your bar, gazing into your eyes, while you poured the whisky and uncorked the small soda.'

'Oh, Tubby!'

'And later, when I watched you wading into that Ambrosia Chiffon Pie, obviously enjoying it, I mean to say *understanding* it, not pecking at it the way most of these dashed women would have done but plainly getting its inner meaning and all that, I said to myself "My mate!" I realized that we were twin souls and that was all there was about it.'

'Oh, Tubby!'

Sir Gregory took a moody salted almond, frowning as he ate it.

'You keep saying, "Oh, Tubby!" but a fat lot of use that is. I said we were twin souls, and we are twin souls, but under prevailing conditions what's the *good* of our being twin souls? Where do we go from there? I mean, you can't get away from the fundamental fact that you're married.'

'No, I'm not.'

'Pardon me. You must have forgotten. I distinctly heard Binstead announce you as "Mrs Stubbs".'

'But Cedric's dead.'

'I'm sorry to hear that,' said Sir Gregory politely. 'Here today and gone tomorrow, what? Who is Cedric?'

'My husband.'

Sir Gregory, who had taken another salted almond, held it poised in air. He looked at her with a wild surmise.

'Your husband?'

'Yes.'

'He's *dead*?'

'He died five years ago.'

Sir Gregory was so moved that he returned the salted almond to its dish untasted.

'Let's get this straight,' he said, his voice and chins shaking a little. 'Let's keep our heads and thresh this thing out calmly and coolly. You say your husband is no longer with us? He has handed in his dinner pail? Then, as I see it, this means that you're at a loose end, like me.'

'Yes.'

'Nothing in the world to stop us getting married any dashed moment we care to.'

'No.'

Sir Gregory reached out for her hand as if it had been a portion of Ambrosia Chiffon Pie.

'Then how about it, old girl?'

'Oh, Tubby!' said Maudie.

3

Most men, having started out in a car with a lady friend and discovered at journey's end that she was no longer there, would have felt a certain surprise at this shortage and probably asked a lot of tedious questions. To Lord Emsworth, woken with a respectful prod in the ribs by Alfred Voules at the door of Blandings Castle and finding himself alone, it never occurred to wonder what had become of Maudie en route. He seldom worried about things like that. If women vanished out of cars, they vanished. There was nothing you could do about it, and no doubt all would be explained in God's good time. So he merely blinked, said 'Eh? What? We're there, are we? Quite. Capital,' and tottered in, sneezing. And Gally, who was passing through the hall with Jerry, stared at him, concerned.

'That's a nasty cold you've got, Clarence,' he said, and Jerry thought so, too.

'That *is* a nasty cold you've got, Lord Emsworth,' said Jerry.

Beach appeared, took one look at his employer and formed a swift diagnosis.

'Your lordship has a nasty cold,' he said.

Lord Emsworth, who had subsided into a chair, sniffed without speaking, and the three men looked at one another.

'There's only one thing to do for a cold,' said Gally. 'Boil the feet and slap on an onion poultice.'

'I should have said vinegar tea and a lump of sugar soaked in kerosene,' said Jerry.

'If I might offer a suggestion, Mr Galahad,' said Beach, 'I was reading in the paper this morning of a new American cereal called Cute Crispies. It contains sixty-two per cent of nutro-glutene, and one tablespoonful, I understand, provides nourishment equal to that of a pound and a half of steak. Such a preparation might prove efficacious.'

'I'll tell you what,' said Jerry. 'Suppose I dash off to Market Blandings and collect a few things at that chemist's in the High Street?'

'An excellent idea. Bulstrode's you mean. It'll be shut, but the blighter lives over the shop, so hammer at the door till he comes down and place your order. What do you think you're doing, Clarence?' asked Gally sternly, for the sufferer had risen and seemed about to accompany Jerry into the great open spaces.

'I was going down to have a look at the Empress.'

Gally and Beach exchanged glances. 'Secrecy and silence!' said Gally's. 'Yes, sir. Precisely, sir,' said that of Beach.

'You're crazy,' said Gally. 'Do you want to get pneumonia? Bed's the place for you. Beach will bring your dinner on a tray. Won't you, Beach?'

'Certainly, Mr Galahad.'

'And not a word to Lady Constance. We don't want her coming fussing over the poor devil and driving him off his rocker. The one thing a man with a cold in the head must avoid is the woman's touch.'

'Her ladyship is not at home, sir. She has gone to attend the weekly meeting of the Literary Society at the Vicarage.'

'That's good. It removes a grave threat. Upsy-daisy, Clarence.'

'But, Galahad, the Empress.'

'What about her?'

'I want to see how she is.'

Once more that significant glance passed between Gally and Beach.

'Don't you worry about the Empress. I was down taking a look at her only just now, and she's fine. Sparkling eyes. Rosy cheeks. You come along to bed, my dear chap,' said Gally, and a short while later Lord Emsworth was between the sheets, a hot water bottle at his toes, a dinner tray on his lap, and at his side a couple of Edgar Wallaces, donated by Beach in case he felt like reading. On his departure for America, Lord Emsworth's younger son, Freddie Threepwood, had bequeathed to Beach his library of who-dun-its, generally supposed to be the most complete in Shropshire, and he was always glad to give of his plenty.

But Lord Emsworth was in no mood for *Faceless Fiends* and *Things In The Night*. A glance at the first of the two volumes had told him that there was a gorilla in it which went climbing up waterpipes, snatching girls with grey eyes and hair the colour of ripe wheat out of their beds in the small hours, but he was a man who could take gorillas or leave them alone. He closed the book and lay there sneezing softly and thinking of Maudie. It saddened him to look back and reflect that by going to sleep in the car he had missed an opportunity which might not occur again of pouring burning words of love into her alabaster ear.

In the matter of pouring burning words of love into people's alabaster ears, Lord Emsworth was handicapped. Blandings Castle was full to bursting point of Nosey Parkers who seemed to have nothing to do except interrupt private conversations, and this rendered it difficult ever to get the desired object alone. Every time you had the stage set for an intimate exchange of ideas, along came somebody breaking it up, and all the weary work to do over again.

It was at this point in his meditations that his eye fell on the desk across the room, and it suddenly struck him that modern civilization has provided other methods of communication between person and person than the spoken word. In the pigeon-holes of that desk were single sheets of notepaper, double sheets of notepaper, postcards, envelopes, telegraph forms, and some of those little pads which enable you to jot down bright thoughts on life in general, while on the desk itself were pens, ink, indiarubber, sealing wax, and what looked like an instrument for taking stones out of horses' hooves. Rising from his sick bed, and ignoring the indiarubber, the sealing wax, and the horses' hooves instrument, Lord Emsworth took pen and paper and began to compose a letter.

It came out splendidly. He was not a very ready letter-writer as a rule, but after a couple of false starts the impassioned prose began gushing up like a geyser. When he had finished, he read the thing over and was stunned by his virtuosity. Just the right note of respectful fervour, he considered, and felt that that drowsiness in the car had been all for the best, for he could never have hoped to speak half as fluently as he had written. What he had got down on four sides of a double sheet of notepaper was the sort of thing that would have earned him a brotherly pat on the back from the author of the Song of Solomon.

As he was licking the envelope, Jerry came in, laden with parcels like a pack mule.

'I've brought you cinnamon, aspirin, vapex, glycerine of thymol, black currant tea, camphorated oil, a linseed poultice, and some thermogene wool,' said Jerry. 'A wide selection is always best, don't you think? And old Pop Bulstrode says you ought to drink hot milk and wear flannel next your skin.'

Lord Emsworth agreed that this sounded like an interesting and even amusing way of passing the time, but his mind was on his letter.

'Er,' he said.

'Yes?' said Jerry eagerly, in pursuance of his policy of hanging on his employer's lightest word.

'I wonder,' said Lord Emsworth, 'if you would do something for me, my dear fellow.'

'Anything, anything,' said Jerry heartily. 'Give it a name.'

'I have written a letter . . . a letter . . . in short, a letter –'

'I see,' said Jerry, following him so far. 'You mean a letter.'

'Exactly. A letter. A letter to Mrs – ah – Bunbury. I want it delivered as soon as possible, and I thought you might convey it to her.'

'Of course, of course. What a splendid idea! Nothing simpler. I'll slip it to her the moment I see her.'

'No, don't do that. There's sure to be someone hanging about watching your every move. You know how it is in this house. Put it in her room.'

'Pinned to the pincushion?'

'Precisely. Pinned to the pincushion. An excellent suggestion.'

'Which is her room?'

'The second on the right as you go along this corridor.'

'Consider it done,' said Jerry.

As simple a way of endearing himself to the boss, he felt, as could have been thought of. He trotted off, feeling that things were moving.

He was extremely curious to know what the dickens the old boy was writing letters to Mrs Bunbury about, but he could hardly ask, and if the idea of steaming the thing open with a kettle presented itself to his mind, he dismissed it resolutely. Like Lord Vosper, he was an Old Harrovian.

Chapter 8

Lord Emsworth lay back in bed. His letter on its way, he was wondering, like all authors who have sent their stuff off, if it could not have been polished a bit and given those last little touches which make all the difference. However, again like all authors, he knew that what he had written, even without a final brush-up, was simply terrific, and it was with a mind at rest that he took up his Edgar Wallace once more.

And he was just thinking that he personally would not have cared to be a gorilla in the employment of a master criminal ... broken sleep, no regular hours, always having to be shinning up water pipes and what not ... when a cheery 'Bring out your dead!' interrupted his meditations, and his brother Galahad came in.

'Hullo, Clarence,' said Gally. 'How are you feeling now? I've been thinking about that cold of yours, and I'll tell you the stuff to give it. You want to take a deep breath and hold it as long as you possibly can. This traps the germs in your interior, and not being able to get fresh air, they suffocate. When you finally exhale, the little sons of guns come out as dead as doornails and all you have to do is buy a black tie and attend the funeral. But what profits it to get rid of germs,' he went on, a grave note creeping into his voice, 'when at any moment you are going to have a super-bacillus like Connie at your throat?'

'Eh?'

'That's what I came to tell you. I think you will be receiving a visit from Connie shortly.'

'Oh, dash it!'

'I know just how you feel.'

'She's back, then?'

'With her hair in a braid. And they tell me she is considerably hotted up. I haven't seen her myself, but Beach, who had an extended interview with her, describes her as resembling a gorilla roaring and beating its chest and preparing to rip the stuffing out of the citizenry.'

Lord Emsworth was struck by a coincidence.

'I was reading a story about a gorilla when you came in. A curious animal.'

'What did it do?'

'Well, it seemed to spend most of its time climbing up water pipes and snatching girls from their beds.'

Gally was not impressed. He sneered scornfully.

'Sissy stuff. Obviously a mere amateur. Wait till you meet Connie.'

'But what is the matter with Connie?'

'Ah!' said Gally. 'I'm glad you asked me that. I'd have told you long ago, only you wouldn't let me get a word in edgeways.'

He sat down on the bed, adjusted his monocle and proceeded to tell a tale of strange happenings.

'Omitting birth, early education, and all that sort of thing, we start the Connie Story with her returning to the house at the conclusion of the weekly meeting of the Market Blandings Literary Society. It had been an interesting meeting, and she was in excellent spirits. She walked with a springy step. It wouldn't surprise me if she wasn't singing a snatch of song. In short, at that moment a child could have played with her, and she would probably have given it twopence to buy sweets with.'

Lord Emsworth, as nearly always when listening to a story, was a little fogged.

'I thought you said she was hotted up.'

'So she was ... a couple of minutes later, and I'll tell you why. On the table in the hall was lying a telegram. Well, when I say telegram, it was actually a cable, shot off from Long Island City in the United States of America by old man Donaldson, the dog biscuit despot. It was about Mrs Bunbury.'

'I believe they're old friends.'

'Donaldson doesn't. The gist of his cable was that he had never heard of her in his life.'

'Well, I'll be damned!'

'Exactly what Connie said, and she went off to find Mrs Bunbury and ask her for further particulars. She discovered her eventually in the passage near the stairs which lead to Beach's pantry. She was folded in Beach's arms, and he was kissing her fondly on both cheeks.'

Lord Emsworth sneezed.

'*Beach* was?'

'I appreciate your surprise. Strongly anti-traditional, you are feeling. Butlers, you say to yourself, don't kiss guests. Chauffeurs, perhaps. Gamekeepers, possibly. But butlers, never. In extenuation of his odd behaviour, however, I must mention that he is her uncle.'

'Her *uncle*?'

'Yes. Her Uncle Sebastian. I ought to have told you before, and I don't know how it happened to slip my mind, but Mrs Bunbury isn't Mrs Bunbury. She is the widow Stubbs. Her maiden name was, of course, Beach, though when I knew her in the old days as a barmaid at the Criterion, she called herself Maudie Montrose.'

Lord Emsworth looked as if he were about to pick at the coverlet.

'She is a *barmaid*?'

'She was a barmaid. Later, she married the proprietor of a private detective agency, now residing with the morning stars, and it was Beach's revelation of the fact that she was connected with the gumshoe industry that gave me the idea of getting her down here in order to keep an eye on young Parsloe and foil his machinations regarding the Empress. It seemed to me that she would have the trained mind. She hasn't as a matter of fact, but she can't help that, poor soul, and it's been delightful having her here and swopping stories of the old days. A fascinating companion. But don't let me wander from the main issue. Resuming the run of the scenario, Connie, already sent rocking back on the heels of her short French vamps by that cable, was naturally stirred even further by the spectacle of butlers bounding about the place embracing people. Is this Blandings Castle, she asked herself, or is it the *Folies Bergères*? She reeled off to her boudoir, rang for Beach and started a probe or quiz.'

Gally waited courteously for Lord Emsworth to finish groaning, and resumed.

'It was during this chat that Beach was struck by her resemblance to a gorilla with stomach ulcers, and we can hardly blame him for cracking under the strain. No more loyal fellow than Sebastian Beach ever swigged port, but every man has his breaking-point. Connie, when she comes down like a wolf on the fold with her cohorts all gleaming with purple and gold, is pretty hot stuff, and I'm not surprised that after she had given him the treatment for about a couple of minutes he threw in his hand and spilled the beans. You spoke?'

Lord Emsworth shook his head. He had merely groaned once more.

'Now while Connie realizes, of course, that I was the spearhead of the movement, for I gather that Beach gave me away fairly completely, it is quite possible that she may be suspecting you of complicity in the affair. You know what Connie's like. She takes in a wide field. So I thought the friendly thing was to come and warn you to be prepared. Have your story all planned out. Get tough with her. Talk out of the side of your mouth. For heaven's sake, Clarence, don't keep groaning like that. She can't eat you. And I don't suppose she'll want to,' said Gally, 'for anything more closely resembling a condemned food product I never saw in my life.' And with a final 'Tails up!' he went out, explaining that while he was not actually afraid of Connie there were moments when women are better avoided till they have come off the boil a bit. One did not, said Gally, want a vulgar brawl.

He left Lord Emsworth frozen where he lay, like a male Lot's wife turned into a pillar of salt.

But he was no longer sneezing. It is a remarkable fact, and one which will interest medical men, that of all the remedies for the common cold which had been suggested to him that night, the shock he had received from Gally's revelations was the only one that had done him any real good. Quite suddenly he had become a well man. It was as though after a course of vinegar tea and Cute Crispies he had taken a deep breath and asphyxiated every germ in his system, regardless of age or sex.

But though physically so greatly improved, spiritually he was in the poorest shape. It is a sad thing to have to record, but his love for Maudie had died as swiftly as if someone had taken it down a dark alley and hit it over the head with a blackjack. All he could think of now was what his sister Constance, always an outspoken woman, would say when she learned that he had written a letter proposing marriage to an ex-barmaid linked by ties of blood to the family butler.

No, not quite all. He was also thinking that after Connie had stopped talking – if she ever did – two alternatives would lie before him . . . one, to be sued for breach of promise; the other, to have to go through life calling Beach 'Uncle Sebastian'.

It was at this moment that Jerry entered, all of a glow. He had just met Penny in the corridor and received renewed assurance of her undying love. True, she was still betrothed to another, but she had flung herself into his arms and kissed him, and that was enough to make his evening. He beamed on Lord Emsworth.

'I deposited the letter,' he said, like a Boy Scout reporting his day's act of kindness.

Lord Emsworth came to life. From a pillar of salt he turned into a semaphore.

'Get it back!' he cried, waving his arms emotionally.

Jerry was perplexed. He could not follow his employer's thought processes.

'Get it back?'

'Yes.'

'You mean unpin it from the pincushion?'

'Yes, yes, yes. I cannot explain now, for every moment is precious, but hurry and bring it back to me.'

If Jerry had any comment to make on this strange attitude, he was unable to give it utterance, for the door had opened and Lady Constance was coming in to join the party.

He thought she eyed him rather frostily on seeing him there, as though any affection she might have been feeling for him had waned a good deal, but a man who has just been kissing dream girls in corridors pays little attention to frosty looks from prominent Society hostesses. He gave her a friendly smile, and said he would be going off and getting that paper.

'What paper?'

'Just a paper Lord Emsworth wanted me to bring him.'

'Why do you want Mr Vail to bring you papers, Clarence?'

'Dash it all,' said Lord Emsworth, panic lending him a weak belligerency. 'Why shouldn't he bring me papers? It's his job, isn't it? He's my secretary, isn't he?'

Lady Constance followed Jerry, as he left the room, with an eye that was bleaker than ever.

'He will not be your secretary long, if I have my way,' she said grimly.

Lord Emsworth was enchanted at this opportunity of steering the conversation away from butlers and their nieces.

'Why won't he be my secretary long, if you have your way?'

'Because I strongly suspect him of making love to Penelope Donaldson and trying to lure her away from Orlo Vosper.'

'Vosper? Vosper? Vosper? Ah, yes, Vosper,' said Lord Emsworth, just in time. A 'Who is Vosper?' might have had the worst results. 'What makes you think he's doing that?'

'I will tell you. When we were in London, a mysterious man rang up on the telephone, asking for Penelope. He gave his name as Gerald Vail and had apparently had a clandestine dinner engagement with her. Next day he arrives here as your secretary, obviously having followed her in accordance with a prearranged plan. And just now, as I was coming along the corridor, I saw them together. Close together,' said Lady Constance significantly.

'God bless my soul! What, *clinched* together?'

'When I saw them, they were not actually embracing, if that is what you mean by that peculiar expression,' said Lady Constance coldly. 'But Penelope's face was flushed, and I suspected the worst. If I can find the slightest excuse, I shall dismiss that young man. Really, with all these things happening, Blandings Castle has become a mad-house. Secretaries kissing girls entrusted to my care, butlers kissing –'

'Ah, yes,' said Lord Emsworth airily. 'Galahad was speaking to me about that. He was saying something, if I recollect rightly, about Mrs Bunbury not being Mrs Bunbury.'

'Her name is Stubbs, and she is Beach's niece.'

'Yes, I seem to recall him mentioning that. I remember thinking at the time that it was curious that a woman should say she was Mrs Bunbury if she wasn't Mrs Bunbury. Seemed a silly thing to do. You don't happen to know what the thought at the back of that was, do you?'

Lady Constance eyed him narrowly.

'Do *you*?'

'Me?'

'Were you in this plot, Clarence?'

Lord Emsworth stiffened his sinews and summoned up the blood.

'What do you mean, was I in this plot? Which plot? What plot? I haven't been in any plots. Do you suppose a busy man like me has time to waste being in plots? Tchah! Bah! Preposterous!'

A lesser woman might have wilted beneath his stern wrath. Lady Constance bore it with fortitude.

'No, I don't think you were. I am sure it was Galahad who was responsible for the whole thing, aided and abetted by Penelope Donaldson, who told me this Mrs Bunbury was an old friend of her father's. I must say I am shocked at the way Penelope has behaved. I thought her such a nice girl, and she has turned out to be thoroughly sly and untrustworthy. If I had not had a cable from Mr Donaldson saying that he had never met a Mrs Bunbury in his life, I might never have discovered what was going on. Of course, my first impulse was to turn the woman out of the house.'

'She's leaving, is she?' said Lord Emsworth, feeling that all things were working together for good.

'No, she is not leaving. Impossible as the situation is, after what Beach told me I have no option but to allow her to remain. I can't offend Sir Gregory.'

'You mean Parsloe?'

'He is the only Sir Gregory we know, I believe.'

'But what's Parsloe got to do with it?'

Lady Constance's expression seemed to suggest that she was swallowing a bitter pill and not liking it.

'According to Beach, this woman and Sir Gregory became engaged to be married this evening.'

'What!'

'I don't wonder you're surprised.'

'I'm amazed. I'm astonished. Dash it, I'm stunned.'

'So was I when Beach told me. I could hardly believe my ears.'

'You mean Parsloe met her for the first time this evening and asked her to marry him?' said Lord Emsworth, with a mild man's respect for a quick worker.

'Of course he did not meet her for the first time this evening. They appear to have known each other in the days before Sir Gregory came into the title. I found Beach kissing her, and he explained that she had just told him the news and he was congratulating her and wishing her happiness. Obviously, if this Mrs Bunbury or Mrs Stubbs or whoever she is is going to marry Sir Gregory, I cannot insult him by turning her out of the house. Life in the country is impossible if you are not on good terms with your neighbours.'

A horrid thought struck Lord Emsworth.

'Are you going to sack Beach?'

'I don't know.'

'I do. I'm dashed if you're going to sack Beach, because ... because I'm dashed if you are,' said Lord Emsworth stoutly. Life without Beach was a thing he did not care to contemplate.

'No,' said Lady Constance, after a moment's thought. 'No, I shall not dismiss Beach. I take the view that he was led astray by Galahad. Galahad! I remember, when we were children,' said Lady Constance wistfully, 'seeing Galahad fall into that deep pond in the kitchen garden. And just as he was sinking for the last time, one of the gardeners came along and pulled him out,' she added, speaking with a sort of wild regret. It was plain that she was in agreement with the poet that of all sad words of tongue or pen the saddest are these: 'It might have been'. She paused a moment, brooding on the thoughtless folly of that chuckle-headed gardener. 'Well,' she said, 'I am going to my room to bathe my temples with eau-de-Cologne. I don't know whether I am standing on my head or my heels.'

She went out, and Lord Emsworth, sinking back on his pillows, gave himself up to the first agreeable thoughts he had had for what seemed to him a lifetime.

Engaged to Parsloe, was she? Then at the eleventh hour he was saved and need no longer dread that breach of promise action or its even ghastlier alternative. What happier ending could there be to a good man's vicissitudes? Lord Emsworth had often speculated as to whether there were really such things as guardian angels, and this evening's happenings convinced him of their existence. Only a thoroughly efficient guardian angel who knew his job backwards could have snatched him from the soup with this amazing dexterity just when he had supposed himself to be getting down in it for the third time, like Galahad in his pond.

He regretted that there was presumably no way of getting in touch with his benefactor. It would have been a real pleasure to have sought him out and shaken him by the hand.

2

In houses of the size of Blandings Castle there are always plenty of nooks which might have been specially designed for the convenience of men desirous of avoiding angry women. The billiard-room was Gally's selection on leaving Lord Emsworth. Connie, he felt, whatever her faults, and they were numerous, was not likely to come poking her head into billiard-rooms.

The first thing he saw on entering was Lord Vosper practising cannons in a distrait sort of way, as if his mind were elsewhere. There was a preoccupied look on his handsome face, and the fact that he was bringing off some nice shots appeared to give him little pleasure. On seeing Gally, he brightened, like a shipwrecked mariner sighting a sail.

Lord Vosper, as has been said, considered Gally frivolous and found much to disapprove of in his attitude to life, but he had a solid respect for him as a man of the world who knew what was what, and it was a man of the world who knew what was what that he was in need of now. Problems had arisen in Orlo Vosper's life, and he felt unequal to coping with them alone.

'Oh, hullo,' he said. 'I say, Mr Threepwood, could I speak to you about something?'

'Touch on any topic that comes into your head, my boy, and you will find in me a ready listener,' said Gally cordially. 'What is on your mind? Are you worrying about the situation in the Far East?'

'Not so much the situation in the Far East,' said Lord Vosper, 'as the one right here in Blandings Castle. Some rather disturbing things have been happening and I should very much like your advice. If you have a moment?'

'My time is at your disposal.'

'It's a longish story.'

'Your stories can never be too long, my dear fellow,' said Gally courteously. 'Suppose we park ourselves on this settee and you get it off your chest.'

Seated on the settee with Gally at his side, his face registering sympathetic interest, Lord Vosper seemed to find a difficulty in beginning his story.

'Do you play tennis?' he said at length.

'I was wondering if you were going to ask me that,' said Gally. 'I suppose you're going to ask me next if I've read any good books lately?'

Lord Vosper blushed apologetically. He saw that he had selected the wrong opening for his narrative.

'I don't mean so much Do you play tennis as Would you believe that a great romance could be wrecked on the tennis court?'

'Ah, now you're talking. Good heavens, yes. My old friend Buffy Struggles was at one time engaged to a girl who was a keen tennis player, and she returned the ring and letters because, when they were partnered in the mixed doubles one day, he insisted on charging into her half of the court and poaching her shots. And before he could effect a reconciliation, he was run over by a hansom cab in Piccadilly and killed instantaneously.'

'Great Scott!' Lord Vosper was staring, amazed. 'Why, that's exactly what happened to me.'

'Were you killed by a hansom cab?'

'No, but I was engaged to a girl, and she broke it off because I poached her shots.'

'Ah, I see. I misunderstood you. When did this happen?'

'About two months ago.'

'But you've only been engaged to Penny Donaldson two or three days.'

'I'm not talking about Penny Donaldson, I'm talking about Gloria Salt.'

'You mean you were engaged to Gloria Salt?'

'I still am.'

'But you're engaged to Penny Donaldson.'

'I know. That's the trouble. I'm engaged to both of them.'

Gally removed his monocle and polished it. He found his companion's story, though full of human interest, a little difficult to follow.

'Intricate,' he said.

'It is a bit,' agreed Lord Vosper. 'I'd better take you through it step by step. I was engaged to Gloria, and she gave me the push. You've got that?'

'I've got it.'

'I then became engaged to Penny. All straight so far?'

'Quite straight. By way of a defiant sort of gesture, I suppose?'

'Well, more or less by way of a defiant sort of gesture, no doubt, though of course I'm very fond of her. Nice girl.'

'Very.'

'I asked her to marry me in London, when I was giving her a bite of dinner at Mario's, and she seemed to like the idea, so that was the position when we got back here. And all might have been well, had not Gloria suddenly blown in.'

'I begin to understand. Seeing her once more, you found that the old love still lingered?'

'That's right. And it had lingered in her, too. Like the dickens, apparently. I didn't know it till tonight, but she also was racked with remorse because she felt that she had chucked away a life's happiness.'

'How did it happen to dawn on you tonight?'

'I was taking a stroll in the garden, and I came upon her weeping bitterly in the moonlight. Well, naturally that struck me as odd, so I said "Oh, hullo. Is anything up?" and she said "Oh, Orlo!" and it all came out. And then . . . well, one thing led to another, don't you know, and before we knew where we were, we were in each other's arms.'

'Murmuring brokenly?'

'That's right, and I don't mind telling you I hope you will have something to suggest, because at the moment you wouldn't be far out in describing me as nonplussed.'

Gally nodded.

'I see your difficulty. You are a man of honour, and you feel that you are bound to Penny?'

'That's right.'

'But your heart belongs to Daddy.'

'Eh?'

'I mean to Gloria. You love this Salt?'

'That's right.'

'Well, these things happen. Nobody is to blame. There's only one thing for you to do, as I see it. You will have to explain the situation to Penny.'

'I suppose so. I hope she won't mind.'

'I hope not. Still, she should be informed, I think.'

'So does Gloria. She told me to go and tell her.'

'Not a pleasant job having to give a warm-hearted young girl the push.'

'No.'

'Perhaps you would prefer that some kindly third party broke the news?'

Lord Vosper started.

'I say! Would you?'

'I was not thinking of myself. The man I had in mind was ... Ah, here he is in person, right on cue,' said Gally, as the door opened and Jerry entered. 'Jerry, our friend Vosper here is in something of a dilemma, or quandary, as it is sometimes called. He has become betrothed to Gloria Salt, and, as you are aware, he is also betrothed to Penny Donaldson, and he is looking for a silver-tongued intermediary to take on the job of explaining to Penny that he will not be at liberty to go through with his commitments to her. I thought you might be just the man, you being a mutual friend of both parties. I will leave you to discuss it. If you want me, you will find me on the terrace.'

3

The moon, shining down on the terrace, illuminated a female figure seated in a deck chair, and Gally's heart, though a stout one, skipped a beat. Then he saw that it was not, as for a moment he had supposed, his sister Constance, but his young friend Penny Donaldson.

'Hullo there, Penny,' he said, taking the chair at her side. 'Well, we are living in stirring times these days. Did Beach tell you about that pig of Parsloe's?'

'Yes.'

'He got it away all right and put it in the house Fruity Biffen used to have.'

'Yes.'

'Extraordinary bit of luck Wellbeloved thinking I was Parsloe and pouring out his heart to me over the telephone.'

'Yes,' said Penny.

Gally gave her a quick look. Her voice had had a dull, metallic note, and eyeing her he saw that her brow was clouded and the corners of her mouth drawn down as though the soul were in pain.

'What's the matter?' he asked. 'You seem depressed.'

'I am.'

'Well, I've got some news for you that will cheer you up. I've just been talking to my Lord Vosper.'

'Oh?'

'And what do you think? He wants to call the whole thing off.'

'To do what?'

'Cancel the engagement, countermand the wedding cake. He's going to marry the Salt girl. It seems that they were like ham and eggs before you entered his life, but the frail bark of love came a stinker on the rocks. It has now been floated off and patched up and a marriage has been arranged and will shortly take place. He was a bit apologetic about it, and hoped you wouldn't mind, but he made it quite clear that that was how matters stood. So you are back in circulation and free to carry on with Jerry along the lines originally planned.'

'I see.'

Gally was hurt. He was feeling as the men who brought the good news from Aix to Ghent would have felt if the citizens of Ghent had received them at the end of their journey with a yawn and an 'Oh, yes?'

'Well, I'm dashed!' he said disapprovingly. 'I must say I expected a little more leaping about and clapping the hands in girlish glee. I might be telling you it's a nice evening.'

Penny heaved a sigh.

'It's the most loathsome evening there ever was. Do you know what's happened, Gally? Jerry's been fired.'

'Eh?'

'Given the gate. Driven into the snow. Lady Constance says if he isn't out of the place first thing tomorrow morning –'

'What?'

'– she'll set the dogs on him.'

Gally's monocle, leaping from the parent eye socket, flashed in the moonlight. He drew it in like an angler gaffing a fish, and having replaced it stared at her uncomprehendingly.

'What on earth are you talking about?'

'I'm telling you.'

'But it doesn't make sense. What's Connie got against Jerry?'

'She didn't like it when she found him in her closet.'

'In her *what*?'

'Well, cupboard, then, if you prefer it. The cupboard in her bedroom.'

'What the dickens was he doing in the cupboard in Connie's bedroom?'

'Hiding.'

Gally gaped.

'Hiding?'

'Yes.'

'In the cupboard?'

'Yes.'

'In Connie's bedroom?'

'Yes.'

A theory that would cover the facts came to Gally.

'This young man of yours isn't a little weak in the head, is he?'

'No, he isn't a little weak in the head. Lord Emsworth seems to be.'

'Quite,' said Gally, conceding this obvious truth. 'But how does Clarence come into it?'

Penny began to explain in a low, toneless voice. One cannot expect of a girl whose hopes and dreams have been shattered that her voice shall be resonant and bell-like.

'Jerry has been telling me about it. It started with Lord Emsworth writing a letter to your friend Maudie.'

'W –?' began Gally, and checked himself. Much as he would have liked to know what his brother had been writing letters to Maudie about, this was no time for interruptions.

'He gave it to Jerry and told him to put it in her room. Jerry asked which was her room, and he said the second on the right along the corridor. So Jerry put the letter there, and then Lord Emsworth told him to go and bring it back.'

Gally was obliged to interrupt.

'Why?'

'He didn't say why.'

'I see. Go on.'

'Well, Jerry went to get the letter, and he'd just got it when he heard someone outside the door. So of course he hid. Naturally he didn't want to be found there. He dived into the cupboard, and I suppose he must have made a noise, because the cupboard door was whipped open, and there was Lady Constance.'

'But what was Connie doing in Maudie's room?'

'It wasn't Maudie's room. It was Lady Constance's room. After he had finished talking to Lady Constance – or after she had finished talking to him – Jerry went back to Lord Emsworth, and Lord Emsworth, having heard the facts, smote his brow and said "Did I say the second door on the right? I meant second door on the left. That is how the mistake arose."'

Gally clicked his tongue.

'There you have Clarence in a nutshell,' he said. 'There is a school of thought that holds that he got that way from being dropped on his head when a baby. I maintain that when you have a baby like Clarence, you don't need to drop it on its head. You just let Nature take its course and it develops automatically into the sort of man who says "right" when he means "left". I suppose Jerry was annoyed?'

'A little. Not too well pleased. In fact, he called Lord Emsworth a muddleheaded old ass and said he ought to be in a padded cell. And if you're going to ask me if that annoyed Lord Emsworth, the answer is in the affirmative. They parted on distant terms. So Jerry's chances of ingratiating himself with the dear old man with a view to leading up to saying "Brother, can you spare two thousand pounds?" seem pretty dim, don't you feel? Well, I think I'll be strolling along to the lake.'

'What are you going to do there?'

'Just drown myself. It'll pass the time.'

Before Gally could ask her if this was the old Donaldson spirit – he had only got as far as a pained 'Tut, tut' – a figure came droopingly along the terrace.

'Ah, Jerry,' said Gally. 'Finished your chat? I've just been telling

Penny about the Vosper-Salt situation, and she has been telling me about your misadventure. Too bad. What are you planning to do now?'

Jerry stared dully.

'I'm going back to London.'

'Ridiculous.'

'What else can I do?'

Gally snorted. It seemed to him that the younger generation was totally lacking in the will to win.

'Why, stick around, of course. You're not licked yet. Who knows what the morrow may bring forth? London, forsooth! You're going to take a room at the Emsworth Arms and wait to see what turns up.'

Jerry brightened a little.

'It's not a bad idea.'

'It's a splendid idea,' said Penny. 'You can come prowling about the grounds, and I'll meet you.'

'So I can.'

'The rose garden would be a good place.'

'None better. Expect me among the roses at an early date. You'll be there?'

'With bells on.'

'Darling!'

'Angel!'

'I was rather thinking that the conversation might work round to some such point before long,' said Gally. 'So there you are, my boy. It's always foolish to despair. You ought to know that. Penny has been giving me some of your stories to read, and a thing that struck me about them was that on every occasion, despite master criminals, pock-marked Mexicans, shots in the night, and cobras down the chimney, true love triumphed in the end. Do you remember a thing of yours called 'A Quick Bier for Barney'? Well, the hero of that story got his girl though up against a bunch of thugs who would have considered my sister Constance very small-time stuff. And now, as the last thing you'll want at a moment like this is an old gargoyle like me hanging around, I'll say good night.'

He toddled off. He was feeling at the top of his form again and thinking that now would be an admirable time to go and see Connie and put it across her properly. His prejudice against vulgar brawls had vanished. He felt just in the mood for a brawl, and the vulgarer it was, the better he would like it.

4

At nine o'clock on the following night Beach, seated in his pantry, was endeavouring with the aid of a glass of port to still the turmoil which recent events at Blandings Castle had engendered in his soul, and not making much of a go of it. Port, usually an unfailing specific, seemed for once to have lost its magic.

Beach was no weakling, but he had begun to feel that too much was being asked of one who, though always desirous of giving satisfaction, liked to draw the line somewhere. A butler who has been compelled to introduce his niece into his employer's home under a false name and on top of that to remove a stolen pig from a gamekeeper's cottage in a west wood and convey it across country to the detached villa Sunnybrae on the Shrewsbury road is a butler who feels that enough is sufficient. There were dark circles under Beach's eyes and he found himself starting at sudden noises. And it did not improve his state of mind that he had a tender heart and winced at the spectacle of all the sadness he saw around him.

A conversation he had had with Penny this evening had affected him deeply, and the sight of Lord Emsworth at dinner had plunged him still further in gloom. It had no longer been possible to withhold from Lord Emsworth the facts relating to Empress of Blandings, and it had been obvious to Beach, watching him at the meal, that the various courses were turning to ashes in his mouth.

Even Mr Galahad had seemed moody, and Maudie, who might have done something to relieve the funereal atmosphere, had been over at Matchingham Hall. The only bright spot was the non-appearance of Lady Constance, who had caught Lord Emsworth's cold and had taken her dinner in bed.

Beach helped himself to another glass of port, his third. It was pre-phylloxera, and should have had him dancing about the room, strewing roses from his hat, but it did not so much as bring a glow to his eye. For all the good it was doing him, it might have been sarsaparilla. And he was just wondering where he could turn for comfort, now that even port had failed him, when he saw that his solitude had been invaded. Gally was entering, and on his expressive face it seemed to Beach that there was a strange new light, as if hope had dawned.

Nor was he in error. Throughout the day and all through dinner Gally had been bringing a brain trained by years of mixing with the members of the Pelican Club to bear on the problems confronting his little group of serious thinkers. What Beach, watching him at the table, had mistaken for moodiness had in reality been deep thought. And now this deep thought had borne fruit.

'Port?' said Gally, eyeing the decanter. 'You can give me some of that, and speedily. My God!' he said, sipping. 'It's the old '78. You certainly do yourself well, Beach, and who has a better right to? If I've said once that there's nobody like you, I've said it a hundred times. Staunch and true are the adjectives I generally select when asked to draw a word-portrait of you. Beach, I tell people when they come inquiring about you, is a man who . . . well, how shall I describe him? Ah yes, I say, he is a man who, if offered an opportunity of doing a friend a good turn, will leap to the task, even if it involves going through fire and water. He –'

It would be incorrect to say that Beach had paled. His was a complexion, ruddier than the cherry, which did not readily lose its vermilion hue. But his jaw had fallen, and he was looking at his visitor rather in the manner of the lamb mentioned by the philosopher Schopenhauer when closeted with the butcher.

'It . . . It isn't anything else, is it, Mr Galahad?' he faltered.

'Eh?'

'There is nothing further you wish me to do for you, sir?'

Gally laughed genially.

'Good heavens, no. Not a thing. At least –'

'Sir?'

'It did, I admit, cross my mind that you might possibly care to kidnap George Cyril Wellbeloved and tie him up and force him to reveal where the Empress is hidden by sticking lighted matches between his toes. Would you?'

'No, sir.'

'Merely a suggestion. You could keep him in the coal cellar.'

'No, sir. I am sorry.'

'Quite all right, my dear fellow. It was just a random thought that occurred to me while reading one of those gangster stories in the library before dinner. I had an idea that it might have appealed to you, but no. Well, we all have our likes and dislikes. Then we must think of something else, and I believe I have it. It's true, is it, that Maudie is going to marry young Parsloe?'

'Yes, sir. I had the information from her personal lips.'

'And he loves her?'

'She inferred as much from his attitude, sir.'

'In that case, I should imagine that her lightest wish would be law to him.'

'One assumes so, Mr Galahad.'

'Then everything becomes quite simple. She must wheedle the blighter.'

'Sir?'

'You must take her aside, Beach, and persuade her to ask young Parsloe where the Empress is and use her feminine wiles till she has got the secret out of him. She can do it if she tries. Look at Samson and Delilah. Look at –'

Whatever further test cases Gally had been about to mention were wiped from his lips by the sudden ringing of the telephone, a strident instrument capable of silencing the stoutest talker. Beach, who had leaped in the air, returned to earth and took up the receiver.

'Blandings Castle. Lord Emsworth's butler spe ... Oh, good evening, sir ... Yes, sir ... Very good, sir ... Mr Vail, Mr Galahad,' said Beach, aside. 'He wishes me to inform Miss Donaldson that he has left the Emsworth Ar –'

It is not easy to break off in the middle of a single syllable word like 'Arms', but Beach had contrived to do so. Like a cloud across the moon, a look of horror and consternation was spreading itself over the acreage of his face.

Gally frowned.

'Left the Emsworth Arms?' he said sharply. A man who has taken the trouble to give the younger generation the benefit of his advice does not like to have that advice rejected. 'Let me talk to him.'

Slowly Beach replaced the receiver.

'The gentleman has rung off, sir.'

'Did he say where he was going?'

Beach tottered to the table, and reached out a feeble hand to his glass of port.

'Yes, Mr Galahad. He has taken a furnished house.'

'Eh? Where? What furnished house?'

Beach drained his glass. His eyes were round and bulging.

'Sunnybrae, sir,' he said in a low voice. 'On the Shrewsbury road.'

Chapter 9

The Pelican Club trains its sons well. After he has been affiliated to that organization for a number of years, taking part week by week in its informal Saturday night get-togethers, a man's moral fibre becomes toughened, and very little can happen to him that is capable of making him even raise his eyebrows. Gally, as he heard Beach utter those devastating words, did, it is true, give a slight start, but a member of the Athenaeum or the National Liberal would have shot six feet straight up in the air and bumped his head against the ceiling.

When he spoke, there was no suggestion of a quiver in his voice. The Club would have been proud of him.

'Are you trying to be funny, Beach?'

'No, sir, I assure you.'

'You really mean it? Sunnybrae?'

'Yes, sir.'

'What on earth does he want to go to Sunnybrae for?'

'I could not say, sir.'

'But he's on his way there?'

'Yes, sir.'

'And when he gets there ...' Gally paused. He polished his monocle thoughtfully. 'Things look sticky, Beach.'

'Extremely glutinous, Mr Galahad. I fear the worst. The gentleman, on arriving at Sunnybrae, will find the pig in residence –'

'And what will the harvest be?'

'Precisely, sir.'

Gally nodded. He was a man who could face facts.

'Yes, sticky is the word. No good trying to conceal it from ourselves that a crisis has arisen. Jerry Vail is an author, and you know as well as I do what authors are. Unbalanced. Unreliable. Fatheads, to a man. It was precisely because he was an author that I did not admit this Vail to our counsels in the matter of the Parsloe pig. Informed of the facts, he would have spread the story all over Shropshire. And he'll be spreading it all over Shropshire now, if we don't act like lightning. You agree?'

'Yes, indeed, sir.'

'Authors are like that. No reticence. No reserve. You or I, Beach, finding a pig in the kitchen of a furnished villa in which we had just hung up our hats, would keep calm and wait till the clouds rolled by. But not an author. The first thing this blighted Vail will do, unless nipped in the bud, will be to rush out and grab the nearest passer-by and say "Pardon me for addressing you, sir, but there appears to be a pig in my kitchen. Have you any suggestions?" And then what? I'll tell you what. Doom, desolation, and despair. In next to no time the news will have reached Parsloe, stirring him up like a dose of salts and bringing him round to Sunnybrae with a whoop and a holler. We must hurry, Beach. Not an instant to lose. We must get the car out immediately and fly like the wind to the centre of the vortex, trusting that we shall not be too late. Come on, man, come on. Don't just stand there. A second's delay may be fatal.'

'But I have to take the tray of beverages into the drawing-room at nine-thirty, Mr Galahad.'

'The what?'

'The tray of beverages, sir. For the ladies and gentlemen. Whisky and, for those who prefer it, barley-water.'

'Give it a miss. Let 'em eat cake. Good heavens, is this a time to be thinking of whisky and babbling of barley-water? I never heard such nonsense.'

Beach stiffened a little. In his long and honourable years of office at Blandings Castle, allowing deduction for an annual holiday by the sea, he had taken the tray of beverages into the drawing-room at nine-thirty a matter of six thousand six hundred and sixty-nine times, and to have the voice of the Tempter urging him to play hooky and not bring the total to six thousand six hundred and seventy was enough to make any butler stiffen.

'I fear I could not do that, Mr Galahad,' he said, coldly. 'Professional intregrity constrains me to perform my allotted task. It is a matter of principle. I shall be happy to join you at Sunnybrae directly I am at liberty. I will borrow the chauffeur's bicycle.'

Gally wasted no time in fruitless argument. You cannot reason with a butler whose motto is Service.

'All right,' he said. 'Come on as soon as you can, for who knows what stern work may lie before us this night!'

And with a crisp 'You and your blasted trays of beverages!' he hurried out, heading for the garage.

2

Jerry Vail's sudden decision to move from the Emsworth Arms and start housekeeping for himself had been due to certain shortcomings in the general set-up of that in many respects admirable hostelry. The Emsworth Arms, like most inns in English country towns, specialized in beer, and when it came to providing its patrons with anything else was rather inclined to lose interest and let its attention wander.

Beds for instance. It did not worry much about beds. You could have one, if you wanted to, but Jerry, having inspected the specimen offered to him, shrank from the prospect of occupying it for an indefinite series of nights. If he had been an Indian fakir, accustomed from childhood to curling up on spikes, he could have wished for nothing better, but he was not an Indian fakir accustomed from childhood to curling up on spikes.

There was also the drawback that nowhere in the place was it possible for a man to write. The Emsworth Arms' idea of a writing-room was an almost pitch dark cubby-hole with no paper, no pens, and in the ink-pot only a curious sediment that looked like something imported from the Florida Everglades. And when he discovered that in addition to these defects the room was much infested by commercial travellers, talking in loud voices about orders and expense accounts, it is not difficult to understand why the quiet evenfall found him in the offices of Caine and Cooper, house agents, High Street, Market Blandings, inquiring about houses.

He was delighted when Mr Lancelot Cooper, the firm's junior partner, informed him that by a lucky chance there happened to be available a furnished villa ready for immediate occupancy, and he was still further pleased to learn that the residence in question had only recently been vacated by Admiral C. J. Biffen. Admiral Biffen, he told Mr Cooper, was a very old and valued friend of his, which would make any villa he had recently vacated seem like home, and the notorious tidiness of naval men gave assurance that everything would have been left in apple-pie order. Nice going, was his verdict, and Mr Cooper agreed with him.

'You intend to remain long in these parts?' he asked.

'Till the sands of the desert grow cold, if necessary,' said Jerry, thinking of Penny, and taking the keys he went off to the Emsworth Arms to pack and have a bite of dinner before settling in.

His new home, when he beheld it at about twenty minutes past nine, came at first glance as a disappointment. True, Mr Cooper had spoken of it throughout as a villa and the name Sunnybrae should have prepared him, but subconsciously Jerry had been picturing something with a thatched roof and honeysuckle and old Mister Moon climbing up over the trees, and it was disconcerting to find a red brick building which might have been transferred from the suburbs of London. Market Blandings itself was old and picturesque, but, as in other country towns, the speculative builder had had his way on the outskirts.

Still, it improved when you got inside. There was a cosy living-room, and in the corner of the living-room a good firm desk. And a good firm desk was what he particularly wanted, for in the intervals of sneaking up to Blandings Castle and meeting Penny among the rose bushes he planned to start composing what he was convinced was going to be his masterpiece.

The inspiration for it had hit him like a bullet the moment he had set eyes on Mr Lancelot Cooper. The junior partner of Caine and Cooper, though a man of blameless life, had one of those dark, saturnine faces which suggest a taste for the more sinister forms of crime, and on one cheek of that dark, saturnine face was a long scar. Actually it had been caused by the bursting of a gingerbeer bottle at a YMCA picnic, but it gave the impression of being the outcome of battles with knives in the cellars of the underworld. And on top of all that he had been wearing lavender gloves.

It was those gloves that had set Jerry tingling. His trained mind saw them as the perfect box office touch. There is nothing so spine-chilling as a dressy assassin. All murderers make us shudder a bit, but when we encounter one who, when spilling human gore, spills it in lavender gloves, our backbone turns to ice. Mr Cooper, talking pleasantly of rent and clauses and deposits, had had no notion of it, but right from the start of their interview his client was seeing him as Lavender Joe, the man for whom the police had for years – vainly – been spreading a drag-net. Jerry had begun to jot down notes within two minutes of his departure from the Caine and Cooper offices, and he was still jotting down notes as he left the living-room and went upstairs to have a look at the bedroom.

The bedroom was all right. Quite a good bedroom, the bed springy to the touch. His spirits rose. A man, he felt, could be very happy and get through a lot of work in a place like this. He could see himself toiling far into the night, with nothing to disturb the flow.

Well, practically nothing. From the point of view of a writer who wanted peace and quiet so that he could concentrate on a goose-flesher about murderers in lavender gloves, Sunnybrae was nearly ideal. Its one small defect was that it appeared to be haunted.

From time to time, as he moved about his new home, Jerry had been aware of curious noises, evidently supernatural. If asked by the Committee of the Society of Psychical Research to describe these noises, he would have been rather at a loss. Well, sort of grunting noises, he would have told them.

Grunting?

Yes.

When you say grunting, do you mean *grunting*?

That's right. It doesn't go on all the time, of course. For a while there will be a kind of lull, as if the spectre were thinking things over and resting its vocal chords. Then, refreshed, off it goes again . . . grunting, if you see what I mean.

Upon which, the Committee of the Society of Psychical Research would have said 'Well, Lord-love-a-duck!', grunting ghosts being new in their experience.

It was in the living-room that the sounds were most noticeable. Back there now, he was startled by a series of five or six almost at his elbow. The poltergeist, for such he assumed it to be, appeared to have holed up behind the door that led presumably to the kitchen, the only part of the house he had not yet inspected.

He opened the door.

3

It is not easy to state offhand what is the last thing a young man starting out in life would wish to find on the premises of the furnished villa ready for immediate occupancy which he had just begun to occupy. Bugs? Perhaps. Cockroaches? Possibly. Maybe defective drains. One cannot say. But a large black pig in the kitchen would unquestionably come quite high up on the list of undesirable objects, and Jerry, as he gazed at Queen of Matchingham, was conscious of that disagreeable sensation which comes to those who, pausing to tie a shoelace while crossing a railway line, find themselves struck in the small of the back by the Cornish express.

It was the unexpectedness of the thing that had unnerved him. It had caught him unprepared. If Lancelot Cooper, handing him the keys, had said 'Oh, by the way, when you get to Sunnybrae, you will find the kitchen rather full of pigs, I'm afraid,' he would have known where he was. But not a word had been spoken on the subject. The animal had come upon him as a complete surprise, and he sought in vain for an explanation of its presence. It was not as though it had been a corpse with a severed head. A corpse with a severed head in the kitchen of Sunnybrae he could have understood. As a writer of mystery thrillers, he knew that you are apt to find corpses with severed heads pretty well anywhere. But why a pig?

It was just after he had closed his eyes, counted twenty and opened them again, hoping to find that the apparition had melted into thin air, that the front door bell rang.

The moment was not one which Jerry would have chosen for entertaining a visitor, and the only thing that made him go and answer the bell was the thought that this caller might have something to suggest which would help to clarify the situation. Two heads, unless of course severed, are so often better than one. He opened the door, and found standing on the steps a large policeman, who gave him one of those keen, penetrating looks which make policemen so unpopular.

'Ho,' he said, in the sort of voice usually described as steely.

He was tough and formidable, like the policemen in Jerry's stories. Indeed, if Jerry had been capable at the moment of thinking of anything except pigs, he might have seen in his visitor an excellent model for Inspector Jarvis, the Scotland Yard man whom he was planning to set on the trail of Lavender Joe. He pictured Inspector Jarvis as a man who might have been carved out of some durable substance like granite, and that was the material which seemed to have been used in assembling this zealous officer.

'Ho!' said the policeman. 'Resident?'

'Eh?'

'Do you live in this house?'

'Yes, I've just moved in.'

'Where did you get the keys?'

'From Caine and Cooper in the High Street.'

'Ho.'

The policeman seemed to soften. His suspicions lulled, he relaxed. He tilted his helmet and passed a large hand over his forehead.

'Warm tonight,' he said, and it was plain that he was now regarding this as a social occasion. 'Thought at one time this afternoon we were in for a thunderstorm. Well, I must apologize for disturbing you, sir, but seeing a light in the window and knowing the house to be unoccupied, I thought it best to make inquiries. You never know. Strange occurrences have been happening recently in Market Blandings and district, and I don't like the look of things.'

This was so exactly what Jerry was feeling himself that he began to regard this policeman as a kindred soul, one to whose sympathetic ear he could confide his troubles and perplexities. And he was about to do so, when the other went on.

'Down at the station the boys think there's one of these crime waves starting. Two milk cans abstracted from doorsteps only last week, and now all this to-do up at Matchingham Hall. You'll have heard about Sir Gregory Parsloe's pig, no doubt, sir?'

Jerry leaped an inch or two.

'Pig?'

'His prize pig, Queen of Matchingham. Stolen,' said the policeman impressively. 'Snitched out of its sty and so far not a trace of the miscreant. But we'll apprehend him. Oh yes, we'll apprehend him all right, and then he'll regret his rash act. Very serious matter, pig stealing. I wouldn't care to be in the shoes of the fellow that's got that pig. He's laughing now,' said the policeman, quite incorrectly, 'but he won't be laughing long. Making an extended stay here, sir?'

'It may be some time.'

'Nice little house,' said the policeman tolerantly. 'Compact, you might call it. Mind you, you don't want to treat it *rough* . . . not go leaning against the walls or anything like that. I know the fellow that built this little lot. Six of them there are – Sunnybrae, Sunnybrow, Sunnywood, Sunnyfields, Sunnycot, and Sunnyhaven. I was having a beer with this chap one night – it was the day Sunnycot fell down – and he started talking about mortar. Mortar? I says. Why, I didn't know you ever used any. Made me laugh, that did. Well, I'll be getting along, sir. Got my round to do, and then I have to go and report progress to Sir Gregory. Not that there is any progress to report, see what I mean, but the gentleman likes us to confer with him. Shows zeal. Mortar!' said the policeman. 'Why, I didn't know you ever used any, I said. You should have seen his face.'

He passed into the night, guffawing heartily, and Jerry, tottering back to the living-room, sat down and put his head between his hands. This is the recognized posture for those who wish to think, and it was obvious that the problems that had arisen could do with all the thinking he was at liberty to give them. Fate, he perceived, had put him in a tight spot. At any moment he was liable to be caught with the goods and to become, as so many an innocent man has become, a victim of circumstantial evidence.

This sort of thing was no novelty to him, of course. He could recall at least three stories he had written in the past year or so in which the principal characters had found themselves in just such a position as he was in now, with the trifling difference that what they had discovered in their homes had been, respectively, a dead millionaire with his head battered in, a dead ambassador with his throat cut, and a dead dancer known as La Flamme with a dagger of Oriental design between her fourth and fifth ribs. Whenever the hero of a Vail story took a house, he was sure to discover something of that sort in it. It was pure routine.

But the fact that the situation was a familiar one brought no comfort to him. He continued agitated. *Vis-à-vis* with the corpses listed above, his heroes had never known what to do next, and he did not know what to do next. The only thing he was sure he was not going to do was answer the front-door bell, which had just rung again.

The bell rang twice, then stopped. Jerry, who had raised his head, replaced it between his hands and gave himself up to thought once more. And he was wishing more earnestly than ever that something even remotely resembling a plan of action would suggest itself to him, when he seemed to sense a presence in the room. He had an uncanny feeling that he was not alone. Then there sounded from behind him a deferential cough, and turning he perceived that his privacy had been invaded by a long, lean, red-haired man with strabismus in his left eye, a mouth like a halibut's, a broken nose, and lots of mud all over him.

He stood gaping. Hearing that cough where no cough should have been he had supposed for an instant that this time it really was the official Sunnybrae ghost reporting for duty, though what ghosts were doing, haunting a red-brick villa put up at the most five years ago by a speculative builder, he was at a loss to understand. Reason now told him that no spectre would be likely to be diffusing such a very strong aroma of pig, as was wafted from this long, lean, red-haired man, and his momentary spasm of panic passed, leaving behind it the righteous indignation of the householder who finds uninvited strangers in the house which he is holding.

'Who on earth are you?' he demanded, with a good deal of heat.

The intruder smirked respectfully.

'Wellbeloved is the name, sir. I am Sir Gregory Parsloe's pig man. Sir?'

Jerry had not spoken. The sound that had proceeded from him had been merely a sort of bubbling cry, like that of a strong swimmer in his agony. With one long, horrified stare, he reeled to a chair and sank into it, frozen from the soles of the feet upwards.

Chapter 10

It was that light shining in the window that had brought George Cyril Wellbeloved to Sunnybrae, just as it had brought the recent officer of the Law. Happening to observe it as he passed along the road, he had halted spell-bound, his heart leaping up as that of the poet Wordsworth used to do when he saw rainbows. He felt like a camel which, wandering across a desert, comes suddenly upon a totally unexpected oasis.

The fact has not been mentioned, for, as we have explained, a historian cannot mention everything, but during the period of the former's tenancy of Sunnybrae relations of considerable cordiality had existed between Admiral G. J. Biffen and Sir Gregory Parsloe's pig man. They had met at the Emsworth Arms one night, and acquaintance had soon ripened into friendship. Admiral Biffen liked telling long stories about life on the China station in the old days, and no story could be too long for George Cyril Wellbeloved to listen to provided beer was supplied, as on these occasions it always was. The result was that many a pleasant evening had been passed in this living-room, with the gallant Admiral yarning away in a voice like a foghorn and George Cyril drinking beer and saying 'Coo!' and 'Lumme' and 'Well, fancy that!' at intervals. The reader will be able to picture the scene if he throws his mind back to descriptions he has read of the sort of thing that used to go on in those *salons* of the eighteenth century.

His host's abrupt departure had come as a stunning blow to George Cyril Wellbeloved. He would not readily forget the black despair which had gripped him that memorable night when, arriving at Sunnybrae in confident expectation of the usual, he had found the house in darkness and all the windows shuttered. It was as if a hart, panting for cooling streams when heated in the chase, had come to a cooling stream and found it dried up.

And then he had seen that light shining in the window, and had assumed from it that his benefactor had returned and that the golden age was about to set in anew.

All this he explained to Jerry as the latter sat congealed in his chair.

'Far be it from me to intrude on a gentleman's privacy,' said George Cyril Wellbeloved in his polished way. 'It is the last thing I would desire. But seeing a light in the window I thinks to myself "Coo! It's the Admiral come back," so I ring the bell, and then I ring it again, and then, when no reply transpires, I remember that the Admiral is a little hard of hearing, as is only natural in a gentleman of his advanced years, and I see the door on the jar as if someone had forgotten to close it, so I took the lib of barging in. I'm sorry to discover that it's not the Admiral come back, after all, though very glad to make your acquaintance, sir,' said George Cyril politely, 'and I'll tell you why I'm sorry. On a warm night like this, his kind heart melted by the thought that I'd been toiling all day at my numerous duties, Admiral Biffen would have given me a bottle of beer. And I don't mind telling you, sir,' said George Cyril, frankly laying his cards on the table, 'that what with it being a warm night and what with me all worn out from toiling at my numerous duties, a bottle of beer is what I'm fairly gasping for.'

He paused for a reply, but no reply came. Not, that is to say, from Jerry. But Queen of Matchingham, hearing that loved voice, had just uttered a cordial grunt of welcome. It seemed to Jerry's strained senses to ring through the room like the Last Trump, and he was surprised that his companion appeared not to have heard it.

'Admiral Biffen,' said George Cyril Wellbeloved, throwing the information out casually, though with perhaps a certain undertone of significance, 'used to keep his bottles of beer in a bucket of cold water in the kitchen.'

And so saying, he moved a step towards the door, as if anxious to ascertain whether his present host pursued that same excellent policy.

For an instant, Jerry sat rigid, like a character in one of his stories hypnotized by a mad scientist. Then, leaping to his feet, he sprang across the room. In doing so, he overturned a small table on which were a bowl of wax fruit, a photograph in a pink frame of the speculative builder to whom Sunnybrae owed its existence, the one who never used mortar, and a china vase bearing the legend 'A Present From Llandudno'. It also contained the notebook in which he had been jotting down his notes for the story of Lavender Joe, and as his eye fell on it, inspiration came to him.

He looked at George Cyril Wellbeloved, and was encouraged by what he saw. He took another look, and was still more encouraged.

The world may be roughly divided into two classes – men who, when you tell them a story difficult to credit, will not believe you, and men who will. It was to this latter and far more likeable section of the community that, judging by his fatuous expression, George Cyril Wellbeloved belonged. He had the air, which Jerry found charming, of being a man who would accept without question whatever anybody cared to tell him. His whole aspect was that of one who believed everything he read in the Sunday papers.

'Listen,' said Jerry.

It was an unfortunate word to have used, for at this moment Queen of Matchingham uttered another grunt. But again the visitor appeared not to have noticed it. Like Admiral Biffen, he seemed to be hard of hearing.

'I suppose,' said Jerry, proceeding rapidly, 'you're wondering what I'm doing in this house?'

With an old-world gesture, George Cyril Wellbeloved disclaimed any such vulgar curiosity.

'I presume,' he said politely, 'that you live here, sir? Or, putting it another way, that this is your residence?'

Jerry shook his head.

'No. I live in London.'

'Sooner you than me,' said George Cyril Wellbeloved. 'Nasty noisy place.'

'And why do I live in London?'

'You like it, I suppose, sir. Some do, I'm told.'

'No. I live in London because I have to. To be handy for the Yard.'

'Sir?'

'Scotland Yard. I'm a Scotland Yard man.'

'Well, strike me pink,' said George Cyril Wellbeloved, properly impressed. 'Might I venture to inquire what you're doing here, sir?'

'I'm on duty. Working on a case. I was sent to watch out for a dangerous criminal known as Lavender Joe. So called because he always wears lavender gloves. From information received, we know that this man will be arriving tonight on the train from London that reaches Market Blandings at ten-fifteen, and we think that he will come to this house.'

George Cyril Wellbeloved asked what had put that idea into their heads, and Jerry said he was unable to tell him because of the Official Secrets Act, and George Cyril said 'Ah, there was always something, wasn't there.'

'But it is possible,' Jerry went on, 'that before coming to Sunny-brae he will go somewhere else, and it is essential that I know where. I ought to be at the station, watching his every move, but I have to remain here. You see my difficulty?'

George Cyril Wellbeloved thought for a moment.

'You can't be in two places at once,' he hazarded.

'Exactly. You've hit it. My God, you're shrewd. So I need your help. I want you to take my place at the station. Go there, meet the train that gets in at ten-fifteen and follow Lavender Joe wherever he goes. But mark this. It is quite possible that he will not come on the ten-fifteen train.'

'That'll be a bit of a mix-up. What they call an amparse. What do I do then?'

'You will have to meet all the other trains from London, even if it means staying there all night.'

'All night?'

'Yes.'

'Coo! Then I'd better have a bottle of beer first. Where d'you keep it?'

'I haven't any beer.'

George Cyril's jaw fell.

'No beer?'

'No. What do you think this place is? A pub? Come, come, man, we have no time to waste talking about beer. It's settled, then, that you go to the station and remain there as long as is necessary, and you ought to be starting right away. Thank you, Wellbeloved. You are a public-spirited citizen, and I'm proud of you. You're doing a fine job, and the Yard will not forget it. Your heroism will be brought to the notice of the men up top.'

George Cyril blinked.

'Heroism? How do you mean heroism?'

'Lavender Joe is a very dangerous man,' explained Jerry. 'He carries weapons, and never hesitates to use them. So you must be careful. I wouldn't like you to have your liver ripped out by a dagger of Oriental design.'

'I wouldn't like it myself.'

'Well, we'll hope it won't come to that,' said Jerry briskly. 'Any questions you want to ask before you go?'

'Yes,' said George Cyril, equally brisk, if not more so. 'What is there in it for me?'

Jerry stared.

'How do you mean, what is there in it for you? You'll be assisting Scotland Yard.'

'Well, I think Scotland Yard ought to assist me,' said George Cyril Wellbeloved.

A grunt from the kitchen seemed to suggest that Queen of Matchingham thoroughly approved of this business-like attitude, and Jerry, leaping as he heard it, felt it best not to argue.

'It might run to a quid,' he conceded.

'Ten quid,' corrected George Cyril Wellbeloved.

'Three quid.'

'Well, I'll tell you,' said George Cyril. 'I don't want to be hard on the Yard. Call it five.'

Jerry felt in his pocket.

'All I have on me is three pounds two and twopence.'

'Write a cheque.'

'I haven't a cheque book.'

'You could use a slip of paper and stick a stamp on.'

'I haven't a stamp.'

George Cyril Wellbeloved sighed. He seemed to be feeling that Jerry was armed at all points.

'All right. Three pounds two and tuppence.'

'Here you are.'

'Hoy!' cried George Cyril Wellbeloved. 'Where's the tuppence?'

A sordid scene, and one feels thankful that it is over. A minute later, Jerry was alone.

Five minutes later, the front-door bell rang again.

2

It seemed to Jerry, whom recent events had left a little peevish, that he had been doing nothing since he was a small boy in a sailor suit but listen to the tinkling of the front door bell of this infernal villa ready for immediate occupancy. The moment one ringer left, another took his place. In all his experience he had never been associated with such a gregarious crowd as the residents of Market Blandings and district. Whenever time hung heavy on their hands, it was as though the cry went up 'Let's all go round to Vail's'.

The current pest, he felt morosely, was probably the Vicar, come to try to touch him for a subscription to his church's organ fund, and he had resolved to stay where he was and let the reverend gentleman go on ringing till his thumb wore out, when he abruptly changed his mind. A voice had called his name, and he recognized it as the voice of the Hon. Galahad Threepwood, the one person in the world he most desired to see. Gally might have his defects – his sister Constance, his sister Dora, his sister Julia, and all his other sisters could have named you hundreds – but he was sure to be a mine of information on what to do when you discovered a stolen pig in your kitchen one jump ahead of the police.

He opened the door and finding Gally on the top step, practically flung himself on his bosom.

'Mr Threepwood –'

'Mr Threepwood be blowed. Call me Gally. I'm not Mr Threepwood to a nephew of Plug Basham's. Is there something on your mind, my boy? You seem agitated. Or am I wrong?'

'No, you're not wrong. I'm on the verge of a nervous breakdown. There's a pig in the kitchen.'

'Ah, you've noticed that?'

Jerry started.

'You knew it was there?'

'It's what I've come about. This is no idle social call. Let us go inside and talk the whole thing over in a calm and detached spirit.'

He led the way to the living-room and settled himself comfortably in a chair.

'I can't understand why Fruity Biffen didn't like this place,' he said, gazing about him. 'Pretty snug, it looks to me. Wax fruit, presents from Llandudno . . . I don't see what more a man could ask. But Fruity always was a peculiar chap. Odd. Temperamental. Did I ever tell you the story of Fruity and –'

Jerry broke in on the reminiscence. A host ought not, of course, to interrupt a visitor, but then, looking at it another way, a visitor ought not to put pigs in a host's kitchen. And a monstrous suspicion had begun to take root in Jerry's mind.

'Was it you who put that pig there?' he demanded, clothing it in words.

'Why, yes,' said Gally. 'That's right. Or, rather, Beach did, acting on my instructions. You see, a good deal of what you might call cut-and-thrust has been going on these last few days, and your pig –'

'I wish you wouldn't call it my pig.'

'The pig under advisement,' amended Gally, 'is one of the pawns in the game. To get a clear, over-all picture of the state of affairs, you must realize that my brother Clarence's porker, Empress of Blandings, and Parsloe's nominee, Queen of Matchingham, are running neck and neck for the Fat Pigs medal at the forthcoming Shropshire Agricultural Show, and Parsloe is a ruthless and unscrupulous man with a soul as black as the ace of spades who will resort to the lowest forms of crime to gain his ends. And so, knowing that it would be merely a question of time before he tried to pinch our pig, I thought it judicious to strike first by pinching his. Attack, as a thinker of my acquaintance pointed out not long ago, is the best form of defence. So we snitched the Queen while he on his side snitched the Empress. You always get a lot of this sort of wholesome give and take on these occasions. We put the Queen in a disused gamekeeper's cottage in the west wood, but with fiendish cunning the opposition traced it there, so we had to find another haven in a hurry. I fortunately remembered that Sunnybrae was unoccupied.'

'Unoccupied!'

'Well, I thought it was.'

Jerry did not attempt to conceal his displeasure.

'You might have told me.'

'Yes, I suppose one should have done.'

'I would have been spared a very nasty shock. When I opened that door and saw pigs in the kitchen as far as the eye could reach,' said Jerry, with a shudder as he relived that high spot in his career, 'I thought the top of my head had come off.'

Gally murmured sympathetically.

'Quite a surprise it must have been, I should imagine.'

'It was.'

'Too bad. I can readily understand it tickling you up a bit. Though it is a very moot point whether such shocks aren't good for one. They stimulate the adrenal glands.'

'Well, I like my adrenal glands the way they are.'

'Quite, quite. Heaven forbid that I should try to dictate to any man about his adrenal glands. Have them exactly as you wish, my boy. This is Liberty Hall. But you appear a little vexed with me, and I cannot see how I can be blamed for what has occurred. How was I to know that you would be coming to roost at Sunnybrae? Why did you, by the way?'

'I didn't like the Emsworth Arms.'

'Bed not up to your specifications?'

'No. Hard lumps all over it.'

'You young fellows think too much of your comfort,' said Gally reprovingly. 'Why, when I was your age, I frequently slept on billiard tables. I remember on one occasion Plug Basham, Puffy Benger, and I shared two chairs and an ironing board. It was when –'

Again Jerry interrupted, once more probably missing something good.

'Touching on this pig –'

'Ah, yes, the pig. I know the pig you mean. Go on, my boy.'

'It may interest you to learn that the police have been here, hot on its trail.'

'The police?'

'Well, a policeman. He saw the light in the window and came to make inquiries.'

'You didn't show him over the house, I hope?'

'No, we talked on the steps.'

'Good.'

'He was full of the stolen pig –'

'Courting dyspepsia.'

'Eh?'

'I merely meant it sounded rather indigestible. Go on. This policeman was full of the stolen pig, you were saying.'

'And he expects to make an early arrest.'

'One smiles.'

'I don't.'

'I do, and mockingly at that. I also laugh with a light tinkle in my voice. Have no anxiety about the local flatties, my boy. They couldn't find a bass drum in a telephone booth. What became of him?'

'He left. Shortly afterwards a man called Wellbeloved arrived.'

Gally gave a little jump.

'Wellbeloved?'

'He said he was Sir Gregory Parsloe's pig man. He, too, had seen the light in the window and thought it was Admiral Biffen come back. He and Admiral Biffen used to swig beer together, it seems.'

Gally nodded.

'That part about Fruity swigging beer rings true, but I should have thought he would have been more careful in his choice of friends. This Wellbeloved is a man of wrath, a deliberate and systematic viper if ever there was one. Did you talk to him on the steps?'

'No. He came in.'

'What on earth did you let him in for?'

'I didn't let him in. Apparently I had left the front door open. I was sitting wondering what to do for the best, and I sensed a presence and there he was.'

'What, in here? With only that door separating him from the pig?'

'He didn't see the pig.'

'But he has ears. Didn't the animal grunt?'

'Yes, several times. I was surprised he didn't hear it.'

Gally rose. His face was a little twisted, as a man's face so often is in the bitter hour of defeat.

'He heard it,' he said shortly. 'A good pig man can hear his personal pig grunt ten miles away in the middle of a thunderstorm and recognize its distinctive note even if a thousand other pigs are giving tongue simultaneously. He knew that pig was there, all right. I wonder he didn't denounce you on the spot. What did happen?'

'I got rid of him.'

'How?'

'I thought up a story to tell him.'

'What story?'

'Oh, just a story.'

Gally sniffed.

'Well, whatever it was, I'll bet he didn't swallow it.'

'He seemed to.'

'He would. Just humouring you, of course. He's probably squeal-ing to Parsloe at this very moment. Ah, well, this is the end. I'll have to take the creature back to its sty. The secret of a happy and successful life is to know when things have got too hot and cut your losses. It's galling. One hates to admit defeat. Still, there it is.'

Jerry hesitated.

'You won't want me, will you?'

'To help with the pig? No, I can manage.'

'Good. I'm feeling a little unstrung.'

'You'd better wait here and entertain Beach. He will be arriving shortly.'

'Walking?'

'Bicycling,' said Gally. 'And it will be a lasting grief to me that I was not able to see him doing it. Well, bung-o.'

With a set face, he opened the door and strode into the kitchen.

It was about ten minutes after he had gone that there came from the great outdoors the unmistakable sound of a butler falling off a bicycle.

3

The years rob us of our boyish accomplishments. There had been a time, back in the distant past, when Sebastian Beach had yielded to none as a performer on the velocipede – once, indeed, actually emerging victorious in the choirboys' handicap at a village sports meeting, open to all whose voices had not broken before the second Sunday in Epiphany. But those days were gone for ever.

Only the feudal spirit, burning brightly within him, and the thought that Mr Galahad was relying on his co-operation had nerved him to borrow Alfred Voules's machine and set out on the road to Sunnybrae. Right from the start he had had misgivings, and they had proved to be well founded. It is a widely held belief that once you have learned to ride a bicycle, you never lose the knack. Beach had exploded this superstition. It was a bruised and shaken butler whom Jerry greeted at the front door and escorted to the living-room.

Having deposited him in a chair, Jerry found himself embarrassed. Excluded from Gally's little group of plotters, he had had no opportunity of seeing this man's more human side, and to him throughout this sojourn beneath Lord Emsworth's roof Beach had been an aloof, supercilious figure who had paralysed him with his majesty. He was paralysing him now. It is a very intrepid young man who can see an English butler steadily and see him whole without feeling a worm-like humility, and all Jerry's previous encounters with Beach – in corridors, in the hall, at lunch and at dinner – had left him with the impression that his feet were too large, his ears too red and his social status something in between that of a Dead End kid and a badly dressed leper. There were cats on the premises of Blandings Castle, and those gooseberry eyes had always made him feel that he might have been some unsavoury object dragged in by one of these cats, one of the less fastidious ones.

However, he was a host, and it was for him to set the conversation going.

'Have a nice ride?' he asked.

A shudder made the butler's body ripple like a field of wheat when a summer breeze passes over it.

'Not very enjoyable, sir,' he replied in a toneless voice. 'I have not cycled since I was a small lad, and I found it trying to the leg muscles.'

'It does catch you in the leg muscles, doesn't it?' said Jerry sympathetically.

'Yes, sir.'

'In the calves, principally.'

'Yes, sir.'

'You came a purler, didn't you?'

'Sir?'

'I thought I heard you falling off on arrival.'

'Yes, sir. I sustained several falls.'

'Unpleasant, falling off a bicycle. Shakes up the old liver.'

'Precisely, sir,' said Beach, closing his eyes.

Rightly feeling that this was about all his guest would wish to hear on the cycling theme, Jerry relapsed into silence, trying to think of some other topic which would interest, elevate and amuse.

'Mr Threepwood's taken that pig back,' he said at length.

He had struck the right note. The butler's eyes opened, and one could see hope dawning in them.

'Indeed, sir?'

'Yes, he deemed it best. Too many people were nosing round the place – policemen, pig men, and so on. He said the wisest move was to cut his losses before things got too hot. He left about a quarter of an hour ago, so the animal's probably in its sty now.'

Beach expelled a deep breath.

'I am extremely glad to hear that, sir. I was nervous.'

The news that a man like Beach could be nervous encouraged Jerry and put him at his ease. It was the first intimation he had had that human emotions lurked beneath that bulging waistcoat. Things were going with a swing, he felt, and he became chatty.

'Have you known Mr Threepwood long?' he asked.

'Nearly twenty years, sir.'

'As long as that? A weird old buster, don't you think?'

'Sir?'

'Well, I mean charging about the place, stealing pigs. Eccentric, wouldn't you say?'

'I fear you must excuse me from venturing an opinion, sir. It is scarcely fitting for me to discuss the members of my employer's household,' said Beach stiffly, and closed his eyes again.

The hot blush of shame mantled Jerry's cheek. He had never been snubbed by a butler before, and the novel experience made him feel as if he had been walking in the garden in the twilight and had stepped on a rake and had the handle jump up and hit him on the tip of the nose. It was difficult to know what to say next.

He ran through a few subjects in his mind.

The weather?

The crops?

The prospects at the next General Election?

Lord Emsworth, his treatment in sickness and in health?

Then he saw with profound relief that no further conversational efforts would be needed. A faint snore, followed by a series of louder ones, told him that his visitor was asleep. Worn out by his unaccustomed exertions in the saddle, Beach was knitting up the ravelled sleave of care.

Jerry rose noiselessly, and tiptoed out of the room. He was glad to go. He was a fair-minded young man and realized that he had probably not been seeing the other at his best and sunniest, but he preferred not to wait on the chance of improved relations in the future. What he wanted at the moment was a breath of fresh air.

The air was nice and fresh in the road outside Sunnybrae's little front garden, and he was drinking it in and gradually becoming restored to something like tranquillity, when the stillness of the summer night was broken by the sound of an approaching car, and Gally drove up. He was accompanied by a large pig.

It was difficult to be sure in the uncertain light of the moon, but Jerry had the impression that the animal gave him a friendly nod, and the civil thing to have done, of course, would have been to return it. But in moments of agitation we tend to forget the little courtesies of life. He stood staring, his lower jaw drooping on its hinge. Like Othello, he was perplexed in the extreme. That tranquillity to which we alluded a moment ago had been induced by the healing thought that, even if he had had to undergo the spiritual agony of being put in his place by a butler, he was at least free from pigs of every description. And here they were, back in his life again, bigger and better than ever.

He pointed a trembling finger.

'W – w – w . . .?'

He had intended to say 'What?' but the word would not come. Gally cocked an inquiring monocle at him.

'W – w – w . . .?'

'I had a dog that used to make a noise just like that when he was going to be sick,' said Gally. 'A dog named Towser. Parsloe once nobbled him with surreptitious steak and onions on the night when he was to have gone up against his dog Banjo in a rat contest. I must tell you all about it when we are more at leisure, for it will give you a rough idea of the lengths to which the man can go when he plants his footsteps on the deep and rides upon the storm. There isn't time now. It's a longish story, and we have to get the Empress indoors before the enemy discovers she's here and can do her a mischief. Her life would not be worth a moment's purchase if Parsloe knew where she was. He would have his goons out after her with sawn-off shotguns before she could wiggle her tail.'

Jerry was still dazed.

'I don't understand,' he said. 'Why do you say the Empress?'

'Why shouldn't I say the Empress? Oh, I see what you mean. I forgot to tell you, didn't I? I was just going to when you started making noises like my dog Towser about to give up all. It's quite simple. This is the Empress I've got here. When I got to Matchingham and had sneaked round to the sty, she was the first thing I saw in it. Parsloe, with a cunning for which one feels a reluctant admiration, was keeping her there, right on the premises where nobody would ever have dreamed of looking. Naturally I had been thinking in terms of lonely outhouses and underground cellars, never supposing for an instant that the man would put her practically out in the open. It was the same principle, of course, as Edgar Allan Poe's Purloined Letter and, as I say, one feels a grudging respect. So I picked her up and brought her along. But we mustn't waste time standing and talking. Is Beach here?'

'Yes, he's asleep in the living-room.'

'Then we won't disturb him,' said Gally considerately. 'Let the good man get his sleep. We'll take her in the back way.'

A few minutes later, though to Jerry it seemed longer, he stood rubbing his hands with a contented smile.

'And now,' he said, 'to notify Clarence of the happy ending. If you feel like coming to Blandings and having a word with Penny, I'll drive you there.'

4

Whatever a critic of aesthetic tastes might have found to say against Sunnybrae, and this was considerable, he would have been obliged to concede that it was a handy place from which to get to Blandings Castle. Only a mile or so of good road separated the two residences, and it was consequently not much more than a few minutes later that Gally's car drew up again at the Sunnybrae front door, this time with Lord Emsworth aboard.

Lord Emsworth, deeply stirred by Gally's news, had been twittering with excitement and ecstasy from the start of the journey. He was still twittering as they entered the living-room, and stopped twittering only when, thinking to see Beach, he observed Sir Gregory Parsloe. The Squire of Matchingham was seated in a chair, looking fixedly at the photograph of the speculative builder in the pink frame. He plainly did not think highly of the speculative builder. Indeed, if questioned, he would have said that he had never seen such a bally bounder in his life. And it must be admitted that, as speculative builders go, this one, considered from the angle of personal beauty, was not much of a speculative builder.

As Gally and Lord Emsworth entered, he transferred his gaze to them, and it was an unpleasant gaze, in quality and intentness not unlike the one the policeman had directed at Jerry in the opening stages of their conference on the front steps.

'Ha!' he said nastily. 'The Master of the Vultures! I had an idea you would be coming along. If you're looking for that bloodstained butler of yours, you're too late.'

Lord Emsworth replaced his pince-nez, which, pursuing their invariable policy at moments when their proprietor was surprised and startled, had leaped from his nose like live creatures of the wild.

'Parsloe! What are you doing here?'

'Yes,' said Gally warmly. 'Who invited you to stroll in and make yourself at home? Of all the crust! I rather think this constitutes a trespass, and I shall advise young Vail that an action may lie.'

'Who's Vail?'

'The lessee of this house.'

'Oh, that chap? Action, did you say? He won't be bringing any actions. He'll be in prison, like Beach.'

'Beach?' Gally stared. 'Beach isn't in prison. You must be thinking of a couple of other fellows.'

'Constable Evans is probably locking him in his cell at this very moment,' said Sir Gregory with offensive gusto. 'He fortunately happened to be at my house when Wellbeloved came with his news.'

'What news?'

Sir Gregory swelled, like a man who knows that he has a good story to tell.

'I was sitting in my study,' he began, 'enjoying a cigar and chatting with my fiancée, when Binstead, my butler, informed me that Wellbeloved wished to speak to me. I told him to tell him I would see him out on the drive, for I prefer to converse with Wellbeloved in the open air. I joined him there, and he had an amazing story to relate. He said he had been in this house, talking to this fellow Vail, who, I take it, is one of the minor cogs in your organization, and while they were talking, he suddenly heard Queen of Matchingham grunt.'

'But it isn't — '

'Wait, Clarence,' said Gally. 'I want to hear this. I can't make head or tail of it so far. Go on.'

Sir Gregory proceeded.

'Well, he thought for a moment, quite naturally, that he must have imagined it, but then the sound came again, and it was Queen of Matchingham all right. He recognized her grunt, and this time he was able to locate it. It had come from the kitchen. There was plainly a pig there.'

'But that's — '

'Clarence, please! Yes?'

'So he said to himself "Oho!"'

'O what?'

'Ho.'

'Right. Carry on.'

'He had noticed, he said, from the start of their conversation, that this fellow Vail seemed very nervous, and now he appeared to lose his head completely. He attempted to get rid of Wellbeloved with some absurd story about something or other which Wellbeloved says would not have deceived a child. I suppose these inexperienced crooks always do lose their heads in a crisis. No staying power. I don't know who this Vail is — '

'He's my secretary,' said Lord Emsworth.

'In your pay, is he? I thought so.'

'No, he isn't, now I come to think of it,' said Lord Emsworth. 'Connie sacked him.'

'Well, whether he's still your secretary or not is beside the dashed point,' said Sir Gregory impatiently. 'The thing that matters is that he's a minion whom you have bought with your gold. To go on with what I was saying, this bally Vail told Wellbeloved this bally story, straining every nerve to get him out of the house, and Wellbeloved very shrewdly pretended to swallow it and then came and reported to me. I drove here immediately with the constable, heard my pig in the kitchen, found Beach on guard, and directed the officer to take him into custody and haul him off to a prison cell. At the next session of the bench of magistrates I shall sentence him to whatever the term of imprisonment is that a bounder gets for stealing pigs. I shall have to look it up. I shall be much surprised if it isn't six months or a year or something like that. Nor is that all. You, Emsworth, and you, Threepwood, will be up to your necks in the soup as accessories before the fact. With the evidence at my disposal, I shall be able to net the whole gang. That,' said Sir Gregory, after a keen glance at Lord Emsworth and another keen glance at Gally, 'is how matters stand, and I don't wonder you're trembling like leaves. You're in a very nasty spot, you two pig purloiners.'

He ceased, and Gally shook his head, perplexed.

'I don't get it,' he said. 'I thought I was a fairly intelligent man, but this defeats me. It sounds absurd, but the way it looks to me is that you are accusing us of having stolen your pig.'

Sir Gregory stared.

'You haven't the nerve to deny it?'

'Of course I deny it.'

'You are trying to tell me there isn't a pig in that kitchen? Listen, dammit! I can hear it grunting now.'

'My dear fellow, of course you can. A deaf adder could. But that's the Empress.'

'What!'

'You are surprised to find her here? The explanation is quite simple. It seemed to Clarence that she was looking a bit peaked, and he thought a change of air and scenery might do her good. So he asked Vail to put her up for a day or two, and Vail of course said he would be delighted. That was what happened, wasn't it, Clarence?'

'Eh?'

'He says yes,' said Gally.

Sir Gregory stood for a moment staring incredulously, then he strode to the kitchen door and flung it open, and Lord Emsworth, unable to restrain himself any longer, shot through. Grunts and endearing exclamations made themselves heard. Gally closed the door on the sacred reunion.

Sir Gregory was puffing in a distraught sort of way.

'That's not my pig!'

'Of course it isn't,' said Gally soothingly. 'That's what I keep telling you. It's the Empress. You see now how groundless those charges of yours were. I don't want to be censorious, Parsloe, but I must say that when you go about accusing the cream of the British aristocracy of pinching pigs purely on the strength of a chap like George Cyril Wellbeloved having heard one grunt, it looks like the beginning of the end. If that sort of thing is to become habitual, it seems to me that the whole fabric of Society must collapse. The thing I can't understand is how you ever got the idea into your head that Queen of Matchingham had been stolen. Bizarre is the word that springs to the lips. You must have known that she has been in her sty right along.'

'What!'

'Well, all I can tell you is that I was round at your place this afternoon, and she was there then. I thought I would look you up and have a friendly chat, because I feel so strongly how important pleasant neighbourly relations are in the country. When I got to Matchingham, you were out, so I took a turn about the grounds, just to see how your flowers were doing, and I noticed her in her sty. I'd have given her a potato, only I didn't happen to have one on me. But if you still feel doubtful, let's go to Matchingham now, and you can see for yourself.'

The drive to Matchingham Hall was a silent one, and so was the quick walk through the grounds to the Parsloe piggeries. Only when the sty had been reached and its occupant inspected did Sir Gregory speak.

When he did so, it was in a strangled voice.

'That pig wasn't here this morning!' he cried hoarsely.

'Who says so?'

'Wellbeloved.'

Gally gave a light laugh. He was amused.

'Wellbeloved! Do you think any credence is to be attached to what a chap like that tells you? My dear fellow, George Cyril Wellbeloved is as mad as a March hatter. All the Wellboloveds have been. Ask anyone in Market Blandings. It was his grand-father, Ezekiel Wellbeloved, who took off his trousers one snowy afternoon in the High Street and gave them to a passer-by, saying he wouldn't be needing them any longer, as the end of the world was coming that evening at five-thirty sharp. His father, Orlando Wellbeloved –'

Sir Gregory interrupted to say that he did not wish to hear about George Cyril's father, Orlando Wellbeloved, and Gally said that was quite all right, many people didn't.

'I was only trying to drive home my point that it is foolish ever to listen to the babblings of any Wellbeloved. Especially George Cyril. He's the dottiest of the lot. I understand that he's always being approached with flattering offers by the talent scouts of Colney Hatch and similar institutions.'

Sir Gregory gave him a long look, a look fraught with deep feeling. His mind was confused. He was convinced that there was a catch in this somewhere, if one could only put one's finger on it, but he was a slow thinker and it eluded him.

'Ha!' he said.

Gally tut-tutted.

'Surely that is not all you are going to say, my dear fellow,' he said mildly.

'Eh?'

'I should have thought a touch of remorse would have been in order. I mean to say, you have been throwing your weight about a bit, what?'

Sir Gregory struggled with his feelings for a moment.

'Yes. Yes, I see what you mean. All right. I apologize.'

Gally beamed.

'There spoke the true Gregory Parsloe!' he said. 'You will, of course, immediately telephone to the cops that Beach is to be released without delay. It would be a graceful act if you sent your chauffeur down in your car to bring him home. I'd do it myself, only I have to take Clarence and the Empress back to Blandings. Now that she has had this rest cure at Sunnybrae, he will want her back in her old quarters.'

Chapter 11

Having deposited Lord Emsworth in his library and the Empress in her headquarters, Gally returned to his car and drove it into the garage of Blandings Castle. He almost collided with another which was coming out with Lord Vosper at its wheel.

'Hullo,' said Gally, surprised. 'You off somewhere?'

'That's right.'

'A little late, isn't it?'

'It is a bit, I suppose.'

Lord Vosper seemed to hesitate for a moment. Then he remembered that this was the man in whom he had confided. As such, he was entitled to hear the latest news.

'As a matter of fact, Gloria and I are driving to London to get married.'

'Well, I'll be dashed. You are?'

'That's right. We both rather shrank from the thought of explaining things to Lady Constance, so we decided we'd just slide off and spring the news in our bread-and-butter letters.'

'Very sensible. "Dear Lady Constance. How can we thank you enough for our delightful visit to your beautiful home? Such a treat meeting your brother Galahad. By the way, we're married. Yours faithfully, The Vospers." Something on those lines?'

'That's right. We shall drive through the silent night, hitting the metropolis about dawn, I imagine. A couple of hours' sleep, a quick shower, the coffee, the oatmeal, the eggs and bacon, and then off to the registrar's.'

'It sounds a most attractive programme.'

'So Penny was saying. She was wishing that she and Jerry Vail could do the same.'

'They may be able to ere long. You've seen Penny, then?'

'Just now.'

'I'm looking for her.'

'She's looking for you. Between ourselves, she seems a bit disgruntled.'

'I'm sorry to hear that. What about?'

'Ah, there you rather have me. Pigs entered into it, I remember, but if you ask me if I definitely got a toe-hold on the gist, I must answer frankly that I didn't. But you appear to have been upsetting Jerry Vail in some way somehow connected with pigs, and, as I say, she's looking for you. She struck me as being a shade below par, and she spoke with a good deal of animation of skinning you with a blunt knife.'

Gally remained calm.

'She won't want to do that when she hears my news. Her only thought will be to dance about the premises, clapping her little hands. Where is she?'

'In Beach's pantry. At least, I left her there five minutes ago.'

'Beach is back, then?'

'I didn't know he'd gone anywhere.'

'Yes, I believe he went into Market Blandings about something.'

'Oh? Well, he's back, all right. I was looking for him, to tip him, and finally located him in his pantry. He was having a spot of port with Penny and Jerry Vail. Which struck me as odd, as I understood Jerry had got the push.'

'He had. But he bobbed up again. Well, I'll be running along and seeing them. Good luck to your matrimonial venture. I wish you every happiness.'

'Thanks.'

'You'll enjoy being married. Whoso findeth a wife findeth a good thing. It was King Solomon who said that, and he knew, eh! I mean, nothing much you could tell *him* about wives, what?'

'That's right,' said Lord Vosper.

2

It seemed to Gally, who was quick to notice things, that there was a certain strain in the atmosphere of Beach's pantry when he entered it a few minutes later. The port appeared to be circulating, as always when the hospitable butler presided over the revels, but he sensed an absence of the mellow jollity which port should produce. Beach had a dazed, stunned look, as if something hard and heavy had recently fallen on his head. So had Jerry. Penny's look, which came shooting in his direction as he crossed the threshold, was of a different quality. It was like a death ray or something out of a flame-thrower, and he saw that in describing her as disgruntled Orlo Vosper had selected the *mot juste*.

'Oh, there you are!' she said, speaking from between pearly teeth.

'And just in time for a drop of the right stuff, it seems,' said Gally genially. 'How pleasant a little something is at this hour of the day, is it not, and how much better a firkin of port than the barley-water which our good host takes into the drawing-room at nine-thirty each night on the tray of beverages. Thank you,' he said, accepting his glass.

Penny continued to glare.

'I'm not speaking to you, Gally Threepwood,' she said. 'I suppose you know,' she went on, with feminine inconsistency, 'that you've reduced my poor darling Jerry and my poor precious Beach to nervous wrecks?'

'They look all right to me,' said Gally, having inspected her poor darling Jerry and her poor precious Beach.

'Outwardly,' said Jerry coldly. 'Inside, I'm just a fluttering fawn.'

'So is Beach,' said Penny. 'Say Boo.'

'Boo!'

'There! See him jump. Now drop a plate or something.'

Beach quivered.

'No, please, miss. My nerves could not endure it.'

'Nor mine,' said Jerry.

'Come, come,' said Gally. 'This is not the spirit I like to see. You were made of sterner stuff when we three fought side by side at the battle of Agincourt. Well, I must say this surprises me. Who would have thought that a mere half hour in the jug would have affected you so deeply, Beach? Why, in my hot youth I frequently spent whole nights in the oubliettes of the old Vine Street police station, and came out rejoicing in my strength. And you, Jerry. Fancy you being so allergic to pigs.'

'I should prefer not to have the word pig mentioned in my presence,' said Jerry stiffly. He brooded for a moment. 'I remember,' he went on, 'hearing my uncle Major Basham once speak of you. I cannot recall in what connexion your name came up, but he said: "If ever you find yourself getting entangled with Galahad Threepwood, my boy, there is only one thing to do – commend your soul to God and try to escape with your life." How right he was, how terribly right!'

'He knew!' said Penny. 'He, too, had suffered.'

Gally seemed puzzled.

'Now why would he have said a thing like that? Ah!' He brightened. 'He must have been thinking of the time when Puffy Benger and I put old Wivenhoe's pig in his bedroom the night of the Bachelors' Ball at Hammer's Easton.'

Jerry frowned.

'I think I expressed a wish that that word –'

'Quite, quite,' said Gally. 'Let us change the subject. I've just been talking to young Vosper,' he said, doing so.

'Oh?' said Penny coldly.

'Orlo Vosper,' said Gally, 'is not what I would call one of our brightest intellects, but he does occasionally get good ideas. His latest, as you know, is to drive up to London tonight with that dark-eyed serpent, Gloria Salt, and get married at a registrar's, and he was saying that you were wishing you could do the same. Why don't you? You could borrow the small car.'

Jerry gave him a frigid look.

'You are suggesting that Penny and I should go to London and get married?'

'Why not?'

Jerry laughed bitterly.

'Let me supply you with a few statistics relating to my financial position,' he said. 'My income last year, after taxes, was –'

'Yes, yes, I know. But Penny was telling me of this magnificent opening you've got with this health cure place. She stunned me with her story of its possibilities. It is not too much to say that I was electrified. You may argue that you cannot be both stunned *and* electrified, but I say you can, if the conditions are right. "Stap my vitals!" I said to myself. "I must keep in with this fellow Vail, endear myself to him in every possible way, so that in time to come I shall be in a position to get into his ribs for occasional loans. A young man with a future."'

Penny regarded him with distaste.

'Go on. Twist the knife in the wound.'

'I don't follow you, my dear.'

'You know perfectly well that Jerry has to raise two thousand pounds and hasn't a hope of getting it.'

'Why not?'

'Who's going to give it to him?'

Gally's eyebrows rose.

'Why, Clarence, of course.'

'Lord Emsworth?'

'Who else?'

Penny stared.

'You're crazy, Gally. There isn't a hope. I told you about him and Jerry straining their relations. Don't you remember?'

'Certainly, I remember. That point came up in the course of conversation as we were driving back from Matchingham. I mentioned Jerry's name, and he drew in his breath sharply. "He called me a muddleheaded old ass," he said. "Well, you are a muddleheaded old ass," I pointed out, quick as a flash, and he seemed to see the justice of this. He didn't actually say "Egad, that's true," but he drew in his breath sharply, and seeing that I had got him on the run, I pressed my advantage. Didn't he realize, I said, that it was entirely through Jerry's efforts that the Empress had been restored to him? He would be showing himself a pretty degenerate scion of a noble race, I said, if he allowed a few heated words spoken under the stress of emotion to outweigh a signal service like that. He drew in his breath sharply. "Was it young Vail who recovered the Empress?", his voice a-quaver and his pince-nez a-quiver. "Of course it was," I said. "Who the dickens did you think it was? How on earth do you suppose she got into that kitchen at Sunnybrae, if Vail didn't put her there – at great personal peril, I may add," I added. "God bless my soul!" he said, and drew in his breath sharply. It was one of those big evenings for sharp-breath-drawers.'

Gally paused, and accepted another glass of port. He was experiencing the quiet satisfaction of the raconteur who sees that his story is going well. A good audience, Beach and these two young people, he felt. Just the right hushed silence, and the eyes protruding just the correct distance from their sockets.

'I saw now,' he resumed, 'that I had touched the spot and got him where I wanted him. You have probably no conception off Clarence's frame of mind, now that he has got that blighted pig off his back. Exalted ecstasy is about the nearest I can come to it. I should imagine that you felt rather the same, Jerry, when you asked Penny to marry you and her shy response told you that you had brought home the bacon. You leaped, I presume. You sang, no doubt. You scoured the countryside looking for someone to do a good turn to, I should suppose – it is the same with Clarence. As the car drove in at the gate, we struck a bumpy patch, and I could hear the milk of human kindness sloshing about inside him. So I hesitated no longer. I got him to the library, dumped him in a chair, and told him all about your hard case. "Here are these two excellent young eggs, Clarence," I said, "linked in the silken fetters of love, and unable to do anything constructive about it because the funds are a bit low. Tragic, eh, Clarence?" "Dashed tragic," he said. "Brings the bally tear to the eye. Can nothing be done about it before my heart breaks?" "The whole matter can be satisfactorily adjusted, Clarence," I said, "if somebody, as it might be you, slips Jerry Vail two thousand pounds. That is the sum he requires in order to unleash the clergyman and set him bustling about his business." He stared at me, amazed. "Two thousand pounds?" he said. "Is that all? Why, I feed such sums to the birds. You're sure he doesn't need more?" "No, two thousand will fix it," I said. "Then I'll write him a cheque immediately," he said. And to cut a long story short, he did, grumbling a little because he wasn't allowed to make it larger, and here it is.'

Jerry and Penny stared at the cheque. They could not speak. In moments of intense emotion words do not come readily.

'He made but one stipulation,' said Gally. 'That you were not to thank him.'

Penny gasped.

'But we must thank him!'

'No. He is a shy, shrinking, nervous fellow. It would embarrass him terribly.'

'Well, we can thank you.'

'Yes, you can do that. I enjoy that sort of thing. You can kiss me, if you like.'

'I will. Oh, Gally!' said Penny, her voice breaking.

'There, there,' said Gally. 'There, there, there!'

It was some little time later that Gally, a good deal dishevelled, turned to Beach. The door had closed, and they were alone.

'Ah, love, love!' he said. 'Is there anything like it? Were you ever in love, Beach?'

'Yes, sir, on one occasion, when I was a young under-footman. But it blew over.'

'Nice, making the young folks happy.'

'Yes, indeed, Mr Galahad.'

'I feel all of a glow. But what of the old folks?'

'Sir?'

'I was only thinking that you don't seem to have got much out of this. And you ought to have your cut. You don't feel like bringing an action against Parsloe?'

Beach was shocked.

'I wouldn't take such a liberty, Mr Galahad.'

'No, I suppose it would be awkward for you, suing your future nephew by marriage. But you certainly are entitled to some compensation for all you have been through, and I think with a little tact I can get it for you. About how much would you suggest? A hundred? Two hundred? Five hundred is a nice round sum,' said Gally. 'I'll see what I can do about it.'

3

In her bedroom on the first floor, the second on the right – not the left – as you went along the corridor, Lady Constance, despite her nasty cold, was feeling, on the whole, pretty good.

There is this to be said for a nasty cold, that when you get it, you can go to bed and cuddle up between the sheets and reflect that but for this passing indisposition you would have been downstairs, meeting your brother Galahad. After all, felt Lady Constance philosophically, kneading the hot water bottle with her toes, a couple of sniffs and a few sneezes are a small price to pay for the luxury of passing an evening away from a brother the mere sight of whom has always made you wonder if Man can really be Nature's last word.

It was consequently with something of the emotions of a character in a Greek Tragedy pursued by the Fates that she saw the door open and observed this brother enter in person, complete with the monocle which had always aroused her worst passions. Lying awake in the still watches of the night, she had sometimes thought that she could have endured Gally if he had not worn an eyeglass.

'Go away!' she said.

'In due season,' said Gally. 'But first a word with you, Connie.' He seated himself on the bed, and ate one of the grapes which loving hands had placed on the table. 'How's your cold?'

'Very bad.'

'Clarence's recent cold was cured, he tells me, by a sudden shock.'

'I am not likely to get a sudden shock.'

'Oh, aren't you?' said Gally. 'That's what *you* think. Beach is bringing an action against Sir Gregory Parsloe, claiming thousands of pounds damages. Try that one on your nasal douche.'

Lady Constance sneezed bitterly. She was feeling that if there was one time more than another when this established blot on the family exasperated her, it was when he attempted to be humorous.

'Is this one of your elaborate jokes, Galahad?'

'Certainly not. Straight, serious stuff. A stark slice of life.'

Lady Constance stared.

'But how can Beach possibly be bringing an action against Sir Gregory? What for?'

'Wrongful arrest. Injury to reputation. Defamation of character.'

'Wrongful *arrest*? What do you mean?'

Gally clicked his tongue.

'Come, come. You know perfectly well what wrongful arrest is. Suppose you were doing a bit of shopping one afternoon at one of the big London stores and suddenly a bunch of store detectives piled themselves on your neck and frog's-marched you off to the coop on a charge of shoplifting. It happening to be one of the days when you weren't shoplifting, you prove your innocence. What then? Are you satisfied with an apology? You bet you're not. You race off to your lawyer and instruct him to bring an action against the blighters and soak them for millions. That's Beach's position. Parsloe, for some reason known only to himself, got the idea that

Beach had pinched his pig, and instead of waiting like a sensible man and sifting the evidence had him summarily arrested and taken off to Market Blandings prison, courtesy of Constable Evans. Beach now, quite naturally, proposes to sue him.'

The full horror of the situation smote Lady Constance like a blow.

'The scandal!' she wailed.

Gally nodded.

'Yes, I thought of that.'

Lady Constance's eyes flashed imperiously.

'I will speak to Beach!'

'You will not speak to Beach,' said Gally firmly. 'Start giving him that *grande dame* stuff of yours, and you'll only put his back up worse.'

'Then what is to be done?'

Gally shrugged his shoulders.

'Nothing, as far as I can see. The situation seems hopeless to me. It would all be simple, if Parsloe would only agree to a settlement out of court, but he refuses to consider it. And Beach wants five hundred pounds.'

Lady Constance stared.

'Five hundred? You said thousands of pounds.'

'Just a figure of speech.'

'You really mean that Beach would consent to drop this action of his for five hundred pounds?'

'It's a lot of money.'

'A lot of money? To avoid a scandal that would make us all the laughing stock of the county? Give me my cheque book. It's in the drawer over there.'

Amazement showed itself on every feature of Gally's face.

'You aren't telling me that *you* are going to brass up?'

'Of course I am.'

Gally, infringing Lord Emsworth's copyright, drew in his breath sharply.

'Well, this opens up a new line of thought,' he said. 'I'm bound to say that that solution of the problem never occurred to me. And yet I ought to have known that you would prove equal to the situation. That's you!' said Gally admiringly. 'Where weaker vessels like myself lose their heads and run round in circles, wringing their hands and crying "What to do? What to do?" you act. Just like that! It's character. That's what it is – character. It comes out in a crisis. Make the cheque payable to Sebastian Beach, and if you find any difficulty in spelling it, call on me. Were you aware that Beach's name is Sebastian? Incredible though it may seem, it is. Showing, in my opinion, that one half of the world never knows how the other half lives, or something of that sort.'

4

Blandings Castle was preparing to call it a day. Now slept the crimson petal and the white, and pretty soon the sandman would be along, closing tired eyes.

Maudie, in her bedroom, was creaming her face and thinking of her Tubby.

Lady Constance, in hers, was having the time of her life. Lord Emsworth, being in no further need of it, had passed on to her his store of cinnamon, aspirin, vapex, glycerine of thymol, black currant tea, camphorated oil and thermogene wool, and she was trying them one by one. As she did so, she was feeling that pleasant glow of satisfaction which comes to women who, when men are losing their heads and running round in circles, wringing their hands and crying 'What to do? What to do?' have handled a critical situation promptly and well. She was even thinking reasonably kindly of her brother Galahad, for his open admiration of her resourcefulness had touched her.

Beach was in his pantry. From time to time he sipped port, from time to time raised his eyes thankfully heavenwards, He, too, was thinking kindly of Gally. Mr Galahad might ask a man to steal rather more pigs than was agreeable, but in the larger affairs of life, such as making cheques for five hundred pounds grow where none had been before, he was a rock to lean on.

Gally, in the library, was having a last quick one with his brother Clarence. He was planning to turn in before long. It was some hours before his usual time for bed, but he had had a busy day and was not so young as he had been. Fighting the good fight takes it out of a man.

He heaved himself out of his chair with a yawn.

'Well, I'm off,' he said. 'Oddly fatigued, for some reason. Have you ever been kissed by the younger daughter of an American manufacturer of dog biscuits, Clarence?'

'Eh? No. No, I don't think so.'

'You would remember, if you had been. It is an unforgettable experience. What's the matter?'

Lord Emsworth was chuckling.

'I was only thinking of something that girl Monica Simmons said to me down at the sty,' he replied. 'She said "Oh, Lord Emsworth, I thought I was never going to see the piggy-wiggy again!" She meant the Empress. She called the Empress a piggy-wiggy. Piggy-wiggy! Most amusing.'

Gally gave him a long look.

'God bless you, Clarence!' he said. 'Good night.'

Down in her boudoir by the kitchen garden, Empress of Blandings had just woken refreshed from a light sleep. She looked about her, happy to be back in the old familiar surroundings. It was pleasant to feel settled once more. She was a philosopher and could take things as they came, but she did like a quiet life. All that whizzing about in cars and being dumped in strange kitchens didn't do a pig of regular habits any good.

There seemed to be edible substances in the trough beside her. She rose, and inspected it. Yes, substances, plainly edible. It was a little late, perhaps, but one could always do with a snack. Whiffle, in his monumental book, had said that a pig, if aiming at the old mid-season form, should consume daily nourishment amounting to not less than fifty-seven thousand eight hundred calories, and what Whiffle said today, Empress of Blandings thought tomorrow.

She lowered her noble head and got down to it.

5

In the tap-room of the Emsworth Arms a good time was being had by all. It was the hour when business there was always at its briskest, and many a sunburned son of the soil had rolled up to slake a well-earned thirst. Strong men, their day's work done, were getting outside the nightly tankard. Other strong men, compelled by slender resources to wait for someone to come along and ask them to have one, were filling in the time by playing darts. It was a scene of gay revelry, and of all the revellers present none was gayer than George Cyril Wellbeloved, quaffing at his ease in the company of Mr Bulstrode, the chemist in the High Street. His merry laugh rang out like the voice of the daughter of the village blacksmith, and on no fewer than three occasions G. Ovens, the landlord, had found it necessary to rebuke him for singing.

Carpers and cavillers, of whom there are far too many around these days, will interrupt at this point with a derisive 'Hoy cocky! Aren't you forgetting something?' thinking that they have caught the historian out in one of those blunders which historians some-times make. But the historian has made no blunder. He has not forgotten Sir Gregory Parsloe's edict that no alcoholic liquors were to be served to George Cyril Wellbeloved. It is with a quiet smile that he confounds these carpers and cavillers by informing them that as a reward to that faithful pig man for his services in restoring Queen of Matchingham to her sty the edict had been withdrawn.

'Go and lower yourself to the level of the beasts of the field, if you want to, my man,' Sir Gregory had said heartily, and had given George Cyril a princely sum to do it with. So now, as we say, he sat quaffing at his ease in the company of Mr Bulstrode, the chemist in the High Street. And Mr Bulstrode was telling him a story which would probably have convulsed him, if he had been listening to it, when through the door there came the jaunty figure of Herbert Binstead.

In response to George Cyril's 'Oi! Herb!' the butler joined him and his companion, but it speedily became apparent that he was to prove no pleasant addition to the company. Between him and Mr Bulstrode there seemed to be bad blood. When the latter started his story again and this time brought it to a conclusion, Herbert Binstead sneered openly, saying in a most offensive manner that he had heard that one in his cradle. And when Mr Bulstrode gave it as his opinion that the current spell of fine weather would be good for the crops, Herbert Binstead said No, it wouldn't be good for the crops, adding that he did not suppose that the other would know a ruddy crop if he saw one. In short, so un-cooperative was his attitude that after a short while the chemist said 'Well, time to be getting along, I suppose,' and withdrew.

George Cyril Wellbeloved found himself at a loss.

'What's the trouble?' he inquired. 'Have you two had a row?'

Binstead shrugged his shoulders.

'I would not describe it as a row. We did not see eye to eye on a certain matter, but I was perfectly civil to the old geezer. "If that's the way you feel about it, Mr Bulstrode," I said, "righty-ho," and I walked out of the shop.'

'Feel about what?'

'I'm telling you. I must begin by saying that a few days ago Sir Gregory Parsloe said to me "Binstead," he said, "a distant connexion of mine wants me to get him some of this stuff Slimmo. So order a half-dozen bottles from Bulstrode in the High Street, the large economy size." And I done so.'

'Slimmo? What's that?'

'Slimmo, George, is a preparation for reducing the weight. It makes you thin. Putting it in a nutshell, it's an anti-fat. You take it, if you see what I mean, and you come over all slender. Well, as I was saying, I got this Slimmo from Bulstrode, and then Sir Gregory says he doesn't want it after all, and I can have it, and if I can get Bulstrode to refund the money, I can keep it.'

'Bit of luck.'

'So I thought. Five bob apiece those bottles cost, so I naturally estimated that that would be thirty bob for me, and very nice, too.'

'Very nice.'

'So I went to Bulstrode's and you could have knocked me down with a feather when he flatly refused to cough up a penny.'

'Coo!'

'Said a sale was a sale, and that was all there was about it.'

'So you're stuck with the stuff?'

'Oh, no. I've passed it on.'

'How do you mean passed it on? Who to?'

'A lady of our acquaintance.'

'Eh?'

Binstead chuckled quietly.

'You know me, George. I'm the fellow they were thinking about when they said you can't keep a good man down. It was a bit of a knock at first, I'll admit, when I found myself landed with six bottles of anti-fat medicine the large economy size, and no way of cashing in on them, but it wasn't long before I began to see that those bottles had been sent for a purpose. Here are you, Herbert Binstead, I said to myself, with a lot of money invested on Queen of Matchingham for the Fat Pigs event at the Agricultural Show, and there, in a sty at your elbow as you might say, is Empress of Blandings, the Queen's only rival. What simpler, Herbert, I said to myself, than to empty those large economy size bottles of Slimmo into the Empress's trough of food . . .'

He broke off. A loud, agonized cry had proceeded from his companion's lips. George Cyril Wellbeloved was gaping at him pallidly.

'You didn't?'

'Yes, I did. All six bottles. A man's got to look after his own interests, hasn't he? Here, where are you off to?'

George Cyril Wellbeloved was off to get his bicycle, to pedal like a racing cyclist to Matchingham Hall, trusting that he might not be too late, that there might still be time to snatch the tainted food from Queen of Matchingham's lips.

It was an idle hope. The Queen, like the Empress, was a pig who believed in getting hers quick. If food was placed in her trough, she accorded it her immediate attention. George Cyril, leaning limply on the rail of the sty, gave a low moan and averted his eyes.

The moon shone down on an empty trough.

6

(From the *Bridgnorth, Shifnal and Albrighton Argus*, with which is incorporated the *Wheat Growers' Intelligencer and Stock Breeders' Gazetteer*.)

It isn't often, goodness knows, that we are urged to quit the prose with which we earn our daily bread and take to poetry instead. But great events come now and then which call for the poetic pen. So you will pardon us, we know, if, dealing with the Shropshire Show, we lisp in numbers to explain that Emp. of Blandings won again.

This year her chance at first appeared a slender one, for it was feared that she, alas, had had her day. On every side you heard folks say 'She's won it twice. She can't repeat. 'Twould be a super-porcine feat.' 'Twas freely whispered up and down that Fate would place the laurel crown this time on the capacious bean of Matching-ham's up-and-coming Queen. For though the Emp. is fat, the latter, they felt, would prove distinctly fatter. 'Her too, too solid flesh,' they said, ''ll be sure to cop that silver medal.'

Such was the story which one heard, but nothing of the sort occurred, and, as in both the previous years, a hurricane of rousing cheers from the nobility and gentry acclaimed the Blandings Castle entry as all the judges – Colonel Brice, Sir Henry Boole and Major Price (three minds with but a single thought whose verdict none can set at naught) – announced the Fat Pigs champ to be Lord Emsworth's portly nominee.

With reference to her success, she gave a statement to the Press. 'Although,' she said, 'one hates to brag, I knew the thing was in the bag. Though I admit the Queen is stout, the issue never was in doubt. Clean living did the trick,' said she. 'To that I owe my victory.'

Ah, what a lesson does it teach to all of us, that splendid speech!

SERVICE WITH A
SMILE

Chapter 1

The morning sun shone down on Blandings Castle, and the various inmates of the ancestral home of Clarence, ninth Earl of Emsworth, their breakfasts digested, were occupying themselves in their various ways. One may as well run through the roster just to keep the record straight.

Beach, the butler, was in his pantry reading an Agatha Christie; Voules, the chauffeur, chewing gum in the car outside the front door. The Duke of Dunstable, who had come uninvited for a long visit and showed no signs of ever leaving, sat spelling through *The Times* on the terrace outside the amber drawing-room, while George, Lord Emsworth's grandson, roamed the grounds with the camera which he had been given on his twelfth birthday. He was photo-graphing – not that the fact is of more than mild general interest – a family of rabbits down by the west wood.

Lord Emsworth's sister, Lady Constance, was in her boudoir writing a letter to her American friend James Schoonmaker. Lord Emsworth's secretary, Lavender Briggs, was out looking for Lord Emsworth. And Lord Emsworth himself, accompanied by Mr Schoonmaker's daughter Myra, was on his way to the headquarters of Empress of Blandings, his pre-eminent sow, three times silver medallist in the Fat Pigs class at the Shropshire Agricultural Show. He had taken the girl with him because it seemed to him that she was a trifle on the low-spirited side these days, and he knew from his own experience that there was nothing like an after-breakfast look at the Empress for bracing one up and bringing the roses back to the cheeks.

'There is her sty,' he said, pointing a reverent finger as they crossed the little meadow dappled with buttercups and daisies. 'And that is my pig man Wellbeloved standing by it.'

Myra Schoonmaker, who had been walking with bowed head, as

if pacing behind the coffin of a dear and valued friend, glanced listlessly in the direction indicated. She was a pretty girl of the small, slim, slender type, who would have been prettier if she had been more cheerful. Her brow was furrowed, her lips drawn, and the large brown eyes which rested on George Cyril Wellbeloved had in them something of the sadness one sees in those of a dachshund which, coming to the dinner table to get its ten per cent, is refused a cut off the joint.

'Looks kind of a plugugly,' she said, having weighed George Cyril in the balance.

'Eh? What? What?' said Lord Emsworth, for the word was new to him.

'I wouldn't trust a guy like that an inch.'

Enlightenment came to Lord Emsworth.

'Ah, you have heard, then, how he left me some time ago and went to my neighbour, Sir Gregory Parsloe. Outrageous and disloyal, of course, but these fellows will do these things. You don't find the old feudal spirit nowadays. But all that is in the past, and I consider myself very fortunate to have got him back. A most capable man.'

'Well, I still say I wouldn't trust him as far as I can throw an elephant.'

At any other moment it would have interested Lord Emsworth to ascertain how far she could throw an elephant, and he would have been all eager questioning. But with the Empress awaiting him at journey's end he was too preoccupied to go into the matter. As far as he was capable of hastening, he hastened on, his mild eyes gleaming in anticipation of the treat in store.

Propping his back against the rail of the sty, George Cyril Wellbeloved watched him approach, a silent whistle of surprise on his lips.

'Well, strike me pink!' he said to his immortal soul. 'Cor chase my aunt Fanny up a gum tree!'

What had occasioned this astonishment was the fact that his social superior, usually the sloppiest of dressers and generally regarded as one of Shropshire's more prominent eyesores, was now pure Savile Row from head to foot. Not even the *Tailor and Cutter*'s most acid critic could have found a thing to cavil at in the quiet splendour of his appearance. Enough to startle any beholder accustomed to seeing him in baggy flannel trousers, an old shooting coat with holes in the elbows, and a hat which would have been rejected disdainfully by the least fastidious of tramps.

It was no sudden outbreak of foppishness that had wrought this change in the ninth earl's outer crust, turning him into a prismatic sight at which pig men blinked amazed. As he had explained to Myra Schoonmaker on encountering her mooning about in the hall, he was wearing the beastly things because he was going to London on the 10.35 train, because his sister Connie had ordered him to attend the opening of Parliament. Though why Parliament could not get itself opened without his assistance he was at a loss to understand.

A backwoods peer to end all backwoods peers, Lord Emsworth had a strong dislike for London. He could never see what pleasure his friend Ickenham found in visiting that frightful city. The latter's statement that London brought out all the best in him and was the only place where his soul could expand like a blossoming flower and his generous nature find full expression bewildered him. Himself he wanted nothing but Blandings Castle, even though his sister Constance, his secretary Lavender Briggs and the Duke of Dunstable were there and Connie, overriding his veto, had allowed the Church Lads' Brigade to camp out by the lake. Many people are fond of church lads, but he was not of their number, and he chafed at Connie's high-handedness in letting loose on his grounds and messuages what sometimes seemed to him about five hundred of them, all squealing simultaneously.

But this morning there was no room in his mind for morbid thoughts about these juvenile pluguglies. He strongly suspected that it was one of them who had knocked his top hat off with a crusty roll at the recent school treat, but with a visit to the Empress in view he had no leisure to brood on past wrongs. One did not think of mundane things when about to fraternize with that wonder-pig.

Arriving at her GHQ, he beamed on George Cyril Wellbeloved as if on some spectacle in glorious technicolor. And this was odd, for the OC Pigs, as Myra Schoonmaker had hinted, was no feast for the eye, having a sinister squint, a broken nose acquired during a political discussion at the Goose and Gander in Market Blandings, and a good deal of mud all over him. He also smelt rather strongly. But what enchanted Lord Emsworth, gazing on this son of the soil, was not his looks or the bouquet he diffused but his mere presence. It thrilled him to feel that this prince of pig men was back again, tending the Empress once more. George Cyril might rather closely resemble someone for whom the police were spreading a drag-net in the expectation of making an arrest shortly, but nobody could deny his great gifts. He knew his pigs.

So Lord Emsworth beamed, and when he spoke did so with what, when statesmen meet for conferences, is known as the utmost cordiality.

'Morning, Wellbeloved.'

'Morning, m'lord.'

'Empress all right?'

'In the pink, m'lord.'

'Eating well?'

'Like a streak, m'lord.'

'Splendid. It is so important,' Lord Emsworth explained to Myra Schoonmaker, who was regarding the noble animal with a dull eye, 'that her appetite should remain good. You have of course read your Wolff-Lehmann and will remember that, according to the Wolff-Lehmann feeding standards, a pig, to enjoy health, must consume daily nourishment amounting to fifty-seven thousand eight hundred calories, these to consist of proteids four pounds five ounces, carbohydrates twenty-five pounds.'

'Oh?' said Myra.

'Linseed meal is the secret. That and potato peelings.'

'Oh?' said Myra.

'I knew you would be interested,' said Lord Emsworth. 'And of course skimmed milk. I've got to go to London for a couple of nights, Wellbeloved. I leave the Empress in your charge.'

'Her welfare shall be my constant concern, m'lord.'

'Capital, capital, capital,' said Lord Emsworth, and would probably have gone on doing so for some little time, for he was a man who, when he started saying 'Capital', found it hard to stop, but at this moment a new arrival joined their little group, a tall, haughty young woman who gazed on the world through harlequin glasses of a peculiarly intimidating kind. She regarded the ninth earl with the cold eye of a governess of strict views who has found her young charge playing hooky.

'Pahdon me,' she said.

Her voice was as cold as her eye. Lavender Briggs disapproved of Lord Emsworth, as she did of all those who employed her, particularly Lord Tilbury of the Mammoth Publishing Company, who had been Lord Emsworth's predecessor. When holding a secretarial post, she performed her duties faithfully, but it irked her to be a wage slave. What she wanted was to go into business for herself as the proprietress of a typewriting bureau. It was the seeming impossibility of ever obtaining the capital for this venture that interfered with her sleep at night and in the daytime made her manner more than a little forbidding. Like George Cyril Wellbeloved, whose views were strongly communistic, which was how he got that broken nose, she eyed the more wealthy of her circle askance. Idle rich, she sometimes called them.

Lord Emsworth, who had been scratching the Empress's back with the ferrule of his stick, an attention greatly appreciated by the silver medallist, turned with a start, much as the Lady of Shalott must have turned when the curse came upon her. There was always something about his secretary's voice, when it addressed him unexpectedly, that gave him the feeling that he was a small boy again and had been caught by the authorities stealing jam.

'Eh, what? Oh, hullo, Miss Briggs. Lovely morning.'

'Quate. Lady Constance desiah-ed me to tell you that you should be getting ready to start, Lord Emsworth.'

'What? What? I've plenty of time.'

'Lady Constance thinks othahwise.'

'I'm all packed, aren't I?'

'Quate.'

'Well, then.'

'The car is at the door, and Lady Constance desiah-ed me to tell you –'

'Oh, all right, all right,' said Lord Emsworth peevishly, adding a third 'All right' for good measure. 'Always something, always something,' he muttered, and told himself once again that, of all the secretarial assistants he had had, none, not even the Efficient Baxter of evil memory, could compare in the art of taking the joy out of life with this repellent female whom Connie in her arbitrary way had insisted on engaging against his strongly expressed wishes. Always after him, always harrying him, always popping up out of a trap and wanting him to *do* things. What with Lavender Briggs, Connie, the Duke and those beastly boys screaming and yelling beside the lake, life at Blandings Castle was becoming insupportable.

Gloomily he took one last, lingering look at the Empress and pottered off, thinking, as so many others had thought before him, that the ideal way of opening Parliament would be to put a bomb under it and press the button.

2

The Duke of Dunstable, having read all he wanted to read in *The Times* and given up a half-hearted attempt to solve the crossword puzzle, had left the terrace and was making his way to Lady Constance's sitting-room. He was looking for someone to talk to, and Connie, though in his opinion potty, like all women, would be better than nothing.

He was a large, stout, bald-headed man with a jutting nose, prominent eyes and a bushy white moustache of the type favoured by regimental sergeant majors and walruses. In Wiltshire, where he resided when not inviting himself for long visits to the homes of others, he was far from popular, his standing among his neighbours being roughly that of a shark at a bathing resort – something, that is to say, to be avoided on all occasions as nimbly as possible. A peremptory manner and an autocratic disposition combined to prevent him winning friends and influencing people.

He reached his destination, went in without knocking, found Lady Constance busy at her desk, and shouted 'Hoy!'

The monosyllable, uttered in her immediate rear in a tone of voice usually confined to the hog-calling industry of western America, made Lady Constance leap like a rising trout. But she was a hostess. Concealing her annoyance, not that that was necessary, for her visitor since early boyhood had never noticed when he was annoying anyone, she laid down her pen and achieved a reasonably bright smile.

'Good morning, Alaric.'

'What do you mean, good morning, as if you hadn't seen me before today?' said the Duke, his low opinion of the woman's intelligence confirmed. 'We met at breakfast, didn't we? Potty thing to say. No sense to it. What you doing?'

'Writing a letter.'

'Who to?' said the Duke, never one to allow the conventions to interfere with his thirst for knowledge.

'James Schoonmaker.'

'Who?'

'Myra's father.'

'Oh, yes, the Yank I met with you in London one day,' said the Duke, remembering a *tête-à-tête* luncheon at the Ritz which he had joined uninvited. 'Fellow with a head like a pumpkin.'

Lady Constance flushed warmly. She was a strikingly handsome woman, and the flush became her. Anybody but the Duke would have seen that she resented this loose talk of pumpkins. James Schoonmaker was a very dear friend of hers, and she had sometimes allowed herself to think that, had they not been sundered by the seas, he might one day have become something more. She spoke sharply.

'He has not got a head like a pumpkin!'

'More like a Spanish onion, you think?' said the Duke, having weighed this. 'Perhaps you're right. Silly ass, anyway.'

Lady Constance's flush deepened. Not for the first time in an association which had lasted some forty years, starting in the days when she had worn pigtails and he had risked mob violence by going about in a Little Lord Fauntleroy suit, she was wishing that her breeding did not prohibit her from bouncing something solid on this man's bald head. There was a paper-weight at her elbow which would have fitted her needs to a nicety. Debarred from physical self-expression by a careful upbringing at the hands of a series of ladylike governesses, she fell back on hauteur.

'Was there something you wanted, Alaric?' she asked in the cold voice which had so often intimidated her brother Clarence.

The Duke was less susceptible to chill than Lord Emsworth. Coldness in other people's voices never bothered him. Whatever else he had been called in the course of his long life, no one had ever described him as a sensitive plant.

'Wanted someone to talk to. Seems impossible to find anyone to talk to in this blasted place. Not at all sure I shall come here again. I tried Emsworth just now, and he just yawped at me like a half-wit.'

'He probably didn't hear you. You know how dreamy and absent-minded Clarence is.'

'Dreamy and absent-minded be blowed! He's potty!'

'He is not!'

'Of course he is. Do you think I don't know pottiness when I see it? My old father was potty. So was my brother Rupert. So are both my nephews. Look at Ricky. Writes poetry and sells onion soup. Look at Archie. An artist. And Emsworth's worse than any of them. I tell you he just yawped at me without uttering, and then he went off with that girl Clarissa Stick-in-the-mud.'

'Myra Schoonmaker.'

'Same thing. She's potty, too.'

'You seem to think everybody potty.'

'So they are. Very rare to meet anyone these days with the intelligence of a cockroach.'

Lady Constance sighed wearily.

'You may be right. I know so few cockroaches. What makes you think that Myra is mentally deficient?'

'Can't get a word out of her. Just yawps.'

Lady Constance frowned. She had not intended to confide her young guest's private affairs to a man who would probably spread them far and near, but she felt that the girl's reputation for sanity should be protected.

'Myra is rather depressed just now. She has had an unfortunate love affair.'

This interested the Duke. He had always been as inquisitive as a cat. He blew his moustache up against his nose and allowed his eyes to protrude.

'What happened? Feller walk out on her?'

'No.'

'She walk out on him?'

'No.'

'Well, somebody must have walked out on someone.'

Lady Constance felt that having said so much she might as well tell all. The alternative was to have the man stand there asking questions for the rest of the morning, and she wanted to finish her letter.

'I put a stop to the thing,' she said curtly.

The Duke gave his moustache a puff.

'You did? Why? None of your ruddy business, was it?'

'Of course it was. When James Schoonmaker went back to America, he left her in my charge. I was responsible for her. So when I found that she had become involved with this man, there was only one thing to do, take her away to Blandings, out of his reach. He has no money, no prospects, nothing. James would never forgive me if she married him.'

'Ever seen the chap?'

'No. And I don't want to.'

'Probably a frightful bounder who drops his aitches and has cocoa and bloaters for supper.'

'No, according to Myra, he was at Harrow and Oxford.'

'That damns him,' said the Duke, who had been at Eton and Cambridge. 'All Harrovians are the scum of the earth, and Oxonians are even worse. Very wise of you to remove her from his clutches.'

'So I thought.'

'That's why she slinks about the place like a funeral mute, is it? You ought to divert her mind from the fellow, get her interested in somebody else.'

'The same idea occurred to me. I've invited Archie to the castle.'

'Archie who?'

'Your nephew Archie.'

'Oh, my God! That poop?'

'He is not a poop at all. He's very good-looking and very charming.'

'Who did he ever charm? Not me.'

'Well, I am hoping he will charm her. I'm a great believer in propinquity.'

The Duke was not at his best with long words, but he thought he saw what she was driving at.

'You mean if he digs in here, he may cut this bloater-eating blighter out? Girl's father's a millionaire, isn't he?'

'Several times over, I believe.'

'Then tell young Archie to get after the wench with all speed,' said the Duke enthusiastically. His nephew was employed by the Mammoth Publishing Company, that vast concern which supplies the more fatheaded of England's millions with their daily, weekly and monthly reading matter, but in so minor a capacity that he, the Duke, was still obliged to supplement his salary with an allowance. And if there was one thing that parsimonious man disliked, it was supplementing people's salaries with allowances. The prospect of getting the boy off his payroll was a glittering one, and his eyes bulged brightly as he envisaged it. 'Tell him to spare no effort,' he urged. 'Tell him to pull up his socks and leave no stone unturned. Tell him – Oh, hell! Come in, curse you.'

There had been a knock at the door. Lavender Briggs entered, all spectacles and efficiency.

'I found Lord Emsworth, Lady Constance, and told him the car was in readiness.'

'Oh, thank you, Miss Briggs. Where was he?'

'Down at the sty. Would there be anything furthah?'

'No thank you, Miss Briggs.'

As the door closed, the Duke exploded with a loud report.

'Down at the sty!' he cried. 'Wouldn't you have known it! Whenever you want him, he's down at the sty, gazing at that pig of his, absorbed, like somebody watching a strip-tease act. It's not wholesome for a man to worship a pig the way he does. Isn't there something in the Bible about the Israelites worshipping a pig? No, it was a golden calf, but the principle's the same. I tell you . . .'

He broke off. The door had opened again. Lord Emsworth stood on the threshold, his mild face agitated.

'Connie, I can't find my umbrella.'

'Oh, Clarence!' said Lady Constance with the exasperation the head of the family so often aroused in her, and hustled him out towards the cupboard in the hall where, as he should have known perfectly well, his umbrella had its home.

Left alone, the Duke prowled about the room for some moments, chewing his moustache and examining his surroundings with popping eyes. He opened drawers, looked at books, stared at pictures, fiddled with pens and paper-knives. He picked up a photograph of Mr Schoonmaker and thought how right he had been in comparing his head to a pumpkin. He read the letter Lady Constance had been

writing. Then, having exhausted all the entertainment the room had
to offer, he sat down at the desk and gave himself up to thoughts of
Lord Emsworth and the Empress.

Every day in every way, he was convinced, association with that
ghastly porker made the feller pottier and pottier. And, in the
Duke's opinion, he had been quite potty enough to start with.

3

As the car rolled away from the front door, Lord Emsworth inside
it clutching his umbrella, Lady Constance stood drooping wearily
with the air of one who has just launched a battleship. Beach, the
butler, who had been assisting at his employer's departure, eyed her
with respectful sympathy. He, too, was feeling the strain that always
resulted from getting Lord Emsworth off on a journey.

Myra Schoonmaker appeared, looking, except that she was not
larded with sweet flowers, like Ophelia in Act Four, Scene Five, of
Shakespeare's well-known play *Hamlet*.

'Oh, hello,' she said in a hollow voice.

'Oh, there you are, my dear,' said Lady Constance, ceasing to be
the battered wreck and becoming the hostess. 'What are you planning to do this morning?'

'I don't know. I might write a letter or two.'

'I have a letter I must finish. To your father. But wouldn't it be
nicer to be out in the open on such a lovely day?'

'Oh, I don't know.'

'Why not?'

'Oh, I don't know.'

Lady Constance sighed. But a hostess has to be bright, so she
proceeded brightly.

'I have been seeing Lord Emsworth off. He's going to London.'

'Yes, he told me. He didn't seem very happy about it.'

'He wasn't,' said Lady Constance, a grim look coming into her
face. 'But he must do his duty occasionally as a member of the
House of Lords.'

'He'll miss his pig.'

'He can do without her society for a couple of days.'

'And he'll miss his flowers.'

'There are plenty of flowers in London. All he has to do . . . Oh, Heavens!'

'What's the matter?'

'I forgot to tell Clarence to be sure not to pick the flowers in Hyde Park. He will wander off there, and he will pick the flowers. He nearly got arrested once for doing it. Beach!'

'M'lady –?'

'If Lord Emsworth rings up tomorrow and says he is in prison and wants bail, tell him to get in touch immediately with his solicitors. Shoesmith, Shoesmith, Shoesmith and Shoesmith of Lincoln's Inn Fields.'

'Very good, m'lady.'

'I shan't be here.'

'No, m'lady. I quite understand.'

'He's sure to have forgotten their name.'

'I will refresh his lordship's memory.'

'Thank you, Beach.'

'Not at all, m'lady!'

Myra Schoonmaker was staring at her hostess. Her voice trembled a little as she said:

'You won't be here, Lady Constance?'

'I have to go to my hairdresser's in Shrewsbury, and I am lunching with some friends there. I shall be back for dinner, of course. And now I really must be going and finishing that letter to your father. I'll give him your love.'

'Yes, do,' said Myra, and sped off to Lord Emsworth's study, where there was a telephone. The number of the man she loved was graven on her heart. He was staying temporarily with his old Oxford friend, Lord Ickenham's nephew, Pongo Twistleton. But until now there had been no opportunity to call it.

Seated at the instrument with a wary eye on the door, for though Lord Emsworth had left, who knew that Lavender Briggs might not pop in at any moment, she heard the bell ringing in distant London, and presently a voice spoke.

'Darling!' said Myra. 'Is that you, darling? This is me, darling.'

'Darling!' said the voice devoutly.

'Darling,' said Myra, 'the most wonderful thing has happened, darling. Lady Constance is having her hair done tomorrow.'

'Oh, yes?' said the voice, seeming a little puzzled, as if wondering whether it would be in order to express a hope that she would have a fine day for it.

'Don't you get it, dumb-bell? She has to go to Shrewsbury, and she'll be away all day, so I can dash up to London and we can get married.'

There was a momentary silence at the other end of the wire. One would have gathered that the owner of the voice had had his breath taken away. Recovering it, he said:

'I see.'

'Aren't you pleased?'

'Oh, rather!'

'Well, you don't sound as if you were. Listen, darling. When I was in London, I did a good deal of looking around for registry offices, just in case. I found one in Wilton Street. Meet me there tomorrow at two sharp. I must hang up now, darling. Somebody may come in. Good-bye, darling.'

'Good-bye, darling.'

'Till tomorrow, darling.'

'Right ho, darling.'

'Good-bye, darling.'

And if they're listening in at the Market Blandings exchange, thought Myra, as she replaced the receiver, that'll give them something to chat about over their tea and crumpets.

Chapter 2

'And now,' said Pongo Twistleton, crushing out his cigarette in the ashtray and speaking with a note of quiet satisfaction in his voice, 'I shall have to be buzzing along. Got a date.'

He had been giving his uncle, Lord Ickenham, lunch at the Drones Club, and a very agreeable function he had found it, for the other, who like Lord Emsworth had graced the opening of Parliament with his presence, had been very entertaining on the subject of his experiences. But what had given him even more pleasure than his relative's mordant critique of the appearance of the four pursuivants, Rouge Croix, Bluemantle, Rouge Dragon and Portcullis, as they headed the procession, had been the stimulating thought that, having this engagement, he ran no risk at the conclusion of the meal of being enticed by his guest into what the latter called one of their pleasant and instructive afternoons. The ordeal of sharing these in the past had never failed to freeze his blood. The occasion when they had gone to the dog races together some years previously remained particularly green in his memory.

Of Frederick Altamont Cornwallis Twistleton, fifth Earl of Ickenham, a thoughtful critic had once said that in the late afternoon of his life he retained, together with a juvenile waistline, the bright enthusiasms and fresh, unspoiled outlook of a slightly inebriated undergraduate, and no one who knew him would have disputed the accuracy of the statement. As a young man in America, before a number of deaths in the family had led to his succession to the title, he had been at various times a cowboy, a soda-jerker, a newspaper reporter and a prospector in the Mojave Desert, and there was not a ranch, a drug-store, a newspaper office or a sandy waste with which he had been connected that he had not done his best to enliven. His hair today was grey, but it was still his aim to enliven, as far as lay within his power, any environment in which he found himself. He liked, as he often said, to spread sweetness and light or, as he sometimes put it, give service with a smile. He was a tall distinguished-looking man with a jaunty moustache and an alert and enterprising eye. In this eye, as he turned it on his nephew, there was a look of disappointment and reproach, as if he had expected better things from one of his flesh and blood.

'You are leaving me? Why is that? I had been hoping for –'

'I know,' said Pongo austerely. 'One of our pleasant and instructive afternoons. Well, pleasant and instructive afternoons are off. I've got to see a man.'

'About a dog?'

'Not so much about a dog as –'

'Phone him and put him off.'

'I can't.'

'Who is this fellow?'

'Bill Bailey.'

Lord Ickenham seemed surprised.

'He's back, is he?'

'Eh?'

'I was given to understand that he had left home. I seem to remember his wife being rather concerned about it.'

Pongo saw that his uncle had got everything mixed up, as elderly gentlemen will.

'Oh, this chap isn't really Bill. I believe he was christened Cuthbert. But if a fellow's name is Bailey, you've more or less got to call him Bill.'

'Of course, *noblesse oblige*. Friend of yours?'

'Bosom. Up at Oxford with him.'

'Tell him to join us here.'

'Can't be done. I've arranged to meet him in Milton Street.'

'Where's that?'

'In South Kensington.'

Lord Ickenham pursed his lips.

'South Kensington? Where sin stalks naked through the dark alleys and only might is right. Give this man a miss. He'll lead you astray.'

'He won't jolly well lead me astray. And why? Because for one thing he's a curate and for another he's getting married. The rendezvous is at the Milton Street registry office.'

'You are his witness?'

'That's right.'

'And who is the bride?'

'American girl.'

'Nice?'

'Bill speaks well of her.'

'What's her name?'

'Schoonmaker.'

Lord Ickenham leaped in his seat.

'Good heavens! Not little Myra Schoonmaker?'

'I don't know if she's little or not. I've never seen her. But her name's Myra all right. Why – do you know her?'

A tender look had come into Lord Ickenham's handsome face. He twirled his moustache sentimentally.

'Do I know her! Many's the time I've given her her bath. Not recently, of course, but years ago when I was earning my living in New York. Jimmy Schoonmaker was my great buddy in those days. I don't get over to God's country much now, your aunt thinks it better otherwise, and I've often wondered how he was making out. He promised, when I knew him, to become a big shot in the financial world. Even then, though comparatively young, he was able to shoot a cigar across his face without touching it with his fingers, which we all know is the first step to establishing oneself as a tycoon. I expect by this time he's the Wolf of Wall Street, and is probably offended if he isn't investigated every other week by a Senate commission. Well, it all seems very odd to me.'

'What's odd?'

'His daughter getting married at a registry office. I should have thought she would have had a big choral wedding with bridesmaids and bishops and all the fixings.'

'Ah, I see what you mean.' Pongo looked cautiously over his shoulder. No one appeared to be within earshot. 'Yes, you would think so, wouldn't you? But Bill's nuptials have got to be solemnized with more than a spot of secrecy and silence. The course of true love hasn't been running too smooth. Hell-hounds have been bunging spanners into it.'

'What hell-hounds would those be?'

'I should have said one hell-hound. You know her. Lady Constance Keeble.'

'What, dear old Connie? How that name brings back fragrant memories. I wonder if you recall the time when you and I went to Blandings Castle, I posing as Sir Roderick Glossop, the loony doctor, you as his nephew Basil?'

'I recall it,' said Pongo with a strong shudder. The visit alluded to had given him nightmares for months.

'Happy days, happy days! I enjoyed my stay enormously, and wish I could repeat it. The bracing air, the pleasant society, the occasional refreshing look at Emsworth's pig, it all combined to pep me up and brush away the cobwebs. But how does Connie come into it?'

'She forbade the banns.'

'I still don't follow the scenario. Why was she in a position to do so?'

'What happened was this. She and Schoonmaker are old pals – I got all this from Bill, so I assume we can take it as accurate – and he wanted his daughter to have a London season, so he brought her over here and left her in Lady C.'s charge.'

'All clear so far.'

'And plumb spang in the middle of their London season Lady C. discovered that the beazel was walking out with Bill. Ascertaining that he was a curate, she became as sore as a gumboil.'

'She does not like curates?'

'That's the idea one gets.'

'Odd. She doesn't like me, either. Very hard to please, that woman. What's wrong with curates?'

'Well, they're all pretty hard up. Bill hasn't a bean.'

'I begin to see. Humble suitor. Curious how prejudiced so many people are against humble suitors. My own case is one in point. When I was courting your Aunt Jane, her parents took the bleakest view of the situation, and weren't their faces red when one day I suddenly became that noblest of created beings, an Earl, a hell of a fellow with four Christian names and a coronet hanging on a peg in the downstairs cupboard. Her father, scorning me because I was a soda-jerker at the time, frequently, I believe, alluded to me as "that bum", but it was very different when I presented myself at his Park Avenue residence with a coronet on the back of my head and a volume of Debrett under my arm. He gave me his blessing and a cigar. No chance of Bill Bailey becoming an earl, I suppose?'

'Not unless he murders about fifty-seven uncles and cousins.'

'Which a curate, of course, would hesitate to do. So what was Connie's procedure?'

'She lugged the poor wench off to Blandings, and she's been there ever since, practically in durance vile, her every movement watched. But this Myra seems to be a sensible, level-headed girl, because, learning from her spies that Lady C. was to go to Shrewsbury for a hair-do and wouldn't be around till dinner time, she phoned Bill that she would be free that day and would nip up to London and marry him. She told him to meet her at the Milton Street registry office, where the project could be put through speedily and at small expense.'

'I see. Very shrewd. I often think these runaway marriages are best. No fuss and feathers. After all, who wants a lot of bishops cluttering up the place? I often say, when you've seen one bishop, you've seen them all.' Lord Ickenham paused. 'Well,' he said, looking at his watch. 'I suppose it's about time we were getting along. Don't want to be late.'

Pongo started. To his sensitive ears this sounded extremely like the beginning of one of their pleasant and instructive afternoons. In just such a tone of voice had his relative a few years earlier suggested that they might look in at the dog races, for there was, he said, no better way of studying the soul of the people than to mingle with them in their simple pastimes.

'We? You aren't coming?'

'Of course I'm coming. Two witnesses are always better than one, and little Myra –'

'I can't guarantee that she's little.'

'And Myra, whatever her size, would never forgive me if I were not there to hold her hand when the firing squad assembles.'

Pongo chewed his lower lip, this way and that dividing the swift mind.

'Well, all right. But no larks.'

'My dear boy! As if I should dream of being frivolous on such a sacred occasion. Of course, if I find this Bill Bailey of yours unworthy of her, I shall put a stopper on the proceedings, as any man of sensibility would. What sort of a chap is he? Pale and fragile, I suppose, with a touch of consumption and a tendency to recite the collect for the day in a high tenor voice?'

'Pale and fragile, my foot. He boxed three years for Oxford.'

'He did?'

'And went through the opposition like a dose of salts.'

'Then all should be well. I expect I shall take the fellow to my bosom.'

His expectation was fulfilled. The Rev. Cuthbert Bailey met with his instant approval. He liked his curates substantial, and Bill proved to be definitely the large economy size, the sort of curate whom one could picture giving the local backslider the choice between seeing the light or getting plugged in the eye. Amplifying his earlier remarks, Pongo on the journey to Milton Street had told his uncle that in the parish of Bottleton East, where he had recently held a cure of souls, Bill Bailey had been universally respected, and Lord Ickenham could readily appreciate why. He himself would have treated with the utmost respect any young man so obviously capable of a sweet left hook followed by a snappy right to the button. A captious critic might have felt on seeing the Rev. Cuthbert that it would have been more suitable for one in holy orders to have looked a little less like the logical contender for the world's heavy-weight championship, but it was impossible to regard his rugged features and bulging shoulders without an immediate feeling of awe. Impossible, too, not to like his manifest honesty and simplicity. It seemed to Lord Ickenham that in probing beneath the forbidding exterior to the gentle soul it hid his little Myra had done the smart thing.

They fell into pleasant conversation, but after the first few exchanges it was plain to Lord Ickenham that the young man of God was becoming extremely nervous. Nor was the reason for this difficult to divine. Some twenty minutes had elapsed, and there were still no signs of the bride-to-be, and nothing so surely saps the morale of a bridegroom on his wedding day as the failure of the party of the second part to put in an appearance at the tryst.

Ten minutes later, Bill Bailey rose, his homely features registering anguish.

'She isn't coming?'

Lord Ickenham tried to comfort him with the quite erroneous statement that it was early yet. Pongo, also anxious to be helpful, said he would go out and cock an eye up and down the street to see

if there were any signs of her. His departure from the room synchronized with a hollow groan from the suffering young man.

'I must have put her off!'

Lord Ickenham raised a sympathetic but puzzled eyebrow.

'I don't think I understand you. Put her off? How?'

'By the way I spoke on the phone. You see, I was a bit doubtful
of this idea of hers. It didn't seem right somehow that she should be
taking this terrifically important step without thinking it over. I
mean, I've so little to offer her. I thought we ought to wait till I get
a vicarage.'

'I follow you now. You had scruples?'

'Yes.'

'Did you tell her so?'

'No, but she must have noticed something odd in my voice,
because she asked me if I wasn't pleased.'

'To which you replied –?'

'"Oh, rather!"'

Lord Ickenham shook his head.

'You should have done better than that. Or did you say "Oh,
ra-a-a-ther!", emphasizing it and dragging it out, as it were? Joyously, if you know what I mean, with a sort of lilt in the voice?'

'I'm afraid I didn't. You see –'

'I know. You had scruples. That's the curate in you coming out.
You must fight against this tendency. You don't suppose Young
Lochinvar had scruples, do you? You know the poem about Young
Lochinvar?'

'Oh, yes. I used to recite it as a kid.'

'I, too, and to solid applause, though there were critics who
considered that I was better at "It wath the schcooner Hesperuth
that thailed the thtormy thea". I was rather short on front teeth in
those days. But despite these scruples you came to this marriage
depot.'

'Yes.'

'And the impression you have given me is that your one desire is
to have the registrar start doing his stuff.'

'Yes.'

'You overcame your scruples?'

'Yes.'

'I quite understand. I've done the same thing myself. I suppose if the scruples I've overcome in my time were laid end to end, they would reach from London to Glasgow. Ah, Pongo,' said Lord Ickenham, as his nephew appeared in the doorway. 'Anything to report?'

'Not a thing. Not a single female as far as the eye could reach. I'll tell you what occurred to me, Bill, as I was scanning the horizon.'

'Probably the very thing that has just occurred to me,' said Lord Ickenham. 'You were thinking that Lady Constance must have changed her mind about going to Shrewsbury for that hair-do.'

'That's right. And with her on the premises, the popsy – '

Bill's rugged features registered displeasure.

'I wish you wouldn't call her a popsy.'

'With her on the premises, your ball of worsted would naturally be unable to make her getaway. You'll probably receive a letter tomorrow explaining the situation and making arrangements for the next fixture.'

'Yes, that must be it,' said Bill, brightening a little. 'Though you'd have thought she would have wired,' he added, sinking into the depths again.

Lord Ickenham patted his burly shoulder paternally.

'My dear chap! How could she? The Market Blandings post office is two miles from the castle and, as Pongo says, her every movement is watched. She'll be lucky if she gets so much as a letter through the lines without having it steamed open and intercepted. If I were you, I wouldn't worry for a moment.'

'I'll try not to,' said Bill, heaving a sigh that shook the room. 'Well, anyway, there's no sense in hanging around here. This place gives me the creeps. Thanks for coming along, Pongo. Thanks for coming along, Lord Ickenham. Sorry your time was wasted.'

'My dear fellow, time is never wasted when it is passed in pleasant company.'

'No. No. There's that, of course. Well, I'll be off.'

As the door closed behind him, Lord Ickenham sighed, not so vigorously as Bill had done but with a wealth of compassion. He mourned in spirit for the young cleric.

'Too bad,' he said. 'It is always difficult for a bridegroom to key himself up to going through the wedding ceremony, an ordeal that taxes the stoutest, and when he's done it and the bride doesn't meet him halfway, the iron enters into the soul pretty deeply. And no knowing when the vigilance of the authorities will be relaxed again, I suppose, if ever. You don't make prison breaks easily when Connie is holding the jailer's keys.'

Pongo nodded. He, too, mourned in spirit for his stricken friend.

'No,' he said. 'I'm afraid Bill's in a spot. And what makes the situation stickier is that Archie Gilpin's at Blandings.'

'Who?'

'The Duke of Dunstable's nephew.'

'Ricky Gilpin's brother?'

'That's right. You ever met him?'

'Never. I know Dunstable, of course, and I know Ricky, but this Archibald is a sealed book to me. Who told you he was at Blandings?'

'He did. In person. I ran into him yesterday and he said he was off there on the afternoon train. Pretty sinister, it seemed to me.'

'Why is that?'

'Well, dash it, there he'll be closeted with the girl, and who knows she won't decide to switch from Bill to him? He's a very good-looking bloke. Which you can't say Bill is.'

'No, I would call Bill's an interesting rather than a beautiful face. He reminds me a little of one of my colleagues on the Wyoming ranch where I held a salaried position in my younger days as a cow-puncher, of whom another of my colleagues, a gifted phrasemaker, said that he had a face that would stop a clock. No doubt Bill has stopped dozens. But surely the little Myra I used to wrap in a bath towel and dandle on my knee can't have grown up into the sort of girl who attaches all that importance to looks.'

'You never know. Girls do go for the finely-chiselled. And apart from his looks, he's an artist, and there's something about artists that seems to act on the other sex like catnip on cats. What's more, I happen to know, because I met a fellow who knows a chap who knows her, that Archie's girl has just broken their engagement.'

'Indeed?'

'A girl called Millicent Rigby. Archie works on one of those papers Lord Tilbury runs at the Mammoth Publishing Company, and she's Tilbury's secretary. This fellow told me that the chap had told him that he had had it direct from the Rigby wench that she had handed Archie the black spot. You see what that means?'

'Not altogether.'

'Use your bean, Uncle Fred. You know what you do when your girl gives you the push. You dash off and propose to another girl, just to show her she isn't the only onion in the stew.'

Lord Ickenham nodded. It was many years since he had acted in the manner described, but he, too, had lived in Arcady.

'Ah, youth, youth!' he was saying to himself, and he shuddered a little as he recalled the fearful female down Greenwich Village way, all beads and bangles and matted hair, at whose sandalled feet he had laid his heart the second time Pongo's Aunt Jane had severed relations with him.

'Yes, I follow you now. This does make Archibald a menace, and one cannot but feel a certain anxiety for Bill. Where can I find him, by the way?'

'He's staying with me at my flat. Why?'

'I was thinking I might look in on him from time to time and try to cheer him up. Take him to the dog races, perhaps.'

Pongo quivered like an aspen. He always quivered like an aspen when reminded of the afternoon when he had attended the dog races in Lord Ickenham's company. Though on that occasion, as his uncle had often pointed out, a wiser policeman would have been content with a mere reprimand.

2

The canny peer of the realm, when duty calls him to lend his presence to the ceremony of the Opening of Parliament, hires his robes and coronet from that indispensable clothing firm, the Brothers Moss of Covent Garden, whose boast is that they can at any time fit anyone out as anything and have him ready to go anywhere. Only they can prevent him being caught short. It was to their emporium that, after leaving his nephew, Lord Ickenham repaired, carrying a suitcase. And he had returned the suitcase's contents and paid his modest bill, when there entered, also carrying a suitcase, a tall, limp, drooping figure, at the sight of which he uttered a glad cry.

'Emsworth! My dear fellow, how nice to run into you again. So you too are bringing back your sheaves?'

'Eh?' said Lord Emsworth, who always said 'Eh?' when anyone addressed him suddenly. 'Oh, hullo, Ickenham. Are you in London?'

Lord Ickenham assured him that he was, and Lord Emsworth said so was he. This having been straightened out, 'Were you at that thing this morning?' he said.

'I was indeed,' said Lord Ickenham, 'and looking magnificent. I don't suppose there is a peer in England who presents a posher appearance when wearing the reach-me-downs and comic hat than I do. Just before the procession got under way, I heard Rouge Croix whisper to Bluemantle "Don't look now, but who's that chap over there?", and Bluemantle whispered back, "I haven't the foggiest, but evidently some terrific swell." But it's nice to get out of the fancy dress, isn't it, and it's wonderful seeing you, Emsworth. How's the Empress?'

'Eh? Oh, capital, capital, capital. I left her in the care of my pig man Wellbeloved, in whom I have every confidence.'

'Splendid. Well, let's go and have a couple for the tonsils and a pleasant chat. I know a little bar round the corner,' said Lord Ickenham, who, wherever he was, always knew a little bar round the corner. 'You have rather a fatigued air, as if putting on all that dog this morning had exhausted you. A whisky with a splash of soda will soon bring back the sparkle to your eyes.'

Seated in the little bar round the corner, Lord Ickenham regarded his companion with some concern.

'Yes,' he said. 'I was right. You don't look your usual bonny self. Very testing, these Openings of Parliament. Usually I give them a miss, as no doubt you do. What brought you up today?'

'Connie insisted.'

'I understand. There are, I should imagine, few finer right-and-left-hand insisters than Lady Constance. Charming woman, of course.'

'Connie?' said Lord Emsworth, surprised.

'Though perhaps not everybody's cup of tea,' said Lord Ickenham, sensing the incredulity in his companion's voice. 'But tell me, how is everything at Blandings Castle? Jogging along nicely, I

hope. I always look on that little shack of yours as an earthly Paradise.'

It was not within Lord Emsworth's power to laugh bitterly, but
he uttered a bleating sound which was as near as he could get to a
bitter laugh. The description of Blandings Castle as an earthly
Paradise, with his sister Constance, the Duke, Lavender Briggs, and
the Church Lads' Brigade running around loose there, struck him as
ironical. He mused for a space in silence.

'I don't know what to do, Ickenham,' he said, his sombre train of
thought coming to its terminus.

'You mean now? Have another.'

'No, no, thank you, really. It is very unusual for me to indulge in
alcoholic stimulant so early in the day. I was referring to conditions
at Blandings Castle.'

'Not so good?'

'They are appalling. I have a new secretary, the worst I have ever
had. Worse than Baxter.'

'That seems scarcely credible.'

'I assure you. A girl of the name of Briggs. She persecutes me.'

'Get rid of her.'

'How can I? Connie engaged her. And the Duke of Dunstable is
staying at the castle.'

'What, again?'

'And the Church Lads' Brigade are camping in the park, yelling
and squealing all the time, and I am convinced that it was one of
them who threw a roll at my top hat.'

'Your top hat? When did you ever wear a top hat?'

'It was at the school treat. Connie always makes me wear a top
hat at the school treat. I went into the tent at teatime to see that
everything was going along all right, and as I was passing down the
aisle between the tables, a boy threw a crusty roll at my hat and
knocked it off. Nothing will persuade me, Ickenham, that the
culprit was not one of the Church Lads.'

'But you have no evidence that would stand up in a court of
law?'

'Eh? No, none.'

'Too bad. Well, the whole set-up sounds extraordinarily like
Devil's Island, and I am not surprised that you find it difficult to

keep the upper lip as stiff as one likes to see upper lips.' A strange light had come into Lord Ickenham's eyes. His nephew Pongo would have recognized it. It was the light which had so often come into them when the other was suggesting that they embark on one of their pleasant and instructive afternoons. 'What you need, it seems to me,' he said, 'is some rugged ally at your side, someone who will quell the secretary, look Connie in the eye and make her wilt, take the Duke off your hands and generally spread sweetness and light.'

'Ah!' said Lord Emsworth with a sigh, as he allowed his mind to dwell on this utopian picture.

'Would you like me to come to Blandings?'

Lord Emsworth started. His pince-nez, which always dropped off his nose when he was deeply stirred, did an adagio dance at the end of their string.

'Would you?'

'Nothing would please me more. When do you return there?'

'Tomorrow. This is very good of you, Ickenham.'

'Not at all. We earls must stick together. There is just one thing. You won't mind if I bring a friend with me? I would not ask you, but he's just back from Brazil and would be rather lost in London without me.'

'Brazil? Do people live in Brazil!'

'Frequently, I believe. This chap has been there some years. He is connected with the Brazil nut industry. I am a little sketchy as to what his actual job is, but I think he's the fellow who squeezes the nuts in the squeezer, to give them that peculiar shape. I may be wrong, of course. Then I bring him with me?'

'Certainly, certainly, certainly. Delighted, delighted.'

'A wise decision on your part. Who knows that he may not help the general composition? He might fall in love with the secretary and marry her and take her to Brazil.'

'True.'

'Or murder the Duke with some little-known Asiatic poison. Or be of assistance in a number of other ways. I'm sure you'll be glad to have him about the place. He is house-broken and eats whatever you're having yourself. What train are you taking tomorrow?'

'The 11.45 from Paddington.'

'Expect us there, my dear Emsworth,' said Lord Ickenham. 'And not only there, but with our hair in a braid and, speaking for myself, prepared to be up and doing with a heart for any fate. I'll go and ring my friend up now and tell him to start packing.'

3

It was some hours later that Pongo Twistleton, having a tissue-restorer before dinner in the Drones Club smoking-room, was informed by the smoking-room waiter that a gentleman was in the hall, asking to see him, and a shadow fell on his tranquil mood. Too often when gentlemen called asking to see members of the Drones Club, their visits had to do with accounts rendered for goods supplied, with the subject of remittances which would oblige cropping up, and he knew that his own affairs were in a state of some disorder.

'Is he short and stout?' he asked nervously, remembering that the representative of the Messrs Hicks and Adrian, to whom he owed a princely sum for shirting, socks and underlinen could be so described.

'Far from it. Tall and beautifully slender,' said a hearty voice behind him. 'Svelte may be the word I am groping for.'

'Oh, hullo, Uncle Fred,' said Pongo, relieved. 'I thought you were someone else.'

'Rest assured that I am not. First, last and all the time yours to command Ickenham! I took the liberty of walking in, my dear Pongo, confident that I would receive a nephew's welcome. We Ickenhams dislike to wait in halls. It offends our pride. What's that you're having? Order me one of the same. I suppose it will harden my arteries but I like them hard. Bill not with you tonight?'

'No. He had to go to Bottleton East to pick up some things.'

'You have not seen him recently?'

'No, I haven't been back to the flat. Do you want me to give you dinner?'

'Just what I was about to suggest. It will be your last opportunity for some little time. I'm off to Blandings Castle tomorrow.'

'You're . . . *what*?'

'Yes, after I left you I ran into Emsworth and he asked me to drop down there for a few days or possibly longer. He's having trouble, poor chap.'

'What's wrong with him?'

'Practically everything. He has a new secretary who harries him. The Duke of Dunstable seems to be a fixture on the premises. Lady Constance has pinched his favourite hat and given it to the deserving poor, and he lives in constant fear of her getting away with his shooting jacket with the holes in the elbows. In addition to which, he is much beset by Church Lads.'

'Eh?'

'You see how full my hands will be, if I am to help him. I shall have to devise some means of ridding him of this turbulent secretary –'

'Church Lads?'

'– shipping the Duke back to Wiltshire, where he belongs, curbing Connie and putting the fear of God into these Church Lads. An impressive programme, and one that would be beyond the scope of a lesser man. Most fortunately I am not a lesser man.'

'How do you mean, Church Lads?'

'Weren't you ever a Church Lad?'

'No.'

'Well, many of the younger generation are: they assemble in gangs in most rural parishes. The Church Lads' Brigade they call themselves. Connie has allowed them to camp out by the lake.'

'And Emsworth doesn't like them?'

'Nobody could, except their mothers. No, he eyes them askance. They ruin the scenery, poison the air with their uncouth cries, and at the recent school treat, so he tells me, knocked off his top hat with a crusty roll.'

Pongo shook his head censoriously.

'He shouldn't have worn a topper at a school treat,' he said. He was remembering functions of this kind into which he had been lured at one time and another by clergymen's daughters for whose charms he had fallen. The one at Maiden Eggesford in Somerset, when his great love for Angelica Briscoe, daughter of the Rev. P. P. Briscoe, who vetted the souls of the peasantry in that hamlet, had led him to put his head in a sack and allow himself to be prodded with sticks by the younger set, had never been erased from his memory. 'A topper! Good Lord! Just asking for it!'

'He acted under duress. He would have preferred to wear a cloth cap, but Connie insisted. You know how persuasive she can be.'

'She's a tough baby.'

'Very tough. Let us hope she takes to Bill Bailey.'

'Does what?'

'Oh, I didn't tell you, did I? Bill is accompanying me to Blandings.'

'What!'

'Yes, Emsworth very kindly included him in his invitation. We're off tomorrow on the 11.45, singing a gypsy song.'

Horror leaped into Pongo's eyes. He started violently, and came within an ace of spilling his martini with a spot of lemon peel in it. Fond though he was of his Uncle Fred, he had never wavered in his view that in the interests of young English manhood he ought to be kept on a chain and seldom allowed at large.

'But my gosh!'

'Something troubling you?'

'You can't . . . what's the word . . . you can't subject poor old Bill to this frightful ordeal.'

Lord Ickenham's eyebrows rose.

'Well, really, Pongo, if you consider it an ordeal for a young man to be in the same house with the girl he loves, you must have less sentiment in you than I had supposed.'

'Yes, that's all very well. His ball of fluff will be there, I agree. But what good's that going to do him when two minutes after his arrival Lady Constance grabs him by the seat of the trousers and heaves him out?'

'I anticipate no such contingency. You seem to have a very odd idea of the sort of thing that goes on at Blandings Castle, my boy. You appear to look on that refined home as a kind of Bowery saloon with bodies being hurled through the swing doors all the time, and bounced along the sidewalk. Nothing of that nature will occur. We shall be like a great big family. Peace and good will everywhere. Too bad you won't be with us.'

'I'm all right here, thanks,' said Pongo with a slight shudder as he recalled some of the high spots of his previous visit to the castle. 'But I still maintain that when Lady Constance hears the name Bailey –'

'But she won't. You don't suppose a shrewd man like myself would have overlooked a point like that. He's calling himself Cuthbert Meriwether. I told him to write it down and memorize it.'

'She'll find out.'

'Not a chance. Who's going to tell her?'

Pongo gave up the struggle. He knew the futility of arguing, and he had just perceived the bright side to the situation – to wit, that after tomorrow more than a hundred miles would separate him from his amiable but hair-bleaching relative. The thought was a very heartening one. Going by the form book, he took it for granted that ere many suns had set the old buster would be up to some kind of hell which would ultimately stagger civilization and turn the moon to blood, but what mattered was that he would be up to it at Lord Emsworth's rural seat and not in London. How right, he felt, the author of the well-known hymn had been in saying that peace, perfect peace is to be attained only when loved ones are far away.

'Let's go in and have some dinner,' he said.

Chapter 3

One of the things that made Lord Emsworth such a fascinating travelling companion was the fact that shortly after the start of any journey he always fell into a restful sleep. The train bearing him and guests to Market Blandings had glided from the platform of Paddington station, as promised by the railway authorities, whose word is their bond, at 11.45, and at 12.10 he was lying back in his seat with his eyes closed, making little whistling noises punctuated at intervals by an occasional snort. Lord Ickenham, accordingly, was able to talk to the junior member of the party without risk, always to be avoided when there is plotting afoot, of being overheard.

'Nervous, Bill?' he said, regarding the Rev. Cuthbert sympathetically. He had seemed to notice during the early stages of the journey a tendency on the other's part to twitch like a galvanized frog and allow a sort of glaze to creep over his eyes.

Bill Bailey breathed deeply.

'I'm feeling as I did when I tottered up the pulpit steps to deliver my first sermon.'

'I quite understand. While there is no more admirably educational experience for a young fellow starting out in life than going to stay at a country house under a false name, it does tend to chill the feet to no little extent. Pongo, though he comes from a stout-hearted family, felt just as you do when I took him to Blandings Castle as Sir Roderick Glossop's nephew Basil. I remember telling him at the time that he reminded me of Hamlet. The same moodiness and irresolution, coupled with a strongly marked disposition to get out of the train and walk back to London. Having become accustomed to this kind of thing myself, so much so that now I don't think it quite sporting to go to stay with people under my own name, I have lost the cat-on-hot-bricks feeling which I must have had at one time, but I can readily imagine that for a novice an experience of this sort cannot fail to be quite testing. Your sermon was a success, I trust?'

'Well, they didn't rush the pulpit.'

'You are too modest, Bill Bailey. I'll bet you had them rolling in the aisles and carried out on stretchers. And this visit to Blandings Castle will, I know, prove equally triumphant. You are probably asking yourself what I am hoping to accomplish by it. Nothing actually constructive, but I think it essential for you to keep an eye on this Archibald Gilpin of whom I have heard so much. Pongo tells me he is an artist, and you know how dangerous they are. Watch him closely. Every time he suggests to Myra an after-dinner stroll to the lake to look at the moonlight glimmering on the water – and on the Church Lads' Brigade too, of course, for I understand that they are camping out down there – you must join the hikers.'

'Yes.'

'That's the spirit. And the same thing applies to any attempt on his part to get the . . . popsy is the term you use, is it not?'

'It is not the term I use. It's the term Pongo uses, and I've had to speak to him about it.'

'I'm sorry. Any attempt on his part, I should have said, to get the girl you love into the rose garden must be countered with the same firmness and resolution. But I can leave that to you. Tell me, how did you two happen to meet?'

A rugged face like Bill Bailey's could never really be a mirror of the softer emotions, but something resembling a tender look did come into it. If their host had not at this moment uttered a sudden snort rather like that of Empress of Blandings on beholding linseed meal, Lord Ickenham would have heard him sigh sentimentally.

'You remember that song, the Limehouse Blues?'

'It is one I frequently sing in my bath. But aren't we changing the subject?'

'No, what I was going to say was that she had heard the song over in America, and she'd read that book *Limehouse Nights*, and she was curious to see the place. So she sneaked off one afternoon and went there. Well, Limehouse is next door to Bottleton East, where my job was, and I happened to be doing some visiting there for a pal of mine who had sprained an ankle while trying to teach the choirboys to dance the carioca, and I came along just as some-one was snatching her bag. So, of course, I biffed the blighter.'

'Where did they bury the unfortunate man?'

'Oh, I didn't biff him much, just enough to make him see how wrong it is to snatch bags.'

'And then?'

'Well, one thing led to another, sort of.'

'I see. And what is she like these days?'

'You know her?'

'In her childhood we were quite intimate. She used to call me Uncle Fred. Extraordinarily pretty she was then. Still is, I hope?'

'Yes.'

'That's good. So many attractive children lose their grip and go all to pieces in later life.'

'Yes.'

'But she didn't?'

'No.'

'Still comely, is she?'

'Yes.'

'And you would die for one little rose from her hair?'

'Yes.'

'There is no peril, such for instance as having Lady Constance Keeble look squiggle-eyed at you, that you would not face for her sake?'

'No.'

'Your conversational method, my dear Bill,' said Lord Ickenham, regarding him approvingly, 'impresses me a good deal and has shown me that I must change the set-up as I had envisaged it. I had planned on arrival at the Castle to draw you out on the subject of Brazil, so that you could hold everybody spellbound with your fund of good stories about your adventures there and make yourself the life of the party, but I feel now that that is not the right approach.'

'Brazil?'

'Ah, yes, I didn't mention that to you, did I? I told Emsworth that there was where you came from.'

'Why Brazil?'

'Oh, one gets these ideas. But I was saying that I had changed my mind about featuring you as a sparkling raconteur. Having had the pleasure of conversing with you, I see you now as the strong, silent man, the fellow with the far-away look in his eyes who rarely speaks except in monosyllables. So if anybody tries to pump you about Brazil, just grunt. Like our host,' said Lord Ickenham, indicating Lord Emsworth, who was doing so. 'A pity in a way of course, for I had a couple of good stories about the Brazilian ants which would have gone down well. As I dare say you know, they go about eating everything in sight, like Empress of Blandings.'

The sound of that honoured name must have penetrated Lord Emsworth's slumbers, for his eyes opened and he sat up, blinking.

'Did I hear you say something about the Empress?'

'I was telling Meriwether here what a superb animal she was, the only pig that has ever won the silver medal in the Fat Pigs class three years in succession at the Shropshire Agricultural Show. Wasn't I, Meriwether?'

'Yes.'

'He says Yes. You must show her to him first thing.'

'Eh? Oh, of course. Yes, certainly, certainly, certainly,' said Lord Emsworth, well pleased. 'You'll join us, Ickenham?'

'Not immediately, if you don't mind. I yield to no one in my appreciation of the Empress, but I feel that on arrival at the old shanty what I shall need first is a refreshing cup of tea.'

'Tea?' said Lord Emsworth, as if puzzled by the word. 'Tea? Oh, tea? Yes, of course, tea. Don't take it myself, but Connie has it on the terrace every afternoon. She'll look after you.'

2

Lady Constance was alone at the tea-table when Lord Ickenham reached it. As he approached, she lowered the cucumber sandwich with which she had been about to refresh herself and contrived what might have passed for a welcoming smile. To say that she was glad to see Lord Ickenham would be overstating the case, and she had already spoken her mind to her brother Clarence with reference to his imbecility in inviting him – with a friend – to Blandings Castle. But, as she had so often had to remind herself when coping with the Duke of Dunstable, she was a hostess, and a hostess must conceal her emotions.

'So nice to see you again, Lord Ickenham. So glad you were able to come,' she said, not actually speaking from between clenched teeth, but far from warmly. 'Will you have some tea, or would you rather . . . Are you looking for something?'

'Nothing important,' said Lord Ickenham, whose eyes had been flitting to and fro as if he felt something to be missing. 'I had been expecting to see my little friend, Myra Schoonmaker. Doesn't she take her dish of tea of an afternoon?'

'Myra went for a walk. You know her?'

'In her childhood we were quite intimate. Her father was a great friend of mine.'

The rather marked frostiness of Lady Constance's manner melted somewhat. Nothing would ever make her forget what this man in a single brief visit had done to the cloistral peace of Blandings Castle while spreading sweetness and light there, but to a friend of James Schoonmaker much had to be forgiven. In a voice that was almost cordial she said:

'Have you seen him lately?'

'Alas, not for many years. He has this unfortunate habit so many Americans have of living in America.'

Lady Constance sighed. She, too, had deplored this whim of James Schoonmaker's.

'And as my dear wife feels rightly or wrongly that it is safer for me not to be exposed to the temptations of New York but to live a quiet rural life at Ickenham Hall, Hants, our paths have parted, much to my regret. I knew him when he was a junior member of one of those Wall Street firms. I suppose he's a monarch of finance now, rolling in the stuff?'

'He has been very successful, yes.'

'I always predicted that he would be. I never actually saw him talking into three telephones at the same time, for he had not yet reached those heights, but it was obvious that the day would come when he would be able to do it without difficulty.'

'He was over here not long ago. He left Myra with me. He wanted her to have a London season.'

'Just the kindly sort of thing he would do. Did she enjoy it?'

Lady Constance frowned.

'I was unfortunately obliged to take her away from London after

we had been there a few weeks. I found that she had become involved with a quite impossible young man.'

There was a shocked horror in Lord Ickenham's 'Tut-tut!'

'She insisted that they were engaged. Absurd, of course.'

'Why absurd?'

'He is a curate.'

'I have known some quite respectable curates.'

'Have you ever known one who had any money?'

'Well, no. They don't often have much, do they? I suppose a
curate who was quick with his fingers would make a certain amount
out of the Sunday offertory bag, but nothing more than a small,
steady income. Did Myra blow her top?'

'I beg your pardon?'

'Is she emotionally disturbed at being parted from the man of her
choice?'

'She seems depressed.'

'What she needs is young society. How extremely fortunate that I
was able to bring my friend Meriwether with me.'

Lady Constance started. She had momentarily forgotten his friend
Meriwether.

'Emsworth took him off to look at the Empress, feeling that it
would have a tonic effect after the long railway journey. You'll like
Meriwether.'

'Indeed?' said Lady Constance, who considered this point a very
moot one. She was strongly of the opinion that any associate of
Frederick, fifth Earl of Ickenham, would be as unfit for human
consumption as that blot on the peerage himself. The slight flicker
of friendliness resulting from the discovery that he had at one time
been on cordial terms with the man who meant so much to her had
died away, and only the memory of his last visit to the castle
remained. She wished she did not remember that visit so clearly.
Like quite a number of those whose paths Lord Ickenham had
crossed, she wanted to forget the past. Pongo Twistleton would
have understood how she felt.

'You have known Mr Meriwether a long time?' she said.

'From boyhood. His boyhood, of course, not mine.'

'He comes from Brazil, I hear.'

'Yes, like Charley's Aunt. But –' Here Lord Ickenham's voice took on a grave note, '– on no account mention Brazil to him if you don't mind. It was the scene of the great tragedy of his life. His young wife fell into the Amazon and was eaten by an alligator.'

'How dreadful!'

'For her, yes, though not of course for the alligator. I thought I had better give you this word of warning. Pass it along, will you? Oh, hullo, Dunstable.'

The Duke had lumbered on to the terrace and was peering at him in his popeyed way.

'Hullo, Ickenham. You here again?'

'That's right.'

'You've aged.'

'Not spiritually. My heart is still the heart of a little child.'

'Pass what along?'

'Ah, you overheard what I was saying? I was speaking of my friend Meriwether, whom Lady Constance very kindly invited here with me.'

It would be too much, perhaps, to say that Lady Constance snorted at this explanation of Bill's presence in the home, but she unquestionably sniffed. She said nothing, and ate a cucumber sandwich in rather a marked manner. She was thinking that she would have more to say to her brother Clarence on this subject when she got him alone.

'What about him?'

'I was urging Lady Constance not to speak to him of Brazil. Will you remember this?'

'What would I want to speak to him of Brazil for?'

'You might on learning that that was where he had spent much of his life. And if you did, a far-away look would come into his eyes and he would grunt with pain. His young wife fell into the Amazon.'

'Potty thing to do.'

'And was eaten by an alligator.'

'Well, what else did the silly ass expect would happen? Connie,' said the Duke, dismissing a topic that had failed from the start to grip him, 'stop stuffing yourself with food and come along. Young George wants to take some pictures of us with his camera. He's out on the lawn with Archibald. You met my nephew, Archibald?'

'Not yet,' said Lord Ickenham. 'I am looking forward eagerly to making his acquaintance.'

'You're *what*?' said the Duke incredulously.

'Any nephew of yours.'

'Oh I see what you mean. But you can't go by that. He's not like me. He's potty.'

'Indeed?'

'Got less brain than Connie here, and hasn't the excuse for pottiness that she has, because he's not a woman. Connie's hoping he'll marry the Stick-in-the-Mud girl, though why any girl would want to tie herself up with a poop like that, is more than I can imagine. He's an artist. Draws pictures. And you know what artists are. Where is the Tiddlypush girl, Connie? George wants her in the picture.'

'She went down to the lake.'

'Well, if she thinks I'm going there to fetch her, she's mistaken,' said the Duke gallantly. 'George'll have to do without her.'

3

On a knoll overlooking the lake there stood a little sort of imitation Greek temple, erected by Lord Emsworth's grandfather in the days when landowners went in for little sort of imitation Greek temples in their grounds. In front of it there was a marble bench, and on this bench Myra Schoonmaker was sitting, gazing with what are called unseeing eyes at the Church Lads bobbing about in the water below. She was not in the gayest of spirits. Her brow, indeed, was as furrowed and her lips as drawn as they had been three days earlier when she had accompanied Lord Emsworth to the Empress's sty.

A footstep on the marble floor brought her out of her reverie with a jerk. She turned and saw a tall, distinguished-looking man with grey hair and a jaunty moustache, who smiled at her affectionately.

'Hullo there, young Myra,' he said.

He spoke as if they were old friends, but she had no recollection of ever having seen him before.

'Who are you?' she said. The question seemed abrupt and she wished she had thought of something more polished.

A reproachful look came into his eyes.

'You usedn't to say that when I soaped your back. "Nobody soaps like you, Uncle Fred," you used to say, and you were right. I had the knack.'

The years fell away from Myra, and she was a child in her bath again.

'Well!' she said, squeaking in her emotion.

'I see you remember.'

'Uncle Fred! Fancy meeting you again like this after all these years. Though I suppose I ought to call you Mr Twistleton.'

'You would be making a serious social gaffe, if you did. I've come a long way since we last saw each other. By pluck and industry I've worked my way up the ladder, step by step, to dizzy heights. You may have heard that a Lord Ickenham was expected at the Castle today. I am the Lord Ickenham about whom there has been so much talk. And not one of your humble Barons or Viscounts, mind you, but a belted Earl, with papers to prove it.'

'Like Lord Emsworth?'

'Yes, only brighter.'

'I remember now Father saying something about your having become a big wheel.'

'He in no way overstated it. How is he?'

'He's all right.'

'Full of beans?'

'Oh, yes.'

'More than you are, my child. I was watching you sitting there, and you reminded me of Rodin's *Penseur*. Were you thinking of Bill Bailey?'

Myra started.

'You don't –?'

'Know Bill Bailey? Certainly I do. He's a friend of my nephew Pongo's and to my mind as fine a curate as ever preached a sermon.'

The animation which had come into the girl's face at this reunion with one of whom she had such pleasant memories died away to be replaced by a cold haughtiness like that of a princess reluctantly compelled to give her attention to the dregs of the underworld.

'You're entitled to your opinion, I suppose,' she said stiffly. 'I think he's a rat.'

It seemed to Lord Ickenham that he could not have heard correctly. Young lovers, he knew, were accustomed to bestow on each other a variety of pet names, but he had never understood 'rat' to be one of them.

'A *rat*?'

'Yes.'

'Why do you call him that?'

'Because of what he did.'

'What was that?'

'Or didn't do, rather.'

'You speak in riddles. Couldn't you make it clearer?'

'I'll make it clearer, all right. He stood me up.'

'I still don't get the gist.'

'Very well, then, if you want the whole story. I phoned him that I was coming to London to marry him, and he didn't show up at the registry office.'

'What!'

'Had cold feet, I suppose. I ought to have guessed from the way he said "Oh, rather", when I asked him if he wasn't pleased. I waited at the place for hours, but he never appeared. And he told me he loved me!'

It was not often that Lord Ickenham was bewildered, but he found himself now unequal to the intellectual pressure of the conversation.

'He never appeared? Are we talking of the same man? The one I mean is an up-and-coming young cleric named Bill Bailey, in whose company I passed fully three-quarters of an hour yesterday at the registry office. I was to have been one of his witnesses, lending a tone to the thing.'

Myra stared.

'Are you crazy?'

'The charge has sometimes been brought against me, but there's nothing in it. Just exuberant. Why do you ask?'

'He can't have been at the registry office. I'd have seen him.'

'He's hard to miss, I agree. Catches the eye, as you might say. But I assure you –'

'At the registry office in Wilton Street?'

'Say that again.'

'Say what again?'

'Wilton Street.'

'Why?'

'I wanted to test a theory that has just occurred to me. I think I have the solution of this mystery that has been perplexing us. Someone, especially if a good deal agitated hearing somebody say "Wilton" over the telephone, could easily mistake it for "Milton". Some trick of the acoustics. It was at the Milton Street registry office that Bill, my nephew Pongo and I kept our vigil. We all missed you.'

The colour drained from Myra Schoonmaker's face. Her eyes, as they stared into Lord Ickenham's, had become almost as prominent as the Duke's.

'You don't mean that?'

'I do, indeed. There were we, waiting at the church – '

'Oh, golly, what an escape I've had!'

Lord Ickenham could not subscribe to this view.

'Now there I disagree with you. My acquaintance with Bill Bailey has been brief, but as I told you, it has left me with a distinctly favourable impression of him. A sterling soul he seemed to me. I feel the spiritual needs of Bottleton East are safe in the hands of a curate like that. Don't tell me you've weakened on him?'

'Of course I've not weakened on him.'

'Then why do you feel that you have had an escape?'

'Because I came back here so mad with him for standing me up, as I thought, that when Archie Gilpin proposed to me I very nearly accepted him.'

Lord Ickenham looked grave. These artists, he was thinking, work fast.

'But you didn't?'

'No.'

'Well, don't. It would spoil Bill's visit. And I want him to enjoy himself at Blandings Castle. But I didn't tell you about that, did I? It must have slipped my mind. I've brought Bill here with me. Incognito, of course. I thought you might like to see him. I always strive, when I can, to spread sweetness and light. There have been several complaints about it.'

Chapter 4

It was the practice of Lord Ickenham, when visiting a country house to look about him, before doing anything else, for a hammock to which he could withdraw after breakfast and lie thinking deep thoughts. Though, like Abou ben Adhem a man who loved his fellow men, he made it an invariable rule to avoid them after the morning meal with an iron firmness, for at that delectable hour he wished to be alone to meditate. Whoever wanted to enjoy the sparkle of his conversation had to wait till lunch, when it would be available to all.

Such a hammock he had found on the lawn of Blandings Castle, and on the morning after his arrival he was reclining in it at peace with all the world. The day was warm and sunny. A breeze blew gently from the west. Birds chirped, bees buzzed, insects droned as they went about the various businesses that engage the attention of insects in the rural districts. In the stable yard, out of view behind a shrubbery, somebody — possibly Voules the chauffeur — was playing the harmonica. And from a window in the house, softened by distance, there sounded faintly the tap-tap-tap of a typewriter, showing that Lavender Briggs, that slave of duty, was at work on some secretarial task and earning the weekly envelope. Soothed and relaxed, Lord Ickenham fell into a reverie.

He had plenty to occupy his mind. As a man who specialized in spreading sweetness and light, he was often confronted with problems difficult of solution, but he had seldom found them so numerous. As he mused on Lady Constance, on Lavender Briggs, on the Duke of Dunstable and on the Church Lads, he could see, as he had told Pongo, that his hands would be full and his ingenuity strained to the uttermost.

He was glad, this being so, that he had not got to worry about Bill Bailey, who had relieved whatever apprehensions he may have had by fitting well into the little Blandings circle. True, Lady Constance had greeted him with a touch of frost in her manner, but that was to be expected. The others, he had been happy to see, had made him welcome, particularly Lord Emsworth, to whom he appeared to have said just the right things about the Empress during yesterday evening's visit to her residence. Lord Emsworth's approval did not, of course, carry much weight at Blandings Castle, but it was something.

It was as he lay meditating on Lord Emsworth that he observed him crossing the lawn and sat up with a start of surprise. What had astonished him was not the other's presence there, for the proprietor of a country house has of course a perfect right to cross lawns on his own premises, but the fact that he was wet. Indeed, the word 'wet' was barely adequate. He was soaked from head to foot and playing like a Versailles fountain.

This puzzled Lord Ickenham. He was aware that his host sometimes took a dip in the lake, but he had not known that he did it immediately after breakfast with all his clothes on, and abandoning his usual policy of allowing nothing to get him out of his hammock till the hour of the midday cocktail, he started in pursuit.

Lord Emsworth was cutting out a good pace, so good that he remained out of earshot, and he had disappeared into the house before Lord Ickenham reached it. The latter, shrewdly reasoning that a wet man would make for his bedroom, followed him there. He found him in the nude, drying himself with a bath towel, and immediately put the question which would have occurred to anyone in his place.

'My dear fellow, what happened? Did you fall into the lake?'

Lord Emsworth lowered the towel and reached for a patched shirt.

'Eh? Oh, hullo, Ickenham. Did you say you had fallen into the lake?'

'I asked if you had.'

'I? Oh, no.'

'Don't tell me that was merely perspiration you were bathed in when I saw you on the lawn?'

'Eh? No, I perspire very little. But I did not fall into the lake. I dived in.'

'With your clothes on?'

'Yes, I had my clothes on.'

'Any particular reason for diving? Or did it just seem a good idea at the time?'

'I had lost my glasses.'

'And you thought they might be in the lake?'

Lord Emsworth appeared to realize that he had not made himself altogether clear. For some moments he busied himself with a pair of trousers. Having succeeded in draping his long legs in these, he explained.

'No, it was not that. But when I am without my glasses, I find a difficulty in seeing properly. And I had no reason to suppose that the boy was not accurate in his statement.'

'What boy was that?'

'One of the Church Lads. I spoke to you about them, if you remember.'

'I remember.'

'I wish somebody would mend my socks,' said Lord Emsworth, deviating for a moment from the main theme. 'Look at those holes. What were we talking about?'

'This statement-making Church Lad.'

'Oh yes. Yes, quite. Well, the whole thing was very peculiar. I had gone down to the lake with the idea of asking the boys if they could possibly make a little less noise, and suddenly one of them came running up to me with the most extraordinary remark. He said, "Oh, sir, please save Willie!"'

'Odd way of starting a conversation, certainly.'

'He was pointing at an object in the water, and putting two and two together I came to the conclusion that one of his comrades must have fallen into the lake and was drowning. So I dived in.'

Lord Ickenham was impressed.

'Very decent of you. Many men who had suffered so much at the hands of the little blisters would just have stood on the bank and sneered. Was the boy grateful?'

'I can't find my shoes. Oh yes, here they are. What did you say?'

'Did the boy thank you brokenly?'

'What boy?'

'The one whose life you saved.'

'Oh, I was going to explain that. It wasn't a boy. It turned out to be a floating log. I swam to it, shouting to it to keep cool, and was very much annoyed to find that my efforts had been for nothing. And do you know what I think, Ickenham? I strongly suspect that it was not a genuine mistake on the boy's part. I am convinced that he was perfectly well aware that the object in the water was not one of his playmates and that he had deliberately deceived me. Oh yes, I feel sure of it, and I'll tell you why. When I came out, he had been joined by several other boys, and they were laughing.'

Lord Ickenham could readily imagine it. They would, he supposed, be laughing when they told the story to their grandchildren.

'I asked them what they were laughing at, and they said it was at something funny which had happened on the previous afternoon. I found it hard to credit their story.'

'I don't wonder.'

'I feel very indignant about the whole affair.'

'I'm not surprised.'

'Should I complain to Constance?'

'I think I would do something more spirited than that.'

'But what?'

'Ah, that wants thinking over, doesn't it? I'll devote earnest thought to the matter, and if anything occurs to me, I'll let you know. You wouldn't consider mowing them down with a shotgun?'

'Eh? No, I doubt if that would be advisable.'

'Might cause remark, you feel?' said Lord Ickenham. 'Perhaps you're right. Never mind. I'll think of something else.'

2

When a visitor to a country house learns that his host, as to the stability of whose mental balance he has long entertained the gravest doubts, has suddenly jumped into a lake with all his clothes on, he cannot but feel concern. He shakes his head. He purses his lips and raises his eyebrows. Something has given, he says to himself, and strains have been cracked under. It was thus that the Duke of Dunstable reacted to the news of Lord Emsworth's exploit.

It was from the latter's grandson George that he got the story. George was a small boy with ginger hair and freckles, and between him and the Duke there had sprung up one of those odd friendships which do sometimes spring up between the most unlikely persons. George was probably the only individual in three counties who actually enjoyed conversing with the Duke of Dunstable. If he had been asked wherein lay the other's fascination, he would have replied that he liked watching the way he blew his moustache about when he talked. It was a spectacle that never wearied him.

'I say,' he said, coming on to the terrace where the Duke was sitting, 'have you heard the latest?'

The Duke, who had been brooding on the seeming impossibility of getting an egg boiled the way he liked it in this blasted house, came out of his thoughts. He spoke irritably. Owing to his tender years George had rather a high voice, and the sudden sound of it had made him bite his tongue.

'Don't come squeaking in my ear like that, boy. Blow your horn or something. What did you say?'

'I asked if you'd heard the latest?'

'Latest what?'

'Front-page news. Big scoop. Grandpapa jumped into the lake.'

'What are you talking about?'

'It's true. The country's ringing with it. I had it from one of the gardeners who saw him. Grandpapa was walking along by the lake, and suddenly he stopped and paused for a moment in thought. Then he did a swan dive,' said George, and eyed the moustache expectantly.

He was not disappointed. It danced like an autumn leaf before a gale.

'He jumped into the lake?'

'That's what he did, big boy.'

'Don't call me big boy.'

'Okay, chief.'

The Duke puffed awhile.

'You say this gardener saw him jump into the water?'

'Yes, *sir*.'

'With his clothes on?'

'That's right. Accoutred as he was, he plunged in,' said George, who in the preceding term at his school had had to write out a familiar passage from Shakespeare's *Julius Caesar* fifty times for bringing a white mouse into the classroom. 'Pretty sporting, don't you think, an old egg like Grandpapa?'

'What do you mean – old egg?'

'Well, he must be getting on for a hundred.'

'He is the same age as myself.'

'Oh?' said George, who supposed the Duke had long since passed the hundred mark.

'But what the deuce made him do a thing like that?'

'Oh, just thought he would, I suppose. Coo – I wish I'd been there with my camera,' said George, and went on his way. And a few moments later, having pondered deeply on this sensational development, the Duke rose and stumped off in search of Lady Constance. What he had heard convinced him of the need for a summit meeting.

He found her in her sitting-room. Lavender Briggs was with her, all spectacles and notebook. It was part of her secretarial duties to look in at this hour for general instructions.

'Hoy!' he boomed like something breaking the sound barrier.

'Oh, Alaric!' said Lady Constance, startled and annoyed. 'I do wish you would knock.'

'Less of the "Oh, Alaric!"' said the Duke, who was always firm with this sort of thing, 'and where's the sense in knocking? I want to talk to you on a matter of the utmost importance, and it's private. Pop off, you,' he said to Lavender Briggs. He was a man who had a short way with underlings. 'It's about Emsworth.'

'What about him?'

'I'll tell you what about him, just as soon as this pie-faced female has removed herself. Don't want her muscling in with her ears sticking up, hearing every word I say.'

'You had better leave us, Miss Briggs.'

'Quate,' said Lavender Briggs, withdrawing haughtily.

'Really, Alaric,' said Lady Constance as the door closed, speaking with the frankness of one who had known him for a lifetime, 'you have the manners of a pig.'

The Duke reacted powerfully to the criticism. He banged the desk with a hamlike hand, upsetting, in the order named, an inkpot, two framed photographs and a vase of roses.

'Pig! That's the operative word. It's the pig I came to talk about.'

Lady Constance would have preferred to talk about the inkpot, the two photographs and the vase of roses, but he gave her no opportunity. He had always been a difficult man to stop.

'It's at the bottom of the whole thing. It's a thoroughly bad influence on him. Stop messing about with that ink and listen to me. I say it's the pig that has made him what he is today.'

'Oh, dear! Made whom what he is today?'

'Emsworth, of course, ass. Who do you think I meant? Constance,' said the Duke in that loud, carrying voice of his, 'I've told you this before, and I tell it to you again. If Emsworth is to be saved from the loony bin, that pig must be removed from his life.'

'Don't shout so, Alaric.'

'I will shout. I feel very strongly on the matter. The pig is affecting his brain, not that he ever had much. Remember the time when he told me he wanted to enter it for the Derby?'

'I spoke to him about that. He said he didn't.'

'Well, I say he did! Heard him distinctly. Anyway, be that as it may, you can't deny that he's halfway round the bend, and I maintain that the pig is responsible. It's at the root of his mental unbalance.'

'Clarence is not mentally unbalanced!'

'He isn't, isn't he? That's what you think. How about what happened this morning? You know the lake?'

'Of course I know the lake.'

'He was walking beside it.'

'Why shouldn't he walk beside the lake?'

'I'm not saying he shouldn't walk beside the lake. He can walk beside the lake till his eyes bubble, as far as I'm concerned. But when it comes to jumping in with all his clothes on, it makes one think a bit.'

'What!'

'That's what he did, so young George informs me.'

'With his *clothes* on?'

'Accoutred as he was.'

'Well, really!'

'Don't know why you seem surprised. It didn't surprise me. I was saddened, yes, but not surprised. Been expecting something like this for a long time. It's just the sort of thing a man would do whose intellect had been sapped by constant association with a pig. And that's why I tell you that the pig must go. Eliminate it, and all may still be well. I'm not saying that anything could make Emsworth actually sane, one mustn't expect miracles, but I'm convinced that if he hadn't this pig to unsettle him all the time, you would see a marked improvement. He'd be an altogether brighter, less potty man. Well, say something, woman. Don't just sit there. Take steps, take steps.'

'What steps?'

'Slip somebody a couple of quid to smuggle the ghastly animal away somewhere, thus removing Emsworth from its sphere of influence.'

'My dear Alaric!'

'It's the only course to pursue. He won't sell the creature, though if I've asked him once, I've asked him a dozen times. "I'll give you five hundred pounds cash down for that bulbous mass of lard and snuffle," I said to him. "Say the word," I said, "and I'll have the revolting object shipped off right away to my place in Wiltshire, paying all the expenses of removal." He refused, and was offensive about it, too. The man's besotted.'

'But you don't keep pigs.'

'I know I don't, not such a silly ass, but I'm prepared to pay five hundred pounds for this one.'

Lady Constance's eyes widened.

'Just to do Clarence good?' she said, amazed. She had not credited her guest with this altruism.

'Certainly not,' said the Duke, offended that he should be supposed capable of any such motive. 'I can make a bit of money out of it. I know someone who'll give me two thousand for the animal.'

'Good gracious! Who . . . Oh, Clarence!'

Lord Emsworth had burst into the room, plainly in the grip of some strong emotion. His mild eyes were gleaming through their pince-nez, and he quivered like a tuning-fork.

'Connie,' he cried, and you could see that he had been pushed just so far. 'You've got to do something about these infernal boys!'

Lady Constance sighed wearily. This was one of those trying mornings.

'What boys? Do you mean the Church Lads?'

'Eh? Yes, precisely. They should never have been let into the place. What do you think I just found one of them doing? He was leaning over the rail of Empress's sty, where he had no business to be, and he was dangling a potato on a string in front of her nose and jerking it away when she snapped at it. Might have ruined her digestion for days. You've got to do something about it, Constance. The boy must be apprehended and severely punished.'

'Oh, Clarence!'

'I insist. He must be given a sharp lesson.'

'Changing the subject,' said the Duke, 'will you sell me that foul pig of yours? I'll give you six hundred pounds.'

Lord Emsworth stared at him, revolted. His eyes glowed hotly behind their pince-nez. Not even George Cyril Wellbeloved could have disliked dukes more.

'Of course I won't. I've told you a dozen times. Nothing would induce me to sell the Empress.'

'Six hundred pounds. That's a firm offer!'

'I don't want six hundred pounds. I've got plenty of money, plenty.'

'Clarence,' said Lady Constance, also changing the subject, 'is it true that you jumped into the lake this morning with all your clothes on?'

'Eh? What? Yes, certainly. I couldn't wait to take them off. Only it was a log.'

'What was a log?'

'The boy.'

'What boy?'

'The log. But I can't stand here talking,' said Lord Emsworth impatiently, and hurried out, turning at the door to repeat to Lady Constance that she must do something about it.

The Duke blew his moustache up a few inches.

'You see? What did I tell you? Definitely barmy. Reached the gibbering stage, and may get dangerous at any moment. But I was speaking about this fellow who'll give two thousand for the porker. I used to know him years ago when I was a young man in London. Pyke was his name then. Stinker Pyke we used to call him. Then he made a packet by running all those papers and magazines and things and got a peerage. Calls himself Lord Tilbury now. You've met him. He says he's stayed here.'

'Yes, he was here for a short time. My brother Galahad used to know him. Miss Briggs was his secretary before she came to us.'

'I'm not interested in Miss Briggs, blast her spectacles.'

'I merely mentioned it.'

'Well, don't mention it again. Now you've made me forget what I was going to tell you. Oh, yes. I ran into Stinker at the club the other day, and we got talking and I said I was coming to Blandings, and the subject of the pig came up. It appears that he keeps pigs at his place in Buckinghamshire, just the sort of potty thing he would do, and he has coveted this ghastly animal of Emsworth's ever since he saw it. He specifically told me that he would give me two thousand pounds to add it to his piggery.'

'How extraordinary!'

'Opportunity of a lifetime.'

'Clarence must be made to see reason.'

'Who's going to make him? I can't. You heard him just now. And you won't pinch the creature. The thing's an impasse. No co-operation, that's what's wrong with this damned place. Very doubtful if I'll ever come here again. You'll miss me, but that can't be helped. Only yourself to blame. I'm going for a walk,' said the Duke, and proceeded to do so.

3

Lord Emsworth was a man with little of the aggressor in his spiritual make-up. He believed in living and letting live. Except for his sister Constance, his secretary Lavender Briggs, the Duke of Dunstable and his younger son Frederick, now fortunately residing in America, few things were able to ruffle him. Placid is the word that springs to the lips.

But the Church Lads had pierced his armour, and he found resentment growing within him like some shrub that has been treated with a patent fertilizer. He brooded bleakly on the injuries he had suffered at the hands of these juvenile delinquents.

The top-hat incident he could have overlooked, for he knew that when small boys are confronted with a man wearing that type of headgear and there is a crusty roll within reach, they are almost bound to lose their calm judgement. The happy laughter which had greeted him as he emerged from the lake had gashed him like a knife, but with a powerful effort he might have excused it. But in upsetting Empress of Blandings' delicately attuned digestive system by dangling potatoes before her eyes and jerking them away as she snapped at them they had gone too far. As Hamlet would have put it, their offence was rank and smelled to heaven. And if heaven would not mete out retribution to them – and there was not a sign so far of any activity in the front office – somebody else would have to attend to it. And that somebody, he was convinced, was Ickenham. He had left Ickenham pondering on the situation, and who knew that by this time his fertile mind might not have hit on a suitable method of vengeance.

On leaving Lady Constance's boudoir, accordingly, he made his way to the hammock and bleated his story into the other's ear. Nor was he disappointed in its reception. Where a man of coarser fibre might have laughed, Lord Ickenham was gravity itself. By not so much as a twitch of the lip did he suggest that he found anything amusing in his host's narrative.

'A potato?' he said, knitting his brow.

'A large potato.'

'On a string?'

'Yes, on a string.'

'And the boy jerked it away?'

'Repeatedly. It must have distressed the Empress greatly. She is passionately fond of potatoes.'

'And you wish to retaliate? You think that something in the nature of a countermove is required?'

'Eh? Yes, certainly.'

'Then how very fortunate,' said Lord Ickenham heartily, 'that I can put you in the way of making it. I throw it out merely as a suggestion, you understand, but I know what I would do in your place.'

'What is that?'

'I'd bide my time and sneak down to the lake in the small hours of the morning and cut the ropes of their tent, as one used to do at the Public Schools Camp at Aldershot in the brave days when

I was somewhat younger. That, to my mind, would be the retort courteous.'

'God bless my soul!' said Lord Emsworth.

He spoke with sudden animation. Forty-six years had rolled away from him, the forty-six years which had passed since, a junior member of the Eton contingent at the Aldershot camp, he had been mixed up in that sort of thing. Then he had been on the receiving, not the giving, end. Some young desperadoes from a school allergic to Eton had cut the ropes of the guard tent in which he was reposing, and he could recall vividly his emotions on suddenly finding himself entangled in a cocoon of canvas. His whole life – some fifteen years at that time – had passed before him, and in suggesting a similar experience for these Church Lads Ickenham, he realized, had shown his usual practical good sense.

For a moment his mild face glowed. Then the light died out of it. Would it, he was asking himself, be altogether prudent to embark on an enterprise of which Connie must inevitably disapprove? Connie had an uncanny knack of finding out things, and if she were to trace this righteous act of vengeance to him . . .

'I'll turn it over in my mind,' he said. 'Thank you very much for the suggestion.'

'Not at all,' said Lord Ickenham. 'Ponder on it at your leisure.'

Chapter 5

The Duke's walk took him to the Empress's sty, and he lit a cigar and stood leaning on the rail, gazing at her as she made a late breakfast.

Except for a certain fullness of figure, the Duke of Dunstable and Empress of Blandings had little in common. There was no fusion between their souls. The next ten minutes accordingly saw nothing in the nature of an exchange of ideas. The Duke smoked his cigar in silence, the Empress in her single-minded way devoted herself to the consumption of her daily nourishment amounting to fifty-seven thousand five hundred calories.

Lord Emsworth would not have believed such a thing possible, but the spectacle of this supreme pig was plunging the Duke in gloom. It was not with admiration that he gazed upon her, but with a growing fury. There, he was saying to himself, golloped a Berkshire sow which, if conveyed to his Wiltshire home, would mean a cool two thousand pounds added to his bank balance, and no hope of conveying her. The thought was like a dagger in his heart.

His cigar having reached the point where, if persevered with, it would burn his moustache, he threw it away, straightened himself with a peevish grunt and was about to leave the noble animal to her proteids and carbohydrates, when a voice said 'Pahdon me', and turning he perceived the pie-faced female whom he had so recently put in her place.

'Get out of here!' he said in his polished way, 'I'm busy.'

Where a lesser woman would have quailed and beaten an apologetic retreat, Lavender Briggs stood firm, her dignified calm unruffled. No man, however bald his head or white his moustache, could intimidate a girl who had served under the banner of Lord Tilbury of the Mammoth Publishing Company.

'I would like a word with Your Grace,' she said in the quiet, level voice which only an upbringing in Kensington followed by years of secretarial college can produce. 'It is with refahrence,' she went on, ignoring the purple flush which had crept over her companion's face, 'to this pig of Lord Emsworth's. I chanced to overhear what you were saying to Lady Constance just now.'

A cascade of hair dashed itself against the Duke's Wellingtonian nose.

'Eavesdropping, eh? Listening at keyholes, what?'

'Quate,' said Lavender Briggs, unmoved by the acidity of his tone. In her time she had been spoken acidly to by experts. 'You were urging Lady Constance to pay somebody to purloin the animal. To which her reply' – she consulted a shorthand note in her notebook – '"My dear Alaric!", indicating that she was not prepare-ahed to consid-ah the idea-h. Had you made the suggestion to me, you would not have received such a dusty answer.'

'Such a what?'

A contemptuous light flickered for an instant behind the harlequin glasses. Lavender Briggs moved in circles where literary allusions were grabbed off the bat, and the other's failure to get his hands to this one aroused her scorn. She did not actually call the Duke an ill-read old bohunkus, but this criticism was implicit in the way she looked at him.

'A quotation. "Ah, what a dusty answer gets the soul when hot for certainties in this our life." George Meredith, "Modern Love," stanza forty-eight.'

The Duke's head had begun to swim a little, but with the sensation of slight giddiness had come an unwilling respect for this goggled girl. Superficially all that stanza forty-eight stuff might seem merely another indication of the pottiness which was so marked a feature of the other sex, but there was something in her manner that suggested that she had more to say and that eventually something would emerge that made sense. This feeling solidified as she proceeded.

'If we can come to some satisfactory business arrangement, I will abstract the pig and see that it is delivered at your address.'

The Duke blinked. Whatever he had been expecting, it was not this. He looked at the Empress, estimating her tonnage, then at Lavender Briggs, in comparison so fragile.

'You? Don't be an ass. You couldn't steal a pig.'

'I should, of course, engage the service of an assistant to do the rough work.'

'Who? Not me.'

'I was not thinking of Your Grace.'

'Then who?'

'I would prefer not to specify with any greatah exactitude.'

'See what you mean. No names, no pack-drill?'

'Quate.'

A thoughtful silence fell. Lavender Briggs stood looking like a spectacled statue, while the Duke, who had lighted another cigar, puffed at it. And at this moment Lord Emsworth appeared, walking across the meadow in that jerky way of his which always reminded his friends and admirers of a mechanical toy which had been insufficiently wound up.

'Hell!' said the Duke. 'Here comes Emsworth.'

'Quate,' said Lavender Briggs. It was obvious to her that the conference must be postponed to some more suitable time and place. Above all else, plotters require privacy. 'I suggest that Your Grace meet me later in my office.'

'Where's that?'

'Beach will direct you.'

The secretary's office, to which the butler some quarter of an hour later escorted the Duke, was at the far end of a corridor, a small room looking out on the Dutch garden. Like herself, it was tidy and austere, with no fripperies. There was a desk with a typewriter on it, a table with a tape-recording machine on it, filing cabinets against the walls, a chair behind the desk, another chair in front of it, both hard and business-like, and – the sole concession to the beautiful – a bowl of flowers by the window. As the Duke entered, she was sitting in the chair behind the desk, and he, after eyeing it suspiciously as if doubtful of its ability to support the largest trouser-seat in the peerage, took the other chair.

'Been thinking over what you were saying just now,' he said. 'About stealing that pig for me. This assistant you were speaking of. Sure you can get him?'

'I am. Actually, I shall requiah two assistants.'

'Eh?'

'One to push and one to pull. It is a very large pig.'

'Oh, yes, see what you mean. Yes, undoubtedly. As you say, very large pig. And you can get this second chap?'

'I can.'

'Good. Then that seems to be about it, what? Everything settled, I mean to say.'

'Except terms.'

'Eh?'

'If you will recall, I spoke of a satisfactory business arrangement? I naturally expect to be compensated for my services. I am anxious to obtain capital with which to start a typewriting bureau.'

The Duke, a prudent man who believed in watching the pennies, said, 'A typewriting bureau, eh? I know the sort of thing you mean. One of those places full of machines and girls hammering away at them like a lot of dashed riveters. Well, you don't want much money for that,' he said, and Lavender Briggs, correcting this view, said she wanted as much as she could get.

'I would suggest five hundred pounds.'

The Duke's moustache leaped into life. His eyes bulged. He had the air of one who is running the gamut of the emotions.

'Five . . . *what?*'

'You were thinking of some lesser fig-ah?'

'I was thinking of a tenner.'

'Ten pounds?' Lavender Briggs smiled pityingly, as if some acquaintance of hers, quoting Horace, had made a false quantity. 'That would leave you with a nice profit, would it not?'

'Eh?'

'You told Lady Constance that you had a friend who was prepared to pay you two thousand pounds for the animal.'

The Duke chewed his moustache in silence for a moment, regretting that he had been so explicit.

'I was pulling her leg,' he said, doing his best.

'Oh?'

'Harmless little joke.'

'Indeed? I took it *au pied de la lettre.*'

'*Au* what *de* what?' said the Duke, who was as shaky on French as he was on English literature.

'I accepted the statement at its face value.'

'Silly of you. Thought you would have seen that I was just kidding her along and making a good story out of it.'

'That was not the impression your words made on me. When' – she consulted her notebook – 'when I heard you say "I know someone who'll give me two thousand for the animal", I was quate convinced that you meant precisely what you said. Unfortunately at that moment Lord Emsworth appeared and I was obliged to move from the door, so did not ascertain the name of the friend to whom you referred. Otherwise, I would be dealing with him directly and you would not appear in the transaction at all. As matters stand, you will be receiving fifteen hundred pounds for doing nothing – from your point of view, I should have supposed, a very satisfactory state of aff-ay-ars.'

She became silent. She was thinking hard thoughts of Lord Emsworth and feeling how like him it was to have intruded at such a vital moment. Had he postponed his arrival for as little as half a minute, she would have learned the identity of this lavish pig-lover and would have been able to dispense with the middleman. A momentary picture rose before her eyes of herself, armed with a stout umbrella, taking a full back swing and breaking it over her employer's head. Even though she recognized this as but an idle dream, it comforted her a little.

The Duke sat chewing his cigar. There was, he had to admit, much in what she said. The thought of parting with five hundred pounds chilled him to his parsimonious marrow, but after all, as she had indicated, the remaining fifteen hundred was nice money and would come under the general heading of velvet.

'All right,' he said, though it hurt him to utter the words, and Lavender Briggs' mouth twitched slightly on the left side, which was her way of smiling.

'I was sure you would be reasonable. Shall we have a written agreement?'

'No,' said the Duke, remembering that one of the few sensible remarks his late father had ever made was 'Alaric, my boy, never put anything in writing'. 'No, certainly not. Written agreement, indeed! Never heard a pottier suggestion in my life.'

'Then I must ask you for a cheque.'

As far as it is possible for a seated man to do so, the Duke reeled. 'What, in advance?'

'Quate. Have you your cheque-book with you?'

'No,' said the Duke, brightening momentarily. For an instant it seemed to him that this solved everything.

'Then you can give it me tonight,' said Lavender Briggs. 'And meanwhile repeat this after me. I, Alaric, Duke of Dunstable, hereby make a solemn promise to you, Lavender Briggs, that if you steal Lord Emsworth's pig, Empress of Blandings, and deliver it to my home in Wiltshire, I will pay you the sum of five hundred pounds.'

'Sounds silly.'

'Nevertheless, I must insist on a formal agreement, even if only a verbal one.'

'Oh, all right.'

The Duke repeated the words, though still considering them silly. The woman had to be humoured.

'Thank you,' said Lavender Briggs, and went off to scour the countryside for George Cyril Wellbeloved.

2

George Cyril was having his elevenses in the tool-shed by the kitchen garden when the rich smell of pig which he always diffused enabled her eventually to locate him. As she entered, closing the door behind her, he lowered the beer bottle from his lips in some surprise. He had seen her around from time to time and knew who she was, but he had not the pleasure of her acquaintance, and he was wondering to what he owed the honour of this visit.

She informed him, but not immediately, for there was what are called *pourparlers* to be gone through first.

'Wellbeloved,' she said, starting to attend to these, 'I have been making inquiries about you in Market Blandings, and everyone to whom I have mentioned your name tells me that you are thoroughly untrustworthy, a man without scruples of any sort, who sticks at nothing and will do anything for money.'

'Who – me?' said George Cyril, blinking. He had frequently had much the same sort of thing said to him before, for he moved in outspoken circles, but somehow it seemed worse and more wounding coming from those Kensingtonian lips. For a moment he debated within himself the advisability of dotting the speaker one on the boko, but decided against this. You never knew what influential friends these women had. He contented himself with waving his arms in a passionate gesture which caused the aroma of pig to spread itself even more thickly about the interior of the shed. 'Who – me?' he said again.

Lavender Briggs had produced a scented handkerchief and was pressing it to her face.

'Toothache?' asked George Cyril, interested.

'It is a little close in here,' said Lavender Briggs primly, and returned to the *pourparlers*. 'At the Emsworth Arms, for instance, I was informed that you would sell your grandmother for twopence.'

George Cyril said he did not have a grandmother, and seemed a good deal outraged by the suggestion that, if that relative had not long since gone to reside with the morning stars, he would have parted with her at such bargain-basement rates. A good grandmother should fetch at least a couple of bob.

'At the Cow and Grasshopper they told me you were a – petty thief of the lowest description.'

'Who – me?' said George Cyril uneasily. That, he told himself, must be those cigars. He had not supposed that suspicion had fallen on himself regarding their disappearance. Evidently the hand had not moved sufficiently quickly to deceive the eye.

'And the butler at Sir Gregory Parsloe's, where I understand you were employed before you returned to Lord Emsworth, said you were always pilfering his cigarettes and whisky.'

'Who – me?' said George Cyril for the fourth time, speaking now with an outraged note in his voice. He had always thought of Binstead, Sir Gregory's butler, as a pal and, what is more, a staunch pal. And now this. Like the prophet Zachariah, he was saying to himself, 'I have been wounded in the house of my friends.'

'Your moral standards have thus been established as negligible. So I want you,' said Lavender Briggs, 'to steal Lord Emsworth's pig.'

Another man, hearing these words, might have been stunned, and certainly a fifth 'Who – me?' could have been expected, but in making this request of George Cyril Wellbeloved the secretary was addressing one who in the not distant past actually had stolen Lord Emsworth's pig. It was a long and intricate story, reflecting great discredit on all concerned, and there is no need to go into it now. One mentions it merely to explain why George Cyril Wellbeloved did not draw himself to his full height and thunder that nothing could make him betray his position of trust, but merely scratched his chin with the beer bottle and looked interested.

'Pinch the pig?'

'Precisely.'

'Why?'

'Never mind why.'

George Cyril did mind why.

'Now use your intelligence, miss,' he pleaded. 'You can't come telling a man to go pinching pigs without giving him the griff about why he's doing it and who for and what not. Who's after that pig this time?'

Lavender Briggs decided to be frank. She was a fair-minded girl and saw that he had reason on his side. Even the humblest hired assassin in the Middle Ages probably wanted to know, before setting out to stick a poignard into someone, whom he was acting for.

'The Duke of Dunstable,' she said. 'You would be requiahed to take the animal to his house in Wiltshire.'

'Wiltshire?' George Cyril seemed incredulous. 'Did you say Wiltshire?'

'That is where the Duke lives.'

'And how do we get to Wiltshire, me and the pig? Walk?'

Lavender Briggs clicked her tongue impatiently.

'I assume that you have some disreputable friend who has a motor vehicle of some kind and is as free from scruples as yourself. And if you are thinking that you may be suspected, you need have no uneasiness. The operation will be carried through early in the morning and nobody will suppose that you were not asleep in bed at the time.'

George Cyril nodded. This was talking sense.

'Yes, so far so good. But aren't you overlooking what I might call a technical point? I can't pinch a pig that size all by myself.'

'You will have a colleague, working with you.'

'I will?'

'Quate.'

'Who pays him?'

'He will not requiah payment.'

'Must be barmy. All right, then, we've got that straight. We now come to the financial aspect of the thing. To speak expleasantly, what is there in it for me?'

'Five pounds.'

'*Five?*'

'Let us say ten.'

'Let us ruddy well say fifty.'

'That is a lot of money.'

'I like a lot of money.'

It was a moment for swift decisions. Lavender Briggs shared the Duke's views on watching the pennies, but she was a realist and knew that if you do not speculate, you cannot accumulate.

'Very well. No doubt I can persuade the Duke to meet you on the point. He is a rich man.'

'R!' said George Cyril Wellbeloved, so far forgetting himself as to spit out of the side of his mouth. 'And how did he get his riches? By grinding the face of the poor and taking the bread out of the mouths of the widow and the orphan. But the red dawn will come,' he said, warming up to his subject. 'One of these days you'll see blood flowing in streams down Park Lane and the corpses of the oppressors hanging from lamp-posts. And His Nibs of Dunstable'll be one of them. And who'll be there, pulling on the rope? Me, and happy to do it.'

Lavender Briggs made no comment on this. She was not interested in her companion's plans for the future, though in principle she approved of suspending Dukes from lamp-posts. All she was thinking at the moment was that she had concluded a most satisfactory business deal, and like a good business girl she was feeling quietly elated. She stood to make four hundred and fifty pounds instead of five hundred, but then she had always foreseen that there would be overheads.

The conference having been concluded and terms arranged, George Cyril Wellbeloved felt justified in raising the beer bottle to his lips, and the spectacle reminded her that there was something else that must be added.

'There is just one thing,' she said. 'No more fuddling yourself with alcoholic liquor. This is a very delicate operation which you will be undertaking, and we cannot risk failure. I want you bright and alert. So no more drinking.'

'Except beer, of course.'

'No beer.'

If George Cyril had not been sitting on an upturned wheel-barrow, he would have reeled.

'No beer?'

'No beer.'

'When you say no beer, do you mean no *beer*?'

'Quate. I shall be keeping an eye on you, and I have my way of finding out things. If I discover that you have been drinking, you will lose your fifty pounds. Do I make myself clear?'

'Quate,' said George Cyril Wellbeloved gloomily.

'Then that is understood,' said Lavender Briggs. 'Keep it well in mind.'

She left the shed, glad to escape from its somewhat cloying atmo-sphere, and started to return to the house. She was anxious now to have a word with Lord Ickenham's friend Cuthbert Meriwether.

3

Lying in his hammock, a soothing cigarette between his lips and his mind busy with great thoughts, Lord Ickenham became aware of emotional breathing in his rear and realized with annoyance that his privacy had been invaded. Then the breather came within the orbit of his vision and he saw that it was not, as for an instant he had feared, the Duke of Dunstable, but only his young friend, Myra Schoonmaker. He had no objection to suspending his thinking in order to converse with Myra.

It seemed to him, as he rose courteously, that the child was steamed up about something. Her eyes were wild, and there was in her manner a suggestion of the hart panting for cooling streams when heated in the chase. And her first words told him that his diagnosis had been correct.

'Oh, Uncle Fred! The most awful thing has happened!'

He patted her shoulder soothingly. Those who brought their troubles to him always caught him at his best. Such was his magic that there had been times – though not on the occasion of their visit to the dog races – when he had even been able to still the fluttering nervous system of his nephew Pongo.

'Take a hammock, my dear, and tell me all about it,' he said. 'You mustn't let yourself get so agitated. I have no doubt that when we go into it we shall find that whatever is disturbing you is simply the ordinary sort of thing you have to expect when you come to Blandings Castle. As you have probably discovered for yourself by now, Blandings Castle is no place for weaklings. What's on your mind?'

'It's Bill.'

'What has Bill been doing?'

'It's not what he's been doing, poor lamb, it's what's being done to him. You know that secretary woman?'

'Lavender Briggs? We're quite buddies. Emsworth doesn't like her, but for me she has a rather gruesome charm. She reminds me of the dancing mistress at my first kindergarten, on whom I had a crush in my formative years. Though when I say crush, it wasn't love exactly, more a sort of awed respect. I feel the same about Lavender Briggs. I had a long chat with her the other day. She was telling me she wanted to start a typewriting bureau, but hadn't enough capital. Why she should have confided in me, I don't know. I suppose I have one of those rare sympathetic natures you hear about. A cynic would probably say that she was leading up to trying to make a touch, but I don't think so. I think it was simply . . . Swedish exercises?' he asked, breaking off, for his companion had flung her arms out in a passionate gesture.

'Don't *talk* so much, Uncle Fred!'

Lord Ickenham felt the justice of the rebuke. He apologized.

'I'm sorry. A bad habit of mine, which I will endeavour to correct. What were you going to say about La Briggs?'

'She's a loathsome blackmailer!'

'She's *what*? You astound me. Who – or, rather, whom – is she blackmailing?'

'Bill, the poor angel. She's told him he's got to steal Lord Emsworth's pig.'

It took a great deal to make Lord Ickenham start. These words, however, did so. The rule by which he lived his life was that the prudent man, especially when at Blandings Castle, should be ready at all times for anything, but he had certainly not been prepared for this. His was a small moustache, not bushy and billowy like the Duke's, and it did not leap as the Duke's would have done, but it quivered perceptibly. He stared at his young friend as at a young friend who has had a couple.

'What on earth do you mean?'

'I'm telling you. She says Bill has got to steal Lord Emsworth's pig. I don't know who's behind her, but somebody wants it and she's working for him, and she's drafted my poor darling Bill as her assistant.'

Lord Ickenham whistled softly. Never a dull moment at Blandings Castle, he was thinking. At first incredulous, he now saw how plausible the girl's story was. People who employ people to steal pigs know that the labourer is worthy of his hire, and the principal in this venture, whoever he was, would undoubtedly reward Lavender Briggs with a purse of gold, thus enabling her to start her typewriting bureau. All that was plain enough, and one could understand the Briggs enthusiasm for the project, but there remained the perplexing problem of why she had selected the Rev. Cuthbert Bailey as her collaborator. Why, dash it, thought Lord Ickenham, they hardly knew one another.

'But why Bill?'

'You mean Why *Bill*?'

'Exactly. Why is he the people's choice?'

'Because she's got the goods on him. Shall I tell you the whole thing?'

'It would be a great help.'

Prefacing her remarks with the statement that if girls like Lavender Briggs were skinned alive and dipped in boiling oil, this would be a better and sweeter world, Myra embarked on her narrative.

'Bill was out taking a stroll just now, and she came along. He said, "Oh, hello. Nice morning."'

'And she said "Quate"?'

'No, she said, "I should like a word with you, Mr Bailey."'

'Mr *Bailey*? She knew who he was?'

'She's known from the moment he got here. Apparently when she lived in London, she used to mess about in Bottleton East, doing good works among the poor and all that, so of course she saw him there and recognized him when he showed up at the Castle. Bill's is the sort of face one remembers.'

Lord Ickenham agreed that it did indeed stamp itself on the mental retina. He was looking grave. Expecting at the outset to be called on to deal with some trifling girlish malaise, probably imaginary, he saw that here was a major crisis. If defied, he realized, Lavender Briggs would at once take Lady Constance into her confidence, with the worst results. Hell has no fury like a woman scorned, and very few like a woman who finds that she has been tricked into entertaining at her home a curate at the thought of whom she has been shuddering for weeks. Unquestionably Lady Constance would take umbrage. There would be pique on her part, and even dudgeon, and Bill's visit to Blandings Castle would be abruptly curtailed. In a matter of minutes the unfortunate young pastor of souls would be slung out of this Paradise on his ear like Lucifer, son of the morning.

'And then?'

'She said he had got to steal the pig.'

'And what did he say?'

'He told her to go to hell.'

'Strange advice from a curate.'

'I'm just giving you the rough idea.'

'Quate.'

'Actually, he said Lord Emsworth was his host and had been very kind to him, and he was very fond of him and he'd be darned if he'd bring his grey hairs in sorrow to the grave by pinching his pig, and apart from that what would his bishop have to say, if the matter was drawn to his attention?'

Lord Ickenham nodded.

'One sees what he meant. Curates must watch their step. One false move, like being caught stealing pigs, and bang goes any chance they may have had of rising to become Princes of the Church. And she –?'

'Told him to think it over, the –'

Lord Ickenham raised a hand.

'I know the word that is trembling on your lips, child, but don't utter it. Let us keep the conversation at as high a level as possible. Well, I agree with you that the crisis is one that calls for thought. I wonder if the simplest thing might not be for Bill just to fold his tent like the Arabs and silently steal away.'

'You mean leave the castle? Leave me?'

'It seems the wise move.'

'I won't have him steal away!'

'Surely it is better to steal away than a pig?'

'I'd die here without him. Can't you think of something better than that?'

'What we want is to gain time.'

'How can we? The –'

'Please!'

'The woman said she had to have his answer tomorrow.'

'As soon as that? Well, Bill will have to consent and tell her that she must give him a couple of days to nerve himself to the task.'

'What's the good of that?'

'We gain time.'

'Only two days.'

'But two days during which I shall be giving the full force of the Ickenham brain to the problem, and there are few problems capable of standing up to that treatment for long. They can't take it.'

'And when the two days are up and you haven't thought of anything?'

'Why, then,' admitted Lord Ickenham, 'the situation becomes a little sticky.'

Chapter 6

Among other notable observations, too numerous to mention here, the poet Dryden (1631–1700) once said that mighty things from small beginnings grow, and all thinking men are agreed that in making this statement he called his shots correctly.

If a fly had not got into his bedroom and started buzzing about his nose in the hearty way flies have, it is improbable that Lord Emsworth would have awoken on the following morning at twenty minutes to five, for he was as a rule a sound sleeper who seldom failed to enjoy his eight hours. And if he had not woken and been unable to doze off again, he would not have lain in bed musing on the Church Lads. And if he had not mused on the Church Lads, he would not have recalled Lord Ickenham's advice of the previous day. Treacherous though his memory habitually was, it all came back to him.

Sneak down to the lake in the small hours of the morning and cut the ropes of the boys' tent, Ickenham had said, and the more he examined the suggestion, the more convinced he became that this was the manly thing to do. These fellows like Ickenham, he told himself, cautious conservative men of the world, do not make snap decisions; they think things over before coming to a conclusion, and when they tell you how to act, you know that by following their instructions you will be acting for the best.

No morning hour could be smaller than the present one, and in his library, he knew, there was a paper-knife of the type with which baronets get stabbed in the back in novels of suspense, and having cut his finger on it only two days ago he had no doubts of its fitness for the purpose he had in mind. Conditions, in short, could scarcely have been more favourable.

The only thing that held him back was the thought of his sister Constance. No one knew better than he how high was her standard of behaviour for brothers, and if the pitiless light of day were to be thrown on the crime he was contemplating, she would undoubtedly extend herself. She could, he estimated, be counted on for at least ten thousand words of rebuke and recrimination, administered in daily instalments over the years. In fact, as he put it to himself, for he was given to homely phrases, he would never hear the end of it.

If Connie finds out . . . he thought, and a shudder ran through him.

Then a voice seemed to whisper in his ear.

'She won't find out,' said the voice, and he was strong again. Filled with the crusading spirit which had animated ancestors of his who had done well at the battles of Acre and Joppa, he rose from his bed and dressed, if putting on an old sweater and a pair of flannel trousers with holes in the knees could be called dressing. When he reached the library his mood was definitely that of those distant forebears who had stropped their battle-axes and sallied out to fight the Paynim.

As he left the library, brandishing the paper-knife as King Arthur had once brandished the sword Excalibur, a sudden hollowness in his interior reminded him that he had not had his morning cup of tea. Absent-minded though he was, he realized that this could be remedied by going to the kitchen. It was not a part of the castle which he ever visited these days, but as a boy he had always been in and out – in when he wanted cake and out when the cook caught him getting it, and he had no difficulty in finding his way there. Full of anticipation of the happy ending, for though he knew he had his limitations he was pretty sure that he could boil a kettle, he pushed open the familiar door and went in, and was unpleasantly surprised to see his grandson George there, eating eggs and bacon.

'Oh, hullo, Grandpa,' said George, speaking thickly, for his mouth was full.

'George!' said Lord Emsworth, also speaking thickly, but for a different reason. 'You are up very early.'

George said he liked rising betimes. You got two breakfasts that way. He was at the age when the young stomach wants all that is coming to it.

'Why are you up so early, Grandpapa?'

'I . . . er . . . I was unable to sleep.'

'Shall I fry you an egg?'

'Thank you, no. I thought of taking a little stroll. The air is so nice and fresh. Er – good-bye, George.'

'Good-bye, Grandpapa.'

'Little stroll,' said Lord Emsworth again, driving home his point, and withdrew, feeling rather shaken.

2

The big story of the cut tent ropes broke shortly before breakfast, when a Church Lad who looked as if he had had a disturbed night called at the back premises of the castle asking to see Beach. To him he revealed the position of affairs, and Beach despatched an underling to find fresh rope to take the place of the severed strands. He then reported to Lady Constance, who told the Duke, who told his nephew Archie Gilpin, who told Lord Ickenham, who said, 'Well, well, well! Just fancy!'

'The work of an international gang, do you think?' he said, and Archie said, 'Well, anyway, the work of somebody who wasn't fond of Church Lads', and Lord Ickenham agreed that this might well be so.

Normally at this hour he would have been on his way to his hammock, but obviously the hammock must be postponed till later. His first task was to seek Lord Emsworth out and offer his congratulations. He was feeling quite a glow as he proceeded to the library, where he knew that the other would have retired to read Whiffle on *The Care Of The Pig* or some other volume of porcine interest, his invariable procedure after he had had breakfast. It gratified the kindly man to know that his advice had been taken with such excellent results.

Lord Emsworth was not actually reading when he entered. He was sitting staring before him, the book on his lap. There are moments when even Whiffle cannot hold the attention, and this was one of them. It would be too much, perhaps, to say that remorse gripped Lord Emsworth, but he was undoubtedly in something of a twitter and wondering if that great gesture of his had been altogether well-advised. His emotions were rather similar to those of a Chicago businessman of the old school who has rubbed out a competitor with a pineapple bomb and, while feeling that that part of it is all right, cannot help speculating on what the FBI are going to do when they hear about it.

'Oh – er – hullo, Ickenham,' he said. 'Nice morning.'

'For you, my dear Emsworth, a red-letter morning. I've just heard the news.'

'Eh?'

'The place is ringing with the story of your exploit.'

'Eh?'

'Now come,' said Lord Ickenham reproachfully. 'No need to dissemble with me. You took my advice, didn't you, and pulled a sword of Gideon on those tented boys? And I imagine that you are feeling a better, cleaner man.'

Lord Emsworth was looking somewhat more guilty and apprehensive than good, clean men usually do. He peered through his pince-nez at the wall, as if suspecting it of having ears.

'I wish you wouldn't talk so loudly, Ickenham.'

'I'll whisper.'

'Yes, do,' said Lord Emsworth, relieved.

Lord Ickenham took a seat and sank his voice.

'Tell me all about it.'

'Well –'

'I understand. You are a man of action, and words don't come to you easily. Like Bill Bailey.'

'Bill Bailey?'

'Fellow I know.'

'There was a song called "Won't You Come Home, Bill Bailey?" I used to sing it as a boy.'

'It must have sounded wonderful. But don't sing it now. I want to hear all about your last night's activities.'

'It was this morning.'

'Ah, yes, that was the time I recommended, wasn't it? With dawn pinking the eastern sky and the early bird chirping over its early worm. I had a feeling that you would be in better shape under those romantic conditions. You thoroughly enjoyed it, no doubt?'

'I was terrified, Ickenham.'

'Nonsense. I know you better than that.'

'I was. I kept thinking what my sister Constance would say, if she found out.'

'She won't find out.'

'You really think so?'

'How can she?'

'She does find out things.'

'But not this one. It will remain one of those great historic mysteries like *The Man in the Iron Mask* and the *Mary Celeste*.'

'Have you seen Constance?'

'For a moment.'

'Was she – er – upset?'

'One might almost say she split a gusset.'

'I feared as much.'

'But that's nothing for you to worry about. Your name never came up. Suspicion fell immediately on the boy who cleans the knives and boots. Do you know him?'

'No, we have never met.'

'Nice chap, I believe. Percy is his name, and apparently his relations with the Church Lads have been far from cordial. They tell me he is rather acutely alive to class distinctions and being on the castle payroll has always looked down on the Church Lads as social inferiors. This has led to resentment, thrown stones, the calling of opprobrious names and so forth, so that when the authorities were apprised of what had happened, he automatically became the logical suspect. Taken into the squad room and grilled under the lights, however, he persisted in stout denial and ultimately had to be released for lack of evidence. That is the thing that is baffling the prosecution, the total lack of evidence.'

'I'm glad of that.'

'You ought to be.'

'But I keep thinking of Constance.'

'You're not afraid of her?'

'Yes, I am. You have no notion how she goes on about a thing. On and on and on. I remember coming down to dinner one night when we had a big dinner party with a brass paper-fastener in my shirt front, because I had unfortunately swallowed my stud, and she kept harping on it for months.'

'I see. Well, I'm sure you need have no uneasiness. Why should she suspect you?'

'She knows I have a grievance against these boys. They knocked off my top hat at the school treat and teased the Empress with a potato on a string. She may put two and two together.'

'Not a chance,' said Lord Ickenham heartily. 'I'm sure you're in the clear. But if she does start anything, imitate the intrepid Percy and stick to stout denial. You can't beat it as a general policy. Keep telling yourself that suspicion won't get her anywhere, she must have proof, and she knows perfectly well that there is none that would have a hope of getting past the Director of Public Prosecutions. If she pulls you in and wants you to make a statement, just look her in the eye and keep saying "Is zat so?" and "Sez you", confident that she can never pin the rap on you. And if she tries any funny business with a rubber hose, see your lawyer. And now I must be leaving you. I am long overdue at my hammock.'

Left alone, Lord Emsworth, though considerably cheered by these heartening words, still did not feel equal to resuming his perusal of Whiffle on *The Care Of The Pig*. He sat staring before him, and so absorbed was he in his meditations that the knock on the door brought him out of his chair, quivering in every limb.

'Come in,' he quavered, though reason told him that this could not be his sister Constance, come to ask him to make a statement, for Connie would not have knocked.

It was Lavender Briggs who entered. In her bearing, though he was too agitated to observe it, there was an unaccustomed jauntiness, a jauntiness occasioned by the fact that after dinner on the previous night the Duke had handed her a cheque for five hundred pounds and she was going to London for the night to celebrate. There are few things that so lend elasticity to a girl's step as the knowledge that in the bag swinging from her right hand there is a cheque for this sum payable to herself. Lavender Briggs was not actually skipping like the high hills, but she came within measurable distance of doing so. On her way to the library she had been humming a *morceau* from one of the avant-garde composers and sketching out preliminary plans for that typewriting bureau for which she now had the requisite capital.

Her prospects, she felt, were of the brightest. She could think off-hand of at least a dozen poets and as many whimsical essayists in her own circle of friends who were always writing something and having to have it typed. Shade her prices a little in the first month or so, and all these Aubreys and Lionels and Lucians and Eustaces would come running, and after them – for the news of good work soon gets around – the general public. Every red-blooded man in England, she knew, not to mention the red-blooded women, was writing a novel and would have to have top copy and two carbons.

It was consequently with something approaching cheeriness that she addressed Lord Emsworth.

'Oh, Lord Emsworth, I am sorry to disturb you, but Lady Constance has given me leave to go to London for the night. I was wondering if there was anything I could do for you while I am there?'

Lord Emsworth thanked her and said No, he could not think of anything, and she went her way, leaving him to his thoughts. He was still feeling boneless and had asked himself for the hundredth time if his friend Ickenham's advice about stout denial could be relied on to produce the happy ending, when a second knock on the door brought him out of his chair again.

This time it was Bill Bailey.

'Could I see you for a moment, Lord Emsworth?' said Bill.

3

Having interviewed Lavender Briggs and given her permission to go to London for the night, Lady Constance had retired to her boudoir to look through the letters which had arrived for her by the morning post. One of them was from her friend James Schoonmaker in New York, and she was reading it with the pleasure which his letters always gave her, when from the other side of the door there came a sound like a mighty rushing wind, and Lord Emsworth burst over the threshold. And she was about to utter a rebuking 'Oh, Clarence!', the customary formula for putting him in his place, when she caught sight of his face and the words froze on her lips.

He was a light mauve in colour, and his eyes, generally so mild, glittered behind their pince-nez with a strange light. It needed but a glance to tell her that he was in one of his rare berserk moods. These occurred perhaps twice in each calendar year, and even she, strong woman though she was, always came near to quailing before them, for on these occasions he ceased to be a human doormat

whom an 'Oh, Clarence!' could quell and became something more
on the order of one of those high winds which from time to time
blow through the state of Kansas and send its inhabitants scurrying
nimbly to their cyclone cellars. When the oppressed rise and start
setting about the oppressor, their fury is always formidable. One
noticed this in the French Revolution.

'Where's that damned Briggs woman?' he demanded, snapping
out the words as if he had been a master of men and not a craven
accustomed to curl up in a ball at the secretary's lightest glance.
'Have you seen that blasted female anywhere, Constance? I've been
looking for her all over the place.'

Normally, Lady Constance would have been swift to criticize
such laxity of speech, but until his belligerent mood had blown over
she knew that the voice of authority must be silent.

'I let her go to London for the night,' she replied almost meekly.

'So you did,' said Lord Emsworth. He had forgotten this, as he
forgot most things. 'Yes, that's right, she told me. I'm going to
London, she said, yes, I remember now.'

'Why do you want Miss Briggs?'

Lord Emsworth, who had shown signs of calming down a little,
returned to boiling point. His pince-nez flew off his nose and
danced at the end of their string, their practice whenever he was
deeply stirred.

'I'm going to sack her!'

'What!'

'She doesn't stay another day in the place. I've just been sacking
Wellbeloved.'

It would be putting it too crudely to say that Lady Constance
bleated, but the sound that proceeded from her did have a certain
resemblance to the utterance of a high-strung sheep startled while
lunching in a meadow. She was not one of George Cyril Wellbeloved's warmest admirers, but she knew how greatly her brother
valued his services and she found it incredible that he should
voluntarily have dispensed with them. She could as readily imagine
herself dismissing Beach, that peerless butler. She shrank a little in
her chair. The impression she received was that this wild-eyed man
was running amok, and there shot into her mind those ominous
words the Duke had spoken on the previous afternoon. 'Definitely

barmy,' he had said. 'Reached the gibbering stage and may become dangerous at any moment.' It was not too fanciful to suppose that that moment had arrived.

'But, Clarence!' she cried, and Lord Emsworth, who had re-covered his pince-nez, waved them at her in a menacing manner, like a retarius in the Roman arena about to throw his net.

'It's no good sitting there saying "But, Clarence!"' he said, replacing the pince-nez on his nose and glaring through them. 'I told him he'd got to be out of the place in ten minutes or I'd be after him with a shot-gun.'

'But, Clarence!'

'Don't keep saying that!'

'No, no, I'm sorry. I was only wondering why.'

Lord Emsworth considered the question. It seemed to him a fair one.

'You mean why did I sack him? I'll tell you why I sacked him. He's a snake in the grass. He and the Briggs woman were plotting to steal my pig.'

'What!'

'Are you deaf? I said they were plotting to steal the Empress.'

'But Clarence!'

'And if you say "But, Clarence!" once more, just once more,' said Lord Emsworth sternly, 'I'll know what to do about it. I suppose what you're trying to tell me is that you don't believe me.'

'How can I believe you? Miss Briggs came with the highest testimonials. She is a graduate of the London School of Economics.'

'Well, apparently the course she took there was the one on how to steal pigs.'

'But, Clarence!'

'I have warned you, Constance!'

'I'm sorry. I meant you must be mistaken.'

'Mistaken be blowed! I had the whole sordid story from the lips of Ickenham's friend Meriwether. He told it me in pitiless detail. According to him, some hidden hand wants the Empress and has bribed the Briggs woman to steal her for him. I would have suspected Sir Gregory Parsloe as the master-mind behind the plot, only he's in the South of France. Though he could have made the preliminary arrangements by letter, I suppose.'

Lady Constance clutched her temples.

'Mr Meriwether?'

'You know Meriwether. Large chap with a face like a gorilla?'

'But how could Mr Meriwether possibly have known?'

'She told him.'

'*Told* him?'

'That's right. She wanted him to be one of her corps of assistants, working with Wellbeloved. She approached him yesterday and said that if he didn't agree to help steal the Empress, she would expose him. Must have been a nasty shock to the poor fellow. Not at all the sort of thing you want to have women coming and saying to you.'

Lady Constance, who had momentarily relaxed her grip on her temples, tightened it again. She had an uneasy feeling that, unless she did so, her head would split.

'Expose him?' she whispered hoarsely. 'What do you mean?'

'What do I mean? Oh, I see. What do I mean? Yes, quite. I ought to have explained that oughtn't I? It seems that his name isn't Meriwether. It's something else which I've forgotten. Not that it matters. The point is that the Briggs woman found out somehow that he was here under an alias, as I believe the expression is, and held it over him.'

'You mean he's an imposter?'

Lady Constance spoke with a wealth of emotion. In the past few years Blandings Castle had been peculiarly rich in imposters, notable among them Lord Ickenham and his nephew Pongo, and she had reached saturation point as regarded them, never wanting to see another of them as long as she lived. A hostess gets annoyed and frets when she finds that every second guest whom she entertains is enjoying her hospitality under a false name, and it sometimes seemed to her that Blandings Castle had imposters the way other houses had mice, a circumstance at which her proud spirit rebelled.

'Who is this man?' she demanded. 'Who is he?'

'Ah, there I'm afraid you rather have me,' said Lord Emsworth. 'He told me, but you know what my memory's like. I do remember he said he was a curate.'

Lady Constance had risen from her chair and was staring at him as if instead of her elder brother he had been the Blandings Castle spectre, a knight in armour carrying his head in his hand, who was generally supposed to be around and about whenever there was going to be a death in the family. Ever since she had discovered that Myra Schoonmaker had formed an attachment to the Reverend Cuthbert Bailey, any mention of curates had affected her profoundly.

'What! What did you say?'

'When?'

'Did you say he was a curate?'

'Who?'

'Lord Ickenham's friend, Mr Meriwether.'

'Oh, ah, yes, quite, Mr Meriwether, to be sure.' Lord Emsworth's fury had expended itself, and he was now his amiable, chatty – or, as some preferred to call it, gibbering – self once more. 'Yes, he's a curate, he tells me. He doesn't look like one, but he is. That was why he refused to be a party to the purloining of my pig. Being in holy orders, his conscience wouldn't let him. I must say I thought it very civil of him to come and warn me of the Briggs woman's foul plot, knowing that it would mean her exposing him to you and you cutting up rough. But he said he had these scruples, and they wouldn't allow him to remain silent. A splendid young man, I thought, and very sound on pigs. Odd, because I didn't know they had pigs in Brazil, or curates either, for that matter. By the way, I've just remembered his name. It's Bailey. You want to keep this very clear, or you'll get muddled. He's got two names, one wrong, the other right. His wrong name's Meriwether, and his right name's Bailey.'

Lady Constance had uttered a wordless cry. She might have known, she was feeling bitterly, that Lord Ickenham would never have brought a friend to Blandings Castle unless with some sinister purpose. That much could be taken as read. But she had never suspected that even he would go to such lengths of depravity as to introduce the infamous Bailey into her home. So that, she told herself, was why Myra Schoonmaker had suddenly become so cheerful recently. Her lips tightened. Well, she was reflecting grimly, it would not be long before Blandings Castle saw the last of Lord Ickenham and his clerical friend.

'Yes, Bailey,' said Lord Emsworth. 'The Reverend Cuthbert Bailey. I was telling Ickenham just now that there was a song years ago called "Won't you come home, Bill Bailey?" I used to sing it as a boy. But why he should have brought the chap here under the name of Meriwether and told me he was in the Brazil-nut industry, I can't imagine. Silly kind of thing to do, wouldn't you say? I mean, if a fellow's name's Bailey, why call him Meriwether? And why say he's come from Brazil when he's come from Bottleton East? Doesn't make sense.'

'Clarence!'

'About that song,' said Lord Emsworth. 'Very catchy tune it had. The verse escapes me – in fact, I don't believe I ever sang it – but the chorus began "Won't you come home, Bill Bailey, won't you come home?" Now, how did the next line go? Something about "the whole day long", and you had to make the "long" two syllables. "Lo-ong", if you follow me.'

'Clarence!'

'Eh?'

'Go and find Lord Ickenham.'

'Lord who?'

'Ickenham.'

'Oh, you mean Ickenham. Yes, certainly, of course, delighted. I think he usually goes and lies in that hammock on the lawn after breakfast.'

'Well, ask him if he will be good enough to leave his hammock, if it is not inconveniencing him, and come and see me immediately,' said Lady Constance.

She sank into her chair, and sat there breathing softly through the nostrils. A frozen calm had fallen on her. Her lips had tightened, her eyes were hard, and even Lord Ickenham, intrepid though he was, might have felt, had he entered at this moment, a pang of apprehension at the sight of her, so clearly was her manner that of a woman about to say to her domestic staff, 'Throw these men out, and see to it that they land on something sharp.'

Chapter 7

Breakfast concluded, the Duke of Dunstable had gone to the terrace, where there was a comfortable deck-chair in the shade of a spreading tree, to smoke the first cigar of the day and read his *Times*. But scarcely had he blown the opening puff of smoke and set eye to print when his peace was destroyed by the same treble voice which had disturbed him on the previous day. Once more it squeaked in his ear, and he saw that he had been joined by Lord Emsworth's grandson George, who, as on the former occasion, had omitted to announce his presence by blowing his horn.

He did not strike the lad, for that would have involved rising from his seat, but he gave him an unpleasant look. Intrusion on his sacred after-breakfast hour always awoke the fiend that slept in him.

'Go away, boy!' he boomed.

'You mean "Scram!", don't you, chum?' said George, who liked to get these things right. 'But I want to confer with you about this tent business.'

'What tent business?'

'That thing that happened last night.'

'Oh, that?'

'Only it wasn't last night, it was this morning. A mysterious affair. Have you formed any conclusions?'

The Duke stirred irritably. He was regretting the mistaken kindness that had led him to brighten Blandings Castle with his presence. It was the old story. You said to yourself in a weak and sentimental moment that Emsworth and Connie and the rest of them led dull lives and needed cheering up by association with a polished man of the world, so you sacrificed yourself and came here, and the next thing you knew everyone was jumping into lakes and charging you five hundred pounds for stealing pigs and coming squeaking in your ear and so on and so forth – in short, making the place a ruddy inferno. He gave an animal snarl, and even when filtered through his moustache the sound was impressive, though it left George unmoved. To George it merely seemed that his old friend had got an insect of some kind in his thoracic cavity.

'What do you mean, have I formed any conclusions? Do you think a busy man like myself has time to bother himself with these trifles? Scram, boy, and let me read my paper.'

Like most small boys, George had the quiet persistence of a gadfly. It was never easy to convince him that his society was not desired by one and all. He settled himself on the stone flooring beside the Duke's chair in the manner of one who has come to stay. Limpets on rocks could have picked up useful hints from him in the way of technique.

'This is a lot hotter news than anything you'll read in the paper,' he squeaked. 'I have a strange story to relate.'

In spite of himself, the Duke found that he was becoming mildly interested.

'I suppose you know who did it, hey?' he said satirically.

George shrugged a shoulder.

'Beyond the obvious facts that the miscreant was a Freemason, left-handed, chewed tobacco and had travelled in the east,' he said, 'I have so far formed no conclusion.'

'What on earth are you talking about?'

'I only put that in to make it sound better. As a matter of fact, it was Grandpapa.'

'What do you mean, it was Grandpapa? Who was Grandpapa?'

'The miscreant.'

'Are you telling me that your grandfather –'

Words failed the Duke. His opinion of Lord Emsworth's IQ was, as we know, low, but he was unable to credit him with the supreme pottiness necessary for the perpetration of an act like the one they were discussing. Then, thinking again, he felt that there might be something in what the boy said. After all, from making an exhibition of oneself by maundering over a pig to sneaking out at daybreak and cutting tent ropes is but a step.

'What makes you think that?' he said, now definitely agog.

George would have liked to say, 'You know my methods. Apply them,' but it would have wasted time, and he was anxious to get on with his story.

'Shall I tell it you from the beginning, omitting no detail, however slight?'

'Certainly, certainly,' said the Duke, and would have added, 'I am all ears,' if the expression had been familiar to him. He wished the boy had a voice in a rather lower register, but in consideration of the importance of what he had to communicate he was willing to be squeaked at.

George marshalled his thoughts.

'I was in the kitchen at five o'clock this morning –'

'What were you doing there at such an hour?'

'Oh, just looking around,' said George guardedly. He knew that there was a school of thought that disapproved of these double breakfasts of his, and nothing to be gained by imparting information which might be relayed to Lady Constance, the head of that school. 'I sort of happened to go in.'

'Well?'

'And I hadn't been there more than about a couple of ticks when Grandpapa entered. He had a knife on his person.'

'A knife?'

'A whacking great scimitar.'

'How do you mean, on his person?'

'Well, actually he was brandishing it. His manner was strange, and there was a wild glitter in his eyes. So I said to myself, "Ho!"'

'You said what?'

'Ho!'

'Why "Ho!"?'

'Well, wouldn't you have said "Ho!"?'

The Duke considered the question, and saw that the lad had a point there.

'No doubt I should have been surprised,' he admitted.

'So was I. That's why I said "Ho!"'

'To yourself?'

'Of course. You can't go about saying "Ho!" to people out loud. So when he went out, I followed him.'

'Why?'

'Use your loaf, big boy,' pleaded George. 'You know my methods. Apply them,' he said, happy to get it in at last. 'I wanted to see what he was up to.'

'Of course. Yes, quite understandable. And –?'

'He headed for the lake. I trickled after him, taking advantage of every inch of cover, and he made a beeline for that tent and started sawing away at the ropes.'

A sudden suspicion darted into the Duke's mind. He puffed a menacing moustache.

'If this is some silly joke of yours, young man –'

'I swear it isn't. I tell you I was watching him the whole time. He didn't see me because I was well concealed behind a neighbouring bush, but I was an eye-witness throughout. Did you ever read *The Hound of the Baskervilles?*'

For an instant the Duke received the impression that the pottiness of Lord Emsworth had been inherited by his grandson, with an assist from the latter's father, the ninth Earl's elder son, Lord Basham, whom he knew to be one of England's less bright minds. You don't, he reasoned, read hounds, you gallop after them on horses, shouting 'Yoicks!' or possibly 'Tally-ho!' Then it occurred to him that the lad might be referring to some book or other. He inquired whether this was so, and received an answer in the affirmative.

'I was thinking of the bit where Holmes and Watson are lurking in the mist, waiting for the bad guy to start things moving. It was rather like that, only there wasn't any mist.'

'So you saw him clearly?'

'With the naked eye.'

'And he was cutting the ropes?'

'With the naked knife.'

The Duke relapsed into a gloomy silence. Like many another thinker before him, he was depressed by the reflection that nothing ever goes just right in this fat-headed world. Always there is the fatal snag in the path that pulls you up sharp when the happy ending seems in sight.

A man of liberal views, he had no objection whatsoever to a little gentlemanly blackmail, and here, you would have said, the luck of the Dunstables had handed him the most admirable opportunity for such blackmail. All he had to do was to go to Lord Emsworth, tell him that his sins had found him out, demand the Empress as the price of his silence, and the wretched man would have no option but to meet his terms. The thing was a walkover. In the bag, as he believed the expression was nowadays.

Such had been his thoughts as he listened to the boy's story, but now despondency had set in. The whole project, he saw, became null and void because of one small snag – that proof of the crime depended solely on the unsupported word of the witness George. If Emsworth, as he was bound to do, pleaded not guilty to the charge, who was going to believe the testimony of a child with ginger hair and freckles, whose reputation as a teller of truth had never been one to invite scrutiny? His evidence would be laughed out of court, and he would be dashed lucky if he were not sent to bed without his supper and deprived of his pocket money for months and months.

Engrossed in these sombre thoughts, he was only dimly aware that the squeaky voice was continuing to squeak. It seemed to be saying something about motion pictures, a subject in which he had never taken even a tepid interest.

'Shut up, boy, and pop off,' he grunted.

'But I thought you'd like to know,' said George, pained.

'If you think I want to hear about a lot of greasy actors grinning on a screen, you are very much mistaken.'

'But this wasn't a greasy, grinning actor, it was Grandpapa.'

'What's that?'

'I was telling you I took pictures of Grandpapa with my camera.'

The Duke quivered as if he had been the sea monster he rather closely resembled and a harpoon had penetrated his skin.

'In the act of cutting those ropes?' he gasped.

'That's right. I've got the film upstairs in my room. I was going to take it into Market Blandings this afternoon to have it developed.'

The Duke quivered again, his emotion such that he could scarcely speak.

'You must do nothing of the sort. And you must not say a word of this to anyone.'

'Well, of course, I won't. I only told you because I thought you'd think it was funny.'

'It is very far from funny. It is extremely serious. Do you realize what would happen when the man developed that film, as you call it, and recognized your grandfather?'

'Coo! I never thought of that. You mean he'd blow the gaff? Spread the story hither and thither? Squeal on him?'

'Exactly. And your grandfather's name in the county would be –'

'Mud?'

'Precisely. Everyone would think he was potty.'

'He *is* rather potty.'

'Not so potty as he would seem if that film were made public. Dash it, they'd certify him without blinking an eye.'

'Who would?'

'The doctors, of course.'

'You mean he'd be put in a loony bin?'

'Exactly.'

'Coo!'

George could see now why his companion had said it was serious. He was very fond of Lord Emsworth, and would have hated to find him winding up in a padded cell. He felt in his pocket and produced a bag of acid drops, always a great help to thought. Chewing one of these, he sat pondering in silence. The Duke resumed his remarks.

'Do you understand what I am saying?'

George nodded.

'I dig you, Chief.'

'Don't say "I dig you" and don't call me "Chief". Bring the thing to me, and I'll take care of it. It's not safe in the hands of a mere child like you.'

'Okay, big boy.'

'And don't call me big boy,' said the Duke.

2

There was a contented smile on Lord Ickenham's face as he settled himself in his hammock after leaving Lord Emsworth. It gratified him to feel that he had allayed the latter's fears and eased his mind. Nothing like a pep talk, he was thinking, and he was deep in a pleasant reverie when a voice spoke his name and he perceived Lord Emsworth at his side, drooping like a tired lily. Except when he had something to prop himself against, there was always a suggestion of the drooping floweret about the master of Blandings

Castle. He seemed to work on a hinge somewhere in the small of his back, and people searching for something nice to say of him sometimes described him as having a scholarly stoop. Lord Ickenham had become accustomed to this bonelessness and no longer expected his friend to give any evidence of possessing vertebrae, but the look of anguish on his face was new, and it shocked him. He rose from the hammock with lissom leap, full of sympathy and concern.

'Good heavens, Emsworth! What's the matter? Is something wrong?'

For some moments it seemed as though speech would prove beyond the ninth earl's powers and that he would continue indefinitely to give his rather vivid impersonation of a paralysed deaf mute. But eventually he spoke.

'I've just seen Dunstable,' he said.

Lord Ickenham remained perplexed. The situation did not appear to him to have been clarified. He, personally, would always prefer not to see the Duke, a preference shared by the latter's many acquaintances in Wiltshire and elsewhere, but it did not disturb him unduly when he had to, and he found it strange that his companion should be of less stern stuff.

'Unavoidable, don't you think, when he's staying in the house?' he said. 'There he is, I mean to say, and you can't very well help running into him from time to time. But perhaps he said something to upset you?'

The anguished look in Lord Emsworth's eyes became more anguished. It was as if the question had touched an exposed nerve. He gulped for a moment, reminding Lord Ickenham of a dog to which he was greatly attached, which made a similar sound when about to give up its all after a too busy day among the fleshpots.

'He said he wanted the Empress.'

'Who wouldn't?'

'And I've got to give her to him.'

'You've *what*?'

'The alternative was too terrible to contemplate. He threatened, if I refused, to tell Constance that it was I who cut those tent ropes.'

Lord Ickenham began to feel a little impatient. He had already told this man, in words adapted to the meanest intelligence, what course to pursue, should suspicion fall upon him.

'My dear fellow, don't you remember what I said to you in the library? Stick to stout denial.'

'But he has proof.'

'Proof?'

'Eh? Yes, proof. It seems that my grandson George took photographs of me with his camera, and Dunstable now has the film in his possession. And I gave George that camera for his birthday! "This will keep you out of mischief, George, my boy," I remember saying. Out of mischief!' said Lord Emsworth bitterly, his air that of a grandfather regretting that he had ever been so foolish as to beget a son who in his turn would beget a son of his own capable of using a camera. There were, he was feeling, far too many grandsons in the world and far too many cameras for them to take pictures of grandfathers with. His view of grandsons was, in short, at the moment jaundiced, and as, having told his tale, he moved limply away, he was thinking almost as harshly of George as of the Duke of Dunstable.

Lord Ickenham returned to his hammock. He always thought more nimbly when in a recumbent position, and it was plain to him that a considerable amount of nimble thinking was now called for. Hitherto, his endeavours to spread sweetness and light and give service with a smile had been uniformly successful, but a man whose aim in life it is to do the square thing by his fellows is never content to think with modest pride of past triumphs; it is the present on which he feels the mind must be fixed, and it was to Lord Emsworth's problem that he gave the full force of his powerful intellect.

It was a problem which undoubtedly presented certain points of interest, and at the moment he confessed himself unable to see how it was to be solved. Given the unhappy man's panic fear of having Lady Constance's attention drawn to his recent activities, there seemed no course for Lord Emsworth to pursue but to meet the Duke's terms. It was one of those occasions, more frequent in real life than on the television and motion picture screens, when the bad guy comes out on top and the good guy gets the loser's end. The Duke of Dunstable might not look like a green bay tree, but everything pointed to the probability of him flourishing like one.

He was musing thus, and had closed his eyes in order to muse the better, when a stately figure approached the hammock and stood beside it. Shrewdly realizing that there was but the slimmest chance of her brother Clarence remembering to tell Lord Ickenham that his presence was desired in her boudoir, Lady Constance had rung for Beach and sent him off to act as a substitute messenger. The butler coughed respectfully, and Lord Ickenham opened his eyes.

'Pardon me for disturbing you, m'lord –'

'Not at all, Beach, not at all,' said Lord Ickenham heartily. He was always glad to chat with this pillar of Blandings, for a firm friendship had sprung up between them during his previous sojourn at the castle, and this second visit had cemented it. 'Something on your mind?'

'Her ladyship, m'lord.'

'What about her?'

'If it is convenient to you m'lord, she would be glad to see you for a moment in her boudoir.'

This struck Lord Ickenham as unusual. It was the first time his hostess had gone out of her way to seek his company, and he was not sure that he liked the look of things. He had never considered himself psychic, but he was conscious of a strong premonition that trouble was about to raise its ugly head.

'Any idea what she wants?'

Butlers rarely display emotion, and there was nothing in Beach's manner to reveal the sympathy he was feeling for one who, in his opinion, was about to face an ordeal somewhat comparable to that of the prophet Daniel when he entered the lion's den.

'I rather fancy, m'lord, her ladyship wishes to confer with you on the subject of Mr Meriwether. With reference to the gentleman's name being in reality the Reverend Cuthbert Bailey.'

Once in his cowboy days Lord Ickenham, injudiciously standing behind a temperamental mule, had been kicked by the animal in the stomach. He felt now rather as he had felt then, though only an involuntary start showed that he was not his usual debonair self.

'Oh,' he said thoughtfully. 'Oh. So she knows about that?'

'Yes, m'lord.'

'How did you come to get abreast?'

'I was inadvertently an auditor of his lordship's conversation with her ladyship. I chanced to be passing the door, and his lordship had omitted to close it.'

'And you stopped, looked and listened?'

'I had paused to tie my shoelace,' said Beach with dignity. 'I found it impossible not to overhear what his lordship was saying.'

'And what was he saying?'

'He was informing her ladyship that Miss Briggs, having discovered Mr Meriwether's identity, was seeking to compel the gentleman to assist her in her project of stealing his lordship's pig, but that Mr Meriwether refused to be a party to the undertaking, having scruples. It was in the course of his remarks on this subject that his lordship revealed that Mr Meriwether was not Mr Meriwether, but Mr Bailey.'

Lord Ickenham sighed. In principle he approved of his young friend's rigid code of ethics, but there was no denying that that high-mindedness of his could be inconvenient, lowering as it did his efficiency as a plotter. The ideal person with whom to plot is the furtive, shifty-eyed man who stifled his conscience at the age of six and would not recognize a scruple if you served it up to him on an individual blue plate with béarnaise sauce.

'I see,' he said. 'How did Lady Constance take this piece of hot news?'

'She appeared somewhat stirred, m'lord.'

'One sees how she might well be. And now she wants to have a word with me?'

'Yes, m'lord.'

'To thresh the thing out, no doubt, and consider it from every angle. Oh, what a tangled web we weave, Beach, when first we practise to deceive.'

'We do, indeed, m'lord.'

'Well, all right,' said Lord Ickenham, rising. 'I can give her five minutes.'

3

The time it had taken Beach to deliver his message and Lord Ickenham to make the journey between lawn and boudoir was perhaps ten minutes, and with each of those minutes Lady Constance's wrath had touched a new high. At the moment when her guest entered the room she had just been thinking how agreeable it would be to skin him with a blunt knife, and the genial smile he gave her as he came in seemed to go through her nervous system like a red-hot bullet through butter. 'My tablets – Meet it is I set it down that one may smile and smile and be a villain. At least, I'm sure it may be so in Blandings Castle,' she was saying to herself.

'Beach says you want to see me, Lady Constance,' said Lord Ickenham, smiling another affectionate smile. His manner was that of a man looking forward to a delightful chat on this and that with an attractive woman, and Lady Constance, meeting the smile head on, realized that in entertaining the idea of skinning him with a blunt knife she had been too lenient. Not a blunt knife, she was thinking, but some such instrument as the one described by the poet Gilbert as looking far less like a hatchet than a dissipated saw.

'Please sit down,' she said coldly.

'Oh, thanks,' said Lord Ickenham doing so. His eye fell on a photograph on the desk. 'Hullo, this face seems familiar. Jimmy Schoonmaker?'

'Yes.'

'Taken recently?'

'Yes.'

'He looks older than he used to. One does, of course, as the years go on. I suppose I do, too, though I've never noticed it. Great chap, Jimmy. Did you know that he brought young Myra up all by himself after his wife died? With a certain amount of assistance from me. The one thing he jibbed at was giving her her bath, so he used to call me in of an evening, and I would soap her back, keeping what the advertisements call a safe suds level. It was a little like massaging an eel. Bless my soul, how long ago it seems. I remember once –'

'Lord Ickenham!' Lady Constance's voice, several degrees below zero at the outset, had become even more like that of a snow queen. The hatchet that looked like a dissipated saw would not have seemed to her barely adequate. 'I did not ask you to come here because I wished to hear your reminiscences. It was to tell you that you will leave the castle immediately. *With*,' added Lady Constance, speaking from between clenched teeth, 'your friend Mr Bailey.'

She paused, and was conscious of a feeling of flatness and disappointment. She had expected her words to bathe this man in confusion and shatter his composure to fragments, but he had not turned a hair of his neatly brushed head. He was looking at another photograph. It was that of Lady Constance's late husband, Joseph Keeble, but she gave him no time to ask questions about it.

'Lord Ickenham!'

He turned, full of apology.

'I'm sorry. I'm afraid I let my attention wander. I was thinking of the dear old days. You were saying that you were about to leave the castle, were you not?'

'I was saying that *you* were about to leave the castle.'

Lord Ickenham seemed surprised.

'I had made no plans. You're sure you mean me?'

'And you will take Mr Bailey with you. How dare you bring that impossible young man here?'

Lord Ickenham fingered his moustache thoughtfully.

'Oh, Bill Bailey. I see what you mean. Yes, I suppose it was a social solecism. But reflect. I meant well. Two young hearts had been sundered in springtime . . . well, not in springtime, perhaps, but as near to it as makes no matter, and I wanted to adjust things. I'm sure Jimmy would have approved of the kindly act.'

'I disagree with you.'

'He wants his ewe lamb to be happy.'

'So do I. That is why I do not intend to allow her to marry a penniless curate. But there is no need to discuss it. There are –'

'You'll be sorry when Bill suddenly becomes a bishop.'

'– good trains –'

'Why did I not push this good thing along, you'll say to yourself.'

'– throughout the day. I recommend the 2.15,' said Lady Constance. 'Good morning, Lord Ickenham. I will not keep you any longer.'

A nicer-minded man would have detected in these words a hint – guarded, perhaps, but nevertheless a hint – that his presence was no longer desired, but Lord Ickenham remained glued to his chair. He was looking troubled.

'I agree that you are probably right in giving this plug to the 2.15 train,' he said. 'No doubt it is an excellent one. But there are difficulties in the way of Bill and me catching it.'

'I see none.'

'I will try to make myself clearer. Have you studied Bill Bailey at all closely during his visit here? He's an odd chap. Wouldn't hurt a fly in the ordinary way, in fact I've known him not to do so –'

'I am not interested in Mr –'

'But, when driven to it, ruthless and sticking at nothing. You might think that, being a curate, he would suppress those photographs, and of course I feel that that is what he ought to do. But even curates can be pushed too far, and I'm afraid if you insist on him leaving the castle, however luxurious the 2.15 train, that that is how he will feel he is being pushed.'

'Lord Ickenham!'

'You spoke?'

'*What* are you talking about?'

'Didn't I explain that? I'm sorry. I have an annoying habit of getting ahead of my story. I was alluding to the photographs he took of Beach and saying that, if driven out into the snow, he will feel so bitter that he will give them wide publicity. Vindictive, yes, and not at all the sort of thing one approves of in a clerk in holy orders, but that is what will happen, I assure you.'

Lady Constance placed a hand on a forehead which had become fevered. Not even when conversing with her brother Clarence had she ever felt so marked a swimming sensation.

'Photographs? Of Beach?'

'Cutting those tent ropes and causing alarm and despondency to more church lads than one likes to contemplate. But how foolish of me. I didn't tell you, did I? Here is the thing in a nutshell. Bill Bailey, unable to sleep this morning possibly because love affects him that way, started to go for a stroll, saw young George's camera lying in the hall, picked it up with a vague idea of photographing some of the local fauna and was surprised to see Beach down by the lake, cutting those ropes. He took a whole reel of him and I understand they have come out splendidly. May I smoke?' said Lord Ickenham, taking out his case.

Lady Constance did not reply. She seemed to have been turned into a pillar of salt, like Lot's wife. It might have been supposed that, having passed her whole life at Blandings Castle, with the sort of things happening that happened daily in that stately but always somewhat hectic home of England, she would have been impervious to shocks. Nothing, one would have said, would have been able to surprise her. This was not so. She was stunned.

Beach! Eighteen years of spotless buttling, and now this! If she had not been seated, she would have reeled. Everything seemed to her to go black, including Lord Ickenham. He might have been an actor, made up to play Othello, lighting an inky cigarette with a sepia lighter.

'Of course,' this negroid man went on, 'one gets the thought behind Beach's rash act. For days Emsworth has been preaching a holy war against these Church Lads, filling the listening air with the tale of what he has suffered at their hands, and it is easy to understand how Beach, feudally devoted to him, felt that he could hold himself back no longer. Out with the knife and go to it, he said to himself. It will probably have occurred to you how closely in its essentials the whole set-up resembles the murder of the late St Thomas à Becket. King Henry, you will remember, kept saying, "Will no one rid me of this turbulent priest?" till those knights of his decided that something had to be done about it. Emsworth, perhaps in other words, expressed the same view about the Church Lads, and Beach, taking his duties as a butler very seriously, thought that it was part of them to show the young thugs that crime does not pay and that retribution must sooner or later overtake those who knock top hats off with crusty rolls at school treats.'

Lord Ickenham paused to cough, for he had swallowed a mouthful of smoke the wrong way. Lady Constance remained congealed. She might have been a statue of herself commissioned by a group of friends and admirers.

'You see how extremely awkward the situation is? Whether or not Emsworth formally instructed Beach to take the law into his hands, we shall probably never know, but it makes very little difference. If those photographs are given to the world, it is inevitable that Beach, unable to bear the shame of exposure, will hand in his portfolio and resign office, and you will lose the finest butler in Shropshire. And there is another thing. Emsworth will unquestionably confess that he inflamed the man and so was directly responsible for what happened, and one can see the County looking very askance at him, pursing their lips, raising their eyebrows, possibly even cutting him at the next Agricultural Show. Really, Lady Constance, if I were you, I think I would reconsider this idea of yours of giving Bill Bailey the old heave-ho. I will leave the castle on the 2.15, if you wish, though sorry to go, for I like the society here, but Bailey, I'm afraid, must stay. Possibly in the course of time his winning personality will overcome your present prejudice against him. I'll leave you to think it over,' said Lord Ickenham, and with another of his kindly smiles left the room.

For an appreciable time after he had gone Lady Constance sat motionless. Then, as if a sudden light had shone on her darkness, she gave a start. She stretched out a hand towards the pigeonholes on the desk, in which reposed notepaper, envelopes, postcards, telegraph forms and cable forms. Selecting one of the last named, she took pen in hand, and began to write.

James Schoonmaker
1000 Park Avenue
New York

She paused a moment in thought. Then she began to write again:

'*Come immediately. Most urgent. Must see you . . .*'

4

It is always unpleasant for a man of good will to be compelled, even from the best of motives, to blacken the name of an innocent butler, and his first thought after he has done so is to make amends. Immediately after leaving Lady Constance, therefore, Lord Ickenham proceeded to Beach's pantry, where with a few well-chosen words he slipped a remorseful five-pound note into the other's hand. Beach trousered the money with a stately bow of thanks, and in answer to a query as to whether he had any knowledge of the Reverend Cuthbert Bailey's whereabouts said that he had seen him some little time ago entering the rose garden in company with Miss Schoonmaker.

Thither Lord Ickenham decided to make his way. He was sufficiently a student of human nature to be aware that, when two lovers get together in a rose garden, they do not watch the clock, and he presumed that, if Bill and Myra had been there some little time ago, they would be there now. They would, be supposed, be discussing in gloomy mood the former's imminent departure from Blandings Castle, and he was anxious to relieve their minds. For there was no doubt in his own that Lady Constance, having thought things over, would continue to extend her hospitality to the young cleric. Her whole air, as he left her, had been that of a woman unable to see any alternative to the hoisting of the white flag.

He had scarcely left the house when he saw that he had been mistaken. So far from being in the rose garden, Myra Schoonmaker was on the gravel strip outside the front door, and so far from being in conference with Bill, she was closeted, as far as one can be closeted in the open air, with the Duke of Dunstable's nephew, Archie Gilpin. As he appeared, Archie Gilpin moved away, and as Myra came towards him, he saw that her face was sombre and her walk the walk of a girl who can detect no silver lining in the clouds. This did not cause him concern. He had that to tell which would be a verbal shot in the arm and set her dancing all over the place and strewing roses from her hat.

'Hullo there,' he said.

'Oh, hullo, Uncle Fred.'

'You look pretty much down among the wines and spirits, young Myra.'

'That's the way I feel.'

'You won't much longer. Where's Bill?'

The girl shrugged her shoulders.

'Oh, somewhere around, I suppose. I left him in the rose garden.'

Lord Ickenham's eyebrows shot up.

'You *left* him in the rose garden? Not a lovers' tiff, I hope?'

'If you like to call it that,' said Myra. She kicked moodily at a passing beetle, which gave her a cold look and went on its way. 'I've broken our engagement.'

It was never easy to disconcert Lord Ickenham, as his nephew Pongo would have testified. Even on that day at the dog races his demeanour, even after the hand of the Law had fallen on his shoulder, had remained unruffled. But now he could not hide his dismay. He looked at the girl incredulously.

'You've broken the engagement?'

'Yes.'

'But why?'

'Because he doesn't love me.'

'What makes you think that?'

'I'll tell you what makes me think that,' said Myra passionately. 'He went and told Lord Emsworth who he was, knowing that Lord Emsworth was bound to spill the beans to Lady Constance, and that Lady Constance would instantly bounce him. And why did he do it, you ask? Because it gave him the excuse to get away from me. I suppose he's got another girl in Bottleton East.'

Lord Ickenham twirled his moustache sternly. He had often in the course of his life listened patiently to people talking through their hats, but he was in no mood to be patient now.

'Myra,' he said. 'You ought to have your head examined.'

'Oh, yes?'

'It would be money well spent. I assure you that if all the girls in Bottleton East came and did the dance of the seven veils before him, Bill Bailey wouldn't give them a glance. He told Emsworth who he was because his conscience wouldn't let him do otherwise. The revelation was unavoidable if he was to make his story of the Briggs' foul plot convincing, and he did not count the cost. He knew that it meant ruin and disaster, but he refused to stand silently by and allow that good man to be deprived of his pig. You ought to be fawning on him for his iron integrity, instead of going about the place breaking engagements. I have always held that the man of sensibility should be careful what he says to the other sex, if he wishes to be numbered among the *preux chevaliers*, but I cannot restrain myself from telling you, young M. Schoonmaker, that you have behaved like a little half-wit.'

Myra, who had been staring at the beetle as if contemplating having another go at it, raised a startled head.

'Do you think that was really it?'

'Of course it was.'

'And he wasn't just jumping at the chance of getting away from me?'

'Of course he wasn't. I tell you, Bill Bailey is about as near being a stainless knight as you could find in a month of Sundays. He's as spotless as they come.'

A deep sigh escaped Myra Schoonmaker. His eloquence had convinced her.

'Half-wit,' she said, 'is right. Uncle Fred, I've made a ghastly fool of myself.'

'Just what I've been telling you.'

'I don't mean about Bill. I could have put that right in a minute. But I've just told Archie Gilpin I'll marry him.'

'No harm that I can see in confiding your matrimonial plans to Archie Gilpin. He'll probably send you a wedding present.'

'Oh, don't be so dumb, Uncle Fred! I mean I've just told Archie, I'll marry *him*!'

'What, *him*?'

'Yes, *him*.'

'Well, fry me for an oyster! Why on earth did you do that?'

'Oh, just a sort of gesture, I suppose. It's what they used to write in my reports at Miss Spence's school. "She is often too impulsive", they used to say.'

She spoke despondently. Ever since that brief but fateful conversation with Archie, an uneasy conviction had been stealing over her that in a rash moment she had started something which she would have given much to stop. Her emotions were somewhat similar to those of a nervous passenger on a roller coaster at an amusement park who when it is too late to get off feels the contraption gathering speed beneath him.

It was not as if she even liked Archie Gilpin very much. He was all right in his way, a pleasant enough companion for a stroll or a game of tennis, but until this awful thing had happened he had been something completely negligible, just some sort of foreign substance that happened to be around. And now she was engaged to him, and the announcement would be in *The Times*, and Lady Constance would be telling her how pleased her father would be and how sensible it was of her to have realized that that other thing had been nothing but a ridiculous infatuation, and she could see no point in going on living. She was very much inclined to go down to the lake and ask one of the Church Lads if he would care to earn a shilling by holding her head under water till the vital spark expired.

'Oh, Uncle Fred!' she said.

'There, there!' said Lord Ickenham.

'Oh, Uncle Fred!'

'Don't talk, just cry. There is nothing more therapeutic.'

'What shall I do?'

'Break it off, of course. What else? Tell him it's been nice knowing him, and hand him his hat.'

'But I can't.'

'Nonsense. Perfectly easy thing to bring into the conversation. You're strolling with him in the moonlight. He says something about how jolly it's going to be when you and he are settled down in your little nest, and you say, "Oh, I forgot to tell you about that. It's off." He says, "What!" You say, "You heard," and he reddens and goes to Africa.'

'And I go to New York.'

'Why New York?'

'Because that's where I'll be shipped back to in disgrace when they hear I've broken my engagement to a Duke's nephew.'

'Don't tell me Jimmy's a stern father?'

'That would make him stern enough. He's got a thing about the British aristocracy. He admires them terrifically.'

'I don't blame him. We're the salt of the earth.'

'He would insist on taking me home, and I'd never see my angel Bill again, because he couldn't possibly afford the fare to New York.'

Lord Ickenham mused. This was a complication he had not taken into his calculations.

'I see. Yes, I appreciate the difficulty.'

'Me, too.'

'This opens up a new line of thought. You'd better leave everything to me.'

'I don't see that you can do anything.'

'That is always a rash observation to make to an Ickenham. As I once remarked to another young friend of mine, this sort of situation brings out the best in me. And when you get the best in Frederick Altamont Cornwallis Twistleton, fifth Earl of good old Ickenham, you've got something.'

Chapter 8

If you go down Fleet Street and turn into one of the side streets leading to the river, you will find yourself confronted by a vast building that looks something like a county jail and something like a biscuit factory. This is Tilbury House, the home of the Mammoth Publishing Company, that busy hive where hordes of workers toil day and night, churning out reading matter for the masses. For Lord Tilbury's numerous daily and weekly papers are not, as is sometimes supposed, just Acts of God; they are produced deliberately.

The building has its scores of windows, but pay no attention to those on the first two floors, for there are only editors and things behind them. Concentrate the eye on the three in the middle of the third floor. These belong to Lord Tilbury's private office, and there is just a chance, if you wait, that you may catch a glimpse of him leaning out to get a breath of air, than which nothing could be more calculated to make a sightseer's day.

This morning, however, you would have been out of luck, for Lord Tilbury was sitting motionless at his desk. He had been sitting there for some little time. There were a hundred letters he should have been dictating to Millicent Rigby, his secretary, but Millicent remained in the outer office, undictated to. There were a dozen editors with whom he should have been conferring, but they stayed where they were, unconferred with.

He was deep in thought, and anyone seeing him would have asked himself with awe what it was that was occupying that giant mind. He might have been planning out some pronouncement which would shake the chancelleries, or pondering on the most suitable line to take in connexion with the latest rift in the Cabinet, or even, for he took a personal interest in all his publications, considering changes in the policy of *Wee Tots*, the journal which has done so much to mould thought in the British nursery. In actual fact, he was musing on Empress of Blandings.

In the life of every successful man there is always some little something missing. Lord Tilbury had wealth and power and the comforting knowledge that, catering as he did for readers who had all been mentally arrested at the age of twelve, he would continue to enjoy these indefinitely, but he had not got Empress of Blandings: and ever since the day when he and that ornament of her sex had met he had yearned to add her to his Buckinghamshire piggery. That was how the pig-minded always reacted to even the briefest glance at the Empress. They came, saw, gasped and went away unhappy and discontented, ever after, to move through life bemused, like men kissed by goddesses in dreams.

His sombre thoughts were broken in upon by the ringing of the telephone. Moodily he took up the receiver.

'Hoy!' shouted a voice in his ear, and he had no difficulty in identifying the speaker. He had a wide circle of acquaintances, but the Duke of Dunstable was the only member of it who opened conversations with this monosyllable in a booming tone reminiscent of a costermonger calling attention to his blood oranges. 'Is that you, Stinker?'

Lord Tilbury frowned. There were only a few survivors of the old days who addressed him thus. Even in the distant past he had found the name distasteful, and now that he had become a man of distinction, it jarred upon him even more gratingly. In addition to frowning, he also swelled a good deal. He was a short, stout man who swelled readily when annoyed.

'Lord Tilbury speaking,' he said curtly, emphasizing the first two words. 'Well?'

'What?' roared the Duke. He was a little deaf in the right ear.

'Well?'

'Speak up, Stinker. Don't mumble.'

Lord Tilbury raised his voice to an almost Duke-like pitch.

'I said "Well?"'

'Well?'

'Yes.'

'Damn silly thing to say,' said the Duke and Lord Tilbury's frown deepened.

'What is it, Dunstable?'

'Eh?'

'What *is* it?'

'What is what?'

'What do you want?' Lord Tilbury rasped, the hand gripping the receiver about to crash it back on its cradle.

'It's not what I want,' bellowed the Duke. 'It's what you want. I've got that pig.'

'What!'

'What?'

Lord Tilbury did not reply. He had stiffened in his chair and presented the appearance of somebody in a fairy story who had had a spell cast upon him by the local wizard. His silence offended the Duke, never a patient man.

'Are you there, Stinker?' he roared, and Lord Tilbury thought for a moment that his eardrum had gone.

'Yes, yes, yes,' he said, removing the receiver for a moment in order to massage his ear.

'Then why the devil don't you utter?'

'I was overcome.'

'What?'

'I could hardly believe it. You have really persuaded Emsworth to sell you Empress of Blandings?'

'We came to an arrangement. Is that offer of yours still open?'

'Of course, of course.'

'Two thousand, cash down?'

'Certainly.'

'What?'

'I said certainly.'

'Then you'd better come here and collect the animal.'

'I will. I'll –'

Lord Tilbury paused. He was thinking of all the correspondence he should have been dictating to Millicent Rigby. Could he neglect this? Then he saw the solution. He could take Millicent Rigby with him. He pressed a bell. His secretary entered.

'Where do you live, Miss Rigby?'

'Shepherd Market, Lord Tilbury.'

'Take a taxi, go and pack some things for the night, and come back here. We're driving down to Shropshire.' He spoke into the telephone. 'Are you there, Dunstable?'

Something not unlike an explosion in an ammunition dump made itself heard at the other end of the line.

'Are *you* there, blast your gizzard? What's the matter? Can't get a word out of you.'

'I was speaking to my secretary.'

'Well, don't. Do you realize what these trunk calls cost?'

'I'm sorry. I am motoring down immediately. Where can I see you? I don't want to come to the castle.'

'Put up at the Emsworth Arms in Market Blandings. I'll meet you there.'

'I'll be waiting for you.'

'What?'

'I said I'll be waiting for you.'

'What?'

Lord Tilbury gritted his teeth. He was feeling hot and exhausted. That was the effect the other's telephone technique often had on people.

2

Lavender Briggs had caught the 12.30 train at Paddington. It set her down on the platform of Market Blandings station shortly after four.

The day was warm and the journey had been stuffy and somewhat exhausting, but her mood was one of quiet contentment. She had enjoyed every minute of her visit to the metropolis. She had deposited the Duke's cheque. She had dined with a group of earnest friends at the Crushed Pansy, the restaurant with a soul, and at the conclusion of the meal they had all gone on to the opening performance at the Flaming Youth Group Centre of one of those avant-garde plays which bring the scent of boiling cabbage across the footlights and in which the little man in the bowler hat turns out to be God. And she was confident that when she saw him the Reverend Cuthbert Bailey would have made up his mind, rather than be unmasked, to lend his services to the purloining of Lord Emsworth's pig. It seemed to her that a cup of tea was indicated by way of celebration, and she made her way to the Emsworth Arms. There were other hostelries in Market Blandings – one does not forget the Goose and Gander, the Jolly Cricketers, the Wheatsheaf, the Waggoner's Rest, the Beetle and Wedge and the Stitch in Time – but the Emsworth Arms was the only one where a lady could get a refined cup of tea with buttered toast and fancy cakes. Those other establishments catered more to the George Cyril Wellbeloved type of client and were content to say it with beer.

At the Emsworth Arms, moreover, you could have your refreshment served to you in the large garden which was one of the features of Market Blandings. Dotted about with rustic tables, it ran all the way down to the river, and there were few of the rustic tables that did not enjoy the shade of a spreading tree or a clump of bushes. The one Lavender Briggs selected was screened from view by a green mass of foliage, and she had chosen it because she wanted complete privacy in which to meditate on the very satisfactory state of her affairs. Elsewhere in the garden one's thoughts were apt to be interrupted by family groups presided over by flushed mothers telling Wilfred to stop teasing Katie or Percival to leave off making faces at Jane.

She had finished the cakes and the buttered toast and was sipping her third cup of tea, when from the other side of the bushes, where she had noticed a rustic table similar to her own, a voice spoke. All it said was 'Two beers', but at the sound of it she stiffened in her chair, some sixth sense telling her that if she listened, she might hear something of interest. For it was the Duke's voice that had shattered the afternoon stillness, and there was only one thing that could have brought the Duke to Market Blandings, the desire for a conference with the mystery man who was prepared to go as high as two thousand pounds to acquire Lord Emsworth's peerless pig.

A moment later a second voice spoke, and if Lavender Briggs had stiffened before, she stiffened doubly now. The words it had said were negligible, something about the warmth of the day, but they were enough to enable her to recognize the speaker as her former employer, Lord Tilbury of the Mammoth Publishing Company. She had taken too much dictation from those august lips in the past to allow of any misconception.

Rigid in her chair, she set herself to listen with, in the Duke's powerful phrase, her ears sticking up.

3

Conversation on the other side of the bushes was for awhile desultory. With a waiter expected back at any moment with beer, two men who have serious matters to discuss do not immediately plumb the deeps, but confine themselves to small talk. Lord Tilbury said once more that the day was warm, and the Duke agreed. The Duke said he supposed it had been even warmer in London, and Lord Tilbury said Yes, much warmer. The Duke said it wasn't the heat he minded so much as the humidity, and Lord Tilbury confessed that it was the humidity that troubled him also. Then the beer arrived, and the Duke flung himself on it with a grunt. He must have abandoned rather noticeably the gentlemanly restraint which one likes to see in Dukes when drinking beer, for Lord Tilbury said:

'You seem thirsty. Did you walk from the castle?'

'No, got a lift. Bit of luck. It's a warm day.'

'Yes, very warm.'

'Humid, too.'

'Very humid.'

'It's the humidity I don't like.'

'I don't like the humidity either.'

Silence followed these intellectual exchanges. It was broken by a loud chuckle from the Duke.

'Eh?' said Lord Tilbury.

'What?' said the Duke. 'Speak up, Stinker.'

'I was merely wondering what it was that was amusing you,' said Lord Tilbury frostily. 'And I wish you wouldn't call me Stinker. Somebody might hear.'

'Let them.'

'What the devil are you giggling about?' demanded Lord Tilbury, as a second chuckle followed the first. He had never been fond of the Duke of Dunstable, and he felt that having to put up with his society, after a fatiguing journey from London, was a heavy price to pay even for Empress of Blandings.

The Duke was not a man who made a practice of disclosing his private affairs to every dashed Tom, Dick and Harry, and at another time and under different conditions would have been blowed if he was going to let himself be pumped by Stinker Pyke, or Lord Tilbury, as he now called himself. He mistrusted these newspaper fellers. You told them something in the strictest confidence, and the next thing you knew it was spread all over the gossip page with a six-inch headline at the top and probably a photograph of you, looking like someone the police were anxious to question in connexion with the Dover Street smash-and-grab raid.

But he was now fairly full of the Emsworth Arms beer, and, as everybody who has tried it knows, there is something about the home-brewed beer purveyed by G. Ovens, landlord of the Emsworth Arms, that has a mellowing effect. What G. Ovens put into it is a secret between him and his Maker, but it acts like magic on the most reticent. With a pint of this elixir sloshing about inside him, it seemed to the Duke that it would be churlish not to share his happiness with a sympathetic crony.

'Just put one over on a blasted female,' he said.

'Lady Constance?' said Lord Tilbury, jumping to what suggested itself to him as the obvious conclusion. His visit to Blandings Castle had been a brief one, but it had enabled him to become well acquainted with his hostess.

'No, not Connie. Connie's all right. Potty, but a good enough soul. This was Emsworth's secretary, a frightful woman of the ghastly name of Briggs. Lavender Briggs,' said the Duke, as if that made it worse.

Something stirred at the back of Lord Tilbury's mind.

'Lavender Briggs? I had a secretary named Briggs, and I seem to have a recollection of hearing someone address her as Lavender.'

'Beastly name.'

'And quite unsuited to a woman of her appearance, if it's the same woman. Is she tall and ungainly?'

'Very.'

'With harlequin glasses?'

'If that's what you call them.'

'Large feet?'

'Enormous.'

'Hair like seaweed?'

'Just like seaweed. And talks rot all the time about dusty answers.'

'I never heard her do that, but from your description it must be the same woman. I sacked her.'

'You couldn't have done better.'

'She had a way of looking at me as if I were some kind of worm, and I frequently caught her sniffing. Well, I wasn't going to put up with that sort of thing. She was an excellent secretary as far as her work was concerned, but I told her she had to go. So she is with Emsworth now? He has my sympathy. But you were saying that you had – ah – put one over on her. How was that?'

'It's a long story. She tried to get five hundred pounds out of me.'

Lord Tilbury seemed for a moment bewildered. Then he understood. He was a quick-witted man.

'Breach of promise, eh? Odd that you should have been attracted by a hideous woman like Lavender Briggs. Her glasses alone, one would have thought . . . However, there is no accounting for these sudden infatuations, though one would have expected a man of your age to have had more sense. No fool like an old fool, as they say. Well, if she could prove this breach of promise – had letters and so forth – I think you got off cheap, and it should be a valuable lesson to you.'

There is just this one thing more to be said about G. Ovens' home-brewed beer. If you want to preserve that mellow fondness for all mankind which it imparts, you have to go on drinking it. The Duke, having had only a single pint, was unable to retain the feeling that Lord Tilbury was a staunch friend from whom he could have no secrets. He was conscious of a vivid dislike for him, and couldn't imagine why a gracious sovereign had bestowed a barony on a man like that. Lavender Briggs, leaning forward, alert not to miss a word, nearly fell out of her chair, so loud was the snort that rang through the garden. When the Duke of Dunstable snorted, he held back nothing but gave it all he had.

'It wasn't breach of promise!'

'What was it, then?'

'If you want to know, she said she knew where she could lay her hands on a couple of willing helpers who would pinch Emsworth's pig for me, so I engaged her services, and she demanded five hundred pounds for the job, cash down in advance, and I gave her a cheque for that sum.'

'Well, really!'

'What do you mean, Well, really? She wouldn't settle for less.'

'Then so far it would seem that she is the one who has put something over, as you express it.'

'That's what she thought, but she was mistaken. Immediately after coming to that arrangement I spoke of with Emsworth I got in touch with my bank and stopped the cheque. I telephoned the blighters and told them I'd scoop out their insides with my bare hands if they coughed up so much as a penny of it. I'd like to see her face when it comes back marked "Refer to drawer".'

It seemed to Lord Tilbury that from somewhere near at hand, as it might have been from behind those bushes near which he was sitting, there had come a sudden gasping sound as if uttered by some soul in agony, but he paid little attention to it. He was following a train of thought.

'So you have not had to pay anything for the pig?'

'Not a bean.'

'Then you ought to let me have it cheaper.'

'You think so, do you? Well, let me tell you, Stinker,' said the Duke, who had been deeply offended by his companion's remark about old fools, 'that my price for that pig has gone up. It's three thousand now.'

'What!'

'That's what it is. Three thousand pounds.'

A sudden hush seemed to have fallen on the garden of the Emsworth Arms. It was as though it and everything in it had been stunned into silence. Birds stopped chirping. Butterflies froze in mid-flutter. Wasps wading in strawberry jam paused motionless, as if they were having their photographs taken. And the general paralysis extended to Lord Tilbury. It was an appreciable time before he spoke. When he did, it was in the hoarse voice of a man unable to believe that he has heard correctly.

'You're joking!'

'Like blazes I'm joking.'

'You expect me to pay three thousand pounds for a pig?'

'If you want the ruddy pig.'

'What about our gentlemen's agreement?'

'Gentlemen's agreements be blowed. If you care to meet my

terms, the porker's yours. If you don't, I'll sell it back to Emsworth.
No doubt he'll be glad to have it, even if the price is stiff. I'll leave
you to think it over, Stinker. No skin off my nose,' said the Duke,
'whichever way you decide.'

Chapter 9

A man who has built up a vast business, starting from nothing, must of necessity be a man capable of making swift decisions, and until this moment Lord Tilbury had never had any difficulty in doing so. His masterful handling of the hundred and one problems that arise daily in a concern like the Mammoth Publishing Company was a byword in Fleet Street.

But as he sat contemplating the dilemma on the horns of which the Duke's parting words had impaled him, he was finding it impossible to determine what course to pursue. The yearning to enrol the Empress under his banner was very powerful, but so also was his ingrained dislike for parting with large sums of money. There was, and always had been, something about signing his name to substantial cheques that gave him a sort of faint feeling.

He was still weighing this against that and balancing the pros and cons, when a shadow fell on the sunlit turf before him and he became aware that his reverie had been intruded on. Something female was standing beside the rustic table, and after blinking once or twice he recognized his former secretary, Lavender Briggs. She was regarding him austerely through her harlequin glasses.

If Lavender Briggs' gaze was austere, it had every reason for being so. No girl enjoys hearing herself described as tall and ungainly with large feet and hair like seaweed, especially if the description is followed up by the revelation that the five hundred golden pounds on which she had been counting to start her off as a proprietress of a typewriting bureau have gone with the wind, never to return. If she had not had a business proposition to place before him, she would not have lowered herself by exchanging words with this man. She would much have preferred to hit him on the head with the tankard from which the Duke had been refreshing himself. But a business girl cannot choose her associates. She has to take them as they come.

'Good afternoon, Lord Tilbury,' she said coldly. 'If you could spay-ah me a moment of your time.'

To any other caller without an appointment the owner of the Mammoth Publishing Company would have been brusque, but Lord Tilbury could not forget that this was the girl who had come within an ace of taking five hundred pounds off the Duke of Dunstable, and feeling as he did about the Duke he found his surprise at seeing her mingled with an unwilling respect. It would be too much to say that he was glad to see her, for he had hoped to continue wrestling undisturbed with the problem which was exercising his mind, but if she wanted a moment of his time, she could certainly have it. He even went so far as to ask her to take a seat, which she did. And having done so she came, like a good business-woman, straight to the point.

'I heard what the Duke of Dunstable was saying to you,' she said. 'This mattah of Lord Emsworth's pig. His demand for three thousand pounds was preposterous. Quate absurd. Do not dream of yielding to his terms.'

Lord Tilbury found himself warming to this girl. He still felt that the words in which he had described her hair, feet and general appearance had been well chosen, but we cannot all be Miss Americas and he was prepared to condone her physical defects in consideration of this womanly sympathy. Beauty, after all, is but skin deep. The main thing a man should ask of the other sex is that their hearts be in the right place, as hers was. 'Preposterous' . . . 'Quate absurd' . . . The very expressions he would have chosen himself.

On the other hand, it seemed to him that she was overlooking something.

'But I want that pig.'

'You shall have it.'

Enlightenment dawned on Lord Tilbury.

'Why, of course! You mean you'll – er –'

'Purloin it for you? Quate. My arrangements are all made and can be put into effect immediately.'

Lord Tilbury could recognize efficiency when he saw it. Here, he perceived, was a girl who thought on her feet and did it now. A genial glow suffused him. Almost as sweet as the thought of obtaining possession of the Empress was the knowledge that, to employ the latter's phrase, he would be putting one over on the Duke.

'Provided,' Lavender Briggs went on, 'that we agree on terms. I should requiah five hundred pounds.'

'Later, you mean?'

'Now, I mean. I know you always carry your cheque-book with you.'

Lord Tilbury gulped. Then the momentary sensation of nausea passed. Nothing could make him enjoy writing a cheque for five hundred pounds, but there are times when a man has to set his teeth and face the facts of life.

'Very well,' he said, a little huskily.

'Thank you,' said Lavender Briggs, a few moments later, placing the slip of paper in her bag. 'And now I ought to be getting back to the castle. Lady Constance may be wanting me for something. I will go and telephone for the station cab.'

The telephone by means of which residents of the Emsworth Arms put themselves in touch with the station cab (Jno. Robinson, propr.) was in the bar. Proceeding thither, Lavender Briggs was about to go in, when she nearly collided with Lord Ickenham, coming out.

2

Lord Ickenham had come to the bar of the Emsworth Arms because the warmth of the day had made him want to renew his acquaintance with G. Ovens' homebrew, of which he had many pleasant memories. It would have been possible – indeed, it would have been more seemly – for him to have taken tea on the terrace with Lady Constance, but he was a kindly man and something told him that after their recent get-together his hostess would prefer to be spared anything in the nature of peaceful co-existence with him. Moments come in a woman's life, he knew, when her prime need is a complete absence of Ickenhams.

He was glad to see Lavender Briggs. He was a man who made friends easily, and in the course of this visit to the castle, something approaching a friendship had sprung up between himself and her. And though he disapproved of her recent activities, he could understand and sympathize with the motives which had actuated them. He was a broad-minded man, and it was his opinion that a girl who needs five hundred pounds to set herself up in business for herself is entitled to stretch a point or two and to forget, if only temporarily, the lessons which she learned at her mother's knee. Thinking these charitable thoughts and knowing the reception that awaited her at Blandings Castle, he was happy to have this opportunity of warning her against completing her journey there.

'Well, well,' he said. 'So you're back?'

'Yayess. I caught the twelve-thirty train.'

'I wonder how it compares with the two-fifteen.'

'I beg your pardon?'

'Just a random thought. It was simply that I have heard the two-fifteen rather highly spoken of lately. Did you have a nice time in London?'

'Quate enjoyable, thank you.'

'I hope I didn't stop you going into that bar for a quick one?'

'I was merely intending to telephone for the station cab to take me to the castle.'

'I see. Well, I wouldn't. Are you familiar with the poem "Excelsior"?'

'I read it as a child,' said Lavender Briggs with a little shiver of distaste. She did not admire Longfellow.

'Then you will recall what the old man said to the fellow with the banner with the strange device. "Try not the pass," he said. "Dark lowers the tempest overhead." That is what an old — or rather, elderly but wonderfully well-preserved — man is saying to you now. Avoid station cabs. Lay off them. Leave them alone. You are better without them.'

'I don't know what you mean!'

'There are many things you do not know, Miss Briggs,' said Lord Ickenham gravely, 'including the fact that you have got a large smut on your nose.'

'Oh, have I?' said Lavender Briggs, opening her bag in a flutter and reaching hurriedly for her mirror. She plied the cleansing tissue. 'Is that better?'

'Practically perfect. I wish I could say as much for your general position.'

'I don't understand.'

'You will. You're in the soup, Miss Briggs. The gaff has been blown, and the jig is up. The pitiless light of day has been thrown on your pig-purloining plans. Bill Bailey has told all.'

'What!'

'Yes, he has squealed to the FBI. Where you made your mistake was in underestimating his integrity. These curates have scruples. The Reverend Cuthbert Bailey's are the talk of Bottleton East. Your proposition revolted him, and only the fact that you didn't offer him any kept him from spurning your gold. He went straight to Lord Emsworth and came clean. That is why I suggest that you do not telephone for station cabs in that light-hearted way. Jno. Robinson would take you to your destination for a reasonably modest sum, no doubt, but what would you find there on arrival? A Lord Emsworth with all his passions roused and flame coming out of both nostrils. For don't deceive yourself into thinking that he will be waiting on the front doorstep with a "Welcome to Blandings Castle" on his lips. In his current role of sabre-toothed tiger he would probably bite several pieces out of your leg. I have seldom seen a man who had got it so thoroughly up his nose.'

Lavender Briggs' jaw had fallen. So, slipping from between her nerveless fingers, had her bag. It fell to earth, and from it there spilled a powder compact, a handkerchief, a comb, a lipstick, a matchbox, an eyebrow pencil, a wallet with a few pound notes in it, a small purse containing some shillings, a bottle of digestive pills, a paperback copy of a book by Alfred Camus and the Tilbury cheque. A little breeze which had sprung up sent the last-named fluttering across the road with Lord Ickenham in agile pursuit. He recovered it, glanced at it, and brought it back to her, his eyebrows raised.

'Your tariff for stealing pigs comes high,' he said. 'Who's Tilbury? Anything to do with Tilbury House?'

There was good stuff in Lavender Briggs. Where a lesser woman would have broken down and wept, she merely hitched up her fallen jaw and tightened her lips.

'He owns it,' she said, taking the cheque. 'I used to be his secretary. Lord Tilbury.'

'Oh, that chap? Good heavens, what are you doing?'

'I'm tearing up his cheque.'

Lord Ickenham stopped her with a horrified gesture.

'My dear child, you mustn't dream of doing such a thing. You need it in your business.'

'But I can't take his money now.'

'Of course you can. Stick to it like glue. He has far too much money, anyway, and it's very bad for him. Look on adhering to this five hundred as a kindly act in his best interests, designed to make him a better, deeper man. It may prove a turning point in his life. I would take five hundred pounds off Tilbury myself, if only I could think of a way of doing it. I should feel it was my duty. But if you have scruples, though you haven't any business having any, not being a curate, look on it as a loan. You could even pay him interest. Not too much, of course. You don't want to spoil him. I would suggest a yearly fiver, accompanied, as a pretty gesture, by a bunch of white violets. But you can think that over at your leisure. The problem that presents itself now, it seems to me, is Where do you go from here? I take it that you will wish to return to London, but you don't want another stuffy journey in the train. I'll tell you what,' said Lord Ickenham, inspired. 'We'll hire a car. I'll pay for it, and you can reimburse me when that typewriting bureau of yours gets going. Don't forget the bunch of white violets.'

'Oh, Lord Ickenham!' said Lavender Briggs devoutly. 'What a help you are!'

'Help is a thing I am always glad to be of,' said Lord Ickenham in his courteous way.

3

As he turned from waving a genial hand at the departing car and set out on the two-mile walk back to the castle, Lord Ickenham was feeling the gentle glow of satisfaction which comes to a man of goodwill conscious of having acted for the best. There had been a moment when his guardian angel, who liked him to draw the line somewhere, had shown a disposition to become critical of his recent activities, whispering in his ear that he ought not to have abetted Lavender Briggs in what, in the guardian angel's opinion, was pretty raw work and virtually tantamount to robbery from the person, but he had his answer ready. Lavender Briggs, he replied in rebuttal, needed the stuff, and when you find a hard-up girl who needs the stuff, the essential thing is to see that she gets it and not to be fussy about the methods employed to that end.

This, moreover, he pointed out, was a special case. As he had reminded La Briggs, it was imperative for the good of his soul that Lord Tilbury should receive an occasional punch in the bank balance, and to have neglected this opportunity of encouraging his spiritual growth would have been mistaken kindness. His guardian angel, who could follow a piece of reasoning all right if you explained it carefully to him, apologized and said he hadn't thought of that. Forget the whole thing, the guardian angel said.

With the approach of evening the day had lost much of its oppressive warmth, but Lord Ickenham kept his walking pace down to a quiet amble, strolling in leisurely fashion and pausing from time to time to inspect the local flora and fauna: and he had stopped to exchange a friendly glance with a rabbit whose looks he liked, when he became aware that there were others more in tune than himself with the modern spirit of rush and bustle. Running footsteps sounded from behind him, and a voice was calling his name. Turning, he saw that the Duke of Dunstable's nephew, Archie Gilpin, was approaching him at a high rate of m.p.h.

With Archie's brother Ricky, the poet, who supplemented the meagre earnings of a minor bard by selling onion soup in a bar off Leicester Square, Lord Ickenham had long been acquainted, but Archie, except for seeing him at meals, he scarcely knew. Nevertheless, he greeted him with a cordial smile. The urgency of his manner suggested that here was another fellow human being in need of his advice and counsel, and, as always, he was delighted to give it. His services were never confined to close personal friends.

'Hullo there,' he said. 'Getting into training for the village sports?'

Archie came to a halt, panting. He was a singularly handsome young man. Pongo at the Milton Street registry office had described him as good-looking, but Lord Ickenham, now that he had met him, considered this an understatement. Tall and slim and elegant, he looked like a film star of the better type. He also, Lord Ickenham was sorry to see, looked worried, and he prepared to do all that was in his power to brighten life for him.

Archie seemed embarrassed. He ran a hand through his hair, which was longer than Lord Ickenham liked hair to be. A visit to a hairdresser would in his opinion have done this Gilpin a world of good. But artists, he reminded himself, are traditionally shy of the scissors, and to do the lad justice he did not wear sideburns.

'I say,' said Archie, when he had finished panting. 'Could you spare me a moment?'

'Dozens, my dear fellow. Help yourself.'

'I don't want to interrupt you, if you're thinking about something.'

'I am always thinking about something, but I can switch it off in a second, just like that. What seems to be the trouble?'

'Well, I'm in a bit of a jam, and my brother Ricky once told me that if ever I got into a jam of any kind, you were the man to get me out of it. When it comes to fixing things, he said, you have to be seen to be believed.'

Lord Ickenham was gratified as any man would have been. One always likes a word of praise from the fans.

'He probably had in mind the time when I was instrumental in getting him the money that enabled him to buy that onion soup bar of his. Oddly enough, it was not till I had it explained to me by my nephew Pongo that I knew what an onion soup bar was. My life is lived in the country, and we rustics so soon get out of touch. Pongo tells me these bars abound in the Piccadilly Circus and Leicester Square neighbourhoods of London, staying open all night and selling onion soup to the survivors of bottle parties. It sounds the ideal life. Is Ricky still gainfully employed in that line?'

'Oh, rather. But may I tell you about my jam?'

Lord Ickenham clicked an apologetic tongue.

'Of course, yes. I'm sorry. I'm afraid we old gaffers from the country have a tendency to ramble on. When I start talking you must stop me, even if you haven't heard it before. This jam of yours, you were saying. Not a bad jam, I trust?'

Once more, Archie Gilpin ran a hand through his hair. The impression he conveyed was that if the vultures gnawing at his bosom did not shortly change their act, he would begin pulling it out in handfuls.

'It's the dickens of a jam. I don't know what to do about it. Have you ever been engaged to two girls at the same time?'

'Not to my recollection. Nor, now I come to think of it, do I know of anyone who has, except of course King Solomon and the late Brigham Young.'

'Well, that's what I am.'

'You? Engaged to two girls? Half a second, let me work this out.'

There was a pause, during which Lord Ickenham seemed to be doing sums in his head.

'No,' he said at length. 'I don't get it. I am aware that you are betrothed to my little friend Myra Schoonmaker, but however often I tot up the score, that only makes one. You're sure you haven't slipped up somewhere in your figures?'

Archie Gilpin's eye rolled in a fine frenzy, glancing from heaven to earth, from earth to heaven, though one would more readily have expected that sort of thing from his poetic brother.

'Look here,' he said. 'Could we sit down somewhere? This is going to take some time.'

'Why, certainly. There should be good sitting on that stile over there. And take all the time you want.'

Seated on the stile, his deportment rather like that of a young Hindu fakir lying for the first time on the traditional bed of spikes, Archie Gilpin seemed still to find a difficulty in clothing his thoughts in words. He cleared his throat a good deal and once more disturbed his hair with a fevered hand. He reminded Lord Ickenham of a nervous after-dinner speaker suddenly aware, after rising to his feet, that he has completely forgotten the story of the two Irishmen, Pat and Mike, on which he had been relying to convulse his audience.

'I don't know where to begin.'

'At the beginning, don't you think? I often feel that that is best. Then work through the middle and from there, taking your time, carry on to the end.'

This appeared to strike Archie Gilpin as reasonable. He became a little calmer.

'Well, it started with old Tilbury. You know I had a job on one of old Tilbury's papers?'

'Had?'

'He fired me last week.'

'Too bad. Why was that?'

'He didn't like a caricature I'd drawn of him.'

'You shouldn't have shown it to him.'

'I didn't, not exactly. I showed it to Millicent. I thought she would get a laugh out of it.'

'Millicent?'

'His secretary. Millicent Rigby. Girl I was engaged to.'

'That you *were* engaged to?'

'Yes. She broke it off.'

'Of course, yes,' said Lord Ickenham. 'I remember now that Pongo told me he had met a fellow who knew a chap who was acquainted with Miss Rigby, and she had told him – the chap, not the fellow – that she had handed you the pink slip. What had you done to incur her displeasure? You showed her this caricature, you say, but why should that have offended her? Tilbury, if I followed you correctly, was its subject, not she.'

A curious rumbling sound told Lord Ickenham that his companion had uttered a hollow groan. It occurred to him, as the other's hand once more shot to his head, that if this gesture was to be repeated much oftener, Archie, like Lady Constance, would have to go to Shrewsbury for a hair-do.

'Yes, I know. Yes, that's right. But I ought to have mentioned that, thinking Tilbury was out at lunch, I went and showed it to her in his office. I put it on his desk, and we were looking at it with our heads together.'

'Ah,' said Lord Ickenham, beginning to understand. 'And he wasn't out at lunch? He came back?'

'Yes.'

'Saw your handiwork?'

'Yes.'

'Took umbrage?'

'Yes.'

'And erased your name from the list of his skilled assistants?'

'Yes. It was his first move. And later on Millicent ticked me off in no uncertain manner for being such a fool as to bring the thing into the old blighter's office, because anyone but a perfect idiot would have known that he was bound to come in, and hadn't I any sense at all, and . . . Oh, well, you know what happens when a girl starts letting a fellow have it. One word led to another, if you know what I mean, and it wasn't long before she was breaking the engagement and telling me she didn't want to see or speak to me again in this world or the next. She didn't actually return the ring, because I hadn't given her one, but apart from that she made the thing seem pretty final.'

Lord Ickenham was silent for a moment. He was thinking of the six times his Jane had done the same thing by him years ago, and he knew how the other must be feeling.

'I see,' he said. 'Well, my heart bleeds for you, my poor young piece of human wreckage, but this bears out what I was saying, that the sum total of your fiancées is not two, but one. It's nice to have got that straight.'

Another hollow groan escaped Archie Gilpin. His hand rose, but Lord Ickenham caught it in time.

'I wouldn't,' he said. 'Don't touch it. It looks lovely.'

'But you don't know what happened just now. You could have knocked me down with a toothpick. I was coming along by the Emsworth Arms, and I saw her.'

'Miss Rigby?'

'Yes.'

'Probably a mirage.'

'No she was there in the flesh.'

'What in the world was she doing in Market Blandings?'

'Apparently old Tilbury came here for some reason . . .'

Lord Ickenham nodded. He knew that reason.

'. . . and he brought her with him, to do his letters. She had popped out for a breath of air, and I came along, and we met, face to face, just about opposite the Jubilee Memorial watering-trough in the High Street.'

'Dramatic.'

'I was never so surprised in my life.'

'I can readily imagine it. Was she cold and proud and aloof?'

'Not by a jugful. She was all over me. Remorse had set in. She said she was sorry she had blown a fuse, and wept a good deal and . . . well, there we were, so to speak.'

'You folded her in your embrace, no doubt?'

'Yes, quite a good deal, actually, and the upshot of the whole thing was that we got engaged again.'

'You didn't mention that you were engaged to Myra?'

'No, I didn't get around to that. The subject didn't seem to come up somehow.'

'I quite understand. So the total is two, after all. You were perfectly right, and I apologize. Well, well!'

'I don't see what you're grinning about.'

'Smiling gently would be a more exact description. I was thinking how absurdly simple these problems are, when you give your mind to them. The solution here is obvious. You must at once tell Myra to make no move in the way of buying the trousseau and pricing wedding cakes, because they won't be needed.'

Only a sudden clutch at the rail on which he was seated prevented Archie Gilpin from falling off the stile. It seemed for a moment that he was about to reach for his hair again, but he merely gaped like a good-looking codfish.

'Tell her it's all off, you mean?'

'Precisely. Save the girl a lot of unnecessary expense.'

'But I can't. I admit that I asked her to marry me because I was feeling pretty bitter about Millicent and had some sort of rough idea of showing her — '

'That she was not the only onion in the stew?'

'Something on those lines. And I was considerably relieved when she turned me down. A narrow escape, I felt I'd had. But now that on second thoughts she's decided that she's in favour of the scheme, I don't see how I can possibly just stroll in and tell her I've changed my mind. Well, dash it, is a shot like that on the board? I ask you!'

'You mean that once a Gilpin plights his troth, it stays plighted? A very creditable attitude to take, though it's a pity you plight it so often. But if you are thinking you may break that gentle heart, have no uneasiness. I can state authoritatively that, left to herself, she wouldn't marry you with a ten-foot pole.'

'Then why did she tell me she would?'

'For precisely the reason that made you propose to her. Relations were strained between her and her betrothed, just as they were between you and Miss Rigby, and she did it as what is known as a gesture. She thought, in a word, that that would teach him.'

'She's got a betrothed?'

'And how! You know him. My friend Meriwether.'

'Good Lord!' Archie Gilpin seemed to blossom like a rose in June. 'Well, this is fine. You've eased my mind.'

'A pleasure.'

'Now one begins to see daylight. Now one knows where one is. But, look here, we don't want to do anything . . . what's the word?'

'Precipitate?'

'Yes, we want to move cautiously. You see, on the strength of getting engaged to the daughter of a millionaire I'm hoping to extract a thousand quid from Uncle Alaric.'

Lord Ickenham pursed his lips.

'From His Grace the pop-eyed Duke of Dunstable? No easy task. His one-way pockets are a byword all over England.'

Archie nodded. He had never blinded himself to the fact that anyone trying to separate cash from the Duke of Dunstable was in much the same position as a man endeavouring to take a bone from a short-tempered wolf-hound.

'I know. But I have a feeling it will come off. When I told him I was engaged to Myra, he was practically civil. I think he's ripe for the touch, and I've simply got to get a thousand pounds.'

'Why that particular sum?'

'Because that's what Ricky wants, to let me into his onion soup business. He's planning to expand, and has to have more capital. He said that if I put in a thousand quid, I could have a third share of the profits, which are enormous.'

'Yes, so Pongo told me. I got the impression of dense crowds of bottle-party addicts charging into Ricky's bar night after night like bisons making for a water-hole.'

'That's right, they do. There's something about onion soup that seems to draw them like a magnet. Can't stand the muck myself but there's no accounting for tastes. Here's the set-up, as I see it,' said Archie, with mounting enthusiasm. 'We coast along as we are at present, Myra engaged to me, me engaged to Myra, and Uncle Alaric fawning on me and telling me I can have any-thing I want, even unto half his kingdom. I get the thousand quid. Myra gives me the push. I slide off and marry Millicent. Myra marries this Meriwether chap, and everybody's happy. Any questions?'

A look of regret and pity had come into Lord Ickenham's face. It pained him to be compelled to act as a black frost in this young man's garden of dreams, but he had no alternative.

'Myra can't give you the push.'

Archie stared. It seemed to him that this kindly old buster, until now so intelligent, had suddenly lost his grip.

'Why not?'

'Because the moment she did, she would be shipped back to America in disgrace and would never see Bill Bailey again.'

'Who on earth's Bill Bailey?'

'Oh, I forgot to tell you, didn't I? That – or, rather, the Reverend Cuthbert Bailey – is Meriwether's real name. He is here incognito because Lady Constance has a deep-seated prejudice against him. He is a penniless curate, and she doesn't like penniless curates. It was to remove Myra from his orbit that she took her away from London and imprisoned her at Blandings Castle. Let her break the engagement, and she'll be back in New York before you can say What ho.'

Silence fell. The light had faded from the evening sky, and simultaneously from Archie Gilpin's face. He sat staring bleakly into the middle distance as if the scenery hurt him in some tender spot.

'It's a mix-up,' he said.

'It wants thinking about,' Lord Ickenham agreed. 'Yes, it certainly wants thinking about. We must turn it over in our minds from time to time.'

Chapter 10

The Duke of Dunstable was not a patient man. When he had business dealings with his fellows, he liked those fellows to jump to it and do it now, and as a general rule took pains to ensure that they did so. But in the matter of Lord Tilbury and the Empress he was inclined to be lenient. He quite understood that a man in the position of having to make up his mind whether or not to pay three thousand pounds for a pig, however obese, needs a little time to think it over. It was only on the third day after the other's return to London that he went to the telephone and having been placed in communication with him opened the conversation with his customary 'Hoy!'

'Are you there, Stinker?'

If the Duke had not been a little deaf in the right ear, he might have heard a sound like an inexperienced motorist changing gears in an old-fashioned car. It was the proprietor of the Mammoth Publishing Company grinding his teeth. Sometimes, when we hear a familiar voice, the heart leaps up like that of the poet Wordsworth when he beheld a rainbow in the sky. Lord Tilbury's was far from doing this. He resented having his morning's work interrupted by a man capable of ignoring gentlemen's agreements and slapping an extra thousand pounds on the price of pigs. When he spoke, his tone was icy.

'Is that you, Dunstable?'

'What?'

'I said, Is that you?'

'Of course it's me. Who do you think it was?'

'What do you want?'

'What?'

'I said What do you want? I'm very busy.'

'What?'

'I said I am very busy.'

'So am I. Got a hundred things to do. Can't stand talking to you all day. About that pig.'

'What about it?'

'Are you prepared to meet my terms? If so, say so. Think on your feet, Stinker!'

Lord Tilbury drew a deep breath. How fortunate, he was feeling, that Fate should have brought him and Lavender Briggs together and so enabled him to defy this man as he ought to be defied. He had heard nothing from Lavender Briggs, but he presumed that she was at Blandings Castle, working in his interests, framing her subtle schemes, and strong in this knowledge he proceeded to answer in the negative. This took some time for in addition to saying 'No' he had to tell the Duke what he thought of him, indicating one by one the various points on which his character diverged from that of the ideal man. Whether it was right of him to call the Duke a fat old sharper whose word he would never again believe, even if given on a stack of Bibles, is open to debate, but he felt considerably better when he had done so, and it was with the feeling of having fought the good fight that several minutes later he slammed down the receiver and rang for Millicent Rigby to come and take dictation.

Nothing that anyone could say to him, no matter how derogatory, ever had the power to wound the Duke. After that initial 'No', indeed, he had scarcely bothered to listen. He could see that it was just routine stuff. All he was thinking, as he came away from the telephone, was that he would now sell the Empress back to Lord Emsworth, who he knew would prove co-operative, and he was proceeding in search of him when a loud squeak in his rear told him that little George was with him again.

'Hullo, big boy,' said George.

'How often have I told you not to call me big boy?'

'Sorry, chum, I keep forgetting. I say, frightfully exciting about Myra, isn't it?'

'Eh?'

'Getting engaged to Archie Gilpin.'

In the interest of his conversation with Lord Tilbury, the Duke had momentarily forgotten that his nephew had become betrothed to the only daughter of a millionaire. Reminded of this, he beamed, as far as it was within his ability to beam, and replied that it was most satisfactory and that he was very pleased about it.

'Her father arrives tomorrow.'

'Indeed?'

'Gets to Market Blandings station, wind and weather permitting, at four-ten. Grandpapa's gone to London to meet him, all dressed up. He looked like a city slicker.'

'You must not call your grandfather a city slicker,' said the Duke, too happy at the way his affairs were working out for a sterner rebuke. He paused, for a sudden thought had struck him, and George, about to inquire whose grandfather he *could* call a city slicker, found himself interrupted. 'What made him get all dressed up and go to London to meet this feller?' he asked, for he knew how much his host disliked the metropolis and how great was his distaste for putting on a decent suit of clothes and trying to look like a respectable human being.

'Aunt Connie told him he jolly well had to or else. He was as sick as mud.'

The Duke puffed at his moustache. His nosiness where other people's affairs were concerned was intense, and Connie's giving this Yank what amounted to a civic welcome intrigued him. It meant something, he told himself. It couldn't be that she was trying to sweeten the feller in the hope of floating a loan, for she had ample private means, bequeathed to her by her late husband, Joseph Keeble, who had made a packet out East, so it must be that she entertained towards him feelings that were deeper and warmer than those of ordinary friendship, as the expression was. He had never suspected this, but it occurred to him now that when a woman keeps a photograph of a man with a head like a Spanish onion on her writing table, it means that her emotions are involved, in all probability deeply. There was that occasion, too, when he had joined them at luncheon at the Ritz. Their heads, he remembered, had been very close together. By the time he had succeeded in shaking off George, declining his invitation to come down to the lake and chat with the Church Lads, he was convinced that he had hit on the right solution, and he waddled off to find Lord Ickenham and canvass his views on the subject. He was not fond of Lord Ickenham, but there was nobody else available as a confidant.

He found him in his hammock, pondering over the various problems which had presented themselves of late, and lost no time in placing the item on the agenda paper.

'I say, Ickenham, this fellow who's coming here tomorrow. This chap Stick-in-the-mud.'

'Schoonmaker. Jimmy Schoonmaker.'

'You know him?'

'One of my oldest friends. I shall like seeing him again.'

'So will somebody else.'

'Who would that be?'

'Connie, that's who. Let me tell you something, Ickenham. I was in Connie's room yesterday, having a look round, and there was a cable on the writing table. "Coming immediately", it said, and a lot more I've forgotten. It was signed Schoonmaker, and was obviously a reply to a cable from her, urging him to come here. Now why was she in such a sweat to get the feller to Blandings Castle, you ask.'

'So I do. Glad you reminded me.'

'I'll tell you why. It sticks out a mile. She's potty about the chap. Sift the evidence. In spite of his having a head like a Spanish onion, she keeps his photograph on her writing table. She sends him urgent cables telling him to come immediately. And what is even more significant, she makes Emsworth put on a clean collar and go all the way to London to meet him. Why, dash it, she didn't do that for *me*! Would she go to such lengths if she wasn't potty about the ... Get out, you!'

He was addressing Beach, who had approached the hammock and uttered a discreet cough.

'What you want?'

'I was instructed by her ladyship to inquire of his lordship if he would be good enough to speak to her ladyship in her ladyship's boudoir, your Grace,' said Beach with dignity. He was not a man to be put upon by Dukes, no matter how white-moustached.

'Wants to see him, does she?'

'Precisely, your Grace.'

'Better go and find out what it's all about, Ickenham. Remember what I was saying. Watch her closely!' said the Duke in a hissing whisper. 'Watch her like a hawk.'

There was a thoughtful look in Lord Ickenham's eye as he

crossed the lawn. This new development interested him. He was aware how sorely persecuted Lord Emsworth was by his sister Constance – the other's story of the brass paper-fastener had impressed him greatly – and he had hoped by his presence at the castle to ease the strain for him a little, but he had never envisaged the possibility of actually removing her from the premises. If Lady Constance were to marry James Schoonmaker and go to live with him in America, it would be the biggest thing that had happened to Lord Emsworth since his younger son Frederick had transferred himself to Long Island City, NY, as a unit of the firm of Donaldson's Dog Biscuits, Inc. There is no surer way of promoting human happiness than to relieve a mild man of the society of a sister who says, 'Oh, Clarence!' to him and sees life in the home generally as a sort of *Uncle Tom's Cabin* production, with herself playing Simon Legree and her brother in the supporting role of Uncle Tom.

Of course, it takes two to make a romance, and James Schoonmaker had yet to be heard from, but Lord Ickenham regarded his old friend's instant response to Lady Constance's cable as distinctly promising. A man in Jimmy's position, a monarch of finance up to his eyes all the time in big deals, with barely a moment to spare from cornering peanuts or whatever it might be, does not drop everything and come bounding across the Atlantic with a whoop and a holler unless there is some great attraction awaiting him at the other end. It would be a good move, he decided, when Jimmy arrived, to meet him at Market Blandings station, hurry him off to the Emsworth Arms and fill him to the brim with G. Ovens' home-brewed beer. Mellowed by that wonder fluid, he felt, it was more than likely that he would cast off reserve, become expansive and give a sympathetic buddy what George Cyril Wellbeloved would have called the griff.

Lady Constance was seated at her writing table, tapping the woodwork with her fingers, and Lord Ickenham had the momentary illusion, as always when summoned to her presence, that time had rolled back in its flight and that he was once more *vis-à-vis* with his old kindergarten mistress. The great question in those days had always been whether or not she would rap him on the knuckles with a ruler, and it was with some relief that he noted that the only weapon within his hostess's reach was a small ivory paper-knife.

She was not looking cordial. Her air was that of somebody who, where Ickenhams were concerned, could take them or leave them alone. A handsome woman, though, and one well calculated to touch off the spark in the Schoonmaker bosom.

'Please sit down, Lord Ickenham.'

He took a chair, and Lady Constance remained silent for a moment. She seemed to be searching for words. Then, for she was never a woman who hesitated long when she had something to say, even when that something verged on the embarrassing, she began.

'Myra's father is arriving tomorrow, Lord Ickenham.'

'So I had heard. I was saying to Dunstable just now how much I shall enjoy seeing him again after all these years.'

A slight frown on Lady Constance's forehead seemed to suggest that his emotions did not interest her.

'I wonder if Jimmy's put on weight. He was inclined to bulge when I last saw him. Wouldn't watch his calories.'

Nor, said the frown, was she in a mood to discuss Mr Schoonmaker's poundage.

'He has come because I asked him to. I sent him an urgent cable.'

'After we had had our little talk?'

'Yes,' said Lady Constance, shuddering as she recalled that little talk. 'I intended to put the whole matter in his hands and advise him to take Myra back to America immediately.'

'I see. Did you say so?'

'No, I did not, and I am particularly anxious that he shall know nothing of her infatuation. It would be difficult to explain why I had allowed Mr Bailey to stay on at the castle.'

'Very difficult. One can see him raising his eyebrows.'

'On the other hand, I must give him some reason why I sent that cable, and I wanted to see you, Lord Ickenham, to ask if you had anything to suggest.'

She sank back in her chair, stiffened in every limb. Her companion was beaming at her, and his kindly smile affected her like a blow in the midriff. She was in a highly nervous condition, and the last thing she desired was to be beamed at by a man whose very presence revolted her finer feelings.

'My dear Lady Constance,' said Lord Ickenham buoyantly, 'the matter is simple. I have the solution hot off the griddle. You tell him that his daughter has become engaged to Archie Gilpin and you wanted him to look in and give the boy the once-over. Perfectly natural thing to suggest to an affectionate father. He would probably have been very hurt, if you hadn't cabled him. That solves your little difficulty, I think?'

Lady Constance relaxed. Her opinion of this man had in no way altered, she still considered him a menace to one and all and his presence an offence to the pure air of Blandings Castle, but she was fair enough to admit that, however black his character might be, and however much she disliked having him beam at her, he knew all the answers.

2

The 11.45 train from Paddington, first stop Swindon, rolled into Market Blandings station, and Lord Emsworth stepped out, followed by James R. Schoonmaker of Park Avenue, New York, and The Dunes, Westhampton, Long Island.

American financiers come in all sizes, ranging from the small and shrimp-like to the large and impressive. Mr Schoonmaker belonged to the latter class. He was a man in the late fifties with a massive head and a handsome face interrupted about halfway up by tortoiseshell-rimmed spectacles. He had been an All-American footballer in his youth, and he still looked capable of bucking a line, though today he would have done it not with a bull-like rush but with an authoritative glance which would have taken all the heart out of the opposition.

His face, as he emerged, was wearing the unmistakable look of a man who has had a long railway journey in Lord Emsworth's company, but it brightened suddenly when he saw the slender figure standing on the platform. He stared incredulously.

'Freddie! Well, I'll be darned!'

'Hullo there, Jimmy.'

'You here?'

'That's right.'

'Well, well!' said Mr Schoonmaker.

'Well, well, well!' said Lord Ickenham.

'Well, well, well, *well*!' said Mr Schoonmaker.

Lord Emsworth interrupted the reunion before it could reach the height of its fever. He was anxious to lose no time in getting to the haven of his bedroom and shedding the raiment which had been irking him all day. His shoes, in particular, were troubling him.

'Oh, hullo, Ickenham. Is the car outside?'

'Straining at the leash.'

'Then let us be off, shall we?'

'Well, I'll tell you,' said Lord Ickenham. 'I can readily understand your desire to hasten homeward and get into something loose –'

'It's my shoes, principally.'

'They look beautiful.'

'They're pinching me.'

'The very words my nephew Pongo said that day at the dog races, and his statement was tested and proved correct. Courage, Emsworth! Think of the women in China. You don't find them beefing because their shoes are tight. But what I was about to say was that Jimmy and I haven't seen each other for upwards of fifteen years, and we've a lot of heavy thread-picking-up to do. I thought I'd take him to the Emsworth Arms for a quick one. You'd enjoy a mouthful of beer, Jimmy?'

'Ah!' said Mr Schoonmaker, his tongue flickering over his lips.

'So we'll just bung you into the car and walk over later.'

The process of bunging Lord Emsworth into a car was never a simple one, for on these occasions his long legs always took on something of the fluid quality of an octopus's tentacles, but the task was accomplished at last, and Lord Ickenham led his old friend to a table in the shady garden where all those business conferences between Lord Tilbury, the Duke of Dunstable and Lavender Briggs had taken place.

'Ah!' said Mr Schoonmaker again some little time later, laying down his empty tankard.

'Have another?'

'I think I will,' said Mr Schoonmaker, speaking in the rather awed voice customary with those tasting G. Ovens' home-brewed for the first time. He added that the beverage had a kick, and Lord Ickenham agreed that its kick was considerable. He said he thought G. Ovens put some form of high explosive in it, and Mr Schoonmaker agreed that this might well be so.

A considerable number of threads had been picked up by this time, and it seemed to Lord Ickenham that it would not be long now before he would be able to divert the conversation from the past to the present. From certain signs he saw that the home-brewed was beginning to have its beneficent effect. Another pint, he felt, should be sufficient to bring his companion to the confidential stage. In one of the cosy talks he had had with George Cyril Wellbeloved before Lord Emsworth had driven him with a flaming sword from his garden of Eden, the pig man had commented on the mysterious properties of a quart of the Ovens output, speaking with a good deal of bitterness of the time when that amount of it had caused him to reveal to Claude Murphy, the local constable, certain top secrets which later he would have given much to have kept to himself.

The second pint arrived, and Mr Schoonmaker quaffed deeply. His journey had been a stuffy one, parching to the throat. He looked about him approvingly, taking in the smooth turf, the shady trees and the silver river that gleamed through them.

'Nice place, this,' he said.

'Rendered all the nicer by your presence, Jimmy,' replied Lord Ickenham courteously. 'What brought you over here, by the way?'

'I had an urgent cable from Lady Constance.' A thought struck Mr Schoonmaker. 'Nothing wrong with Mike, is there?'

'Not to my knowledge. Nor with Pat. Mike who?'

'Myra.'

'I didn't know she was known to the police as Mike. You must have started calling her that after my time. No, Myra's all right. She's just got engaged.'

Mr Schoonmaker started violently, always a dangerous thing to do when drinking beer. Having stopped coughing and dried himself off, he said:

'She has? What made her do that?'

'Love, Jimmy,' said Lord Ickenham with a touch of reproach. 'You can't expect a girl not to fall in love in these romantic surroundings. There's something in the air of Blandings Castle that brings out all the sentiment in people. Strong men have come here without a thought of matrimony in their minds and within a week have started writing poetry and carving hearts on trees. Probably the ozone.'

Mr Schoonmaker was frowning. He was not at all sure he liked the look of this. His daughter's impulsiveness was no secret from him.

'Who is the fellow?' he demanded, not exactly expecting to hear that it was the boy who cleaned the knives and boots, but prepared for the worst. 'Who's this guy she's got engaged to?'

'Gilpin is the name, first name Archibald. He's the nephew of the Duke of Dunstable,' said Lord Ickenham, and Mr Schoonmaker's brow cleared magically. He would have preferred not to have a son-in-law called Archibald, but he knew that in these matters one has to take the rough with the smooth, and he had a great respect for Dukes.

'Is he, by golly! Well, that's fine.'

'I thought you'd be pleased.'

'When did this happen?'

'Oh, recently.'

'Odd that Lady Constance didn't mention it in her cable.'

'Probably wanted to keep the expense down. You know what they charge you per word for cables, and a penny saved is a penny earned. Do you call her Lady Constance?'

'Of course. Why not?'

'Rather formal. You've known her a long time.'

'Yes, we've been friends for quite a while, very close friends as a matter of fact. She's a wonderful woman. But there's a sort of cool aristocratic dignity about her ... a kind of aloofness ... I don't know how to put it, but she gives you the feeling that you'll never get to first base with her.'

'And you want to get to first base with her?' said Lord Ickenham, eyeing him narrowly. Mr Schoonmaker had just finished his second pint, and something told him that this was the moment for which he had been waiting. It was after his second pint that George Cyril Wellbeloved had poured out his confidences to Constable Claude Murphy, among them his personal technique for poaching pheasants.

For an instant it seemed that Mr Schoonmaker would be reticent, but the Ovens' home-brewed was too strong for him. A pinkness spread itself over his face. The ears, in particular, were glowing brightly.

'Yes, I do,' he said, glaring a little as if about to ask Lord Ickenham if he wanted to make something of it. 'Why shouldn't I?'

'My dear fellow, I'm not criticizing. I'm all sympathy and understanding. Any red-blooded man would be glad to get to first base with Connie.'

Mr Schoonmaker started.

'Do you call her Connie?'

'Of course.'

'How do you manage it?'

'Just comes naturally.'

'I wish it did to me.' Mr Schoonmaker looked into his tankard, saw that it was empty and heaved a long sigh. 'Yes, sir, I wish I had your nerve. Freddie, if I could get that woman to marry me, I'd be the happiest man on earth.'

With the exception, Lord Ickenham thought, as he laid a gentle hand on his friend's arm, of her brother Clarence.

'Now you're talking, Jimmy. Relay that information to her. Women like to hear these things.'

'But I told you. I haven't the nerve.'

'Nonsense. A child of six could do it, provided he hadn't got the dumb staggers.'

Mr Schoonmaker sighed again. G. Ovens' home-brewed tends as a rule to induce joviality – sometimes, as in the case of George Cyril Wellbeloved, injudicious joviality – but it was plain that today it had failed of its mission.

'That's just what I have got. When I try to propose to her, the words won't come. It's happened a dozen times. The sight of that calm aristocratic profile wipes them from my lips.'

'Try not looking at her sideways.'

'I'm not in her class. That's the trouble. I'm aiming too high.'

'A Schoonmaker is a fitting mate for the highest in the land.'

'Who says so?'

'I say so.'

'Well, I don't. I know what would happen. She'd be very nice about it, but she would freeze me.'

Lord Ickenham, who had removed his hand from the arm, replaced it.

'Now there I'm sure you're wrong, Jimmy. I happen to be certain that she loves you. Connie has few secrets from me.'

Mr Schoonmaker stared.

'You aren't telling me she told you she did?'

'Not in so many words, of course. You could hardly expect that, even to an old friend like myself. But that way she has of drawing her breath in sharply and looking starry-eyed whenever your name is mentioned is enough to show me how things stand. The impression I received was of a woman wailing for her demon lover. Well, perhaps not actually wailing, but making quite a production number of it. I tell you I've seen her clench her hands till the knuckles stood out white under the strain, just because your name happened to come up in the course of conversation. I'm convinced that if you were to try the Ickenham system, you couldn't fail.'

'The Ickenham system?'

'I call it that. It's a little thing I knocked together in my bachelor days. It consists of grabbing the girl, waggling her about a bit, showering kisses on her upturned face and making some such remark as "My mate!". Clench the teeth of course, while saying that. It adds conviction.'

Mr Schoonmaker's stare widened.

'You expect me to do that to *Lady Constance*?'

'I see no objection.'

'I do.'

'Such as –?'

'I couldn't even get started.'

'Where's your manly courage?'

'I don't have any, not where she's concerned.'

'Come, come. She's only a woman.'

'No, she isn't. She's Lady Constance Keeble, sister of the Earl of Emsworth, with a pedigree stretching back to the Flood, and I can't forget it.'

Lord Ickenham mused. He recognized the fact that an obstacle had arisen, but a few moments' thought told him that it was not an impasse.

'What you need, Jimmy, is a pint or two of May Queen.'

'Eh?'

'It is a beverage which I always recommend to timorous wooers when they find a difficulty in bringing themselves to try the Ickenham system. Its full name is "Tomorrow'll be of all the year the maddest, merriest day, for I'm to be Queen of the May, mother, I'm to be Queen of the May", but the title is generally shortened for purposes of convenience in ordinary conversation. Its foundation is any good dry champagne, to which is added liqueur brandy, kümmel and green chartreuse, and I can assure you it acts like magic. Under its influence little men with receding chins and pince-nez have dominated the proudest beauties and compelled them to sign on the dotted line. I'll tell Beach to see that you get plenty of it before and during dinner tonight. Then you take Connie out on the terrace under the moon and go into the Ickenham routine, and I shall be vastly surprised if we don't shortly see an interesting announcement in *The Times*.'

'H'm.' Mr Schoonmaker weighed the suggestion, but it was plain that he was none too enthusiastic about it. 'Grab her?'

'That's it.'

'Waggle her about?'

'That's the idea.'

'And say "My mate!"?'

'Unless there is some other turn of phrase which you prefer,' said Lord Ickenham, always ready to stretch a point. 'You needn't stick too closely to the script if you feel like gagging, but on no account tamper with the business. That is of the essence.'

3

On the morning following his old friend's arrival, Lord Ickenham had settled himself in his hammock when a husky voice spoke his name and he found Mr Schoonmaker at his side. Sitting up and directing a keen glance at him, he did not like what he saw. James Schoonmaker was looking pale and careworn, and there was in his bearing no suggestion whatsoever that he was the happiest man on earth. He looked, indeed, far more like that schooner Hesperus of which Lord Ickenham in his boyhood had recited so successfully, on the occasion when it swept like a sheeted ghost to the reef of Norman's Woe. Give him a skipper and a little daughter whom he had taken to bear him company, thought Lord Ickenham, and he could have made straight for the reef of Norman's Woe, and no questions asked.

But he was too well-bred to put this sentiment into words. Instead, he affected an eager animation which he was far from feeling.

'Jimmy! I was hoping you would come along. Have you good news to report? Everything pretty smooth? I start saving up for the wedding present?'

Mr Schoonmaker shook his head and simultaneously uttered a sharp cry of anguish. As Lord Ickenham had suspected, he was in no shape to shake heads. To the dullest eye it would have been plain that this hand across the sea was in the grip of a hangover of majestic proportions.

'That May Queen is kind of powerful stuff,' said Mr Schoonmaker, endorsing this view.

'It sometimes brings regrets with the dawning of a new day,' Lord Ickenham agreed. 'It's the chartreuse mostly, I think. Still, if it has produced results . . .'

'But it hasn't.'

'Come, come, Jimmy. With my own eyes I saw you lead Connie out on to the terrace, and the moon was shining like billy-o.'

'Yes, and what happened? What always happens, and what's always going to happen. I lost my nerve.'

Lord Ickenham sighed. This was a set-back, and though he knew that these disappointments are sent to us to make us more spiritual, he could never bring himself to like them.

'You didn't ask her to marry you?'

'I didn't come within a mile of it.'

'What *did* you talk about? The weather?'

'We talked about Mike and this boy she's engaged to. I asked her why she hadn't mentioned him in her cable.'

'What did she say to that?'

'She said she wanted to wait till I could see him for myself. Seems strange.'

'Nothing strange about it. She could hardly tell you that she sent the cable because she couldn't endure being away from you for another minute. Modesty forbade.'

For a moment Mr Schoonmaker brightened.

'You really think that was it?'

'Of course it was. She loves you with every fibre of her being. She's crazy about you. So cheer up, Jimmy, and have another pop when you're feeling better. My experience is that a May Queen hangover soon wears off after one has had a little sleep. Try this hammock.'

'Don't you want it?'

'Your need is greater than mine.'

'Well, thanks,' said Mr Schoonmaker. The momentary brightness seemed to ooze out of him as he climbed into the hammock, leaving him the pessimist he had been. He heaved a sigh. 'Of course, you're all wrong, Freddie. There's no hope for me. I know when I'm licked.'

'Scarcely the spirit of '76.'

'She would never consider me for a moment. We don't play in the same league. Oh well,' said Mr Schoonmaker, heaving another sigh, 'there's always one's work.'

A sudden gleam came into Lord Ickenham's eye. It was as if a thought had occurred to him.

'What are you working on now, Jimmy? Something big, of course?'

'Fairly big. Do you know Florida?'

'Not very well. My time in America was spent out west and in New York.'

'Then you probably don't know Jupiter Island.'

'I've heard of it. Sort of a winter home from home for millionaires, isn't it?'

'That kind of idea. Club, golf links, tennis, bathing. You rent a cottage for the season.'

'And pay pretty high for it, no doubt?'

'Yes, it comes high. This thing I'm promoting is the same sort of set-up farther down the coast. The Venus Island Development Corporation, it's called. There'll be a fortune in it.'

'You aren't looking for capital, I suppose?'

'No difficulty there. Why?'

'I was only thinking, Jimmy, that as your daughter is marrying his nephew, it would be a graceful act to let the Duke in on the ground floor. He's rolling in money, but he can always do with a bit more. There's something about the stuff that fascinates him.'

Mr Schoonmaker was on the verge of sleep, but he was sufficiently awake to reply that he would be glad to do the Duke this good turn. He thanked Lord Ickenham for the suggestion and Lord Ickenham said he always made a point of doing his day's kind deed. His mother, he said, had been frightened by a Boy Scout.

'I expect to pass through this world but once, Jimmy. Any good thing, therefore, that I can do, let me do it now, as the fellow said. How's the hammock?'

Mr Schoonmaker snored gently, and Lord Ickenham went off to have a word with the Duke.

Chapter 11

The Duke of Dunstable was sitting on the terrace, and not only on the terrace but on top of the world with a rainbow round his shoulder. Counting his blessings one by one, he was of the opinion that he had never had it so good. He had not yet approached Lord Emsworth in the matter of the Empress, but he knew that when he did he would be in the pleasant position of dealing in a seller's market. And he had the comforting thought that, whatever the figure arrived at, it would be all clear profit, with none of the distasteful necessity of paying agent's commission. The recollection of how nearly he had come to parting with that five hundred pounds to Lavender Briggs still made him shudder.

And in addition to this, showing that when Providence starts showering its boons on a good man, the sky is the limit, his nephew Archibald, until now a sad burden on his purse, was engaged to be married to the only daughter of a millionaire. How the young poop had done it, he was at a loss to understand, but there it was, and so deep was his contentment that when Lord Ickenham dropped into a chair beside him, he did not even puff at his moustache. He disliked Lord Ickenham, considering him a potty sort of feller whose spiritual home was a padded cell in some not too choosy lunatic asylum, but this morning he was the friend of all the world.

Lord Ickenham was looking grave.

'Hope I'm not interrupting you, Dunstable, if you were doing the crossword puzzle.'

'Not at all,' said the Duke amiably. 'I was only thinkin' a bit.'

'I'm afraid I've come to give you more food for thought,' said Lord Ickenham, 'and not very agreeable thought, either. It's very saddening, don't you feel, how people change for the worse as the years go on?'

'Who does? I don't.'

'No, not you. You always maintain a safe suds level. I was thinking of poor Schoonmaker.'

'What's poor about him?'

There was a look of pain on Lord Ickenham's face. He was silent
for a moment, musing, or so it seemed, on life's tragedies.

'Everything,' he said. 'When I knew James Schoonmaker fifteen
years ago in New York, he was a man with a glittering future, and
for a time, I understand, he did do extremely well. But that's all in
the past. He's gone right under.'

'Under what?' said the Duke, who was never very quick at the
uptake.

'He's a pauper. Down to his last thirty cents. Please don't mention this to anyone, but he's just been borrowing money from me.
It was a great shock.'

The Duke sat up. This time he did not neglect to puff at his
moustache. It floated up like a waterfall going the wrong way.

'But he's a millionaire!'

Lord Ickenham smiled sadly.

'That's what he'd like you to believe. But I have friends in New
York who keep me posted from time to time about the fellows I
used to know there, and they have told me his whole story. He's
down to his last dollar, and his bankruptcy may be expected at any
moment. You know how it is with these American financiers. They
over-extend themselves. They bite off more than they can chew,
and then comes the inevitable smash. A fiver means a lot to
Schoonmaker at this moment. A tenner was what he wanted just
now, and I gave it to him, poor devil. I hadn't the heart to refuse.
This is strictly between you and me, of course, and I wouldn't like
it to be spread about, but I thought I ought to warn you about
him.'

The Duke's eyes were protruding like a snail's. His moustache
was in a constant state of activity. Not even little George had ever
seen it giving so sedulously of its best.

'Warn me? If the feller thinks he's going to get tuppence out of
me, he'll be disappointed.'

'He's hoping for more than tuppence. I'm afraid he's planning to
try to talk you into putting up money for some wild-cat scheme he's
got. As far as I could make out, it's some sort of land and building

operation down in Florida. The Venus Island Development Corporation he calls it. The very name sounds fishy, don't you think? Venus
Island, I mean to say! There probably isn't such a place. What's
worrying me is that you may feel tempted to invest, because he'll
make the thing sound so good. He's very plausible. But don't
dream of doing it. Be on your guard.'

'I'll be on my guard,' said the Duke, breathing heavily.

Lord Ickenham waited a moment in case the other might wish to
thank his benefactor, but as he merely continued to breathe heavily,
he made his way back to the hammock. He found Mr Schoonmaker
sitting up and looking brighter. He was glad to hear that his nap
had done him good.

'Headache gone?'

Mr Schoonmaker considered this.

'Well, not gone,' he said. He was a man who liked exactness of
speech. 'But it's a lot better.'

'Then what I wish you would do, Jimmy, is go and see the Duke
and tell him all about that Venus Island thing of yours. I've just
been talking to him, and oddly enough, he was saying he wished he
could find some business opportunity which would give him the
chance of having a little flutter. He's a great gambler at heart.'

Mr Schoonmaker disapproved of his choice of words. A man
with a hangover of the dimensions of the one from which he was
suffering finds it difficult to bridle, but he did his best.

'Gambler? What do you mean, gambler? The Venus Island Development Corporation's as sound as Fort Knox.'

'I'm sure it is,' said Lord Ickenham soothingly. 'Impress that on
him. Give him a big sales talk.'

'Why?' said Mr Schoonmaker, still ruffled, 'I don't want his
money.'

'Of course you don't. You'll be doing him a great favour by
allowing him to buy in. But for goodness' sake don't let him see
that. You know how proud these dukes are. They hate to feel under
an obligation to anyone. Seem eager, Jimmy.'

'Oh, all right,' said Mr Schoonmaker grudgingly. 'Though it's
funny having to wheedle someone into accepting shares in something that'll quadruple his money in under a year.'

'We'll have a good laugh about it later,' Lord Ickenham assured him. 'You'll find him on the terrace,' he said. 'I told him you might be looking in.'

He nestled into the vacated hammock, and was in the process of explaining to his guardian angel, who had once more become critical, that there is no harm in deviating from the truth a little, if it is done in a good cause, and that the interview which Mr Schoonmaker was about to have with the Duke of Dunstable, though possibly wounding to his feelings, would make him forget his headache, when he became aware of Archie Gilpin at his side.

Archie was looking as beautiful as ever, but anxious.

'I say,' he said. 'I saw you talking to Uncle Alaric.'

'Yes, we had a chat.'

'What sort of mood is he in?'

'He seemed to me a little agitated. He was annoyed because an attempt was being made to get money out of him.'

'Oh, my God!'

'Or, rather, he was expecting such an attempt to be made. That always does something to the fine old man. Did you ever read a book called *The Confessions of Alphonse*, the reminiscences of a French waiter? No, I suppose not, for it was published a number of years ago, long before you were born. At one point in it Alphonse says "Instantly as a man wishes to borrow money of me, I dislike him. It is in the blood. It is more strong than me." The Duke's like that.'

Archie Gilpin reached for his hair and was busy for awhile with the customary scalp massage. There was a bleakness in his voice when at length he spoke.

'Then you wouldn't recommend an immediate try for that thousand?'

'Not whole-heartedly. But what's your hurry?'

'I'll tell you what's my hurry. I had a letter from Ricky this morning. He says he can only give me another week to raise the money. If I don't give it him by then, he'll have to get somebody else, he says.'

'A nuisance, I agree. That kind of ultimatum is always unpleasant. But much may happen in a week. Much, for that matter, may happen in a day. My advice to you – '

But Archie was not destined to receive that advice, which would probably have been very valuable, for at this moment Mr Schoon-maker appeared, and he sidled off. The father of his betrothed, now that he had made his acquaintance, always gave him a sort of nervous feeling akin to what are sometimes called the heeby-jeebies and he was never completely at his ease in his presence. It was the tortoiseshell-rimmed spectacles principally that did it, he thought, though possibly the square jaw contributed its mite.

Mr Schoonmaker stood looming over the hammock like a thunder-cloud.

'You and your damned Dukes!' he said and Lord Ickenham raised his eyebrows.

'My dear Jimmy! It may be my imagination, but a certain half-veiled something in your manner seems to suggest that your confer-ence with Dunstable was not an agreeable one. What happened? Did you broach the subject of the Venus Island Development Cor-poration?'

'Yes, I did,' said Mr Schoonmaker, taking time out for a snort similar in its resonance to the shot heard round the world. 'And he acted as if he thought I was some sort of con man. Did you tell him I'd borrowed money from you?'

Lord Ickenham's eyes widened. He was plainly at a loss.

'Borrowed money from me? Of course not.'

'He said you did.'

'How very extraordinary. How much am I supposed to have lent you?'

'Ten pounds.'

'What a laughable idea! The sort of sum a man like you leaves on the plate for the waiter when he's had lunch. What on earth can have put that into his head?' Lord Ickenham's face cleared. 'I'll tell you what I think must have misled him, Jimmy. I remember now that I was talking to him about the old days in New York, when we were both young and hard up and I would sometimes sting you for a trifle and you would sometimes sting me for a trifle, according to which of us happened to have anything in his wallet at the moment, and he got it all mixed up. Very muddle-headed man, the Duke. His father, I believe, was the same. So were his sisters and his cousins and his aunts. Well, I must say the thought of someone of your eminence panhandling me for a tenner is a very stimulating one. It isn't everyone who gets his ear bitten by a millionaire. How did you leave things with Dunstable?'

'I told him he was crazy and came away.'

'Very proper. And what are you planning to do now?'

A faint blush spread itself over Mr Schoonmaker's face.

'I thought I might go and see if Lady Constance would like a stroll in the park or something.'

'Connie,' Lord Ickenham corrected. 'You won't get anywhere if you don't think of her as Connie.'

'I won't get anywhere if I do,' said Mr Schoonmaker morosely.

The morning was now pleasantly warm and full of little soothing noises, some contributed by the local insects, others by a gardener who was mowing a distant lawn, and it was not long after Mr Schoonmaker's departure before Lord Ickenham's eyes closed and his breathing became soft and regular. He was within two breaths of sleep, when a voice spoke.

'Hoy!' it said, and he sat up.

'Hullo, Dunstable. You seem upset.'

The Duke's eyes were popping, and his moustache danced in the breeze.

'Ickenham, you were right!'

'About what?'

'About that Yank, that feller Stick-in-the-Mud. Not ten minutes after you'd warned me he was going to do it, he came to me and started trying to get me to put up money for that Tiddlypush Island scheme of his.'

Lord Ickenham gave a low whistle.

'You don't say!'

'That's what he did.'

'So soon! One would have expected him to wait at least till he had got to know you a little better. He was very plausible, of course?'

'Yes, very.'

'He would be. These fellows always specialize in the slick sales talk. You weren't taken in, I hope?'

'*Me?*'

'No, of course not. You're much too level-headed.'

'I sent him off with a flea in his ear, by Jove!'

'I see. I don't blame you. Still, it's very embarrassing.'

'Who's embarrassed? I'm not.'

'I was only thinking that as your nephew is going to marry his daughter . . .'

The Duke's jaw fell.

'Good God! I'd forgotten that.'

'I should try to bear it in mind from now on, if I were you, for it is a matter that affects you rather deeply. It's lucky you're a rich man.'

'Eh?'

'Well, you're going to have to support Archie and the girl, and not only them but Schoonmaker and his sisters. I believe he has three of them.'

'I won't do it!'

'Can't let them starve.'

'Why not?'

'You mean you think we all eat too much nowadays? Quite true, but it won't do you any good if they go about begging crusts of bread and telling people why. Can't you see the gossip columns in Tilbury's papers? They'd really spread themselves.'

The Duke clutched at the hammock, causing Lord Ickenham to oscillate and feel a little seasick. He had overlooked this angle, and none knew better than he how blithely, after what had occurred between them, the proprietor of the Mammoth Publishing Company would spring to the task of getting a certain something of his own back.

A thought struck him.

'Why should Archibald beg crusts of bread?'

'Wouldn't you, if suffering from the pangs of hunger?'

'He has a salaried position.'

'No longer.'

'Eh?'

'They handed him his hat.'

'His hat? How do you mean, his hat?'

'Putting it another way, his services were dispensed with last week.'

'What!'

'So he told me.'

'He never said anything about it to me.'

'Probably didn't want to cause you anxiety. He's a very considerate young man.'

'He's a poop and a waster!'

'I like his hair, though, don't you? Well, that's how matters stand, and I'm afraid it's going to cost you a lot of money. I don't see how you're going to do it under two or three thousand a year. For years and years and years. Great drain on your resources. What a pity it isn't possible for you just to tell Archie to break the engagement. That would solve everything. But of course you can't do it.'

'Why can't I? It's an excellent idea. I'll go and find him now, and if he raises the slightest objection, I'll kick his spine up through his hat.'

'No, wait. You still haven't got that toehold on the situation which I should like to see. You're forgetting the breach of promise case.'

'What breach of promise case?'

Lord Ickenham's manner was that of a patient governess explaining a problem in elementary arithmetic to a child who through no fault of its own had been dropped on the head when a baby.

'Isn't it obvious? If Archie were to break the engagement, the girl's first move would be to start an action for breach of promise. Even if the idea didn't occur to her independently, a man like Schoonmaker would see that she did it, and the jury would give her heavy damages without leaving the box. Archie tells me he has written her any number of letters.'

'How can he have written her letters when they're staying in the same dashed house?'

'Notes would perhaps be a better term. Fervid notes slipped into her hand by daylight or pushed under her door at night. You know what lovers are.'

'Sounds potty.'

'But is frequently done, I believe, when the heart is young.'

'He may not have mentioned marriage.'

'I wouldn't build too much on that. I know he asked me once how to spell "honeymoon", which shows the trend his thoughts were taking. You can't speak of honeymoons in a letter to a girl without laying up trouble for yourself. When you consider what a mere reference to chops and tomato sauce did to Mr Pickwick –'

'Who's Mr Pickwick?'

'Let it pass. I'm only saying that when those notes are read out in court, you'll be for it.'

'Why me? If Archibald is fool enough to get involved in a breach of promise case, blast his idiotic eyes. I don't have to pay his damages.'

'It won't look well in the gossip columns, if you don't. He's your nephew.'

The Duke uttered a bitter curse on all nephews, and Lord Ickenham agreed that they could be trying, though his own nephew Pongo, he said, held the view that all the trouble in the world was caused by uncles.

'I can see only one ray of hope.'

'What's that?' asked the Duke, who was unable to detect even one. His prominent eyes gleamed a little. He was saying to himself that this feller Ickenham might be potty, but apparently he had lucid intervals.

'It may be possible to buy the girl off. We have this in our favour, that she isn't in love with Archie.'

'Who could be in love with a poop like that?'

'Hers is rather a sad case. You know Meriwether?'

'The feller with the face?'

'A very accurate description. He has a heart of gold, too, but you don't see that.'

'What about him?'

'He is the man she wants to marry.'

'Meriwether is?'

'Yes.'

'Then why did she get engaged to Archibald?'

'My dear Dunstable! A girl whose father is on the verge of bankruptcy has to look out for herself. She isn't in a position to let her heart rule her head. When she has the opportunity of becoming linked by marriage to a man like you, you can't expect her not to grab it.'

'That's true.'

'She would much prefer not to make a marriage of convenience, but she sees no hope of happiness with the man she loves. What stands in the way of her union to Meriwether is money.'

'Hasn't he got any? You told me he came from Brazil. Fellers make money in Brazil.'

'He didn't. A wasting sickness struck the Brazil nuts, and he lost all his capital.'

'Silly ass.'

'Your sympathy does you credit. Yes, his lack of money is the trouble. And the reason I think Myra Schoonmaker would jump at any adequate offer is that he has just got the chance of buying into a lucrative onion soup business.'

The Duke started as if stung. The last three words always stirred him to his depths.

'My nephew Alaric runs an onion soup business.'

'No, really?'

'That's what he does. Writes poetry and sells onion soup. It embarrasses me at the club. Fellers come up to me and ask, "What's that nephew of yours doing now?", thinking I'm going to say he's in the diplomatic service or something, and I have to tell them he's selling onion soup. Don't know which way to look.'

'I can understand your emotion. The stuff is very nourishing, I believe, but, as far as I know, no statue has ever been erected to a man who sold onion soup. Still, there's lots of money in it, and this chap I'm speaking of is doing so well that he wants to expand. He has offered Meriwether a third share in his business for a thousand pounds. So if you were to offer the girl that . . .'

'A thousand pounds?'

'That's what Meriwether told me.'

'It's a great deal of money.'

'That's why the chap wants it.'

The Duke pondered. His was a slow mind, and it was only gradually that he ever grasped a thing. But he had begun to see what this Ickenham feller was driving at.

'You think that if I give the girl a thousand pounds, she'll pass it on to this gargoyle chap, and then she'll hand Archibald his hat and marry the gargoyle?'

'Exactly. You put it in a nutshell.'

A sudden healing thought came to the Duke. It was that if he bought the dashed girl off for a thousand and got three thousand from Emsworth for that appalling pig, he would still be comfortably ahead of the game. If it had been within his power to give people grateful looks, he would have given Lord Ickenham one, for it appeared to him that he had found the way.

'I'll go and write the cheque now,' he said.

2

It seemed to Lord Ickenham, drowsing in his hammock after the Duke's departure, that an angel voice was speaking his name, and he speculated for a moment on the possibility of his having been snatched up to heaven in a fiery chariot without noticing it. Then reason told him that an angel, punctilious as all angels are, would scarcely on so brief an acquaintance be addressing him as Uncle Fred, and he sat up, brushing the mists of sleep from his eyes, to see Myra Schoonmaker standing beside him. She was looking as attractive as always, but her clothes struck him as unsuitable for a morning in the country.

'Hullo, young Myra,' he said. 'Why all dressed up?'

'I'm going to London. I came to ask if there was any little present I could bring you back.'

'Nothing that I can think of except tobacco. What's taking you to London?'

'Father has given me a big cheque and wants me to go and buy things.'

'A kindly thought. You don't seem very elated.'

'Not much to be elated about these days. Everything's such a mess.'

'Things will clear up.'

'Says you!'

'I would call the outlook rather promising.'

'Well, I don't know where you get that idea, but I wish you would sell it to Bill. He needs a bracer.'

'Morale low?'

'Very low. He's all jumpy. You know how you feel when you're waiting for something to explode.'

'Apprehensive?'

'That's the word. He can't understand why Lady Constance has said nothing to him.'

'Was he expecting a chat with her?'

'Well, wouldn't you in his place? He told Lord Emsworth who he was, and Lord Emsworth must have told her.'

'Not necessarily. Perhaps he forgot.'

'Could he forget a thing like that?'

'There is no limit to what Emsworth can forget, especially when he's distracted about his pig.'

'What's wrong with the pig? She looked all right to me when I saw her last.'

'What's wrong is that the Duke has taken her from him.'

'How?'

'It's a long story. I'll tell you about it some other time. What train are you catching?'

'The ten-thirty-five. I wanted Bill to sneak down to the station and come with me. I thought we might get married.'

'Very sensible. Wouldn't he?'

'No. He had scruples. He said it would be a low trick to play on Archie.'

Lord Ickenham sighed.

'Those scruples! They do keep popping up, don't they? Tell him to relax. Archie's dearest wish is to marry a girl named Millicent Rigby. He's engaged to her.'

'But he's engaged to me.'

'He's engaged to both of you. Very awkward situation for the poor boy.'

'Then why doesn't he just break it off?'

'He wants to get a thousand pounds out of the Duke to buy into an onion soupery, and he felt that if he jilted the daughter of a millionaire, his chances would be slim. His only course seemed to him to be to sit tight and hope for the best. And you can't break the engagement because Jimmy would take you back to America. Until this morning the situation was an extraordinarily delicate one.'

'What happened this morning?'

'The Duke somehow or other got the curious idea that your father was on the verge of bankruptcy, and he saw himself faced with the prospect of having to support not only you and Archie but

the whole Schoonmaker family. His distaste for this was so great
that he left me just now to go and write a cheque for a thousand
pounds, payable to you. He hopes to buy you off.'

'Buy me off?'

'So that you won't sue Archie for breach of promise. When you
see him, accept the cheque in full settlement, endorse it to Archie,
and pay it into his bank. You'll just have time, if the train isn't late.
Be sure to do it today. The Duke has a nasty habit of stopping
cheques. Then, if you explain the situation to him, it is possible that
Bill might see his way to joining you on that 10.35 train, and you
and he could look in at the registry office tomorrow, being very
careful this time to choose the same one. It would wind everything
up very neatly.'

There was a silence. Myra drew a deep breath.

'Uncle Fred, did you work this?'

Lord Ickenham seemed surprised.

'Work it?'

'Did you tell the Duke Father was broke?'

Lord Ickenham considered.

'Well, now you mention it,' he said, 'it is just possible that some
careless word of mine may have given him that impression. Yes,
now that I think back, I believe I did say something along those
lines. It seemed to me to come under the head of spreading sweetness and light. I thought I would be making everybody happy,
except perhaps the Duke.'

'Oh, Uncle Fred!'

'Quite all right, my dear.'

'I'm going to kiss you.'

'Nothing to stop you, as far as I can see. Tell me,' said Lord
Ickenham, when this had been done, 'do you think you can now
overcome those scruples of Bill's?'

'I'll overcome them.'

'Just as well, perhaps, that he'll be leaving Blandings Castle.
Never outstay your welcome, I always say. Then all that remains is
to write a civil note to Lady Constance, thanking her for her
hospitality, placing the facts before her and hoping that this finds
her in the pink, as it leaves you at present. Give it to Beach. He'll
see that she gets it. Why the light laugh?'

'It was more a giggle. I was thinking I'd like to see her face, when she reads it.'

'Morbid, but understandable. I'm afraid she may not be too pleased. There is always apt to be that trouble when you start spreading sweetness and light. You find there isn't enough to go around and someone has to be left out of the distribution. Very difficult to get a full hand.'

3

In supposing that, having given audience to the Duke, Mr Schoonmaker, Archie Gilpin and Myra, he would now be allowed that restful solitude which was so necessary to him when digesting the morning eggs and bacon, Lord Ickenham was in error. This time it was not an angel voice that interrupted his slumber, but more of a bleat, as if an elderly sheep in the vicinity had been endowed with speech. Only one man of his acquaintance bleated in just that manner, and he was not surprised, on assuming an upright pose, to find that it was Lord Emsworth who had been called to his attention. The ninth earl was drooping limply at his side, as if some unfriendly hand had removed his spinal column.

Having become reconciled by now to being in the position of a French monarch of the old régime holding a levee, Lord Ickenham showed no annoyance, but greeted him with a welcoming smile and said that it was a nice day.

'The sun,' he said, indicating it.

Lord Emsworth looked at the sun, and gave it a nod of approval.

'I came to give you something.'

'The right spirit. It's not my birthday, but I am always open to receive presents. What sort of something?'

'I'm sorry to say I've forgotten.'

'Too bad.'

'I shall remember it in time, I expect.'

'I'll count the minutes.'

'And there's something I wanted to tell you.'

'But you've forgotten it?'

'No, I remember that. It is about the Empress. I have been thinking it over, Ickenham, and I have decided to buy the Empress from Dunstable. I admit I hesitated for a while, because his price was so stiff. He is asking three thousand pounds.'

It took a great deal to disturb Lord Ickenham's normal calm, but at these words he could not repress a gasp.

'Three thousand *pounds*! For a pig?'

'For the Empress,' Lord Emsworth corrected in a reverent voice.

'Kick him in the stomach!'

'No, I must have the Empress, no matter what the cost. I am lost without her. I'm on my way to see her now.'

'Who's attending to her wants now that Wellbeloved's gone?'

'Oh, I've taken Wellbeloved back,' said Lord Emsworth, looking a little sheepish, as a man will who has done the weak thing. 'I had no alternative. The Empress needs constant care and attention, and no pig man I have ever had has understood her as Wellbeloved does. But I gave him a good talking to. And do you know what he said to me? He said something that shocked me profoundly.'

Lord Ickenham nodded.

'These rugged sons of the soil don't always watch their language. They tend at times to get a bit Shakespearian. What did he call you?'

'He didn't call me anything.'

'Then what shocked you?'

'What he said. He said that Briggs woman who bribed him to steal the Empress was in the pay of Dunstable. It was Dunstable she was working for. I was never so astounded in my life. Should I tax him about it, do you think?'

'In the hope of making him shave his price a bit?' Lord Ickenham shook his head. 'I doubt if that would get you anywhere. He would do what I always advise everyone to do, stick to stout denial. All you have to go on is Wellbeloved's word, and that would not carry much conviction. I like George Cyril Wellbeloved and always enjoy exchanging ideas with him, but I wouldn't believe his word if he brought it to me on a plate with watercress round it. On this occasion he probably deviated from the policy of a lifetime and told the truth, but what of that? You know and I know that Dunstable is a man who sticks at nothing and would walk ten miles in the snow to chisel a starving orphan out of tuppence, but we are helpless without proof. If only he had written some sort of divisional orders, embodying his low schemes in a letter, it would be –'

'Oh!' said Lord Emsworth.

'Eh?' said Lord Ickenham.

'I've just remembered what it was I came to give you,' said Lord Emsworth, feeling in his pocket. 'This letter. It got mixed up with mine. Well, I'll be getting along and seeing the Empress. Would you care to come?'

'Come? Oh, I see what you mean. I think not, thanks. Later on, perhaps.'

Lord Ickenham spoke absently. He had opened the letter, and a glance at the signature had told him that its contents might well be fraught with interest.

His correspondent was Lavender Briggs.

Chapter 12

The door of Lady Constance's boudoir flew open and something large and spectacled shot out, so rapidly that it was only by an adroit *pas seul* that Beach, who happened to be passing at the moment, avoided a damaging collision.

'Oops!' said Mr Schoonmaker, for the large spectacled object was he. 'Pardon me.'

'Pardon me, sir,' said Beach.

'No, no, pardon me,' said Mr Schoonmaker.

'Very good, sir,' said Beach.

He was regarding this man who had so nearly become his dancing partner with a surprise which he did not allow to appear on his moonlike features, for butlers are not permitted by the rules of their guild to look surprised. Earlier in the day he had viewed Mr Schoonmaker with some concern, thinking that his face seemed pale and drawn, as if he were suffering from a headache, but now there had been a magical change and it was plain that he had made a quick recovery. The cheeks glowed, and the eyes, formerly like oysters in the last stages of dissolution, were bright and sparkling. Exuberant was the word Beach would have applied to the financier, if he had happened to know it. He had once heard Lord Ickenham use the expression 'All spooked up with zip and vinegar', and it was thus that he was mentally labelling Mr Schoonmaker now. Unquestionably spooked up, was his verdict.

'Oh, Beach,' said Mr Schoonmaker.

'Sir?' said Beach.

'Lovely day.'

'Extremely clement, sir'

'I'm looking for Lord Ickenham. You seen him anywhere?'

'It was only a few moments ago that I observed his lordship entering the office of Lord Emsworth's late secretary, sir'

'Late?'

'Not defunct, sir. Miss Briggs was dismissed from her post.'

'Oh, I see. Got the push, did she? Where is this office?'

'At the far end of the corridor on the floor above this one. Should I escort you there, sir?'

'No, don't bother. I'll find it. Oh, Beach.'

'Sir?'

'Here,' said Mr Schoonmaker, and thrusting a piece of paper into the butler's hand he curvetted off like, thought Beach, an unusually extrovert lamb in springtime.

Beach looked at the paper, and being alone, with nobody to report him to his guild, permitted himself a sharp gasp. It was a ten-pound note, and it was the third piece of largesse that had been bestowed on him in the last half hour. First, that charming young lady, Miss Schoonmaker, giving him a missive to take to her ladyship, had accompanied it with a fiver, and shortly after that Mr Meriwether had pressed money into his hand with what looked to him like a farewell gesture, though he had not been notified that the gentleman was leaving. It all seemed very mysterious to Beach, though far from displeasing.

Mr Schoonmaker, meanwhile, touching the ground only at odd spots, had arrived at Lavender Briggs' office. He found Lord Ickenham seated at the desk, and burst immediately into speech.

'Oh, Freddie. The butler told me you were here.'

'And he was quite right. Here I am, precisely as predicted. Take a chair.'

'I can't take a chair, I'm much too excited. You don't mind me walking about the room like this? I wanted to see you, Freddie. I wanted you to be the first to hear the news. Do you remember me telling you that if I could get Lady Constance to be my wife, I'd be the happiest man on earth?'

'I remember. Those were your very words.'

'Well, I am.'

Something of the bewilderment recently exhibited by Beach showed itself on Lord Ickenham's face. This was a totally unexpected development. A shrewd judge of form, he had supposed that only infinite patience and a compelling series of pep talks would have been able to screw this man's courage to the sticking point and

turn him, as he appeared to have been turned, into a whirlwind
wooer. Very unpromising wedding bells material his old friend had
seemed to him in the previous talks they had had together, and he
had almost despaired of bringing about the happy ending. For if a
suitor's nerve fails him every time he sees the adored object sideways, it is seldom that he can accomplish anything constructive. Yet
now it was plain that something had occurred to change James
Schoonmaker from the timorous rabbit he had been to a dasher
with whom Don Juan would not have been ashamed to shake
hands. It struck him instantly that there could be but one solution
of the mystery.

'Jimmy, you've been at the May Queen again.'

'I have not!'

'You're sure?'

'Of course I'm sure.'

'Well, I'm glad to hear that, for it is not a practice I would
recommend so early in the day. And yet you tell me that you have
been proposing marriage with, I am glad to hear, great success.
How did you overcome that diffidence of yours?'

'I didn't have to overcome it. When I saw her sitting there in
floods of tears, all my diffidence vanished. I felt strong and protect-
ive. I hurried to where she sat.'

'And grabbed her?'

'Certainly not.'

'Waggled her about?'

'Nothing of the kind. I bent over her and took her hand gently in
mine. "Connie," I said.'

'Connie?'

'Certainly.'

'At last! I knew you would get around to it sooner or later. And
then?'

'She said, "Oh, James!"'

'Well, I don't think much of the dialogue so far, but perhaps it
got brighter later on. What did you say after that?'

'I said, "Connie, darling. What's the matter?"'

'One can understand how you must have been curious to know.
And what was the matter?'

Mr Schoonmaker, who had been pacing the floor in the manner

popularized by tigers at a zoo, suddenly halted in mid-stride, and the animation died out of his face as though turned off with a switch. He looked like a man suddenly reminded of something unpleasant, as indeed he had been.

'Who's this guy Meriwether?' he demanded.

'Meriwether?' said Lord Ickenham, who had had an idea that the name would be coming up shortly. 'Didn't Connie tell you about him?'

'Only that you brought him here.'

Lord Ickenham could understand this reticence. He recalled that his hostess, going into the matter at their recent conference, had decided that silence was best. It would have been difficult, as she had said, were she to place the facts before her betrothed, to explain why she had allowed Bill to continue enjoying her hospitality.

'Yes, I brought him here. He's a young friend of mine. His name actually is Bailey, but he generally travels incognito. He's a curate. He brushes and polishes the souls of the parishioners of Bottleton East, a district of London, where he is greatly respected. I'll tell you something about Bill Bailey, Jimmy. I have an idea he's a good deal attracted by your daughter Myra. Not easy to tell for certain because he wears the mask, but I wouldn't be at all surprised if he wasn't in love with her. One or two little signs I've noticed. Poor lad, it must have been a sad shock for him when he learned that she's going to marry Archie Gilpin.'

Mr Schoonmaker snorted. This habit of his of behaving like a bursting paper bag was new to Lord Ickenham. Probably, he thought, a mannerism acquired since his rise to riches. No doubt there was some form of unwritten law that compelled millionaires to act that way.

'She isn't,' said Mr Schoonmaker.

'Isn't what?'

'Going to marry Archie Gilpin. She eloped with Meriwether this morning.'

'You astound me. Are you sure? Where did you hear that?'

'She left a note for Connie.'

'Well, this is wonderful news,' said Lord Ickenham, his face lighting up. 'I'm not surprised you're dancing about all over the place on the tips of your toes. He's a splendid young fellow. Boxed three years for Oxford and, so I learn from a usually reliable source, went through the opposition like a dose of salts. I congratulate you, Jimmy.'

Mr Schoonmaker seemed to be experiencing some difficulty in sharing his joyous enthusiasm.

'I call it a disaster. Connie thinks so, too – that's why she was in floods of tears. And she says you're responsible.'

'Who, me?' said Lord Ickenham, amazed, not knowing that the copyright in those words was held by George Cyril Wellbeloved. 'What had I got to do with it?'

'You brought him here.'

'Merely because I thought he looked a little peaked and needed a breath of country air. Honestly, Jimmy,' said Lord Ickenham, speaking rather severely, 'I don't see what you're beefing about. If I hadn't brought him here, he wouldn't have eloped with Myra, thus causing Connie to burst into floods of tears, thus causing you to lose your diffidence and take her hand gently in yours and say "Connie, darling." If it hadn't been for these outside stimuli, you would still be calling her Lady Constance and wincing like a salted snail every time you saw her profile. You ought to be thanking me on bended knee, unless the passage of time has made you stiff in the joints. What's your objection to Bill Bailey?'

'Connie says he hasn't a cent to his name.'

'Well, you've enough for all. Haven't you ever heard of sharing the wealth?'

'I don't like Myra marrying a curate.'

'The very husband you should have wished her. The one thing a financier wants is a clergyman in the family. What happens next time the Senate Commission has you on the carpet and starts a probe? You say "As proof of my respectability, gentlemen, I may mention that my daughter is married to a curate. You don't find curates marrying into a man's family if there's anything fishy about him," and they look silly and apologize. And there's another thing.'

'Eh?' said Mr Schoonmaker, who had been musing.

'I said there was another thing you ought to bear in mind. Have you considered what would have happened if Myra had married the Duke of Dunstable's nephew? You would never have got Dunstable out of your hair. A Christmas present would have been expected yearly. You would have had to lunch with him, dine with him, be constantly in his society. He would have come over to New York to spend long visits with you. The children, if any, would have had to learn to call him "Uncle Alaric". I think you've been extraordinarily lucky, Jimmy. Imagine a life with Dunstable like a sort of Siamese twin.'

It is possible that Mr Schoonmaker would have had much to say in reply to this, for Lord Ickenham's reasoning, though shrewd, had not wholly convinced him that everything was for the best in the best of all possible worlds, but at this moment the air was rent by a stentorian 'Hoy!' and they perceived that the Duke of Dunstable was in their midst.

'Oh, *you're* here?' said the Duke, pausing in the doorway and giving Mr Schoonmaker a nasty look.

Mr Schoonmaker, returning the nasty look with accrued interest, said he was.

'I hoped you'd be alone, Ickenham.'

'Jimmy was just going, weren't you, Jimmy? This is your busy day, isn't it? A thousand things to attend to. So what,' said Lord Ickenham, as the door closed, 'can I do for you, Dunstable?'

The Duke jerked a thumb at the door.

'Has he been trying to touch you?'

'Oh, no. We were just talking.'

'Oh?'

The Duke transferred his gaze to the room, regarding it with dislike and disapproval. It had unpleasant memories for him. He took in the desk, the typewriter, the recording machine and the chairs with a smouldering eye. It was in this interior set, he could not but remember, that that woman with the spectacles had so nearly deprived him of five hundred pounds.

'What you doing here?' he asked, as if revolted to find Lord Ickenham in such surroundings.

'In Miss Briggs' office? I had a letter from her this morning asking me to look in and attend to a number of things on her behalf. She left, if you recall, in rather a hurry.'

'Why did she write to you?'

'I think she felt that I was her only friend at Blandings Castle.'

'You a friend of hers?'

'We became reasonably matey.'

'Then I'd advise you to choose your friends more carefully, that's what I'd advise you. Matey, indeed!'

'You don't like the divine Briggs?'

'Blasted female.'

'Ah, well,' said Lord Ickenham tolerantly, 'we all have our faults. Even I have been criticized at times. But you were going to tell me what you wanted to see me about.'

The Duke, who had been scowling at the typewriter, as if daring it to start something, became more composed. A curious gurgling noise suggested that he had chuckled.

'Oh, that? I just came to say that everything's all right.'

'Splendid. What's all right?'

'About the pipsqueak.'

'What pipsqueak would that be?'

'The Tiddlypush girl. She took the cheque.'

'She did?'

'In full settlement.'

'Well, that's wonderful news.'

'So there won't be any breach of promise case. She's gone to London.'

'Yes, I saw her for a moment before she left. You bought her off, did you?'

'That's what I did. "Here you are," I said, and I dangled the cheque in front of her. She didn't hesitate. Grabbed at it like a seal going after a slice of fish. I knew she would. They can't resist the cash. I've just been telling Archibald that she has ... what's that expression you used when you told me he'd been sacked from that job of his?'

'Handed him his hat?'

'That's right. I told him she's handed him his hat.'

'Was he very distressed?'

'Didn't seem to be.'

'Easy come, easy go, he probably said to himself.'

'I shouldn't wonder. He's gone to London, too.'

'On the same train as Miss Schoonmaker?'

'No, he went in that little car of his. Said he was going to take a friend to dinner. Fellow of the name of Rigby.'

'Ah, yes, he has spoken to me of his friend Rigby. I believe they are very fond of each other.'

'Chap must be a silly ass if he's fond of a poop like Archibald.'

'Oh, we all have our likes and dislikes. You'll be leaving soon yourself, I take it?'

'Me? Why?'

'Well, it won't be very comfortable for you here now that Emsworth knows it was you who engaged Miss Briggs to steal his pig. Creates a strain, that sort of thing. Tension. Awkward silences.'

The Duke gaped. The shock had been severe. If a meteorite had entered through the open window and struck him behind one of his rather prominent ears, he might have been more taken aback, but not very much so. When he was able to speak, which was not immediately, he said:

'What . . . what you talking about?'

'Isn't it true?'

'Of course it's not true.'

Lord Ickenham clicked his tongue reprovingly.

'My dear Dunstable, I am always a great advocate of stout denial, but I'm afraid it is useless here. Emsworth has had the whole story from George Cyril Wellbeloved.'

The Duke was still feeling far from at his best, but he rallied sufficiently to say 'Pooh!'

'Who's going to believe him?'

'His testimony is supported by Miss Briggs.'

'Who's going to believe her?'

'Everybody, I should say. Certainly Emsworth, for one, after he hears this record.'

'Eh?'

'I told you I had received a letter from the divine Briggs this morning. In it she asked me to turn on her tape recording machine . . . this is the tape recording machine . . . because, she said, that would give the old bounder . . . I fancy she meant you . . . something to think about. I will now do so,' said Lord Ickenham. He pressed the button, and a voice filled the room.

'I, Alaric, Duke of Dunstable, hereby make a solemn promise, to you, Lavender Briggs . . .'

The Duke sat down abruptly. His jaw had fallen, and he seemed suddenly to have become as boneless as Lord Emsworth.

'. . . that if you steal Lord Emsworth's pig, Empress of Blandings, and deliver it to my home in Wiltshire, I will pay you five hundred pounds.'

'That,' said Lord Ickenham, 'is you in conference with La Briggs. She naturally took the precaution of having this instrument working at the time. It's always safer with these verbal agreements. Well, I don't know what view you take of the situation, but it seems to me that you and Emsworth are like two cowboys in the Malemute Saloon who have got the drop on each other simultaneously. You have young George's film, he has this Scotch tape or whatever it's called. I suggest a fair exchange. Or would you rather I brought Emsworth in here and played this recording to him? It's not a thing I would recommend. One feels that the consequences would be extremely unpleasant for you.'

The Duke froze, appalled. The feller was right. Let this get about, and not only would his name be a hissing and a byword, so that when he invited himself to houses in the future, his host and hostess would hasten to put their valuables away in a stout box and sit on the lid, but Emsworth would bring an action against him for conspiracy or malice aforethought or whatever it was and mulct him in substantial damages. With only the minimum of hesitation he thrust a hand in his pocket and produced the spool which had never left his person since little George had given it to him.

'Here you are, blast you!'

'Oh, thanks. Now everybody's happy. Emsworth has his pig, Myra her Bill, Archie his Millicent Rigby.'

The Duke started.

'His *what* Rigby?'

'Oh yes, I should have told you that, shouldn't I? He's gone to London to marry a very nice girl called Millicent Rigby, at least he says she's very nice, and he probably knows. By the way, that reminds me. There's one thing I wish you would clear up for me before you go. Why was it that you were so anxious that Archie shouldn't marry Myra Schoonmaker? It has puzzled me from the first. She's charming, and apart from being charming she's the heiress of one of the richest men in America. Don't you like heiresses?'

The Duke's moustache had become violently agitated. He was not normally quick-witted, but he had begun to suspect that fishy things had been going on. If this Ickenham had not been deliberately misleading him, he was very much mistaken.

'You told me Schoonmaker was broke!'

'Surely not?'

'You said he touched you for a tenner.'

'No, no, I touched *him* for a tenner. That may be where you got confused. What would a man like James Schoonmaker be doing, borrowing money from people? He's a millionaire, so Bradstreet informs us.'

'Who's Bradstreet?'

'The leading authority on millionaires. A sort of American Debrett. Bradstreet is very definite on the subject of James Schoonmaker. Stinking rich is, I believe, the expression it uses of him.'

The Duke continued to bend his brain to the problem. He was more convinced than ever that he had been deceived.

'Then why did she take that cheque?'

'Ah, that we shall never know. Just girlish high spirits, do you think?'

'I'll give her girlish high spirits!'

'I'll tell you a possible solution that has occurred to me. She knew that Archie was planning to get married and needed money, so being a kind-hearted girl she took the cheque and endorsed it over to him. Sort of a wedding present from you. Where are you going?'

The Duke had lumbered to the door. He paused with a hand on the handle, regarded Lord Ickenham balefully.

'I'll tell you where I'm going. I'm going to get to the telephone and stop that cheque.'

Lord Ickenham shook his head.

'I wouldn't. I still have the tape, remember. I was just about to give it to you, but if you are going to stop cheques, I shall have to make an agonizing reappraisal.'

There was a silence, as far as silence was possible in a small room where the Duke was puffing at his moustache.

'You shall have it tomorrow night after the cheque has gone through. It's not that I don't trust you, Dunstable, it's simply that I don't trust you.'

The Duke breathed stertorously. He did not like many people, but he searched his mind in vain for somebody he disliked as much as he was disliking his present companion.

'Ickenham,' he said, 'you are a low cad!'

'Now you're just trying to be nice. I bet you say that to all the boys,' said Lord Ickenham, and rising from his chair he went off to tell Lord Emsworth that though he had lost Lavender Briggs and was losing a sister and the Duke of Dunstable, he would be gaining a pig which for three years in succession had won the silver medal in the Fat Pigs class at the Shropshire Agricultural Show.

There was a smile on his handsome face, the smile it always wore when he had given service.